O9-BRY-644

Ronen Lalena

SHIMON ADAF
TAKE UP AND READ
Translated by Yardenne Greenspan

Shimon Adaf was born in Sderot, Israel, and now lives in Holon. A poet, novelist, and musician, Adaf worked for several years as a literary editor at Keter Publishing House and has also been a writer-in-residence at the University of Iowa. He leads the creative writing program and lectures on Hebrew literature at Ben-Gurion University of the Negev. Adaf received the Yehuda Amichai Prize for Hebrew Poetry (2010) for the collection *Aviva-No*; the Sapir Prize (2012) for the novel *Mox Nox*, the English translation of which, by Philip Simpson, won the Jewish Book Council's 2020 Paper Brigade Award for New Israeli Fiction in Honor of Jane Weitzman; and the I. and B. Neuman Prize for Hebrew Literature (2017).

Yardenne Greenspan is a writer and Hebrew translator born in Tel Aviv and based in New York. Her translations have been published by Restless Books, St. Martin's Press, Akashic Books, Syracuse University Press, New Vessel Press, Amazon Crossing, and Farrar, Straus and Giroux. Her translation of Yishai Sarid's novel *The Memory Monster* was selected as one of *The New York Times* 100 Notable Books of 2020. Greenspan's writing and translations have appeared in *The New Yorker*, *Haaretz*, *Guernica*, *Literary Hub*, *Blunderbuss Magazine*, *Apogee*, *The Massachusetts Review*, *Asymptote*, and *Words Without Borders*, among other publications. She has an MFA from Columbia University and is a regular contributor to *Ploughshares*.

By
SHIMON ADAF

Aviva-No

TAKE UP
AND READ

Take Up and Read

TRANSLATED FROM THE HEBREW
BY YARDENNE GREENSPAN

Shimon Adaf

PICADOR | NEW YORK

Picador
120 Broadway, New York 10271

Originally published in Hebrew in 2017 by Kinneret Zmora-Bitan, Israel,
as קום קרא (*Kum Kra*)
English translation published in the United States by Picador
First American edition, 2022

Library of Congress Cataloging-in-Publication Data
Names: Adaf, Shimon, author. | Greenspan, Yardenne, translator.
Title: Take up and read / Shimon Adaf ; translated by Yardenne Greenspan.
Other titles: Ḳum ḳera. English
Description: First American edition. | New York : Picador, 2022. | Series: The
    lost detective trilogy ; 3
Identifiers: LCCN 2022013322 | ISBN 9780374277970 (paperback)
Subjects: LCGFT: Detective and mystery fiction. | Novels.
Classification: LCC PJ5055.2.D44 K8613 2022 | DDC 892.43/7—dc23/
    eng/20220318
LC record available at https://lccn.loc.gov/2022013322

Designed by Janet Evans-Scanlon

For book club information, please visit facebook.com/picadorbookclub or
email marketing@picadorusa.com.

picadorusa.com · instagram.com/picador
twitter.com/picadorusa · facebook.com/picadorusa

10   9   8   7   6   5   4   3   2   1

To my friends

TAKE UP
AND READ

In the middle of comp class, one of my enemies stood up, no, in the middle of comp class my sworn enemy stood up and recited ridiculous rhymed couplets that swept away the boys in the religious classroom. The topic of the essay we were instructed to write was a frightening event in our lives. What had we encountered at that age other than fear and some muffled, insinuated desire? But in grade 7D the world began to open. For some of us. The world was televised evidence. The world was secret dreams of fame. The world was the battle for the role of cantor during morning prayer. In the beginning of the school year we fought against the sleep that beckoned during High Holiday prayers. Now, at the top of the month of Adar, we competed for who could sing the Passover songs the loudest, those of us whose voices had already dropped and who had control over them. Then we snuck furtive glances at the teacher on duty, the gym teacher, the geography teacher, the bleary-eyed Talmud teacher. I saw myself as separate from the others. Most of them inspired in me a kind of limp resentment, a kind of reservation that had taken over me that year. Suddenly, at the end of summer, these feelings assaulted me. I walked through the gates of the religious high school, trading in a kingdom of silence for a kingdom of mobs, screaming, scampering, sweaty boys. I knew right away that the sweat within the religious classroom was different. Twenty-something other boys sitting at desks in pairs. It contained a pungency and an urgency. I recognized the pungency. But the other element, it was as if they were raring to embark on a journey that I hadn't been invited to join. I barely traversed the path from the gate to the classroom. In spite of the immense space, the curved space, the margins of which grazed the edges of the universe, I rubbed against swarms of people.

When I walked inside I saw that the desks in the front of the room were mostly occupied. I found an empty chair. Our home-room teacher was all buttoned up. Brown, doughy face and near-inflamed irises. The bit of skin that peeked through her layers of clothing, the skin of an ankle among the many folds of a skirt, a strip of elbow, was marble-like, ivory. My desk mate lowered his head while the teacher explained our scholarly duties. I looked at him. His cheeks were flushed, his lips pursed, his hands balled into fists, reaching for his knees. The front of his shorts was swollen. I looked away quickly. The teacher walked stiffly along the aisles. Occasionally, she paused to jot down an important point on the blackboard. I tried to concentrate on what she was saying, but my eyes wandered from her repetitive motions to my desk mate's erection. With a start, I thought, The bell will ring soon to mark the end of class, what will he do then, how will he stand up in front of everybody while his thing is standing too? His lips moved silently in some invisible plea, echoing the illusion of calm he attempted to summon. He thought about clear, frozen lakes, bluing icy tundras, cracks of frost in windowpanes, snow on coniferous trees.

His well of images invaded me. I was seized by the whirlpool of dropping temperatures, an abyss of motionlessness. There was serenity there, a promise of serenity, but not of the kind I knew. No. My fingers were already numb, frozen, my control of them diminishing, and the frozenumbness crawled slowly up my arms and down my legs. I, meaning I, can say that a silence was cast into the veins, tendrils of frost. Bam—one of the hooks anchoring the soul in its natural dwelling bursts, and then another, the metals breaking near absolute zero.

I called out, Miss, Miss, I have to go outside, I'm suffocating in here.

Didn't you hear what I said at the beginning of class? asked the teacher.

I did, but.

No buts, you're no longer in elementary school. In here you're accountable for every error or misdemeanor. Her voice screeched. How had I not noticed before the screeches of her voice, her voice-creeches, scroice, voichees, scroice—in the icy barrenness there are no bugs, only the whips of wind and storm, scroice, scroice. But I.

No ifs, ands, or buts. What did I say? Raise your hand before you speak. You aren't a donkey who brays every morning just because the sun comes up, are you?

I'm not sure, I said. I'm not so sure.

I'm beginning to have my doubts too, said the teacher.

I said, We're all donkeys.

Speak for yourself, somebody said.

Name, said the teacher.

Ehud Barda, miss, said the kid.

And you, said the teacher.

Farkash, I said.

Farkash who?

Ha, said Ehud Barda, just like the criminal.

He's probably related to him, someone else said. I heard he's got relatives in Sder—then another voice cut him off from some depths: They say he was hiding in the burrows here, not far from—but then he was cut off too by gleeful cheers of Nachman the king.

Such quality upbringing, said the teacher. I'll make sure to root out this savagery. Are all your heroes criminals?

Ehud Barda said, That guy gave the cops the runaround.

Quiet, said the teacher. I'm starting to think Farkash was right when he said you were all donkeys.

I regained control of my limbs. My desk mate was a meek, impure twinkle in the corner of my field of vision. I said, It wasn't me who said it; it's in the Talmud.

You must be expecting applause, she said.

The bell rang. Thirty-something systems of pistons and coils jumped up from their seats. Barda and Farkash, come see me, said the teacher. I felt a wave of pleasure for the mere response, the possibility of movement. Someone patted my back. I turned around. It was my desk mate. His cheeks had gone back to pink.

THERE WAS A CHANGE, UNDOUBTEDLY, IN THE SWEAT. IT WAS NO longer the sweat of the month of Elul with its boiling mornings. The air stood still in spite of the windows that were open onto the cracked, tiled yard. Beyond it rose a sandy slope. A fence separated the school from the hurdle of trees. Beyond that was a field and eolianite hills with a network of burrows in their stomachs. I sat at the front desk, beside Ehud Barda, under the murky gaze of Ms. Dadon. Her voice buzzed all around. During the summer vacation, I discovered an ability that had not been known to me beforehand, the ability to ride on the humming of other people's conversations. I was not yet seasoned in it. It had yet to obey my wishes. I listened to the words until their barren side appeared, until their meaning evaporated, and only the music of speech floated through the air like a scent. Sometimes this required a lot of noise. Last Shavuot, at the synagogue, the prayer became a hypnotizing tune, and I sunk into a life-swarming silence out of which rose gorgeous, meaningless images. At times, single sounds were enough—my father's sighs over the past months as he tossed and turned in his bed. When I was lucky, my sisters' chatter from the next room mixed in as well.

My two younger sisters wore me out all summer long with their inane conflicts. In the morning, they experienced a camaraderie as they headed together to camp, but upon their return, something of the fury of the sun rubbed off on them, and they began to quarrel. One day, Tova bit the skin of her right arm, pointed at the circle of divots made by her teeth, and told Chantal,

Look, I've got a watch. Chantal, who was chubbier, was unable to mimic the trick. Tova suggested she might bite Chantal's arm for her. Chantal cried out as Tova's mouth locked around her arm. She pushed Tova, but Tova's jaws remained tight. Chantal began to weep. Tova let go and sat down on the couch. She watched contentedly as Chantal attempted to scrub off the bite marks. Chantal ran to the bathroom, and her halting sobs broke the sound of running water. Simo Farkash stared at his daughters throughout this row, his empty gaze fixed. Once Chantal fled, his eyes wandered to other parts of the house. I went over to Chantal. She was sitting on the lid of the toilet, the water running in vain, landing on the inside of the sink, spinning with the revolutions of the earth toward the drain. I watched the pooling for a few moments as well. Then I turned off the faucet. Chantal stopped crying and stared at me, her eyes glistening with tears. With the fingers of her left hands she continued to massage the injury. I asked her to show it to me.

You don't care, said Chantal. You don't care about anything. If I was big like you, I'd slap her so hard she'd see stars.

I told her it wasn't about size.

What do you know, anyway? said Chantal. It hurts.

I said it would pass.

Chantal started crying again, silently this time. I kneeled down and touched her chin. Her head sprang back, as if from an electric spark. What makes the pain go away? I asked.

Chantal said, Revenge.

She walked silently out of the bathroom. I watched her from the doorway. Tova sprawled out on the couch. Chantal snuck up on her from behind. I assumed Tova would notice her approach momentarily, but Tova's senses were aimed at something else. Chantal pounced on her, sinking her teeth into Tova's neck. Tova screamed. Our father, from his submissive seat in front of the kitchen window, jumped to attention. For several seconds I was convinced that I recognized in him the same terrible force he contained up until eighteen months ago, in the final days of his heroism. For a moment, his eyes focused, burnishing. Then he collapsed back to his chair. Again those hollow sockets, barely able to see, meek vowels rising like vapor from his lips. My sisters, ages seven and eight and a half, wore their old, everyday image. Maturity came over Tova whenever she rushed to our father's aid. She walked over, worried, Chantal following behind, secretly pinching Tova's butt cheeks as Tova offered to pour him some water, slice him up some watermelon, call him a doctor.

I peeked from the doorway until I was convinced a cease-fire had taken effect, then retired. Behind my back, I heard Chantal chiding that our mother had instructed us to stay home until she returned, but I knew our mother would be walking through the door in a matter of minutes, or—

I applaud your confidence, said Ms. Dadon.

I returned a panicked look. Con-confidence, I said.

She leaned in and tapped her finger against my forehead. The beats ran down like a chill, aspiring to my feet. You trust your brain to record every detail of the class, don't you? she said.

How odd, my notebook was closed and pushed off to the corner of the desk, away from me. Ehud Barda put down his pencil to rest from its race across the pages of his own notebook. I nodded slowly.

Good, said Ms. Dadon. So perhaps you can tell us a little about the important regulation made by Ezra the Scribe during the days of the Return to Zion. Just a little, not too much; we don't want to put you out, heaven forbid.

The sandy slope and the hurdle of trees were locked by the window frame. I, meaning I, would like to point out that the outdoors were trapped by this blow of the window being made of glass, one of the materials of this world.

With effort, I said, He changed the script.

Changed the script?

Yes, I said. There was a hint of memory in my words. Where

did I hear that Ezra the Scribe changed the script? Maybe while reading the Mishnah at synagogue before the Minchah prayer. Yes, I said, until then they used a different, Canaanite script, these lines, and he changed it into the square script we use now, Assyrian script.

That's a great innovation, said Ms. Dadon. Look at this innovator. Apparently, we write Assyrian.

Her eyes moved away from me, examining the other students with amusement. Ehud pulled on my sleeve. His notebook was open, the final page reading, in huge letters, Torah reading on Mondays and Thursdays and during Shabbat Minchah prayer.

Again, Ms. Dadon's eyes, which had cleared, slammed into me. I heard the rage making the edges of her words tremble, striving underneath the sounds. So, she said, you know how to make things up, but listening is beneath you. Maybe you aren't a good enough student for this classroom.

Yes, I said, I mean, no, miss, I'm a big fool, a big fool.

MY FATHER ONCE TOLD ME THAT THE FARKASH CLAN WAS NOT meant to live in houses. We live facing the outside, the window is our comfort, then the door. The problem is we must be always on the run, which sometimes means we must create our own pursuers. I didn't find any logic in his words. They were spoken on a whim, out of context. My father took me to a soccer game one Saturday. In the middle of the game, right smack in the middle of a long line of juicy curse words regarding the femininity and cuntiness of the goalie and the forward, my father said what he said. He used the same hard, cursed, crude language I practiced in hiding. I nodded. I recalled the wispy respect with which anyone in the crowd addressed Mr. Farkash during a Saturday game. In his early days of heroism, my father was the head of the local soccer team—Hapoel Sderot—and led the team through a series of victories, at the end of which they went up a league. My father said I should have seen how they celebrated that year. But why, actually? he wondered. As if going from the fourth to third league helped anybody. He retired when he enlisted into a combat unit, then defected, served time in a military prison, and was discharged. Once, as my father retold his stories, my mother said that's how Simo Farkash was—Simo Farkash couldn't live unless he was ruining his own life.

Last night my father called me over. He didn't speak, only smacked his knee. I dragged over a chair and sat down beside him. After a few moments' silence, Mr. Farkash said, Be good. He rested his hand on my head. He said, Don't show your smarts at school. You'll only spoil it, like me. I'm not one of those blessers. And then, tenderly, he kissed the top of my head. The warmth of the kiss descended through my hair. I, meaning I, can tell that the warmth of the kiss kept going down, through the skull bones, through the blood-brain barrier, through tissues and neuron traps. It became a thought, open like an electric flower. I got up, choked. I left the chair behind me and hurried off to my room. Chantal was standing in the hallway, mouth slightly open. Even in the darkness that had fallen over the space, the glaze on her eyeballs still glimmered. She moved her lips in anticipation of some word that her throat had already processed, but Tova emerged behind her, coming out of the bathroom, rubbing her damp hands in one final wiping motion, then pushed her. What are you standing in the way for? she said. Move it, you cow.

I walked past them, sat down on my bed, and wondered if it wasn't too late for one last visit to the burrows, if it wouldn't be nightfall by the time I arrived. What would I find in the hour of the concealed lunar face, even with the flashlight I'd taken from my father's toolbox? I left the room. My father looked out the window, in the dirtying light, toward the backyard and beyond, to the wall separating our home from that of the neighbors. The chair I'd set beside him had been returned to its place. Lucky, because my mother just walked through the door. How she hated the deviation of furniture from its rightful place.

Tova, she said, did you remember the shopping?

Yes, Tova answered from deep inside the house.

Good, then, our mother said, come over here and help me with dinner.

Tova came in, reluctantly dragging her feet. Chantal followed, asking if she could help as well. But our mother gave her usual response: You're too young.

Mom, Chantal whined, we're going back to school tomorrow and my first-grade book bag is ripped.

You're going back to school tomorrow?

What, you don't know? said Tova. Even Dad remembered.

A spasm of hostility raced through our mother's expression, and her beauty was apparent, the murky beauty of the former Miss Sderot, which only emerged when she allowed her face to disclose her sorrow and disgruntlement. It vanished as swiftly as it had appeared, along with the emotion that had ignited it. Her features were hardened into their newfound tenseness. She said, So why are you wasting my time with this babbling right now? We'll go get some new school gear tomorrow.

She left Tova to watch the meat pot and make sure the sauce didn't bubble over. Chantal stayed with her as well. Our mother pulled me aside. What do you mean, your father remembered? she said.

I said, He wanted me to sit with him, he wanted to tell me not to stand out, that I'll just spoil it.

He talked to you?

Not much, he talked quietly, he barely had—

Nonsense, my mother said. All your dad has in his head is nonsense.

I pushed her protest out of my mind, and the edge of Simo Farkash's words poked at my throat when I admitted my foolishness in class. But the boys interpreted my admission as a joke. A wave of laughter ran through them. Ms. Dadon asked me to come see her after class.

Ehud Barda waited for me on the bench outside of class. He asked, What did the little worm want, wriggling the *W* sound in his mouth. He was holding a sandwich wrapped in wax paper and sealed inside a bag. I knew I'd forgotten something in the haste of leaving for school—I'd forgotten to pack lunch for my sisters and myself. Our mother had left for work early. I'd risen from heavy dreams quickly into wakefulness. I lay on the mattress, my body beating its gray pulses. I hurried to my father, shaking him awake. He was sprawled with his eyes open. Perhaps he too was crushed between the weights of the changing hours. My mother had instructed me not to leave him lying there. That one, she said, he can hang out in bed all day like a dead fish.

I'm fine, my father whispered, go about your business.

But I wouldn't leave him alone until he sat up. I pulled on his arms and called out to Tova and Chantal to get up already, we were late. They were combing each other's hair. Chantal said, She's doing it on purpose, she's combing too hard on purpose.

Nothing, I told Ehud. She warned me not to interrupt her for the rest of the day, or she'd make sure I got kicked out of the religious classroom.

She's all talk, said Ehud, that Ms. Ahuva Dadon. You want to go out to the yard?

Her name is Ahuva? I asked.

Yeah, doesn't suit her, though. Beloved? More like hated. She teaches at the girls' school too.

I followed him outside. He pointed at a small stone wall at the base of the eolianite hills. A painful glow invaded through the leaves of the tree over our head. Poinciana, said Ehud. The summer flowers had already fallen. The ground beneath us was stained with reddish rot.

Ehud slowly peeled the wax paper from his sandwich. He held

the sandwich in one hand and spread the paper on his knees with the other, patting it smooth. He placed the sandwich on the center of the paper, examined it, turned it ninety degrees, looked it over again, raised it to eye level. What do you think is the best way to cut to make two equal halves? he asked.

Why do you need to cut it? I asked.

You didn't pack a lunch.

Oh, I said, don't worry about that, I'm not hungry. And I thought, But Chantal will be hungry all day.

Ehud returned the sandwich to the wax paper on his lap, ran his fingernail through it lengthwise, and folded it in half. The sandwich cracked along the fraction line he'd created. Here, he said. He handed me half.

I'm really not—

Bshala, said Ehud. You'll get me back tomorrow. He mumbled the Hamotzi prayer and bit into his half. I thought, Should I walk all the way to the bathroom now to do the hand-washing prayer? I repeated after him, mumbling quickly, and gnawing on the crust. Hunger erupted inside of me, urging me to shove the entire half sandwich into my mouth and down my throat until I threw it up, spreading vomit all the way to the wounds of ripe poinciana flowers. Ehud took small bites off of his half, chewing them ponderously. We said nothing. The egg, the cheese, the vegetables, the bread itself, were shockingly delicious. In the distance I saw Dudi and Pini running in the basketball court. I'd shed them over the course of the summer. I have no idea why. Every remnant of intimacy seemed planted in the thicket of a past grown wild, entry forbidden. I didn't pick up the phone when they called. When they stopped by to get me I came outside but said I was otherwise engaged. Pini and I attended the same synagogue. One Shabbat, after the morning prayer, he approached me. His hand was full of Jordan almonds he'd swiped out of the Kiddush plates. The pink, powder blue, and white sugar coatings had melted into his palm. Why is he so gross? I thought. Pini asked if I wanted to join them at the game that afternoon. I told him I had Mishnah class.

You're still going to that? Pini marveled. Why? You're going to the religious homeroom, isn't that enough?

I shrugged. Pini asked why I was wandering so much. I told him I had no idea what he was talking about. He said he came by to get me on Tuesday and Tova told him I was out, that I was wandering outside all day long. I said she was just talking, the most incessant nagger. Pini licked the colorful roux from his sweaty palm. Then he slipped a piece of candy into his mouth with a quick, snaky motion. The sound of its grinding traveled from one end of the synagogue to the next.

I like plants, Ehud finally said. He collected the crumbs that had fallen onto his clothes and gathered them in the wax paper. Then he kissed the bundle. We both muttered a quick, truncated food blessing. Ehud said, I would eat nothing but plants, but my father says it goes against religion.

AT THE END OF THE DAY I CONCLUDED THAT SO FAR EHUD WAS only better than me at math. I surpassed him in every other important subject, like Gmarah and Jewish history. But Ehud suspected nothing. I lowered myself. Why motivate Ehud to work harder than he already was, that nerd? I took the long way home. Not that I wanted to evade Dudi and Pini, who were waiting at the quad outside the middle school. It seemed like they were only waiting so they could turn their backs on me anyway. A silence fell between us, a stifled silk of words. I turned around and walked the other way.

Ahuva knew my father in his final days of heroism. That's what she said. Her husband worked for the rabbinate, for the venerable Rabbi Avisror, she said. He also volunteered in Naftaly Spector's mayoral campaign. It's too bad he lost, she said. We got stuck with that old posse again, she said. This whole town is headed for devastation, she said. How can we expect change? she said. Is this where we hoped our children would grow up? she said. But her husband, she said, was a lowly activist, not like Simo Farkash. They should have found someone like my father to run the rec center, she said. He came to their house once, she said. What a man, she said, he walked in and the house lit up, she said. A man's man, she said. Like a lion, she said. People like him are one in a million, she said. The kind that know how to rule with an iron fist at the right time, she said. She was so sorry to hear about what happened, she said. She remembered exactly where she was when she heard it, she said. It was at the grocery store that had just opened, she said. Waiting in line for the delicatessen, she said. They have amazing pickles, she said. Even better than how her mother made them, she said. She felt weak at the knees, she said. She never knew what that meant before, she said, her knees were the strongest bones in her body. But then she felt that faintness, in line at the delicatessen, standing there with her knees trembling. Her knees buckled, meaning they were swept up from under her, she said. She almost fell down, she said. She knew things weren't easy at home, she said. But that's no excuse, she said. She wouldn't accept any unruliness on my part, she said. Even though she was aware of my situation she wouldn't play favorites, she said. You have to get ahold of yourself, she said. Whips and scorpions, she said. Redemption can only be bought through suffering, she said. Go out to the quad now, she said, you've taken up half of my recess with your disruptions.

I climbed up the sandy slope. I walked along the fence until I found an opening. As soon as a fence is erected in Sderot, along comes a breach. They appear of their own volition, by virtue of the mere existence of the fence. No human agency is involved in the misdemeanor, but another agency must be. That's how it goes.

The municipal pool, the tennis court, the rec center yard—a hole in the metallic layers flanking them is torn as soon as they are rolled out.

I WENT TO EHUD'S HOUSE AFTER THE SUKKOT DINNER. EHUD said, Why don't you come over? It would be the first year I didn't play Rummikub with Dudi and Pini. They didn't bother inviting me, but there was no need for an invitation. We'd kept the ritual ever since first grade, when Sabah, Dudi, and I involuntarily fought back against the six graders. We'd been sitting on the benches in the gym, waiting for the phys ed teacher. Four older kids came in, one of them holding a soccer ball. They were huge. Two of them guarded the door, and one, skinnier and shorter than the rest, yelled at the boys from my class to line up against the wall. The one carrying the ball placed it on the floor, pointed at it, and said, The ugly one on the left with the Gonzo nose.

He gained momentum and kicked the ball, which hit the boy he'd targeted in the stomach. The boy doubled over, fell to the floor, and screamed.

Shut your mouth, said the kicker, shut your mouth and sit back down.

My classmate walked away, submissive and hunched. His hand was anesthetizing his stomach, swirling around the spot of the blow. The kicker walked over to the two guards at the door and switched places with one of them. That entire time, the evil gaze of the short, skinny one kept us frozen in place. The former guard reached the ball and rolled it back to the front of the gym with swift kicks.

Kick it over here, said the skinny short guy.

Give me a break, said the former guard, it's my turn now.

Kick it, kick, before I jump on you, said the short, skinny one.

Ugh, you suck balls, said the former guard, kicking the ball over.

You see that little twerp in the middle? said the short, skinny one.

Which one, said the former guard, that chubster? You're picking an easy target.

Ha, said the short, skinny one. Easy, dickwad? I'm going to get him in the balls.

He moved back and put his whole body into the kick. The sound of the side of his shoe meeting the leather patch of the ball as it shot through the air toward the rotund classmate echoed through the empty gym. The classmate moved aside. The ball smacked against the wall behind him and flew back.

You see the insolence? said the former guard.

Roll that ball over here and stand where we tell you, said the short, skinny one.

My eyes magnetized onto the rotund classmate. On the verge of tears, he said, I don't feel like it.

Held breath fluttered against my chest. I felt as if a chain that had been wrapped around my body had melted away in the fallen silence, in the heart of horror, in the heart of horrid obedience, in the heart of the power that governed my limbs. And out of the spot of quiet, the howling of the other classmates rose. They screamed and began to scamper around the gym. The giddiness of the older students exacerbated. The former guard kicked the ball, hard. It hit the feet of a classmate, who faceplanted.

You better not let me catch someone who already got hit still standing, the short, skinny one yelled, or I'll kick their asses.

The ball got another kid in the back and shot him forward. In the chaos, I searched for the rebellious classmate. He was standing with another classmate on the sidelines, examining the hunt. I flanked a few boys and walked over to them. They were whispering. From within the racket rose the call of the short, skinny guy, Leave me the chubster, cross my heart and hope to die I'm going to blow him away, heaven can't help him right now, I'm not leaving until I tear him a new one.

I said, They're not allowed to do this, someone should call the princi—

The rebellious classmate said, They won't let us out. He watched the chaos some more and said, We need to get their ball.

The other classmate said, And then what?

I said, Run away with it.

Yeah, said the rebellious classmate, but they won't let us out. Up there, that window is open.

I looked toward where the rebellious classmate pointed. He was right. Almost. We would have to pass at least two of the older students on the way to the staircase leading to the balcony seats.

We need bait, I said.

Yeah, said the rebel, try to pull them in and—

But he wants you, I said, he want—

Yeah, said the other classmate, he won't chase us.

The rebellious classmate looked over the gym. Then he said quietly, Okay.

I joined the other classmates in their helpless running. I passed by another kid who'd been intercepted, zigzagged between two older students, and paused at the bottom of the staircase. Then I hid behind it. The rebellious classmate burst into the center of the gym, waving his arms.

A smile emerged on the lips of the short, skinny one, spreading, stretching, jagged. Someone threw the ball to him. He gained momentum again and kicked. The ball hit the rebel in the shoulder, then bounced to the floor of the gym, spasmodic little bounces toward the other classmates. He snatched it and ran to the staircase, straight toward two of the older boys. Their bodies hardened in place. I was already climbing up the stairs, almost at the balcony. The other classmate paused, ducked, and threw the ball at me as hard as he could. The ball hit my arm, but as Nahum, I was unable to take hold of it. It rolled along the balcony, its trajectory blocked by the pile of green exercise mats.

Get him, the short, skinny one shouted, why are you standing there like lemons?

I grabbed the ball and looked over my shoulder. The two older students were bounding up the stairs. I rushed to the open window. A blue sheet speckled with white mold stretched against an aluminum frame, and somewhere in the distance was a dull antenna, a disruption to the field of vision. I threw the ball. The two older students paused beside me and stared outside. I turned to look as well. The ball flew into the courtyard. For some reason, the principal was standing right at the center of the yard, looking around, smoking.

IT WAS STRANGE TO WALK INTO EHUD'S ROOM DURING A HOLI-day. A kind of still set, an array of objects rendered unusable by the sacred occasion. Ehud pointed at his computer, a keyboard connected to a small, blackened screen, adjacent to a small tape recorder. That's where he saved his programs. He learned BASIC last year. The silenced splendor the room was immersed in, the familiar scent of fresh linens, made me sick. I said, What are these programs?

Ehud said, I'm programming. You know what sine and cosine are?

I nodded.

Ehud said, Tri-go-no-met-ric func-tions.

I said, Why are you talking like a retard?

Ehud said, Those are hard words, I couldn't pronounce them at first either.

I said, What do they do, these words?

Ehud said, Don't you think they're pretty words?

I said, Pretty words? What's pretty about words?

Ehud said, The way they sound.

I said, But what are they?

Ehud said, It's like a relationship between a triangle's sides. It's too bad it's a holiday, I would have drawn you a picture.

I said, I still don't get what it's good for.

Ehud said, It's a little complicated. You can use them in programming to make repeating shapes, like flower shapes. That's why I got a computer. My uncle said that . . . in nature there are all sorts of shapes that . . . I can't explain it well. It's too bad it's a holiday, I would have shown you on my computer.

I continued to examine the room. The walls were anointed midnight blue, and the wall with the window was strewn with artificial stars. The wall across from it had an artful drawing of a series of ovals surrounding the sun, each of them shining, in the hushed lights of the space, with a celestial body over its name. I lingered over the drawing. I said, Isn't this star worship, like the pagans do?

No way, said Ehud, my uncle's religious, but he's also a scientist. He said the Jews were masters of star theory. Astrologers.

I said, Go out of your astrology.

What, said Ehud.

I said, God told Abraham, go out of your astrology.

Oh, said Ehud, I didn't know.

He led me into the kitchen. The counter twinkling in place, the rinsed dishes upside down in their rack, the porcelain burning in its harsh white. I wanted to touch, to touch, to feel their reality. Ehud pulled on the screen door that led outside, then pushed the door out. I was spat after him onto a treaded path, a yard, a sukkah.

But before, when I was about to step outside, when I was hesitating like the door between inside and out, I spotted the glowing of the sukkah. Palatial light emerged through the dark fabrics, beaming out of the frond roof. A moon glared in the heavenly well, wrapped with the melancholic halo of the month of Tishrei. I paused on the path. Ehud turned around and urged me to move on. He pushed the curtain aside for me. The light erupted, spilling

out. Tacky streamers hung from the roof, cheap glass pomegranates, shabby paper chandeliers, each surrounding an electric furnace slaving to make heat. The fabric walls, on the other hand, were
adorned with drawings. No, some kind of small, white engravings.
I easily identified the biblical occasions they depicted. Adam and
Eve, Cain and Abel, the binding of Isaac, Jacob's ladder, Joseph in
the pit, Joseph interpreting the pharaoh's dreams, Mount Sinai,
delicate, developed, dedicated laces. I could look at them for
hours, tracing every detail, Elijah and the prophets of Ba'al, David
and Goliath, Daniel in the lion's den, a wall from which—

Ehud touched my back, poking his finger between my verte-
brae. Bone against bone without the mediation of flesh. I jumped.
He said with pleasure, Pretty, isn't it?

I asked if the engravings were store-bought. Where did they
get them?

Ehud said, My aunt made them, papercutting. He pointed at
the opening and whispered, Let's go outside.

Hang on, I want to—

Ehud pulled on my shirt. Come on.

A figure stood between the house and the sukkah. She was the
size of a young girl, but there was a weight of years about her
stance. I, meaning I, am saying it was as if the skeleton had de-
spaired of supporting the body, the accumulated time within it,
each cell carrying within it, densely, the history of the cells it had
replaced, and the futures it had to look forward to, emerging into
the world and vanishing from it almost simultaneously, separated
by the splitting of seconds, elementary particles whose accumulated mass was capable of crumbling tissues, calcium, and colla-
gen fibers. But how could I-Nahum notice anything in the passage
from great light to partial darkness? Of course I could not.

THE REBELLIOUS CLASSMATE AND THE OTHER ONE SHARED THE
same name, David. For the first time, I listened when the teacher

took attendance. I didn't dare address them. I watched them fighting by the water fountain in the yard for the right of first drink. Round David pushed Long David, and Long David stumbled before lunging at Round David's back, wrapping his arms around his neck, until Round David kneeled onto the dirt. Long David let go, skipped ahead, and leaned over the push button on the edges of the concrete basin. His chin reached for the tap. Round David pulled on the ends of his pants, hard, dragging him down to the floor tiles. An older girl walked over their recumbent bodies and leaned over for a drink. The two of them burst out laughing, a balling, smooth laughter against a coarse, panting laughter. They exchanged meek blows. I was sitting on the top step, near the gate.

They didn't stay on the ground for long. All of a sudden, Long David jumped up, slapped the back of Round David's neck, and broke into a run. Round David didn't lag behind. I was surprised he wasn't out of breath, marveled at the speed with which he caught up with Long David. At the end of the school day, on my way back home, I found them walking just a few meters ahead of me. I kept my distance. I wondered if our paths would diverge when we reached the large thicket, the start of the shortcut into the neighborhood. I preferred not to go there. A gorge cut through the thicket, deep and jagged. At its bottom was a constant, dampish, reeking scum. Two thick spill pipes, bound with tar and asbestos, bridged over it. They emerged from one dirt wall and were swallowed into each another, suspended in air, exposed to the cruelty of gravity and the fluctuations of climate. One pipe stretched over the narrow edge of the gorge, the other hovered over a gaping pit, crosswise.

My father showed me the thicket shortcut at the end of summer break. On rainy days, he told me to walk through proper streets. But as long as it was dry, he instructed me not to waste any time, taking the short way home. He pulled me behind him all the way to the pipe, ordering me to cross the gorge over the short pipe, which he nicknamed the little bridge. I stared into the abyss. Simo Farkash, in his final days of heroism, gave me a push, saying, *Yallah*, we haven't got all day, with Baby Tova and the new baby on the way, I had to figure things out on my own. I thought, Baby Tova and the new baby on the way, that's all I ever hear about. Once, in a moment of disobedience drawn from self-pity, I answered, but that isn't my fault. I, meaning I, know for sure that I-Nahum would believe in my own fault for many years to come, insinuated and joked about, as if giving birth to me had blocked my mother's womb until that putrid Baby Tova came along, gathering into her all the bitterness experienced by Msodi Farkash in her four years of infertility. I tried to plant my feet in the ground and my father said that was too bad, that I wouldn't be coming back home until I crossed to the other side of the gorge, the one closer to school. It didn't matter if I cried, or even if an angel came down from the sky to plead my case. Because I did cry. I really cried.

Mihlo'a, said my father. How did I, Simo Farkash, get such a *mihlo'a* kid?

I measured the bottom of the gorge with my eyes. There was a story about a kid from a previous generation who'd fallen in. When he climbed back up he was covered in mire that never came off. He was exempt from military service because of the greenish glow of his skin. How could he lie in ambush, all glittering? Go on, *ya mihlo'a*, do it sitting down if you have to, my father said.

I sat down on the pipe and stretched my arms along it. I lowered onto my stomach and crawled carefully to the other end. Simo Farkash, in his final days of heroism, did not disguise his contempt. In the days that followed, he nicknamed me, with a tone of sneaky affection, worm boy. And I felt the flush, the tingling, the bristling of tar and asbestos refilling the flesh of my chest, my stomach, my arms.

Be that as it may, David and David paused at the entrance to the thicket and turned around. Their tanness almost blended into the darkness of the thicket. They sloughed off their detailed images, turning into abstract sketches of shadow. Together, I remember thinking, they looked like a soccer score, 1 0, missing only the colon. My father often said there was nothing better than 1:0 games. The games where one team schools the other, you could shove up your ass. In 1:0 games there's none of that luck bullshit or uneven bullshit, no way one team is strong and the other weak. Talent only shows when hardly any difference exists.

You coming? Long David shouted needlessly. I was already standing next to them. I forced my feet to keep still, but they walked on. A wave of gratitude washed over me, and I knew it would soon be replaced with tears, so I just nodded my head vigorously.

Yes or no? said Round David.

I was taken aback. I'd agreed enthusiastically, failing only to speak. I walked all the way over and stood in line with them.

Got any marbles? asked Round David.

I shook my head no.

You can borrow mine, said Long David. You can borrow them, but . . . only for one game, okay? I already owe Sabah and Pini.

Pini's name fell out of the ring choking my throat. I was mystified.

Yeah, Pini Pita, said Long David. He removed the yarmulke from his head, folded it, and slipped it into his back pocket. The two of you are neighbors, right?

Pini Pita, I said.

We moved deeper into the thicket. The eucalyptuses emitted the saltiness of summer, the thickness of tense sunny hours, the bright dimness of the night of the soil, in which their roots sang.

Long David said, Sabah came up with that name. He's good with names. Maybe he'll give you one too.

I'm fine with Nahum, I said.

Long David looked at Round David and said, No, something else.

I told Round David, And you, what name did he give you?
Long David laughed. He's Sabah, you idiot.

I said nothing. I thought they'd switched laughs. The balling laughter should have been Round David's, not Long David's. Through a trembling mouth, Long David added, I'm Dudi and he's Sabah.

THEY SAID THE FIRST RAIN WOULD COME AROUND THE SECOND festival of Sukkot. Chantal ran amok between different sukkahs and reported back to me. It's going to rain, she said, agitated, and all the sukkahs will get wrecked. She added that she and Tova had to go see Barda's sukkah, which had won the best-looking sukkah award, and how come ours never wins, forget how much work the Barda family puts into it, Tova says the contest is rigged. I asked what Barda family she was talking about. Chantal said, The one on Ron Shukrun Street, what, haven't you heard, where've you been, they wrote about it in the *Southern Wind.*

I thought about the crude streamers my sisters made, the clumsy poster board cuttings.

Chantal said, Is it true Ron Shukrun was a soldier who jumped on a grenade to save his soldier friends?

I nodded, but I didn't really have any idea. I said I knew Ehud Barda, that I would give him a call.

Chantal narrowed her eyes at me. I said, He's in my homeroom.

Chantal said, And you'd really do that, for us, because we were going to climb up their neighbors' fence to peek.

We crossed the villa neighborhood on the way to the Bardas'. In one front yard, behind a black iron gate, roses had begun to die in their beds. The petals of other flowers glistened. Chantal ran to the gate and pushed her face against the bars. A little girl was sitting on the doorstep, watching the three of us. I tried to pull Chantal away, but her body resisted. Tova persisted in her nagging, which had begun the moment we left home, about how I'd failed to tell them I was Ehud's friend, and why I never invited him over, and why was that gross Pini the only one who ever came by, and how most of the time when he comes over I pretend not to be home and she has to lie to him for me. I switched from pulling to persuading, Chantal frozen-limbed in her refusal, her eyes drinking in the sights while Tova hummed. This lasted long minutes, until finally the little girl began to bleat, Mommy, mommy, there are scary kids out here.

Chantal tore off the gate at once, turning toward Tova. Shut up, she said, shut up, all you do is complain, if I were Nahum I'd send you home.

I don't think so, said Tova. You're not going to do that, right, Nahum?

I said nothing. Ehud waited by the gate to his house, mighty, hard wooden planks, reinforced with lead. He led us down the path that went around the house. At the edge of the path was an empty doghouse. Chantal asked what happened to the dog. Ehud said they had to get rid of him. He used to bark at Ehud's mother like mad. They tolerated that, but when his aunt came over he jumped on her and would have bitten her if his father hadn't pulled him by the collar.

Did you kill him? Tova asked with excitement.

No, Ehud cried. Why would we kill Geiseric? He stood in place, staring at the doghouse. They took their places alongside him.

What kind of dog was he? Chantal asked.

Bor-der Col-lie, said Ehud, softly this time. One of his ears was broken, he was really smart, but we couldn't train him to tell friends from intruders, that's what my dad said.

When I grow up and have a house, said Chantal, I'll have six, no, seven dogs, and they'll live upstairs, and if . . . if one of them acts out he'll have to go to his room.

She gasped at the end of her sentence and looked at Ehud. Her tongue ran over a loose baby tooth and the empty spaces in her smile.

In your dreams, said Tova. Disgusting animals. All they do is bark and bite, why did God even create them?

Ehud said, It's a shame we had to give Geiseric over to a shelter.

I would have taken him, Chantal said, but I wouldn't give him a name that sounds like "geyser."

What name would you give him? said Ehud.

Cocoa, said Chantal. Cocoa Pup.

Ehud laughed and kept on walking. Chantal's cheeks flushed. In daylight the sukkah appeared less ominous, less defiant. Ehud walked inside with my sisters. Big deal, I thought, it's just pieces of paper. And again I saw her, the figure appeared out of nowhere, a worldly swell of skin and bones. I, meaning I, can be more accurate here and say she was devoid of the weight of existence of Sukkot, the density of history, which was merely a spasm in time, the outburst of matter's pretense to resist chaos. I could assess her age. She must have been younger than my mother and Ms. Ahuva Dadon, only slightly older than the soldier-teachers that for some reason were swarming through town. Suddenly, I realized she was looking back at me, no, that more than I was examining her, I was the object of her examination. I lowered my head. She asked, Why don't you go into the sukkah too?

I said I was just chaperoning my sisters.

She asked if I wasn't interested in the papercuttings, they seemed to be the talk of the town, at least among the religious crowd.

I wanted to ask why the papercuttings were arranged in the same order as they were in the Bible. When I walked into the sukkah on the holiday eve, I looked to the right out of force of habit, and the sequence started with the story of Eden and continued counterclockwise. I restrained myself and said, Not really, looking up at her.

The aunt smiled, her lips stretching. A crack in her façade was somewhat revealed. I, meaning I, can say that the same thread of emptiness that was stretched through Simo Farkash's eyes was revealed. As if he, back in his heroism days, was concealed inside of a perfect double of himself, wearing a wax mask of his face; only in the irises, in a budding of a gaze, could one detect the gap between the man and the man's cloaking. The aunt said she'd heard about my father's collapse at Spector's campaign headquarters eighteen months earlier. She said, What exactly happened to him?

I pursed my lips.

She said I didn't have to tell her if I didn't want to.

I called out, Tova, Chantal, we're going home.

Tova walked quickly out of the sukkah. Ugly pictures, she grumbled, they look like lumps of poop, our sukkah is a thousand times—

Her words were snatched out of her mouth when she noticed the aunt. The aunt shot Tova a ridiculing look and turned away from us. She took measured steps down the path back into the house, as if every step involved risk and calculation. Her hips swayed.

But it's true, Tova said once the aunt was swallowed into the house, it's true, ours is much nicer, Chantal and I did it ourselves, without help from grown-ups, it isn't fair.

I wanted to ask the aunt more questions—why the final papercutting showed the ghost hand emerging out of the wall in Belshazzar's feast, why the hand alone without the letters? Chantal, I said again.

Tova said, She's sucking up to Ehud, that idiot.

I hardened my voice. Chantal.

What, what, she said from inside. I want to look a little longer.

Ehud stepped outside. He asked if I could stay. I said I couldn't let my sisters walk home all by themselves.

I GOT HOME THAT AFTERNOON LOOKING WILD FROM PLAYING IN the thicket with Sabah and Dudi, whom I'd just met, and with

Pini, who joined us. My school T-shirt got stained with whatever stained it, and my mother looked me over with restraint. She was busy weaning Tova, who cried bitterly whenever our mother attempted to feed her vegetable puree or baby cereal. The new pregnancy imbued my mother with a new strength and patience. I heard people saying she was glowing. Neighbors and random friends who ran into her at the old shopping center, at the grocery store, said she looked healthier than she'd been in years, even prettier than she was in her golden age, when she was seventeen. But simultaneously she was alert to any signal of change, as if sensing that her luck would not last long. She placed Tova in her bassinet. Tova punched the walls of the bassinet and screamed.

How she yells, this kid, our mother repeated. Nahum was such an easy baby. Our father once said she didn't live up to her name—Tova, Hebrew for "good"—but that she might grow into it. Our mother said nature was nature, and no matter how much nurture and rules you heap over it, it always breaks through, and this one, just wait and see what she's going to put us through when she hits puberty.

What's wrong? she asked. Did somebody beat you up?

No, I said, I was playing with friends.

Friends, she said. I saw a spark of suspicion lighting her eyes.

Yes, I said, Sabah and Dudi and Pini.

Pini Lazmi, said my mother, so now he's your friend.

No, I said, he's friends with Dudi and Sabah.

I don't know a Sabah family, my mother said, are they new in town?

With sweeping enthusiasm, I told her about how I'd finally managed to cross that small bridge on the way home, standing up. I'd hid the fact that I'd still been taking the long way home through the neighborhoods and the projects from my father. When I confirmed to him on the first day of school that I'd taken the shortcut, my mother could tell I was lying. She kept my secret. She told my father she wouldn't let me take that big a risk just to save fifteen minutes. Now I refrained from showing her the note from the vice principal that I had in my bag.

Yes, I said, Sabah showed me how. What's for lunch?

I kept my stained clothes on as I sat down to do my homework. I leaned over the exercise book I'd opened on the dining table and traced my pencil over the square letters and the vowelization below them. I shaped my lips around their pronunciation soundlessly. There was something else in me. The letters and the vowelization ran through my body, their heat making me shiver. The name Farkash blazed through them and died out within them, losing its shape and finding it once more. Sabah had decided that's what they'd call me, before Pini even got there. Back in the thicket, he said, You're half this and half that.

I said nothing.

Dudi turned to him, his voice tensing, lingering. Half this and half that?

Sabah said, Like half a fart and half a cashmere sweater.

They both laughed their confused laugh, their switched laugh. I tried the name out on the margins of my notebook, in unsteady lines, over and over, rolling it down from my mind through the etching fingers. I didn't notice my father when he entered. In his final days of heroism, his presence used to fill the place. He patted the back of my neck. I flinched. The purrs of pleasure quickly evaporated out of my blood vessels and nervous system.

What are you doing, sitting in this filth? my father said.

I widened my eyes. I'd forgotten to clean the table. Reddish drops of oil tinged the plastic cover of my textbook.

Get a cloth, my father said.

When I got up he must have noticed the marks of dirt and eucalyptus on my shirt. He grabbed my arm. Who hit you? he asked.

I said, Nobody.

I saw signs of hunger in Simo Farkash's features, the scrunching of the nose and the tensing of the jaw. I knew there was no way of alleviating them. I depicted my day—the game of marbles, Sabah's sudden announcement of boredom with marbles, how he'd split us up into pairs, picking me as his partner, and how we had to find bendy eucalyptus branches and sneak about through the trees, ambushing, deflecting, and swatting one another by surprise, and how Sabah had turned out to be a master of strategy, because he and I, using all sorts of methods he'd taught me, continuously surprised our opponents, evading almost all of their lashings. I marveled at the urgency that accompanied the events as I recounted them. I, meaning I, know how to be accurate. Before my Nahum eyes, the heat of noon in the thicket, the exposed area where we played, the light stretched between the leaves as I looked up at the sky, the smell of dirt, the roughness of tree trunks, the wild weeds itching and scratching the ankles, all reappeared at full force. Every detail received greater concreteness than what I-Nahum was aware of at the time, when I was immersed in action, in attentiveness toward others' intentions. Perhaps because I-Nahum seemed to be watching it all from the outside, knowing that without the dubbing skills of the viewer I'd become against my will, the force of my gaze that gripped them, the events would have lost their vitality. But there may have not been any vitality in the first place, it being added now only by virtue of my attention to the changing expressions on Simo Farkash's face, the way the actions reflected in his mask of muscle and twitches.

I carried on in decisive sentences, about the gym, the note in my bag, like smoldering coal scorching the notebooks and writing implements.

Sabah, huh, said my father. I don't know him.

My flow of words dwindled. My tongue was imprisoned in my mouth once more.

He's not an imaginary friend, is he?

I shook my head. I could feel the ring of tears tightening around my breath. My father rummaged through my bag and fished out the note that informed my parents of a disruption during gym class, warning that the school would not tolerate any similar behavior in the future. He pulled a pen from his pocket and sketched his signature in the margins. Don't tell Mom, he said, rubbing my head.

THE SOUND OF AVALANCHES, THE THUNDER OF TUMBLING ROCKS rolled through the hollow space of the dream. I startled awake, sitting up. In the evening, boulder clouds, shale clouds, were standing in the sky. In the middle of the night, the clouds cracked, roots of light and beats of glimmer. Those striving and crumbling from within, those shattering their hardness from without. Within the blur, a corpuscle of thought formed, Belshazzar's palace with the gold and silver dishes stolen by his father, Nebuchadnezzar, from the Jewish temple, his wife and mistresses around the feast. Then the thought turned into a cascade. I envisioned the first rain. Its hesitant drops were already drizzling through the air of Sderot. I imagined it washing the papercuttings in the Barda sukkah, first breaking through the roof, the dense leaves, wetting the wooden beams, the palm fronds, then trickling to the innards of burning flares, shorting them, bathing the glass pomegranates and crystal chandeliers with the dust it collected on the way, and finally ripping off the papercuttings in the order in which they'd been hung, letting them fall from the rain-drenched fabric to the damp ground, wounded, the perforations and light and shadow tricks that afforded them depth and life deforming, wrinkling, the slaughtering knife, the ladder, the tablets of stone, the shofars of Jericho, all the powerful objects of the mighty ministers of Israel breaking in the thunder of water, the miracles and acts of redemption dissolving in puddles, and only the final papercutting, with the ghost hand emerging from the wall of the banquet hall of the Chaldean king, survives, stamped into the fabric by the force of the flood.

I was titillated by the changing images. A tickle rose from my diaphragm to my vocal cords, poured into my jaw muscles. I almost laughed out loud, but then I heard the pacing around the house, which stopped as soon as it invaded my consciousness. I wondered if I was dreaming this wakefulness. And I listened, I listened. Only my mother's punctuated snores. Air pulled with an effort, then the silence of a slow exhalation. And my father's sighs were gone. My attentiveness toward the house weakened, then turned outward, to the deluge short-changing summertime. The pacing—energetic, determined—sounded once again. The rhythm of my father's pacing in his final days of heroism. I pricked my ears again. Only the sounds of sleep, excepting Simo Farkash's sighs, filled the house. Within this alertness, my consciousness resumed its wandering toward the orphaned, unreal realms of sleep.

MY PARENTS HAD GROWN USED TO SABAH'S AND DUDI'S PRESences in our home. My mother loathed Pini. Pini's mother, she claimed, was the town gossip, a contentious woman, and her husband supported her without question. Mrs. Lazmi had made many enemies. My mother would never forget the day when Mrs. Lazmi spread a rumor at the market that Simo Farkash was infertile, and how my mother, having investigated and questioned and tracked down the source of the slander, was astounded when she carefully asked Pini's father to instruct his wife to correct her error and admit her lie to her friends. The husband chuckled and said his wife had yet to be wrong, trust him, he knew from experience.

But Pini was friends with everybody, and he was an inseparable part of our group. He was the best soccer player out of all of us, as it turned out when Simo Farkash decided to coach us. Simo walked into my room without warning, soccer ball in hand. He said we were spending too much time on our asses, not moving

our bodies. I followed the calculating look Sabah fixed on my father. I knew him. A plan or scheme was coming together in the
back of his mind. Either that, or he did not appreciate the disruption. We were deep into a game of Go Fish that Sabah had convinced us to make. We used Garbage Pail Kids cards, scratching
out the original character names and pasting the names of our
classmates instead. I did not understand the logic according to
which our classmates were divided into categories.

Dudi got up first. I glanced around the room before we left.
The cards were polluting the design of the carpet with their disorder, some facedown, the bits of paper glued to them peeking out
around the edges.

Dudi was fast and agile, but his long legs bumped into the ball
constantly. Sabah huffed dramatically, dragging himself around
the makeshift field. I did my best. Pini's kicks were precise, his
limbs coordinated. Simo Farkash soon began referring to us as
shoelace, lardball, wimp, and Pelé, firmly ordering us around. The
sky above burned, a white canopy of autumn afternoon glare.
At some point, Sabah grabbed his side, paused for a long moment,
then threw up. My father said, Such a *dbeih*, it's disgusting.

But Dudi was the one to inform me the next day that we
weren't going to hang out at my place anymore, and that soccer
was a lame game, and they'd decided to start practicing basketball, and that I could stick around if I wanted to. At first we stumbled ungracefully, trying to master dribbling, failing in our
attempts to shoot the ball into the basket in motion. Dudi pretended to teach us the drills. Maybe because he was tall he
thought he would show a natural knack for the game. Sabah gave
up first, standing around, sweating. Pini and I followed suit. Dudi
continued in his efforts until finally Sabah yelled at him, Shoelace, and Dudi answered, Lardball. The two of them doubled over
with laughter on opposite sides of the court. Their laughters
crashed into each other, ringing and echoing, metallic clanging.
They practiced shooting hoops from different distances. In the

course of ongoing trial, beneath the thin cloudiness, one said, Shoelace, and the other responded, Lardball, and they chuckled. When I came home that night, Dad asked why I was late and where my friends were. He'd returned early from work especially to continue our coaching sessions. I said, We prefer basketball. Simo Farkash muttered, Oh, and his green eyes hardened into two pieces of flint.

During fourth-grade Passover break, Sabah told us his family was going to leave Sderot at the end of the school year. They were moving to Netanya. Dudi looked down, and I watched the movement in his throat, which corresponded with how I felt. Pini said he knew it already, his mom had told him two months ago. Sabah said that was nonsense, his father had only been told about the promotion and the transfer a few days before Purim.

Then why are you only telling us now? Dudi yelled.

Because I didn't know, said Sabah.

During that vacation, we transferred our center of activity from the big thicket to a denser thicket across the road that flanked the soccer field, bordering Sderot from that side. The new thicket was enormous, unending, clung to by a fear of danger, some fecundity of growth, and water that had been standing in puddles since winter, dirt paths twisting constantly. Herons parked on the branches, swaying in the light breeze. Other birds chirped crookedly.

In our tours, we made it all the way to the outskirts of Sderot, where Dudi and Sabah taunted Pini to cross the deserted road and enter between the trees to bring back some testimony, a souvenir.

Big deal, said Pini, just another thicket. He walked slowly. I dawdled behind him with a pounding heart. Dudi and Sabah cheered from behind. Pini was swallowed among the tree trunks. I entered behind him. I slowly crossed from sunlight to pleasant shade. I, meaning I, know how each footstep carries its other quality, the warmth peeling off the skin, the dimming of the gaze,

the light chill of darkness contained within the blood, in the pro-
teinaceous codes, answering the darkness outside. Pini's voice as
he whispered my name startled me with its crudeness. My senses
opened up to take in the aerial movement of leaves, the deep
scent of nature left to its own devices for long enough.

Pini leaned down and picked up an old bottle of detergent
from the ground. He patted it a few times, bits of dirt falling off.
All right, I said, can we go back now?

No, Pini said, let's walk around a little more.

They're waiting for us, I said.

Let them wait, said Pini. Let's see if they come looking for us.

I froze in place and turned my head toward the road.

Come on, said Pini, those two are all talk.

I followed him in silence, occasionally glancing over my shoulder. The trees were all confusingly similar. Not like in the large
thicket, where experience garbed them in familiarity and uniqueness. Eventually, we arrived at some closed, asymmetrical clearing.
At the far end from where we came from, to our left, was a wide,
mossy, moldy eucalyptus stump. It was grazed by the brightness
that greened from its passage through foliage. The trees flanking
the bald space seemed to be retreating unevenly and uncoordinat-
edly from the stump, each according to its own level of dread.

Feel that power, said Pini. This is not the kind of place you
forget. With the detergent bottle in his hand, he tapped the trunks
around him. The sound of his tapping startled me. I heard a distant flutter of wings. Pini did not seem concerned, either about
losing our way or about disrupting the rustling peace. On the
contrary—with his round, milky face, his small ears and fleshy
snout, his orange hair that was buzzed almost down to the scalp,
Pini was in his rightful place, bathed in the ancient nature of the
thicket. He said, They're probably arguing right now about whether
or not to come in here. Sabah is saying no and Dudi is saying yes.

How do you know, I said.

I know them, said Pini, especially Sabah.

Me too, I said.

You don't know them at all, he said, you're excited about them.

So what?

So, Pini said, Sabah is friends with no one.

That's not true, I said, he's—

Pita, Farkash, Dudi's call cut through the air, more frightening than Pini tapping the tree trunks.

Pini placed a finger against his lips. We paused motionlessly, waiting with tense muscles.

Get out already, Dudi shouted, where are you?

I pulled on Pini's arm. He nodded. We followed the voice until we saw Dudi. His figure sketched against the backdrop of the glimmer pent up by the trees on the edges of the thicket. My eyes adjusted easily to the glare of the month of Nissan. Sabah was standing across the road, within Sderot borders, gesticulating.

On the way back Dudi reported in a whisper that the place was safe. Sabah announced we would be taking a tour the next day in the place he called the outer thicket, but we ought to bring water and maybe food, otherwise he had no problem spending all day in the outer thicket. When Dudi and Sabah parted from us, Pini said, I told you.

What, I said.

That he's got his head up his ass, that Sabah. Even when we were just kids in the pool or on the slides he was a sneak. He'd wait on the side and watch to see which kid fell down and who pushed who and how it all happened. And then he'd join in. And the grown-ups would say, *Sabah al'hir ya* Dudu, we see you finally woke up.

AND AFTER THESE THINGS CAME TO PASS, IN AN AFTERNOON IN Marcheshvan, the final days of Simo Farkash's heroism had reached their end. The world was preparing for rain, for the year's purification from summer. At Naftaly Spector's campaign headquarters, fears exacerbated that the odds were against them. Rumors flowed in from the streets by sweaty messengers that rushed over to whisper in his ear. The Gabai familia, the pillar of the Spector voting public, had been cooking a covert deal with Spector's main opponent, then-mayor Eli Fahima. People said that Simo Farkash was enraged, they said he cursed God, they said he flipped tables over, they said he attacked Hannan Malka, his secret consultant and loyal spy at the Fahima headquarters, breaking one of his ribs. They said that all of a sudden, in the middle of the hubbub, his body went limp and he fell to the floor. He was rushed to the hospital in Ashkelon. I was sitting in the back seat of the car Spector sent to drive our mother to the hospital. The route passed by both thickets, the large thicket and the outer thicket. They both shrank in the window, blending into one tangle of trees, body odor, sun shards, accelerated heart rate.

Simo Farkash was bound to the bed. The nurse my mother tracked down with difficulty reported that he'd begun to go wild when he regained consciousness and found himself in a hospital. Simo Farkash opened his eyes the moment my mother touched him. What had he seen in his delusions during the brief sleep cast on him by the tranquilizers?

I saw, through the skin, how the skeleton anguished under the burden of the body. He grabbed my mother's hand and murmured, Msodi, get me out of here, don't let them operate.

Operate, said Msodi Farkash, what operate, you just got dehydrated from the effort.

Swear to me, Msodi.

She pulled her hand out of his with revulsion and ordered me to wait by the bed while she went to the front desk to find out what was going on.

I looked at my father, who was staring at the ceiling. It was as if his muscles had been emptied and then filled with mush or rubber. Then the print on the curtains around his hospital bed caught my attention. My eyes skipped from one spot to the next. Not spots—tiny, greenish, insignificant flowers. I pulled on the curtains until they closed around the two of us. A fragile but shut-off chamber.

What are you doing? my father sighed.

I said, So you can have some peace and quiet.

My father's expression was clean of any emotion or will. I was startled. Simo Farkash said, I'm not going to have a moment's peace.

At the cafeteria, waiting for our ride back, Msodi Farkash said, Your father's just exhausted, that's what they said. Mental frailty, have you ever heard of that?

My father's features were nothing more than high-end flesh machines put together without a blueprint. They were etched onto an interior panel that emerged in my mind without warning in the next few days. I thought miasma had invaded him.

At the synagogue it was as if I'd received permission. I woke up of my own volition on Saturday morning, washed my face and eyes of my own volition, rinsed my hands, and said a prayer. Of my own volition I grabbed my *tallit* and hurried out to the morning prayer. My organs were shaken during prayer time of their own volition. During break, Rabbi Amar approached me and asked how my mother was doing. I looked at him wordlessly. The rabbi said I would have to help out at home. Pini emerged from someplace and offered his hand.

Oh, Lazmi, said the rabbi. He searched his pocket and placed a piece of candy in Pini's palm. He looked me over and pulled out another piece of candy. I shook my head.

Come today, said the rabbi, come to read the Mishnah before the Minha prayer, it brings good health.

I continued to say nothing.

The rabbi said, I can see you're hesitating. Lazmi's going to be there too, aren't you, Lazmi?

Pini's teeth clicked against the candy.

The rabbi left. I stood before Pini wordlessly. He and Dudi and

I had spent election morning together, running from one polling place to the next, gathering ballots, then attending the older kids' basketball tournament. Then all of a sudden I was called home. But it seemed now as if we hadn't seen one another in an eternity, maybe even since the beginning of summer, when Sabah's family left Sderot, taking Sabah with them. That was the feel of it, judging by the words' refusal to form, the lingering of thought itself about what ought to be said. Maybe Pini didn't share this abyss of time and paralysis. He said reading the Mishnah was fun and that he'd convince Dudi to come too.

And Dudi did come. Slowly, we read words that were difficult to pronounce and to perceive, all about oaths and scapegoats and atonements. Rabbi Amar chose a volunteer from the veteran kids, someone I didn't know, to start the first Mishnah, then pointed at another kid. Ten kids, ten voices, ten different types of stutter. When my turn came, I read with trepidation about the malice in defiling the temple and its sacred objects, a scapegoat made on the inside and the atonement of Yom Kippur. The syllables were released into space, simultaneously hovering through me, and my spirit lifted the more my voice forged its path among the rocky utterances, a scapegoat sent out of its village.

EVER SINCE MY FATHER'S FINAL DAYS OF HEROISM CAME TO AN end, our mother forbade us from bringing up Sylvia, his younger sister. Simo Farkash lost his father before his mandatory military service, and his mother remarried and moved to Beit She'an. Simo Farkash would recount in a factual tone how he went to his stepfather's house immediately after he was honorably discharged to say goodbye to his sister and assure his mother that he would not say the Kaddish prayer for her. He told his sister that the moment she was old enough to leave home she was invited to come live in Sderot, where he was returning to start a life. I couldn't fathom what he was trying to prove by telling us this story. Perhaps he was attempting to offer evidence of his willpower, his decisiveness, the total loyalty he demanded of others and undertook to offer in return. All that mattered was that Simo Farkash kept both parts of his oath—to pay his sister's way through college and not to set foot at his stepfather's home. His mother wasn't even invited to his wedding.

All I have left of Sylvia is little shards of memory. Flickers and bursts of images. When I try to fish them out, they slip away. Then my thought turns sideways, and I think Sylvia's there, on the outskirts, standing before a gate leading into a past that had evaded me. I, meaning I, understand what this was about, an animal that could only be noticed through senses yet to be created. But once those senses were created, I would no longer be the I who wished to know it. And that's how one becomes trapped in memory's vise grip. To remember, one must transform into another, someone to whom that memory is a stranger.

I remember Sylvia had long, dark hair, always well brushed. It smelled warm and fresh when she leaned over me to help me with my homework. I remember her eyes, enormous, as dark as her hair, a flame of wonder whispered in their depths. I once heard her say, in response to my father's boasting, that the fluttering, unsteady essence of the extant is always discovered, and we are on our way to that discovery too. I remember she was short, and that over the course of third grade I almost caught up with her height. I remember she urged me to join her on her walks on summer evenings. Sabah referred to her simply as the aunt. Whenever I scored higher than him on a test he grumbled softly, It isn't his doing, it's the aunt. I remember the shock of her death.

In the month of Elul, a few months before Simo Farkash collapsed, she caught a peculiar flu, a fever that wouldn't relent, and dizziness. Her feet swelled. A few days later, she was rushed to the hospital, and at the hospital, what happened at the hospital, a virus discovered too late, complications, system failure. Sylvia wasn't hospitalized for long. She died twenty-four hours later.

My father was at her side the entire time. My mother said, What's Simo got to do there, she's in intensive care, he must be pacing the hallways like a madman, driving the doctors crazy. When he returned home with the news, his face was dried out, an ancient parchment mask cracked to reveal skull, sunken eye sockets, an exposed bit of cheekbone. He said, We should have taken her to the hospital sooner.

And that was it. She was unmarried. We sat shiva in our house, in the living room, the furniture pushed aside and mattresses spread along the walls. I watched the legions of neighbors toiling to rearrange the house, conducted by our mother. The burning of Elul was present inside, beaming from the bodies. The air steaming with their breath. The clean skies cut into the windows, and the screen door scorched like metal panels. Simo Farkash refused to receive condolences. Meaning he performed mourning customs, got up for prayer, said Kaddish, read the Mishnah over her grave, but he didn't answer condolence visitors' questions about what had happened. Even those who remembered or were persuaded to remember Sylvia's childhood in Sderot were not able to get him to cooperate in reminiscing. Their description of her sweetness and even-keeled temper, the halo of holiness their words formed, all remained unanswered. Parents who'd hired her to prepare their children for their high school finals came by to sing her praises. Simo Farkash listened in silence.

He only spoke about a single topic, and he kept it brief. He had no intention of resigning from Naftaly Spector's campaign, he announced to Spector himself and his colleagues. After visiting the grave and rising from shiva, Simo took me for a dip in the *mikveh* bath. For the first time since I was a toddler, I saw him completely naked. His thighs thick, the skin of the genitals purpling in contact with the air, his ribs arranged like wings under a hard chest split by a thin fuzz. His biceps swelled when his hands gripped the railing as he descended into the bubbling stream that moved against the stainless steel bottom. The hair that fell from his body flickered blackly against the water, cell growths carried away on the flow as he rose, glistening, from the dip.

I would awake with a stinging esophagus from visions that hadn't been maintained in my mind, lying in bed. At first it was as if I had no body, made of void. Then all at once heaviness pounced at me, the weight of blood in my arms and legs pulling me to the ground. The resistance of the mattress and the wooden plank underneath it crushed me, pushing the air out of my lungs. The cry I'd been meaning to emit was slammed back from the sides of my skull. Slowly, the blood would wake and start moving again, beating at the rhythms of wakefulness, and I would cry in complete silence so as not to inconvenience anyone, my sisters and parents and that other being, lurking in the background, dripping from one wall to the next, simmering between the cracks, alert to the moment in which it had to become time and action again.

By some instinct, I concealed my nightly suffering from my parents, even when my mother interrogated me about my tired state in the mornings. I put out feelers with Dudi and Pini. I stuttered about how I sometimes felt like I was suffocating. Dudi wrapped his hands around his throat and asked, Like this? Then he pulled on an imaginary rope tied around his neck and asked, Or like this? Pini made the same face he'd made when he talked about Sabah back at the outer thicket.

The Ten Days of Repentance arrived, and with them the revealing of the tombstone. A large crowd gathered, forced voters, whom Simo Farkash had wooed and persuaded until they felt a sense of camaraderie, an identification with his position in the wave of bereavement, the courage he'd demonstrated for lunging at life and its pitfalls. And Marcheshvan ticked by and Simo Farkash was sent from the hospital to the sanatorium for convalescence. Spector took care of all our needs during that time. He sent food. Women who helped Msodi care for the young girls visited us daily. On the Tenth of Tevet I fasted from early in the morning. My innards were purified by sword, polished by fire. I felt that my soul, that forlorn, filthy cloud, was whitening and glowing from my eyes. That afternoon, my mother told us that Simo would be home the next day. With the wave of that news, our mother retrieved me into that dark, dusty, unholy existence from which I'd just fled.

And not a word about Sylvia, said our mother. Not a peep.

I'd learned to keep my mouth shut anyway. Occasionally, I whispered her name to myself when I was unable to summon her image, which would erase, erase, and the whisper was no good. But just as it was falling out of my consciousness, it manifested again in all its glory in my mind's eye. On the second Saturday that I attended the Mishnah reading, I was on my own. Pini and Dudi didn't attend. I hadn't expected them to. It didn't matter to me. All that mattered was the inner accumulation of words, their echoing in the world, and the tension that silenced my thoughts. Inside of them, all of a sudden, Sylvia erupted. And once she appeared, she began to slowly disappear again, her voice dissipating, her countenances blending into each other to form a random array of features. And thus, cyclically, she ebbed and flowed within me.

I had no need for the one-year memorial we held, the first and last one. Among the month of Av thickening around the house, a canopy of vapor and lament and the scrubbing of disasters and suns clutching at the sides of the earth, I sat at the long table out in the yard. Men I didn't know were sitting there too, digging up nuts from paper plates and sipping soft drinks. A boy walked by, handing out booklets with Idra Rabba chapters. His Majesty Spector, deputy mayor, steered Simo Farkash to the table and sat him down beside me. Without knowing why, I grabbed my father's hand and directed it toward the booklet rested before me. The mumblings of men reading their booklets rose from all directions. The Aramaic sounds were like the brashness of summer, an enchanting siege ring. My father's hand coiled up, except for his forefinger, which remained erect. I used it to point at the lines as I joined in the reading.

✷ ✷ ✷

IT'S ODD THAT ONLY AFTER SUKKOT WAS OVER DID I NOTICE HOW
the other kids sought Ehud out constantly. Not because the Bardas won the award for the best-looking sukkah, certainly, but because something elusive, unattainable about him captivated
everyone around. One testament to this was his effect on Chantal. Since the afternoon when she met him, she never stopped
asking when he'd come by for a visit. Her eyes filled with a tense
mist when she chatted with the same breath about her desire for
a border collie she would name Cocoa Pup and about Ehud's aunt's
skilled papercuttings, until finally our mother frowned and said,
What's so exciting about those Bardas? Just Moroccans with
their noses up in the air. And Therese? I wouldn't be too proud of
that *agunah*.

   The word "*agunah*"—a woman whose husband has disappeared, who is neither divorcée nor widow—was lashed from one
side of the holiday table to the other. It seemed to be aimed at me
or my father. He sat up without warning, his face on alert, and
started devouring the plate of couscous placed in front of him.
The lumps of steamed semolina absorbed the soup that had been
poured over them, anointed with an oil that cast a glimmer on
the chickpeas and vegetables and bits of chicken mixed into it.
One spoonful after another, Simo Farkash raked the food into
his mouth. We abandoned our own plates, watching this binge
with astonishment, this lively delving into self-forced-feeding.
Like an overgrown baby, pushing the spoon inaccurately into his
mouth as scraps clung to the corners of his lips and the front of
his shirt.

   Tova was the first to shake off the stupor, grabbing a napkin
and leaning in to clean the fallout and the stains.

   Leave him alone, our mother commanded. Don't you dare
touch him.

   Tova sat back down heavily.

Simo Farkash finished the couscous in his plate and exhaustion took over him at once. His face turned gray, and the wrinkles of experience, temporarily erased by the act of eating, reappeared.

Help him up, our mother told Tova.

Chantal jumped to her feet.

Where do you think you're going, young lady? our mother asked.

To help Dad, said Chantal.

You talked so much you haven't eaten a bite. *Yalla.*

Tova said, She'll be just fine if she missed a few meals, look at what a piece of veal she's become.

What do you mean? I asked.

What? said Tova as she toiled around our father, encouraging him to stand up. A piece of veal, like on television.

Not you. Mom. What did you mean when you said "*agunah*"?

My mother gave me a long look. Why do you ask.

No reason, I said. I didn't know they really existed. I thought it was from the Gmarah.

My mother said, Her husband disappeared last year.

Halfway to the bedroom, Simo Farkash, who was leaning against Tova, turned his head. Perhaps the hint of a smile on his lips was merely an optical illusion. Perhaps the faint promise in the verdance of his irises, which I felt like a pat against my skin, did not stem from an ancient, nameless terror I'd always managed to keep at bay.

I stepped out onto the porch. Chantal followed me. She asked about Ehud again.

I asked what exactly interested her about him.

She recoiled.

What, spit it out or shut up already.

Chantal plopped into a chair across from me and looked out into the street. The first rain stuck out a clear, polished abrasion of sky through the armor of dust the cypresses had grown accustomed to. The colorless birds biting off an opening for them to sing. Occasionally, a gust of wind shifted the heat.

Why are you so mean? said Chantal.

I didn't mean it, I said.

Chantal looked at her foot, which she was rubbing against the floor. The crookedness of insult was still etched into her features. Sometimes you're just like them, she said.

Just like who, he asked.

Like them, she said, gesturing at the door leading inside.

I said, You're more spoiled, that's your problem.

Chantal said, No, I'm not.

I said, Yes, you are.

Chantal said, Am not.

I said, Prove it, then.

Chantal said, What.

Prove you aren't spoiled and that you don't only care about yourself.

Chantal looked into the street again. Two panting street dogs limped along the asphalt. One of them climbed up the step outside our house, shoved half his body between the iron gate and the doorjamb, and paused. The other remained on the road, his tongue dangling out of his jaws, its shrunken chest rising and falling like a bellows. Tova ran out the door carrying a small bucket. She emptied it over the dog stuck in the gate, the racket of breaking water. The dog yelped, a long, thin howl, and released itself from the iron grip. She watched the two dogs fleeing down the asphalt, let out a chuckle, then startled at the sight of Chantal, who screamed along with the dog, as if the liquid poured on it were acid that had splashed on her too. Tova broke into song, With joy you will draw water from the wells of salvation, singing with a precise, delicate purity, just like the solos she sang at the school choir, an angelic voice, lilting gracefully and effortlessly.

Chantal walked inside. Tova came over. She said, Dad'll be up soon, you'll see, he'll be just the way he used to be.

What are you talking about?

What, didn't you see what just happened? she asked. Didn't you see him get all healthy?

That's nothing, I said. Something else crawled over from the street now, blocked by the gate. It came closer, kissing my skin.

Nothing, said Tova, but what about what happened at the memorial two months ago?

I racked my brain, but all I could see was our father's hollow hand that gave me free rein and his forefinger traveling over the letters of the Idra Rabba. What? I said.

What a *huvul*, said Tova.

Furious, I thought, How dare she speak to me that way, this little girl. How rude.

Huvul, she said. They have eyes but do not see. Didn't you see him reading out loud at the men's table?

A murky wall of water crashed inside of me, flowing through my muscles and tendons. My hand rose of its own volition, gathering momentum. Rude, rude, the word pulsed through my head.

Let's see if you dare, Tova yelled, Moooooooooom.

I rushed outside into a burning white sheet of light.

THAT SCORCHING AFTERNOON DURING SUMMER VACATION, I left my sisters to dance around our father, taking care of all his needs. I wandered without aim or method. My body followed only one rule—seeking out shaded areas. I moved from one spot of shade to the next with the curve of the street, the thinning of houses, or the spraining of the angle of the sun. I vaguely remember the weight of the light, though evening was near, a kind of pressure of radiation against my back, a charge my neck could not withstand. There was no focal point to the gleaming glare. It didn't break into rays but prevailed over all. Only in the shade was there brief respite. No, the combination of movement and shade. The shopping center was empty. The ragged stores grew into fortresses of darkness. Concrete fortifications separated the dimness of inside from the steamroller of gleam outside. But the stores were closed. For some reason, I recalled the synagogue where Sabah and Dudi prayed. They told me the place had a *minyan* for Minha and Arvit prayers even on weekdays. I visited once, on the Shabbat before Dudi's brother's wedding. My father was in his final days of heroism and couldn't stand to miss a social gathering of that magnitude. On his mother's side, Dudi was related to the large clan that supported Spector, the candidate for whom Simo Farkash served as central vote contractor.

I touched the yarmulke on my head. The pin that fastened it to my hair was scorching hot. All around, the flames of a solar assault. But when I stood before the gates of the synagogue I didn't walk in. My field of vision narrowed into tunnels of whiteness, chimneys with a few children flickering in their ends. Dudi must be among them, I thought and kept moving. I was blinded when I reached the harvested field. The straw was packed in its heaps that were tossed here and there like remnants of an ancient era, inflamed gold gnawing whitely into the tunnels of my vision. It mottled my retinas with glittering spots, also boiling anciently. I dragged my feet through the field, crushing bugs and straw. Such an abundance of extinction was contained in the light aspiring for the mass of land. I heard that in the eolianite hills, a ways away, was a punctured web of burrows. I might have made up the rumors. Or perhaps Sabah or Dudi told me. Or maybe Pini, who always popped up from someplace carrying news from another, closed and mysterious world. Yes, Pini, who on that Shabbat at the synagogue said, with his patent carelessness, that Nachman Farkash once hid in those burrows, and asked me if I was named after him. Dudi chuckled, and Pini said that either way he wouldn't go near there because there was a herd of porcupines living in there. Dudi said, A family of porcupines maybe, they don't live in herds. Pini said it didn't matter, that everyone knew porcupine spines were toxic. He asked if they thought Farkash grilled and ate porcupines. I asked Pini if he didn't know that people in caves survived on carob pods. Dudi said nothing.

I thought about the cool air in the burrows and no image floated into my mind. Inside the glimmer, which had trickled into my skull, the glimmer that burned every thought in the bud, the word "burrows" sparkled with black blaze. Eventually, I reached them. The hill humps loosened something in the vise grips of summer. A tangled fence separated me from the entrance to the network of burrows. What was it made of? I licked my chapped lips. My fingers felt through the tangles. A fog solid enough to serve as a barrier. My brain blurred. I paced along the fence until I found the opening. Of course alarms sounded. Of course my muscles and tendons tensed in objection. But I still walked through.

SO, EHUD WHISPERED IN CLASS, ARE YOU COMING OVER AFTER school?

Ms. Dadon's ruler slammed on the table between us. We quickly drew away our vulnerable arms.

When are the two of you going to stop clucking like a couple of chickens? said Ms. Dadon. Clucking and clucking from morning till night. Haven't you tired yet?

A weak wave of laughter rose and fell at once. The last time we laughed at something Dadon said she attacked us with a pop quiz about material we hadn't even learned yet. Ehud told those seeking his good graces and hovering around him like a cloud that I got an A+.

Obviously, one of them said. He spends all Saturday reading the Mishnah, so he doesn't mind interrupting, he doesn't care if we get screwed.

But it was my fault, Ehud said, I'm the one who started talking.

His admission did not convince those seeking his good graces. A few of them kicked my backpack, crushing the lunch packed inside it.

Forget it, said Ehud, they'll get used to you being a real whiz. They aren't psy-cho-lo-gi-ca-lly developed.

At the end of the school day, Ehud demonstrated his programming skills with excessive meticulousness. He explained routines, loops, co-or-di-nates, and how he started with the co-or-di-nates of one point on the screen's invisible latitudes and longitudes, used tri-go-no-met-ric func-tions to calculate the co-or-di-nates of a second point, then stretched lines between the two points, and the func-tions produced the complicated patterns presented on his television screen. Nice, isn't it?

I asked what good it was for. I asked it out of boredom.

Ehud said, with excitement, that this was a way of understanding shapes in nature.

I said nothing.

Ehud said, My uncle showed me. He, he works for the Weizmann Institute, he . . .

The sentence died, but its echo rang and twirled around the room. The shock of knowledge, the shock of the guess, like a punch to the bones, a tremble.

I said, Your uncle who disappea . . . But I never finished speaking. I, meaning I, know the word was too heavy. Without any warning, it sloughed off experience and habit, and the void inside gaped, a perforation through which I-Nahum could look at a foreign landscape in which the human was defeated. But I-Nahum didn't want to. My senses gripped at the tangible, as usual. The smell of socks that emanated from Ehud's room, in spite of the open window. The strips of light the shifting of the shutters painted over the wall and wiped out alternately. Ehud himself, paling and chewing on his lip. His smattering of freckles that resembled small holes in his cheeks.

Is he Therese's husband? I said. I, meaning I, see how these words matched the intent, shoved off of the tangible, soft and rolling in electric pulses.

Yes, said Ehud.

Show me that book you mentioned.

Oh, yeah, the *Flora*.

Ehud opened the *Flora*. Calyxes, petals, stamens, stems, cross sections of plants, lengthwise, diagonal, which made me recoil from the secret that burst forth, taunting me, black sketches against pearly paper, crowded lettering.

Do you read all of this? I asked.

Not all of it, said Ehud, it isn't a regular book.

He pulled a small bag from his desk drawer. Inside of it were heaped small white flowers with yolk-yellow centers, an inflorescence that erupted from a crudely green wand of a stem, spherical growths around thickening into a hornlike calyx. With a nod of his chin, Ehud signaled for me to open my hand. A light tingle accompanied the silky touch of his skin.

This is the first flower I ever learned how to define, said Ehud, so I'll show you how to do the definition process with the new book and you'll see.

Ehud embarked on a series of questions, which, in order to answer I had to look at the plant from every side. The shape of the petals, the interior organization, the structure of the stem. According to the answers I gave, Ehud flipped through the *Flora* until he reached the corresponding descriptions. Then he said out loud, Family, Compositae. Then, Stem, polygonal. Then, Leaf, simple. Then, Petal, regular. Then, Sepal, entire.

He took the flower from me and handed over the book. My eyes pored over the images on the left page until they located the flower. The number underneath it led me to the corresponding paragraph. Balsam aster is a bald late bloomer . . . It is an immigrant in Israel, hailing from North America, and has become prevalent in Israel starting in the mid-twentieth century . . . It mostly invades disturbed habitats, junkyards, irrigated fields, ditches, as well as humid habitats. The stem is polygonal and dark. The leaves are dark green. Balsam asters bloom for a long time, all throughout summer and even later, from April to

November. The capitula are small and many. The involucel bracts are imbricate. The ray florets are only slightly longer than the disc florets . . . Their color ranges from white to pale purple, and they are female or barren. The disc florets are fewer, yellow with crimson tips, and are androgynous . . . The seed is discoid, beakless, small, with a bristly pappus, disperses well in wind . . . Balsam ast . . .

I stopped reading and told Ehud I didn't understand most of the words, so what was the point?

They dry out, said Ehud, the flowers, like dandelions and thorns, and the seeds fly in the wind, they've got little parachutes.

I think I've seen them, I said.

There are tons of them, said Ehud, they're everywhere.

Like Jews, I said.

Ehud looked at me, startled. Why do you say that?

I don't know. No reason.

Ehud placed the flower and stem between the pages of the *Flora* that imbued them with a name, an image, a purpose, and shut the book. He said, That's what my uncle did when he taught me with his old *Flora*.

So it's kind of like a ritual, I said.

Kind of, said Ehud.

Was he a—

Not was, said Ehud, is.

Is he a plant expert?

No, said Ehud, it's his hobby. He's an im-mu-no-lo-gist.

I nodded.

He studies vaccines for different diseases. And also the human immune system.

Is he religious?

Why?

I don't know, no reason.

Because he studies things about the body?

Yeah, maybe.

So what, did you know the Jews advanced science because they operated on dead bodies, you know it's allowed because—

Impurity of the dead, I said, yes, because there's no red cow and no way to purify, so—

And did you know that the Jews were always the greatest doctors?

I didn't answer. From inside, my throat tingled. From inside.

So that's the thing, he said, that my uncle is—

What's his name?

What's his name? Ehud repeated with wonder. What, didn't I tell you already, he's very famous, you must have heard of him, Eldad Kavillio.

EHUD AND I CHATTED AS WE WALKED ALONG THE SCHOOLYARD during recess. Boys from different classrooms mixed together, splitting into groups and playing an especially violent version of tag. I was talking with too much enthusiasm about *Blackstar*, an animated series that played on Sundays during Arabic broadcasting. Ehud didn't understand what drew me to that series. An astronaut lands on a wild, primitive planet ruled by an evil wizard. A sorceress grants him half a mythical sword with great powers and sends him to rescue the planet from the claws of the cruel tyrant. How did I get swept up in idolatry? I thought Ehud would understand. Meaning, Ehud must have understood, just like I understood him. A light flutter accompanied my thoughts about him ever since we sat in his room on Sukkot, and the conversation seemed to be opening up, revealing a danger zone. Ehud listened to me all the way through and said, That isn't idolatry. Idolatry is believing in Jesus, may his name and memory be erased.

And in statuettes and idols, I said.

Yes, said Ehud, so the Christians create statues of Jesus, may his name and memory be erased, and they pray. What are they thinking, praying to a person? And the Indians make statues of their Buddha and give it food. That's why they say stupidity originates with gentiles.

Who says? I asked.

They say, said Ehud.

So you don't think *Blackstar*–

No, said Ehud. Star is English for *kokhav*, right? I know because that flower, the aster, looks like a star.

Yeah, I said, the *Flora* said aster–

Did you manage? Ehud asked. It works, doesn't it?

Yeah, yeah, I said, I found a bindweed in our yard, and a musk stork's bill. Did you ask Therese?

Sure, said Ehud, she–

Two kids ran over to us, racing each other. They invited Ehud to join their game with voices that rose in their attempt to overtake each other. Ehud shrugged a refusal. They turned their reddening, sweaty faces toward their temporary masters, who encouraged them with hand gestures. They tried to persuade him, saying it would be fun and they'd definitely win if they had Ehud on their team, because–

A hand touched my shoulder. Pini was standing behind me. A cunning, spacious smile of pleasure spilled across his face. I flinched. I knew Pini was already indulging in the shock I had to look forward to when I heard his news.

Calm down, said Pini, I tried to get ahold of you all through the holiday and before too.

I tried to mumble something. Pini cut me off.

He said, Listen, Sabah is coming back.

What?

Yeah, yeah, said Pini. Dudi's already losing it. I told him. Pini's smile widened. He was starting to bulk up, and the cheek curves added to his pita face, the *h'dudim*, as Msodi Farkash called them, stood out in their milkiness. He had grown his hair out. The woolly kinks, which seemed to have been carefully brushed, going by their orange sheen, did not support the knit yarmulke atop his head. I guessed at Dudi's astonishment. Sabah hadn't kept in touch with any of us, in spite of the letters we sent to the new address, at least until last summer.

How do you know? I asked. I had no hope that Pini was pulling my leg as a tiny form of revenge. The thought passed through my mind. I pushed it away. Pini wasn't lying.

How do I know? How long have you known me?

Lazmi intel, I murmured.

The chill the first rain spread through the air of Sderot evaporated. The afternoon lit up. Every oxygen molecule was a small-scale torch that our lungs fought pointlessly to put out. Every oxygen molecule was a tiny furnace binding to the iron in our blood.

Who's Sabah, Ehud asked.

Just a guy who went to elementary school with us. The word "us" and its artificial volume. Pini had already taken off, practically prancing toward the middle school building.

Oh, Ehud said, so why—

Forget it, I said. What was the conversation we were having before being interrupted by different messengers of misdemeanor? *Blackstar*, aster, *Flora*, micro—I said, Are you sure our money is going to be enough?

Yes, said Ehud, I asked Therese, she got a little mad because she already promised and she doesn't like to repeat her promises. Ya'akobowitz will definitely get us a discount on a microscope.

I went to the library, I told him, and read a book about Israeli medicine and immunology. They mentioned your uncle.

Really, Ehud said, pursing his lips. Now it was as if Ehud was shown to me in all his glory and I was allowed to look at him. Each of his eyes had its own will. The "Bekhorot" tractate that we read last Saturday at synagogue listed the defects that rule out a priest from service, and I wondered how I would define Ehud's defect, one eye looking upward and the other looking downward, seeing the ventricle and the atrium as one, or perhaps the number of eyes or their axes. The words switched around on Ehud's forehead like signs outside of stores.

Yes, I said. I touched the ends of my school T-shirt, which had come loose from the grip of my pants. I'm thinking of wearing a *tallit katan*, I added.

There's no obligation, said Ehud, no obligation, you didn't have your bar mitzvah yet.

Still, I said, it's soon. Then, without warning, Simo Farkash and the small signs of recovery he'd demonstrated over the past week, since that lunch, invaded my thoughts. Or perhaps they began before that lunch, according to Tova, who tracked our father, documenting the signs of health in a new notebook. Loud voice for a few seconds, stable stance for a moment, an old, burning vitality for a flicker—

So what did you read? asked Ehud.

That's he's an expert on a vaccination for a disease called typhus, and that it's a disease that hardly exists anywhere in the world anymore.

Yes, yes, said Ehud, that's true. He said that—

The metallic ringing eviscerated recess, the promise of autumn returned to the afternoon, the unfinished sentence.

THE BURROWS WERE EMPTY, BUT ONLY BY FORCE OF INVASION. That was my sense, that I was invading, intruding. I, meaning I, prefer to be more precise and say that I-Nahum had to strain against the foreign tangibility of the space, against the change in the level of reality. Inside, I was plagued with walking pains. I turned the spotlight of consciousness and examined one pain after the other. The burning of the skin, the indefinition of the burned areas, the narrow scorch along the chapped lips, demarcated nicely as gashings, the burning of the eyes in their sockets, the pricking shooting from them to the skull in a measured beat, the pulsing army of nails, the granularity of thirst in the throat, layered with the suffocating softness of dust hanging in the air. I lingered over every one of them until they moved away, as if they existed in another body, which was loosely tied to this one with cords and nerves that transmitted messages, facts, updates.

What was the new flesh? That conundrum was still far from me. A quiet, rather than a void, fell upon me. A middle ground with its own qualities, air, ether. It was familiar to me from those rare moments at night in bed, at synagogue. Their intensity grew ever since I began praying with great intention, ever since I began praying with devotion, putting my whole heart into my pleas.

ONCE AGAIN, LAZMI'S INTEL HAD BEEN RIGHT. SABAH APPEARED in the classroom on Sunday morning. I walked into the religious classroom and saw him sitting in the back row. He was taller, and his rotundness had been replaced with a width that worked in his favor. He was waiting on the threshold of a robust body in which he would reveal himself, arms splayed with indifferent confidence, almost unflappable, on the back of the chair next to his, legs spread ahead, stretched in jeans of a deep blue that betrayed their newness, with eyes the color of molasses darkening and refilling with light. His backpack was tossed on the desk with intentional carelessness as he looked over the thronging of kids into the classroom. It was lucky I'd lingered. It was lucky Tova had insisted, like Chantal did, on watching our father walk to the fridge to choose food. Simo still moved heavily, purposelessly, but there was the beginning of will in his actions, a demand for an acknowledgment of his independence.

You see, said Tova, and poison bubbled in her victorious glee. It dripped into me through the ears. It perforated my ear canals and my nerves. Chantal suggested that one of us stay with our father. Before, when all he did was stare out the window, there was no problem leaving him alone, but now he might go outside and get lost. And Tova said, It's about time you catch up, what did you think I was planning on doing? I had to steer my sisters out of the house and force them to walk to school. I arrived huffing, a minute before class started. I was the last to walk into the room. I imagined Sabah had arrived early on purpose, to spy, to calculate, to stake out. Ehud sat tensely at the desk, calling me over. In the space of the classroom, in the tumult of boys screeching the legs of chairs and desks, a sharp, urgent sound accompanied my name, like a nail file. But it was sufficient to confirm my grip on the classroom, my place in the existing order. I smiled drily at Sabah and nodded lightly. On the short walk to my seat, my thoughts hung on the racket of the outside and then evaporated.

So this is that Sabah guy your friend was talking about? Ehud asked in a whisper, gesturing with his thumb.

He isn't my friend, I said.

Ms. Dadon walked in with her typical authority. The boys fell silent. She instructed us to open our Jewish history textbooks. The temple in the days of Herod the Great. She spoke, and I, suddenly enveloped with silence, a satiating silence, was shut off by the power of the tune. Ms. Dadon had to pull me out with an unusually intense slap of her ruler. I stared at the ruler, then at her. She said, Read your answer to question four of the homework. It looks like your friends don't know enough about Herod's horrors, or won't do any reading themselves.

With a steady voice, I read about the execution of Hezekiah by Herod, and about Herod's insolence before the Sanhedrin when he was summoned to receive his sentence, that Hezekiah rebelled against the empire and only a king had the authority to execute him, and how he persecuted the Hasmonean dynasty and killed them off, one by one.

Go back to your daydreaming, said Ms. Dadon. The kids laughed meekly.

During recess, the shards of conversation between Ehud and me died out quickly, and as much as he tried to come up with subjects, his eyes kept turning to the spot I was evading. The gathering around Sabah in the yard. Come on, said Ehud, that guy's definitely showing off.

When we came closer, we picked up bits of conversation. They revolved around me, of all things. Sabah was asking with a kind of nonchalance why Farkash received such special status with the teacher, who oozed evil by the gallon. One of the kids said I knew all sorts of Talmudic chapters and stories that nobody else did, and that I even knew more than Ms. Dadon, because I was a book nerd. And Sabah said, offhandedly, with a chuckle, But it isn't him, his aunt tells him everything.

Ehud looked at me quizzically. His lips shaped the word "aunt" voicelessly. The muscles of my legs bounced uncontrollably. I crouched down to sit. I touched the sand, the silicon sharpenings, the granularity, the lazy warmth absorbed within it. Ehud pulled me up. Gmarah class is about to start, he said, we'd better get back.

THE START OF THE MONTH OF KISLEV GLISTENED ON THE HORIzon, an enormous, threatening moon pulled on the water with its weight, swelling and releasing the blood. These gusts ran through me, an unbearable wakefulness at nights replaced at once with endless exhaustion, the two extremes of sleeplessness. Tova was right, Simo Farkash's heroism had intensified. He was already leaving the house, sitting at the edge of the group of men who played games at the old shopping center, outside the seed and nut shop, underneath the Bauhinia trees with their butterfly foliage. I worked hard with the *Flora* until I tracked down their name. Their bloom would have to wait for summer, but I remembered it—the bloom—the energy and savagery with which the purple petals gaped and the stamens erected with all this glowing silk. What was the use of knowing its name? It did nothing to lessen the screeching sound I heard within the footsteps of Simo Farkash, the scattering of his mastery throughout the house, the renewal of his old covenants with the walls and the floor tiles, the vents and the doors, the streaming of water through the pipes, the rips and apertures in the structure that invite the light in. It did nothing to alleviate the choking, the burning of the esophagus, which plagued me as the house regained its ordinances.

Sylvia Gozlan studied at a religious girls' school outside school grounds. Though I'd seen the girls crossing the quad before, always in groups, I'd never truly noticed them before. Just as I hadn't noticed the eighth graders. They were in a sort of empty middle ground, not prominent enough for stories to be told about them, and lacking any real influence on my life. And really, the girls from the other seventh-grade homerooms were also cloaked with this distance of disinterest and disconnection. And suddenly, Sylvia Gozlan came on her own, walking through the gate through which crossing was forbidden during school hours, between the middle school and the girls' school, mixing territories, blending one species with another, with her long skirts, her haughty, crushing separateness. How ugly she was, a kind of hard swirl of hair and an enormous, stubbly mole beside a crooked nose, needlessly buggy eyes, and those fatty balls curving against her chest, and her deviant habit of covering her mouth when she laughed, and her overly white and straight teeth, and her inappropriate giggles. Sylvia, who promised to change her name to Ya'ara when she was grown-up, because she'd heard that the name Sylvia originated from the word for "forest" in foreign, distant languages, the languages of gentiles, God help us.

Ehud checked and confirmed that the name Tran-syl-va-nia meant beyond the forests, and Syl-va meant forest, probably in Romanian, and maybe she was half-Romanian. I said that Sylvia was a common name among Moroccans. Not that it mattered. We both watched closely as her whispering with Sabah charged him with an electric current. Those who sought Ehud's closeness were ripped away, and the constant cloud of their bustling at the edges of consciousness gradually lessened. One day, toward the end of Marcheshvan, that same cloud reformed around Sabah. That's where it seemed to find its internal organizations, concentric circles of proximity.

Sabah and I spoke occasionally, sharing news with tense voices, consulting about homework and test answers. Obviously, we were old friends. Sylvia Gozlan asked questions too. She caught me in the yard. One afternoon, halfway home, I startled, thinking I'd forgotten something important, that I'd left my math textbook, which I needed for my homework, on my desk in the classroom. She couldn't have been waiting around for me in the yard. It was only a coincidence that I went back. It was only a coincidence that I startled, within that swell of breathlessness and a tingling in the back and fingertips, within that race of thoughts feeling around toward the future, for the estimated consequences of that forgetfulness. I did not bother to check my backpack. I could see clearly in my mind how the book was spreading its slow glow of knowledge in the orphaned classroom.

Sylvia Gozlan waved at me from her spot on a crumbling stone wall in front of the middle school building. I ignored her. I climbed the short flight of stairs. As soon as I set foot in the hallway the image of the forgotten book was replaced with another. I remembered how I'd raked it hastily into my backpack. I removed the pack and peeked through the partially open zipper. The math textbook was inside.

Now the heat struck me, the heat of embarrassment and of the speedy walk back. Now I could sense the floating of my bones when whatever abandoned my veins abandoned them even more strongly, and the sweat dammed underneath my skin erupted. I took the stairs down, attentive to the dying racket of my pulse.

Wow, said Sylvia Gozlan, you look like a squeezed lemon.

I narrowed my eyes at her. What do you want? I asked.

Nothing, she said, I stayed a little later, it's boring at home.

But I thought you had a long school day at the girls' school.

Yeah, those extra Mishnah classes are a drag.

You should be in class right now.

So? said Sylvia Gozlan. What are you trying to say?

That . . . You just said that at home . . .

What's your problem?

The collar of her school T-shirt was covered with dark stains. I lingered over them. It's a shame, Sylvia Gozlan said, I can't drink chocolate milk around David.

How come? I said.

When David makes me laugh, the chocolate milk flies out of my mouth.

Who's David? I asked.

Your friend, said Sylvia Gozlan, and in spite of her skeletal hand covering her mouth, her laugh was a swarm of clear bubbles.

I thought, Sabah, Sabah, I haven't called him David since the day we met.

Have you really been friends since first grade? she asked.

So-so, I said.

I hope it's more so than so. She accompanied her words with gestures, with the first "so" she turned her right hand to the sky, and with the second "so" she flipped it over. The back of her hand was dark, the blue map of veins visible.

I nodded. Sylvia embarked on her investigation. What did David like, which TV shows, which music, did he have a girlfriend in elementary school, who else was he friends with, who did he keep in touch with while he was in Netanya, why did his family leave, why did they come back, was he always a good student? To my surprise, I could answer too few of her questions. Sabah was Sabah. He liked making up games and scheming schemes, and liked even more to see his friends obeying the rules he'd invented, enjoyed witnessing them loyally fulfilling the roles to which he'd appointed them. We talked a lot about *Wonder Woman*, and Sabah was allowed to stay up late and watch *Dynasty*. And the ninja movies his father procured on VHS. They had a VCR. And I think

Sabah followed the news too. He listened to the same music everybody else did. Sylvia Gozlan listed names I didn't recognize, and she said that she and David listened to the biggest hits countdown together.

WHY SHOULD I FEEL LIKE I'VE BEEN TRAPPED IN THE BEAM OF A black flashlight, that I am looking inward in search for a bit of memory that had escaped me and finding murky islands, sandbanks, and broken ships? A similar beam crossed my path that morning. For the first time in two years, my father laughed. The rows of his yellowing teeth, rotting and silvering as they became swallowed in the darkness of his mouth, parted, and a bubble of air pushed its way out, full of miniscule trembling sand shocks. Tova joined in with her bellowing, with a giddiness that seemed to be ripped off from Chantal. Something was taken away from me too, the faith that the dwelling of the body was safe and familiar.

I knew that the indirect path that opened before me passed close to the Lazmi house, of course I knew. And I knew, as if I were watching my future self, disconnected from me and shoved two minutes ahead in the flow of time, that I would stop and call for Pini, and that his pita face would appear instantly, appear from someplace, from the street or from the doorway, from the window or materializing out of the air, with his plump smiling and that conniving gleam. A piercing of longing shot through me, longing for the thing about to happen.

He came to ask about Crispel, huh, said Pini's mother, who followed him out onto the porch. A wild-haired woman in clothes that reminded me of rags, a skirt and top sewn or adjusted to her size with an unskilled hand, without paying any mind to appropriate fabrics.

Don't butt in, said Pini.

What'd I tell you, said his mother, that he'd come to ask about

Crispel. The mom changed her name from Rosa to Varda, like what, no one's heard about Moroccans in Netanya? Garbage people.

Go inside, Pini told her, you don't want people thinking you're crazy again.

Like I care what people think, she huffed, shifting a lock of hair away from her face, revealing eyes as narrow as slits, but only because she was squinting. A flame threatened to burst through them. She said, They should be afraid of what I might think about them.

We heard you, we heard you, said Pini. Then, turning to me, he said, Did you come to ask about Sabah?

I said nothing.

Pini said, So come on, *ta'al l'hon*, come over already, what do you want to know?

With a tense hand, I took the glass of Coke he offered me. I had to think about the actions of the fingers, how to wrap them around the glass cylinder.

Why did they come back? I asked.

Because his dad was fired.

Who's he in touch with?

Nobody. Dudi tried talking to him, came over, called him, but he ignored him. Didn't you notice he only walks around with new friends at school?

So do I, I said and hushed.

You don't say, I didn't notice.

I smiled lightly. I told myself, stretch your lips, pucker them a little, think pleasant thoughts, show it in your eyes.

Snap out of it, said Pini.

Snap out of what?

Snap out of whatever nonsense you just fell into.

What nonsense?

Sitting there like a baby doll. *Tkun hfif.*

This expression, spoken exactly the way my father used to say it in his final days of heroism, typically along with a pat on the back, it was like oil, smoothing out pistons and cogs. I loosened all at once.

That's better, said Pini.

How do you know?

Know what?

Know everything that's going on, know how . . .

It's just how I am. I got it from my mother.

I nodded.

Pini said, Don't think it hurts my feelings to see you hanging out with Barda. It makes sense for you to be friends.

Yeah? I asked.

Yeah, said Pini.

I said, You know about his aunt?

His mother's sister whose husband disappeared?

Yeah.

Poor girl.

Because she's *agunah*?

Pini laughed. Mom, he yelled.

What, what, Mrs. Lazmi answered from inside. Now that you need me I should come out?

Yeah, come on, we know your tricks.

Her torso emerged through the door, leaning toward us, skull and collarbones and breasts. From up close, her scent was intoxicating, intense blossom, thick in the nostrils.

Pini said, Barda's aunt.

Therese Kavillio? Poor thing. She was his student. He left his wife for her. A few months into their marriage, he disappeared. She's like twenty years younger than him. I'm surprised the Bardas accepted her like that, that homewrecker.

Where did he disappear to? I asked.

The flickers of flame in her eyes were visible beyond the locks of hair that fell on her face when she leaned forward. She said, He went to that country, *shu isma*, that Ashkenazi country, Poland. And that's it. Darkness.

That's it? I said.

Not that's it, she said. That's it. Darkness. She retreated into the house.

Pini smiled with pleasure. I placed the half-full glass on the floor and grabbed my backpack. I have to get back, I said.

Pini said, Do me a favor, next time you see Dudi, at least say hello.

I nodded.

I was already passing through the gate when Pini called after me, And don't worry about Sabah, he came over when they got back too. He's updated on everything.

I turned back to face him. Everything? I asked.

Yeah, everything that happened over the last two years, when Dudi broke his leg the day before the big game at school, and how we wrote dirty words about the teachers on his cast and then drew over them with a marker, and whenever he was in a bad mood he'd touch one of the dirty words and only we knew.

Everything? I asked again.

Yeah, what, why should I hide anything?

About me too?

What d'you mean, he asked about you first. I told him about your father, about what happened on election day.

Everything?

Yes, said Pini. About your aunt Sylvia too, I'm telling you, everything.

THE BOX SABAH CARRIED WITH HIM HAD NOTHING TO DO WITH checkers, as Ehud had guessed when we saw him pulling out a checkered plastic board folded into quarters. Sabah said he'd joined a chess club in Netanya. He asked me to play with him during recess. He said, I think you'd pick it up easily. The board spread open between us. From the box rose first black pieces, molded from polished plastic, tiny yet full of details, rook and knight and bishop and pawns, and a king and queen, a green circle of felt on the bottom of each piece. Sabah said that magnets anchored the pieces in place on the metal board. One by one, he set them on the side of the board closer to him, and explained their moves thoroughly, what was permitted and what was forbidden, and the purpose of the game. Ehud was tense behind my back, holding back from leaning down to touch the pieces and the board. Sabah handed me the white pieces and I copied the arrangement, with the help of Ehud's directions, which he offered with a trembling voice, perforating the remarks of the other kids who gathered around us.

White starts, said Sabah.

I moved one of my pawns one square forward.

No, said Ehud. A pawn starts by moving two squares. You weren't listening.

I glanced at Sabah. His eyes were trained on the board. More accurately, his eyes were evading mine.

Go on, said Ehud.

I thought he was wrong. But it didn't matter. I pushed the pawn one more square forward. Sabah moved his own pawn. After that I couldn't get anything. A few more moves were made hastily, the queen was beaten down by a knight, the king was threatened and taken. From within the blur, I might have heard Ehud say, I told you not to move the bishop. The tense silence that filled the air broke into a thousand chatters.

Sabah looked at his watch, a jagged metal ring surrounding a dark screen of digits. Waterproof, he'd boasted a few days earlier. He no longer wore digital watches, sophisticated as they may be. The next day Ehud showed up at school no longer wearing his calculator watch that he got from Therese when she moved in with them. We've got time for another game, he said.

I nodded. I figured I'd be on guard this time. We switched colors. Sabah, the winner, started the game with the white camp. Ten moves, Sabah said poignantly.

What ten? I said.

Checkmate in ten moves.

I moved carefully, focused, trying to consider the consequences of every move, to predict something. But the board was opaque, and my thoughts seemed to be spraying off it. I, meaning I, know that for me, Nahum, time tore into shreds. Each shred and the action contained within it like a seed. The wait for the hand reaching out, moving the piece, releasing me, Nahum, out of the petrification of watch hands, the narrow gap, space for breathing, of Sabah's hand movement, snaky and energetic, and another shred formed, a crystal of deviation. And yet, time was a leap between two points over a gaping abyss, on one side the opening move, and on the other the felled king falling against the board with a tap. The soul drew to a halt and all at once a hole tore up into it, the minutes taken away from it, ripped away from knowing.

There's time for another game, there's time for another game, Ehud's voice was choked, embalmed in a plastic wrapping of emotion.

But a boy from another seventh-grade homeroom leaned in to whisper something in Sabah's ear. Sabah nodded and hastily packed up the board, miniscule, dull thumps of metal against plastic as they were swallowed into the box. Some of the kids followed him.

Ehud said, Whoa.

I shrugged.

Throughout the day, Ehud pleaded with Sabah to open the box and play against him, but Sabah said he didn't have time, maybe tomorrow. Convince him, Ehud told me, please.

I waved him off, saying, You can't convince Sabah, he must be planning something.

What? said Ehud.

I don't know, I said, he's always planning something.

I was too exhausted to go to Ehud's at the end of the school day. I was too tired to go home, with the revitalizing reign of Simo Farkash and Tova's rise to greatness. The school quad emptied. Marcheshvan was breathlessly fleeing. The knockings of the horses of rain arriving from some aquatic kingdom burst forth from seas and ponds. That same sensual blurring of the chess game was poured into me. I knew Sylvia Gozlan appeared, that she got me talking, asking again about Sabah's friends and old acquaintances, and I stared at her stubbly mole and the lumpy mending of her nose, which emphasized the symmetrical fracture of the human face. I listed names that pushed their way into my thoughts in no particular order. I didn't pay any mind to the notepad in which she jotted these down as I spoke. But when I fish these events from memory, Sylvia Gozlan's image as an older girl, sixteen years old, developed, beaming with adolescence, fresh, erases the image of the girl she used to be. And she stands before me, writing in her open notepad, then pausing, closing it, and inserting the pen into the metallic spiral, saying, Farkash, you really, but I mean really, nailed it.

I knew also that I'd climbed up the incline and passed through the opening in the fence, crossed the barrier of trees. Still, only a fence, only an opening, only eucalyptuses layered with the promise of autumn, only a plowed field in which the pores of dust were parched for some kind of liquid, only a long way of languid beauty that posed no difficulty, only burrows in the eolianite hills, clawed by who knows what kind of precipitation or creatures. Just like at the end of summer vacation, the flavor of lingering in them was taken away, gone was the denseness of quiet, the possibility of expansiveness they carried. Only a musty odor of dirt animals, the rot of their feed, mold, and the fallout of porcupines, elongated antler-like cylinders striped black and white.

✼ ✼ ✼

MY PROLONGED ABSENCES WERE UNACCEPTABLE TO SIMO FAR-kash. He sat me down in front of him. What was that quality, without which he was hollow, his image drained of substance? And how had it been returned? The muscles were the same muscles, so why did they seem lifeless just a month ago? The eyes were now certainly surfaces of glimmer but used to be murky pools. And the lips too, no longer weights that had to be ordered to move, but pliable flesh that shaped words as it pleased. Hatred, I thought, that was the thing. Like Therese Kavillio told me when we were alone in Ehud's room. Man hates helplessness. The sole human art is the extinction of anything or anyone that reminds man of his powerlessness.

I assumed she was quoting from a book, but didn't ask. A chess board was set on a small table in Ehud's bedroom, and Therese was sitting cross-legged on the rug beside it. Ehud went into the kitchen to replenish the stock of small chocolates individually wrapped in textured silver paper. Therese said chocolate was good for mental acuity and could help us during tests, as well as help Ehud with his chess practice.

The day after my defeat, Ehud said dramatically, David cheated. Then he elaborated, whispering through rounded palms held against his mouth, that there are all sorts of loopholes and stra-te-gies in chess that ensure the victory of those familiar with them. The opening moves, he said, allow control of the board. It isn't about smarts, just about memorization. He just happened to ask Therese yesterday and she showed him. It's a shame I hadn't come over, because I would have seen, and I should come today.

But I found little interest in openings. Even when I performed them well, I did so mechanically. Excited, Ehud said, It's like programming, you just have to learn what every command does, and then— Therese cut him off brashly, saying, absolutely not, chess is a game of intuition and creativity. It's built first and foremost on resistance to obvious rules. As soon as you know the rules, you forget about them. All that's left is the board and you pounce inside of yourself. You see the board.

I couldn't see it, hard as I tried. There were pieces, there were squares, there were rules. The pounce inside of myself, which made the game a living event, evaded me, and with it the will to pounce at all. I sat in a chair and watched Therese as she corrected Ehud's wild gambles, interrogating him on the rationale behind them and proposing alternatives. She was young in the light softening through the lampshade. An angular, chiseled face, every feature in place, especially when I tried to compare it in my mind to the portrait of Sylvia Gozlan, like an image marred by acid.

And we were on our own. Therese examining the board set for a new game, trapped unknowingly within my gaze. A cloud or a twitch of awkwardness or a wrinkle of ponder in the forehead or the shift of the lampshade flickering against her skin and her smooth arms in short sleeves, something, and she was revealed to me. Not the possibly young Therese, but Therese the *agunah*. Therese in which a forsaken land opened up, its soil rich with strips of life that crumbled into their carbon elements, and with the pressure of eons, and the shifts of the continent, tectonic forces, became crystals and precious stones with no one to extract them, not even her. I knew the mining delusions her consciousness bore. Perhaps in bed, before falling asleep, she crossed the deserted, cracked land. I knew the hatchet thoughts, the digging thoughts, the drilling thoughts, which added up to nothing, to broken utensils, to fractured iron, to wood chips. In the margins of my senses I was aware of Ehud's entrance, of his eyes that hovered between her head, which was lowered toward the chessboard, and my beam of vision, and his emerging Adam's apple shifted, and I could hear that gurgling, the dry throat rolling through sounds, drythroat, droat, droat, droat, and I couldn't bear the gnawing of my being, another bite taken by Therese Kavillio the *agunah*, the first time she saw Eldad Kavillio was stamped into one precious stone, the shock of the touch in another, and droat, droat, droat, and now here she was alone, reading and nodding to herself with understanding, and on the horizon were the phone call, the letter, the delayed messages from a foreign country, droat, droat, and I got up and yelled, But I have to run home, and my limbs were paralyzed by the attack, aching from motion, and yet I managed to walk out of the room without stepping on a single one of the chocolates scattered over the rug and the floor.

I sat before my father. Simo said I had to spend more time at home, helping Mom and watching Chantal. He said, It took you a long time to stop being a baby, don't let it take you that long to become a man. But in the accumulation of the day's events, Simo Farkash's voice was missing its pressure and didn't send chills through me.

PINI TOLD ME HE WASN'T GOING. WHAT DID HE HAVE TO GO there for, he wasn't friends with any of them, but at least they invited Dudi, so he didn't feel like a leper, that telephone pole, did you see the size of his Adam's apple?

Not going where? I asked.

I, meaning I, can say that Pini seemed to gather into my thoughts as I-Nahum sat on a rock in the school quad behind the gym, and spoke inside of them, or at least an internal copy of him did. But no, the foreign presence of the voice, its invasive quality, pulled me out. I-Nahum opened my eyes. The charged air, the dimness that a weak sun insisted on disrupting, its radiation reaching the body like a touch, the intensity of those lessened upon the return of vision. But a wind wafted through, a Kislev wind, the rain that drenched last week would be back soon.

Sylvia Gozlan's Hanukkah party, said Pini. His round face glowed above me with that same knowing smile.

I nodded.

Are you going?

Where? To the party?

Yeah.

I wasn't invited.

You weren't invited?

No.

But she invited everyone, that Sylvia.

Maybe she forgot.

I don't think so, said Pini.

I cleaned the damp sand from the seat of my pants and went back to the classroom.

I didn't ask Ehud if he'd been invited. Of course he had. He was now Sabah's regular chess opponent. They played at recess every day, and one of the other kids always volunteered to keep track of the results. Even in their first games, Sabah's lips drew together as he realized that Ehud knew the opening moves he used, and that he'd have to come up with new ruses. He adapted quickly. It was incredible that in a little over two weeks Ehud would draw level with Sabah, who had two years' experience of playing at the flagship club of the Israeli chess capital—the city of Netanya. But it was a fact. With his signature compulsiveness, Ehud spent every free moment with the board, the chess riddles that appeared in the weekend papers, and with Therese and the chess book she bought him.

I came home every evening obediently. On my way, I collected random plants and flowers that broke through the pavement and the asphalt after the rain and sat down with the *Flora.* When I reminded Ehud about the microscope he said that he'd decided instead to use the money he'd saved to buy a fancy chess set, top-of-the-line. And I said, "Top-of-the-line" is just a bunch of everyday words pushed together.

What, said Ehud.

I said, Nothing, never mind.

With you everything is nothing and never mind, Farkash, said Ehud.

I said, Some things aren't.

Like what, asked Ehud, *Blackstar?*

Don't call me Farkash.

But that's your name, isn't it, Nahum, Farkash is your name.

HE GOT UP JUST LIKE HE FELL, SAID MSODI FARKASH, SUMMING up the past two years as far as she was concerned. Now it's my turn to rest, she said. No more slipping dried figs into Simo's mouth at lunchtime. No more freezing mangoes and feeding him a slice every day. Dried figs and mangoes, the two fruits she craved during her pregnancy, therefore attributing healing powers to them. The flame of the sun flickered and wavered in the menorah on the windowsill. A breeze infiltrated through the cracks in the sealing of the window frame. The first candle lit unwaveringly, with ridiculous boldness. Tova was the one who lit it. Simo Farkash said the blessing with a steady voice. The yarmulke on his head seemed foreign, a fabric sediment that had bumped against an exposed network of roots. My fingers distractedly combed the strands of the *tallit katan* fringes. I'd decided to wear it that morning. Last Saturday I consulted with the venerable Rabbi Amar after the reading of the Mishnah. He confirmed that though there was no obligation for me to wear it, anyone who meticulously followed fringe mitzvahs welcomed the divine presence of God, which was of equal merit as following all 613 commandments.

Chantal let out a whimper and didn't join us in singing "Maoz Tzur" after the blessings. She rejected the donuts too, because why was Tova chosen to light the first candle?

You, said Tova, you have a black heart. You get everything and you're always the favorite, and then I get one thing and you start crying.

And you didn't let me sing either, said Chantal.

Because you're off-key, said Tova.

So what if you're in the choir? said Chantal.

La la la la, sang Tova.

No fighting on Hanukkah, said Msodi.

Weakness went in and out of Simo Farkash. He looked over his daughters, making no comment, but to me he said, What are you doing, playing with your fringes like some girl.

I said, Girls don't wear fringes.

Fringes, a dress, it's all the same, isn't it? You shouldn't overdo anything. We're religious, but we don't want to be orthodox, like those guys in black that we saw around here with their suits. What do they have to do with Judaism?

Rabbi Amar said—

Rabbi Amar, my father said, is going orthodox because the Ashkenazi got it into his head that they're more Jewish than he is. Tell me, when did you ever see blond Jews in the Bible? In the Mishnah? In the Gmarah?

I nodded.

Dad seemed to be exhausted by his bursts of preaching. He said, Nahum, when I said you should be home I didn't mean for you to lock yourself in your room. He licked his lips and heaved. You and your friends should go out and enjoy Hanukkah.

I lowered my eyes to the fringes. The lie cut through my throat. I said, I made plans to meet Pini in thirty minutes, we're going to some party.

So now I had to go, but where, I'd wander around on my own, of course I'd stop by Pini's, Pini told me clearly that he had no intention of going to Sylvia Gozlan and her group's party.

Something in me shivered at the sight of Pini's smile as he welcomed me on the porch. Pini asked me to give him a few minutes, he was getting dressed, and he was planning on walking around the old shopping center.

But it's closed at night, I said.

The boys from Mekif Klali High School are sitting there.

I said, The secular kids?

Yeah, they're a thousand times better than the kids at our religious school.

I wanted to leave, but I couldn't back out. In my pocket was the note of money my father had given me to buy something for myself, it's no good, wasting youth, you should have fun so long as you don't have any worries, Simo Farkash's mantra during his final days of heroism. But what is life made of, and when did concern ever not gnaw during his years of collapse? I remained in the covered porch. A loaded laundry rack stood there. Mrs. Lazmi walked out with a laundry basket, humming to herself. She cut her tune short when she saw me. Nahum, Nahum, she said, your name means comfort. What kind of comfort were you born to offer?

I said nothing, staring at her. Her hair was more orderly. Those swollen, reddish eyelids couldn't compete with the glow in her eyes. She kept that glow on me, even as she removed the clothes from the rack and dropped them in the basket at her feet. She returned to her singing, this time more clearly, the Moroccan syllables of the tune legible, rising from her lungs and throat, boiling in the chill of the outside. I couldn't understand the language, but I recognized the longing and the heartbreak that motivated the words. From within the melody, my straining ears caught hold of one sentence, accumulated from consonants and vowels closer to Hebrew, And there shall be no more death in the Land of Shadow. My hand reached frantically, of its own volition, to the strands of my fringes, combing them with my fingers, until Pini walked out the door. He was more elegant than I'd ever seen him before, his head bare, his kinky mane smoothed out with gel, glistening, shifting between orange and gold.

His mother let out a quick, happy laugh. *Yimʃhi kapara alik, ya* Pinhas, she said, look at this handsome man growing in my home.

Mom, Pini scolded her indulgently. His plump, milky cheeks were painted a fleeting crimson.

✻ ✻ ✻

TWO DISRUPTIONS. FIRST, WHEN I WOKE UP IN THE MORNING IT occurred to me to check if my *tallit katan* was kosher. I found only seven strands in the front right fringes. Second, Tova took her revenge for the slap I gave her. She'd glued together the pages of the *Flora* that Ehud had lent me.

Wait, wait, when and how did the strand fall off? When I wore the *tallit katan* yesterday morning, when I received it from Rabbi Amar, already flawed, or last night, when I mingled with the secular children? Damn those sinners. No, no, he who suspects the honest suffers an ill body. I sat on my bed in my pajamas, the *tallit* lying on the back of my chair like an animal skin.

Pini hadn't lied. The boys I met the night before had a liberty I wasn't familiar with. It infected Pini too. He even joked with them about his father, who'd left home the previous year to be with another woman. The images that came to mind were glossed over with a crushed, granular glow and some blurry distance, as if the existence trapped within them, the hours that only pulsed around me the previous night, took place in a kingdom of twilight, and an invisible force pulled them away from it, making it hover before me.

The boys who gathered there varied in size and stature, and some of them were eighth graders, but they left their mark on me as a single cluster, a creature breaking up into its components to come together again, a raw being in the midst of its formation. All save for one of them—skinny, his face narrow and thoughtful. Perhaps the down-pulled corners of his lips contributed to that impression. His friends called him Niro.

They talked about music, about their plans for next year, about the girls from class, about teachers, and about television shows, and laughed, they laughed so much, there was no denying the laughter. They laughed with abandon. And perhaps this is where that sense of liberty came from, the giddy intoxication with which I too returned home, and the weight of rising from it that took over my flesh. At some point Niro told Pini, Come on, do the trick.

Pini said no, that he couldn't.

What trick? I asked.

You can talk, one of the boys remarked about me. The others chuckled.

The boy's got a nice voice, he'll grow up to be a singer, said another.

Why do you always have to ruin a good joke with your downer comments? said Niro. To Pini, he said, Why can't you? Because it's Hanukkah?

No, said Pini, I need a pen and paper.

I happen to have those at my disposal, said Niro. He pulled a folded piece of paper from his pants pocket and a pencil stub from his shirt pocket. Always be prepared, he said, how many are we?

Mechanically, I ran my eyes over everyone present. Save thy people, and bless thine—

What's he doing? one of them asked.

Counting, said Pini.

No, said the boy, counting is using numbers, one, two, three, don't you watch *Sesame Street*?

What's your method? asked Niro.

It's forbidden to count Jews, I said, it brings . . . it brings a curse.

So how can you tell how many we are?

For minyan, I said, you count using a Psalms passage with ten words.

Niro nodded. How many are we, do it out loud, I want to hear it.

I bent my finger and tapped the air in their direction, as if tapping the tops of their heads, the yarmulkes I pictured them wearing. Save thy people, and bless thine inheritance: feed them. Nine. I stopped before the word also.

Let's pretend we all speak the same language, said one kid.

The boy who'd tried the unsuccessful joke said, Are you sure he isn't cursing us, it sounds like witchcraft to me.

Niro said, How many times do I have to tell you to stop being a downer? Open your mind, you might learn something. Without Pini there are eight of us, right?

Look who's talking, said the downer kid. *Zrada.*

I was familiar with the nickname, which was used for Chantal when she was a baby. She was tiny back then, and her crying meek and rattling. But it wasn't the Moroccan word for "cricket" that caught my attention but rather the proximity to the word "*zered*"–Hebrew for twig–and the accuracy of that proximity. Niro looked like a mélange of bony, twig-like limbs. I confirmed the number with a nod. He ripped off a piece of paper and handed it to me. Then he did the same for everyone else. It was like the Hamotzi prayer, I thought.

The downer kid said, I came up with a good word this time, Lazmi, you'll never guess it.

Niro wrote something down quickly on the piece of paper in his hand, crushed it into a ball, and passed the pencil to another kid. When the pencil reached me, I stood there, staring at Niro.

Think of a word, said Niro, write it down, and don't show anyone.

All of a sudden, my mind was a blank. I looked around me. Some of the boys were sitting on the steps leading to the orphaned shopping center, in the smoky light spots of the streetlamps, beneath the dying moon, revealing itself for brief moments through the embrasures of cloudiness. Darkness over the two rows of stores, darkness over the spice shop and darkness over the nut and seed stall, darkness over the grocery store, and darkness over the jeweler's shop. I wrote *the Land of Shadow* on the piece of paper and closed my left fist around it.

Line up, said Pini, right to left, from the tallest to the shortest.

I found myself standing all the way to the left. Niro stood to my right. I was surprised he was only slightly taller than me, even though he was a year older. I was convinced he was the tallest of us all. Pini walked down the line, arms behind his back, head somewhat lowered. Finally, he paused in front of one of the boys, looked at him through lowered lids, and said, resolutely, Wheel. The boy smiled and nodded. Good on you, Lazmi, he said, and stepped out of the row. Thus Pini continued, pausing one by one and guessing the words written down: "spoon," "pine," etc. And the boy whose word was revealed left the line. Standing in front of the downer kid, he clicked his tongue and said, Seriously, you wrote "condom"?

The downer kid burst out laughing.

What's a condom? I whispered to Niro.

A smile emerged on Niro's lips, and he fought to restrain it.

Thunder, chafing—on he went down the dwindling line. Only Niro and I were left. Pini stood before us and his eyes, almost unseeing, moved over us. I'd never seen him like that. Pini said, You're both trying to cheat. You, he said, his arm reaching to gesture at Niro. Niro's muscles tensed. The tension infected me too. My tendons answered to that entanglement, to the flesh on the verge of ringing out. I, meaning I, feel that if I'd reached over, my finger, shattering from the torrent of crossing history, would have rescued from that image the sound that would grate the shape of reality.

Tiglath-Pileser, Pini said hotly.

Niro huffed. You're amazing, he said. You should be on television. He unfolded his piece of paper and showed it to me. The name Tiglath-Pileser was written on it in messy, illegible handwriting.

Pini's eyes opened and fixed on me. He shivered with alertness, and something else. My other hand grabbed the strands of my fringes, gripping them. The concentration in Pini's eyes was replaced with sorrow. He swallowed and shook his head lightly, a shake I interpreted as disappointment in me. That is how I would imagine him four years later, when he would call to scold me for the events at the thicket, and though his voice would thicken, and, as it emerged from the phone, would be accompanied by an inconceivable weight of experience and authority, I'd still see him standing before me in the half-light, prepared to turn away and saying, Well, my power to help only goes this far.

AND SECOND, SECOND, OBVIOUSLY TOVA WASN'T GOING TO KEEP quiet about it, and now that she had the necessary protection of our father, she would muster the courage to take her revenge. That's what he would have done too, wasn't it? Yes, Simo Farkash always preached to us in his first and final days of heroism: What heals the soul, revenge, what cures pain, revenge.

The *tallit katan* was abandoned until I could repair it. But the *Flora*. I thought about stopping by Ehud's and returning it. Ehud wouldn't object to a visit. Still, running the evening through my thoughts returned a hint of that expansiveness I'd felt. When Pini and I parted with the others and made our way back to our neighborhood, I asked him how he did that trick and where he'd learned it.

How do you do *your* trick? Pini asked me in turn.

We invaded the better-lit territories of the town, the great commotion of Hanukkah at the new shopping center, lighted faces, lighting bodies, the air rustling with presence, with the ruckus of humanity in which the senses sharpened.

What trick? I asked.

Pulling things no one's ever heard of out of thin air.

I learn them, I said, I learn them.

It doesn't look like you know them, it's like you pluck them, said Pini.

No, I said, is that what happens to you?

Pini smiled.

And lining us up and walking back and forth, I said, Is that how you know?

No, Pini said, that's just for show.

Laughter bubbled through me and erupted, but not in response to Pini and his cunning, but as a kind of embodiment of
the giddy intoxication that filled me. I, meaning I, dare guess the
reason for this intoxication. The burning candles sketched the
night with a constellation of stars that had not been created before us and would not be created after us, on that one of many
Hanukkahs, inside of which I-Nahum laughed, and listened to my
laugh, and realized the laughter was mine, that it was a sound
pulled out of my thoughts and emerging from lungs and a throat
made out of dirt into Nahum Farkash's organs. I thought about
the conversation Niro dragged me into when he asked about my
tallit katan and my yarmulke and about the mitzvahs and prohibitions. One of the boys said Niro knew the Bible by heart. Pini
said, You found your own kind in Nahum.

Niro said, Really?

Yeah, said Pini. Ask him anything.

And Niro asked, trying to trip me up with what he thought of
as minor details, like the tribal symbols in the blessing of Jacob
and the hoshen jewels. And I asked him, with that same thin excitement in which the heart appeases and goes out to another, to
an unexpected intimacy, what Tamar asked Judah. Niro said he
didn't remember, why did I have to ask about this story. But the
longer our wrangling went on, even after the other boys gave up
and turned to their own conversations, the more familiar I became with the nature of Niro's knowledge of Bible stories. Marveling, I said, You only know stories that contain profound
secrets. Because Niro knew all the minutia of angels and revela-
tions and temple service and prophecies.

Yes, said Niro. Have you ever heard of the book *Chariots of the
Gods?*

I shook my head and Niro unfolded some bizarre argument
about creatures from outer space and how all the holy entities in
the Bible are depictions of alien invasions and advanced technology. I said, Nonsense.

Niro shrugged, as if the sentences meeting my ears should have been enough to convince me. The next day, as I held on to the *Flora*, the glued pages like lumps of clay, I wondered if I hadn't enjoyed his words of heresy, therefore inviting all these punishments.

I walked out into the hallway and passed Tova on her way to the bathroom. She was humming in her pure, delicate voice and looked at me askance.

No doubt, I thought. I also thought, I acknowledge the judge as right.

THERESE LET ME IN, AND IN THE HARSH LIGHT OF THE HOUSE, the bulbs burning in the crystals of the living room chandelier, she examined me, as if the change was apparent in me. They're outside, she said, pointing to the back door. I shuffled out into the yard. Sabah, Ehud, and Dudi were sitting around a metal table, speaking enthusiastically. There were teacups and *ſfenj* on the table, and the fourth chair was occupied by Ehud's new chess set.

Sabah's face lit up. Farkash, I'm glad you're here, come on, come on, sit with us.

Ehud got up quickly, picking up his chess set. He rushed back inside and returned with a clean glass. Wordlessly, he poured me some tea. The air filled with a cloud of fresh mint leaves, imbued with the aroma of winter, and awakening other scents—the unripe abrasion of wild vegetation, the bitterness of the drenched earth, the electricity of midday, and the greasy veil of frying emitting from the kitchen windows and the fritters on the table. I looked at the *ſfenj*, their golden appearance, anointed with molten sugar.

Take one, Sabah said, pushing the plate toward me. If I had room for another one I'd shove a finger down my throat.

The three of them laughed, and Sabah added, Don't take it the wrong way, Radio, these *ſfenj* really do rock.

Why Radio, I wondered, because of his eyes? I mumbled the mealtime prayer and took a bite off the fritter. The tart flavor of the dough and the sweet coating lined the roof of my mouth.

No, no, said Ehud, I'm with you, they taste awesome but might not be gastronomically recommended.

What, I said.

Ehud turned to me. Might not be gas-tro-no-mi-cal-ly recommended.

So why'd you blow off the party last night? asked Sabah.

I ran my eyes over them to see which one would disclose the joke at my expense, but all I found were expressions of curiosity. I told them I wasn't invited.

Ehud said, Seriously?

I nodded. Another bite. A sip. My pharynx was clogged by the dough, and the tea helped it slip down my gullet.

Sylvia told me she invited you, said Sabah, she swore she told you. You'll never believe who was there, kids we haven't seen in fifty years.

Dudi nodded his confirmation and joined Sabah in listing the names. I recognized all of them. They lit up and extinguished in my mind. I knew where that list was drawn from. Their faces, the images of the kids, the young men they were becoming, ran through my mind, and in each of them the defects listed by the Mishnah stood out—this one had no eyebrows, that one had only one eyebrow, this one had eyes as big as a calf's, that one's eyes were as small as a goose's, this one's body was larger than his limbs, that one's body was smaller than his limbs, this one's upper lip spilled over his lower lip, and that one's lower lip climbed over his upper lip, one had an oversized Adam's apple, like Dudi, and the other had spongelike ears. And what about Sabah, his defect was hidden, perhaps a single testicle, who knew? Beyond a dull screen, their conversation about the party and the behavior of other children, crude and otherwise, went on. It didn't matter to me. Here was the bowlegged one, and there was the one with the protruding belly button. Sylvia Gozlan's nose was larger than her face. I muttered a blessing and got up. The warmth of the *sfenj* was replaced by pain in my stomach.

Where are you going, said Sabah, you just got here. We—

I've got to go, I said, I only dropped by to return this.

I placed the *Flora* on the table and walked slowly to the door, and as I walked, bits of time pushed their way in, the Tenth of Tevet and wonder of wonders, Simo Farkash went looking for a job with his contacts, who hadn't forsaken him, including Mr. Spector, the deputy mayor, and Tu Bishvat that flew by with its planting, and the sun rising to disinherit the earth from the force of winter, and the month of Adar with its prescribed joy bursting through spring, and Ehud standing before the class to read his deplorable rhymes, about a cry in the kitchen as quick as a cheetah and the fear he felt that flattened him like a pita, and the laughter of the kids, the broken bellow of teenagers, mixed with the pure oil of a castrated childhood, and Ms. Dadon's comment, slicing through the laughter, that since the days of Rabbi Solomon Ibn Gabirol we have not had a poet like Ehud Barda, and the inner loss of fluid inside of me began, cracked blood vessels whose contents spread through the space of my mouth guidelessly, the fingernails digging and scratching, abrasions of hunger, and the shock of its refusal to be consumed, its bottomlessness, passing like a tapeworm within my years from here on out, emerging again, as I came home, for example, with Ehud's image etched into my mind, glowing with the force of the gazes resting on it, their greediness, their thirst, and I pounced at the notebook I left on the desk, writing about the rustle passing through the trees and the movement of some bird, an eternal curse falling from its beak on the world at large, and the disappearance of the spirit of poetry from me the next day, as I awakened to count down the days left before Passover break, while this hole grew in my chest, certainly more real than all the chatter in the notebook about the swelling curse that dimmed the brightness in summer days, until

the sparrow failed to find a nest and doomed itself to homeless-
ness, or about the moment when I pushed away Cocoa Pup as he
dawdled behind me to the thicket, his dog senses failing to deter
him from what was to come, or when I woke up from a nocturnal
emission, my mind filled with lines from *The Cat in the Hat*, or
when I returned from Sylvia Gozlan's home, or when I lay beside
Dalia Shushan, both of us naked and breathless and the tops of
eucalyptuses bisecting the clarity of nighttime as my hand felt
for the yarmulke that had fallen off along with my clothes, or
when I bent down in the street to pick up a coin and told myself,
This will be the sign, this will be the sign, or when I leaned my
iPhone at the lookout point in that crumbling castle overlooking
Heidelberg and a tremble passed by the thatched roofs and the
river and darkened the lens, or when I heard about the death of
Elish Ben Zaken at the end of the Fast of Gedaliah after the Gaza
War, or now, as I adjust my clothes in front of the mirror thirty
years after that classroom moment, and in the reflection I find
that Nahum, the real Nahum, shivering with hunger, while I, Nahum Farkash, no longer know what is causing me to stand there,
confidently planning my actions, as if there were substance to
the years that had gone by, as if their accumulation validated my
experience, the things I have to say, the urgency awakening
within me, that I have to leave already, leave, leave, leave the bedroom, leave the apartment, finally reach the door and go out into
the chilly light storm of morning, lest I miss the train to Tel Aviv.

I NOTICED THE THREE CHILDREN UPON ENTERING. THEY WERE
huddling near the cashier and counting their shared funds. I stood
by the ticket machine and pretended to check my ticket. I had ten
trips left on the Sderot–Tel Aviv line. The sound of the coins hitting
the metal counter pleased me. Two of the children, the boy and the
girl, were older, almost teenagers, and were bickering at a whisper.
It seemed to be a complicated, preplanned, overly smooth dance.

Twins, or two people who knew each other since infancy. As they smiled between whispers, the matching braces on their teeth were revealed, and one dimple corresponded with another. The girl's smile was missing something, no, a shadow fell on it, it never fully materialized. The hair of her companion covered his crude features, his masculine ugliness. In a few years, I thought, this ugliness would work in his favor, becoming an appeal.

The boy standing beside them, a little over ten years of age, heavy-skulled and stout, gripping the strap of his school bag with a fist, looked over the station. I easily wriggled into the boy's wonder. I realized once more, just like on the night the station was dedicated and I was asked to read one of my poems, how needlessly vast this building was, how foreboding. The tall iron canopy, the space trapped within it, the curve of the hallway leading to the platform. Just how much human traffic had the architects of this building expected? They might have fostered hopes that a peace treaty with the Palestinians was close at hand, and that Sderot would grow into a border city and a regional trade center. The child's thoughts must have been far from that. I plopped back into the dwelling of my body. The nearly teenaged girl was lightly patting the boy's back anyway, and he shook himself off and followed her and her maybe-twin. The three of them were carrying backpacks. What were they doing out here on a school day? Outside, a dark bird hovered over the parking lot, over the halfway-erected mall, neither built nor undone. The doors opened and the bird evaporated. Only an insect tempted by the polished glass's illusion of passage. Somewhere out there, November glowed. The children stood beside the turnstiles. The nearly teenaged girl pulled out her smartphone and gestured with it toward the nearly teenaged boy. The smaller boy stared into space. I walked over quickly and said, You have to insert your tickets here, pointing at the slot.

The nearly teenaged girl nodded vigorously. Her black hair fell on her shoulders. She scrunched up her nose gracefully, blue eyes but not a pure blue but rather an earthenware blue, charged with radiation. They hurried away. The little one paused in the hallway in front of the words and pictures printed on the walls. There's no time, the nearly teenaged girl urged him, Oshri, the train'll be here soon.

I sought out the traces of Oshri's gaze. I lingered over the printed words, quotes from famous Sderot-born artists. I arrived at the dedication of the station, bathed with pride to have my words embedded in the walls of that bizarre hall of fame, alongside lines written by Dalia Shushan. But when I stood before them, I experienced the black outburst of mornings when I awake powerless from sleep. I would have erased my own lines and replaced Dalia's with others. Odd choice. And an entire mythology is gathering beneath my fingernails, when I see people, their darkness approaching, it's a pain I can no longer resist. Those were the truest lines she'd ever written, but they didn't characterize the whole of her oeuvre. She lied to me. When she sang her songs, her downtrodden angel's voice imbued them with persuasion and urgency, but when they were naked of music, of performance, the truth was taken away from them, the poetry was taken away. Ultimately, she too worshipped the idol of death against which she'd so often preached to me.

It's a shame no one consulted me when the quotes were chosen. The secretary to the head of the culture department in city hall called me and, in a lifeless voice, announced the honor bestowed on me, to have my creation adorn the walls of the new station. Thousands of people would read my lines on their way to work or back home, And you know, she said, for the first three months residents can ride the train for free, can you imagine the celebration, they'll choke up the train going to Ashdod or the Azrieli Mall in Tel Aviv. Sweetly, she added, No harm in getting a little Farkash between a croissant from Roladin and a top from Zara. She giggled.

The nearly teenaged girl paced the platform restlessly. Her

eyes were fixed on the electronic board listing the train arrival times. The nearly teenaged boy couldn't have been her twin, not considering the spell her image seemed to cast on him. His eyeballs were glued to her. Her restlessness translated into a tenseness in his limbs. Oshri, the smallest of the group, sat on a metal chair, a book open in front of him, indifferent to his surroundings. A voice emerged, announcing the arrival of the train, and the nearly teenaged girl froze in place.

During the train ride I attempted to lose myself in staring. But the outside held its own, fields and trees and roads and cities padded with concrete. In the familiar, tiresome, material landscape, the quality forced by the speed of the train, the foreignness of the distance, the fear of the danger of being on the road did not manifest this time. The three children sat in the same train car as me, or perhaps I made a point of sitting a short distance away from them. They said nothing. Oshri's head was lowered toward the book in his hands. I walked over. I said, Hello.

The two older ones stared at me. Oshri ignored me.

Are you from Sderot? I asked.

None of your business, the nearly teenaged girl said, a bite in her syllables. The earthenware in her eyes heated up.

The possibly teenaged boy nodded lightly.

I said, I'm Nahum Farkash, manager of the public library.

I've never seen you there, said the possible youth.

I can say the same about you, I said.

What do you want? asked the nearly teenaged girl.

I noticed you're riding without a chaperone, I said.

The nearly teenaged girl chewed on her lips. In a small, sleepy voice, Oshri said, We're not allowed to talk to strangers.

I just wanted to ask if you needed any help or guidance, I said.

No, said the nearly teenaged girl. We're going to visit our uncle, he'll meet us at the station.

The possibly teenaged boy turned his head toward the sights passing outside the windows, the fields and electric poles, the shredded speed of the November sky hurtling toward rainy days. Oshri dropped his book in the lap of the nearly teenaged girl, his heavy skull pressing against the upholstery. All of a sudden, he looked lost, without solace.

THE FILM RESEARCHER SAID, HOW ODD, I'VE NEVER SEEN ANY-one walking with crossed arms before. We'd made plans to meet outside the Sarona neighborhood. The Tel Aviv atmosphere was still charged with a humid heaviness though winter was already approaching, but also a clarity, a light cloudiness that glistened over the Azrieli Mall and the twinkling of glass and over the Templar architecture, which was entirely shifted several meters over. The houses were sliced at the foundation and wheeled out, cleared for the purposes of expanding the highway. The beauty that history and longing afforded the stone. It's hard to find a more profound symbol of Israel than this tasteless site, and the half-kilometer radius territory for which it serves as a hub. On one side the Kirya military base, on the other side Azrieli. The lie of history and the lie of security crack as financial forces are pushed to appear in their bold glory. The film researcher said her name was Ohila Vaknin, as if she hadn't already introduced herself in the preliminary conversation, then added, Nice to meet you. She didn't offer her hand in greeting. The hem of her skirt lapped against her ankles, which were covered with socks. She was all fastened and zipped, collar and cuff links.

When she'd told me her name on the phone, I said in response, I shall entreat your favor. Face-to-face, I said, *Hen yikteleni lo ohila.*

She said nothing then. And nothing now. Oh well. She said she'd heard there was a kosher café at Sarona, but couldn't find it on the map. I dragged behind her down the paths, taut concrete and grass, forkings, and trees. She was swallowed inside three different cafés and walked out with pursed lips. I walked into the fourth café and asked the server if he knew a kosher café in the area. He said he did. Ohila asked if it was certified by the major Jewish court. The server shrugged and gave us directions.

We walked into a wooden-and-glass canopy and I already sat down, but Ohila demanded to see the place's kosher certificate and the server led her into the kitchen. With a kind of severity, Ohila said, The certificate is fine. She ordered tea in a glass. I glanced at my watch. Thirty minutes had elapsed.

Do we have a time limit, Ohila asked, I thought—

No, no, it's fine, I was late. I'm free.

Great, Ohila said and stood up. Because I need to use the bathroom. All that walking.

The kids on the verge of adolescence glanced at me the whole ride over, whispering. Bits of sentences reached my ears. Bus number five ... Did you make copies of the right keys? ... He must have left notes, he had a notepad ...

When the train stopped at Ha'Haganah station, I walked over to their seats again. I asked if they were certain I couldn't help them. The nearly teenaged girl said, You're harassing us.

The possibly teenaged boy choked. Oshri looked down at his book.

I asked them to at least tell me their names. I know he, I said, pointing at Oshri, is called Oshri. The nearly teenaged girl shook her head no, a momentum of hair that left some strands clinging to her face. The possibly teenaged boy said his name was Yalon.

Yalon? That's an unusual name. Yalon what?

Yalon Asor.

You don't happen to be—

Yalon nodded, smiling wide.

Well, I know your father.

Who doesn't, said the almost-teenaged girl, every pervert who reads the Sderot papers knows him.

I understand. Anyway, Oshri, we've got some more books by
that author you're reading at the library, you—

I have all three of them, said Oshri.

Don't talk to him, said the almost-teenaged girl, her voice already scorching.

I fluttered my eyes over their different expressions. Yalon's
alertness, the tense muscles, like an animal protecting its prey or
its cubs. Oshri's wonder, the foggy blue of his irises, a slight annoyance for being pulled away from the busy life in the book. The
rebellious expression of the nearly teenaged girl, I was forced to
linger on it. In one of those flashes of reversed history, of future
memory, the woman she would become was revealed to me, the
harder incarnation of those bones, the misleading tenderness of
the skin, the rage congealed to the corneas, resting against the
eyes, waiting.

OHILA WHISPERED OVER THE LIP OF HER GLASS, BLEW ON IT,
and sipped. A small sip, the crimping of lips, the dampening of a
tongue, the swallowing beat in the throat, the descent down the
esophagus. I smiled evenly. While I'd awaited her return from
the bathroom, I felt a tingle on my arm. A small, black ant against
my skin, wandering among the hairs. I pinched it between my
forefinger and thumb and brought it close to my face. Half its
body held by the flesh of my fingers, and the other half, antennas
going wild, shifting here and there, searching for messages, the
jaws I could envision opening and closing. A tiny black machine
whose purpose was lost upon disconnection from headquarters.
I crushed it softly, slowly, between my fingers.

My coffee landed before me. Ohila's order was also placed on
the table, a glass of boiling water and a teabag, and Ohila kept
dawdling. I picked up my teaspoon, placed the ant corpse upon it,
and carefully dipped it in Ohila's water. Carefully, I removed and

dipped it, three times. Then I pulled over the spoon and dropped the corpse into my own cup, into the blackout of the Americano.

Lots of drama you've got down south, Ohila said when she returned.

I asked, You mean the war.

That too, said Ohila, but I'm not just talking about Operation Protective Edge and the missiles. That story about the secretary and the mayor is horrifying.

I said, Heftzi Columbus.

Yes, said Ohila, dropping the teabag into the water. A bright cloud abandoned the paper wrapping, resting for a few moments in the liquid middle ground, swelling. I followed it to a point, until it lost its contours and fully blended into its surroundings.

Did you know her? asked Ohila.

I knew who she was, but I never got a chance to meet her.

But you worked at city hall.

No, I was in charge of events at the rec center, I had nothing to do with the mayor's office.

And he, Yoram Bitton, what—

Is your movie about city hall? About Heftzi Columbus's murder? About the corruption?

No, I'm just interested, she said, tapping on the circumference of her glass. A small ripple opened up on the surface of the tea before becoming absorbed on the edges. She pulled a writing pad and a few printed pages from her bag. She said, But you knew Dalia Shushan well, didn't you?

Depends on how you define knowing someone well.

The piece you published after she—

The elegy.

Yes, the elegy. It seemed like you two were friends.

At some point all artists who grew up in Sderot met one another.

But I read an interview with her where she said she didn't feel like part of the musician group—

94

What does knowing people have to do with belonging? I said.

She took her first sip. I imagined the impurity washed into her gut along with the tea, surviving the acidic assault, striding through her blood vessels.

Tell me about her.

I gave her a long look, then once more through the transparent canopy and its wooden supporting beam. The thundering of cars, the protest of lead and electricity against speed. How it worked to deny the limitations of the body, the violence stuffed into a desire to arrive, to shorten the way, this negation of senses, what for?

I said, I don't really understand the nature of your film.

A small, second sip puckered her lips. It's a very special concept, she said, innovative. A documentary series about the artists that shaped the culture in Tel Aviv since the 1960s. It's called *Midnight Sun*. That's just a working title, but I like it. The series is a combination of archival materials, interviews with the people who knew them, and some scripted reenactments. Like a feature film. We really feel like giving each episode its own language.

Third sip. A sigh of relief.

And you need me for?

Like I explained on the phone, we're in the research phase, but we sort of want to get shooting already, at least the talking-heads parts.

So you're checking what I have to offer.

Look, I spoke to Rami Amzaleg, who was with Dalia in Blasé. Did you hear the album he put out, with the instrumental arrangements of their songs?

Yes.

Amazing album. So Rami agreed to do it. And Debbie Malkieli, her manager, will give an interview too. We ran into a bit of bad luck with—

Elish Ben Zaken.

Uh-huh. Her movements turned hasty, swift. She downed half

the tea before speaking again. I'm such an idiot, I don't know why
I put off talking to him. I had his number right in front of me, and
every time I sat in my office and thought about calling, I found
something else to do. I don't—

I thought about the messages Elish left me two weeks before
he died. He wanted to meet and discuss Heftzi Columbus. He said
he was gathering materials for a book about her life and its forlorn end. I took my time too, not calling him back. Perhaps his
relationship with Dalia, about whom he'd refused to talk to me
back in the day, awakened a small-scale vengefulness. Perhaps
there was another reason I've yet to identify.

I said, Have you read his book?

Which one, the detective novel? No. Does he write about her?

No, *The Sky Is Dust*. His book about Israeli rock.

Yeah, sure.

So I think you can find everything he had to say in there.

But it isn't the same. We wanted him to give an interview himself. He must have had something to say after twelve years. God
help us. He was young.

I can portray him, I said, in the scripted parts.

Ohila smiled derisively and sipped her tea. Why did you stay
in Sderot? she asked.

That whole mass migration to Tel Aviv during the nineties, so
dull. I tried it for a month, but I figured out the scam pretty
quickly.

What scam?

Where are you from originally?

Karnei Shomron.

Hard-core. The Bnei Akiva movement is pretty strong there,
isn't it?

She shrugged.

And you live in Tel Aviv?

Tel Aviv is a settlement too, she said.

I poured some milk into my coffee. The whiteness raining

onto the dimness of the Americano revealed the dead ant. A dark, floating oil stain. Gross, I said, look at that. I tilted the cup toward her.

What is that, said Ohila, a coffee ground?

I fished out the ant with a spoon. I looked at it wallowing in a puddle of milky coffee. An ant, I said.

An ant, Ohila fretted. She picked up her glass and examined it.

I don't think, I said, there's one in your glass too. But there must be a nest somewhere on the ground—

Ohila raised her glass up in the air to trap in the light. The amber fluid gathered the sunrays, growing brighter. She lowered the glass and sniffed it. The tea steam swallowed inside her nostrils.

Calm down, big deal, even if you ingested the impurity of the insect, you did it by error, there's no—

What do you even know? said Ohila. The taut skin of her cheeks grew pale, her nostrils paling. You don't have a clue.

I said nothing.

I've got to wash my mouth, she said. She limped out, a hand covering her mouth.

I shook my spoon this way and that until the ant corpse flew off in some direction. Ohila returned a little while later and sat down across from me. A strained mask of calm. Her fingers dug into the fabric of her skirt that bunched up on her lap. So there's nothing special you can tell me about Dalia Shushan, she said, her words separated, felt around for. Some side of her that only you know?

I invested a lot in analyzing her texts. I can talk about central motifs and so forth.

She considered this for a few moments. Would you be willing to let us film you reading your elegy? I read someplace that occasionally you collaborate and perform with musicians. It could be a nice scene. I need to speak to the director first, because—

I said, My dad ran the rec center for many years. She came in

for a meeting with him once. I mean, I arranged a meeting for her.
I mean, not for her, for a mutual friend, someone I knew. She was
sixteen. She wanted the rec center to offer guitar lessons.

And?

My father said no.

That can also be a fascinating scene, said Ohila, pouncing on
her writing pad. A few quick jots, and she set her iPhone between
us. Do you mind repeating that, I want to record it.

That's all I've got, I said, not a big story.

No, said Ohila. We'll interview you and your father, and we'll
bring her mother too. We'll stage a confrontation with—

Are you crazy, I said, you want to involve Esther Shushan in
this?

She's the last one on our list, said Ohila. Noya said we should
save her for the end, we should go—

Noya?

I already told you on the phone—the director, Noya Resnick,
you must have seen her film, *Labor*, about the Nigerian migrant
workers' children—

Well, sure, I said, how could I have not? I'm always amazed at
how bottomless exploitation is. The exploited can continue to be
exploited endlessly. After they're deprived of their identities,
their rights, after every last shred of humanity is scratched off of
them and it seems like there's nothing left to take, someone
comes by and steals their voice, their cry.

Amazing, amazing, amazing, said Ohila, you can't believe the
responses she's getting. The movie's being shown all over Europe,
people are leaving in tear—

Yeah, I said, I wondered while watching it, before she falls
asleep in a five-star hotel room paid for by the film festival that
invited her, does she even consider the comfort level of the three
Nigerian families she filmed back in that forty-square-meter
apartment in the Shapira neighborhood?

Oh, said Ohila, just so you know, Noya is an awesome person.

Remember that cute kid in the movie, the one she filmed at the day-care center near the Central Bus Station? She used to call him once a week until his father got laid off and they couldn't pay the cell phone bill anymore, and by that time—

No, I said, you have no permission to bother Esther Shushan.

What? said Ohila, the syllable stretching into a bleat. She got ahold of herself. What does that have to do with you, she's—

No, I said.

Why don't you stop cutting me off and let me talk for a minute? Her voice elevated into a screech. She tensed her jaw. I heard the rows of teeth gnashing into each other with a click.

MY REFLECTION WAS CAUGHT IN THE BATHROOM MIRROR AFTER the meeting at the department of education in city hall. I marinated my hands in the stream of water under the softly humming faucet, and leaned in for a closer look. Signs of edema, of putting on flesh. I was fattening up again. I grabbed the side of my stomach to feel for the forming of a gut, but it did not yet show any signs of overflowing. I touched the sides of my chest, feeling for the protruding of my ribs. Still, the face, somewhat bloated, the cheeks, up close, plump. When I twisted my face into a smile, the eyes sank into the padded sockets. What could I have possibly changed in my diet over the past few days? I ate as usual, oatmeal in the morning with a spoonful of honey and some cinnamon, 150 calories. Half a teaspoon of sugar in my black coffee, another ten calories. For lunch all I had was light whole-grain bread sandwiches. Maybe it's that new bread—the calories per slice must have been marked wrong, or else maybe I should avoid gluten. I'd pondered this possibility before, and I would have given it a shot had I not loathed abstainers of all kinds. This whole country is full of Goddamn abstainers, vegans and vegetarians, paleolithians and fruitarians. But they would never abstain from one thing— the violence with which they promote their dietary notions, the violence with which they attempt to enforce them. Even if my digestive system rejected some elemental substance, even if I was missing some enzyme fundamental for its digestion, I would never cut it out. Just like that, for spite. And in the evening, what did I eat, rice and salad, all told about 1,200 calories. I'd been neglecting my treadmill workout, choosing easier sessions. Or maybe I'd just reached that age when the body begins to thicken regardless of calorie intake, rolling muscle cells into fat. I saw it happen to my father. At age forty-three, his movements weakened and his measurements widened. Msodi Farkash grumbled lengthily about how they had to replace his entire wardrobe every few months. None of the prohibitions she placed made any difference. She forbade him from consuming alcohol or sweets, but his metabolism ticked by according to a private clock. One day, I'd lose my grip on my own organs too. For years, I've suspected I was an infiltrator into this body, which others address as Nahum Farkash. Cogs and thin threads are intertwined in my nervous system, rushing to the brain, the command center I'd invaded, stretching to the tips of my fingers. There's no such thing, I thought, it's simple economics, extracting the same amount you consume. I have to be more vigilant. I stood back up and turned off the faucet. My hands were wrinkled, but their skeletal structure was clear to the eye. At least they remained loyal.

I actually liked Alice Shitrit, the head of the department of education. She used to be my pre-K teacher. Or so she claimed, and my mother confirmed. I remember my pre-K and kindergarten days as a long, sweaty marathon under thick trees, in sunny expanses, skipping over stone walls and suddenly converging in sand lots, sinking in, and occasional stairwells, damp with rain, and a deep electric aroma, and sleeps and wakes according to a meaningless, random rhythm, and waiting, waiting, my face buried in the crook of my arm as I lean against a blue door and cry, a crying that seemed, on certain mornings, when the flickers of night refused to die out inside of me, to predict everything that would happen.

Alice asked me to come in for an urgent meeting. She called my cell phone, rather than my office number, the night before, and asked if I could come see her the next morning. I could guess her news from the tenseness of her face and the prolonged small talk. City hall had not approved the additional budget for the program I'd submitted for the coming year.

What do you mean? I said with feigned anger, preparing for a blow but not yet feeling the punch of pain in the beaten limb. What do you mean, Asraf promised the budget would be approved, I—

He didn't make any promises, said Alice.

Yes, he did, in public, no less, a few months ago, during the talent show. He stood onstage and said there would be a bigger variety of cultural events. Didn't he say just that? He did. It's documented. It's contractually binding.

Alice smiled meekly. Nahum, sweetheart, she said, don't get carried away.

Those settlers are taking over the whole town.

He was elected democratically, Alice said flatly. Not in vain had she risen from her stature as a kindergarten teacher. In the past year, she'd added some headscarves and stockings to her wardrobe. She no longer walked outside with her head bare.

Look, I said, you know I'd already made commitments with writers and poets. The program is complete, with scheduled dates and everything.

These things are always taken with a grain of salt, they must know that.

Asraf has no idea how happy they were to hear from me. The opening is in February, and we're already working on publicity.

Alice lowered her head. A pattern on her headscarf was revealed—twisting silver threads, a delicate, white-hot web.

Explain something to me, I said. The public library cultural event budget is supposed to increase according to the government's five-year plan, right? It's supposed to reach its maximum size in the next year. So what is Asraf's interest here? If we don't present the government with a structured plan, we won't get the budget increase and we'll be stuck with this year's budget, which was already half of what we could have gotten. I don't understand. Didn't you read the letter I attached to my plan? I thought—

I have no control over these things, said Alice. There are lots of expenses for renovations and rebuilding, and with the operation in Gaza, there are considerations that have nothing to do—

Considerations, my ass, I said. It's because of me, isn't it?

Alice fell silent. Then she said, Nahum, be smart about this, what can you gain from being pigheaded again?

JUST A FEW MORE MINUTES. THE RED DIGITS ON THE TREADMILL screen beat to the pace of my breathing, forty-five minutes, twenty seconds, six kilometers. My forehead drenched with sweat. My calf muscles ached. I'd chosen a mountain climbing program. The treadmill's incline kept changing. I ascended the mountain, then descended the slope. I switched to the calorie counter, 350 calories, not bad, but that wasn't the point. I'd only gained four hundred grams over the past week, but they showed on my body like several kilos. Softness covered the angularity of my face, the bones of my skull, though the body mass calculator, which was entirely unreliable, placed me close to the underweight extreme for my age and height. No, it wasn't about that. It was the furnace of thoughts that had yet to stand still and cool down. Go on. More. I had another free hour, an empty hour, a hollow, oval hour. I'd given up reading since the war. I didn't give it up, but it lost its point. The smearing of ink and the roughness of paper, and heaps of indecipherable syllables. Poetry lost its flavor too. On Rosh Hashanah, our group of Sderot friends convened as usual in Ma'ayan's mother's home after the holiday meal. Our conversation took its usual form—nostalgia and inside jokes, TV show commentary, and grumbling. And the war, analyzing it, analyzing it, all the horror shifting within our lives, which so rarely we allowed to rear its ugly head, flowed into the work of dismantling and putting back together. We have to take down the government, said Gil. Ma'ayan mentioned for the thousandth time that Gil didn't even vote, and Gil said that was true, but he loved anarchy, and laughed. And Yaron told him to stop yammering, and Ma'ayan talked about how shocked she was about the things people allowed themselves to say on social media, about the cutthroat cancel culture. About the three crimes of Israel and the fourth that could not be taken back. About the Bar-Ilan University professor who asked his students to remember that dead children were dead children regardless of which side they were on, and was subsequently removed from his position under the pretext that he'd violated the ethical code of conduct for a public institution. About the post office clerk who suggested that all left-wing voters be gassed and got off scot-free. About the prime minister fanning the flames of hatred as his main method for garnering support. I hardly pitched in. Eventually, Yaron tired of hearing the complaints and shifted the conversation to an acquaintance of ours who'd grown inured during the war and about an argument he'd gotten into with Gil over Facebook and the swear words the two had typed at each other. Gil defended his behavior, claiming drugs had muddled the brain of said acquaintance, and that the guy's bouts of panic over missiles were fueled by all the coke he was snorting. I said, Fine, but what can we do about it? And Ma'ayan said, Nothing, he's a goner, but Gil should apologize to the poor guy. I said, No, what can we do about this situation, and the conversation returned to parsing out the distress into run-on sentences, the purpose of which was singular—seeking shelter in our old, powerful intimacy.

What I didn't say was, Sure, collapsing houses and burnt

children, but for me, beyond events, the space of resonance of the Hebrew language has been distorted. If I bit words between my teeth they tasted like lead, oxidized. If they fell out of my mouth, their sound grew grating as the airwaves shifted to carry them. More than anything, they looked fake in their written form, their squareness. As if their foreignness, overpowered and domesticated over prolonged eons of debates and questioning, and prayers, and priestly compositions translated into decrees, and purification rituals, and the pulse of life, the redemption of the son, and the dowry of the daughter, and entering under the shelter of the Torah, and marriages and wakes, had finally emerged. Their Assyrian origin sprung up and sabotaged their intentions. Our ancestors were idolaters from the start.

And the irony, I thought, when I retired from the gathering and walked along Sderot's still-scorching lights, the dark, inner glow of the nocturnal texture in its moonless nights, the irony of a library manager who can no longer read books written in his language. "Everyone whose name shall be found written in the book," how bitterly rang the quote in the foyers of my mind.

Before making a plan to meet Snot outside the library, back in ninth grade, I hadn't even noticed the quote. Snot was late. As I waited for him, I examined the exterior wall of the exposed quad. I found it standing against a patchwork of figures and broken quotations praising the power of the book. Bits and shards of glistening, colorful ceramics. A few moments later, Snot skipped up three steps and stopped beside me. His eyes also traveled over the mosaic. He said, I've never looked at that before. His nose was full of snot from walking, and he interspersed his words with moist inhalations.

And many of them that sleep in the dust of the earth shall awake, some to everlasting life, and some to shame and everlasting contempt.

What? said Snot.

I pointed at the quote, "Everyone whose name shall be found

written in the book," and the source in parentheses, Daniel 12:1, and said, That's the next passage, and the previous one says, "And at that time shall Michael stand up." And I pointed at Snot.

Snot huffed, and as he did so he swallowed his snot with a sucking sound.

I said, Everyone whose name shall be found written in the book. Then, at age fifteen, my heart overflowed.

IN THE WEEK FOLLOWING OUR APPOINTMENT, OHILA SENT ME an email reminding me that I'd promised to give them an answer. She also left me a voicemail. I didn't get back to her. Desperate, she called the library. Shifra, the librarian from the adult circulation room, walked into my office with a wide smile on her face. She said that a very lovely young woman was calling for me, her name was Ohila, what a wonderful Hebrew name. I wondered if Shifra was utilizing a measure of mercy or of judgment. If she'd caught on to the fact that I was trying to avoid Ohila and was tripping me up or if she was genuinely trying to help me. Shifra's dream of serving as the library manager was crushed when Simo Farkash intervened, pulled some strings, and arranged for me, with no training or previous experience in library work, to get the job when the former manager retired. Shifra was the veteran, most experienced library employee, and promoting her would have been the natural choice. I felt no scruples for stealing the job away. Shifra treated me with the same fickle manner she'd reserved for me in my youth, when, thanks to Snot, I discovered the library and started spending all my time there. Some days she greeted me warmly, motivating me, even allowing me to borrow an irregular number or type of books from the reference room or the rare collections. Other days she welcomed me with severe, stingy expressions, sparing words and demanding that I comply with the public library decrees that were delivered to Earth by the angel of literature. Her exposed rows of teeth and her lips that stretched to the edges of her face, slicing the two sections of her skull, were equal parts prize and whip.

I asked her to transfer the call, as if I didn't know that she hadn't managed to figure out the technological advances at the library, and transferring calls was beyond her capabilities. Bemusement slashed through her far-apart eyes, a cracking of the glazed irises. A measure of mercy, then. I stood up.

She waited for me to step out of my office, paused for a few moments longer, then hurried after me. I could feel her presence against my back. She asked if the rumors were true, that there were going to be cuts in next year's budget. I turned to face her. She was wringing her fingers.

I said, Over my dead body.

She nodded, but the concern did not disappear from her face. I noted that I must put an end to the rumors. In a place like Sderot they can quickly transform into reality, and who knew if the mayor's office hadn't spread them to apply pressure on me in the first place.

Occasionally, I am assaulted once again with the shock of entering the circulation room. As if a version of myself had been ensconced in an alternate pocket universe where time has no control. It erupts onto me, and I am forced to don it, to enter this hall as I had back then, with the same wonder at the sight of the dense avenues of shelves, sprawled to eternity, carrying their promises, and the trickling of tension down the esophagus, and the nasal cavities filling with the supernatural moldiness of the space.

I grabbed the phone and spoke urgently. Yes, Ohila, how are you?

Hang on, I heard her yelling coming from a distance, the hastiness of her footsteps and the rustling of the skirt around her ankles, then her nearby voice. Thanks for picking up. She settled her breath and added, I need an answer.

You know what my condition is. You won't be bothering Esther Shushan.

Shifra walked behind her counter and took a seat. I assumed she was eavesdropping, though she pretended to busy herself ordering new books. She clicked her tongue at the mention of Esther Shushan's name.

And I told you that was unacceptable, said Ohila.

Then we've got nothing to talk about.

Noya says she heard you performed one of your poems with Antibiotics, and that it could be a nice homage to Dalia—

Forget it, I said and hung up.

What do they want from Esther? said Shifra.

They want to make a movie about Dalia.

At the library?

Why do you say that?

There was a time when you used to come here a lot, you and her.

Oh, well, we lament those that are gone yet linger among us.

But wait, said Shifra.

I paused on the threshold, one foot in and one foot out. What? I said, not turning around to face her.

Hasn't Esther suffered enough? Yossef died of sorrow too, may he rest in peace.

With effort, I removed the foot that still remained inside the circulation room. Sometimes I think someone ought to coin the term "absolute zero hour." Why should we imagine that outlandish measure of distance—the total number of kilometers light can travel in a spatial void over the course of a year—when we are closer in experience to the measure of distance that a single molecule covers in one hour, near absolute zero? There is no physical logic to it, true, but consciousness is familiar with that hour, consciousness knows. My way back to the office was measured by tens and hundreds of absolute zero hours. When I arrived, an email was waiting for me from the mayor's office, summoning me to a meeting early the following week.

✻ ✻ ✻

AFTER WATCHING THE MOVIE, SNOT AND I HAD LONG ARGUMENTS about the ending. Snot was satisfied, but I claimed that if, after all that harrowing training, in the final battle between the new kid, the protagonist, and the local bully, the new kid would have lost, limping away from the ring with bruised bones and swollen face, the film would have been perfect. The moments of greatest pleasure occurred in the beginning of the movie. The irritating new kid had been humiliated by a gang of bikers on the beach. The camera lingered over him, lying on his stomach, his bleeding lips against the sand. Actually, I told Snot, if the movie would have ended with a close-up of the shock on the Japanese master's face as his beaten protégé walked away, it would have been a masterpiece.

But Shoo'i, Chantal's youngest, who watched the remake of *The Karate Kid*, only answered a hasty yes when I asked him if he found the movie interesting. He didn't even turn his head to me. His eyes were planted on the screen. I sat down on the couch beside him. I'd already dragged myself over, as it were, showing up a little late. Chantal called, her whispered voice emerging from the iPhone's speaker. Where are you, she said, Dad's already back from synagogue.

In my apartment, I played my mother's voice in my mind, saying, What's a ten-minute walk, and so what if I come visit in the middle of the week, Shabbat is Shabbat. I played Chantal, claiming that our father had started grumbling that if I couldn't be bothered then I shouldn't come at all, and not to do them any favors. Even those playbacks didn't motivate me to press on the doorknob, to open the door. I didn't want to go there, with the holeache that had lit up within me again. But Chantal's whisper sliced through all of that.

What a guest, said Simo Farkash as I walked in. He was sitting alone at the table, the challahs in their embroidered dresses, the wine bottle corked before him, the goblet still set upside down. Time, which rolls into weight and gravity, was apparent in his body. The goatee that he'd been growing over the past few weeks had reached its full form. It afforded his face a renewed validity.

Sorry, I said, I was reading and lost track of time.

Reading, said Simo, big deal.

My mother was sprawled on the living room couch. Exhausted from preparing for Shabbat. Chantal was toiling over the salads. She said, Nahum, go check on Shoo'i.

Where are the others? I asked.

Ariel had to stay the weekend on base and Sharon's at his girl-friend's, said Chantal, her back still turned to me.

My mother stood up to greet me. I gestured for her to stay seated. I walked over. I leaned down and kissed her cheek. Shabbat Shalom, I said.

Shoo'i was in my childhood bedroom. He was flipping between the different kids' channels. I said, How's it going?

Shoo'i turned his two dark eye pools toward me, chambers of velvet that took up half his face, and said, Cool.

What's cool, how's school, how's judo, what?

Fun, said Shoo'i.

Well, come on, we're having dinner.

I don't feel like it, said Shoo'i, I'm not hungry.

No, no, no, I said, you're not starting with that trick, Grandpa is already mad at me.

What do I care? said Shoo'i.

I plopped onto the pull-out sofa and pulled him into my arms.

Let go, let go, said Shoo'i.

I'm not letting go, I said. I tickled his stomach and his chest. Shoo'i laughed involuntarily, but in between laughter kept saying, Let go, let go.

And that's how Chantal found us—me on the sofa, Shoo'i on my lap, his chubby body twisting away from my tickling and his mouth shifting between bursts of laughter and squeals of Let go.

Great, she said, maybe I should have sent Shoo'i to get you. Her hands were hidden inside a kitchen towel.

During dinner, our mother commented, You're barely touching the salads, and Chantal said I looked a little down.

Problems at work again? asked Simo.

No, I said, it's nothing.

Chantal said she was going to put an offer in for the new neighborhood bid. Music neighborhood, they're unfreezing the land.

Where? I asked.

On the border of Sderot, near the train station, my mother said.

Seriously? I said. The dust hasn't even settled yet over Heftzi Columbus's murder and the corruption at the Lakeside neighborhood, and already they're putting out bids for new zones.

Chantal said, Don't talk about that kind of thing around Shoo'i.

Shoo'i was devouring his special tomato salad. He sponged the soft insides of the challah in the juice from the salad and chewed vigorously. Can I have more Coke? he asked when his mother spoke his name.

No, said Chantal, you have your father's genes, and I need to keep an eye on you.

But it's Saturday, said Shoo'i.

Like you've got any shortage, I said.

Shortage of what, asked Chantal, looking over herself. Even after carrying three children, her body showed no signs of thickening. In the striped dress, her body was youthful, lithe.

Did you forget what a little fritter you used to be as a kid?

She was healthy, said Msodi.

Shoo'i looks healthy to me too.

No, said Msodi. You can tell by the *h'dud*. She reached a hand across the table and gently pinched Shoo'i's cheek. Chantal didn't have a *h'dud* like that.

You Moroccans have invented your own science of medicine, I said.

Very funny, said Chantal. Oh, Mom, I just got a joke on WhatsApp that's perfect for you. Listen. Only a Moroccan woman books a housecleaning and, hang on, how does that joke go?

She stood up.

Where are you going? asked Simo.

Um, said Chantal, Dad, what can I get you?

Simo turned to me and said, You should place a bid too, your apartment is old and your neighborhood is bad.

I always filled with shame whenever Simo brought up the subject of my apartment. When I came back to Sderot after my year at Ben-Gurion University, returning from my voyages in the midnineties, Simo struck a deal with one of the contractors working to expand Sderot by building new neighborhoods. The local population had doubled in size upon receiving immigrants from the former Soviet Union, and there were bids aplenty. Simo had convoluted connections in local government. I only asked once what kind of inducement was offered in exchange for the four-bedroom apartment I received, whether it was information or benefits or some other, more questionable tribute. Dad shushed me furiously, offering an inarguable rationale—that the dark negotiations I was asking after were a necessary evil and none of my business. People like Simo were sentenced to serve as gatekeepers, maintaining the ideal dosage of corruption. Too little, and no plan would ever come to fruition. Too much, and it would constitute a betrayal of city residents.

I was too young, and my father's argument stunned me. Or perhaps I was making an effort, as my mother often beseeched me, to allow my father to give his gifts under his own terms. You're his eldest son, said Msodi Farkash. When you have your own children, you'll realize there are a million ways to give. Don't expect your father to give his gifts the way you want to receive them, let him give them the way he knows how. The shame resurfaced in full force during the summer of 2011, when I organized a protest in front of Sderot city hall. Yoram Bitton, who was the mayor at the time, called me then and said, You've got some nerve, isn't it enough for you to share a protest tent with Gazan protesters, now you dare complain about the financial situation, what finances are troubling you exactly, enlighten me. Is it the financial situation that got you set up with your own apartment?

I told Dad I preferred to stay in my apartment. I liked the neighborhood, the residents, and the proximity to the library.

Yibki alik, what residents? Have you forgotten the club they started outside the library until we finally had to kick them out? All the human garbage they brought over from Russia.

Is the human garbage they brought over from Morocco any better? I asked.

Don't start, my mom said, why'd you come here, all depressed?

We kept eating. Biting into meat and shaking our glasses. When my mother and Chantal cleared the table, Chantal said, So it goes like this, only a Moroccan woman hires a maid, cleans up before the maid comes, helps the maid mop the floor, makes her coffee, pays her, then after she leaves, says, She cleans about as pretty as her face.

Msodi laughed.

Dad and I stayed seated at the table. He glared at me.

I said, What, Dad?

Trouble at work?

A little, I whispered. I glanced into the kitchen. My mother and Chantal were deep in conversation, passing the dishes from one to the other.

Spill it, said Simo.

No big deal, they didn't approve the new program.

Let's go out to the balcony. Simo removed his yarmulke and placed it on the table. On more than one occasion, I've told Dad that the yarmulke isn't God's wire. If Simo believed God was listening, then he should believe that he was never safe, not even in dreams. And Dad said, You've always been radical, even when you were religious. How far are you trying to go with your heresy?

So, Simo said now, I thought this was the way to ensure the increase in the library's annual budget.

Yeah, I said, Asraf knows that.

He wants to get something out of you, said Simo Farkash. That Asraf is a snake.

I nodded.

Leave it to me, said Simo. I'll talk to Rabbi Avisror, he listens to him.

No, I said, I have a meeting with Asraf early next week.

Chantal called out from inside the house, but I knew it was my mother borrowing my sister's throat: Nahum, honey, go check on Shoo'i, he's alone with the TV again.

MAYOR ASRAF'S BALD, TAN HEAD, WHICH WAS NOT CONCEALED by a yarmulke, glistened in the neon lights of his office. Outside the window, an army of clouds was gathering, a charged, shabby dimness. The curls on the sides of his head descended down to the back of his head, just like in Maimonides's halachic definitions of baldness. The narrow electricity of winter and the earthing of Asraf's nasal speech blended together.

The problem wasn't the proposal, he said, which was good and founded in the wise idea of increasing the library budget through government establishments, and if I'd heard his statements I must know that culture was very important to him, as well as the general quality of life in the city and the state of education. The problem was the library had become a hub for subversive activities, and he'd heard rumors of my participation in demonstrations against Operation Protective Edge, and now I wanted to bring all of my bleeding-heart traitor friends from Tel Aviv to Sderot to corrupt minds with their propaganda.

Well, Asraf didn't say that in so many words. None of the people who talked to me used those words, save for Yoram Bitton and his silver tongue. Bitton's word choice had fixed itself in my mind, verbatim. But as for others, I write their words the way I think they ought to be remembered.

I told Asraf, first, the purpose of the demonstration was iden-tification with victims of war. And two, the poets and writers that would be invited to these events would be discussing their work.

You aren't listening to me, said Asraf.

I nodded. I said, You want to interfere with my list.

God forbid, said Asraf, I'm not a dictator.

Then what are you?

You're using public funds, the library's activity should reflect that.

Do you even know what we do at the library?

I know enough.

Then tell me what you think is missing.

Isn't it obvious?

Not to me, unless you're ascribing me some ill intentions.

You used to be religious, didn't you? Your father wears a yar-mulke. I can see your Jewish soul pining for its roots.

You can?

When you walked in here and sat across from me, you had that twinkle in your eyes, I remember that twinkle from the ye-shiva study groups.

Aha, I said.

So I don't need to tell you what's missing.

I said, Jewish heritage.

Asraf said, It's decided, then. You'll submit a detailed proposal for a series of lectures by next week?

AND THERE WAS NOYA RESNICK HERSELF, THE NIGERIAN WHIS-perer, as I referred to her in my tweets, posted under my alias, @TheAbominable. Her voice chopped the narration of the audio-book I was listening to during a brisk, tendon-snapping walk on my treadmill. Two kilometers, 230 calories, an unpassable wilderness of an Israeli novel. It too decried, unknowingly, the great betrayal of Israeli bourgeoisie itself. An existence that had been parsed out into a punctilious narrative, divorce and travels abroad and returns to Israel, and convoluted relationships with the next generations, and revealing secrets from the ever-frothing death camps, and a hint of pioneering heritage suddenly raging into ideological declarations and words of affection and seduction, and beyond all that, an awful anxiety, an approaching ruin. Not the symbolic ruin, the previous generation of writers' despondent, overdone ruin of the nation. The true ruin of the bourgeois being, the foundation of which has always been the chain of production and the accumulation of capital. Puritanical values of sexual policing and birthing supervision were recruited for its preservation, and its power was always apparent in aggrandizing that very foundation into an encompassing, natural social order. But in its Israeli incarnation, the bourgeoisie was deceived by the lie of security and its adoption as a deeper, more tangible foundation than the economic one, and sentenced itself to—

Good evening, may I speak to Nahum?

Speaking.

How are you?

Not too—

Am I interrupting you, you—

Bad.

Sound all . . . breathless.

One minute.

Yes, um, who am I talking to?

The giggle that accompanied the adjective *breathless* emerged again. Sorry, Noya, Noya Resnick.

Hi, nice to meet you.

Let's start over. Good evening.

How are you?

It isn't working out for us, huh?

What isn't?

Fine. You can probably guess why I'm calling.

Why don't you tell me? I'm a little weary of postulating.

Weary of postulating, she repeated, then giggled. I can tell you're a poet.

Poetry's got nothing to do with flowery expressions.

You're a difficult man to compliment.

Why do you need to?

Are you annoyed because of Ohila?

I'm not annoyed. Listen, it isn't your fault, just a long day.

Okay. I understand there's some issue with your participation in the film about Dalia Shushan.

Not really an issue. I'm happy to contribute to any action intended to perpetuate Dalia Shushan's work and heritage, as long as they aren't being sullied.

And you think the film is going to sully them?

I don't know what the division of labor is between you and Ohila, but to me she seems to have screenwriter pretenses.

We're writing it together.

Then why did she introduce herself as a researcher?

Because we're in the development stage, and, look, Nahum, the idea was hers to begin with . . . She heard about the project and fought to be part of it. She wrote the initial outline and talked me into joining, otherwise she didn't stand a chance.

Of course.

I'm not boasting. That's how things work.

All right.

She's shooting in all directions and maybe I ought to restrain her, but I want to promise you that she won't—

Did she tell you about my condition?

Yes, but does that really make sense to you? Making a movie about Dalia Shushan without interviewing her mother?

From what I understand, the project's creative liberty is fairly expansive.

It's like if I made my other film without filming those poor families living around the Central Bus Station.

I said nothing. In one of my @TheAbominable tweets, I wrote that for the Nigerian Whisperer the Nigerians were nothing more than an amplification system for her ego.

Then where's the objection?

Her daughter was murdered. Her husband faded away over the course of a decade until one day he didn't get out of bed anymore. Do you truly believe there's any justification, film or no film, for picking at her scabs?

Noya hummed. The murder is an important aspect of the story, she said.

You don't need Esther Shushan for that.

Yes, I do.

I almost said, Art is the opposite of emotional extortion. But as the words made their way through my throat, I realized I was about to quote another one of @TheAbominable's tweets regarding the work of the Nigerian Whisperer. I quickly said, And why are you insisting on me?

What?

I caught the edge of her panic. She wasn't prepared for this question. Why are you insisting on me?

I . . . I need a contact in Sderot, and you–

That isn't a good enough reason. Some of the artists that left came back to live here in the last few years, and every one of them–

But you knew her.

Again, I'm not the only one.

Okay, I'm going to tell you this in confidence. Promise me this stays between us.

I solemnly swear.

Is that a joke?

No, I solemnly swear. What did you want me to say, upon my honor?

Noya giggled. She must have thought there was a charm to that teenaged sound. She was in her midthirties, to take her Wikipedia page's word for it. She said, Ohila has a reliable source who says that a year after Dalia was murdered, Elish Ben Zaken was walking around Sderot, asking questions.

Elish Ben Zaken? What's he got to do with it? Was he working on a sequel to *The Sky Is Dust*?

No, he was a private investigator by that point.

Okay, so you think he found any new evidence?

Unfortunately, we haven't been able to find out. He—

Is no longer with us.

Yeah, and his accident, it happened just as we were beginning to gather materials.

You think there's a connection between the two events?

Do you think there is? No, no way . . . What's for sure is, Esther Shushan will know more.

That's likely.

So you understand why I need her?

I don't really need an explanation. I've got no questions about the logic or the emotion behind it. I just know where I stand.

Noya sighed.

I said, So far you've danced around the subject beautifully. So how do I fit into all this?

Noya sighed again.

Good night, I said.

Wait, wait, she said.

I listened to the thin rustlings of hesitation, the sibilance that sliced through her shaping and breaking syllables before they formed words. Finally, she said that the production had received an unequivocal message from the Culture Flame Fund, which supported the film, that my appearance was essential.

No concealments, then. No straw owners, no anonymous

donations. The Culture Flame Fund, the charitable enterprise founded by Therese Kavillio-Buganim, one of the owners of Becker-Kavillio-Buganim Medicinal Technologies, Inc.

I READ THE LONG INTERVIEW THERESE HAD GIVEN IN 2012 IN one of the weekend supplements, an interview laden with falsifications and intentional deceptions on her part. I hadn't seen her since military service. Back then, I was standing in a nocturnal barrenness beneath a canopy of concrete strewn with profanities, doodles, expressions of the foolish desire to leave a mark, all under an enormous moon that labored to flow mercurially across the Givati Junction. I was freezing at the bus stop. The dark in-between of the heavenly bodies grew tighter, pressing on my windpipe as the minutes ticked by and thoughts of Amiram did not fade away, did not desert. Bus service had already ended, and not even a dog would pass by in the next few hours, let alone a car. But a car did stop, and behind the wheel was Therese. The shock of her still young, always young eyes passed me by as my soldier image fell down her gaze, in and down, toward my other image, which was reserved within her.

SHE SAID I'D GROWN, AS IF THAT WERE SOMETHING I COULD control. But where would I have stopped if I'd had a choice? No, not stopped, stopping is an illusion that appeases the soul rather than sustaining it. And I, meaning I, think there must be a future in which we are able to gather dead bits of being, our bits of waiting, and plant them in moments requiring the expansion of awareness, until the tangible is tangible in a thickened time, tangible in a dense time, tangible in several dimensions of time. Of course I-Nahum would not have stopped then, that night, with the oxygen-starved holeache in my chest.

What are you standing there for? said Therese. Get in the car.

What could I have said, that I had to digest the change, not of the passage of time, but of sight? She looked younger than I'd remembered her, still caught in my preteen mind. The prominent cheekbones and sunken eyes, contoured by the dark rings on the taut skin, gleaming softly, a final rustle of a dying fire. Just like then, in the outer thicket, Cocoa Pup's grunting. I got into the car. The seat was spacious. My body became lost in the act of sitting.

Do you serve nearby? Therese asked. She lowered the volume on the radio as she spoke. There was a whisper underneath the words.

I looked at my uniform, the corporal ranks sewn to the sleeves. Yes, I said, almost surprised, close.

Open base, jobnick?

I nodded.

I was sure you'd go further.

What's far? I asked.

I don't know, she said. Ehud was accepted into the Talpiot intelligence program, that seems far enough.

I didn't know. We're not in touch.

My throat was dry, as was my esophagus. Amiram was probably eager to get home to Kiryat Gat. His face wore a lustful smile back in the base when he said, I just think of my wife and I get sleepy. Then he yawned big. Amiram's car was old. The rails of the passenger seat had screeched when I tried to adjust it to my size. I trembled at the sound of the metallic discord. I left it as it was, adjusted for a body smaller than his. His wife's, probably. As we rode, the shaking that started in my feet hurried up my legs. I held back from shouting at Amiram to pull over and let me keep going on foot, through the night, through the clarity of night, under the arrangement of stars, a silver embroidery in the black curtain. Look at that strong moon, Amiram said, and I choked. I felt the touch nerving up his arm, the preparation to reach. The burning in my thighs waited, near the knee shoved against the gearbox. He dropped me off at Givati Junction and asked if I was sure I'd be okay. I lied. I told him the last bus was coming in ten minutes. I was in a rush to get out of the car, but I dawdled. I felt like something had to be said. I staked it out, waiting for it to clarify. Amiram asked, with a kind of paternal worry, Is everything all right? I couldn't even mumble a thank-y—

Don't get upset, said Therese, the military isn't the end of the world, I'm sure you've got—

I write poetry, I said.

Poetry, said Therese. The ghost smile was apparent on the edges of her naked lips. As a rule, her face was clean of makeup, sharper and more angular than I'd remembered, in absolute contrast with the rest of her curvy figure. My voice cracked when I spoke the word "poetry," but she couldn't hear the cracks. I asked if she was going to Sderot.

She said she was stopping by Sderot on her way to Beersheba. I meant to ask why she was taking the side roads rather than the highway. She beat me to it and said she was in no rush and thought it was such a lovely night, but there was something else, some longing that urged her, awakening in her as she left Tel Aviv. There was a similar light eight years ago when she arrived in Sderot.

I said I thought she'd arrived in summer, before the High Holy Days. And she said of course she did, but something about the brightness of the moon, the color of the sky. In Israel one can confuse the dying of winter and the dying of summer. If I wrote poetry, then I could definitely understand.

I said, Maybe I write poetry against nature.

For nature, against nature, either way, it's part of the way you look at the world.

I said I was sorry. When I heard about her husband's death he—
She cut me off, she said it was all right.
Did you go there? I asked.
She said, Where? To Lublin? Yes, a few times.

What happened to him?

He was murdered, said Therese. Her jaws locked. I felt a twin tenseness in my own jaw muscles.

I . . . I didn't know, I thought—

There's nothing to know. Eldad wouldn't have caught typhus. He traveled for research purposes. They couldn't find any official lab in the area that grew cultures, no studies about that particular strain of bacteria.

I fell silent. The radio played a faraway, choked song, no, a collection of sounds that didn't come together to form any kind of meaning. Why had I even brought it up? Though I didn't know him, I couldn't help but picture him back then, when stories of him were circulating among the boys at school. They talked about his body being found in an abandoned warehouse somewhere in Poland. They said his right hand had rotted and fallen off before he died, that his body was covered with abscesses. The image didn't let go of me that entire year. The man lying in loneliness, his blackened flesh slowly decaying. We passed the turn into the village of Heletz, a transient spot on the polished glass. In the deserted bus stop, a single lamp did its best to spread a rough aura of light. The eucalyptus hedgerows scratched the skies. Even beyond the shuttered windows, the steel speed of the chassis, their presence penetrated. The thunder of their growth gurgled under the murmur of the air-conditioning.

I shouldn't burden you with these dark thoughts, said Therese.

I said, But all my thoughts are dark.

That's because you're a poet, she said and laughed almost bitterly.

No, I said, just because.

Oh, to be young and in love with pain.

But you're young.

Not as young as I was eight years ago.

I remember the papercutting you made for the Barda sukkah. Do you still—

Are you kidding? That was a onetime thing. That's all I did at their house from the moment I got there. All summer long I cut and cut, I couldn't think about anything else.

Why, I asked, did you make a papercutting of the hand on the wall from Belshazzar's feast?

You really do remember.

I said nothing.

She said, I didn't like being at my sister's. I didn't like the insinuations, the looks, from her, from my brother-in-law.

I said, They looked like nice people to me.

Conservative bourgeoisie, she said. You think I didn't guess what they thought about Eldad leaving his wife for me? The word "homewrecker" was all over their foreheads whenever they looked at me. And the worst part was they never asked what happened and why, and if Eldad was unhappy in his previous marriage, only invited me to stay with them for as long as I needed, and crucified me with mute accusations.

And you, for your part, imagined their punishment.

What, she said.

The papercutting, there was a secret message in it, right? *Mene, mene, tekel, parsin.*

Ehud admired your knowledge. He said there wasn't a single Bible story you didn't–

Kids are easy to impress.

You were a child too. You're still a child.

Maybe that's how Amiram saw me. The weight of age that threatened to take me down, eternal years on my shoulders, even if I was only twenty. But still the pathetic, scared, dirty child who could only be redeemed by the brotherhood of the rejected.

Your fat is childish, anyway. You used to be a twig, all skin and bones.

Am I fat? I asked, startled.

Not actually fat, but you've filled out. She pinched my cheek, my forearm. It looks good on you.

Signs for villages flickered by, glowing from the road as markers of approaching Sderot. I asked if she lived in Beersheba.

She said she didn't, but she had a meeting first thing the next morning with hospital donors, and she hated driving during rush hour. She was raising funds for a lab she was starting with some partners in Heidelberg.

Heidelberg, in Germany? I asked.

She said people had no idea of the massive window of opportunity for biotech developments that was opened up by the fall of the Berlin Wall, now that a large part of the study records from the east had become available. She told me to take her word for it, that those studies' protocols wouldn't have passed any ethics committee, but still.

The car twisted like a fish into Sderot. I guided her to my parents' house. I stood on the porch. The roof that extended over it bit off its hunk of sky. I wasn't sure I remembered how to go inside as myself, wearing the same image with which I'd walked out on Friday morning. Who knew if I hadn't already shed it and what remained of me in its wake.

BUT THE NEXT MORNING I WOKE UP WITH DIFFERENT THOUGHTS. I examined the formation of hands on the clock until the lost knowledge of reading them returned to me. Five thirty. Chantal's hesitant crying had infiltrated my sleep. I almost held on to the butt of the dream when my eyes opened. All that was left was a dull sensation, something to do with Therese, and our long voyage to the ends of the earth. Cappadocia. I chuckled for a moment. Cappadocia, there must be a treasure under the floor tiles that Simo Farkash buried and forgot about. For that word, of all lost visions, to persist. The weeping sound was the movement of water in that Cappadocia river. The mountains in the distance, and Therese's car gliding, pulled toward them. But something else, an enormous, sudden discovery of which only the contours of wonder remained. They were enough to wipe away the sorrow of yesterday. Five thirty in the morning. A strip of damp light behind the shutters. I felt around under the pillow, then on the rug beside the bed, until I found my yarmulke. Washing off the impurities, then *Modeh Ani* and the dawn prayers. A rhythmic, rustling formula. Why won't she stop crying, I thought, and so early in the morning? Then the toxic sting of terror. I hurried to her room.

Even on the bus, Chantal's disagreeable expression appeared before me. She bit her lips and swallowed. Unlike Tova, she'd preserved her childish gracefulness. Youth already gnawed around it, biting into it, and her limbs had thinned out and lengthened. Grown-ups said she was beautiful. Her classmates, who were more equipped to attest to the beauty of a fifteen-year-old girl, did not agree with that statement, Tova claimed. Most of them were deterred. They think she's butt ugly, said Tova. The waifish paleness that captivated the hearts of grown-ups might have been perceived by her peers as a testament of sickness. At any rate, Tova did not elaborate, only scattering the report once in a while in the days when she still wandered the house, inserting suspicion into the hearts of Simo and Msodi Farkash.

I stopped at the guard booth for a brief conversation with Sha'ashu'a. He told me that the previous week he'd gone to a lecture by some legendary guitarist at a music store. He now knew which electric guitar he wanted to buy. He described it in detail— the wooden body, the bridge, the special pickups, the keys, the silver engraving he would get. Out of his detailed vision, all that fixed into my mind was a white, gleaming, curving body. The musicians I knew, whose rehearsals I'd attended, made do with any instrument they could get their hands on. Classic guitars across which metal strings were stretched, emitting a crunchy sound that grew rougher until it went off-key due to the bridge, made crooked by the tautness of strings. Keyboards still programmed to produce outdated electronic sounds. Unsuitable amplifiers that added the weight of distortion and industry to the toylike tone of the instruments.

I didn't tell him any of that. Almost two weeks earlier, I'd walked through the gates of the maintenance base around noon. A slouched soldier was standing in the guard booth, staring blankly at the vehicles passing down the road a short distance away. The first rains had washed summer's nuclear fallout off the leaves. Enormous eucalyptuses unfolded their presence, a sort of roar of growth that took my breath away when I got off at the bus stop. I stood below the paunches of cracked clouds. They were stamped into the exterior boards of the guard booth, fissured wood, drenched with years and brightnesses.

I showed him my ID. He said, What do you want, applause?

I said nothing.

Wow, so serious, he said, you think anyone cares about your objectification card on this base?

Oh, objectification, I said, you said objectification.

So you're not as shocked as you look. Where're you from?

Sderot.

No, what base?

Oh, from here, I was just transferred here.

Cool, so you say you're from Sderot.

Yeah.

You play?

No, I said. In the past two years, in every one of the warehouses that took over the expanses of dust, whenever I said I was from Sderot, people asked, Where's that? I had to make do with a general geographical mark: twenty minutes away from Ashkelon.

I thought everyone played music over there.

Yeah, you could say that.

Except for you.

Except for me.

So what good are you to me?

I don't think I was assigned to this base for you.

But you don't look like one of those bores.

I'm pretty boring.

You know what I mean, all those *arsim* from the Transport Corps. There's a pile of Sderot guys here, no shortage.

And they all play music?

No, none of them is any good.

I'm Nahum, I said.

I saw that on your objectification card, said the guard. I'm Sha'ashu'a. And don't say it's nice to meet me yet.

I told him I had to get to maintenance headquarters. He gave me directions. I walked through the quad. A flag smacking against the top of the pole was beginning to lose its shape and color. The thought of returning home in a few hours glowed around my solar plexus. Heat rose from it, spreading through my fatigued muscles, through the ringing of veins, the squeaking of tendons. Some light was still mixed into the paunches of clouds, glowing amber devoured by vapors.

For two years I sank into the absence in my chest, the outlines of a scrap of life that had gone absent, a breach that I nicknamed "holeache" and that kept contracting and expanding. It resembled the enormous navel in the pictures of power figures from Congo. In the library reference room, Snot and I found a book of photographs: wooden statues of short-legged men, their torsos puffed as they leaned, perhaps preparing to pounce. Their chest and facial hair were made of nails and black iron bits folded into the wood. They too seemed either threatening to erupt and shoot out or striving inward in slow motion through a viscous, honeyed time. And their closed eyes, their captivity eyes, beamed with a call of defiance or a cry of pain, trapped too in a time of a different nature, more mysterious than Snot's and mine. A time that was all history, defeats and victories and monarchy and crisis. Not the gray, impoverished in-between time dripping out of the clocks in our homes, the grandfather clocks of the Sderot that is external.

All of these figures had an enormous, circular protrusion in place of a navel. Two half-moons of a clam, like slightly parted lips, covered its inner space. I thought they were like two wings of a door on the verge of being shut. But Snot said, What did they put that pussy in the middle of their bodies for? I recoiled. My hand reached for my yarmulke of its own volition. I ran my thumb and middle finger over my eyes and gave their tips a fluttering kiss.

Snot laughed at his own crudeness, then repeated, Pussy, pussy, pussy, they put a pussy there. I searched the book for an explanation but found none. The nature of the navels remained unknown. Perhaps the people of Congo believed that power lay in the first testament to a baby's independence, his sign of death, that he was flesh and blood. For two years I sank into that bog of a self refusing to exist. Like a heavenly body, its mass grown tired. Even the poems I wrote—and where haven't I written them? In guard booths, in the bone-crushing cold of the desert at winter, out of layers of sweat drying on the skin in the northern heat, through showerless weeks, that's all I needed, to reveal my pale nakedness to the other soldiers. On one of my first days on one of the bases, when I was an inexperienced quartermaster clerk, I volunteered to stand in for a casualty in a CPR training course. I lay on the ground, bare-chested, supposedly bleeding or shot, waiting for the medic to reach me. Another quartermaster clerk, a Georgian, I think, who constantly boasted about the size of his penis, called the other quartermaster soldiers and said, Look at this worm, finally getting some sun. And he stinks, he must never shower.

It wasn't hard to guess what awakened the hatred in the guy. My observance offered some respite, during which I could get away from my storage work. And when I returned from synagogue, limbs purified, the curves of my veins refined, the quartermaster clerk, the one who was probably Georgian, would say, That guy must take off his yarmulke when he's on break. He's all quiet, but a real trickster, like all those other religious freeloaders.

The first time I heard him say that, I was appalled. Ever since puberty I'd taught myself to become immune to any psychic attacks. I had all my defenses in place so that nobody could invade me without warning. I'd entertained sinful thoughts. I often envisioned myself in a flash image, from the outside, walking bareheaded through the streets of Sderot. I saw myself visiting my friends in the bomb shelters where they met on Saturdays to play music rather than waiting, nerves racked, for the Shabbat to be over, quietly cursing the cantor for taking his time or my mother for indifferently setting the Havdalah table.

I wrote poems. Still, riding through Israel fans the flames. And the soldiers of the headquarters where I served followed the combat soldiers in our battalion to the Lebanese border, the occupied territories, to the Egyptian border. Through the windows of buses crowded with soldiers on Sunday mornings and Thursday evenings, through the windows of the trains gliding down from Nahariya, I saw the speed of growth. The tangle of carrots replaced with thistles, sheep evolving like vitiligo on the hastily greening face of a hill. I saw patterns of the flickers of birds through space, miniscule and swift explosions of flight. I saw the plowed fields, mirrors of the trudging Israeli skies, or the pounding of wheels driving the seats of stars. So I wrote poems. It so happened that the race paused, or that my eyes, for a brief moment, saw beyond the traffic, through slits, frozen-solid clouds. I knew they'd been standing that way since the day they were parted from water at the dawn of creation.

And yet, the hours free of poetry, of the heating of the soul in response to a force not its own, those endless minutes were filled with thoughts of death, the scheme I'd planned back when, when was it, actually, perhaps since I returned from Sylvia Gozlan's, or perhaps since the outer thicket, since Cocoa Pup, or perhaps since I lay beside Dalia Shushan, without clothes on, or perhaps since she came by to say goodbye and offer me a gift the significance of which I did not understand.

I stopped talking to the other quartermaster clerks in my unit. In the warehouses, equipment rested on metal shelves, its aging, its wear and tear, the particles of plastic and rubber and felt thickening their surroundings. I obeyed their orders with a grunt of yes or a grunt of no. I answered with a nod when soldiers wanted to know the size of the uniforms they turned in. I stayed away from the deals cut between the cooks and those in charge of the treasures of the military. The cooks enjoyed new uniforms and state-of-the-art heaters and the quartermaster clerks enjoyed the delicacies set aside by the cupbearers and the bakers for themselves or for the officers' meals.

I WAS ADDED TO AMIRAM NISSIMOV'S QUARTERMASTER UNIT. When he gave me a tour of the warehouses and showed me the heaps of equipment, he smiled wide and said, Rest up today, work starts tomorrow, we need to prepare for the biennial inspection.

What's all this? I asked.

Amiram Nissimov said, Emergency equipment for reserve-duty soldiers.

But why is it so neglected? I asked another soldier, who quickly clarified his identity as a White Russian, not like all that human trash from Bukhara and the Caucasus, perhaps casting aspersions at Amiram Nissimov himself. What could you possibly expect from one of them? he said.

I tried to keep a straight face, not returning the White Russian's smile, as he added, But the whole base is like this, standing army officers scratch their balls all year until they hear about an upcoming inspection, then their balls start shaking.

The Russian's face was scorched with dissatisfaction. His leave was postponed because of preparations for the inspection. At least he wouldn't be on base during the inspection itself. He couldn't give a shit what they found. They wouldn't be putting him on trial again for losing equipment.

Nissimov, as the soldiers referred to him, seemed elderly to me, although he was only fifty years old. He had a hunchback that tilted to the left. A glorious, canine, possibly German mustache dangled down from the corners of his mouth. It was the only testament of his original hair color, a flaming tone that, when touched by the sun, gleamed like a crown. The dwindling locks on his head turned gray, and beyond extinguished eyes, beyond the screen of extinguishing, a flash of annoyance alternated with a flash of vengefulness.

Not that I noticed these flashes right away. The White Russian, Costa, told me, Pay attention to the evil in him when he looks at things. Nissimov was heavy of movement and thought. He rubbed his mustache lengthily before he answered any questions addressed to him, be they offhand or urgent. And yet, occasionally a desire awakened in me to touch the history of those who stood before me. Either that, or they became palpable against my will, lunging at me. I had to keep my distance, inside of myself, from the gluttonous worm of compassion. Nissimov's smile was crooked too.

I asked how the warehouses were organized and Costa spit. Nissimov said, You see, *blat*, someone with motivation, not like that shit the government in Moscow rubbed off the bottoms of their shoes and sent to Israel.

All of Costa's explanations were accompanied by spitting and interjections of "blat" between sentences. He'd wasted two and a half years on that base doing nothing. He wanted to work with Amiram, who would have understood him, because Amiram had a background in competitive swimming, just like him. Costa used to be part of the Ness Ziona swim team, that's why he was serving on an open base, *blat*, he said and laughed, but actually, if he hadn't been on the team he wouldn't have enlisted at all, who needs Israel's two-bit military, nothing like the Russian military, *blat*, they would have killed off people like Nissimov a long time ago.

I thought Nissimov *was* Amiram, I said.

Yeah, but when I say Amiram, I mean somebody else.

I don't get it.

Amiram Alfassi, the other quartermaster officer, *blat*, do I have to spell out everything for you, are you retarded, or what?

Yeah, I, meaning I, have also been wondering if there is any meaning to the overused theme of duality—that life is haunted by doubles, not doubles, seeming doubles, shared names—or if the clarification of the pattern only inspires a brief sigh, drained of the flavor of wonder. Either way, Costa said, at the back of the base, that's where Amiram's warehouses are, but he spends most of his time at the offices or the arsenal and his soldiers do whatever they want. No luck, *blat*, as soon as Nissimov heard Costa was a swimmer he grabbed him, grabbed him in his claws and wouldn't let go.

But I thought the other Amiram was the swimmer.

That's why. These dogs from Bukhara hate us.

He doesn't look Bukharan, I said.

Turkish, Romanian, Bukharan, same thing. They stuck me here and gave Amiram the black guy.

I said nothing. The chaos in the warehouse muddied my thoughts. But I could watch the clock and take comfort in the fact that time was limited. I'd be heading home at four in the afternoon.

It had been with me for two years, the urgency to get back home. It started during basic training. I went to the recruitment center alone, but the day before, my Walkman took its final breath. I sat in the living room at home next to my father's stereo system and listened with headphones to the mixtape Dalia had made me. I didn't know many of the performing artists, and my English wasn't good enough to decipher the lyrics. Instead, I rewrote the lyrics in English in my mind according to proximal Hebrew sounds and the singers' pronunciation. Dalia said that female singers tended to sing more sweetly and indulgently, and because the female voice was naturally clearer than men's, they put little effort into imbuing their voices with character, with the exception of Patti Smith, but that was because she wasn't a singer, she was an artist and had depth. *Horses* played in the headphones. I allowed my mind to get carried away with Smith's voice, the inner stride of the song, to submit to that floating, in which every sound existed on its own, every instrument playing for itself, and I could shift my attention from the bass to the guitar, the drums, the slits and singes in Smith's voice. I pictured a photograph of her that Dalia once showed me. She was leaning against a wall, wearing a man's suit, radiating defiance, but not truly defiant at all. As if the universe, in all its bizarre calculations, bookkeeping, and note-taking, demanded protest, with slightly parted lips, with tense muscles.

Dalia was deeper than she was. I tried to overlay the song Dalia wrote and recorded for me on Smith's voice and pacing: Now you know there shall be no more death in the land of— The words broke up and shuffled. I waited for Smith's song to end. In the pause before the next one, I tried to implant Dalia's voice, a downtrodden voice that emerged from the cumbersome body, from the flawed resonance space of the flesh, transforming, once it abandoned the lips, into a presence, a force among others in the world. A new song emerged, another singer. Dalia edited the songs on the tape to lead into one another, grow from one another. She believed this next song was an homage to Patti Smith. It was simply named "I Love You" and, through dim images, told the story of a guy named Johnny. The sounds of music and voices once again sabotaged my attempt to sing the song. I stopped the tape and went looking for Dalia's demo.

The drawers at the bottom of my closet contained piles of notebooks filled with poems, bits of sentences, bad drawings made with different pens, magazines I thought I'd look at again at some point, a folder of plastic sheets full of newspaper clippings, poems I'd cut out of literary supplements, mementos, writing instruments, a letter opener, postcards, and other notions that had lost their original shape and turned into miscellanea. I rummaged through the bottoms of the drawers, emptied their contents on the floor of the room, then returned them, one item at a time, but the tape evaded me. Again I emptied them and put them back, counting and considering, and the tape was nowhere to be found. Surely one of Tova's small-scale revenges. Though she was already a teenager and had broken the habit, it seemed. I hadn't touched the tape in a year. We'd made it in my bedroom. Dalia showed up with a tape recorder and a guitar. I listened to it once after Dalia left, and that was it, I deposited it in the drawer.

I walked out of the room. More and more possibilities ran through my mind, insults I might have administered to Tova without noticing. There were many. My mother walked inside, carrying an empty laundry basket. She looked me over for a moment and told me not to worry, my clothes would dry out by that evening, what did I need to pack, just underwear, right?

Something disappeared from my room, I said.

No one goes into your room.

Still, I said, something disappeared.

What? she said.

A tape.

Oh, she said, the one that was in the drawer.

Yes.

She went to the kitchen and I followed her there. From the top corner drawer, where she always kept her wallet and purse, she pulled out the sewing box, and from inside of it, the tape. I found it while I was cleaning your room last Passover, she said, and figured you ought to keep it in a safer place.

I stood before her, petrified. How many times have I had the chance to see Msodi Farkash with her dirty-blond hair, with the honey-toned eyes planted in a narrow, tan face, with all the youthfulness burned into them from her year as Miss Sderot? My entire childhood, she was reflected behind my father's shoulder, even during the two years when Simo Farkash collapsed into his somber kingdom. And there she stood, inconceivably real, her being open to an existence I had no idea about, but to which I was indebted. Days of sickness in bed, days when I came home with my heart made of terrible ice, days of sitting in my bedroom and listening to the rain as my limbs swelled by force of their secret plan, days of coming and going without being asked where from or where to, and she was there, what I assumed was a spot in my line of vision but turned out to be a condition for my eyes' proper function.

THAT IMAGE OF MY MOTHER IN THE KITCHEN FOLLOWED ME THE whole ride back to base. In the first few nights I lay awake, pondering all the gestures that had gone unnoticed, which I took for granted. There she was, serving me food as I pored over my books, preparing for finals, and I shifted them aside to make room for the plate without looking at her, and the bare lamp burned in the kitchen, spilling its tungsten glare. There she was, sitting and talking to me, my thoughts turning outward, toward Sabah, toward Snot, toward Sylvia Gozlan, toward Dalia, toward the secret wounds I couldn't imagine anyone in my family experiencing, toward the roots they took inside nerve endings, and onward, striving toward the great darkness of the soul. There she was, urging me to send my poetry to a publisher whose ad was posted in the weekend papers, and when I refused she gathered them without permission, ordering Tova to copy them in her legible handwriting, and sent them, and I shook with anger when she served me the acceptance letter with excitement. There she was, sleeping on the couch in the small hours of the night, all the lights on, when the bus returning from the field trip was late to arrive. That was all given to me without my demanding it, and perhaps because I didn't demand it, I also didn't know how to accept it.

I took the tape from her and slipped it into the stereo. From the rustling of the recording rose Dalia's hesitant opening notes, a few fearful chords, and my near-muted whisper of encouragement in the background. And again, that expressionless sound of the cheap guitar, as if Dalia were strumming on cardboard strings. And still, a metallic hint, a touch of iron, and then that voice. I should be more accurate—Dalia didn't sing, didn't strum the guitar, didn't perform. All of those actions joined together to a music that was her very being, but the seed of recognition was planted in that listening. And I, meaning I, know there is no earlier and later in consciousness. Dalia's playing fell on my ears after the first round of random, unharmonized chords. Dalia told Niro in my presence that she was sick of songs with three major chords, though she'd only been playing for less than a year. She was tired of overused orchestrations.

I turned the volume all the way up.

> Now you know there shall be no more death
> In the Land of Shadow
> To the place you beseech

Dalia's voice broke, or perhaps switching scales made it falter. Either way, the two instruments, the human and the one made of wood and metal, echoed each other.

> You shall not be redeemed by love
> Pain shan't be your savior

And once again, a sharp switch that forced Dalia to purposefully go off-key, descending too low, almost low enough to speak, to whisper.

> All that is will rise to the extant
> And you shan't be brought down
> By the shackles of metaphors
> Free in the web of flesh

Free, I thought within the song. Was that what Dalia saw as the superior purpose, freedom from imagery? And I, meaning I, would add: Is flesh not our superior image, ultimately?

> Your ears are pricked to the depth of silence
> Your eyes torn to see in the dark
>
> And by these signs you shall know
> That your kingdom is nigh
> Son of Man
> Take up and read.

The command "Take up and read" evolved into a scream, a falsetto that blended into the beginning of the harmony, but the end of the song veered so far from it that the scream sounded ludicrous, out of control. I stared at the living room, at the walls, at the pictures hanging on them, at the couch, at the television, at the coffee table, at everything that would soon fall inside of that screaming sound, everything that had already fallen, only kept in place by the delayed perception of time, a loose, flickering memory. Chantal rushed in with a friend. So young and unburdened. She waved at me as they headed to her room. She turned her head before being swallowed through the doorway. Her beauty, inherited from our mother, was prepared to burst through her features. She said, Have a good enlistment, Nahum, don't forget to write to us.

NISSIMOV CALLED COSTA AND ME INTO THE FIRST WAREHOUSE on the left. Whose left? I asked Costa, but Costa told me to stop being a smart-ass, didn't I know that military officers told the sun where to rise in the morning? I told him that maybe in Isaac Babel's army . . .

Costa said, Whose army?

I told him to forget it, sometimes I said nonsense.

Costa said we shouldn't ask the commanders anyway.

Ask them what? I said.

The direction of the sun, said Costa. It shines out of their asses.

At first I saw no logic in the place markers Nissimov employed. The warehouses were arranged in an angular half-circle around a sandlot. In the front of each of them a concrete loading and unloading platform had been cast. Left and right were meant in relation to those standing with their backs to the entry to the warehouse area. The western row of warehouses was the reference point, and left and right really meant north and south. I pointed this out to Nissimov. As was his custom, he rubbed his mustache for a long time and finally waved me off by decisively saying, How is that supposed to help anyone?

Well, he said as we entered, Gideon and Honest John.

I'm Honest John, I said.

Who's that? asked Costa.

What a *muzhik*, said Nissimov. The body of a bull, *blat*, but the brain of a donkey.

Now that Nissimov muttered what he'd muttered, I realized he was correct. Costa hadn't been blessed with a swimmer's body, he was heavy and square-shaped. He was my height, but the breadth of his shoulders and the width of his hips made him look shorter, dense, and robust.

Have we said our prayers yet? Nissimov asked.

I was tired of that joke. I nodded.

Very well, Mr. Compass, said Nissimov, so you can tell me how you think we should organize the warehouse.

Costa shook his head, his face crumpling. I looked around. I said what came to mind. From what I've seen so far, the personal kits are equally dispersed between the different warehouses, and I can't figure out why. Wouldn't it make more sense to dedicate each warehouse to a separate category? For example, this warehouse and the one next door could be dedicated to gas masks and kit bags, providing us with better control over the gear, and simplifying inventory.

After a long pause, Nissimov said, Yes, that was the arrangement until ten years ago, and actually, now that Meshulam, who changed everything on base, has moved on to a different role, why shouldn't we go back to the old ways?

Costa cursed me out later. Why did I have to put all that nonsense in Nissimov's head, *blat*, did I have any idea what kind of a project I just signed us up for?

What do you care, you're going on leave on the day of the inspection anyway.

I don't care, but you should worry, because Meshulam's new method made it easier to hide shortages. What'd you think he made it up for, efficiency?

You're trying to tell me people steal gear here? I said. I pulled an emergency kit off of one of the shelves. The cardboard around the mask was gnawed and perforated, maybe by termites. I picked up a flashlight. The bolts were rusted.

People are thieves, what are you going to do, *blat*, leave a lump of shit on the windowsill and someone'll come steal it.

Is that a Russian proverb? I asked.

What?

About the shit on the windowsill.

You're funny.

Maybe it's better that they steal gear than use it to go to war.

Okay, okay, don't start with the guilt. I knew people like you in Russia.

Like me?

Costa piled up the kit bags, tossed them furiously off the shelves, then arranged the emergency kits on the other side. The cardboard boxes he pulled them out of quickly sucked the air out of the room. I started to fold, stack, and tie them up.

Where'd you learn how to do that? asked Costa.

I used to work at a grocery store, I said, when I was a senior in high school.

Oh, said Costa, so how do you think we should organize the gear?

I paused. The emptiness of the shelves was harder to take as a reality than as an imaginary idea. I counted the shelves. I calculated. Okay, I said and explained it to Costa.

Like you, said Costa after we repacked the kit bags in the warehouses and walked to the nearby warehouse to grab some more, like you, people who carry the truth with them, *blat*, try to control everybody with it.

IN SPITE OF THE DIMNESS OF THE DAY AND THE FORECASTED rain, Costa and I tumbled out of the warehouse area drenched with sweat on the third afternoon of our inspection preparations. An equipment-laden truck paused by the northwestern warehouse. Good, said Nissimov. With his crooked posture and the giddiness that took over his expression, he looked like a wealthy Jewish man rubbing his hands at the sight of his gold ships docking in the harbor.

No questions, said Nissimov. Start unloading.

I told you, said Costa, lightly slapping my shoulder. Nothing but trouble.

The driver rolled down his window, waved through his sideview mirror, and lit a cigarette. Costa spat. An Ethiopian boy stepped out of the passenger seat and walked over, standing tall, almost aloof.

He hasn't been discharged yet, said Costa, and he's got six months seniority on me.

Blat, I said.

What? said Costa.

You were so stunned you forgot to say *blat*.

Blat, said Costa, clearing his throat. The thick spit caught like a gem in a cluster of hawkbit flowers. The petals shone in the fading light.

What's up, Aviel? said Costa.

Avocado, said the young Ethiopian man. To me he said, Are you the new guy?

Yeah, I was assigned here a few days ago.

What's your seniority?

Costa said, What's with the name Avocado now, are you dumb?

Two years, I said.

Avocado nodded. His widening lips stretched a cloak of purity across his face. I followed his eyes. A skinny man walked toward us, his footsteps more measured than Avocado's. His image slowly cleared up. I, meaning I, think it was something different, that the being of distance evaporated, making way for the being of standing up close, the being of the examinable, the one boasting features and expressions, eyes, and the pace of breath.

Amiram, said Costa. For the first time, I saw something of his age twinkling in him.

Amiram paused next to Nissimov. He was taller than him to begin with, and Nissimov's hunch forced him to lower his head. They spoke quietly among themselves.

What's going on? said Costa.

How should I know? said Avocado. I'm leaving in a week, what do I care?

You always know. What, you think I haven't heard you talking to your friends from transportation? Yapping all day like old ladies.

I wondered what Costa was talking about. The Ethiopians I knew in Sderot tended to be taciturn. Chantal's best friend, Shula, barely spoke a word in our presence. She and Chantal were inseparable from the moment Shula joined her classroom. One day at the end of eighth grade she stopped coming over. When Msodi asked, Chantal said that was it, that now that Shula was a big girl she couldn't come by anymore. In a fashion unusual to her, she swallowed her sorrow. It was apparent only in the bruised depth of her eyes. Our mother said, Yes, times never really change, that's what they did to girls in Morocco. They'd take them and marry them off to some old man with money. Chantal made us swear not to tell Tova. The last thing she needed was that one's festival of gloating.

She sober or high off vodka? asked Avocado.

You'd better shut up, said Costa, it would be a shame for you to get discharged with a broken arm or foot.

Hey, I said, what happened?

He should leave my mother out of it, said Costa.

What? said Amiram, who popped up between them. What's going on, the bosses are working and the workers are messing around.

He looked at me and smiled. A beauty fit for women, I thought for some reason. The warehouse Nissimov unlocked was barren, almost completely empty. A whiff of mildew swelled through the air upon the shifting of the metal doors and the squealing of the axes. We slowly unloaded the contents of the truck. I was filled with some kind of fizzing. I narrated as Avocado and Costa wrestled with the burden of unloading and with each other. Yes, I offered, why not, block the entrance with the sleeping bags, that'll make it easier to get everything else in, and really, standing in a line between the truck and the warehouse and passing the equipment from one to the next, that's so inefficient, we should climb up and bring things down one at a time, and maybe you should push that box harder when you put it in lengthwise, it's a shame it goes in so easily when you stack it on its head. There were metal shelving units at the back of the truck. I stood before them. Then I turned around and said, Seriously, what kind of genius loaded the shelving units first?

Amiram's face glanced into the bed of the truck. In a charged voice, he said, Get down here a second. All of a sudden I was aware of myself, sweating, dusty under the tarp cover, reeking from the mold of a history not my own. Amiram ordered Costa and Avocado to finish unloading the shelving units. In the depths of the warehouse, in the yellow boldness of bare bulbs, Nissimov governed over heaps of plastic and leather and fabric.

Amiram pulled me aside. Away from the pale halo of lamps and the wintery pre-rain sunset. Away from the savagery of the cloud strips that delayed the departure of light. Away into the shadow cast by the main warehouse. I couldn't stop thinking about how filthy I probably was, and how I should hurry home to take a shower, and then into the silence of my bedroom, the silence of books, the silence of blood in its insecure vessels. Amiram's arm wrapped around my shoulders, squeezing. My bones popped simultaneously with my realization that Amiram's embrace was light, friendly. Cool it, said Amiram. Sarcasm doesn't help anybody.

THE MORE THE WAREHOUSES TOOK SHAPE, THE MORE COSTA'S mood improved. By the end of the first week of preparations, we already knew the designated spot for every item. When we finished rearranging two of the warehouses and it turned out the amount of equipment matched the inventory in the headquarter offices, Costa was smiling. Amiram stopped by to see the work we'd done. He said that after the inspection he'd be adopting the new-old order. Though he'd been assigned to base during Meshulam's days, a good maintenance NCO didn't remain loyal to any specific system, only to efficiency. About his smile, I can say it was dry. What is it about a smile that causes it to be delayed? In the face of a young man, it reveals the remains of a boy. In the face of a grown man, the remains of an adolescent. Amiram's muscles held up from his swimming days, lithe limbs and a thin, taut figure. He lived in Kiryat Gat. A golden Star of David dangled off a delicate gold chain around his neck, tangling with his meager chest hair. He always left the top few shirt buttons undone. His shoe size was surprising—long feet that added a somewhat ridiculous aspect to his image. Perhaps that's why he made sure to walk slowly and not to throw his feet around. I once saw him hurrying down the hill, at the top of which was headquarters and at the bottom of which were the different corps bases. He waved his legs around. I thought he'd be better off walking on his hands. His body revealed what had already been insinuated by his smile, a concealed clownishness, which exterior force could turn into a frenetic vision.

Costa broke into song one morning as we were working on our own, with a cumbersome voice that got tangled in the vocal cords, too heavy to make them vibrate on the correct frequencies. I stopped working and watched him for the first time. There must be a purpose to all that crudeness, that thickness, that shabbiness. His hidden charm must have revealed itself when he swam, assuming he wasn't lying and was, indeed, a professional swimmer. I, meaning I, must quickly add that the dumbness of flesh can never prevail, that the body's preordained plan, ticking away on its mission, cannot become reality.

Suddenly, Costa noticed me standing there, watching him. You're surprised, he said, aren't you?

What?

To hear me singing.

No.

Don't lie. In Russian we have an expression about people like me—a bear stepped on his ear.

Why a bear?

Russians, *blat*. What do you want them to say, a squirrel or a horse? He laughed. This was the first time I'd heard him laughing, a great, hearty laugh. Baring his teeth. He had straight, pearly white teeth. I had to be more vigilant when we sat down to eat, lest he bite me when I wasn't looking. I asked about the song he was singing.

Vysotsky, you know Vysotsky?

The guy from the teabags?

No. Vysotsky, he was, how do you call it, *blat*, a troubadour.

Is it supposed to be a sad song? I couldn't tell . . .

Because I'm such a bad singer.

No, because I don't know Russian music.

You're too polite, Nahum.

What's the story with Avocado? I was going to ask and—

When we got to this base his name was Aviel. He was supposed to get honorably discharged already, but Amiram recommended that he be recruited to the standing army. He's leaving base soon.

So he must have gone back to his original name.

What, avocado? That's a vegetable.

Maybe the sounds mean something else in Amharic.

What's so bad about "Aviel" that he had to change it?

Why didn't you change your name? Why did you get to keep the name your parents gave you?

Costa isn't just any name, it's short for Constantine. You know who he was?

That Byzantine emperor who converted like a quarter of the world to Christianity.

Good, so you know it's a name for cultured people, not like those savages from Falash Mura.

Can you be any more racist?

I'm telling the truth. I told you, you're too polite.

He's got some nobility about him. I think he's from Addis Ababa.

You suck, *blat*.

I said, You might be named after an emperor, but Avocado looks like an exiled prince.

Costa grabbed his stomach and laughed, a greater laugh this time, all his limbs taking part. I stared at him. I'd read descriptions like this in books, but I've never seen anyone actually melt into laughter. And those teeth, yes indeed, I had to watch out for those canines and incisors.

An exiled prince, said Costa. What is this, *blat*, you've turned him Russian. You know what the song is about?

The Vysotsky song, I said, thinking about the Land of Shadow and Dalia singing about it for me, for my ears only.

Yeah, it's about a man who promises his beloved who lives in a palace inside an enchanted forest that he would get her out of there and take her to live in his castle by the sea, but ultimately reveals that he can only take her to his shack.

Do you know it by heart?

I can sing it.

Can you translate it?

He translated it, Costa did. One line from the original followed by one line of hesitant translation. The Hebrew smacked against his throat and mouth. Almost like in a spell, the miraculous vapor of the words rising from those organs, which twist and harden at its birth, fragile signals of color and shape.

There's some truth to it, I said. The silence at the end of Costa's translation had to be shattered. He stood before me, face flushed with effort or embarrassment.

And he isn't polite, that Vysotsky, said Costa.

You think politeness is the opposite of truth?

Most of the time.

But lying is a kind of impoliteness too.

Costa considered this. He said, Well, we have to finish working at some point.

I leaned down to pick up a plump jumble of bulletproof vests whose zippers got tangled together. After a few minutes of silence, Costa asked, So what is the truth in the song?

I said that the enchanted palace was the dream about being rescued by a prince, not the actual structure where the beloved lived. Because if he promised to get her out of one castle and put her in another, how was she supposed to step out into life? The promise of a castle was a trick intended to gradually get her used to reality.

And the shack is reality?

Reality is the shack.

Looks like you know about romance. You bastard.

I don't know about anything, I said, only poetry.

Like Mayakovsky.

I read his poem "A Cloud in Trousers."

Is that the poem where he writes that the night is big like a woman's ass?

I don't remember that line.

But he's got it, I remember we learned it in class, he was, how do you call it, a *gomo*.

I don't know what that is.

You got a girlfriend, Costa asked.

No, not anymore, I said, and even when I did, she wasn't what I thought she was.

Why, what happened?

Forget it. How about you?

No, but I'm working on it, Costa said and chuckled. Anyway, if impoliteness is a kind of lie, that doesn't mean that politeness is a kind of truth. Right, *blat*.

BUT THERE WAS STILL A LIE IN COSTA. I JUST DIDN'T GRASP WHAT it was. Some detail didn't fit, a crack in the cohesive façade. It just so happened that my father and I found ourselves at the Sderot movie theater and watched *Superman II*. As the man in a leotard flew around, fighting against his enemies, prisoners escaped from Krypton, his home planet. Earth's sun graced them with the same powers as his. One thing led to another, and the prisoners invaded his Fortress of Solitude, an expansive hall paved with crystals somewhere in the Arctic. And our hero, who was, of course, a fearless man, became embroiled in a game of advanced tag. The players had to replicate themselves. Thus spoke Superman: I sucked at this game as a child.

B'shala dilmut, said Simo Farkash. How could he have played this game as a child when he came to Earth as a baby?

But though nothing broke in my memory and the viewing experience remained whole, it contained another mark, of the chase after the disappearing scrap of enchantment. How I kept repeating to myself: What does my father know about movies, he only likes backward Israeli cinema that he quotes to death. "Corny horny." What does "corny horny" even mean? I didn't understand it when I was ten years old, and I still don't understand it years later.

For no reason at all, Costa decided to postpone his leave. He claimed he wanted to take both his leaves in a row and attach them to his discharge leave. Nissimov looked him over with introspective eyes. It was hard to guess what was bouncing inside of them, astonishment or surprise. It wasn't depth. His fingers played with the ends of his beard. He said, What's in it for you?

Costa didn't answer.

We saw Nissimov less and less as we prepared anyway. We didn't need him and he didn't need us. Occasionally, Costa cursed him out as we carried gear from one warehouse to the next. He took on the burden of carrying. He moved me aside gently when he saw how the heavy load was exhausting me. He put his hand on my shoulder. Through my shirt, I felt a well of warmth. I was in charge of matching what we had with our inventory. For this purpose, I would ascend to headquarters. Through the window of the maintenance office, I witnessed the land that was stretched before me and beautiful. The crispness of the air like a crystal sound. And a few branching trees, basins for the draining of light, and they burned within it, amber and patina. The caressing fragrance of a close, electrified winter. And I was in the Land of Israel, and the watchful eyes were not mine, but borrowed from the generations that preceded me, tensing from within the blood.

Every scrap of memory, every hint of a heart's desire lay fully on the reality of things, the draping of eolianite, the granular dirt whose names were shocks awaiting recognition, whose names were detonators of familiarity.

Our warehouses were ready two days before the inspection. Nissimov came by to look at the results. He nodded and told me, Tomorrow you're going to work with Amiram, he needs some help.

He deserves a break, said Costa. We've worked our asses off here, *blat*.

Did I ask for your opinion? said Nissimov. And what do you even care, huh, you ass, you'll be lying around here and resting for two days.

Amiram wasn't in the main warehouse when I showed up the next morning. Just like in Nissimov's warehouse, part of the space has been converted into an office area. A metal bureau painted with silver lacquer, shelves full of folders. It did not contain the abandoned sense that was so apparent in Nissimov's office. Sometimes, during the empty hours of rest, Costa and I felt like forgotten children that had been dropped off the timeline. What imbued things with their fastidious essence, in spite of the dust and fibers that were the nature of storage and to which all that was stored longed to return? Two sets of ironed uniforms hanging on a hanger covered with plastic. The floor tiles were spotless. No food crumbs, no candy wrappers, no sand in the cracks between the tiles. A delicate, invisible hand was apparent in all that was there.

A spotless glass plate was placed over the desk. Photos were trapped underneath it, twitching under the see-through weight, dried insects in a display case, the damp sheen of their creation still about them. My eyes were drawn to two children standing on the lip of a pool. Both dark-haired, one curly, his lips twisted with rebellion, the other wearing a grave expression. Their eyes were narrowed in the sunny waves that swelled someplace and crashed against them. The blue bottom of the pool switched in the back-drop into skies. In the other photographs, the happy family was seen in its moments of happiness. The changing views, desert and sea, sunset, sunrise, midday. The boys moving from infancy into childhood. The parents already at the age when the progress of time is less visible. They were young without knowing how young. And spilled over all was the blurry glory of happiness that renders those who hold it unholdable. Maybe it was not the result of their happiness but its feature, that none but them could influence or control.

In the top left corner was a picture of Amiram standing on his own, looking surprised. The nocturnal quality of the photo was clear. His pupils were red, whispering through the narrow face. He was standing in a room, leaning toward the lens, as if to prevent his image from making its mark on film. He was wearing an unfastened robe, revealing his chest and the meagerness of hair on it. His Star of David pendant glimmered somehow. Perhaps he'd just finished a swim. It's possible that my staring at his portrait was what summoned him. He walked into the main warehouse with soft footsteps. In my haste to rise out of his chair, I pushed off a tray of documents. The order in which they'd been arranged crashed onto the clean floor tiles. I leaned down to pick them up. I gathered one page and another, a flimsy file against a chubby wood-free chart. I piled them back on the desk. Amiram didn't move that entire time. His eyes remained on me.

COSTA DID NOT WALK IN. HE CALLED MY NAME FROM OUTSIDE. Through the gaping door, I saw Amiram emerging from a warehouse behind him. Some ponderous darkness on his face that the light of the approaching storm broke. His fatigues riddled with dust and other black substances. So, he said, did you come to help?

No way, said Costa.

What, then?

Where's Nahum?

Someplace, working.

It isn't like you to work hard, Amiram, *blat*.

Blat, blat, blat, said Amiram. Why don't you learn another word, already. You're in Israel now.

Costa shook his head. His thick, black hair was parted into equal sections. His mane was straightened with some product that added shine. He looked over the three sides of Amiram's warehouse area until he found me. I was sorting and packing atropine syringes in the entirely inefficient gas mask kits. Are you coming to the canteen? he yelled at me. The voice came with the look. There was a dark shock in both of them as they came. I got up.

Ask nicely, said Amiram.

Please, *blat*, said Costa.

It was his egg sandwich day. As was his manner, he kept silent the whole way to the wooden canteen structure. He attacked the sandwich, swallowing half of it down quickly, then suffocating the rest back into its cling film. I looked at the half-moons of his bites in the flesh of the roll, at the sesame seeds trapped in the clear wrapping, the yolk crumbs clinging to the sides of his mouth. The rotting, sulfurous aroma of the sandwich wafted toward me when he said I had to watch out and not let Amiram give me too much work. His problem is that he doesn't do any work all year long, he said.

I asked, What happened between the two of you?

He said, What happened, *blat*.

I said, I mean, like, didn't you want to serve with him?

He's just an ingrate, said Costa, adding, why are you eating that candy, *blat*?

I debated whether or not I should tell him about the time that I showed up to Friday-night dinner at a base down south straight from synagogue, still wearing my service dress. Trays of *bourekas* covered the tables. My veins had already been sanitized by the boiling temperature of the incantations. The voice of the Lord breaketh the cedars, the Lord breaketh the cedars of Lebanon, therefore all they that devour thee shall be devoured; and all thine adversaries, every one of them, shall go into captivity, thou anointest my head with oil, my cup runneth over. And there was the greasiness of the phyllo dough anointed with margarine, and the *bourekas'* filling. My palate was prepared for Msodi Farkash's potato creaminess, but my tongue was met with steaming Spam. And then the wounded purity of the body. I sat, petrified for a few moments, my buttock muscles tensed against the hardness of the bench, and my intestines roiling, and my lips stretched, damming the mouth. I gave in. I ran out and threw up among the oleander bushes. What season was it? I cannot remember if their velvety blossoms were beating through the dark as usual, or if only the foliage rustled.

After that the smell of beef and chicken repulsed me, and a new hunger opened up, for the fishes my mother cooked on Fridays. When I was a child and a teenager I detested them, the maliciousness of the mullet's thorns, the dryness of a tuna drowned in paprika sauce. But how can one escape the delicacies that trickled into them along with uterine fluids, circulating through their bloodstream before their entry could be supervised? And how to control their belated awakening, donning the cloak of an appetite for them? On the weekend after the *bourekas* incident, my mother squinted at me suspiciously when I asked her to serve me some fish, and I detected the stunned tone she always repressed, crushing it underneath words, emerging as she told my father how I'd ripped into the dish. And indeed, in the next few weeks, I couldn't even think about going home without my mouth filling with anticipation for the Friday lunchtime feast of fish. In the meantime, my diet relied mostly on foods whose production did not seem to involve human touch.

I told Costa, I like sweets.

You're like a baby, said Costa. He took long gulps from his Coke can. Burped. You're spoiling your health, he said. What do you even like about it? It's just air.

I tore open the bag. Chocolate-coated wafers. I said, Exactly, that's what I like, the hole, that's the best part of it. I eat the coating first and then shove the hole in all at once.

Costa returned to his eating ritual, the other half of the sandwich. He undid the protective wrapping and took tiny bites. The loudspeakers emitted the distortion assault of Nirvana's "Smells Like Teen Spirit," slicing through the ruckus of the chattering and shouting soldiers. Odd that I only noticed the racket then. It was as if Costa and I were trapped under glass that the guitars shattered with their precise, distorted frequency. Costa said, What's that noise, *blat*, sounds like a truck that can't get started.

I said, Let's get moving, I have that warehouse hanging over my head.

Costa said, You've got a yarmulke hanging over your head, not a warehouse. Let's stay a little longer.

I said I could barely hear him, that his voice was drowning in the tumult. He said, What, what? I said, You're right. We stepped outside. Winter was accumulated in the air. The eucalyptus trees were charged with storm down to their roots. So what kind of music do you like? he asked.

I said, Wounded music. Like poetry. Like—
Like Mayakovsky? he asked.

Enough already with your Mayakovsky, I said, is he the only poet you know?

He wiped his hands and lightly punched my shoulder. You're all right, he said, laughing. Maybe he really is a swimmer, I thought. In moments like these, the clumsiness was absent from Costa's being. His movements were suddenly limber, his body woven with feathers.

☆ ☆ ☆

I, MEANING I, THINK ABOUT THE BLINDING LIGHT OF THE PAST, washing over the details of experience, the present, until they become shadows, until they become chained into shapes, until they are forced to appear as visions swallowed by their own molds. Amiram scolded me for taking a needlessly long lunch. But what is need? Costa and I wandered down the paths of the base. I tried to explain to him what music was for me, a person devoid of any musical talent, to whom music was revealed only through language, through the use of words.

I tried to get him to pronounce syllable sequences whose force deviated from their meaning, whose meaning was a point on a map stretching to both sides. I told him, say *le'ayel pila*.

He said, Lilapilha. Then he said, I don't feel a thing.

I said, What do you hear in *le'ayel pila*?

He said, Blah blahhh.

Ball a-ha, I said. You see how far you can go when you follow language.

He said, Say another word.

I said, *Andrelamusia.*

He said, What did Andre tell Musia?

I said, Blah blahhh.

He slapped my shoulder again with that amiable affection, which, when translated into touch, can arouse dread.

I said, *Saqiyah.*

He said, Sequoia.

I said, Suck a koi fish.

He said, Sack of fishes.

I said, Fishev Anatoly, from transportation.

He said, That primitive idiot, why bring him up?

Why do you hate Caucasians so much?

He said, Those Arabs, *blat.*

I said, People said the same things about my parents.

He said, Not even twenty yet and they already married him off. What's the rush? He should live first.

TAKE UP AND READ

I said, My parents married young too. My mother's seven years younger than my father. She—

Yes, but you're not like them, *blat*, you're . . .

What?

Modern. Just take off that yarmulke and you'll be golden.

I said, This world is like the *saqiyah* well. When it fills up, it empties out; when it empties out, it fills up.

What are you mumbling about?

Nothing, never mind.

Is that one of your poems?

I wish.

Let me read your poetry sometime, maybe then I'll understand better, *blat*.

But Amiram's scolding was just words. I could see it in his detached expression. It insinuated a tenderness. We worked in separate warehouses. He'd informed me in advance that the job would last till evening but that he'd make sure to compensate me. I nodded. It was afternoon and the air grew dim. Swifts screamed the dwindling day. Black wheels of swifts galloping through the sky. Sunset, a fading smear of lighting. The door unraveled the outside into bits of spectacles. Finally, Amiram called me into his warehouse. He stood in the doorway, saying, It looks like it's going to pour tomorrow. With any luck, they'll cancel the inspection.

Don't you think we can pull it off in time? I asked.

They were supposed to assign me two new soldiers, but some idiot at the adjutancy approved a three-day break for them.

We'll do what we can, I said.

He retreated into the warehouse. I followed him. It was equally dim inside. A few bulbs with their defeated glow. He smiled and said, So you're from Sderot.

I nodded. I sat down.

Moroccan? he asked.

Yes.

"Farkash" doesn't sound Moroccan. It sounds Romanian.

Tell that to my father.

There used to be a soccer player with that same name in Hapoel Sderot.

Was he Moroccan?

Well, you know what they say, Romanians are the Moroccans of the Ashkenazi population.

But as the bulbs faded, I could see the beaming of the skin, a nanometer of dull aura over the pores. His pupils dilated in the darkness. All that approached them was swallowed, rolling into something unknown as it descended down those burrows and into his consciousness.

So what are your plans? he asked.

Plans?

Yes. How long do you have before you get discharged?

About a year.

And where did you serve before?

Here and there. A little north, a little south. Headquarters, you know.

Being a maintenance soldier doesn't suit you.

As we spoke, the saliva thickened in my mouth. It threatened to spill out of the corners of my mouth. I had to pronounce the words moderately, with the measured movements of the vocal cords.

And your plans?

Who knows? My mother wants me to go to university.

And you?

I don't know yet.

Nonsense, a twenty-year-old guy who doesn't know what he wants.

So what, did you know?

When I was your age I already knew my wife. By the end of my first year in the standing army I already had a kid.

And the swimming?

I see someone already told you. Sometimes you carry with you something from childhood without understanding why, until you meet someone who shakes you up.

Your wife?

His head moved slowly. He yawned. Just thinking about my wife makes me want to go to bed, he said, winking.

He got up from his chair and stretched. His lithe body took on an intensified tangibility, as if a depth translated into spatial dimensions was added to his being. Then he walked past me and out the door. I sat, listening. The sound of urination carried through the concrete walls or the door, liquid crashing against dirt, the foamy gurgling, a long stream, lilting in homey pleasantness.

AS WE WALKED OUT OF THE BASE, A WIND DROVE THE CLUSTER of clouds, steering them someplace, and a naked, pregnant moon was revealed in the clear sky. Occasionally, I turned to answer one of Amiram's questions and witnessed his profile, bathed in moonlight. The shaded eye sockets, the moving lips sharply sketched. What was he actually asking? I told him something about high school. A dark, twisting strip of asphalt going extinct under the beams of streetlamps. Maybe a little about my family. He seemed to be listening attentively, perhaps even listening to the holes in my words, which I carefully tiptoed around. I sensed the comfort of speaking to someone who shared my language, not normal language, no, the other language present below and above words. I sensed the danger. Amiram cursed the fickle weather. He said, You can't trust anything in this country.

I said, No problem. On the day of the inspection I'll draw a circle in the sand outside the warehouses and stand inside it until it starts to rain.

What is that, some orthodox thing? asked Amiram.

I said, Yes. I said, No. I said, Depends on your perspective.

He said, Look, look how strong the moon is tonight.

The next day Costa came to get me again at lunchtime. Amiram huffed at our backs as we moved away, I want you back here in half an hour, tops.

What's with him, said Costa, he's agitated all of a sudden.

We worked late last night, I said.

Screw those freeloaders.

I said nothing. Costa asked if I was upset about what he'd said the previous day. I couldn't remember what he'd said. I didn't imagine he cared what I thought. I said I wasn't. He said he hadn't meant to offend my parents. His father used to be an engineer but couldn't find work in Israel. His mother had a job at the music conservatory, as a receptionist, not a music teacher, as her training would have dictated. She was lucky. Friends of hers with the same level of education were cleaning homes. I wanted to say, Enough, enough, enough, I've heard millions of stories like this, all with the same laments. I have no idea what to do with them, if compassion is required or if the appropriate response is mockery. We, who migrated from Morocco, have a gift. Nobody wants to hear our stories. They're passed on from parents to children, seeping into our drinking water. They are transferred through meals, in the inflamed dimness of family bonds. That's how they preserve their uniqueness. Enough, I wanted to tell him, enough, enough, I can't think anymore, I'm crowded, I'm crowded. And the consequences, the threads of consequences. I've yet to wean myself of my desire to guess the future. I said, It's awful, yes, but Israel is a young country, there are plenty of immigration problems.

It isn't like you to say that, said Costa.

To say what?

The same nonsense everyone else says.

He was right. Meaning, I wanted to believe he was right. Of all the things he'd told me back then, that one echoed most intensely. Perhaps because a fetal image of it was already resting inside of me. I hadn't told a soul about the assaults I experienced as a child, when an exterior consciousness recruited its power against me, to invade me and disinherit me of my grasp of the body, of my selfhood. I hadn't told a soul besides Dalia. She said nothing for a few moments. Perhaps she wondered if I was trying to impress her, and raised herself up on her left elbow, looking at me among the thicket's bursts of darkness, finding what she found. She said, You should write that down. I said, But there are no words in that void. Dalia said, Who needs words as a starting point? You must still have the feeling, a buzzing on the edge of your brain, your senses, something only you know. Words come later, so much later, and when they show up they're finally yours.

There was a thicket around us too, I mean, when Costa and I were wandering. Not a thicket, but an assembly of eucalyptuses. Once again, storm clouds emerged from someplace, hanging from the walls of the skies and crawling along with the wind. We hadn't intended to stray, but we walked the paths aimlessly, away from the canteen. Costa sat down on a table made up of logs and planks. A crude, transient structure. Years and worms had gnawed through it. He said, I brought you something. He pulled a small black bag from the inner pocket of his jacket and handed it to me.

What's this? I said.

Just a little something, he said, no big deal.

There was a tape inside the bag. On the front of the box was a picture of a red chair dripping anxiety on a black backdrop. Inside a blue strip over the picture he'd written the words *Want to Be and Will Be*, and underneath that: *Arkadi Duchin * Vladimir Vysotsky*. The top left corner was perforated twice.

What's this? I said.

Vysotsky songs, said Costa, a tremble in his voice. In Hebrew, *blat.*

Are you lending it to me?

No, it's for you, to have.

But I—I'll pay you—how much—

Costa chucked. It's just a gift, *blat*.

I, but, you bought it and—

Don't worry, it cost pennies. It's from a store at the Central Bus Station, you see the holes, that means it's a cheap tape that nobody wants to buy.

A special sale, I said.

Yes, what's his name, *blat*, that toy boy told me about that place.

The guard?

Yeah, that Tza'atzu'a guy who thinks about guitars all day. He said you and he talk a lot, that you have friends who play and—

I never told him that.

He said you did, and that you, *blat*, know singers and bands.

I WENT AGAINST MY IMPULSE AND BOUGHT AN AVOCADO SAND-wich. Costa said I was finally eating like a human being. The Vysotsky tape rested in my pocket. I could feel it grazing against my thigh through the fabric of my pants when we sat down. Costa spoke quickly between one swallow and the next through the first half of his sandwich, of his eating ritual. He said, You'll see, Vysotsky will give you thoughts, *blat*. He said, You promised to show me your poetry. He said, Avocado, you see, it's a vegetable.

What ever happened to Aviel? I asked when he took a break.

I told you, he's taking some course.

Who's going to work with Amiram? I asked. Are you transfer-ring over?

His Coke gurgled in the can. I turned my head. Almost whis-pering, he said, He won't take me, I'm about to get discharged, *blat*, you know that. And besides—

Besides, what? The taste of the avocado made me shudder, its creaminess against my tongue, its eruption from its prison of bread. That greenness and that memory of egg. I would have spit it out on the worn parquet floor of the canteen. The coolness of the closed tape's cellophane wrapper conspired with the drop in temperature.

Like you don't know, said Costa.

I don't know.

That Nissimov transferred you to Amiram for good.

What are you talking about?

Don't play naïve. You can't even look at me, *blat*.

I looked up from the floor with difficulty. What are you talking about?

He bit into his sandwich. Isn't that what you wanted? he asked, and hiccupped. And hiccupped. And hiccupped. What a, hiccup, mistake.

I jumped up, stood behind him, and slapped his back. It didn't help. The hiccupping continued, Morse codes from his pharynx. Hold your breath, I said, as if you're diving. His face flushed with a lack of oxygen. Finally, he exhaled and said, Thank you, *blat*. Then he said nothing. Said nothing the whole way back.

His silence merged into another silence. I got home late again that evening. My mother had left a light on in the living room. I took my shoes off and lay down on the couch in my uniform, trying to read. My parents' bedroom door opened. My mother, with her mussed hair, her evening hair, a hint of the sunset's flame blended into its thick darkness, stood in the doorway. Her gaze was fatigued. Her sleep had been disrupted too. She said, I thought you were Simo. Her mouth was heavy, slow-moving. But Nahum, sweetheart, why didn't you change your clothes, and why are you reading in the dark?

Go back to sleep, I said, where's Dad?

You think I have any idea where he goes this late?

He's probably standing outside of Balasko's house, I said.

She said, You want me to heat something up for you, there's meat and rice in the fridge.

I said, I'll figure something out.

At least turn on the water heater, she said. It takes so long for the water to get hot. Simo's promised me a thousand times to re-place it, but that guy, his head isn't screwed on right.

Go to sleep, Mom, I said, walking to the door, I'll go get him.

On the day of the inspection, the heavens had opened, as they say. It was, as they say, raining cats and dogs. Amiram's prayers had been answered, then. The air on base was cut with thrusts of gleaming. The panicking trees, scorched by this light. The birds birthed with the storm wailing about their birth. How did I find time to breathe between mumbling one power and strength shall fill the world blessing and another, and between the bouts of running, through raging waters, as I scampered up and down to the registration office? Because the inspection had not been scrapped, but the forces of nature were working for our redemp-tion. The heads of the entourage—maintenance officers in their padded coats and fur collars, shoved into the main warehouse and sent their emissaries, along with me, to run inventory, one warehouse at a time. After each one was completed, I dashed back to the office to register the inventory of one warehouse after the other, mobilizing the shortages into a warehouse that was found fully loaded, while the soldiers returned to the main warehouse to report back to their commanders.

My odd health held up even in the furious rains. It seemed that during my adolescence my body had revolted against the no-tion of sickness. The rotting was interior, intertwined with my organs, spoiling my blood, the best defense against any exterior threat. From within the barrages and the gusts I recalled Chan-tal's crying. My father argued with me the previous night, refus-ing to come home. The meek beam of a night-light stretched out through Balasko's window. The street was empty, frozen. The flashlight's filament flickered off every few minutes and Simo slapped it back to life. What do you think they're doing in there, he asked me, they're probably already stoned out of their heads. I asked him how he thought standing on the sidewalk would help. He asked how a father could sleep at a time like this. I joined him.

I complained about the cold. You're barely dressed, he finally said, go home. I said I would stay with him. He nodded. He followed me, hunched, mumbling, only a beating'll do it. Chantal's sobs invaded my room as sleep took hold of my limbs, pulling me down. Is it because of Tova? I asked the next day. All of her paleness fixed on me when she said no.

I didn't see Costa all day. I stopped by at Nissimov's twice to have him sign a transfer of equipment to Amiram. I knew exactly what his equipment surpluses were. He didn't question my acts, nor did he resist them. He just signed the form. At the end of the day I dared ask about Costa. Nissimov gave his fiery mustache a long rub. He asked if I was happy at Amiram's and laughed. I asked if it was true that he'd transferred me there for good. I

He said, Of course, he gave me a good amount of equipment in exchange.

Then he added, What are you so shocked about, Mr. Compass, you think I have any reason to keep a bushy-tailed guy like you around? A spark I hadn't seen before lit up in his expressionless eyes. Not a spark. A shard of glass lit up by a stray sunray, a cold, false brightening. Suddenly, I grasped his hatred for me. I don't know how. It was palpable, acidic. He said, Costa didn't feel well, so I sent him home. I know how to treat people who are loyal to me.

THE FISH MEALS WITH MY MOTHER ON FRIDAY AFTERNOONS almost became a tradition that held on even upon my transfer to an open base. She tried different kinds of fish, but we always came back to tilapia and mullet. Tuna was too dry for my taste, but the flesh of the tilapia and the mullet were well suited for absorbing Moroccan spicing—the oil, the garlic cloves, softened enough to squash. We dipped bread in the sauce of the leviathan banquet she'd prepared, and the world all fit into our conversation. Just the two of us at the dining table, me still in uniform, she wearing her own uniform—the sweats she donned when she cooked and cleaned the house. The Friday-afternoon respite, the parlor our conversation created for us. Stories I hadn't been willing to listen to before pleased my ears. About her childhood in a transit camp. About the sword of immigration that sliced her life in two. A game played with a friend on the street in her hometown that ended with a broken leg, and worse, low spirits. Days pale as a plant in water. The glowing face of a righteous man who came out to greet them as they were approaching to ask for his advice. The talisman he wrote for her, which she carried in a fabric pouch for a week, until a snake slithered out of her grandfather's grave to announce her good health. All week long, different perfumes burned in special metal plates all over the house. Thick incense plumed out. Her mother walked around the house and yard, coloring the air with smoke.

That Friday, she returned to her story. But it no longer unfolded before me as a detached tale set in the undefined period of her childhood, in a Morocco whose architecture and landscape I could only imagine. No more borrowed images. Everything was tangible. Her paleness was Chantal's paleness. That righteous man, Baba Baruch, who had inherited his father's powers, though his weren't as great, the beaming of sanctity was held in his eyes. She could recognize it from a distance. They went to see him about Tova. They hadn't managed to reach him, and Simo dragged her there against her will. She didn't believe in that idolatry. But when they reached the yard, the crowd gathering outside with all its illnesses and depressions, they switched hearts. Her heart turned to faith, and Simo's heart turned to bitterness. He grumbled, saying there was nothing for them there, couldn't she see this was a charlatan taking advantage of people's misery? He, being the secret advisor of the leading politicians of Sderot, knew all the tricks, their effect, the symptoms of their workings. And thus, arguing, they returned home empty-handed.

For a full month, rumors and whispers were heard. Chantal

saw Tova associating with Johnny Balasko near the old market. Chantal said nothing happened, they just stood there, talking, and Tova laughed. Her entire skinny body trembled with laughter, to take Chantal's word for it. What was Tova doing, talking to a guy like that, a known junkie, God help us, with a permanent record, who'd spent two and a half of his twenty-five years of age in jails and prisons for drug possession and drug abuse? All of a sudden, the coils in the depths of the house were all pulled tight, coils that hadn't been active ever since Simo Farkash's heroism had returned to him. The cogs that had been gathering dust and cobwebs, rusting inside the walls, all moved with a screech. The lenses were focused and cleaned, and the house became the machine it had been meant to be from the moment of its creation. Eyes tracked, minds took notice, expressions calculated, fingers drummed restlessly on the furniture.

Tova returned from school in the late evening and sneaked out again at night. Simo spoke to the principal of the religious high school, an old acquaintance. He learned that Tova's grades, which had never been a cause for pride, were now plummeting. She was failing her exams. Her mind wandered during classes, and she was atypically dreamy. She was whispering with Johnny Balasko, that stinking leper. Chantal learned this from Tova's friends. At the grocery store in the new shopping center, Eva, one of Msodi's friends, said, Msodi, it's no good, who your daughter's hanging around with.

I only heard all this after the fact. I called my mother whenever I happened upon a phone at base. I begged the signal operators. But the news that I was leaving base, removed from the system of inside trading founded on benefits and services, had already spread. My haggling power as a quartermaster clerk, which I'd never utilized in my time with the battalion, had evaporated. No one had an interest in helping me out. My family's spying, monitoring, and supervision machine ticked away without me. My commander, an NCO only three years my senior who seemed a complete grown-up to me, assigned me to a small guard force. We received the honor of using our own bodies to guard an abandoned military facility in the Golan Heights through frozen nights. A worn, gray stone structure. Trees I didn't recognize grew in the large yard, northern trees, resistant to frost. Now and then I looked up at the jagged thinness of leaves. I saw the clarity of the air. Threads and wicks dangled from the branches, reminding me of hanging people. I was returned to base, from which I was allowed to emerge only in order to meet the mental health officer. I wrote poems about the birds of the sky and the animals of the field. I barely spoke a word.

Had they asked for my advice, I would have told Simo and Msodi Farkash, It's just a phase, let Tova breathe, trust her. Out of all of us, Tova was the most mature, the most skilled for life, with the pleasure she took in harassing and pestering. But they decided to confront her. I wasn't present for the fight either. It was only during Friday fish lunch that my mother recounted everything that happened, Simo's uncontrollable fury. The slap. The disbelief and horror in Tova's eyes. She said she could make her own choices now and he should be thankful she didn't file a complaint with the police. She packed a bag and left. My mother said, She's living with that Balasko kid now. She'll get involved with drugs. She'll get involved with prostitution. And her throat broke into a cry. She said, Nahum, what are we going to do? She didn't touch her fish. Not that Friday either. She held on to her fountain of childhood impressions. For two weeks the girl had been gripped in the talons of that Balasko, damn his name, and Simo couldn't find peace. Every night he went to stand underneath the guy's apartment window.

I wanted to say I knew that already, that I'd been serving on an open base for two weeks now, that I came home every day. And the household's supervision party had rolled into another machine, a machine of sorrow that screeched and moaned as it moved. I was part of it against my will. But my body refused, my blood flowing at a different pace. It wanted to wade in the veins on its own. So I listened to you, Msodi, dipping the challah in the sauce, in the torn pepper that made me choke, and nodded. My mother said, Maybe it's time to perform some rituals to remove the evil eye.

I, MEANING I, BELIEVE, HOWEVER VALID MY BELIEFS MAY BE, that moments are lost only in the sense that they are destined to repeat themselves forever, but never exist again. In the meager hour of the synagogue, the men's voice lowered to a whisper, a mumbling of lips during the Standing Prayer. My father stood before me, closer to the Torah ark, wrapped up in his *tallit*, swaying. He hadn't been there in years, certainly not on a Saturday morning. I had trouble sleeping too. I walked out to the yard after *Nakdishach*. Final trickling, trailing after the storm front. Marigolds clinging to a clover abundance, the broad foliage of the mallow with the dotting of tiny snail shells on top. Mustard lighthouses popped out of crowds of nettles and chicory. A hand gripped and twisted the guts. Children empty of the sediment of time, only the mechanism of its gathering growing through their cells, skipped around small water puddles. They taunted one another to step in them. Once upon a time, I thought, the tables would be set, waiting for the end of prayer time, and we would step out into the aroma of *hamin* and the sweet Kiddush grape wine. I thought about Pini and Dudi, I thought about Snot, I thought about Ehud. I would have even been willing to forgive Sabah had he appeared before me as he once was, with his firm stockiness. Before he left with his family for the first time. Before the years divided and we rushed away through the barren earth.

I went to visit Niro without making plans in advance. I would see him occasionally at the rehearsals of his former band, A Separate Reality, on Saturday nights in moldy basements. The sounds melded in the concrete space into a single roux, a defective mass of vocals and instruments. He left the band because he believed

he'd gone as far as he could go as a guitar player. He told me simply that after a year of playing with the keyboardist who replaced
Hershko, he realized he wasn't growing as a musician, that he was
stuck in his old shtick, the same method of composition. But I saw
how the new guitarist's playing grew cumbersome when he tried
to play Niro's parts. He hadn't gotten much taller since the first
time I met him, on the first night of Hanukkah, at the darkened
shopping center. His limbs lengthened, and with them his fingers,
which grew limber from his daily practice. They stretched unnatu-
rally against the strings. He had his own style. He didn't know how
to play music he hadn't written himself. I understood him.

He was sitting on his porch, smoking. He was wearing shorts
in spite of the cold. His hairy legs were stretched out in front of
him and his head was leaned back toward the top of the pergola.
He must have just woken up. He startled when he spotted me at
the gate, crushing the half cigarette in the ashtray with urgency.
Nahum, he said, what a surprise. Then he wrinkled his forehead.
We didn't make plans to meet, did we?

I told him I could come back in a few minutes if he preferred,
pointing at the cigarette, which was emitting plumes of smoke.

Forget it, he said, it's my second cigarette this morning. He
stretched and yawned. Coffee? he asked.

I shook my head.

Don't worry, he said. We've got a hot plate and a samovar now.
My nagging sister decided to observe the Shabbat.

Mint tea, I said.

So, he said when the cups rested before us. I wrapped my hand
around the cup. I froze in the brief moment of sitting. Drops of
sun and water pooled on the edges of the pergola. They grew
plumper until gravity overcame them. The sound of their popping against the pavement slivered in between our words.

So how are things on the new base? he asked.

Who knows, I said, the same, it's the military. But at least I
come home every evening.

What, no guard duties and all that?

One evening a week.

So why haven't you been coming to rehearsal?

No reason, just tired.

Listen, it's weird that you showed up today. Last night I met someone at a party who knows you.

Me?

Yeah, she said you were close in high school.

Me, no, what, Dalia? You see Dalia around?

Forget her, she's a drag, she'll never snap out of her depression. It was someone else, what was her name, she was tall.

Someone who was close with me in high school? Are you sure?

Yeah, curly black hair, she's hot, but you can tell she used to be an ugly kid and a hanger-on.

How can you tell?

She's got zero confidence. Laughs at stupid jokes. Her nose is crooked too. She was definitely a reject.

Oh, I said.

So what's her name?

Sylvia Gozlan.

That's it, said Niro. So what's the story?

Nothing, she was friends with a good friend of mine. Like you said, a hanger-on.

Isn't she the one who—

What's up with you? I asked.

What do you mean?

Last rehearsal you said we should talk, that you have news.

I'm moving to Tel Aviv.

What?

Yes. That's it, I enrolled in music school for next year.

I said nothing.

Do you know Vadim?

The guy who teaches at Sha'ar Hanegev College? Yeah, Dahan told me about him.

Yeah, he and his friend Igor sit around the editing room at the college all day. Igor is classically trained. They make video art together. They came to see our installation.

What installation?

You were stuck on base then. Eddy and I wrote live music for Dahan's film about the gamblers and the clock and performed it at the rec center. Didn't your dad tell you?

I shook my head.

They talked me into it. Said I had no technique.

I don't get it, since when do you care about technique?

Niro said, What are you getting all worked up about?

I thought about the worlds I was striving so hard to separate. To the left, Niro's world, the open world with its promise of freedom, and the boys inside each of whom there burned a bright dream, a composition, a song, a film, art. To the right, the world of the past, already beginning to cover itself with that faraway veil, embalmed by a yellowing plastic tarp. And I thought about the pointlessness. The worlds had started seeping into each other ever since the thicket. The two sides blending together. The worlds overlapping with a click. Over a year ago, during one of my leaves, Niro and I sat together all afternoon, talking about a plot-based musical piece he wanted to write with Eddy. We broke down the sequence of events. Niro said I should start writing stories. I told him nothing was more foreign to me. I knew only moods, only mental states. Those were the only things I could translate into words. I told him writing stories required a technique I didn't have. And he said, in his knowledgeable tone, that technique was for passionless people. Dalia repeated the same ideas to me back in the day, in her own words. Perhaps she'd heard them from Niro.

I said, But there must be a music school around here, even in Beersheba.

And get stuck for the rest of my life in this place where all people ever want is to get married and have children?

You sound like Dalia.

Don't remind me of her.

I said, I heard Hershko's getting married.

Yeah, well, said Niro, another one bites the dust. He'll end his life as a wedding performer.

She also moved, I said, Dalia.

Moved where?

To Tel Aviv. Everybody leaves.

Don't sweat it, said Niro, you'll get discharged and follow us there, won't you? He reached out and touched the yarmulke on my head. What are you doing still wearing that thing?

He pulled a cigarette from the pack on the table. The scorching scent of the Nobles, the aggressive ring of fire lurking at the tip. I got up.

He said, Sit down, where are you going, I wasn't going to light it. You're a riot. What's going on?

I sat back down. Sipped my tea. The chapel of raindrops dripped around us.

Military service isn't good for you, said Niro. You should have asked the mental health officer to get you discharged. I don't understand why you insisted.

I shrugged.

So are you going to tell me or not?

About what?

From the moment you got here you've been looking, I don't know, on edge. No, disturbed.

It's nothing. We had an inspection on base and they worked me like a dog. Just tired.

Listen, said Niro, I've got a solution for you.

OF COURSE I STAYED AWAY FROM THE DUNGEONS & DRAGONS meetup that Niro suggested. He said he'd joined a group opened by the other Sderot poet just the previous week. I hadn't heard about him until that day. I didn't know there was another poet

walking around Sderot. Niro said, Listen, he's like your doppelgänger from a parallel universe. You have no idea how alike you
are. And he's a terrific dungeon master.

Then he explained the rules of role play. The players are all
assigned roles: wizard, rogue, fighter, druid. Dice determine their
different abilities: constitution, strength, dexterity, charisma,
and so forth. They are part of a group that embarks on adventures
in an unknown land in order to locate enchanted objects, destroy
sources of evil, save their reality and themselves. They change according to their proclivities, gain experience and skills. Their ability scores improve. The bonds strengthen, or, alternatively, inner
rivalries form. Niro said, You won't believe it. We met in the afternoon and brought snacks and drinks. We didn't move for like six
hours. It's like a trip. You get in and you never want to get out.

It was only natural for a game like that to work its magic on
Niro. He was an avid reader of Castaneda, performed lucid dreaming experiments, and meditated for a while.

He said, I'm telling you, this guy came up with an amazing
campaign setting.

I asked him what a campaign setting was.

Niro said, A world, with rules and maps.

Long story short, according to Niro, this poet invented a full,
detailed, precise campaign setting. A world blending together elements of science fiction and fantasy, advanced technology and
magic, a patchwork of imaginary countries and segments of familiar geography, all alternative versions of Sderot. The other
guys in the group visited one of the Sderotae, as he called them, in
a previous adventure. It was half futuristic city, buildings made of
metals and conductors controlled by human brains that were implanted inside them, and half wild, barren wasteland filled with
hiding places and flickers of some raw power and wondrous animals. You understand, said Niro, in this multiverse, some time
disruptions occurred whose origins are unknown, meaning, to us,
the players. He, the dungeon master, knows why they occurred,

but anyway, different Sderotae were torn off of their timelines, some from the future, others from a mythological past, and they were distinguished by borders with openings called seeping points, and there are all sorts of hybrids born of couplings between futuristic creatures, and there are others that are genetically engineered or mutated, and demons and ghouls and other monsters that you definitely know from that Jewish world of yours. He was religious, like you were.

I'm still religious.

You know what I mean, said Niro.

I nodded.

Niro said, Besides, you know who he is, he wrote the poems for Sealed and Leased.

ON SUNDAY MORNING THE GROUND ON BASE WAS POKED WITH puddles, expanses of mud that even invaded the paved paths. Amiram said he loved the smell of rain. He saw his children charging with energy when it rained, like watered plants, and it reminded him of being young.

I said, You are young.

He said, I could be younger.

Where have I heard that tone in his voice before, in the depths of which words, words of comfort, words of concern, spreading like healing oil through the organs? His eyes turned outward.

So what now, I asked, that we've passed inspection?

He said, Now the real work begins.

I asked if he meant routine. He didn't answer. He walked to the door, stood cross-armed in the light of the new morning, bathed by the previous days. Outside that same synagogue vegetation savaged. I wondered what routine was made of.

First, said Amiram, confirm shortage refill.

I asked how.

He turned his face to me. A spot of shade. Perhaps I caught a smile. But I, meaning I, know that the spot of shade was, in fact, the sudden tangibility of distance, a hint of the being's flinching away from the world.

Amiram said, We submit applications for gear replenishments. We'll have to be creative. He glanced at his watch. The registration NCO should be here already, he said, let's go up to see her.

His feet waved up the incline with his typical clownish strut. I wondered if he could be included in one of the alternative Sderotae, and under what title. What metamorphosis gave birth to those ridiculous feet? Perhaps he had fins in his shoes. I asked Niro the previous day if they had aliens in their game world. He laughed and said he hoped they did, and that they were the reason for the timeline disruptions. For now, the other poet's character was Cybccult, a portmanteau the he made up. Just like cyborg is short for "cyber organism," Cybccult is short for "cyber occult." Niro plays a demon called Kordiakos who was infected by an artificial intelligence virus.

I said, You already have wings like a ministering angel, and you fly between both ends of the world like a ministering angel, and hear everything the future holds from behind the curtain like a ministering angel, what could the virus possibly add?

He said, I'm learning my character slowly. Plus, I know all the secrets.

I smiled meekly.

Niro said, So you do remember we used to be kids once, it isn't just my hallucination.

I said, No, the hallucination is mine. Niro and everybody else are my fever dreams. I said I'd think about coming. I said we'd see what the future holds. Niro gave me the address. I thought to myself, Seeping shmeeping. I felt a hubbub of laughter that I instantly stifled. A babyish, backward hubbub. I knew the address, of course. It was where Snot's family used to live.

✳ ✳ ✳

COSTA FOUND ME ON THE BANKS OF THE RAVINE BEHIND AMI-
ram's warehouse area. An enormous puddle pooled at the bottom.
On its periphery and along the slopes, a tangle of wild vegetation
erupted. I recognized the skillful etchings of daisies whose yellow
glow was still buttoned up at the tips of their stems. I recognized
a stork's bill. I recognized the inflamed petals of dandelions,
burst stars, dripping with energy. There was a purple flicker between them. I shifted them aside for a better view. I hadn't been
mistaken. Anchusa. I hadn't seen that weed, with its stubbly
stems and leaves, in years. It used to bloom every winter in our
yard, near the fence bordering the neighbors' house. Tova and
Chantal once glued the purple flowers to their faces, and the
neighbor, who stepped outside to fan the flames of the frena clay
oven fire she'd built in her yard, panicked and spat at them. Simo
Farkash was in his early days of heroism. The neighbor's husband's skull had the pleasure of meeting the sole of Simo's shoe.
The memory came back to me like a middle-of-the-night muscle
spasm.

What are you looking for down there? asked Costa. He was
standing between me and the sun. I felt his shadow before he
spoke.

My pants turned green around the knees from kneeling. Are
you all right? I asked. I slapped the fabric clean.

Take your time, he said. He was a little hoarse. The usual
thunder of his voice was gone.

I haven't seen you since the inspection, I said. For some reason I didn't stand up. And I didn't turn to look at him. I liked being
close to the ground, the rich scent, the bitter vitality that rose
from it.

It's only been a week, said Costa.

He touched my back. I turned to face him. He offered me a
hand, and from it fell a tissue. It dropped down to the bottom of
the valley. The rivulets swirled at its touch under their cover
of cloud. The tissue lay like a lily on the surface of the water,

glistening. Costa pulled me up to my feet. What are you holding? he asked.

I showed him the anchusa.

He said, Oh, a plant.

I said, Anchusa. Bull's tongue.

He said, You know the names?

I said, Sometimes. If I'm lucky.

Why is it called bull's tongue?

I pointed at the fleshy leaves and short stubble.

What is that good for? he asked.

Aesthetics, I think.

You should show it to Anatoly, his mom can probably cook a spell out of it, *blat*.

There's a similar plant, alkanet, steer's tongue.

What's the difference between a bull and a steer?

There's no difference, but that plant, the steer tongue is good for—

For what?

I can't say, it's crude.

What?

It gives men potency.

To fuck, *blat*.

I said nothing.

So how did the inspection go?

Exhausting, I said. I told him about my conversation with Nissimov. I said, You think I'm overeager?

That's an exaggeration, he said. What are you listening to Nissimov for?

I like my corner, I said.

Yeah, but sometimes you don't hold back. You taunt.

I what?

You make, *blat*, inappropriate comments.

Like what?

What difference does it make.

No, no, tell me.

Like when you told Nissimov it was a good thing there was a twice-yearly inspection because if there wasn't the gear would fall apart when reserve-duty soldiers tried to use it in the next war.

But I'm right, aren't I? What are these warehouses for?

What do you care? What has this country ever done for you, *blat*, it can go to hell.

Easy for you to say. You came here and found paradise. Do you have any idea what people gave to make this a country?

Are you nuts?

Well, that's because you're not really Jewish, you don't know what Shabbat and the High Holy Days mean. You don't know what happened here, you can't feel the sanctity of the Land of Israel.

Costa said nothing.

You pull a flower out of the ground, and that flower might remember the footsteps of Rabbi Shimon bar Yochai. His eyes and his son's eyes might have burned the thorns growing around it two thousand years ago. You touch a rock, and it's still sharp, maybe Solomon's *shamir* crawled over it, cutting it into bricks for the temple.

He placed his hand on my forehead. Nope, he said, no fever. What's going on, Nahum?

I don't know, I said, I don't know anymore.

Come on, let's go to the canteen. Maybe some candy will fix you up.

I'm not hungry.

So just walk with me.

From the drawer in Amiram's bureau I pulled out the pages with the typed-up poems. They'd been lying there since the day of the inspection, folded up. My father brought me colorful paper from city hall, red, blue, green, purple. I saved up my money all summer long to buy an electric typewriter before I enlisted. I coveted it as soon as it appeared in the window of the stationery and gift store at the shopping center. It waited for me for two months. It emitted an electric hum when we hooked it up at home. For two days, I couldn't even type on it, I was so pleased.

Costa looked at the pictures trapped under the glass plate over the desk. He leaned down and took a close look at the portrait of Amiram in the top left corner. He slapped it and laughed. That's from the vacation at Olga, he said. This guy has some balls to put that picture here.

Why? I asked.

He said, That Amiram is a bastard. He definitely doesn't need your plant. He spread out the papers and touched them. He brought them to his nose. They smell like alcohol, he said.

I nodded.

He read the poems while I chewed on the faded chocolate bar I'd bought. His half a tuna sandwich with the bite marks rested between us. He said, I don't understand some of these words. It's from the *Biblia*, no?

I said, From the *Biblia*, *blat*.

He cleared his throat, then coughed a series of dry coughs. He held his fist against his mouth. In the break between the coughs he said, Can I keep them?

What is it about his body, I wondered, that doesn't hesitate to make itself present? I, meaning I, believe that thought is inaccurate. There is something more profound about Costa, just as in existence, in the overall existence, higher matters enslave lower matters, turning them into their own substance, but do not extinguish them, and the inferior matters undermine them, scheming to return to their original essence, which is the presence of the body, a scheme to return to the flesh.

There are some nice poems about love here, he said. Maybe I could use them sometime.

For what? To send to your girlfriend?

Who knows? said Costa. Who did you write them about?

You were so pale before, I said.

He said, I needed to eat, I'm feeling a little weak. That asshole doctor wouldn't give me any more sick days.

I said nothing.

He said, How about you, are you better?

I said, Yes. Difficult days.

What, he said, is Amiram working you hard? The new soldiers arrive tomorrow. The burden will be eased.

I said, No, at home.

He said, What's at home?

I wanted to tell him about Tova, but the yearning on his face, as if expecting me to disclose some secret, something that would provide him with, what, actually? What could I possibly give him? I told him about Chantal crying and refusing to reveal the reason.

He said, Girls, what do you expect? At some point their hormones start going crazy. You can't talk to them.

Do you have sisters?

Older ones, he said. He was an only son from his parents' current marriage. The father of his three sisters left his mother after they immigrated to Israel. But I shouldn't get confused, just because they're women and mothers doesn't make them any less crazy. Maybe that's why you're a little crazy, he said, you caught your sister's craziness.

IT'S FUNNY HOW THE TABLES TURN. I, WHO SPENT THE FIRST two years of my military service just yearning to go home, now ached for some respite from the stress of evenings at the house. Tova hadn't returned yet. She had some angry words with my mother. They met in public, on the street, or at the shopping center or at the market. My mother begged, pleaded with Tova to tell her something, to explain. Tova told our mother she didn't understand anything. What did we do to her to make her turn her back on us? Msodi said to me. I couldn't bear the tears trembling on the edge of her voice. I said that perhaps what Tova was looking for had nothing to do with them and everything to do with herself, the process she was going through.

Process, process, said my mother. What's wrong with your generation, everything with you is a process. We didn't treat our parents like this.

I told her that Tova was her own person, and they couldn't force their parenting on her if she'd had enough of it.

My mother said, You don't have a heart either.

I liked the guard tower on the outskirts of the base, the startling silence inside, the coldness of iron that penetrated every fabric while one climbed up. I was sent up there on my first and second guard duties. The floor was coated with nut shells and food wrappers. It was an injustice to answer the existence insinuated by it with silence. Dense time, dead time that necessitated the movement of life, that forced speech. The songs that played through my head sang back to me from the metal walls, from the hard plastic plates covering the windows.

I volunteered for my third guard duty. Costa was pacing and moping when he found out he'd been scheduled for guard duty that night. He had plans to go out with friends, he told me. Though it was no big loss, Amiram was on duty too, and things were always simpler with him. He didn't suck the blood out of soldiers the way some of the other commanders did.

I told him I had no problem replacing him. He'd regained his strength. We wandered the paths during our lunch break, and his flesh was a quiet bellows of energy. He stopped in his tracks. He said, Really, you'd switch with me?

No, I said, I'm willing to take your shift.

But then you'll have duty two weeks in a row, *blat*.

I told him not to worry. He became restless. He leaned a little toward me, as if wishing to translate his gratitude into a physical gesture, but another force prevented him, the hidden knowledge of my natural recoiling. Finally, he rested a hand on my shoulder. Thank you, he said, you're a true friend.

I hated the ritual of receiving the weapon, the needless weight and the smell of oil, and the false promise of maturity it suggested. I also hated the evening formation, the lowering of the flag. Amiram seemed also to find it despicable. Flawed boys putting on a production of military in the center of the country, within the safe noose of a reserve-duty base. There was an air of self-awareness and mockery in the way he carried out the formation, in the voice he used to bark at soldiers to stand up straight, with the worn tone of content employed by boot camp instructors, in the supposedly withering glare he shot us when he read the assignations. That time, I was assigned to the entry gate.

Amiram's hand shook me awake before midnight. A rough blanket was pulled up over my head for protection against cold and female mosquitos, mosquitas, who swarmed in flocks from the puddles left by the rain. Costa warned me against the puddles when he saw me searching for more childhood plants on their banks. He said, First the gnats will come, *blat*, and then the mosquitos. When that happens you'll be cursing that water. I was already awake. When I lowered the blanket, Amiram moved on to the next soldier on duty.

I tried to imagine what Sha'ashu'a saw as he sat in his guard booth every day. The eucalyptus trees, in their journey toward eternity, and cars on the road on their short, shortening journey. I couldn't think of poetry. I turned on the transistor radio Sha'ashu'a left there for his nightly replacements.

The radio announcer, in his shattered voice, vanquished by white noise, translated the lyrics of the song he was about to play. I don't want to get out of bed, I don't want to go to school, I don't know why, but the dolphins make me cry. Such a simple loss in even simpler words. The music was their engine, a muted lamentation in the singing voice. Somewhere a piano, the soft distortion of an electric guitar in the background, or maybe it was the frequency slicing of the appliance's tiny speakers. I don't want to get out of bed, I don't want to go to school. But dolphins. Once, in his bedroom, in the sealed space of age fifteen, Snot said that dolphins were disgusting animals, rapists and whatnot. They did some experiments, Snot said, they did experiments, they put a woman in a house with a dolphin. She had to give him hand jobs to keep him from mounting her.

What's wrong with you? I asked. Lately every time you open your mouth, filth comes out.

Why not, am I telling the truth or what? I don't lie, that's life.

But how can a woman and a dolphin be in the same house?

Who knows, half the house was full of water.

And she slept in the water?

Why are you getting hung up on nonsense, the important thing is he tried to—

But you said this was life, so I need to know the details.

Walla, that Gmarah class really messed with your mind. You can't see the point of things anymore. It's all the same to you.

And are dolphins the point?

You know five boy-dolphins gang up on one girl-dolphin and screw her silly?

His cheeks crumpled when he laughed. The pus-topped pimples glistened on his skin. I couldn't remember how we got to talking about dolphins. Different conversations mixed in, echoes of evaporating, amorphous hours. Snot's features from different moments of our acquaintance joined together to form a reproachful, threatening expression.

All at once, my consciousness clarified. A man towered over me, bare-chested, muscular, kinky hair twisting around dark nipples. A few gray hairs in his temples, and those golden spots of rage in his eyes. How could he bear to stand in the cold without a shirt on? He said, Very nice, asleep on duty. Give me your name and ID number.

The digits stuttered in my mouth. My name was a collection of hollow syllables.

So, Corporal Nahum Farkash, you think the military is like boarding school?

I said I didn't think that, my mind had just wandered.

And your eyes closed. Do you have any idea how seriously you endangered all the soldiers on this base?

I was afraid to ask who he was. He said I'd be put on trial the following day. I didn't return to the guard room. Instead, I climbed up to the offices, to the officer on duty's room. I opened the door carefully. Amiram had managed to get back from waking up the next round of guards and slip back into bed. His breathing was soft and steady. The force of sleep ruled the room, odor, presence. I thought, The world is falling apart, and this guy couldn't care less. Asleep.

FOUR HOURS OF WAKEFULNESS UNTIL MY NEXT SHIFT. ALERT underneath the blanket weaved out of the fibers of some unknown material, a combination of scabies and the stench of soldiers' dreams. I had a new Walkman I hardly ever used. I put on my headphones and slipped in the *Want to Be and Will Be* tape. A man decrying the fact that he had to share his vodka with his friends. Vodka was meant to be like a bride. But a woman could very well belong to more than one man. Then came Costa's song. Poetic, faraway forest landscapes, a castle. Snows hover in the air, idiotic kingdoms collapse. As does the flesh, fatigued from fighting against gravity. Then I changed the tape to John Cale's *Paris 1919*. He sang, "You're a ghost, la la la la la la la la la la, you're a ghost, I'm the church and I've come to claim you with my iron drum, la la la la la la la la la la." Dalia loved that album. She asked me who I liked better, John Cale or Lou Reed. I didn't know what to answer. I wasn't familiar with either.

I, meaning I, though I don't have a personal recollection of this conversation, call it a lie, a falsehood. From what I've learned about Dalia so far, she can't have loved John Cale. His harmonies were too pure for her taste. Even the song "Macbeth"—all of a sudden I, meaning I, know—in said album, with its furious rock guitar, contains no grit, no discord.

Eventually, Amiram came by to send me back to my guard post. He touched me and moved on. I said, Hold on, hold on. It's the freezing hour of the night, I didn't say. I said, Amiram, I'm in big trouble.

He walked with me half the way to the guard post. I had a prepared speech, an apology. But the uniting thought was methodless. I said what I said. He stopped me. He said, The base commander caught you sleeping on duty?

There wasn't enough light where we were standing. His expression evaded me. I quickly recognized a hint of the same mockery from formation in his tone. I said, I know, it's serious, I'm sorry.

Amiram nodded and turned to leave.

My wakefulness was a nature of its own. My façade was made up of muscle tension, eyes peering into the dark. From behind this façade, bits of pondering, unstructured exaggerations came and went. Here Snot and I were talking heatedly. There Sabah looked at me calculatingly and joked with Ehud. Here Dalia with her apparently hesitant playing and her singing that breached all defenses. They haunted me out of nowhere, I didn't even miss any of them.

Later, I waited outside of the warehouse. In the dizziness that plagued me, the nervous energy of sleep deprivation was already building up. I followed the peeling of darkness, the pinkness of dawn, until the sun came out. When I wrapped the *tefillin* around my arm I suddenly let out a howl. Like a gag reflex, the tears spilled out. Talk no more so exceeding proudly, let not arrogance come out of your mouth. The letters of the prayer book grew fuzzy.

Amiram walked into the warehouse. The door faced the east. He darkened the rectangle of light on the floor tiles. I was gripped in the elation of *aleynu leshabe'ach*. Perhaps he noticed my still damp eyes. He said, *Amen selah*.

I nodded and continued mumbling as I folded the *tallit*. He watched me for several moments. Then he said, I took care of it, there won't be a trial, only a reprimand.

He'd already disappeared when he leaned his head back through the doorway and added, And you're grounded next Saturday, that's from me, in case you wondered.

In the hour I had left before morning formation, I sat down at his desk, staring at the photos pressed under the glass steamroller. My eyes kept wandering back to the photograph on the top left corner. What did Costa mean when he talked about Amiram's courage? I cleared the glass plate, pushed a letter opener underneath, and shifted it until the photo emerged into the air. I removed the corner of a form that covered its bottom part.

Amiram was standing in a bathroom, his robe opened, his flesh exposed. The thin chest, the ribs visible, the skin gilded with tan, and the thin line of hair descending and thickening to form the bush of the loins. Around his groin, on his waistline, on the tops of his thighs, his skin was whitened, a negative of his bathing suit sketched onto his body. From within the tangle of hair, his member pulled downward. It was long and narrow. The expression on his face was surprised yet defiant. As if in that fraction of a second he'd turned his nudity into an advantage. I don't know how long I lingered over the image before returning the photograph to its place.

Simo Farkash told me that night, *Isha bekayah*, you wanted to be a jobnik, you wanted the mental health officer, you wanted to serve close to home, now reap what you sow and stop complain-

ing. I didn't dare ask about Tova. Earlier that evening, when Chantal asked for some money to get pizza at the new place with her
friends, he said, I've had it up to here with you, up to here, you
hear me?

She sat on the porch, pouting. I went out to talk to her. I said,
It's still sunny in the daytime, but the evenings are freezing.

She said, Why am I being punished for what Tova did?

I shoved a twenty-shekel note into her hand. I said, Be back by
eight, you don't want Simo losing it on you now.

She looked at me. She said, What are you doing, clearing your
conscience?

What conscience?

As if you don't know you're the only one Tova would listen to.

What? I said.

Chantal stood up. She said, I'll pay you back, don't worry.

I lay down in bed, reading an anthology of translated German
poetry. What did I have to do with those gentiles? One of the poets
quoted the New Testament. The pleasant lead of sleep was approaching. The book fell out of my hands. In my dream, I was lying in the same bed, in the navel of another room. It expanded to
the size of a parlor, but my youth still clung to the walls. Our great
Rabbi Maimonides stood over me, wearing a sword. My heart was
resting in one of his hands, and in the other was a burning prayer
book. He was feeding the flames with the blood that dripped out
of the torn heart. Then he walked out.

I WOULD CONVENE NIRO, COSTA, AND AMIRAM FOR A MORNING
prayer and announce to them, *Helma tava hazai.* I have dreamed
a good dream. But what could those absolute sinners, those vile
converts, possibly say to me in response? I hurried off to morning
prayer so that I could at least mutter the priestly blessing, I have
dreamed a dream whose nature I do not know. And more so out of
a pointless anxiety to say, to tell, to have words to describe the

image that occurred, because what did Maimonides want from me now, looking like his portrait on money bills and in textbooks, with his turban and his chubby face, contoured by an overly quaffed beard and Eurasian features? My spirits are low, our great master, my spirits are heavy.

Too many soldiers got detention that Saturday–transportation soldiers who disappeared for hours with a military truck, a medic who was caught, God help us, masturbating in the infirmary, and soldiers punished for all sorts of mischief and whimsy whose nature I didn't bother to find out. The only one I knew was Anatoly, who was a thick-bearded brute of a father, and only my age. Though he was punished for his brashness, it seemed he'd been excessively punished. I told Amiram, who was the officer on duty that day. I assumed he had the authority to let Anatoly go. Amiram widened his eyes at me and said nothing.

It didn't matter that someplace, however many days and weeks away, the holiday of Tu Bishvat was preparing to turn over the force of the sun. It was only mid-Tevet and winter was already unraveling. I was exempt from guard duty. Just myself. There wasn't even a minyan at synagogue. The five young men who utilized it were forced, like me, to pray on their own. I wandered the base, in the areas where the savagery of vegetation collapsed the order of things. All of a sudden, the expanses of childhood appeared before me. The two thickets and fields and the streets of the town beaten by the afternoon light and the porcupine lairs I imagined to be a network of burrows spread underneath Sderot, perforating the ground.

I saw Amiram sitting on a large dirt heap, nearly a small-scale hill. I emerged out of a thin cluster of trees, out of the shade. He was closed off in his position. Legs crossed. Head between his hands. I froze in place. I couldn't retreat for fear that my footsteps would make a racket, and I didn't want to advance toward him, lest I invade his territory of pondering. I waited. Under the force of the gaze, the years-long layers of granite cracked, the rock split, and Amiram the boy was revealed, trapped inside. Gaunt, prepared for the world to take place around him. All of a sudden, he noticed me there. He waved at me and stirred himself. Time returned to pounce on him, wrapping its stone cerecloth around him. But in his eyes were remnants of that fragile, shape-shifting being. I saw it in him, the holeache that I had inside too, whose movement was often a contraction and suckling of the existent, and often an expansion and gushing of bitter waters.

He said, Don't worry about it, it's public property.

I said I understood, that I also sometimes needed to get away from everything and let my thoughts flow. Amiram leaned down to pick up a dry branch. He bent it between his hands. The shattering of the fracture shattered. What could I say about that, that the simple sound made me choke? A kind of super-sound that allowed words to play on the correct frequency. I said that some days weren't as simple.

He said, Tell me about it.

I said, I went through some hard months at my old base.

He nodded. With indifference, he said, I read in your case file that your profile was lowered because of a mental health issue.

I said nothing.

He said, Don't worry about it, there are lots of bummed-out soldiers on this base.

I said, I'm not bummed out.

He said nothing and walked with his measured steps. I slowed my own pace. The quiet of Saturday afternoon tightened around us. Amiram asked, Are you having a hard time here too?

I said, You know, it's an inner thing.

But there must be something that can help.

I said, Being close to home is therapeutic.

I'd told the mental health officer similar things, though I didn't believe them at the time. I told him how for years I'd never realized how at-home I felt at home, and how the distance was now unbearable. I thought it was an ingenious camouflage. What would that bearded, nasally man have done with my truth, had I offered it? I thought I was presenting my façade as my essence, the pus as the thorn infecting the skin, the temporary incarnation of my emptiness as the reason for my emptiness. But I knew more than I let myself, guessing the final shape of things before they became experience. Either way, the mental health officer cut me off, asking, But you get excited about the ass of a woman walking down the street, yes, when you see a pair of juicy breasts, that excites you? I cursed him on the way out, *Inshallah* you'll die painfully of cancer, you Ashkenazi jerk. My cheeks still burned. My yarmulke burned even worse.

But Amiram listened in silence. I could not mistake the beauty enveloping the features of those who understood me deeply. Something inside of him knew my language.

We reached the warehouse. He said, I have to leave once the Shabbat is over to run an errand. He yawned. Can I give you a ride? he asked. There's no reason for you to stick around if you don't have guard duty. The metal in his car gasped as I adjusted the passenger seat to my dimensions. Amiram's hand tensed for a touch. The light swept the sky. Amiram said, Look at that strong moon.

I, MEANING I, PANIC AT NAHUM'S THOUGHT THAT PASSING TIME has a weight, an accumulation. Because if it is secretly sweeping, then where can it be felt? When did any of us receive proof of the invisible flow of blood in the vessels, of the resin dripping under-cover of bark, if not with the wounding, with the piercing of the exterior?

The new soldier who came to serve under Amiram barely registered in my Nahum mind. From the day he arrived, he busied himself with some task in a distant warehouse, while I worked around the main warehouse. Amiram disappeared for hours on end. When I asked Costa if he knew where Amiram disappeared to, he'd say, That bastard has his own affairs. Then he went back to his usual complaint about the new soldier working with him, who drove him mad with his laziness and naysaying. He was a Moroccan like me, the new soldier, but he wasn't educated like me. Mr. Primitivsky. And Costa, who came from a cultured home, had trouble finding a shared language with him. I tell him to go put the kit bags in order and *blat*, the guy laughs and asks what a kit bag is.

The truth was that Costa's complaints were getting on my nerves, which were already agitated. Things at home were so stressful that I could barely breathe. I had dreams of hunger. Dreams in which I was plagued by a desire for odd foods. One dream in particular stayed with me. I was etching words onto round, smooth marble, handing them over someplace, to some agency whose nature was unclear to me. I did this joyfully. In the dream I sensed the joy as a slight push that I could intensify if I wanted to. I did this for years. One time, an inspector came to see me. I can't say who she looked like, only that her eyes were bright, sockets burning with a lucid flame. She stood before me and levitated into the air. I levitated up to the same height, both of us a distance away from the ground. I returned to the workshop, famished. One of the stones began to crumble under the stylus. I pressed it down. The marble veins became cracks. The hardness of the rock crumbled into pieces of canned tuna. I shoved it voraciously into my mouth.

I wandered on my own in the lengthening hours of the evening. The alleys, the side paths, the faulty roads of Sderot resembled an uncharted land, every inch of it awakening a memory. I thought about how much I loved the Israeli landscape, a modesty that turned out to be endless offering. I needed to write poetry, I wanted to write a poetry collection that would capture something of this exterior, which is eternal longing and eternally untouchable. A sort of veil of space stretched over the abyss of time. It prevented me from reuniting with its depths, and with the same breath it was the lens that focused my sight, helping me to observe.

And within the glamour of reality alternately revealing and concealing itself, Costa stood there, talking my head off about the new soldier making his final days of mandatory military service a living hell. And I had to think about Tova, and I had to think about Chantal and her small lamentation, the lamentation of the small hours. I insisted on going back to discussing Amiram's disappearances. And what actually did Amiram want, meaning, did Costa think Amiram was pleased with his life? Clearly something was bothering him. When did he quit swimming, and did Costa think one could just give up an activity one was devoted to throughout their youth, and anyway, swimming was an emotional thing, wasn't it? Costa was a swimmer, he knew.

At the canteen, Costa said, Why are you so interested in that parasite? If I know him, he's probably messing around. Then he told me again, in detail, about how Nissimov laughed at his complaints. He enjoys it, *huy loh. Suka blat.*

Messing around where?

I don't know, there's a new arms officer. They kicked out the old one after she fucked all the career soldiers. I told that *huy loh* new soldier to organize the gas masks, half a day later I went to check. Turns out that loser pulled apart all the masks and put them in a pile on the floor. I tell him, Are you an idiot, and that cretin laughs, *yobani vrot.* He—

An idea flickered through me, to make plans to meet Tova at Tu Bishvat. The holiday would soften her. She was emotional. The intensity of the idea brought tears to my eyes.

What's up with you, man? said Costa.

What arms officer? I asked.

Who, the old one? I told you, she isn't here anymore. Just an ape, as dumb as a dog. She brought a camera to the vacation week at Olga. She walked into the rooms of all the career soldiers who were fucking her on the side and took naked pictures of them.

Oh, I said, that's where Amiram's picture is from.

Costa paused for a few minutes. He asked, Have you been listening to that Vysotsky tape I gave you?

I nodded. He'd asked me more than once, and every time I told him the same thing, Those songs are brilliant.

He's good, that Arkadi Duchin, he said.

I said, You know, Micha Shitrit translated most of the songs, and he's Moroccan.

Moroccans and Russians are the best combination. That's what's going to get this country out of the garbage.

Hey now, I said, what's changed, all of a sudden you like Moroccans?

He said, *Yob tvoyu mat*, you don't understand anything.

So there's a new arms officer, I said.

He said, As ugly as the night. Go see for yourself.

I tried to hold on to Tova's image, awaiting redemption. How miserable she'd looked to me in Balasko's sad apartment. She must not have showered for a week, I thought, it's a known fact that junkies stink. But the image I forced upon myself refused to become real. The same noise and frantic energy stirred within me. It must be the spring, no doubt, spring came early this year.

THERESE SAID THAT IF SHE HADN'T RUN INTO ME ON THE ROAD A month and a half ago she wouldn't have thought to call and let me know, but that meeting brought back memories of the close friendship between me and Ehud when we were children. Ehud was injured in an accident. He went on leave with friends and they went out drinking. Meaning that their designated driver drank too. I thought, The wheels of justice turn so freaking slowly. She asked if I could come visit. I said I'd come in a few days. She said, How about tomorrow?

What was so urgent? His right foot had shattered and his left tibia was broken. He was bedridden anyway. The next day I asked Amiram if I could leave early. He was preoccupied and didn't listen. I tried, as I had throughout recent weeks, to make him listen, to offer not the contents of my words but the emotional tangle that came with them, the spreading of the inner darkness that clung to all. I told him about my friendship with Ehud. I debated aloud whether we were still friends, if we hadn't spoken in four years. People change over the course of that much time, especially at our age.

Amiram said he had no idea what I was talking about. Said he'd consider my request to leave early. We had quite a bit of work now that our equipment replenishment request had been approved. Our warehouses finally had the potential to be properly prepped.

I said, Are you worried about another war?

He said, That's not my job.

I said, But we have a ton of time, what's the rush? Besides, I can teach the new soldier how to organize. What's his name, Warbler, Eagle?

Hawk, said Amiram. I want you to supervise the organization up close. That Hawk guy, he's got problems.

I said, Who doesn't?

Amiram glared at me. His twin darkness appeared in his eyes. I said I understood.

But the afternoon passed, and the evening stretched taut, that silent stakeout of the dim light of Adar. The shadows grew shorter, their edges still soft, the boundaries blurry, and suddenly they came together for an ambiguous hour, defying definition, neither afternoon nor night, neither twilight nor sunset. A glow blinding with its inky thickness.

Then Amiram disappeared as usual. I went off to look for him on base, ascending to the office area and then returning to the lower territories of the warehouses and transportation garages.

The warmth of the day pulled the leaves off an ancient poinciana tree. I thought about the future shock of blossom, that inflammation that summer would bring. I didn't want it to come.
Soldiers were talking about a fun day planned at a pool near
Kiryat Gat. The rumors revolted me.

With no choice left, I went to the arms storage. The arms officer was seated on Amiram's lap as the two of them frolicked. His
snaky hand had a will of its own, and she, the arms officer, was
dark and ugly as the tents of Kedar.

I stood in the doorway. So, I said, the equipment shows up and
you take off. Where's your sense of responsibility?

They flinched, their bodies parting. But she retained her
smile.

Amiram lowered his head. My breath caught in my throat for
several seconds. I waited outside the iron door. The sweet, rich
odor of machine oil assaulted my nostrils and mouth. I left, but
the sickening film of flavor remained in my throat. Amiram arrived thirty minutes later, light-footed and cheerful.

I said, You promised you'd let me off early.

He said, I promised nothing, I said I'd consider it.

I said, When you needed me to stay late, I did. You're such an
ingrate.

Amiram said, Cool it, this is the military, not a members' club,
and I'm not your parents, get it?

Sorry, I said, it's just that I promised I'd visit Ehud, and—

Go get ready to leave, said Amiram, and this is the last time
you use that tone with me.

Therese was restless when I arrived. Ehud's parents wanted a
night to themselves. Ehud required constant supervision, and
she'd volunteered. She greeted me with a nod and hurried out.

Ehud was lying on the bed. His figure was firm. It wasn't just
the muscles he'd grown since he and Sabah joined a pre-military
training team. For some reason, the two of them had been taken
by the instructor's aura. He'd arrived in Sderot by proxy of some

organization established by a graduate of a combat unit who'd decided that the elite unit enlistment percentages in our remote town were too low. He traveled from school to school, lecturing kids about the importance of taking part in the national mission. I told Dalia about him once, I think, in the course of a whispered, intimate conversation. And Dalia laughed. She said she was surprised I hadn't joined the team as well, as a future ultranationalist party voter.

No, it wasn't just the muscles, Ehud was more real, more mature. The shadow of a mustache peeked from underneath his nose. I wondered if being cross-eyed was what had disqualified him from serving in the reconnaissance unit that Sabah had enlisted into.

So, Farkash, said Ehud, it's been years.

Yeah, I said, years.

I let him tell me his tales of achievements and mischief. Such a dull series of plans, intentions that became fulfilled without the obstacles of reality. He didn't say much about his military endeavors. His training was confidential. His stories seemed to hint that a bright future was awaiting him.

How about you? he said.

I said, I'm a bottom-feeder quartermaster clerk.

Oh, he said, that's a shame.

I looked at the casts on his legs and asked if he wanted me to sign them. He said, Write me a poem. I heard you write poetry.

I nodded.

Don't lose hope, you'll make something of yourself.

I told him I was going to college after I got discharged.

He said, We each move at our own pace.

On his cast I wrote, *Get well, a brightly dark shell.*

He had to shift positions to read it. The pillow under his head fell to the floor. I picked it up, fluffed it, and adjusted it under his back. Ehud sighed with relief. You should study nursing, he said.

I said nothing.

What's a darkly bright shell?

I shrugged. I said, You wanted a poem, didn't you?

You're still on your bullshit, huh, Farkash?

I looked at the line I'd written again. I said, It's lucky you have this cast. At least this year you won't have to break the bank buying a costume for Purim. Then I bellowed, once, twice.

What's up, said Ehud, what a *bshala*.

I choked down my laughter. Get it, I said, you don't have to break the bank because you already broke your leg.

Therese, Ehud shouted.

But she was already there, in the room. What's wrong, what happened? she said.

Where'd you disappear to, said Ehud, I'm thirsty.

She poured water from the pitcher and put the glass to his mouth. Sip, swallow, sip. Shards of laughter rattled through my brain at an even pace.

Come, Therese told me, Ehud needs to rest.

His eyes lit up when she reached for the light switch and darkened his space.

I thought to myself, He took off the yarmulke, but he still has the Moroccan accent of our childhood.

THAT LITTLE JACKASS, SHE MUTTERED. WHAT A JACKASS HE'S become. Just like his parents. What good is all his education if his nature keeps breaking through? Therese lit a cigarette. The backyard remained identical to the version that had stamped itself onto my mind four years earlier. But rather than being a model of the familiar, preceding and determining reality, it was one of many reflections, full of intentional errors. It was already etched into that cellophane of pastness. I had to position it against reality, make sure it was valid. Light chills down my spine. I've seen greater beauty than this, broad beauty, less measured vegetation, tears of land more darkened by rain.

I've been with him for two days, letting his parents rest, said Therese. And he won't cut it out. Get me this, get me that, adjust my blanket, I'm cold, I need the bathroom. Seriously, I stage him like a puppet beside the toilet, on the toilet, then stand outside to listen. It's lucky his parents hired an aide to bathe him every morning.

She exhaled, then took another puff.

We got brainwashed with family values, family above everything. No matter what I've achieved in life, when something happens I drop everything and come over. I come myself, I don't send anyone. Otherwise they say I'm condescending, a snob, coldhearted.

I was thinking about how the legs of the white metal table had been sinking into the ground since Ehud and I were children. With each passing month they'd blend in a little more, until the process would be reversed, and the table would rise from the earth, part of the life it sustained. And the chairs, also made of wrought metal, twisted with decorations on the backrest and armrests, contained a denser vitality, moving this way and that, and had someone fast-forwarded the film of everyday life, animation would have been visible, that might of movement. One day, these chairs would be gnawing on the grass.

So like an idiot, I agree, I regress to being a servant.

I said, Yeah, family.

She blew a long, smoky exhale. The lighting was meek, but the early darkness was imbued with clarity. The details were sketched in sharply, even the evaporating white plumes, and the angles of the profile, the down-curved nose, the soft fuzz gathering light on the skin, its negative beam, emerging from the core of her being. Like Ehud, she was firm. She rubbed her left arm gently, the burning ring at the edges of the rub. She said, How about you?

I said, Fine.

I stood beside her, stealing glances. With every look, the change occurred. She hardened back up.

I don't know what happened to me, she said. I don't usually have outbursts like this.

I nodded.

She said, Yes, yes, I know I was bragging just recently about what a success story Ehud was, with the Intelligence Corps and everything. But look at what he's become, a small-scale tyrant. He used to be such a charming boy.

I asked how long it had been since she'd seen him.

She said it had been close to six years. She'd spent four years working on her PhD and two more on her postdoc, which she'd done abroad. It was hard to assess somebody's personality during brief visits and family dinners.

I looked over the yard again. I made me gardens and orchards, I thought for some reason.

A smile flashed across her face. She said, Your joke really is funny. Now that he broke his legs he doesn't need to break the bank.

It was just a fluke, I said.

Don't sell yourself short, she said, people waste too much energy belittling themselves.

I'm sober.

And don't be in such a rush to act like an adult.

And do not separate yourself from the community, do not trust in yourself until the day of your death.

Are you planning on going to college after military service?

More or less.

Don't you want to travel first?

I hadn't thought of that.

Little tip, she said, if you do go, don't go to India or South America like the rest of the sheep, pretending to run away but actually traveling so they can get to meet themselves without the weight of this country and its trauma. Go so you can meet the new.

What's the new?

Each person and their own new. Not the new place, the new you. Go someplace where you can be new.

What did you study?

I was a research assistant in Eldad's lab, didn't you know that? That's how we met. I went back to complete my PhD after Eldad . . . after he was murdered.

The verb "murdered" sounded so ridiculous. It echoed through my mind until, against my will, I blew it back out. Murdered.

Therese went silent for a few moments. Anyway, she said, I . . . I did the same thing he did. I studied typhus.

When I was little I read somewhere that that disease no longer exists.

Not exactly. There's an effective vaccine, but the bacteria itself hasn't been wiped out. There are reserves and outbreaks. Anyway, a parasite that affects the nervous system opens channels for study and understanding of the dynamics between consciousness and reality. Those are soon gone, along with the parasite.

What does that mean?

That statement requires further investigation. It isn't . . . it isn't an immunologist's statement. Her voice trembled. She continued, It's the statement of a mystic with biological training. But it's the kind of thing Eldad somehow studied. Or at least the kind of thing I found in the notes he left behind.

She dropped the cigarette butt and stepped on it. She pulled a thin, gold metal case from her pocket. She slipped the business card into my shirt pocket and patted my chest. If you ever want some advice about college, don't hesitate to call me.

On my way home, I wondered if she was speaking from experience. If she'd traveled someplace where she'd managed to be new. If that was even a worthy aspiration. I'd be happy if the old didn't feel quite so old. I touched the card. Rough, lumpy, indifferent paper.

❧ ❧ ❧

AMIRAM SUGGESTED I GO ON LEAVE DURING PASSOVER. HE claimed that I was hanging out at the main warehouse, following him around. Wherever he turned, there I was, he said. He claimed I was leaving the new soldier—Hawk, I think he was called—unsupervised in remote warehouses, and that now that there was a chance his warehouses might finally be properly equipped and organized, I was spoiling it for him. And that he'd already told me that Hawk had problems. He'd already warned me. True, there was a story going around that this Hawk guy had disappeared from base for two days. He wouldn't come out of his room. His mother called Amiram, summoning him urgently to their home in Bat Yam. Costa gave me the full version. Nissimov had filled him in. Costa said, You should have seen, *blat*, how he smiled, that cretin, like it was a joke. Then he said, What's with the face?

I said, Nothing, never mind. That morning, Amiram and Hawk, was that his name, had whispered with each other for hours. I watched them from a distance with a contracting heart.

Amiram's claims were all lies, of course. He just wanted more time to frolic with his arms officer. What, were these my warehouses? So what if I could take more responsibility?

Amiram said, You're rude, you're ungrateful, I already told you not to utilize that tone with me. Utilize that tone, he said, how pathetic. Why don't you go on leave, he said, cool off.

The Star of David shined golden on his bare chest, which was turning golden itself. I thought about the camera lens freezing the glow bursting out of the same locket in the photo underneath the glass plate. I thought about the posture of his body in that photo, somewhere between recoil and defiance. At first he said, Listen, it'll be hard to keep kosher here during the holiday. As I said, totally pathetic. I had to dig and pester for half a day until he revealed his motives.

You're quiet, said Costa as we wandered toward the canteen.

I said, These aren't good days.

What, why?

I said, I don't get it, what kind of swimming career are you planning to have?

He said, I told you I won a silver medal at the youth championships before I enlisted. And the Haifa Cup. And I'm training for the summer Israeli Olympics. I told you.

Yes, but athletes retire young. You won't be twenty forever.

I'll train kids, *blat*. I'll always swim, I wouldn't be me without swimming. What are you worrying about me for?

I said, I think a lot about the future.

Mine or yours, *pizdiloh*? he said, slapping my shoulder limply again.

I told him I was going on leave during Passover. He nodded curtly. He said, Come to Tel Aviv some night.

MY HEAD WAS DIZZY WITH SONG AND SWEETENED GRAPE JUICE. Tova's chair stood empty at the Seder table. Chantal insisted we keep it there to disgrace us. Tova didn't come, even though she'd promised me. Anonymous culprits had jumped Johnny Balasko, breaking some of his ribs. He was in the hospital in Ashkelon.

My father said, There are too many chairs around the table.

Chantal said, There's still a chance Tova will make it. Tell him, Nahum, isn't there a chance?

I said, Let all who are hungry enter and eat.

Chantal chewed on her lip. The thoughtful expression was foreign to her paleness. So was the vigorous rebellion she posed against our father. I knew she was debating whether to ram into me as well or retain our cold alliance. She needed help. Msodi Farkash didn't take sides. She lost herself in cooking. Occasionally, she consulted with us on amounts. She wasn't used to such a meagerly attended Passover Seder. Why didn't you invite anyone this year? Chantal asked. What are you ashamed of, people asking about Tova, or people seeing her if she comes?

I looked at the covered Seder plate when Dad and I returned

from synagogue. I always feared the shank and egg hidden inside. I wanted to say, We haven't even eaten yet and already you've removed the table from us.

The previous week, Tova had agreed to meet me, in public, at the Gymboree. A few trees, an old *mikveh* building. The Gymboree was deserted. A distant hubbub of children rose, a giddy roar against the thick sky. We sat side by side on twin swings. Our legs were long enough to support themselves against the sandy ground. There was a stupor in our words, an indulgent hammocking. It was as if we were reciting lines from a school play. Tova said she thought I'd understand her and the reasons for her actions.

I said, What are you doing, threatening to marry a junkie?

Are you crazy? she said. He's just giving me a place to stay. I've never touched drugs and I don't plan to.

I said, You found some friend to help you stay away from drugs. A destined criminal.

Our parents are the real criminals.

What are you talking about?

She said, I'm talking about neglect. I'm talking about growing up without a family.

Is that really how you feel?

She said, I see I've made a mistake.

I said, Yes, you're making a mistake.

She said, No, I mean when I thought you'd understand me.

I said, What kind of chance have you given Mom and Dad?

She said, You should ask what chances they've missed.

I said, How come you're so bitter?

She said, How come you and Chantal aren't?

She waved. Up the path forking off the road, by the synagogue, some guy appeared. He seemed about to descend in our direction, then thought better of it and turned another way.

Who's that?

Just a guy, you don't know him. She spoke his name. I recognized the name. The other poet. The syllables sounded like bird-song in her mouth. Only the voice of birdsong, without the knowledge accumulated in it. I told her a friend claimed that guy was my doppelgänger.

I don't see any resemblance between the two yous, said Tova.

What did you say?

I don't see any resemblance between the two of you, none.

What do you have to do with him?

He comes by to smoke with Johnny sometimes. Not just him. And you're sure you don't?

Why should I lie, she said, everyone's convinced I'm a junkie, you think I care? Johnny, he's a gentle guy, he'd never hurt a fly, he's got lots of friends, and for good reason.

I said, Why don't you at least come for Passover?

She said, We'll see how I feel, we'll see.

THERE ARE FACTS WITH JAGGED EDGES IN MY MIND. I FEEL around and the thought flinches, the recollection of the cut is fresh, no matter how many years have gone by. Tova's empty chair at the Passover Seder, for instance. Chantal's paling skin, her loosening in her seat. Simo and Msodi Farkash focusing on tri-fles. Msodi preoccupied with the aftertastes she'd detected in her cooking, the vegetable soup she claimed was sour, the lungs that hadn't been sufficiently marinated, were still bitter. Simo Far-kash bugged me with questions about blessings and leanings. What does it mean if you drink while leaning to the left? he pressed me, flushed with wine.

Or the coin I found on the road when I was circling the town during the holiday that became my leave. Before I left base, Ami-ram told me warmly, Have fun and rest up. I'll call to check on you. But he didn't. I was afraid to go out lest I miss his call. I was afraid to stay home lest I drown in silence. A ten-agorot coin, golden against the asphalt. I told myself, If it's heads that would be a sign. But no fortune for Israel. Heads glimmered at me as I ducked to pick it up. I let the metal burn against my palm, the heat absorbing into my flesh along with a promise. The phone remained silent. At least as far as I was concerned.

Or on Second Passover, when I made plans to meet Niro at his place, and he raved about Tel Aviv and the wonders he discovered there daily, making me swear to come visit him sometime. And when I asked about Johnny Balasko, he answered with an excited nod and said his weed and hash were the best in the area, he couldn't even imagine who his supplier was. He invited me to come by for Mimouna that night. But on my way home, walking up the path not far from the small thicket, I passed through a field struck by spring with all its glory, filled with green thistles. I remembered how, not that many years earlier, Snot taught me how to kick off their heads, how to aim the toe of my shoe to the top of the stem. And how my limbs burst with liveliness all of a sudden, causing me to kick every which way. The shattered thistle skulls spread through the air, heads of purple fuzz. Until a different, cold spirit entered me and I said, Here I am, desecrating a holy day.

Or when Costa stared at me during one of our arguments and said, for no good reason, Why don't you listen, *blat*, I listen to all of your nonsense. And I realized how deeply insulted he was that I couldn't remember any of the details he'd recited about his swim meets and the prizes he'd won. And I thought, What do I want from him, or actually, do I want anything from him at all?

Or when Amiram exiled me to the faraway warehouses, sentencing me to work there in solitude for a week. And when I turned to look at him, a flicker of Iyar light rattled me. In his face, I saw, with a flash, Msodi Farkash's face, hardened into the features of a man, but that same clear dimness of eyes, the same delicate, contoured mouth.

Or on one of the nights afterward, two months after she stopped crying, when Chantal went back to her old ways. But this time I didn't wake up. In my dream I walked out of my room, in my dream I walked into my sisters' shared room, and in that blurry kingdom, where physical figures did not govern, I saw her, still a young woman, sitting at the head of Chantal's bed. Chantal couldn't remember her. She can't have retained her image in memory, and yet she was there, with her soft hair, her short stature, her delicacy, Sylvia Farkash, rubbing Chantal's forehead and offering words of comfort.

EVENTUALLY, I WENT TO VISIT NIRO. BUT ONLY IN THE SUMMER, on a Thursday afternoon. I'd sunk so deeply into the final shape of Amiram's distant warehouses when he suddenly softened and rewarded me with a Friday off, a long weekend. I could no longer look at him, I was so disgusted. He hadn't shaved during the days of Omer, and his beard, which was as thin as his chest hair, spoiled his handsomeness. Costa was gone on his discharge leave, or the regular leave he'd taken in sequence with his discharge leave.

He only came to base for the outing that took place after Shavuot. He sat next to me on the bus traveling south to some fancy swimming pool near Kiryat Gat. We barely spoke. We were clothed in the alert cloaks of parting.

Under my uniform I was wearing a white T-shirt with a cutoff collar decorated with embroidery. The back was embroidered too, with the words *We hear rumors about a different kind of sex.* Dalia gave it to me the last time we met, when she came over, guitar in hand, to tape "The Land of Shadow" on the tape recorder in my room. I hadn't seen her for two months. I used to wait for her on the edge of her neighborhood. Once I even mustered the courage to enter the outer thicket. But she wasn't there. Then one day, all of a sudden, she called to me from the gate of my home. After we made the tape, she handed me a package. A birthday gift, a goodbye gift. I opened it after she left. One of her smart-ass gestures.

But I felt the fabric like armor against my body. The embroidered words drew attention to me. Other soldiers asked me what they meant. They gathered in groups on the chlorine fragrant lawn, some carrying hunks of beef and a grill, others a cooler filled with Popsicles and soda bottles. I lay on my back under one of the sun umbrellas and read. A few soldiers from the arms storage came over, rolled me onto my stomach, and laughed.

I abandoned my book and went to the dressing room. Costa was there, dressed in sweats. He was stretching. I didn't want to take off my shirt around him. I sat down on the wooden bench. In the neon lights, he tuned his limbs, breathing in and out at a mesmerizing pace.

Then he removed his sweats with measured movements. He folded his shirt and pants carefully and stood at the mirror in his swimsuit. His skin was dark and smooth. Even his armpits were smooth. His entire dense body was heavy and massive with muscle. His calves were swollen. I looked up. My eyes met his eyes in the mirror. He bared his teeth with a grin. After he left, I turned my shirt inside out.

Many of the soldiers gathered around the rim of the pool. I walked over too. Costa glided effortlessly through the water. His front crawl formed an aura of spray as he crossed the pool, pushing himself off the wall, then returning to his starting point. He smiled happily at us as we stood around, watching his head resurface with the goggles and shiny cap, his body hovering and distorting with the movements of water beneath, like an ancient animal. Amiram said, He's a natural. He was born to do it. I never got to his level.

He was bare-chested too, his swimsuit shimmering, too tight. The others encouraged him to get in and show off his skills, competing against Costa. He dove in without warning, arms outstretched.

I returned to my recliner to read my book. A shadow hovered

over me. Smiling, Amiram said, Don't your eyes hurt? This isn't what you're supposed to do on these outings. I sat up. Amiram kneeled. He was soaked, eel-like. Tenderly, he said, You've worked hard these past few weeks, I'm lucky to have you, I wish I could give you better perks. Why don't you take Friday off, rest, have a long weekend. He crushed some weeds in his hand. My throat soured with all the conversations we could have had that had gotten cut short. I nodded.

I saw Costa in the parking lot. Anatoly came with his private car. I asked him if he could give me a ride to Sderot. He said, No problem. Costa was back in his uniform. I told him, You're an amazing swimmer.

He said, Why don't you come visit me in Tel Aviv soon? My parents are going to Moscow for two weeks. You can stay over.

I didn't know what I'd talk about with Anatoly. I feared he'd ask me questions I could only evade rather than answer. I was bound by his hospitality, chained by common courtesy. He just grunted occasionally. Only twenty, and already a gloomy, overgrown man. That was a level I would never reach, I thought. He was wearing his thick wedding ring, the gold hoop digging divots into the steering wheel's upholstery. I thought about how Amiram didn't even wear his, his fingers tan, devoid of a white mark. Not even the tracks of a ring. Everyone contained a lie that refused to align.

For no good reason, the car shook, pulled wildly sideways. Anatoly gripped the steering wheel hard. He fought against the tumult and slowed down, gliding onto the shoulder. When we pulled up he cursed. His forehead was damp. He said, Did you see my driving, huh, have you ever seen a driver like me? If that happened to you you'd have lost control.

I asked what happened. He said it was a flat tire, fuck that tire repair shop guy's mother. The guy had replaced his tire two weeks ago, and now his spare tire had a flat too. He had to wait for a tow truck. I proposed to wait with him, but he said there was no need and that I should head home. The bitterness of his tone remained in my ears.

THE AIR-CONDITIONING IN THE SERVICE TAXI HEADED FOR TEL Aviv was broken as well. Open your windows, the driver commanded us. I put on my earphones to silence the protesting cries of the other passengers. I listened to Dalia's tape. It took a few songs before it hit me: What if I ran into her on the street? I replaced her tape with the Vysotsky tape. My hands stopped shaking, the fear tore off and fell into the abyss forever. If only. I'd made plans to visit Costa the next day. When I'd called him on the phone, he'd let out a cry of astonishment, then stifled it.

I followed Niro's directions but must have taken a wrong turn. A busy street beat against my senses. I stood in the heat of the evening. The wheel of the sun ran over the western way, a flow of radiation rising from the sea. What are you looking for, young man? a white-haired man asked. I gave him the address. His hands were gathered behind his back. He rose on tiptoes and tapped his heels against the sidewalk. Then he pointed back at the direction I came from. I, meaning I, wonder at the trifles that pile up in my memory.

Niro was in a tizzy. A kind of swell of the soul, almost gushing. He talked and talked. He said if I wanted to make art I had to leave Sderot. You're living among blind and deaf people, he said.

I said, How about anosmics?

He said, What?

I said, People who lack a sense of smell.

He said, Yeah, but who uses their sense of smell to make art?

I said, I don't know, chefs, maybe.

He said, Funny you should mention food. I've been thinking about how art is like tahini.

I smiled.

He said, No, I'm serious. You know how the tahini you get at restaurants is made out of raw tahini?

I said I did, but asked what he meant.

So you know how at first you have this mush, smooth and oily, right? But it's too thick, you can't eat it. It's so smooth that it gets stuck in your throat.

So?

So that's what artists are like when they start out. They have unprocessed talent. And all you can see is their outburst. They seem ready, but when you take a closer look you realize there's no ripeness, it's only on the surface.

Like tahini?

Like *raw* tahini. Then you start diluting it with water or lemon juice, softening it, and then the tahini becomes lumpy, looking like it's disintegrating. That's the artists' learning phase, when they start adding outside ingredients. At first it looks like they're spoiling it, and they do, until they add enough.

Then the tahini is smooth again.

Forget smooth, it's a delicacy. And that's the third and final phase, when the skill you've learned becomes so absorbed it's a part of you.

If you're the tahini.

Yes, said Niro, if you're the tahini.

He was already drunk, I think. He had had a few glasses of arak. A pauper's drink, he said.

I said, Well, it's *mahya*. Life's water.

He giggled. I didn't drink. He took me out to some bar. One of the cool ones, he claimed. Before we left, he said I might want to ditch the yarmulke. I folded it into quarters and slipped it into my breast pocket. His studio apartment was on the roof of a derelict building with mold and damp stains out front, in a sooty neighborhood that Niro described as "amazing." I think it used to be a shantytown. I strode down the stairs without shivering. It took longer to cross the threshold out into the street. Niro pulled me out. I thought I'd soon be punished.

When we returned, he plopped onto his bed and fell asleep. I tossed and turned on the couch, my thoughts traveling to their random roots, to the whimsy of experience from which they emerged and to which they rushed to drain back. I woke up at dawn. Antennas and concrete covered the tarred roof. Different birds perched along electric wires, the tendons of the city. I wondered if this was a landscape for song. If the fowl would sing the glory and praise of the Lord for me. I'd left my *tallit* and *tefillin* in Sderot. I thought, The burden of Nahum the sinner, son of Simo the Farkashian. The same trembling laugh ambushed at the ends of my limbs.

COSTA WAITED FOR ME AT THE BUS STOP. I NEARLY MISSED IT. Every few stops I got up to remind the driver of the name of my stop. He said Ramat Aviv was far and he wouldn't remember. Costa wore shorts and a T-shirt. His stance was loose, limber. His muscles were galvanized.

He described his training plan at the university pool at length. He'd nearly broken his own records. He would be competing in freeform swimming.

His house was heavily furnished. Wooden furniture and rugs and soft couches upholstered with faux velvet. And wallpaper. Every bit of original construction had been carefully covered. No bare floor or wall tiles to be seen. Dim lighting blocked by curtains. He had to turn on the chandelier even at this late-morning hour.

He asked me about my weekend plans. I told him I had to catch the last bus that afternoon. He fell silent for a moment. He asked if I wanted something to drink. He'd made some lemonade.

Should we go to the beach? he asked.

The glass was cold in my hand. The mixture of sour and sweet on the roof of my mouth. I said, Why not?

There was a plate of cookies on the table. He was sitting across from me, on the armchair. He even listened intently to my dull updates about the torture Amiram was putting me through. His look, veiled with dreaminess, hung on me, followed my fingers as they sketched out my speech, weaving my words, bouncing up to my eyes, lingering on them. I fell silent. I asked, What, what?

Nothing, he said, then got up and leaned over me. I was sunken into the couch, my range of motion limited. His palm rested on the side of my neck and his lips rubbed against mine before I flinched and pushed him away. His breath smelled like mint.

He sat up. What, he said, where's the fire?

I said, What are you doing?

He said, Isn't that what—

What?

He swallowed. The blood drained out of his cheeks. The narrow crack that split the eyes lengthwise since childhood, disclosing inner light, widened. Just like that time he accused me of not listening to him. He said, Don't pretend, *blat*, don't play dumb with me, I saw the way you looked at me in the dressing room by the pool. I saw how you—

No, no, I said, you misunderstood what you saw.

I saw the way you looked at Amiram, at his picture in the warehouse.

What are you—

It's me, then, isn't it? he said. I repel you, right?

No, I said, no.

He said, When you looked at me in the dressing room, I saw it, I'm not stupid.

I don't know what you're talking about.

Maybe you're interested in something else, he said. He undid his pants and dropped his underwear down to his ankles with a quick, nervous gesture. The diamond pattern on his boxers was burned by the gesture. His hand took hold of his penis, his testicles. I marveled. They too, like the rest of his body, were shaved.

Without the tangle of pubic hair the skin was babyish, dark. But his dick was thick, a little hard, and his balls were big. I thought about the shape of my own penis, slightly curved when it was erect, pink and snail-like the rest of the time, about the shape of Amiram's groin in the picture, the testicles concealed by the thighs and the long, dangling dick.

I considered the multiplicity of male penis forms, their unprecedented variety. What greater baselessness could one possibly imagine for personal providence, so much labor devoted to a flesh remaining under wraps, which has no role beyond eliminations and procreation. I saw multitudes of angels shaping cocks and balls, each wiener with its unique, unusable image. The holy spirit which glows in the uselessly aesthetic, in fringes and embellishments. No dick is without its guardian seraph.

And I laughed, I laughed, I laughed. Not the bursting laugh, the animal baying of the moment, but a deep chuckle for which the sound and trembling are the smallest of its expressions, and which gathers echoes from the expanses of time, a sob of lamentation for the disaster I'd brought upon the thicket, the throat's coursing over Dalia Shushan's abandonment, her betrayal of her lovers, the whoosh of the sword passing over the lack of understanding, a chuckle about the sequence of life that others were caught up in, a childhood rolling into youth that transforms into maturity, and which for me was broken, a wailing for the man I would have become had I arranged events according to their appropriate order, and maturity, their logical consequence, would have been fulfilled by their power, a howl for the man I wasn't, a whimper for the possibility, the deception, the future, the pointless world traveling held before me, and my stop in Heidelberg, Therese and her plans, her research which would be revealed to me, and its outcomes, which veered beyond anything I could fathom, a bawl for Elish Ben Zaken, awaiting his emergence in a twist of self, a whine for his niece Tahel, who stands at the center of these incidents, blind to their whimsy, a snivel for her lurking outside my library office wearing a rebellious, disgruntled expression, still a nameless girl, and beside her, Yalon Asor, her companion from the train, the two of them arguing at a whisper.

OH, SAID THE GIRL. YOU'RE THE GUY FROM THE TRAIN. THE ECHO of her hand patting the door to my office vanished into space, blending into the words.

Yeah, obviously, said Yalon Asor, that's why we came to see him.

Yes, said the girl, but you don't have to say that out loud.

So what, said Yalon, you say everything, I can too.

Calm down, I said.

He's the one arguing all the time, said the girl, picking a fight all the time. She bit her lower lip.

Is Oshri not with you? I asked.

The girl's face sealed up. That same fury of hardening irises, the light gone out, leaving them looking metallic, prepared to retreat.

What?

He's sick, said Yalon. He's been tired ever since we got back from—

Don't say it, said the girl. Her voice was measured now, devoid of the heat that colored their whispering outside of my office and the bubbling of rebellion that had been so palpable on the train. I was surprised by her self-control. Her hair was tied in a loose ponytail, her features were quiet, an innocent demonstration of beauty, but one couldn't mistake the thin flame underneath her facial skin, a flame flowing through veins and capillaries. Yalon twisted his neck to return his hair to its place, covering half of his forehead. The ends of his hair touched his eyelids. In that motion, his masculine, crude, hasty charm was revealed to me again.

Tevet glimmered in the window facing the yard. No, I must remember it's January now, and the assaults of watery light, a break from the rains of gloomy January with its naked Persian

lilacs and their fortified trunks, a finer light would only visit
them again in April, or its reflections off the young greenness,
the life they returned to the light showering them, and the shadows not yet sketching in the summer sharpness. For some reason, I thought about the upcoming elections, the prime minister's
infected defeat predicted in the polls. But he would grab the armrests and growl. He would grind his teeth with his bluish-gray
hair. That scoundrel would continue to smear his shit over Israel. Continue to plaster over the poor with their self-hatred. I
asked, with all the indifference I could muster, what I could help
them with.

Yalon said, Tahel and I—

Tahel? I asked.

She nodded.

So we, said Yalon, wanted to ask you about . . . Is it true you're
organizing a protest?

Not a protest, I said, a rally.

Never mind, said Tahel, we read it on the *Southern Wind*'s
Facebook page.

I said nothing.

We wanted to know, said Tahel, if you knew Dalia Shushan.

The reporter also asked me about that at the interview. I told
her that beyond moving in the same circles and occasionally saying hello, I didn't really know Dalia Shushan. I said it was a matter of principle. I said Esther Shushan had a right to privacy, and
that commemorating her daughter in some documentary—the
sole purpose of which was to allow its creators to maintain a hold
of the right to manage cultural memory, local history—meant
stealing Esther's own private recollections. I said that memory
didn't have a fixed form, and that an arbitrary, capricious force
separated the wheat and the chaff in our recollections. Memories
had nothing to do with the importance reality ascribed to the
event that stamped them into consciousness, but with the emotional circumstances. A coin we pick up on a walk glows with all

the intensity of love granted to us at the time, or the love we ached for, and for a fraction of a second it seems we have not been turned away empty-handed, that the glow remains with us, in hiding. Why did Dalia write, why did she sing, if not to offer that glow?

The reporter quoted me verbatim, but typed up in the newspaper my statement appeared self-important and ridiculous. I could imagine my enemies snickering to themselves, That pompous left-wing ass, that fucker. But Simo and Msodi Farkash smiled at me at Shabbat dinner that week. It's easy to tell you're a poet, my mother said with rare generosity. Just like back then, when she collected and mailed my poems to the publisher. She never discussed their quality with me, only the fact that they could be published someplace, that my name could hover in that in-between space, with only the possibility of leaving a mark.

SIMO FARKASH TALKED TO THE OWNER OF THE LOCAL NEWSPAPER, who owed him a favor. Simo convinced him, Simo urged him to fan the flames. He might have said, It's a big story, would be a shame to miss it. The owner finally gave in. First a piece was published in the paper's society pages. *"A Librarian, Not a Sucker."* *Nahum Farkash, the library manager and successful poet, has waged a battle over the legacy of Dalia Shushan. A famous media outlet wishing to produce a film about the life of the late Shushan, the mythological local musician, assumed the people of Sderot would bow down and clear a path for them. Well, they were sorely mistaken.* This ambiguous phrasing was accompanied by a photo of me sitting at my desk, holding Dalia's band Blasé et Sans Lumière's CD *One Mile and Two Days Before Sunset* and smiling dumbly. The piece was placed between a report of an elegant bar mitzvah celebration for the son of a local hairdresser and news of the Sderot Choir's victory in a regional singing contest.

The next Sunday, the paper was bombarded with demands for further information. Who was the media organization, what was the nature of the proposed film, would the production benefit local merchants or offer temporary work for local residents, and why the hell was I objecting to it? These calls even reached the library. Shifra stared anxiously at the ringing phone on her desk. Her eyes assessed me, calculating which position to take. She knew little, only whispered shreds. A week after visiting Therese, I walked into the library and found Ohila Vaknin in the adult circulation room, her head supported by arms that rested on Shifra's desk, leaning in attentively. The childish scent of dust, of worlds clarifying through book covers, enveloped both of them.

But first I met Therese. I stood outside Electra Tower on Yigal Alon Street, walked through the glass door, passed security, a metal detector and hands rummaging through my backpack, and took the elevator to the tenth floor, where the Culture Flame offices were located. My sense of reality loosened with every floor I passed, as if vanishing with the efforts of the soul to cross the rising tangle of years and blurring memories, the tendon stretching of their return. Space is always an image, I thought, a byproduct of the activity of the spirit. The thought was foreign, forced from the outside. But I no longer panicked.

The receptionist smiled at me and gestured toward purple upholstered seats. She's in a meeting, he said. Can I get you anything to drink? I asked for some coffee, and as he prepared it in the kitchenette, I wandered over to her office. The spaciousness, the metal louvers, and the wooden furniture. Before we even met again, I recognized the profundity of change, this glamour that Therese did not hold in the past, the need for it, a beautification that wafted at me from every shining surface in the room. There were printouts, posters, and small copies of street ads on her desk. From them beamed the surprised faces of stars and starlets against the backdrop of a summer night sky, holding small, silver tablet computers that emitted a bluish glow, bathing their features, burning the words *Take Up and Read* on their foreheads with white fire. My heart sped, urged to action, but the blood wasn't sufficient to sustain my limbs. I stood paralyzed, pressed between a rapid pulse and the looseness of the flesh. What is this, I wondered, where did Therese or her employees learn this combination of words and what was it intended to promote? What was she selling, I wondered, what did she have to do with—

What are you doing here? the receptionist asked. Small and energetic, but his mannerisms were soft, attentive.

I swallowed and pointed at the printouts. I said, What's this, what is this in reference to?

He said pleasantly, Mr. Farkash, will you go wait in the lobby?

I didn't touch the coffee. The cup stood before me. It might have been boiling inside. It might not have been. I tried to bind together two thoughts that grated against each other. Therese Kavillio-Buganim wanted to promote a film about the life of Dalia Shushan. Therese Kavillio-Buganim was selling a product with a name that was torn out of a Dalia Shushan song written for me, belonging to me, about which only I knew.

The passage of years was visible in Therese's face. Not her skin, which, of course, was grooved in the spots where the years dug deeper—the base of the neck, the backs of the hands. But more in the depth of her being, an integumentary layering, a roughness of consciousness that transforms into movements and gestures, a clouding of the eye, a kinking of the hair, but not into her appearance, because her limbs were still limber, perhaps even more limber than before, her forehead and her cheeks were smooth and well-fed. Gone were the dark circles around her eyes. The sunken sockets were finally age appropriate. I wondered if this was an incarnation or the appearance of an incarnation, and how to differentiate between the two. Is becoming who we finally are a certainty promised at birth, or delivered in a wallop that distorts our nature, substance, and spirit? She walked past me, wearing stonewashed jeans and a T-shirt, intentionally shabby, striped, all beaming with quiet intensity, not disclosing the fact that we knew each other. A few moments later, the receptionist leaned in and signaled for me to follow him. When I entered her office a second time I was immune to the jolt of the space. I didn't see the printouts anywhere.

ARE YOU HUNGRY? THERESE ASKED ME AS I STUTTERED. IT'S lunchtime. She evaded my questions about the mockups I'd seen. She asked how I was doing, about my exploits, if I could describe them as such. I said curtly that this was not what I'd come for. I said I wanted to hear more about her interest in Dalia Shushan, and why she even had such an interest.

She said, You know, Nahum, for some reason I've always felt comfortable speaking to you. But that doesn't give you the right to take that tone with me.

I said she was right and that I was sorry.

She said, Still, it's surprising that the age difference between us isn't significant.

I said, It's reversed. You've become younger than I am.

She smiled. Rows of shiny teeth emerged, framed by lipstick of such a natural hue that it could have been merely another layer of skin cells. I thought, The wonders of wealth. I thought, Economy is a continuation of biology by different means. I smiled back.

But now, she said, there's nothing odd about this comfort, like . . .

I said, Like time caught up to our conversation.

Yes, she said, that's exactly what I mean.

And yet, I said, we never really knew each other.

She nodded. Smiled again. But the smile was empty. Like a fucking emoticon, supposedly a new way to dress up a long, convoluted statement, but really only marking the moment in which such a statement might be appropriate, its pronunciation already grating, its melody hollow.

No, not exactly, because the smile served as an anchoring

point in all her permutations, a thread that allowed me to pull the new image from my memory of it, or rehouse it in its old flesh lodgings.

And yet, she said, even when you were a boy I didn't feel like we needed any introductions.

I asked what this sense of intimacy was founded upon.

She shrugged. There was grace and sorrow in the gesture. It wasn't her own, but her body was already adept in its language. She said, Sometimes you recognize in another the powers of attention you demand of yourself. So I want to believe. Maybe that's what people mean when they say someone is on the same wavelength.

The same wavelength of being.

Yeah, she said, maybe.

I said, Why are we talking about this?

She said, You want to start at the beginning.

I said nothing.

She said, So, Nahum, what's going on, tell me a little about yourself. Did you ever go to college, did you travel the world, did you lose something, did you find something, or what?

What about you? I asked.

She laid out a chain of facts I already knew from her interview in the paper, in a measured manner, with a nasal tone that disclosed her awareness of the fact that she was reciting, and that the act of recitation amused her. She'd started a small biotechnology company with Yoel Buganim, a young entrepreneur who would end up becoming her husband. The labs were in Poland. In the late nineties they discovered a breakthrough treatment for *Helicobacter pylori* in the digestive system. It's a type of bacteria that causes stomach ulcers, she said, and certain types of cancer. Their company was bought out by a large pharmaceutical corporation, which buried the treatment project. The antibiotic treatment remained the most common choice, and when the helicobacter population did not die out, the corporation chose to supplement treatment with antacids. She asked if I knew what the bacteria looked like.

Like a pea pod with tails, I said.

A green, lumpy cylinder with flagella, she said, but your description isn't bad. She wanted to know when I'd had the chance to witness this wonder of nature.

I asked what the treatment was. She said, Metabolizing the enzyme urease, which allows the bacteria to create a comfortable habitat. It turns urea into . . . She paused.

I said it was fine, I knew the lingo.

She was surprised to hear I'd enrolled in life sciences studies after my discharge, and was even more surprised I'd chosen to do so at Ben-Gurion University. I said I'd left after the first year. I said I'd gone to Europe. I said at some point I'd become filled with revulsion. I thought about that morning when I realized, when it became clear, that there was no more conflict between my wish to die and the fact that I was able to find pleasure and satisfaction at any given moment. On the contrary, my yearning for death was completely detached from any suicidal ideation, and even this avenue, the imagination of the moment of death, its conditions, its circumstances, how it would be achieved, was blocked for me. I realized in a flash that Therese was guiding me away from my questions about the printouts. I began to stutter.

We went downstairs to a small vegan restaurant where she liked to eat lunch. She came to the Culture Flame offices once a week. On the elevator she told me, They have terrific food, a marvelous chef.

I said, Are you one of those new abstainers willing to torture themselves to polish their scruples for living in a society of plenty? Wouldn't it be simpler to donate some of your income to improve the living conditions of the poor, rather than spend a fortune on lavishly spiced straw?

She laughed. I remembered that glassy laughter. Now it

pushed off the metal walls. The sound persisted in my ears. There we were, shoved out into the kingdom of November. There were the lonely trees on the street with their pounding foliage. There was the gold of the afternoon that illuminated even the wretched. There was the chilled, reviving kiss of the heavens. There was the coursing river of traffic on the Ayalon Highway. Even the dull irony that smacked against me only after I'd received my food couldn't darken this burst of liberty that washed over me inexplicably. Lentil stew.

THE TALE OF THAT TRIP IS RESERVED BEHIND A PARTIALLY CLEAR screen. I could list the facts involved, the cities I visited, the transportation, the guesthouses, the sprawled bodies, their odor, their outline, the power of sex to whittle in time, in space, seeds of moments. In Paris I was crowded into a room of ten iron bunk beds. I spent half the night listening to breathing and snoring, to the denseness of flesh. In Rome, after two nights in the attic of a family-owned inn, my skin became irritated, covered with a rash. In my fingertips I can still feel the rough sheets, the obstinate blanket. On a packed train to the Alps, with ravines opening up on both sides of the tracks, snowy cliffs rising, I squatted on my backpack in the corner. They are all with me, details torn from experience, tacks holding them against the corkboard of consciousness. But I want the other memory, the one pulsating uncontrollably, slicing through the present and intermingling into it like the remains of a dream flashing in the middle of the day.

I passed through places that did not leave their mark on me, where I didn't even leave tracks. There was more contained even in a panicked escape. I wasn't panicked. The interior froze. I was witness to a life that was not my own, though it happened to me. In Germany, the temporary rooms I stayed in were overheated. I awoke in them breathless and sweaty, recognizing the scheme to remove me from this world, metal bookcases with loosening wall anchors, heavily framed pictures hanging insecurely over the bed. I wanted to die. I didn't want to. A heartless force pushed me onward, onward.

At the grocery store in Heidelberg, near the produce fridge. A woman wearing a headscarf bent down to feel the goods. Not far from her was a dark, plump, bald young man. He grabbed the handle of his shopping basket hard, following her. I assumed he was her husband, but when she stood up and shot the man an imploring, approval-seeking look, I realized she was older, gaunt, a face chiseled by time, a skin containing experience in cracks and wrinkles, tan like her son's—that's what I assumed, that they were mother and son. The man nodded and a glow washed over her face, her features deepening. The son smiled at her, an awkward twitch, his shoulders dropping, as if he finally sensed the weight of the basket. I lingered over them, watching from afar as the woman sorted, testing a weight in her palm, bringing it to her nose. I guessed the scents of childhood, of homeland, embodied the fruit of the earth, as foreign as they might be, carrying memories of home. Love is given in these measurements, which are the language in which the soul learned to speak before the other organs caught up.

A few days later, as I returned from my wandering to a guesthouse in the Old City in which I was offered a room in exchange for washing dishes and cleaning the kitchen, the road twisted needlessly. I crossed the old bridge over the Neckar with its quiet waters, that liquid languidness, perforated with movement by elongated boats. I looked up at the statue of Carl over the gate, which shared that fever of stony haughtiness common to the statues of famous people, a fever that washed all over the sunny day, even the clouds of summer boiling in its gold. I thought about how I'd yet to visit the castle and fort. Dust collected in my windpipe, growths of dirt on the walls of my lungs, and the nature of European castles is to appear closer than they are. The more you strive to reach them, the farther off they draw, swallowed into the sheets of sky that serve as their background. I knew it, I could sense it. But I tried. I wandered through some streets, but those medieval cobblestones aggravate the modern foot, accustomed to padding and soles.

But the miracle occurred, *kefitzat haderech* happened somehow. This is something literature does not often grasp, how suddenly the space wrinkles, shoved into a membrane punctured up by consciousness. We are born into our desired realms, we do not reach them. At any rate, I was already standing there, in the gardens of the castle. The stairwells translated into tendon sketches, the barriers of stones containing starlight and lunar terror became an effort of limbs. The trees grew tall as trees do on such a fabulous sunny day. I moved from one shaded spot to the next, one story after another in the rings of fortification.

From the quad underneath the turret, the chiseled coil where embrasures evaded the glow of the hour, I saw the thatched-roof houses, neighborhoods bisected by the river, spread over mountainous banks, the bricks basking in their oldness, the culture poured over by nature, bubbling to it and thriving from it, and all that burning vegetation, all the vegetation inflamed with life. Where were the scars of abomination in the unbombed city, its thread of history never broken? Within this plenty, my heart grumbled, a repulsive, despicable sound of a turning stomach, a starved stomach, that's how I experienced that disgusting, oh-so-human muscle, beating its pulse, improvising that humming that emerged for some reason at the grocery store. The visions blurred on me. I cried, first with surprise at the fact that my ability to cry hadn't vanished along with the rest of my emotional capacity, then for the purpose of crying alone, the real, great crying hidden in the distance between the object of crying and the formless sorrow that was its reason.

❖ ❖ ❖

THERESE REFUSED MY OFFER TO HELP NOYA RESNICK AND OHILA Vaknin as much as possible with the film's production. Research, contacting townspeople who could enrich the portrait of Dalia they were hoping to create, in exchange for Therese and Culture Flame agreeing to sponsor the series of talks by writers and poets I was planning for the library. She said, Are you kidding? Noya's an experienced director and Ohila's a fantastic researcher, they don't need you.

I said I'd made the offer as a favor, that the two didn't need to be linked, and that really I was asking her to fund my talk series.

Why is it so important to you? she said.

I told her about Mayor Asraf, about the budget restructuring he'd dictated, allowing him direct control of every project, or at least requiring that every project be approved by his office.

They know how to work, she said, this generation of settlers. They know all the management methods and don't have the same remorse that you do.

That who does? I asked.

You, she said, left-wingers with your philosophy of multiculturalism and respect for others. It's killing you.

You don't know anything about me, I said, and already you're rushing to generalizations.

She nodded slowly. Her profile was washed by the November light, which intensified in the café windows, breaking up the artificial dimness. Still, the hints of age, its bird talons, with all the miracles of technology reserved for the wealthy. Her Thai curry with quinoa was bitten around the edges, orange vegetables and chickpeas dipped in a soft brilliance over the gray heap. Some kind of floral aroma wafted off the stew, like the toasted scent of chrysanthemums before sunset during the months of Adar and Nissan.

Anyway, she said, they're using it against you, and they don't have a hint of cynicism. They just don't have any doubts or second thoughts.

I said I didn't know any people who didn't have doubts or

second thoughts, only ones more skilled at repressing them. The trick was to unburden the individual of them and delegate the work of repression to the social construct.

Her eyes lingered over me. Did something happen to you? she said.

I said, With regards to what?

To the person you thought you'd be.

Then I felt it, the faint feelers of a neighboring being, the shadow of one of the attacks I'd experienced as a child, when an exterior consciousness recruited its power against me, to invade me and disown me of my grip on my body, on my self.

I asked Therese, Are you going to help me or not?

I still don't understand why this is important to you.

I said, And I don't understand why it's important to you that I participate in the film about Dalia Shushan if you have so much faith in those friends of yours.

They aren't my friends.

Your servants.

Okay, you're exaggerating.

What do you have to do with Dalia Shushan, how come you—

I owe a debt to Sderot.

You owe no debt.

Who are you to—

Is everything all right, Ms. Kavillio? a server asked, his voice lilting, as if the question was set to a certain piece of music he'd composed.

Yes, thank you, I'm just not as hungry as I'd thought.

I can bring you something else if the food isn't to your liking.

No, no, tell Elena the curry is wonderful. Smoothly, she added that the quinoa's nuttiness, coupled with the tanginess of the hummus and the sweetness of the pumpkin and coconut milk, was a brilliant orchestration of flavors.

I let out a shard of laughter. The server removed himself fluidly.

I said, Dalia Shushan, what's your interest in her?

How did you deduce I had an interest in her?

The film you're promoting?

It's part of a bigger project. Culture is a business too, in case you haven't noticed. I support projects that have a very big chance of returning the investment. There's great public interest in cultural heroes these days.

Heroes. I chuckled. Figures whose work is turned into advertising material by the culture. Their work isn't necessary, nor is the conflict and dispute and exhaustion and passion and hell and lonesomeness they know, but only the fact that they signify some possibility of a crevasse in the soul, an uncompromising truth. Only the fact that they allow wheeler-dealers to picture themselves as suffering artists simply by learning about them.

Hasn't that always been the case?

No.

You're naïve, she said. At least you've kept your innocence.

So, Dalia Shushan, I said.

What about her?

Why did you agree to meet me? For this small talk? A busy woman like yourself?

I have an interest in Dalia Shushan's work, she said. When I searched for clues as to what happened to Eldad in Lublin and then in Lvov, in Ukraine, at the labs that, for some reason, are still conducting typhus research . . . at some point I gave up any preconception I might have had, any framework of thought, maybe because I finally understood some of Ludwik Fleck . . . She paused and looked me over. Have you heard of him? she asked.

I shook my head.

She said, He's one of two researchers who developed the first typhus vaccine, in Buchenwald, at the camp. Eldad showed great interest in his work. Did you know he spent the final years of his life in Israel? He had a lab at the Weizmann Institute. But it wasn't his research that Eldad was excited about. The man wrote a masterful monograph, *Genesis and Development of Scientific Fact*.

She drummed her fingers against the table. She said, When I was still just his research assistant, Eldad told me it was a book every scientist should read. Fleck says our conceptual worldview affects the nature of the facts we uncover. No, not uncover. Create. The facts we create are a derivative of our world of metaphors. You understand?

Not really, I said.

Anyway, you ought to take a look at that book.

I said nothing.

She went on. Take, for instance, thinking about the relationship between infections and the immune system. Fleck claimed that, in his day, the metaphor of war was so dominant that even science couldn't escape it. He said that's why researchers of the previous century perceived the body as a battleground between the good guys—the immune system—and the bad guys—disease. And that makes them formulate certain assertions and determine them as axioms. He believed a day would come when the metaphor would change, because our experience of the world would be different.

I said, Of course, being determines consciousness.

She said, I mean this plainly, not as a slogan. Today we think about the body differently. Now, all of a sudden, scientists perceive it as an enormous colony of microorganisms that communicates as a collective. A microbiome. Consider the discovery of bacteria populations in the digestive system.

I said, In that case, the war metaphor will be back soon. It's going to make a comeback.

In Ukraine, of all places, she said, when I was already desperate, I sat down in a little café, and a young woman sat down next to me. She was stunned, her face fixed on the door, as if she were waiting for someone. She riveted me. I recognized in her my own sense of loss. Her heart had also been ripped out by some monstrous event. She was wearing headphones and the sounds of the music she was playing leaked out. I touched her shoulder and she jumped out of her seat. I pointed at her headphones. When she took them off, I asked in English what she was listening to.

She said, You wouldn't know it, it's from Israel, with that disgusting sabra accent, like she had a hammer in her mouth and she was grinding gravel. That accent has the rhythm of an army marching over occupied territories. I asked her in Hebrew to tell me the name of the musician. She had a crooked smile, I remember, and her black lipstick stained her teeth. She said the band name wasn't in Hebrew, but the singer, she said, sings from inside my soul.

I said, Dalia Shushan.

Therese said, Yes. The girl, I think her name was Liat or some name like that, something that started with "Li," she let me listen to a few songs. She was right, that Liat. The singer was singing my pain. When I got back to Israel she was all I could listen to for a while. The two Blasé albums and the demo that came out a few years later.

I asked if she'd had a chance to listen to the album of instrumental arrangements that Rami Amzaleg had put out the previous year. She said that was the album her iPhone automatically started playing whenever she got into the car. Then she said we'd talked long enough.

I said I'd come for nothing.

Why do you say that? she asked.

I asked if she remembered the papercutting at the Barda sukkah.

She asked why.

I said, Because if you remember, you must understand my reason for insisting on this lecture series. I said, Therese, I was going to offer you a deal, but instead I'm offering you an alliance.

She shook her head. Neither of us is the person we used to be, she said.

I COULDN'T GET SHIFRA TO TELL ME WHAT OHILA WANTED. SHE said Ohila was just interested in hearing some gossip about me, what I was like as a child. I told her, Shifra said, that you and Dalia used to come here a lot, and that you also came with that friend of yours, what was his name, that fat Kurdish boy.

Her stretched lips sliced her face in half. The flicker in her eyes revealed her pleasure. She came with a measure of judgment today, then.

Michael, I said, his name is Michael.

Who cares? she said. Repulsive child. I was always afraid he'd smear his snot all over the books.

I restrained my laughter. Had she searched the dictionary in the reference room for the definition of "snot," she would have had an unpleasant surprise. Snot had smeared the words under that term with a handsome pull from his nose. He detested the sweetness with which Shifra offered him a tissue whenever she saw us. I told him, May God do so to her, and more also. And Snot said amen, his finger landing on the cluster of letters and paper.

Don't talk to her or to anyone else from the production about the Shushans, is that clear?

Her face froze, the amusement gone. I'd never spoken to her so boldly before. You can't tell me what to do, she said.

With the same severity, I said, Shifra, I'm asking you.

She lowered her head to the book open in front of her. I spoke her name, but she ignored me.

Ohila waited for me outside of my office, her denim skirt kissing her ankles. She was lost in her cell phone, its bell-like bleatings expanding into a ruckus in the silent space of early afternoon.

This is a library, I told her, not a bus stop. I pointed at the sign forbidding cell phone use. Put it on silent.

Whoa, she said, I haven't seen this side of you before. You're a legit librarian.

What are you doing here? I asked. When I spoke to Therese two days ago I got the impression that the film wasn't happening.

A glimmer of mischief flickered across her face. She said, That's not what Noya understood from Therese . . . She got the impression that you were expendable.

Therese?

Noya.

I said nothing.

She said, But now I'm not so sure.

I noticed how skinny she was underneath her layers, the burden of grace she tried to shoulder. Almost skeletal, like a survivor, her thick black hair drawn back, accentuating the fragility of her bones, her eyes like gaping, smoldering discs.

I shrugged. I said, Try to do as you see fit. It would be hard to film here without the residents' cooperation.

You lied to me, she said. You said you didn't really know Dalia Shushan.

I said our acquaintance was superficial.

She, said Ohila, pointing at the adult circulation room, re-members things differently.

I said, Why are we standing in the doorway? Come in.

She leaned back in the chair, refused my offer of coffee or tea, even after I insisted that we kept a kosher kitchen. She pulled out a bottle. Chunks of aloe vera dotted the illusion of clarity of the water inside. She mumbled a blessing and sipped. She placed her arm on the desk, next to the bottle, revealing her wrist. The pale skin was circled by a delicate gold bracelet. I recognized the pat-tern engraved in it, groove by groove, the inner webbings of a leaf and flower. Msodi had inherited five such bracelets from her mother. She wore the three she kept at her disposal on holidays and special occasions. Tova and Chantal each received one for their bat mitzvahs. Tova sold hers a few years ago, after keeping it even through challenging times, when she was a hard-up social work student. Perhaps selling it was the first crack in the rift between her and Chantal, the seed of the animosity that had only grown since.

I lingered on the bracelet for one moment too long. Ohila quickly covered up the fragile bit of skin. How old could she have been, twenty-two or so? I wondered to myself, Wasn't she supposed to be married off to some combat unit graduate by now, someone headed for war with *tefillin* and weapon? But there was a hunger in her, beyond her boniness and waifishness, that wouldn't allow her to remain where she'd come of age. Her whole presence seemed to bite the air. I saw what was gnawing at her, I saw how she was crowned by that hunger. I never notice beauty in women her age. They have parted with the latent innocence of youth, but their limbs have not yet acquired the flexibility of awareness. With the exception of Dalia Shushan. But the beauty of phantoms is different; it is the beauty of a leaking foreignness and the refusal to forget, not the chagrin of a body exiled into time.

Ohila said, We couldn't find any real childhood friends of Dalia's. We didn't imagine she was that lonely.

I said, I don't think she was.

She said, That's what I'm realizing now. Everyone who knew her back then guards her like a secret. There's one guy, Nir Vazana, who I hear—

He's in America.

Yeah, and he won't give an interview anyway. And there's her cousin Ronnit Dgani. So funny, she's married to a guy who went to the same yeshiva as my mother's brother-in-law. My mother's brother-in-law started a *kolel* for newly religious Jews. But she won't talk either.

So you're stuck with me, I said.

And there's Esther Shushan, said Ohila. There's Dalia's mother.

SHE ASKED ABOUT RARE RECORDINGS OF DALIA'S WORK. SHE said that would be an epic win. An epic win, seriously, there had to be some recordings from pre-Blasé days, she didn't only start writing songs with Rami Amzaleg. And if anyone who was close with her was avoiding being in the film, that must mean they've got something to hide, some memento.

I told her that her imagination was getting the better of her, and that mementos from a beloved person were private property, their own inner belongings.

She laughed at the sound of that expression. So young and so sharp. She said, That's nonsense. The function of that concealment is to increase the value of the objects.

I said, You're talking about use value. Don't mistake that for exchange value.

She said, What difference does it make? Ultimately, value is determined by price.

I said, By sorrow. You haven't even learned the first lesson yet. I thought damages was the first lesson, even at a religious girls' school.

Her expression clouded over, a narrowing of the eyes, a pressing against the back of her chair. She sipped her water again.

I told her I was surprised that she, a religious woman, didn't assume in advance a boundary between the territory of the individual and the territory of the public.

She said, You've got lots of biases.

I said, What kind of war are you trying to wage through this Dalia film, and against who—yourself, your family?

She said, Culture doesn't belong to you.

I said, Who's you?

She said, All you left-wingers.

I said, Did you know that Dalia insisted on being exempt from military service for moral reasons? It was important to her that people acknowledge her conscientious objection.

She said, People are complicated. It isn't her songs, it isn't—

I said, Don't look at her teachings, look at her actions.

She said, So what are you trying to prove to me, that you know Judaism?

I said, I thought culture doesn't belong to one specific camp.

She said, Culture, not religion.

I said, I heard the way you talk about Dalia. You talk like a follower, not a fan.

Ha ha, said Ohila, taking a gulp of water, filling her throat with more than she could swallow. The water spilled out of her mouth with a gurgling sound, drops jumping into my coffee, small streams wetting the paper on my desk, crawling over to a book I quickly snatched up, though its cover was protected by the usual library plastic. Ohila stood up, pulled a pack of tissues from her bag, and started blotting.

It's fine, I said, these are just drafts.

She picked one up and read. Gradually, weapons would become smaller. A book of poetry contains enough ammunition for an entire war. Is that yours, she asked, it's nice.

I took it from her, gathered the damp pages, balled them up, and tossed them into the trash can.

But your poems, she said, isn't that a shame.

I said, That which doesn't haunt consciousness, doesn't glom onto thought, perhaps isn't worthy of keeping.

She continued blotting. She said, I'm sorry, I'm sorry.

I said it was no problem. She fidgeted restlessly, shifting her weight from one foot to the other. The movement of her legs behind the denim screen, a gust of wind waving through a finer fabric. Where's the bathroom? she said, startled.

By the time she returned, the desk was dry. I'd wiped it down with a dishcloth. She wrung her hands, took a deep breath, and

SHIMON
ADAF

sat down. A careful sitting, arms against the armrest, torso lean-ing toward me, balancing on the edge of the seat. She said, So, do you have one? A memento from Dalia?

I shook my head. I said, I find it odd that so many of her fans have popped up, people cherishing her memory.

It's a sign of the times, she said.

I asked, What, Dalia Shushan's depression?

She said, No, you know, the way everything's become bar-baric. And superficial.

I said, It's interesting how those who sold their soul for lucre all of a sudden want intellectual validation, are suddenly search-ing for lightbearers to show them through the darkness they brought on all by themselves.

Do you mean Therese?

No, I said. Noya Resnick.

She said, Noya is all good. Totally good.

Who ever said self-love was bad?

She said, You're disingenuous. Dalia Shushan's songs touch different people in different ways, people from all walks of life. Take Therese, for example.

I said, Therese is the oddest variable in this equation. I don't understand her motives.

She's promoting this project to encourage youths to read. It's all inspired by Dalia, in case that wasn't already obvious. What difference do her motives make? She wants to help.

What are you talking about?

She said, I thought you'd discussed this. The project is taking place in public libraries. She wants to launch it here, in Sderot.

How are you connected to it?

I'm the production assistant for Take Up and Read. She hummed to herself. I recognized the tune, the hidden lyrics. What meanest thou, oh sleeper, arise, call upon thy God. But it wasn't the correct, concealed melody of the expression that rolled against her tongue, Take up and read, arise and call. She was intentionally teasing me. She and the one who sent her. She said, Therese told me you used to be religious. So you must recognize . . .

There was no room for her voice within the racket in my head. I said, So, so what?

Tova
10:02 Hi Nahumi, what's up.

I stared at the message on my iPhone screen. It had been cracked ever since the war in Gaza. I told myself I wouldn't repair it until it went dark. When I wrote that in our group chat, Sub-Heroes, Ma'ayan replied, That's a great image for Israel.

                                          10:04 Tova???

Tova
10:04 Yes, Nahumi, Tova, your sister. Remember?

We hadn't been in touch in almost four years. She started it. During the 2011 social justice protests, I was electrified. I went to Tel Aviv, to the tent city on Rothschild Boulevard. I could hear the messiah's approach on my way there. Even in Sderot I could sense him skipping over rooftops, hopping down the street, sounding a massive march. The air was different, the shaking and ember of change. But I left the day I came. I heard the poets born by distress, their murky laments, their juvenile slogans, nothing but an unexamined desire to be washed over by a great vision, to have their experience molded by an awesome fire, their selves welded into a cohesive identity. More victims of the furnaces of ideology. As just as that ideology may be, it was proof of the fact that the only right humans ever fought for was the right to choose their own oppressors.

                                   10:07 Of course. Is anything
                                   wrong?

Tova
10:08 Nothing, so far. Are you good?

                                   10:09 I'm all right.

I read my poems there. Two young women joined me with their guitars in a smiling semi-self-awareness, wearing plastic flower crowns. One of them was wearing a shirt with the print *Wired Is the Lord* arced across her braless breasts. Her strumming was confident, a major key. My throat didn't tremble. I read one of my poems about being repulsed by lyrical poetry that seeks the expression of a faint state of mind, that's laden with fashionable religious references, and about the need for a call to action, to step out into the streets, to viciously shatter the idolatry of national security discourse.

Even as I read, I felt the energy draining from my body and the space around me. Not that there wasn't attention, not that there wasn't alertness, not that there wasn't responsiveness, but that the form in which they were offered was too polished, premade. The wound, the burn, if they even existed, were covered up with patches of imagery. And not that I could formulate this back then. There was merely an alarm beeping in the back of my conscious mind, and in spite of the tumult I inhaled and inside of which I tried to smother myself, it wouldn't stop going off.

I spoke to the protest leaders. The fire was in their eyes, the lightning of action apparent in their irises. They spoke about an apolitical protest intended to unite the people. I said, Justice doesn't care about sectarian or nationalistic definitions. Justice for all or justice for no one.

They said that would only hurt the goals they wanted to promote—a fairer distribution of wealth and resources, a future for people in their twenties, who watched as jobs and homeownership and dignified living conditions grew farther out of reach faster than the years went by.

I said they wanted to treat the symptom rather than remove the cause of illness.

I returned to Sderot and talked to some friends and acquaintances. We put up our own tents, invited representatives of every ethnicity—Moroccans, Iraqis, Kurds, Caucasians, Bukharans,

Ethiopians, Palestinian collaborators who'd been housed in town. We formed protest shifts that marched from the public library quad to city hall, besieging it. I knew some of the police officers who beat us. I spoke to the media. Chantal called to chastise me for shaming Dad, giving him a bad name, ruining his relationships with his friends, former mayors, and current city hall officials, forcing him to confront his loyal friend Yoram Bitton.

Tova

10:12 I need a favor.

10:12 What else?

I told Chantal that I never asked Simo to defend me. I told her she and her children were welcome to visit our tents. It would be an educational experience. She hung up.

Tova came all the way from Acre in her cotton dress, with her skinny body and her face glowing with devotion. She came with her partner, Adam, a social worker just like her, and their adopted children, Comet and Tanita. Their adoption was the reason for her rift with Chantal. Chantal was furious when she'd heard about the decision. For a moment, I saw the tent city we'd erected through their eyes, a space of twists and strange discoveries. They ran around, laughing. Adam chased Tanita with a tissue, trying to wipe the spittle off her chin. Comet waved his hands excitedly in front of a little girl, squealing in a high-pitched voice that sliced through the racket. The girl just stared at him. Adam put his hand on Comet's shoulder and gently pulled him away. Tova and I stood outside the central tent. She looked all around.

Impressive, she said. At least it isn't fake like the one in Tel Aviv.

God forbid, I said.

But there's fakery here too.

I didn't answer.

In a few days, she said, people will go back to their homes with a bitter taste in their mouths. They'll wake up that way the next day. Their lives won't change. What are you trying to achieve with this protest?

I said, A change of consciousness.

She said, Consciousness change is the idle chatter of those with means, those who already know how to talk, who have eyes in their heads. What can you do with the mute, deaf, and blind of the world?

I said nothing again.

Tova

10:17 I know it's a lot to ask. I need to speak to you and Chantal. Face to face.

Tova

10:21 Chantal will listen to you. Don't be a drag, I need you to mediate

In the tent city she said, When have you ever considered giving up your apartment and handing out your money to the less fortunate? When have you ever taken in someone who truly needed help?

I said, There's the rub.

Tova opened her arms. Summer skies have an inner glow even at night. In this light, I saw Adam holding his children's hands as they pulled him in two opposite directions.

You talk about change, said Tova. But, Nahumi, your specialty is sitting on the fence.

I SAW FEMININITY LIGHT UP WITHIN TOVA. SHE DIDN'T OFTEN bring Adam to Shabbat dinner. Perhaps that was the source of the murky stream, the stream of animosity, that divided her and Chantal. I listened to it bubble and gain strength. Tova told us about their plan to adopt Comet. She only told me and Chantal. The three of us were gathered at a Tel Aviv café. On the way, Chantal said, I can't believe she's making us come all the way to that Ashkenazi town. Both of us live in Sderot, don't we? If she wants to talk to us, she can come down and see us. She drove with aggravating slowness in the left lane. Cars used their high beams to urge her along. In the taut afternoon spring light, they twinkled like pins. They honked at her and overtook her from the right, and some even waved or slowed down to align their cars with hers, their lips moving, shaping some curse, I imagined, some rote swear words. Chantal gripped the steering wheel and leaned over it as if she had to harness the full weight of her body just to make the tiny car move. I pointed out drily that Tova lived in Acre and that none of us ever bothered to visit her there. Tel Aviv was the halfway point.

Sometimes, Chantal said, I feel like slapping her out of her daze.

There was no daze in Tova. On the contrary, there was a tender vitality. She'd shed her old weight, and her high, angular cheekbones granted her a typical Moroccan nobility. But her eyes, which radiated darkness, granted her an air of peaceful elation, or an elation brought on by peace. She's a real woman, I thought. Where did that sudden beauty come from, the beauty of life and experience that had nothing to do with our mother's good looks, or with Chantal's haunted, lazy, dumb-luck beauty, the beauty of convoluted nature and hereditary errors? Thus sat the dark sister and the pale sister across from each other, with me in the middle.

Looking around her, Chantal said, Ugh, what a gross city.

I also hate Dizengoff Street. We drove in circles for twenty minutes in the Center's underground parking lot, waiting for someone to leave. When someone did, the driver went the opposite way, blocking us. By the time Chantal backed up to let the other driver pass, another car had grabbed the parking space. When I stepped out of the car to instruct Chantal in her reverse maneuvers, I signaled to them that it was our spot. The man, a young brute, nodded his understanding, but then glided into the space anyway. Chantal pulled up next to him as he got out of the car, on the verge of trembling, rolled down her window, and called out to him. He ignored her. His partner, tall like him, blonde, got out from the passenger-side door, hung her weight against his shoulder, looked at us from the corner of her eye, and giggled.

Tova said, Just look at the energy in this place. Think about how every person walking around here is an entire universe of desire and fear.

She smiled at the server and whispered a thank-you when a pot of boiling water and a cup were placed before her. She mixed her own infusion into the pot. I smelled white Micromeria, rosemary, mint, sage. She offered us some. From within the bitter velvet of sage and the hot fiery tongue of rosemary jumped careful explosions of micromeria, the freshness of mint.

Chantal rejected her offer with contempt. She sipped her milky coffee and said, It's a shame they don't have store-bought instant coffee. Why are they so pretentious?

I told Tova her interpretation was wrong. This was a city of blood, full of lies. Thus it was erected, and thus it shall fall.

You're exaggerating, said Tova. Both of you came here in a bad mood, it looks like.

Chantal laughed. She said, Why were you in such a rush to meet us on a weekday? Couldn't you wait until Friday?

Tova said, I wanted you to meet Comet.

Shu hada, said Chantal. What's that?

My son.

What?

Adam and I adopted a child.

Chantal and I were still for several moments.

A child, said Chantal, you said you and Adam didn't want to—

No, said Tova, we said there was no reason to bring children into a world already overflowing with children who don't have a home or a future or—

What's that got to do with anything? said Chantal. You and Adam have a home, and jobs. Look at me and Maurice, our kids want for nothing.

I'm not talking about anyone specific, said Tova, don't put words in my mouth again. I'm speaking generally.

You never speak generally, said Chantal. What's your problem, don't you want a child of your own, what's Adam's problem, what kind of man is he to—

Hang on, said Tova, are you generally against adoption?

No. If someone has trouble getting pregnant, adoption is a common solution.

And is that the only reason to do it?

If there are no medical issues that the wife or the husband—

Tova glanced at me and Chantal followed suit.

Say something, Chantal told me. I'm right, aren't I? Why bring a stranger into your home, what do you know about his diseases or his parents, you don't just throw away a child, something must be wrong with him or . . .

I stared at Tova. Just don't let her drag me into this discussion. In a moment of weakness, back in the day, I'd shared the details of my Sylvia Gozlan debacle with her.

She nodded at me and said, Nahum, do you agree with her?

I said, I'd love to meet your son. What's his name?

Comet.

Adam showed up after an eternity, which I spent gently questioning Tova about the adoption process and their decision-making and how they knew Comet, who was already five years old, would find a home with them. Tova gave me vague answers while Chantal leaned back in her seat, arms crossed, her paleness growing whiter, her lips pursed. She tensed when she heard those partial sentences—a home for children with special needs, a mother dying of ovarian cancer. When Adam showed up a child was bouncing beside him, skinny, with narrow eyes, one hand gripped in Adam's, the other waving around like a trapped butterfly's wing, his whole being bursting with joy.

THE TABLE WAS NEARLY EMPTY FOR SHABBAT DINNER, JUST Simo, Msodi, and me. Chantal's children were with her ex-husband, Maurice, and she'd gone to visit a friend from her national service days. Simo asked me how things were going with Asraf. Msodi said, Enough, Simo, no work talk at the Shabbat table. She served me a plate of mullet filet in red sauce, its edges golden with oil, a pepper curved from cooking lying beside it, its stomach burst open, slices of potato, polygons with many sides, asymmetrical, almost like delicate flowers, and a heap of hummus, that same glow of an old-time home, the illusion of home. I realized right away it was no mistake. She wasn't distracted. I've avoided fish for several years now, that same childish recoil returning to me inexplicably. But Msodi Farkash knew how to see into people's hearts. I looked up at her. She smiled.

Eat, she ordered me.

I tore off some challah and obediently dipped it in the sauce. The flesh of the fish was tender, its interior paleness revealed.

My father wouldn't relent. At the end of dinner he left his yarmulke on the table and called me to join him out on the porch. I was helping my mother clear the table. He shouted, Leave that to your mother. What's become of you?

I ignored him, raking the leftovers off the plate and into the garbage. I placed the plates down in the meat sink. My mother touched my arm. She said, Nahum, I don't really need any help. What's going on?

I said, The usual, what else?

She said, Have you talked to Tova lately?

Why do you ask?

No reason, I just have a feeling that something's up with her. Why don't you give her a call?

You know why.

She's your daughter.

Yes, she's my daughter, but those kids aren't my grandchildren. Why does she have to spite everyone all the time?

I'm not getting into that argument again, Mom. Why do you think that adopting two children with special needs is spiteful?

You don't know how that woman's head works. She and her husband. Two of a kind.

Mom, I'm really not getting into that.

She touched my arm again. She was wearing one of her inherited bracelets. A spot of gold, I realized. The orange hue of Moroccan gold was different from the yellow hue of local gold, which was a kind of impure boldness, melted and soldered again until any connection between substance and form was undone. The gold of her bracelet was warmer, deeper, gathering a history in its floral engraving. She said, Go out to your father. I'll finish up and join you.

Out on the porch, Simo said, I don't understand your generation. What was so bad about our way of doing things? Why are men today in such a rush to change diapers and help out in the kitchen?

I didn't answer.

So, Nahum, how's work?

It was a bad idea to eat the fish. It putrefied inside of me, that shadow of death from the ocean depths that no amount of cooking could get rid of. The meatballs lay on top of it, clogging my esophagus.

Nothing's moving, I said. I thought I'd go over Asraf's head and get support from a rich philanthropist, but it didn't work.

What does Asraf want?

He wants the speakers to talk a little bit about their connection to Jewish heritage.

What's so bad about some Judaism, a little heritage? asked Simo.

His response was too automatic. I wondered if he'd talked to Asraf or any of his associates in city hall.

I said, Drop it, Dad, there's nothing to explain.

He said, Have you asked the speakers you invited if they have any problem with that?

I had, actually. None of them objected to discussing their work's relationship with Jewish resources, the influence or criticism they experienced with regards to them. But all I told my father was, That's not the point. It's a matter of principle.

What do principles have to do with it?

I said, That's just the first step. I saw what happened in other libraries. Next thing, he'll want us to mark the books.

Simo said nothing.

I said, It's already happening at the Netivot library. You crack open a book and the first page has a scrawl in it, saying it's a dirty book. Is that any way to read? What kind of reading culture are they promoting?

Simo said, If I were a young boy and it was about movies, I would have sought them out. So would you. Young boys are drawn to filth.

I kept silent. Bullets fired through the darkness of my consciousness, seventeen-year-old Sylvia Gozlan, the buzzing and whispering of Sabah and Ehud as their eyes followed the girls.

I said, It's a deeper principle than that.

What, that they're intervening in your business?

No. That people without an ounce of social tolerance are trying to enforce their own values in the name of that tolerance.

Ah, said Simo, you and your leftism again.

I said, How come these days in Israel seeking justice has become a leftist crime?

Simo said, Follow justice and justice alone, huh, Nahum?

I said, It's no mistake that the word "justice" appears twice in that passage. You follow justice after justice, and the following never ends. You bring justice to one scenario and move on to the next. Never stumble. Never rest.

Simo said, Follow justice and justice alone, and you end up dying alone. Isn't it bad enough what happened back at that protest when people tried to burn down the collaborators' tent, and last summer when you were beaten up at the rally? You—

No politics, my mother said, stepping out onto the porch. She shoved the screen door open with her shoulder, carrying a plate of fruit and a plate of nuts and seeds.

I said, I'm not going to give up. That's what the war last summer taught me. It's a financial crisis that disguises itself with the appearance of national security and nationalistic slogans. They figured it out before we did, which is why they're putting so much effort into taking over budgets. I'm not—

What did I just say? my mother said. No politics. Look at these gorgeous apples the grocery store got. Pink Lady, they're called.

Simo said, It's a shame you're so stubborn. Eventually, Asraf will figure out a way to kick you out of the library. That guy is going to make it big in politics.

A snake in the grass, said Msodi. Did you see how quickly he killed the story about the Lakeside neighborhood and that poor soul, Heftzi Columbus, as if there was never any murder or any corruption and city hall wasn't overflowing with human garbage?

HOW IS IT THAT THE WOUNDS IN SDEROT NEVER HEAL, BUT ARE painless at any given moment? I wrote in the group chat.

Gil wrote, You've got to be punished somehow for staying in Sderot

Yaron wrote, Yeah, like Rishon L'Zion is an amusement park every day

Gil wrote, Don't throw shade, we've got a multiplex too

Ma'ayan wrote, So what, Yaron, you're a patriot now

Gil wrote, My mom tells me you're picking a fight with city hall

Ma'ayan wrote, Yeah, Nahum, bad idea

Yaron wrote, The people are behind you, Farkash, I always knew you had what it takes

I wrote, How's cooking for yuppies, Gil? Aren't you sick of it by now?

Ma'ayan wrote, He made us some *moflettas* too

I wrote, Exactly what I said, yuppies

Ma'ayan wrote, Nahum, it looks like you're about to go to Heidelberg again

I left the phone to beep its messages. On Saturday morning I woke up with two lumps on the inside of my lower lip, the warning signs of two canker sores, their early pussing, their sickly white.

At first, the red digits on the treadmill screen couldn't invade or appease the chaos in my mind. Ten kilometers and 350 calories. I did not require the extra effort. Eight hundred grams fell off me of their own accord. I ascribed the weight loss to anxiety. I pushed my muscles, more, more, until I crossed that line where they loosened and the thoughts received a different speed, dangling off one another and roaming according to their own laws, free from density, from the acidic flow in the throat, the choking of the heart.

Things unfurled before me with bizarre clarity, facts, facts. I'd met Elish Ben Zaken during the war. He'd found my cell phone at the rally in the gymnasium. He said his niece unlocked the phone and that he found Dalia's song in my music folder. Her name didn't appear, only her initials, DS, but Elish could easily recognize her voice. He used to write about her and the duo she had with Rami Amzaleg. When I tried to reminisce about her, he cut the conversation short. Could he have copied the song and passed it on to Therese Kavillio?

But how would they know each other?

Ohila and Noya Resnick brought up his name too. What did Noya Resnick say, that a year after Dalia's death Elish was roaming Sderot, asking questions. When was that, 2003, what was I doing in 2003? I was still working at the rec center. I didn't come across him then, and I didn't hear anything about a man investigating her death. Maybe I was too preoccupied with Sylvia Gozlan. But rumors usually spread, especially in Sderot. There hadn't been any rumors. I didn't have to accept Noya Resnick's testimony. I'd seen enough of the Nigerian Whisperer's film to know she spun reality for her own benefit.

What is the connection between Elish Ben Zaken and Therese?

What was Elish doing in Sderot during the war? People said he rented a home in the Lakeside neighborhood to be close to his family, who had just moved here. They also said he was involved with uncovering the corruption surrounding Heftzi Columbus's murder. I read one of his books, from the series about the police detective, Benny Zehaviv or whatever his name was. As if I needed further proof that detective novels are the opposite of poetry. My mother's voice from the previous night echoed through my mind, a snake in the grass, she called Asraf, did you see how quickly he killed the story about the Lakeside neighborhood?

Ohila said Therese was planning to launch her reading promotion project in Sderot. If my eyes hadn't deceived me, and the mockups I saw were indeed meant to promote this project, then it was Culture Flame's flagship enterprise. Perhaps even bigger than *Midnight Sun*, their lust for the spirits of Israeli culture. Then why that name, Take Up and Read? It was a distasteful name, with its superior tone and Latin roots, not to mention the fact that in Hebrew it used male pronouns, which was odd, especially coming from a woman who'd forged her own path. Therese wasn't dim like some other philanthropists whose racism was colored by ignorance.

But if she planned to have the launch in Sderot, she must be seeking a collaboration with city hall. I was such an idiot to turn

to her for help in my battle against Asraf. Such an idiot. What,
didn't I know that war involved countless formations and schemes,
waged on multiple fronts, and that the powers that be nurtured
one another for the sake of promoting their superior interest–the
preservation of the unequal division of wealth–regardless of
the shape that division took on the surface of the everyday, be it
national, cultural, or religious?

I turned off the treadmill. My feet hovered for a moment or
two after I stepped off. My balance was faulty. But now that I'd
removed the screen that blurs the web of powers working to exhaust us, defeat us, and make us compliant, gone too were its
effects–exhaustion, defeat, and compliance.

I opened the document detailing the names of the writers and
poets who were to take part in the lecture series at the public library. I wrote that the talks would revolve around the relationship between their work and canonical Jewish narratives. I titled
the series "Sources of Creation." I thought the expression would
echo to Asraf the phrase *Orot HaTeshuvah* or some other misleading combination by Rabbi Kook, the Heidegger of religious
Zionism. I'd send the document to his office on Sunday morning.

A week passed. I'd left several messages with Therese's personal assistant. He took them all down patiently and politely, having announced to me in a whisper, as if sharing a secret, that she
couldn't be reached at the moment, she was in a meeting, in the
car, at lunch, in a marathon of meetings with senior officials and
business moguls. Therese never got back to me.

Alice Shitrit from the mayor's office wrote me an email. Asraf
was satisfied. The series had been approved. I could begin preparing publicity materials and contracts for the visiting artists.

I came upon Ohila by chance at a poetry reading organized by
Sapir College students at a Sderot pub. I don't often attend open
mic nights, which are a recipe for poisoning one's ears. Even I
draw a line when it comes to pimping out form in favor of content.

But the organizers invited me personally. They were hoping the library would sponsor the following readings.

The pub was busy. A late November still brimming with earliness. Students crowded the tables outside, under the curving Perspex pergola, its milky opacity blocking out the clarity of the sky. They filled the stairs leading up to the old movie theater with its elegant wooden seats and its unending space, abandoned to the city's pigeons and ghosts. I recognized Ohila sitting inside, at the corner of the bar, detached from the rest of the scene. She didn't stand out, really, in her modest outfit, from the other customers. Most of them seemed to me like children playing dress-up with their grandparents' clothes. She spoke to some of them. Her cheeks were turning red, perhaps from the heating, or perhaps from passionate conversation. I carefully backed away, disappearing among the tables.

I wasn't wrong to be cautious. Mighty drizzles of murky poetry, some of it performed to hip-hop beats, some of it an indifferent recitation of distress, narcissistic monologues, grunts of self-love peppered with theoretical clichés. Everybody wants to be victims of some oppressive system, even the ones who really are victims. What a decisive victory for the free market, selling resistance against itself as just another consumer product.

So what did you think? I asked Ohila. She'd left when the reading was over and I followed her outside, turning left into some dark nook where the lights of the outside had no purchase. She recoiled under the no-moon sky, holding her cell phone in front of her face like a shield. A ray of light emitted from it, bathing me. She gasped. Oh, it's you, you idiot, you scared me.

You don't look like the kind that scares easy, I said.

She kept walking. Here and there we came across the terrorizing brightness of the old shopping center. Boarded-up shops. This is where I passed years ago, under a sunny storm, on my way to discover the eolianite burrows and their empty chill. But what was it about this night that brought them back to me, some echo from the depths of consciousness, to which the memory of that day had been banished? I paused, astonished.

Ohila turned to face me. Is something wrong, she said.

I said, Did you move to Sderot?

Only for a few days, for research.

I said, I've been trying to get ahold of Therese. I want to help.

She looked me over and said, But we've already given up on you.

Seriously? I asked. I thought you were looking for Dalia's childhood friends, to fill out the portrait of her that Noya wants to paint.

She said nothing.

I looked at my watch. I've got some time right now, I said. Where are you staying?

She didn't answer. She started walking, more determined now, fast.

I quickened my steps as well.

Why are you following me? she said.

I said, There's another student hangout spot not far from their dorms.

She nodded and moved away. I watched her whispering into her phone as she swayed nervously in place. She waved at me. When I came closer she gave me a tired smile. Fine, she said, Noya okayed it. Mind if I record this?

I TOLD HER ABOUT DALIA. I GAVE MEASURED DETAILS, WELL filtered, which I'd already prepared for my conversation with Therese. I told her about Nir Vazana, who was known as Niro for all the years I knew him, and who was her guitar teacher. He met her at a class at Sha'ar Hanegev College, even though they were both from Sderot. I told her that at the time there was a group of artists active in Sderot—musicians, filmmakers, writers, painters. Actually, they all did everything—writing, painting, playing music, making films. Adolescent energy. But they each knew what their main art form was. Dalia and I were satellite members. She, because she was skittish and stayed away from social gatherings, either because she felt she might get swallowed into them or because she was afraid of rejection, even though she had that aura, even then.

What aura? asked Ohila.

You know. At first glance you see a girl who's kind of chubby, not pretty, an uggo, as your generation likes to say. But after a few minutes of talking to her or listening to her, you see a shining being. The body disappears. There's only a presence.

That's something we'll want you to repeat during shooting.

I said nothing.

She said, And you?

What about me?

You said you were both satellite members.

Oh, I said, I was wearing a yarmulke. A lot of the rehearsals and the shooting and the improvisations and the games happened on Saturday.

Therese told me about that. Did you study at a yeshiva?

No, I said, my family isn't that observant. I hung out with rabbis and religious teachers. I laughed. My father only became more observant recently, when he realized it was politically beneficial.

I heard your father's got connections.

I told you he used to run the rec center.

Yes, and that he wouldn't allot a rehearsal room for musicians.

I said, Allocate.

Yeah, that.

Her wrist became exposed against the table. In the golden cloudiness of the wrinkled interior of the pub, with its embroidered pillows and *bourekas*-movie posters, the whiteness glowed. The beer tingled against my lower lip, the sores had healed, but the tender tissue still tingled.

Ohila smiled. She said, You remind me of the library manager from my childhood. Me and my sisters would go there to borrow books. He had a very precise Hebrew. Every word he spoke sounded like he was tasting a delicacy.

My sisters and I, I said.

Huh?

It's customary to put others before oneself when both are the subject of a sentence.

He would correct us all the time. Like, what?

I said, Do you intend to address Elish Ben Zaken's part of the story in the film as well?

What part?

I don't know. Noya said he investigated Dalia Shushan's death.

Therese has some interest in him, I think, but I'm not sure it's got anything to do with the film.

What if he discovered unpublished facts about her death?

She shrugged and reached for her cider. The cinnamon and the apple freshness and the aroma of mulled wine, the alcoholic thickness, all mixed with her own scent as well as with the pub's moldiness.

We would love to hear about them, Therese and Noya and I, she said, and another smile emerged on her face, but it sounded sort of unconvincing.

Have Therese and Elish ever met?

Not that I know. What else can you tell me about Dalia Shushan?

She had wisdom beyond her years, I said. An ancient wisdom, if that makes sense. She was vulnerable like a girl, but then, all of a sudden, for no apparent reason, she'd change, revealing that side of her. Niro used to joke that she was a *sh'hara*.

Then I thought, But he was only quoting that other poet. Dalia visited one of their Dungeons & Dragons sessions. The other poet couldn't stand her. He asked Niro to make sure she didn't come back.

I said, "*Sh'hara*" means witch.

I know what "*sh'hara*" means, said Ohila. My grandmother uses that word.

Did she give you that bracelet? I asked.

She glanced at her bare wrist. I recognized the dilemma on her face, whether or not to cover it up. She touched the bracelet.

You can't mistake the quality of that gold, I said.

That's what my dad says. He says nothing beats Moroccan gold.

Where is she from, I asked, your grandmother?

I don't know. How many places are there in Morocco?

Are you serious?

Maybe from one of the cities? Casablanca? Rabat?

Does anybody tease her?

Why do you ask?

Because you can infer the hometown of Moroccans by the way other people tease them.

My grandpa used to call me *meraksiya zreyra*.

Got it.

My mother used to say it meant "little Moroccan."

Is your mother of Ashkenazi descent?

Somewhere in Eastern Europe.

It just means that your grandparents came from Marrakech.

Marrakech, she said.

Where in Eastern Europe?

I've never really been able to figure it out. Sometimes they say Ukraine and other times they say Poland.

Galicia?

After a long pause she asked, How did you end up running the library?

Local politics, I said. My father's an old-time *politruk*.

She laughed. You could be a little more subtle.

Why? It's the truth.

I recognized the yearning in her face, the fetters undone by intoxication, or the inner permission incarnated into her expression. She said, I've always wondered what libraries look like at night.

Same way they look during the day, only dark.

No, I'm serious. We would pass the library on our way home at night and my sister would say, I wonder what's going on in there. She made up all sorts of silly stories.

I said, Well, I've got my keys here, if the question is still bugging you.

She nodded. She leaned against the table to help herself up from one of the cushions.

OTHER PROFILES WERE DOUBLED IN OHILA'S PROFILE AGAINST the pillow in my bed when I propped myself up on an elbow to look at her, gathered, the curve of the forehead, the roundness of the nose, its narrow fleshiness, the razor-like wrinkle descending from it, the slight fluff of the lips, the sloping of the chin into the neck. Dalia's profile from the thicket was in there, as was Sylvia Gozlan's mature profile, with the eyelids squeezing shut during her journey toward sleep.

Ohila's mind had grown clearer on the way to the library with the help of the late November air or the glare of the night. She'd regained her posture, anyway. She walked beside me with that stern, fast pace of hers, devoid of any feminine mannerisms like strutting or shaking. I asked if she drank often. She said almost never, and that she'd kill for a cigarette right now. But all of the stores were closed, and she silenced her longing. I asked if she was all right and she said she was, somewhat impatiently, asking how much longer till we got to the library. Then her voice turned softer and she said, The public library.

Structures under the cover of darkness resemble a slumbering animal. The tendons are taut underneath the skin, the pounce blazing somewhere in the muscles. Beneath the expressionless gaze they return from their dark windows hides a second gaze, calculating risks, assessing opportunities. We paused in front of the library. I asked Ohila, Are you brave enough, do you dare?

She nodded and exhaled.

I opened the front door and disarmed the alarm system. The flashlight apps of our cell phones forged a path for us through the lobby. I turned on the light in my office. Ohila stood before me, her still-dilated pupils filling her face with emotion. But her entire body seemed charged up with something. She smiled.

I said, So did reality match your imagination, or are you underwhelmed?

She said she wanted to see the books but without any lights on. I opened the door of the adult circulation room. The smells of the day were gone from the room. Only a chill invaded from the northern windows. Cold metallic strips of nightglow and glass, a chill that had nothing to do with the heavens, but was a level of reality. The metallicness of the bookcases, the paperness of the pages, the nylonness of the protective covers, the stickiness of the parquet, were all in a more primitive phase of their existence, on the verge of being born into matter.

I reached for the light switch. Ohila's hand took hold of mine. She shook her head and headed inside. She took a deep breath. Nothing more than a vanishing shape in the general blindness of the room. Had it not been for her fingers loosely holding on to my wrist, I doubt I'd be aware of her existence at all. But my eyes adjusted. And I saw her. Darkness and fabric, and a flowing softness.

I said, And now?

She whispered, Go out and come back in a minute, and pretend to be surprised to find me here, like you're catching me stealing a book.

I whispered, What? A nervous gurgling escaped my throat.

She whispered, Shh, Nahum, don't leave me hanging.

I stepped out quietly, waited a few seconds, then walked back inside. I sniffed the air, hard, moving my head this way and that, searching for the cause of the disruption. A figure was standing next to one of the bookcases, book in hand. She spotted me and flinched.

Who's there? I called.

She froze.

I hurried over. Little girl, I said, what are you doing here so late?

She said, N . . . nothing, Mr. Lililibrarian, I was just passsssing by and I saw . . . I saw the door open.

I started to laugh.

Don't spoil it, Ohila whispered. The girl said, Mr. Lililibrarian, I'm so, I'm so sorr . . . sorry, I—

It's a little too late for that, I said. What were you planning on doing with the book?

I was rrrreading, sir, I suddenly rereremembered—

You wouldn't have been able to see a mountain in this room, it's so dark. How did you think you'd be able to read the letters?

I'm ssssorry. You're not going tttto tellll my . . . my parents, are you?

God forbid, I said. But you must be punished.

I took the book from her and placed it on the counter. I pulled her after me. She resisted slightly, then gave in. When we got back to my office, she said, It's a shame you don't wear glasses.

I had her arm bent behind her back. I breathed against the back of her neck. What good would glasses do? I said. I loosened my grip and she turned to face me, pressed against my chest. I kissed her. A current ran over my lips, my tongue shifting between metallicness and a living heat.

✳ ✳ ✳

BACK IN MY APARTMENT, WE REMOVED OUR CLOTHES SLOWLY. Well, she did. She undid my belt, pulled down my pants. Took hold of my dick through my underwear. I took off my shirt and the T-shirt I had underneath. Her fingers hovered over my chest and stomach. The tiny gap between them and my skin was a universe of electric activity, as if she'd pierced through my body heat.

I reached for her clothes. She pushed me lightly. Watch, she said.

I leaned against the wall. She stood between me and the bed. One by one, she folded each item and placed it on the dresser, as if requiring a pause to adjust to their parting from her body. Her slim figure was revealed. She removed her bra. Average, citron-shaped breasts. The areolas were dark and narrow, taut. That didn't matter, that wasn't what I wanted to touch. The format of her body parts was gone from my mind. I wanted her hunger, the being raging within her. I wanted her. The desire was soft, the desire was downy in all of my blood vessels, even in my hard dick. I moved toward her. Flatly, she said she was still a virgin and intended to remain one until she married, but that I shouldn't worry, she had experience in other body parts. She said her friend from religious school called it parking in the rear. She turned her back on me as she pulled down her underwear. Her ass was pear-shaped, two plump, elongated cheeks. All my friends are penetration observant, she said. I swallowed the spit balling in my throat. She turned around to face me, one hand covering her crotch. She asked that I turn out the light.

Then she suddenly laughed and said, A mountain in this room.

I said, Well, I'm bad at that sort of improvising.

I asked what he was called, the librarian from her childhood.

She said, Menashe Dalumi. In her sister's stories, he'd grow a second head in the middle of the night, no eyes or eyebrows or nose, just many little mouths with sharp teeth, mouths all over his skulls. In his normal head, his mouth would be toothless, but when he opened up you'd see an eyeball on the tip of his tongue.

I said, Your sister's a real writer.

She said, She's got three children already. How about you, how come you don't have any kids?

I said, It didn't turn out that way. Then I asked, How long have you had that fantasy?

She said, What fantasy?

I didn't answer.

She said, How come you're not married?

I said, It didn't turn out that way either.

She pulled up the blanket and covered her breasts. I'm thirsty, she said.

I got out of bed and picked up my underwear.

She said, Why do you need to get dressed, you're home.

I put them on.

When I got back, she was standing at the window. The building across the street blocked a considerable part of the sky, but the strip above it was perforated with stars, like embers scorching fabric. The blanket was wrapped around her shoulders.

I handed her the glass of water. It's so quiet, she said.

I said, That's how it is here in Sderot, between one war and the next. Isn't it dead quiet in Karnei Shomron? I lay in bed and said, I wanted to ask you, Therese, Noya, and you are all women, so how come you're addressing the reading promotion project to males?

She looked at me. She said, Why are you still wearing your underwear?

What?

Take it off. Your body proportions are interesting. I know how to appreciate male beauty, unlike lots of other women.

I said, You're so young and already so smart.

She lay beside me, rubbing my leg. She said, Am I smart the way Dalia was smart?

I said nothing.

Were you a couple, you and Dalia?

What an odd idea.

She said, Because you told me you were both sort of like rejects.

Satellites.

Rejects, satellites, same shit. Unpopular.

Dalia was unattainable. That's not the same.

Unattainable, she said. I wonder how a person becomes unattainable.

It's congenital.

Put your arms around me. What's wrong with you, can't you see I'm shivering?

I reached my arm under the blanket and wrapped it around her shoulders. She rested her head on my chest. Her sweat had evaporated, and all that was left was the smell of burning from our bodies and some faint honey scent from her shampoo. She said, Your breathing is shallow. You need to learn how to breathe more deeply.

I held the air in my lungs and let it out slowly, a long exhale.

She said, Reading Forward.

I said, Forward what?

Noya isn't connected to the reading project, only to the Dalia Shushan film. But that's the project's name. Take Up and Read is the name of the e-reader.

She shook off my arm and pulled her bag off the dresser, then fished out her cell phone. Some Chinese knockoff. She pulled up one of the posters I'd seen in Therese's office, enlarged the device held by the celebrity in the picture, and handed over her phone.

Why do you care about this? she asked.

A professional interest, I said. People always say that the internet and e-readers are changing reading culture. What kind of future do libraries have?

But that's Therese's plan, to have these e-readers borrowed from libraries. And organize events around them. She already signed contracts with a ton of publishers to donate books to the project. Digital copies, I mean, that kids can download at home or at the library. It's a unique format that can only be used on her device.

There was a black spot on the back of the device. I zoomed in on it. A logo. An open palm out of which shot the stalks of some twisted, forked seedling. At the bottom, in black lettering, the name was engraved: "Take Up and Read."

I asked, Wouldn't it be simpler to develop an app?

She didn't answer.

I asked, Who thought up the name?

Therese, I think. She told me she heard it in a song. She must have meant the Selichot prayers.

Did she tell you directly that she heard it from the Selichot liturgical poem?

She paused, either to ponder my question or take a quick nap.

I said, "A voice says, 'Cry out.' And I said, 'What shall I cry?'"

What? said Ohila, a sleepy, drawn-out syllable.

I said, Sometimes I forget that you plebeian orthodox have no methodical knowledge of the Jewish world. Some *halachas* here, a few well-worn passages there, some quotes from *midrash aggadah*. A partial knowledge, ignorance and trends maintained by the rabbinical establishment to make you more obedient.

Nonsense, said Ohila.

"A voice says, 'Cry out.' And I said, 'What shall I cry?' All people are like grass, and all their faithfulness is like the flowers of the field."

Oh.

Yes, oh. Deutero-Isaiah.

She paused again. Her response came through the blurry in-between of sleep. She said, The connection to the Selichot poem is mine, I made that, all people are like ass and all—

Her voice thickened and sloped. Rhythmic breaths. I thought, But it wasn't just Jonah the Prophet, commanded to arise and call upon his God, and it wasn't just Isaiah with the prophecy burning in his bones, and it wasn't just the Selichot that echoed with the command "kum kera," with its double meaning, "rise and call," and "take up and read." It was also Augustine, the falsest of the sages I'd ever read, lying Augustine, drunk with power, who heard a child in his court saying, take up and read, or, in Latin, of course, *tolle lege*, and the words gave him a change of heart. But Hebrew is smarter than him and it retrieved what had been stolen from it. I pushed up to my side and examined her profile in the room's absent light. When I'd put down the book she randomly pulled out from the library shelf I'd recognized it, the hard yellow cover, the art nouveau illustration—*Froth on the Daydream* by Boris Vian. In one of the last pages, Snot had written in pen, *This is a sick book. If you've read all the way to this page, call 896354. There's a surprise in store for you.* Years later, I opened the book and found the message intact. I marveled at its survival.

BUT THE TRUTH IS I WANTED A DAUGHTER. I WOULD HAVE MADE do with a son. I would tell myself with fake, unconvincing bravery, Why should I have offspring, to have creatures in this world practicing my demise while I practice theirs? Sylvia Gozlan wanted them too.

I met her at the reunion she'd organized. We'd all turned thirty. Like her, I felt the weight of the age and was prepared to disclose it. I hadn't accomplished a thing, had gotten nothing done. I did one year of college at Ben-Gurion University, traveled the world, returned, and since then I'd been moving from one job to the next in different cultural institutions around town, under Simo Farkash's wing. I hadn't married. I hadn't started a family. I'd published some poems here and there. I knew how to cover up my heartbreak with a mature countenance. The sense of failure, the sourness of face, the holeache that often consumed its surroundings almost never slipped out from behind it.

The others declined. Most of them utilized the same trick— recognizing the person standing before them, calculating the signs of the times, where the explosion shattered deeper, where it passed by without taking its toll, a retreat into the boys and girls they once were, standing on the threshold of ignorance. Ehud Barda was there, donning the cloak of arrogance he'd acquired in Sabah's company during our high school years. We exchanged some pleasantries. I was stunned before him. Gone was the time I came to see him while he lay in bed, legs in casts. I was once more the young boy emerging from the thicket who had just served as an instrument of its destruction or an aid to its bitter sentence. And he was the assistant architect, the sly strategist, the snake. I asked him about Sabah. He corrected me by calling him David. David was a project manager for a small start-up. He was out of the country, on a work trip, instructing clients on the product. He couldn't remember where exactly, definitely America, some Midwestern state. Or maybe Hong Kong. They weren't very close, but kept in touch. He, Ehud, had helped him start the company. And he, Ehud, what did he do? What, couldn't I tell, he was a major in the military. Which unit? A secret one.

Dudi patted my back with his *lulav*-like form. The decade and change that had gone by hadn't touched his body but had been hell on his eyes. Something had drained his gaze. He had three children, praise the Lord. They lived in Sde David. Get it? David from Sde David. A few of his teeth had turned brown. No, he didn't come back to Sderot often.

The reunion took place in Sylvia Gozlan's apartment, a garden apartment she'd purchased with her divorce settlement money. At least something good came out of that son of a bitch. Her words. With her signature Moroccan warmth, she said, *B'la faida*, useless. A few fruit trees and barren trees stood in the pre-summer air, the post-spring air, that days-long gap during which the heat waves of late May are still shaky, not yet asserting themselves as a law of climate. Guava trees, pomegranate trees, dry. A branched jacaranda. I took a seat on a bench beneath it, on the edge of the hubbub. Sylvia Gozlan sat down next to me. Earlier, I'd watched her circling around, clinking glasses, assessing her guests' level of enjoyment. She made a habit of tweezing her eyebrows, and now her crude, hook-like, angular nose added charm to her face. The mole was gone, perhaps surgically removed, perhaps fallen off with age. She'd turned her unruly kinky hair into an advantage. Her puffy 'do shifted as her head moved, the ends trembling.

So, Nahum, she said, you've stayed antisocial.

I've stayed in Sderot.

Like that's an achievement.

Returning to Sderot after ten years in Tel Aviv seems more pathetic.

You're up-to-date.

I don't know what ignited between us, maybe the alcohol, maybe the false emotion of a renewed encounter, the promise of youth, of returning to be who we used to be in each other's company, exempt from the future, which was our past. She, not yet married. Me, what? What did I wish to undo?

She said she wasn't the one who'd planted the trees in the garden. A family used to live there before her. The first thing she did was get rid of the swings, dismantle the planks that served as rungs for a ladder leading to even more planks, probably a tree house. She pointed up. I could see the nails in the tree trunk.

She said her husband didn't want any children.

I said, What's wanting children?

She said, What do you mean what's wanting children, wanting children is wanting children.

I said, Yes, but what is that?

She got up and left, mingling among her guests, most of whom were already intoxicated and beginning to leave. I saw her kissing cheeks goodbye. I saw her hugging and being hugged. I saw her spewing hollow promises, performing the agreed-upon gestures for relationships that had been severed and must, simply *must*, be renewed. That entire time, I remained underneath the tree. The last wilted jacaranda petals fluttered on the dark ground. Some might have clung to my clothes, my hair. That fallout, a source for bad metaphors. Sylvia came back, two glasses of wine in her hands. She handed me one and plopped down beside me.

What's wanting children? she said. You're hungry, you're thirsty, you're horny. It's all the same.

I said, It can't be the same.

She said, You fall asleep and hear sounds of games and laughter in your dream, or even a little before the dream starts. You know that?

I said nothing.

She said, And then you wake up and the rooms are empty.

I didn't like her. Perhaps I held a grudge.

She said, Imagine if I'd gotten pregnant that time.

After fucking once?

Yeah, she said. I was a virgin, I was seventeen, it's the most natural thing in the world.

I was careful.

Yeah, right. Careful. Neither of us knew what we were doing. I remember my sister preaching to me about contraception and STDs. You think I remembered any of it? The brain is always slower than horniness. I told my sister after we had sex. She called me every day to ask if I'd gotten my period yet. It's a shame, our kid would have been pretty like me and nerdy like you.

I said, Oh well.

She said, It isn't too late. It isn't too late.

SYLVIA GOZLAN WAS HAUNTED BY THE IDEA THAT HAD OCCURRED to her. She called me every day. She said, You owe me. I considered the fact that her shadow son, born at the time of our loss of virginity, would have had his bar mitzvah this year. My shadow daughter would have been appalled by the transformations of her body. I told her she should have slept with Sabah that night, not me. Her entire life would have been different. She said she didn't believe he could have even gotten it up. That guy could only get excited thinking about himself.

I said, Still, it didn't stop him from ruining my life when he found out we'd made love.

Made love, huh, why not, talk it up like that if it helps you maintain your naïvety.

You know what I meant.

She said she couldn't figure out what the deal was with men, how they made every achievement secondary to whether or not they got laid. Her ex-husband had some single male friends. I should have seen them patting one another's backs when they told one another about a chick they'd picked up at the bar the previous night and how they'd nailed her.

I said it was funny she had to talk like a man in order to criticize men.

She said it wasn't funny, and that if I didn't understand the meaning of the allegory she could explain.

I said there was no allegory.

She said, So listen closely, Nahum Farkash. Your darling Sabah didn't care that you slept with me, but he was destroyed by the fact that you lost your virginity before him. She said, Nahum, I'd never ask you for a thing, I swear to God, we'll sign a contract. What do you care, it's just sperm.

We tried, we really did. She was skilled, Sylvia Gozlan. Skilled like me. She was surprised by how skilled I was. Costa was surprised too, on the one night we spent together after randomly bumping into each other in Tel Aviv, near the Rothschild Boulevard protest tent city. He was still my age, but already older than me. He was married and a father of two. The coach of the Wingate Institute's youth swim team. His life was an accurate execution of a plan formed in his twenty-year-old mind. We went to a hotel that offered rooms by the hour. He asked if I'd slept with a man before. I didn't answer. He wanted me to show him my scars. What scars? I asked. He said, The traces left by those who loved you, where are they? I want to know if a man or a woman touched you like fire, it's what I knew would happen to us. Then he added vaguely, *Blat*, as if conjuring up the word like a spell. Why wouldn't you try it with me back then? He wasn't interested in penetration, said he had enough of that with his wife. He only wanted that proximity between men, without barriers or hesitations. Touching wherever we felt like. I didn't tell him what I already knew, that sex was possible only between distant people. Performed by close souls, it became incest. He kissed me gently, lengthily, almost laboriously. That's what he wanted, for conversations to be disrupted by the pressure of lips, underneath silences, which were meaningless but always had multiple meanings.

Sylvia Gozlan, on the other hand, kissed fervently. There was a small stud in her left nipple. I enjoyed the sour taste of the metal against my lips, poking from the softness of the breast. The touch and the taste sent fire shooting through my limbs, which tended to act out of indifference around her. The first time, she urged me to go lower. There was a dryness in my mouth when the smell of her pussy finally filled my sinuses, and my tongue carefully sampled the flavor within. After that, I preferred to use my fingers. Within a moment, Sylvia Gozlan would announce she was ready, and I would penetrate her. She would turn her head away from me. The mechanic motions of the first time, the strangeness of youth, the seeking, were ensconced in every shift of flesh. Our bodies repeated them, practicing them, improving them, but never deviating from them. The strangeness remained. People tend to exaggerate the importance of the body because the desire mechanism is contained within it, the biology of it. But flesh is finite, its pleasure brief. Not so with words. Complete Eros is contained within speech. We didn't have much to talk about. But two months later, I too was haunted. I pictured every feature in the face of the little girl that would grow in her womb. I have no idea why, but I was convinced we would have a girl.

I was sitting on my apartment balcony. In the distance, a meteorite crossed the darkening heavens. I nicked my finger on the fruit knife in my hand. Three drops of blood fell to the floor. I whispered, I would like a daughter, her skin as honeyed as the bursting of jasmine, her lips thick like these drops of blood, her eyes fiery like this speck of dust crossing the atmosphere. She would probably be chubby like Tova and Chantal were when they were young. I thought if the girl was conceived in summer, she would be born in spring, perhaps around Purim. She would contain a savagery, which in girls stemmed from an ancient sense, a sense of preservation and defensiveness, a wild defiance whose flip side is an equally wild compassion. She would contain childhood, in the original sense our sages meant—boldness, brashness. Her face would always be stained from climbing trees, smeared with a mixture of sand and spit from standing her ground at the jungle gym.

Eventually, we got some fertility tests. Shit out of luck to the bitter end, said Sylvia Gozlan. It's just like me to end up with the only barren man in Sderot.

TOVA WAS THE ONLY ONE I TOLD ABOUT MY ATTEMPTS AT PRO-creation. Chantal heard a rumor somewhere. She said, People are claiming you've been hanging out with Sylvia Gozlan. What are you doing, dumpster diving?

I laughed. I said, Imagine if that were true. What would you gain by insulting me?

She said, I've seen smart-ass men like you, how easily they fall into the trap.

I told Tova in a moment of weakness, maybe. I couldn't get out of bed in the mornings after we received the test results. And Tova called. She said, Nahumi, you've got every reason in the world to feel sad, but just think, this world is full of other reasons too. Do you have any idea how much happiness you could experience, offering kindness to children who've had a hard life?

The grace of her words was reserved for the weak. Whenever she recognized a force within me, the ability to resist, a spine, she insinuated that my secret was safe with her, looking at me askance, using the emphasized tone of double entendre. Not that she wanted to make me her hostage, but that she herself was a victim of her own beliefs.

I implored Chantal to stop shunning Tova. I don't know the source of the rage fermenting in her the day Tova told us about adopting Comet. If she didn't want children of her own, that would be one thing, Chantal said that day as we drove back to Sderot. But why does she have to adopt retarded children?

I corrected, Special needs.

Call it whatever you want, it doesn't change what they are. What's missing in her life, what made her so messed up?

You really don't understand?

No, there's nothing to understand. Look at me, how come I don't have the same problems she does? What's different about how I was brought up?

I said, It's so personal, the interior experience. Her perception of our family is completely different.

Do me a favor, said Chantal, do me a favor, you and your philosophy. How badly can she twist things? Everything? What was so hard for her? Huh? Tell me. Interior experience, my ass.

I said, I can understand the appeal of complete selflessness.

Ibki alekh, ya Nahum. She's been selfish since she was a little girl.

Now she said, She probably wants to adopt another broken child. Why not? I wonder what country the next one will be from.

I said, She asked to meet us two weeks ago, and she's been sending me reminders every day.

Did something happen to her?

That's what I asked.

268

I just hope she doesn't lose it again, the way she did back then, with Johnny.

I didn't answer.

Do Mom and Dad know?

She only wants to talk to the two of us.

Now Chantal didn't answer.

So what do you say? I asked.

When?

I don't know.

Tell her to come to Sderot.

Chantal came to my apartment at the appointed time. She paced restlessly. I just hope she isn't sick, she said, God forbid. Or that Adam is dying, God help us.

I said, Calm down, I don't think that's what this is.

It's serious, said Chantal, I can feel it.

I looked at her cup of coffee on the living room table. I'd slaved over foaming the coffee grounds with sugar and a little water, the way we used to make it as children, in glasses. A creamy layer, its hue revealing the work it required, would form on top of the liquid. The closer it was to an ivory beige, the color of paper fading in the sun, the higher the quality. Chantal took one sip and put the glass down. In her wandering, she walked into my bedroom. She asked, Are you seeing somebody?

What?

She returned to the living room. Are you seeing somebody?

No.

She gave me a long, calculating look. There were words on the tip of her tongue, but the doorbell rang.

Chantal plopped down into the armchair and took a few quick sips. Behind me, she said, Great coffee, Nahum. Her tone was customary, sovereign.

Tova walked in. She was alone, standing tall as usual, wearing a white cotton dress, a shawl around her shoulders. Two thin braids hanging off her head contained the smooth mane, strewn here and there with gray. She hugged me. Chantal remained seated, tense in her seat.

What can I get you to drink? I asked.

Nahumi, she said, I didn't give you any notice, but we're going to spend the weekend in Mitzpe Ramon. Adam's picking me up tomorrow. Would it be okay if I spent the night?

I said it was no problem. I hadn't even noticed the plump duffel bag she was carrying.

Figures, said Chantal, she'd invite herself like that.

Tova took a breath. What kind of tea do you have?

The silence was rough for all of us. Tova broke it first. She said, So. There's this young woman with kidney failure that's only getting worse. A few months ago, I enrolled myself as a kidney donor, and I'm a match. So—

What are you talking about? said Chantal. You're donating a kidney? They're going to take one of your kidneys out?

Yes, said Tova. It's not as awful as it sounds.

They're going to cut out your kidney?

Of course, how else can they remove it?

Chantal glared at me. I looked away.

Sarina Sar, said Tova. That's her name.

Are you serious? I asked.

Tova took a long sip from her tea.

Chantal hummed, Sounds like an Egyptian mosquito's name.

Tova said, It isn't a complicated operation. Two kidneys are too many, anyway.

I don't believe you, said Chantal. You're making it up.

Why would I make it up? What kind of person do you think I am? Nahum?

Too far, I said.

Chantal said, What's that name, sounds like an Egyptian mosquito.

I don't know her, said Tova.

Then why . . . why . . .

I looked at Chantal. She was pressed against the back of her seat, her hands, gripping the half-empty coffee mug, were shaking, the milky liquid swishing against the glass. Though it had cooled, its sweetly singed aroma had not evaporated.

A smile transformed Tova's face. Her eyes filled with a glow that lit up all her features. In a near whisper, she said, Thou shalt love thy neighbor as thyself, right? There's no risk in donating a kidney, and if I can save a life—

Chantal slammed her glass against the table. Why did you come here to tell us that? Why was it so urgent for us to hear your shit? Chantal's beautiful paleness deepened along with her fury. Her slightness sliced through the space. She stood up. I've had it up to here with you, she said, placing her hand on her forehead. Up to here. You've totally lost it. Totally. Risking your life for some girl who . . . Just wait till Mom hears about this . . . Up to here.

BUT REALLY, WHY WAS IT URGENT FOR YOU TO TELL US? I ASKED Tova after Chantal left. You knew exactly how she'd react.

She said, But why, why does generosity make her so angry?

You're playing naïve.

She said she refused to believe Chantal was beyond repair. True, she'd been brought up to be selfish and snatch whatever she could, because she was convinced that people were either predators or prey. But she, Tova, every morning she woke up and saw her children's smiles, their profound happiness, and realized everyone deserved to experience the world this way, as endless giving resulting from endless receiving. Ultimately, we're our own worst enemies, she said. We trap ourselves in structures of hatred and suspicion, then use them to justify any cruelty and injustice and villainy we inflict on others. Instead of waking up.

I told her it was a nice speech, but devoid of any understanding of human psychology. And what was the whole Golden Rule bit about, since when did she speak in clichés?

She said, You too, Nahumi, you think too much instead of trying to feel.

I said, There's a reason the Sanhedrin tractate says about the
Golden Rule, Thou shalt choose for him the easiest possible
execution.

She said, You're still stuck in the Gmarah, with all those insane rabbis. This is the 2000s, go on, snap out of it.

I said, Altruism is a kind of disorder too.

I didn't expect any different from you.

You talk about generosity, about selflessness, but you still
want us to affirm your actions.

I saw Chantal becoming swallowed in Mom and Dad. I could
have saved her, but I didn't. Instead, I ran away. I tried to save
myself.

Wow, are you for real? Chantal was holding on to the edge of
an abyss. You stood there, arms crossed, while she fell into the
Farkash family hell. Poor thing.

Be as cynical as you want, Nahumi, but you know I'm right.

Is there even the possibility of being wrong in your world?

Why are you getting angry now too?

I didn't answer. Instead, I moved the coffee table and opened
the pull-out sofa while Tova slowly sipped her tea. Standing before the open doors of the bedroom closet, in front of the linen
shelves, I remembered the night when I came across Chantal's
dream, her indecipherable crying, and the comfort Sylvia Farkash
had offered her in vain. Looking back, I could fathom the pattern
Tova had embellished on, Chantal's willful surrender of any hint of
independence, her absorption of the familial law, the orders she
inherited, without criticism, without any desire to overturn them.

This pillow is a little hard, I told Tova, but it's comfortable.

I tucked the ends of the sheet under the edges of the sofa.
Tova held two corners of the duvet cover.

I said, I have my own method of getting the blanket inside.

Tova said, Forget it, it's easier to do it together.

I told her not to bother, to get something to eat instead. There wasn't much food in the fridge. We could order a pizza.

She said she'd make do with whatever I had.

My phone beeped. I looked at the screen. A text from Chantal. *Is she still there?*

Yes, I wrote. *She's staying over.*

She wrote, *if I were yoi I would tell her to go to helk*

I wrote, *you forgot to use an emoji.*

What kind

The kind that means you don't mean it.

But I do

I'll talk to you tomorrow.

I swear I would come over right now p

From the kitchen, Tova called out, Nahumi, do you have any onions?

I said, Yes, in the bowl under the microwave.

Chantal wrote, *and slap her, she got on my nervef*

I wrote, *good night, Chantal.*

So what do you want to know? Tova asked over dinner.

I chomped on the salad and asked, How did you reach the verdict?

Reach the verdict. You're a real live librarian, Nahumi.

I said nothing.

She said, After a while you start feeling empty and you don't know why.

A while after what.

Tova said, At first it's like a bug bite. You get up in the morning and go to sleep at night, and all day long you feel an itch but don't know why.

I shook my head silently.

You know what I'm talking about, right?

That depends.

Not that I have a problem with Comet and Tanita, God forbid. I'm crazy about them. But suddenly being a mother isn't enough.

And Adam?

He understands.

No, I mean, isn't he enough?

She ate in silence, sipped the infusion she'd made us, chewed.

I said, In that case, nothing is enough.

She said, I heard about this organization that connects kidney donors with people who need a donation. They always need people. It's so easy to save somebody's life.

Isn't it kind of boring to create more and more debtors for yourself?

She spread her hand on the table, closing and opening a fist. She said, Not everything is about loss and gain.

I told her we lie to ourselves when we say it isn't. That maybe it keeps sorrow away, numbing the helplessness, but reality is founded on the exchange of goods, on supply and demand.

Again that silence, in which the music of the human sounded clear. The bottom of a glass tapping against a wooden table, the metal of a fork against the ceramic of a plate, breathing, lip smacking, the nicking of bone against objects.

Tova placed the dishes in the sink. I said I'd wash them later. Afterward, she stood in my doorway, leaning against the doorjamb. An icon of a woman cut out of the great light of the living room lamp. She said, But what about you, Nahumi, how long can you use your brain to keep out your emotions? I've worked with enough traumatized children. I can easily recognize the signs of a wounded soul.

THEN, IN THE FINAL HOURS OF THE NIGHT, I AWOKE. OHILA'S flesh lay down beside me. I got up and showered in boiling water. But neither the water nor the two cups of coffee I funneled into my body were enough to wipe away my disorientation. I used to think I'd be scalded by warm water, but now I'm not scalded even by boiling water. I turned on my laptop and read the news. More fascist smears in every headline.

Ohila walked over to the dining table with the languid limbs of those who take pleasure in their sleep, stretching and smiling. What's she smiling about?

Good morning, she said.

Morning, I said.

Is there any coffee?

I pointed my chin toward the kitchen. She pressed the back of the laptop screen and said, That's not polite. I'm a guest.

I slammed the laptop shut. I asked, How do you take your coffee?

I didn't have any cookies. The only way for me to avoid temptation was to remove it completely. I offered to go get some. She said it was too early, and that it would probably be nice out on the balcony.

Not really, I said. The balcony faces east, and the Israeli sun is cruel in every season.

Then in the evening, she said.

A hushed sizzle of annoyance ran through my veins. I pursed my lips. I said, I have a long day today. Don't you need to go to work?

She asked if she could get a towel. She wanted to shower. When she returned, bathed, the towel I gave her wrapped around her breasts and the hand towel, which I'd only hung by the sink the previous day, wrapped around her hair, I told her to try to leave quietly, because my neighbors were terrible gossips.

She didn't return my calls in the following days. I called to ask how the research was going. She didn't pick up. My DMs remained unanswered. I called Therese's office. Again, she was unavailable. It was over a month later when Shifra told me that filming was about to start.

I asked if she knew who was going to be interviewed.

She said, They want to film at Esther's.

I spoke to Simo Farkash, who spoke to the owners of the *Southern Wind*. The news and the related interview were outside the *Southern Wind*'s range. A large news website took up the story.

I posted under @TheAbominable's Twitter account: #ParrotNahum. Nahum Farkash, some poet. Just another hipster organizing protests to create an interesting selfie background.

Then I tweeted: #TheNigerianWhisperer. You don't have to make a fortune off of migrant workers. Dead Mizrahis make for a pretty good diving board too.

I spoke to the editor in chief of the *Southern Wind*, who was also the head reporter. I told him I wanted to organize a protest outside of Esther Shushan's house and block the production's access. He asked if I'd lost my mind. I asked him why he'd say that. He said, Don't you know Asraf is supporting the film, that he's promoting the production?

I said, What do you care? You finally have a story that excites people in town and outside it as well.

Yes, he said, the biggest thing to take place here since Heftzi Columbus's body was found. And you saw what happened with that.

What happened? I asked.

Exactly, he said.

I said, I'll make sure to irritate the wound, make it bleed.

He said, Yeah, I've heard you're good at irritating people.

I was sitting in my office, planning agitations and disruptions, when Yalon Asor and the girl from the train appeared at my door. They asked if I knew Dalia Shushan.

Why do you ask? I said.

Tahel, the girl, was holding a book. I tried to catch its name. She noticed me looking and held it to her chest, protecting it with her arms.

We're working on a school project, said Yalon, with all the news and everything going on. We picked her. We read a little about her in this book. He pointed at Tahel and nodded.

Tahel swallowed. She said, So, we're doing a news report about it for media class.

A news report, I said.

There was wildness in the blue of her eyes, which she tried to tame. Her submissive stance, I easily recognized, was a façade. Something wanted to break through. That same predator that moved through her at the train station, during the train ride. Yalon was also alert to its revelation.

She nodded. A news report. We'll film it and if it turns out good we'll put it on YouTube.

And what's your angle?

Tahel said, Five things you never knew about Dalia Shushan.

So you don't care if the film gets made or not.

Why do you? said Tahel.

I said, What do you want to hear?

Yalon said, Anything.

I said, What book did you get, Elish Ben Zaken's *The Sky Is Dust*?

An expression I could not interpret inflamed Tahel's face. She quickly looked away.

Yalon said, Yes, how did you know?

There's no other book about her and Blasé.

Yalon said, We listened to the two CDs. We downloaded them at—

Don't say that, said Tahel, we don't want him to report us.

I laughed. Don't worry, I said, as long as you aren't stealing books from the library, the record labels can go to hell.

They said nothing. Yalon threw his head with that same twitch of the neck. His hair fell on his eyes.

What do you know about him? I asked.

About who? said Tahel.

About Elish Ben Zaken, may he rest in peace.

What does Elish have to do with this? said Yalon, his eyes hidden behind his hair. He reached over to Tahel. I saw the blood rising in her cheeks, her skin catching fire, the flipping heat in her irises.

Come on, he said, this wasn't a good idea.

In the 1990s, after military service, I enrolled in life sciences at Ben-Gurion University. I thought I'd figure out a solution while in college. My whole life, I trusted learning to heal me. I was a religious kid; I don't think I need to explain that to people who live in Sderot.

Religion, faith, offered me shelter, a framework, and answers. Until a certain age. Until a certain point. During military service, I could no longer view them as a source of comfort. I won't exhaust you with the details of the process. It's a familiar story, told thousands of times, the story of losing one's religion. But anyone who goes through it feels like the first person it ever happened to.

As a life sciences student, I was obliged to take four hours' worth of classes outside my major. When I looked over the list of courses on offer, one caught my eye: "The Literature of Possible Worlds: Science Fiction and Critical Thinking." Not that I was particularly interested in science fiction, and though I was a poet and occasionally submitted my poems to be published, I had no use for literature classes. But a rumor circulated among sciences and engineering students that the materials in the course were related to their studies. So I registered. I didn't realize it at the time, but looking back, I'm sure of it—that class changed my life.

The first class was devoted to clarifying the term "science fiction literature." The professor asked us what is real about literature, when it is clearly mostly fictional. What is "real" fiction and what is "unreal" fiction? Suddenly, I realized I had to give up my most basic assumptions, ones that seemed obvious to me. In that course, nothing was obvious, everything needed to be examined. I felt at home.

I remembered those kinds of discussions from Gmarah studies.

Then the professor asked what we thought differentiated literature that announced itself as representative of reality from literature that announced itself as attempting to create a nonexistent reality, but one with laws we can still understand. He said we could think about science fiction like this: as literature that builds on the ramifications of processes in our reality, or literature that takes one of our basic assumptions about the world and changes it.

This literature, he said, is one with a clear principle—each and every detail in the reality it depicts can be different. The reality isn't determined from on high and contains nothing essential. We can replace any truth we know with another and ask, What kind of people would we be then?

I know that sounds a little abstract. So here's an example that's relevant to our times. A significant part of our culture, our rituals, is founded in the fact that we're mortal, that death is an event that occurs to us, around us. What if we had efficient life extension technology that would make death a rare disruption in our existence? What would our retirement plans look like, our procreation, our wars, our economy, our religion?

The same principle also guides critical thinking: everything we accept as truth is incidental.

In spite of the shock the first class caused me, in spite of the professor's enthusiasm, I wasn't taken by the literary works we read. There were nice ideas, there were fascinating discussions, yes. But they were detached. They didn't apply to my questions.

Until one day the professor introduced Marxist theory with regards to the work of two authors. I'm not about to get into that. I just want to describe the shock I experienced. I was offered a way of considering my situation that required me to go back to zero and ask questions about the place where I live, the way society arranges itself, the interests motivating our beliefs and opinions, the division of resources.

I'll just say this: there are some enticing concepts, such as love, or God, or inner wholeness. But all of them are subject to material conditions—how much money we have, how it's divided, who calls the shots, our buying and selling power, who always profits from our staying at the bottom of the ladder, who creates the illusions that leave us unable to act, unable to change our reality.

These questions, which are burning questions in the Israel of recent years, have been catching fully on fire in Sderot. These are questions of awareness, of transparency: Who determines budgets? How does the encouragement of certain activities through financial incentives, and the killing of other activities through draining resources, affect our thinking, our voting patterns, even our biggest question: Is someone intentionally blinding us?

In the Berakhot tractate, we ask, Starting at what time are we allowed to read the morning Shema? Sages say, When there's enough light to distinguish between similar things like a dog and a wolf, or pale tones like powder blue and white or powder blue and the color of leeks. Leeks have a certain greenish hue. And powder blue, in all its varieties, is very close to that color. Powder blue has an important role in Jewish thought, because it is a sign of sunrise, a symbol of parting from black, which is a sign of night, the blending of colors within it. But powder blue still contains the memory of darkness, its secret. Jews are ordered to ask God to listen to them only from the point when they themselves can distinguish dark from bright, confusion from sobriety.

Combining two similar cultural events forces us to ask whether we use culture in order to live in the night or in the day. Next week, the public library will start a series of talks I'm curating with Israeli poets and writers. The role of literature is to make distinctions, to criticize, to make us rethink what we perceive as obvious. But can literature fill this role when the powers that be in city hall wish to castrate us, intervene in our content, and decide in advance which issues our speakers can address?

In a few weeks, filming will begin on a documentary film about the life and death of Dalia Shushan, may her righteous memory be a blessing. There have been quite a few TV cameras in Sderot in recent decades, quite a few news articles on different phenomena. None of that is unfamiliar to us residents. But I'd like to argue that the case of Dalia Shushan is different. Of all the artists and thinkers to grow out of this city, Dalia Shushan is the one closest to our hearts, our most precious possession. It's no coincidence that she's enveloped by an air of mystery. Not long ago, a young boy and girl who only recently discovered her work came to see me at the library. You should have seen the light in their eyes, the excitement with which they spoke about her music. There's no proof greater than this—Dalia Shushan gives voice to latent layers of the soul. She offers an emotional experience the force of which relies on the proximity, the secret, the intimacy, on her being our emotional powder blue.

This film intends to destroy this very quality and turn Dalia into some kind of free-for-all Tel Avivian asset, turning this wonderful spirit of Sderot into a sinful idol. The director Noya Resnick's mode of operation is known to all. She uses the less fortunate for the purposes of glorifying her own name.

Filming cannot take place without support from the Sderot municipality. But what are the interests at work behind the scenes? What funds will be used? Which pockets will be filled? Who stands to gain here? Whose job is it to blind us, to convince us that we would benefit from this robbery of Dalia Shushan?

❋ ❋ ❋

ASRAF SAID, YOU'VE SURPRISED ME. I THOUGHT YOU WERE A
sinner of passion but now it turns out you're a sinner of spite.
What I don't understand is where you're going with this.

The summons to visit his office arrived on Sunday morning.
Alice Shitrit wrote me, He's got a time window between some of
his afternoon meetings. Back at Shabbat dinner, Simo said, I
don't understand what you wrote there, but you pissed Asraf off
good. Did I or did I not tell you to be careful?

I said, I'm tired of threats, explicit or insinuated. So he's dangerous. And what about me? Am I nothing? Have you forgotten
about what you repeated to us all through childhood, about what
heals the soul? Revenge. So now you're telling me to chicken out?
I've had enough, Dad.

To Asraf I said, I was very clear in my newspaper piece.

Maybe, said Asraf, maybe. His almond-shaped eyes lingered
on me. He said, I don't think I fully understood your hints about
corruption in city hall. I don't think they have legs to stand on either. I don't think city hall has ever been cleaner of impertinent
motives, or certainly of shady dealings.

I said, I think residents have a right to know you're camou-
flaging your own private interests as public.

Out of the blue, he laughed. He said, I learned those Marx clichés too, in my social sciences degree.

You're right, that was an unnecessarily derogatory statement.
But still, it wasn't wrong.

He said nothing.

I'd written that piece on the advice of the paper's editor. We
agreed that I'd also post it in Rabble, a leading social activism
blog. People kept sharing it on Facebook over the weekend. It
received some hype. A national newspaper contacted me, asking
me to report on the battle in a special column on their website.
Everyone's become socially conscious all of a sudden. Social
awareness is a hot commodity. And effective bleach for one's
conscience.

I posted a link to the article on Friday through @TheAbominable's Twitter account. I tweeted: #ParrotNahum. I'll buy a parrot and name it Farkash. I'll chatter to it shamelessly, shamelessly.

One hour later: #ParrotNahum. Marxists, Communists, social activists. Ultimately, they always have a sentimental Jewish soul.

To Asraf I said, I know you plan to remove any obstacle from this film's path so that Therese Kavillio-Buganim agrees to launch her reading promotion project here.

He said, You know how much traffic the library is going to get? I'd like to believe that you fight to make every child a reader. Not to mention the employment opportunities this would offer residents.

Have you asked yourself what motive she has to promote a film about Dalia Shushan?

I think she's interested in culture.

You're an experienced politician. I don't think that would satisfy you.

I've got no reason to question her.

That's a fairer answer, but I still don't believe it.

So what do you want?

I said, She can exploit Dalia's public image all she wants. She can appropriate it, turn it into a marketing platform. She's got too much money and too many lawyers to be stopped. Then I fell silent.

On Saturday night I tweeted: #ParrotNahum #TheNigerianWhisperer. Chatter versus whisper. Ooh, I can't stand the suspense.

The user Ohi-V, whose profile photo was a picture of Ohila Vaknin, tweeted in response: You're just picking fights. Disgusting.

I tweeted back: I hate fights where the right side is so lame you feel like supporting the wrong one.

She tweeted: Lame indeed. Takes one to know one.

Other users joined the conversation with the same mixture of glee and poison characteristic of social media arguments.

Asraf asked again, Where are you going with this?

I said, You know how easy it is to start an online fire and how quickly things get out of control. I'm willing to settle things down, but in return I ask that you persuade Therese Kavillio to stop her attempts to interview Esther Shushan or make any thrilling discoveries. People's personal memories of Dalia should remain personal. Juicy details from her past should remain in the past.

Asraf said, I hear Esther Shushan agreed to be in the film. Who are you to decide for her? Did you ask her before you went on this war in her name?

I said, Esther's a smart woman. Her statements are unexpected, and she takes pity on no one. But you know just as well as I do how they'll make her look. Like an elderly, bereaved Moroccan woman whose pain turned her into an eccentric.

He nodded.

And tell Therese I have to meet her. Tell her Elish sends his best.

IT HAD BEEN NEARLY FIFTEEN YEARS SINCE I LAST LISTENED TO "The Land of Shadow." I'd converted it into a digital format when tapes and tape decks went extinct. I burned it onto a CD. That method of storage had also gone the way of the dodo, taking its scratches and fractures with it. When the time arrived, I downloaded it to my phone's music player, and all that was left were magnetic sequences, a genetic code, its shape, the depiction of its behavior as an aural being. And even this simplification contained an excessive presence, a boil that burned someplace, its imagined branches reaching all organs. The exit path was sketched onto my vinyl soul, lumps and rails, with Dalia's performance serving only as the needle, running over the engravings and translating them into a corporeal tangibility. How can I otherwise explain the way in which it was mine more than anything else?

At the end of the day that Tahel and Yalon visited my office, I
put on my headphones back at home. My finger trembled before
I touched the music player icon on the phone's screen. I won't
lie—the volume of time, its silence, stood between me and the
action. The many years the song had absorbed, and which unloaded into the mind upon its playing. Their profiles hovered before me as they turned to leave my office. Tahel shook off Yalon's
arm, which pulled her away, and looked at me. Anxiety, yes, was
contained in her expression, but also a thread of light whitening
within her, its glow bursting through her eyes. Yalon was also
infected by this anxiety, but his enthusiasm was different, some
spark that I attributed to encountering the Blasé albums. It was
hard to miss.

I listened again to the hesitant strumming of the chords, the
break, the background rustles, and the inharmonious harmony,
the smothered sound of a home recording, like slapping cardboard, and yet a harmony nevertheless, and then Dalia's singing,
the low voice that is all seduction and darkness, *Now you know
there shall be no more death in the Land of Shadow, to the place
you beseech*, and then a twist, the rising abyss, *You shall not be
redeemed by love, pain shan't be your savior, all that is will rise to
the extant.* Or the abyss into which singing plummets, *and you
shan't be brought down in the shackles of metaphors, free in the
web of flesh.* I used to think Dalia sang from within an abyss, *your
ears are pricked to the depth of silence, your eyes torn to see in the
dark*, but now I realized she was creating it, so that her voice
could be heard. *And by these signs you shall know that your kingdom is nigh, son of man, arise, take up and read.* There, that cry,
in which the voice runs off-key when freeing itself from the melo-
dious trap. The command to call. But to call in whose name, to
call what?

Tahel and Yalon occupied my mind. The way they recoiled
when I asked about their relationship with Elish Ben Zaken, their
attempt to offhandedly wave away his importance to them, which

only served to further reveal it. Yalon referred to him by his first name alone, as if he were a friend or acquaintance.

I'd been planning this visit for close to fifteen years. Two kilometers as the crow flies. The volume of time, its silence, stood between me and the action. The many years the space had absorbed until it became uncrossable. But I could no longer postpone passing through it. I stood before the gate of the house, not far from the ball field. The weight of the late Kislev rain sped up the earth's growth forces. Birds pecked the ground cozily, foraging and toddling. Among the shaved branches of a poinciana tree, a peacock stood in all its glory, the eyes in its tail glowing in the noon light, outshining the guava tree's eruption of foliage. I stood before the door. Brown, made of thin boards. Esther Shushan opened it.

There was no need to introduce myself. She recognized me. Twenty-seven revolutions of the earth around the sun, three hundred twenty-eight revolutions of the moon around the earth, 9,850 revolutions of the earth around its axis. And the translation of their evaporation into body cells and mind.

She spoke my name. Said she once saw me waiting for her daughter behind the field. Childhood games that required secrecy. As if adults actually cared.

She was different than Dalia as only one family member can be different from another. Their shared nucleus was the starting point, the basis of comparison. Its expressions in the world, in the flesh mold, in the eyeballs, the shine set within them, are what sparked this discussion of difference. I saw her windswept facial features. She said she spent most of her time in the yard. We crossed the house and walked out into a second yard stretching behind it, concealed by curtains of bindweeds, a purple avalanche.

✷ ✷ ✷

I DIDN'T LINGER. I DIDN'T WANT TO STAY LONG. MY HEART WAS damaged with every passing minute. I asked her about the movie.

Someone spoke to her, she said. A cute little Moroccan girl came all the way there to see her. Sat right there, the seat where you're sitting.

I asked if her name was Ohila.

Yes, she said. God help me with all these new names. She said she didn't mind them filming, they could come to the yard.

I asked if it wasn't difficult for her, this snooping.

She said, They made up their own Dalia. It isn't my daughter. Every day I know what she looks like. She's looking more and more like her grandmother. Her kids too. One of them has Yossef's size, kind of little and short with that Alfassi nose. Esther didn't insist they name one of them after him or herself.

I said nothing.

She said, But that other Dalia, the one that sings, the one that swallowed glass, she isn't mine. So what do I care if they want me to talk?

I said, I loved her. The same scream that passed through me the day she died now filled my throat. I had no intention of crying.

Esther said, Go ahead and cry, *ya bnini*, that's what you came here for, isn't it?

Why this boiling, the tears, what survival mechanism did it serve? I kept quiet for as long as I could.

Esther said, Go get yourself some water from the kitchen. I didn't offer you anything. Where's my head today?

I got up. I went inside. The kitchen cabinets were scratched. Crumbling Formica. I stood before them for a few moments. Suddenly, Snot and Niro and Costa and Dalia herself appeared in the space, all of my missing friends, my disappearing friends, the friendships that time cut short, and their presence exacerbated the tears that were crawling up to my ducts. But in the core of those tears, a glint of joy lit up, wild, ruthless, for having had the privilege to know them, for carrying them inside of me, for leading them to the doorways I had to look forward to, for having something of them, for them still being with me, for not having robbed a thing of them, and for not having to steal looks at what I'd been given. Esther called from behind me, on the top shelf, by the fridge.

She sipped the water I offered her.

When the term of silence, the term of suffocation, was over, I said, After Dalia was murd ... after Dalia.

She looked at me, a weak smile on her lips. Her hair was already white, a kind of solid white.

I said, Did someone come to interview you, a guy—

Ben Zaken, she said. Elish, from Ashkelon.

I said, You've got a great memory.

She said, I wouldn't have remembered if my niece hadn't reminded me.

Your niece?

Ronnit. She and Dalia were best friends.

I said, I've never heard about her.

There was a rift between them, but then Dalia moved in with her in Tel Aviv.

Did they meet, Dalia and Elish Ben Zaken?

No. Ronnit met him a few years later. By chance. That's God's handiwork. Never stops fixing, never stops spoiling.

I said, Did you hear that Elish died a few months ago?

She had. She said Ronnit visited the shiva at his mother's house in Ashkelon and then came to see Esther, along with her eldest son and the other child growing in her womb. She's like me, said Esther. Ronnit. She doesn't want anything to do with the Dalia who sings.

I nodded.

She said, She married a newly observant guy, a Russian. I don't know if she's happy. One of them isn't his.

One of who?

The children. The eldest. Not the one in her belly. The one in her belly is his. I told her right away, as soon as I saw the eldest kid. There's a dead part in the boy that hasn't fallen apart yet, it's still there.

I said nothing.

She said, She gave him a religious name. Akiva. Like the word *okev*, following. Who's he following? Maybe his real father. Anyway, they're coming back. They're on their way. She sighed. She said, We'll be helpless to resist them.

I said, Resist who?

She said, Ronnit's been calling me in recent years, bless her heart, to talk. I ask her, Why are you alone, but she doesn't hear me. She calls to talk but doesn't hear what I've got to say.

Elish Ben Zaken, did he tell her something the two of you didn't know?

About Dalia? What is there to tell?

I don't know.

She said, *Allah yerahmo.* Ronnit said he never sat still, always moving around, looking into things. He had the accident because his head was such a mess. But he keeps going, he isn't done dying.

I said, I thought he committed—but I didn't finish the sentence.

The flower beds were neat. A few anemones burned in a delineated green carpet. In another bed there were irises, white and yellow tongues sticking out. Not far from them were mustard flowers and marigolds, a loud, yellow tumult. Esther pointed at a fenced-in plot where wormwood bushes branched out wildly along with the toxic silver of sage. Those are the herbs, she said. She grew them for the fragrance and the abundance. She gave the leaves away to her neighbors.

I asked if the birds didn't threaten her plants. She said that ever since Yossef died she and the birds had an understanding. She allotted them a living area in the front yard, and they stayed out of the backyard. I told her I wanted to stop the movie from filming her. I said Dalia deserved to keep some of her secrets.

She said, He had secrets, Ronnit's friend. I could see her love wasn't gone.

What secrets?

That's what Ronnit said, that in the last month of his life he was looking into the affairs of some guy, Buganim, a Moroccan who got rich. As if Moroccans aren't allowed to have money.

I told her I had to go, but that I had at my disposal an inheritance that was rightfully hers too. A song Dalia wrote for me. Maybe she wrote it for Esther too.

She said, *Ya bnini*, that Dalia who sings, who swallowed glass, that belongs to your grief. If you want to say goodbye, if you want to start remembering the way the living remember, you'd better give it to the person who needs it.

The gate slammed behind me. The idea for the article budded within me. I knew who it would be written for.

I ARRIVED AT THE LIBRARY THAT AFTERNOON AND TOOK MY REGular tour. Oshri was sitting in the children's circulation room, cross-legged, on a cushion, six stacked books on the rug in front of him as he was reading the seventh. I crouched beside him and looked at the books. Good taste, I thought. But they were all complicated coming-of-age stories. *Marius*, *Love That Dog*, *The Jungle Book*, *Skellig*, *The Bartimaeus Sequence*.

He noticed me, glanced my way from the corner of his eye, but didn't move his gaze away from Rolf Docker's *Marius*. I knew the final lines of the book by heart. I hated them.

I asked him if he thought Marius was making it up or if he was really seeing the things he told about. He said, Can you give me permission to borrow all of them? She, he said, pointing at the temporary librarian, said I can only have two.

No problem, I said, I'll run the books through the system myself. I understand you already got a library card.

He didn't answer.

I said, All right, come see me at the office when you want. I imagine your sister and Yalon are already waiting there.

He got up heavily. Weighty skull, thoughtful eyes, turning off and lighting up by the force of a passing thought. The same blue dwelled in his eyes as in Tahel's, but its appearance was tamer, weaker. I wondered if this was a sign of the illness Yalon had mentioned, the meekness of those flaming irises. He picked up the books and followed me. He said, Marius definitely saw Mr. Death. He didn't make that up.

THE TWO WERE SITTING IN MY OFFICE WITH SHIFRA. SHE MUST have made some extrapolations when I interrogated her about Tahel's family. She said she didn't know much, only that they were Moroccan, originally from Ashkelon, and that they moved to the Lakeside neighborhood before Operation Protective Edge. That's when things clicked for me. I met Elish at the home he rented in that neighborhood during the war and he told me he'd come to Sderot to be near his family.

They were ensconced in the leather chairs. Yalon's head was lowered. Tahel stared in front of her. On her lap was a notepad and she was distractedly crushing the top page. Shifra served them hot cocoa, which she found God knows where. The mugs were still steaming. With a natural gesture, she reached over to rub Oshri's hair as he walked in. Do you want some hot cocoa too, sweetheart? she said.

I realized I was suppressing my automatic urge to offer condolences to him and his sister, to rub their hair too, maybe even to wrap them in a hug. No, it was a foreign urge that had gotten into me. Whose was it? My mental defenses snapped into action.

Oshri nodded. I took the books from him and handed them to Shifra. I asked her to run them through the borrowing system.

Shifra left and returned, using her measure of mercy, books, and hot cocoa in hand. Oshri sipped it carefully. Yalon and Tahel remained petrified in their positions. I closed the door behind Shifra and said, Listen to this.

My player was connected to an exterior loudspeaker. Dalia's voice rose from within it, the unappeasable singing with all its yearning to heal. Oshri opened his book upon the first few notes and dove in. Tahel's eyes closed. Yalon tensed in his seat, his entire being aimed at the place from which the song was born into space. I saw the shine that had filled him. I recognized that devotion to music, some inner growth in its early stages.

WHEN THE SONG ENDED I SAID, THIS IS A GIFT. YOU'RE THE FIRST people, besides me, to ever hear this song. I want to give you a copy. I think this is a great discovery. You could write your assignment around it.

Tahel widened her eyes. There was a fragile clarity in them. And suspicion. She said, Why did you play this for us? Why are you giving it to us?

Yalon looked at her. He shifted nervously but didn't speak.

I said, Because the song no longer belongs to me. Dalia left it with me, and I kept it, but it's time for it to move into someone else's hands.

Tahel continued crushing the notepad in her hand. Yalon's eyes burned in his head. His lips wanted to move, but he enforced silence upon them.

Why, said Tahel, why?

I said, I would have given it to Elish. Right now, I think you need it more than I do.

She froze.

Oshri said, with the dreamy tone of one awakening from deep reading, Tahel, tell him.

No, said Tahel.

Yalon said, Yes, tell him.

Oshri said, He needs to know.

She glanced at him and he went back to his book. His finger touched the line where he'd paused in his reading.

Tahel flipped back in her notepad. She handed it to me. A nearly empty, lined page. At the center a sentence appeared in sloppy yet effortful handwriting: *Now you know there shall be no more death in the Land of Shadow.* It was flanked by a frame of thin, black ink lines, like a narrow lattice. I could deduce their repeated scratching, the deciphering work that had been performed as they were sketched.

What's this? I said.

Yalon said, It's Elish's notepad.

Tahel said, We found it in his apartment, when we went looking for clues.

That's when we met you on the train, said Yalon, remember?

That same day? I asked.

Yes, he said. Tahel heard something. A cop talked to her mother—

Don't tell him, said Tahel.

Never mind, said Yalon. We decided to investigate.

So you went to his apartment by yourselves?

I had a key, said Tahel. Elish left us ke— She fell silent. I recognized her struggle against tears.

I'm so sorry to hear that, I said.

Yalon said, He wrote a whole page about Dalia Shushan after this one, about how something in the investigation of her death didn't resolve like he'd thought.

What did he think?

We thought you might know, said Yalon, because you knew her.

I said, But how are you connected to all this?

Tahel signaled to Yalon with her eyes. Her silence extended. She swallowed whenever her mouth opened to answer. Yalon told a bizarre tale about a girl named Kalanit Shaubi, his grandmother's maid's daughter, who'd disappeared for three days, and returned without realizing she'd been gone. She only remembered her bus ride from Beersheba to Sderot. As far as she was concerned, a single hour had gone by. He told me they had followed a shadow man who Yalon had filmed on his phone talking to Kalanit, who claimed she hadn't talked to anyone. He said they'd decided to investigate the case even though it was in the middle of the war, and that Elish helped them.

I asked, Why would he do that?

Tahel whispered, stifled, Because he's a detective. He's an excellent detective. He's the best detective in the world.

I said, But it sounds so far-fetched.

Sleepily, his voice hoarser than before, Oshri said, He didn't come to help because of Kalanit. He came to help because of the thicket.

What thicket?

The thicket by our house, said Tahel.

In the Lakeside neighborhood?

A dimple flickered in Yalon's cheek, and a matching one responded in Tahel's. Two rows of braces emerged over two rows of emotionally bared teeth. In the course of one moment there was tension and relaxation. Perhaps that's why I gave them the song. Their twinning erupted.

Yes, said Tahel, right across from our house. There was a ghost and . . .

Yalon said, Her mother saw her.

Tahel said, She was in the thicket. Not my mom, the ghost of Heftzi Columbus. My mom saw—

A great racket was contained in the word "thicket," and the word "ghost" appeared within it as a ghost in and of itself, the cracking of a twig in the dark, a melody distorted by the earpiece, back then on the landline in my parents' house. On the other end, Pini Pita's voice rushed through the wires. What did you do, he said, are you intent on inviting ghosts?

I laughed.

Why are you laughing? Pini had said. You think I'm joking?

Why are you being so tough all of a sudden? That's no good.

Pini said, Nahum, you're crazy. I felt the aftershock all the way here. Then he continued describing how he was in the middle of a performance and was supposed to guess the thoughts of an audience volunteer. She walked up onstage and the typical tension rose. Then, all of a sudden, he felt a shivering he could barely control, and the hint of her thought about the number, the object, and the person she'd picked, slipped away from him, replaced with entirely different mental impressions.

You remember that time we went, he said, when that idiot Sabah made us walk into the thicket? I saw the same image in my head. The trees, the empty area between them with that chopped trunk in the middle, remember, there was a dead dog there, and the darkness came and ate.

Ate what? I wanted to ask, but I knew Pini would say no more. And there was no need for him to. This expression returned Pini's palpability that the last few years had melted. Someone, maybe one of Niro's friends, had spread the rumor about his powers of conjecture. And it had permeated. Even Sabah asked me, flushed, if it was true, during one of our brief, hostile catch-ups that feigned the affection customary between old friends. I told him I had no idea. I lied. I'd met Pini quite a bit during the year when his name was being passed around, each time in connection with a different marvel. Eventually, a talent agent came to his house, one who was already managing a girl who advised her audience about which of their romances would bear fruit and which were merely fleeting, as well as a young man who brought dead appliances and machines, clocks and electronics of all sorts, back to life. Pini's mother objected. She said it was a hereditary power that was meant to service the community, not for entertainment or moneymaking purposes. They argued inside the house as I waited out on the porch for Pini to come out.

His mother said, This isn't something you take or receive, it's something that just is. You can do it, do it for others, it's out in the world, but it isn't there until it starts activating you and you start activating it. You know just as well as I do. It isn't yours, but it's for you, so it can be for others.

"It," she kept repeating, "it," she didn't say "power," she didn't say "talent," didn't say "gift," didn't say "purpose," didn't say "destiny." "It" contained everything, the thing, its course of action, its subject and object.

Pini didn't listen. He pleaded and pleaded until she agreed to one show at a desolate club in Beersheba, which gave birth to a series of shows, until the permanent style of the performance took shape and he and his mother made enough money to buy a house in Holon. Pini performed all sorts of tricks, secondary expressions of "it." It remained intentionally concealed, its sense of truth. He asked his clients to think of a number, an object, a person. But a choice, as random as it may be, is always a result of a primordial emotion. And the way Pini drew the names out of them stirred up the same emotion. His clients didn't realize he'd shifted a hidden part of them into the light, a part they believed was a surplus of their existence. Sediment. Broken furniture they'd pushed away with the flow of time.

He didn't spare me from it when I refused to listen. He would speak my name, and a particle within me would respond. I didn't bother keeping what had happened from him. I told him about Cocoa Pup, his unbearable barking, and the madness that overtook Sabah and infected Ehud Barda, the violent celebration and how I remained alone with the shattered canine body, beating weakly, dying. He said nothing the whole time I stuttered after less stifled words. I asked what I could do now. He said the years would repair the rift we'd created in the air of the thicket, or not. And that if they didn't, I'd know.

His palpability was returned to me. I held on to the moment on both ends, like a coin with Pini's portrait engraved on each of its faces—ten-year-old Pini with a round, milky face and buzzed ginger hair, whispering, Feel that power, this is not the kind of place you forget, and the estimated Pini of seventeen years old, borrowed from the black-and-white photographs that accompanied advertisements for his performances all over the country, a face whose dimensions were transformed by its frame of fluffy orange hair, looking long and serious, a portrait that whispered, The darkness came and ate.

THAT NIGHT, I SHIFTED FROM RIPS OF ONE CONSCIOUSNESS INTO rips of another. My dreaming self and senses at its disposal, its objection to the shielding of daylight, the ruckus. It may not have been able to bear the storm of sights and had to flee to wakefulness. But waking hadn't rid it of the freshness of memory, and my awake self attempted to wallow in sleep. I innocently cross the *mikveh* yard, a path that is a paved scratch within an overgrown lawn. I know about the murderer roaming Sderot, freely killing boys and girls. But some odd peace comes upon me, the world is still, even the breeze in the fiery foliage with its chubby aphids, swelling among the stems like fruit. I fear that I do not fear enough, I fear that I have good reasons for not fearing. The tranquility crushes my breath inside my chest. There is some movement in the doorway to the *mikveh*, a dip before an engagement celebration, I recall. I hurry over. A frozen strip of metal clings to my leg. Cocoa Pup's wheezing becomes trapped in the interim space of movement, the ease of the animal's soul as it abandons the entanglement of blood vessels through his body, the form falling away from its content, rising to a place where the forms are. Relief is pushed into my hands as they break his neck, becoming a layer of skin, I know. In a house I do not recognize I see Tova and Chantal lying in iron bunk beds without mattresses, Chantal on the top bunk, Tova on the bottom. The legs of the bed are wrapped with bundles of twigs that light up, flames overtaking them. I'm already there, kneeling before the tiny torches, patting them pointlessly. I do not burn. My palms are unable to choke down the fire. I grab the burning sticks and swallow them. My throat smarts. Slowly, my room shrinks. I have no idea which direction my head lies, whether under the window or near one of the walls, but the esophagus smarts. I turn my head and release the acid. These things take place in one of those hours invaded and cleaved by a second hour, the hour echoing with Chantal's crying. She can't find Cocoa Pup.

Tova and I joined her on her search. We looked through the nearby streets, calling his name. Tova was gripped by the same panic as Chantal. A dog like that, a cutie, would definitely get lost, or worse, he's a fool, after all, you always have to keep him on the leash, otherwise you'll find him with his nose shoved into some trash can. How could he have gone out by himself? He might have eaten poison, Abutbul from the grocery store keeps complaining about his barking at night. What barking? He tweets like a bird.

I couldn't bear Tova's blather. I suggested we split up. Only on my own did I realize that Tova had become more attached to the dog than Chantal. For Chantal he was an accessory. An ugly, violent Pekinese that attacked cats bigger than himself, abhorred by his master, who combed his coat and kept it shiny. But Tova was affectionate with him, played with him, talked to him. I imagined the two of them, crying back and forth through the early morning, their voices breaking.

In the chill of late Nissan, the light began to harden into a whole sunrise, a layer of shimmering, crystal medium. Suddenly, I realized I myself was still calling out that hollow name. I turned into the path descending to the synagogue to say the morning prayer. The attendees were already in the *d'zimra* passages, and unlike Saturday, the pacing of the prayer answered to the business of the weekday, a brief prayer before worshippers headed to work. This was the second shift, I knew. The meticulous, wishing not to rush, had already prayed at first light. I found a *tefillin* and a *tallit* for the use of random visitors like myself. In the thin burst of the silence of wrapping myself, I thought about coming in with first light the following day, skipping the obligatory prayer at the school synagogue, with its smelly armpits and bad jokes. But as I stepped out of the elegant safe haven of embroidered *parochet* curtain and wooden benches and leather-bound, gold-lettered prayer books, the hollow name escaped my mouth again. The outside, which was present wherever I turned, and every bird the size of a fist, and every insect with its joints' lacy tangle, announcing its realness, still contained the name Cocoa Pup within it, allowing it to echo, absorbing this corpse as it converted into rot and juices. They rose up the throat upon its sounding, the juices, pausing bitterly in the blockade of teeth I'd set against them.

I returned home and told my mother, who was getting ready to go to work, that I thought I had the flu.

The flu, Msodi said incredulously. Since when do people get the flu after Passover?

I have a temperature, I said. I think. I'm dizzy.

She placed her hand on my forehead. Hard to tell, she said flatly. Go lie down. I'll get you some water and medicine.

I told her not to worry about me, that I'd manage. She said, Have it your way, you're a big boy, thank the Lord.

The fever became evident that evening. My throat dried out and my head pulsated, a flock of burning wasps attacking and retreating. A reddish, rough, keratin aura was added to the desk, the chair, the lampshade, one of a series of identical lampshades that my mother insisted on using on every bulb. So did the outlines of the photographs hanging in my room. My bar mitzvah picture. Tova and Chantal's little heads from the joint birthday party we threw for them two years ago, when Chantal received the Pekinese puppy she'd yearned for, all stared into my delusions, piercing through. As did their crying. And Simo's rebuke as he told them to stop crying and go do something, hang signs on trees and electric poles, organize a search party with their classmates, and Msodi's sighs, her crude condolences, saying there was nothing to be done, it was the way of the world, and they had to accept the fact that Cocoa Pup wouldn't be coming back, that he was probably run over by a car, his body lying on the side of the road. For three whole days I stared at the cool wall.

(I, MEANING I, SUDDENLY HAVE DOUBTS. I DOUBT THIS STORY IS completely fictional, I suspect it might be just as solid as my experience. Some vague memory, something similar happened to me. But before I can hold on to it, it evaporates, and once again I, meaning I, am foggy, become trapped in the story as it passes through me.)

PERHAPS THE CONVERSATION WITH PINI WAS WHAT SUMMONED Niro, or tilted our trajectories toward each other, a slight tilt that forced them to intersect. I regained my physical power at once, waking up refreshed, almost cheerful. Not exactly. My limbs were still spent, but they already burned with the momentum of the victory of spirit over them, even though they were frail enough to move according to its lucidity. I was lucid. I remember the clearheadedness. My mother's expression, a mesmerizing artwork of capillaries and small muscles, an energetic pageant.

Yahsra alai, she said when she saw me coming out of my room.

My face was already washed, and I felt the glistening dew of water against my skin. Good morning, I said. The velvet of the *tallit* and *tefillin* cases and the roughness of the silver embroidery felt good against my palm. I replaced the *tallit* to match the size of my growing body, but kept the case in which it had been given me upon my bar mitzvah. At the end of every prayer I struggled to fit the folded fabric in.

Where are you going? my mother asked. Sit down, I'll make you something to eat, you haven't eaten in three days. She took some vegetables and eggs out of the fridge.

But the agony had boiled the veins, cleaning them out. I said, I'll eat when I get back from synagogue.

Where are you going to find someone to pray with at this hour? The synagogue is empty. And what about school? Aren't you going back?

I looked at the clock. Eight thirty. I shrugged and walked out.

A late Nissan that assaults the senses. I crossed it. Msodi was right. The central synagogue was already empty save for an elderly dues collector, sitting and consulting the Chumash. Probably reading this week's Torah portion, I thought, and if it ought remain until the third day, it shall be burned in the fire, do not turn to mediums or seek out spiritists. But the sensation of writhing flesh, the nerves struggling to act under their pressure, their glove of abomination, dissipated from my hands. Gone. The dues collector looked me over suspiciously as I walked in. White beard, face heavy with blood, withering gaze. His suspicion disappeared when he noticed the *tallit* and *tefillin* I carried with me. He said, There's no *minyan*.

I nodded and took a seat on a long bench in front of the Torah arc. Fatigue plopped down inside of me all throughout my lone-some prayer. I stood up to leave.

The dues collector stopped me. He said, Who are you? You never come here.

I shook my head.

Why don't you come on Saturdays?

I said, I'm Farkash's son.

Farkash from city hall.

I didn't answer.

He said, So bring him with you next time.

He isn't observant.

No such thing. A Jew's a Jew.

My mother had already gone to work. There was a plate of salad, hard-boiled eggs, and sliced bread on the kitchen counter. The gleam of oil on the vegetables made me feel sick. So did the hardened calcium of the eggs. I sat on the porch for a few min-utes, alert to the weight gathering in my muscles. I got up with an effort. I wandered idly through the streets, gritting my teeth. I passed the new event hall, saw wedding preparations, cars un-loading merchandise. I crossed the small park at the foot of the EMT station. There was the usual abundance of flowers and the wild eruption of weeds. I didn't find a point in asking about the point of all these signs of vitality. In the distance, I saw the high school, with its elongated edifices. I hadn't taken my back-pack with me, anyway. I walked around it, lingering between buildings. Birds pecked among the lawns. Laundry hung on lines in the woolly light. So what? A young woman urged a runny-nosed, reluctant tot, dragging him behind her. I kept go-ing. I reached the outskirts of town, Sderot Junction. The honk-ing of cars made me shudder.

Hey, kid, someone yelled, watch where you're going.

The car pulled up next to me. Niro was in the passenger seat, his lips stretched into a wide smile. He said, You, Nahum? I can't believe it. I'm so disappointed in you, skipping school like this.

A green, beat-up Subaru with a shattered headlight, the metal around it bruised. The guy in the driver's seat laughed for no reason. Four years had gone by, but the features of the boy he used to be still burned within him like a filament. The downer kid. I stared at them.

What are you standing there for? he said, pale like I don't know what. Get in already.

I opened the door. I remained paralyzed on the side of the road. I hadn't seen Niro in years either. After that meeting, at Hanukkah, he came to visit me. He looked at the naked walls of my room, save for the bar mitzvah photos and the pictures of my sisters, which my mother had duplicated and framed. Damn, he said, boring as hell. He convinced me to buy some posters. I said that would be idolatry. We argued with growing fury about religion and faith. He was sharper than I was. I could feel his roughness, his flame. Whenever I screened his phone calls, I imagined the conversation I'd just given up, the natural sense of intimacy that had washed over me as early as that evening. It emerged again now in his smile. At least the feeling was mutual. The downer kid honked again, waking me up.

The car was filled with the bitter, accumulated aroma of bodies. The seat covers were old and scratched. It wasn't clear whether the stains on them were remnants of the fabric's original patterns, or random dirt. Where are we going? I asked over the roar of the wind. I couldn't hear Niro and the downer kid's conversation.

Niro yelled, Getting some things for the party tonight. No-good Hershko is enlisting in two weeks.

The downer kid yelled, No-good your mama, what's so bad about being a jobnick?

Niro rolled up his window and turned to face me. So, he said, are you still orthodox?

Who's Hershko? I said.

Niro patted the downer kid's back. Hannan Hershkowitz, he said, the Romanian son of a bitch, at your service.

* * *

WHO'S HONKING OUTSIDE LIKE THAT? SAID TOVA, THEN RAN OUT to the porch to check. Chantal followed her out, then ran back inside. Nahum, she marveled, there are two boys in the car, they're asking for you. So that's why you dressed up like that.

The screen door slammed behind Tova. She said, How handsome, and Chantal giggled. I believed Chantal's giggle, but Tova's over-the-top gesture was colored by a different emotion.

Introduce us to them, said Tova. Especially the one with the long curly hair.

Get out of my face, I said.

Come on, Nahum, she said, invite them in.

I made a mistake earlier and asked Tova for advice on my outfit. All those light transitional sweaters seemed to lack character, and my Shabbat clothes were too fancy, those striped white shirts and pressed slacks. Of course she asked where I was going, trying to stand out like that.

I didn't answer.

But what do you want to look like? she asked. Square, like usual? She was biting the base of her finger. She said, You think we'll find Cocoa Pup?

I told her I thought our mother was right.

She nodded with a gravity that instantly evaporated. She regained the excessive excitement she'd demonstrated when she walked into the room. She rummaged through the closet and tossed a pair of pants at me. These are your most washed-out jeans, she said. Start with these and find a shirt that goes with them. Then she left.

I tried different shirts and sweaters. The evenings were chilly, and I could freeze on the beach. Finally, I settled on a yellow short-sleeved T-shirt over a long-sleeved white undershirt.

Gross, said Chantal as she followed Tova inside. Why are you looking so shabby all of a sudden?

You should have told me you wanted to look like a stoner, said Tova. Anyway, you need to shave.

I fingered the flimsy hair that had started growing on my chin and lip. Two weeks ago, my father bought me an electric razor after I refused to use his razor blades. The fuzz grew without any order, one hair here, a small tangle there. I was convinced that shaving would put some logic into the growth.

Chantal followed me to the bathroom door, which I slammed in her face. From behind the door she cried, Oh, come on already, who are you going out with?

Niro and Hershko were wearing the same clothes they had on that morning. Hershko's pants bore the marks of tahini from the falafel we ate that afternoon at the Ashkelon shopping center. We'd spent the whole morning at the pedestrian mall. We went to a liquor store where the owner knew Hershko. He laughed and said, No need for an ID, I know you're eighteen. Hershko was broad-bodied and limb-swollen, but the chubbiness of his cheeks, the freckles that covered them and his bulbous nose, and the blue, squinting buttons of his eyes made him look younger. His hair was made up of small, tight curls. The store owner called him Steel Wool.

He and Niro filled a cart with six-packs and a few bottles of arak. The owner said, I've got awesome whiskey, a new brand, got it a week ago. Niro nodded.

What about some shandy or Breezers? said the owner. They're'll probably be girls there, right?

Load it up, said Hershko.

How about some reinforcements?

Niro said, No, we're good.

From his back pocket, Hershko pulled out a wad of bills. I addressed a silent question at Niro. Niro shrugged. When Hershko licked his fingertip to separate the bills, a silver ring glimmered on his pinky, studded with a single turquoise.

He spared no expense at the grocery store either, loading

the cart with snacks. I asked if he didn't think he was overdo-ing it.

You only enlist once, said Hershko.

Worst-case scenario, you'll have some left over for Indepen-dence Day, said Niro.

Is Dahan bringing potatoes? asked Hershko.

Niro confirmed and added some bags of marshmallows to the pile of salty snacks.

When we put the bags in the back seat alongside the booze, Hershko said, Nahum, honestly, we weren't planning on picking up hitchhikers. You might have to ride home in the trunk.

Then he pulled up his shirt. A pack of chocolate was tucked between his belt and his white skin. Niro pulled two other candy bars from his sleeve.

The two of them broke out in laughter.

You should see your face, said Niro.

Why, I said, what, you stole it?

Taxes, said Hershko, value added.

But why? I asked. You've got enough money.

It's dessert, said Hershko. Let's go get something to eat. I'm starving.

A few pigeons pounced on the falafel ball Niro tossed onto the ground, then scattered away from the pedestrian traffic. We sat on a bench under the ficus tree. The dense foliage was aflame with noon light. A breeze passed, its core preserving something of the night.

Between bites, Niro told me about this tradition of theirs. Six months ago, they were caught stealing a box of chocolates from the store when they sneaked out of school grounds during recess. They stole it out of boredom. Well, not exactly. Hershko was in the mood for something sweet. Dahan came with them. He was sup-posed to distract the cashier. But he failed. She stopped them at the door. She was furious, threatening to call the police. Niro pretended to fall apart, telling her their friend was in the hospital and they didn't want to come see him empty-handed. They promised to stop by the next day and pay her back. She took their parents' phone numbers.

Then we pooled all the allowance we had left, said Hershko, and went back there the next day. But it wasn't enough for her. She said the chocolates cost twice as much as what we brought. Black-mailing bitch. Said if we didn't pay her back in full she'd tell our parents. To this day, Dahan is convinced those chocolates were expired and that we would have found worms inside.

We were flat broke, said Niro.

My parents would have killed me, said Hershko.

His dad's a cop, said Niro.

Goddamn it, said Hershko. A drop of tahini stained his pants, and when he tried to remove it he ended up smearing it further. He placed his remaining half pita on the bench and got up.

You don't know how to eat, said Niro. You eat like a rhino. He handed him a napkin from the stack. Hershko spat on it and rubbed the expanding stain.

I said, Go clean it with soap. I saw a bathroom behind the stall. It'll come off.

As long as that's all you use the soap for, Niro shouted as Hershko moved away.

We ate in silence for several moments.

Niro said, So that's it, from that day on we decided we'd charge tax from every place we shop, except for Buhris, because he sells us booze without asking too many questions.

So it's a matter of principle, I said.

A ritual, said Niro.

I said, Habit becomes law.

But something good came out of it, said Niro. Hershko discovered how to make a profit off of his playing.

Hershko approached us, hunched. A sorrowful tone invaded

Niro's voice as he said, Maybe it isn't such a good thing, actually. He's grown up too quickly.

WE ARRIVED AT ZIKIM BEACH EARLY. EVEN WITH DAYLIGHT SAVings, it's hard to delay sunset. Hershko cursed the sun for bothering his eyes. It set steeply, plumping and cooling, as we moved west. Hershko told Niro, Let me borrow your shades.

No, said Niro, you've got that big old rhino face, you'll stretch them out.

So you'd rather get into an accident.

I trust you, said Niro.

Goddamn you, said Hershko, stop being so lazy and get a driver's license. I'm sick of being your chauffeur.

Do you have a license? Niro asked.

I said I didn't.

How come? said Niro.

I don't know. How come you don't have yours?

Because he doesn't want to add to the air pollution, said Hershko.

What does that mean?

Greenhouse gas emissions, said Niro. Carbon dioxide. Isn't it bad enough that we're already ruining the ozone layer?

I had no idea what he was talking about.

Hershko said, So because of that hole in the ozone layer, this stink bomb stopped using deodorant.

Niro said, The greenhouse gases cause light reflected from Earth to become trapped in the atmosphere, and Earth is heating up because of it.

At least it made him stop farting, which isn't half-bad, said Hershko, not a bad achievement at all.

A thick strip of hazy sheen stretched over the water, branches of brilliance pulling out of it. Feather clouds held remainders of the light, hovering uteri of radiation. The water itself had already started to dim, its green shade darkening and deep.

Niro left the car door open behind him and hurried off from the asphalt of the parking lot to the depth of the sand. You understand why we had to leave early, he said, this is the most beautiful hour of the day. Birds shot out from someplace, black fireworks, bullets of shadow, screeching a song no less complicated than their flight, pushed back and pausing in unison.

Niro and Hershko sent me to gather stones among the bushes that rose to the south of the strip of sand. In the meantime, they piled up wood to build a fire, a kind of tent of twigs and plywood they'd shipped over in the trunk of the car. We arranged a circle of stones around it.

Gradually, other cars arrived. Boys and girls I didn't know joined us. One of them, dark and wiry, hopped onto Hershko's back as the latter crouched down to light the fire. Maniac Romanian, he said affectionately.

Get off my back, Dahan, or I swear to God I'll throw you into the bonfire and light it up. He stood up suddenly and the boy fell against the sand. What an *afrit* you've become, Hershko, he said.

I searched around with my eyes. In the darkening air, Niro spoke, with bony gesticulations, to a group that had just arrived. A cold object was shoved into my hand. I grabbed it by force of instinct. A bottle of beer.

So, said Dahan, are you the *dos* Niro and Hershko have been talking about?

I looked at my beer silently. I don't drink, I said.

He said, More for me, then. He took the bottle from me and walked on.

The remains of the light, the wrung grayness of post-twilight, came together to form stars, frozen pricks in the moonless space. I leaned against the eolianite nook I'd wandered off to with a plate of snacks, watching the bonfire and the celebrants from afar. Laughter and shouting were swallowed into the music emerging from a tape player one of them had brought. I didn't recognize the songs. The squeaking, electric sounds exploded against my eardrums, the beats sliding over heartbeats, not seeping in. Louder was the tumult of the sea biting against the shore and rolling back to its place, gnawing and retreating. Figures moved against the backdrop of flames. The pieces of dance had a meaning, the pulling out of potatoes slipped into the flame, beaded onto barbed wires. The skewering and toasting of marshmallows. One of the guests passed close to me without noticing me on his way to the parking lot, then returned with a guitar hanging off his chest. He started playing while he walked back to the fire.

Niro hurried over, waving a flashlight. No, no, he said, what are you doing?

Let me through, said the guitarist.

I explicitly said no guitars. I'm sick of amateurs. What is this, a youth movement meetup?

Cool it, Vazana, said the guitarist, this isn't your party, let others have fun.

What, singing old Land of Israel folk songs around the fire?

The guitarist didn't answer. Niro didn't move. He sailed the flashlight this way and that, and the beam fell upon me. He watched me for a few moments. Nahum, he said tenderly, I was sure you were with the others.

My throat was choked, and I didn't know what to say.

Make some room, he said, plopping beside me. He shone a light onto the plate. You're on top of your shit. So how's it going, you having fun yet?

I said, Looks like fun.

That boring-ass Tomer brought his guitar. What a moron.

We listened quietly. The music playing on the tape was cut

off. Strumming was sounded, followed by a clear, ringing voice quickly covered by a group song. The music sounded familiar, the words muffled. Hershko arrived, breathing heavily, and plopped down beside us.

Where's Dahan? asked Niro.

Over there with Tomer, he said. You won't believe it. They're singing Naomi Shemer songs.

Niro spat to the side. I noticed, he said.

So, what, you've started your own competing party? said Hershko. He swigged from his bottle.

Give me a sip, said Niro, I left my bottle by the fire.

Hershko got up and roared, Dahan, get over here and bring something to drink and eat, *bihyat abuk*, Goddamn you.

Does that sound like Romanian to you? said Niro.

No shit-talk, said Hershko. Besides, Nahum doesn't even know he's half-Romanian himself, so how can he tell?

I told you my father's Moroccan.

Yeah, right, said Hershko. Can't bullshit a bullshitter. A Moroccan Farkash.

When I'd walked out of the house toward Niro and Hershko, who were waiting in the car, I saw my father signaling to Niro to roll down his window. He leaned in and spoke to them. Back on the porch, he said to me, New friends?

I nodded.

He said, I thought you'd never get rid of that trashy Barda and Sabah.

In the car, Hershko asked, Are you Farkash from the rec center's kid?

You know him?

The Kakoon Brothers, the ones I play with, he said, are friends of his. He let us use the place to rehearse.

I asked, Kakoon from the weddings?

Yeah, he said, I'm their keyboard player.

Shit music, said Niro, but good money.

I had no idea, I said.

You don't go to the right event halls, said Niro.

Hershko crouched beside us again. For real, I'm going to butcher Dahan if he doesn't leave those nerds.

Niro said, Go figure, maybe they're doing a Kakoon Brothers song now. Give me a sip already, you hog.

Hershko took a spiteful gulp, making a gurgling sound, then wiped his face spitefully, with a sigh. He said, So what, your girlfriend isn't coming?

I told you, said Niro, she's not my girlfriend. She . . . well, you'll see.

Probably a snob like you, said Hershko.

No, said Niro, she's not very social. He pointed the beam of light toward the bonfire. Dahan was walking over, sinking into the sand, moving with effort. His hands were full of drinks. Snacks were shoved into the pockets of his light jacket.

It isn't cool, said Hershko, for you to be so into someone we haven't even met yet.

Yeah, said Dahan, not cool. He handed Niro and me bottles of beer.

But she'll come to our Independence Day show, said Niro. You're coming too, Nahum, there's no special service at the synagogue that day, is there?

A prayer for the safety of Israeli soldiers, said Dahan, a prayer for the safety of Hannan Hershkowitz, the Romanian maniac who'll be joining them soon. *Inshallah* he'll break some of their equipment and the whole military'll fall apart.

I held the beer bottle against my will. I said to Dahan, I told you I don't drink.

What hole did you pull this guy out of? said Dahan. He took out a pack of cigarettes. Tell me you at least smoke.

✳ ✳ ✳

(FORGET ME, NAHUM, HAUNTED BY MEMORIES, SO MUCH SO THAT I-Nahum am forced to re-create one detail after the next in a language other than my own, the language of another. But I, meaning I, what do I have to do with this story into which I sank so deeply that I can no longer remember my own history?)

THE EVENING PRAYER I HADN'T SAID THE PREVIOUS NIGHT pierced the sides of my body when I woke up. The morning prayer is a prayer of the feet and the head, the afternoon prayer can be felt in the lower back. But besides that, I felt the same smooth warmth in my limbs that I'd felt back then, after my first Purim meeting with Pini's and Niro's then-friends, the liberty that was a flexible, sweeping being. I couldn't remember what the *Halachah* said about evening prayer payments, and I hadn't even said a Shema prayer in bed. I washed up and opened the *Shulhan Aruch* in my bedroom. It said I had to speak the *Tahnun* and *Ashrei* after morning prayer. I rushed out with the *tallit* and the *tefillin*. My father, breaking his habit, was sitting at the dining table with my mother. They were eating. Chewing slowly. Sleeping beauty, said Msodi.

A thin laughter awoke within me. That's what I'd said to Niro, that we ought to come home before midnight, because at midnight the magic expired. The Subaru would go back to being a shoebox, and I had to get up for school.

Niro said I hadn't smoked enough to start talking nonsense. How strong was the occasion in my mind, and how sudden, and how clear was its blurring. The fogging of the mind stood before wakefulness, as sharp as glass.

Simo said, Where are you running off to?

I said, To the synagogue for morning prayer.

My parents exchanged looks.

Simo said, We need to talk. He pulled off a bit of bread and wiped the remains of the runny egg white from his plate.

I told him I'd stop by his office at the rec center. He said he'd wait for me at home.

I'd never noticed how high the synagogue's ceiling was. It arched over me. I examined it as the single prayer mumbled between my lips. Behind the worshippers' benches, at second-story height, was the balcony, the exterior extension of the women's section. It made sense. After all, they only came to synagogue to toss candy and gossip. The distance blocks the chatter, and the height of the balcony allows a more equal dispersal of candy among worshippers during *Shabbat Hatan*. The thought that emerged broke the train of prayer, its automatic nature. I looked at the prayer book, flipping through it. Where was I, in *veaya im shemo'a* or in *vayomer*? I looked at my hand. It knew the job. The *tallit* fringes were gathered in it. In *vayomer*, then. I hurried off to *Amidah*. Then, what, was there a singular version of *nefilat apaim*?

There was nobody to ask. The special cigarette Niro had brought with him, what did he call it, a joint, continued to undermine my thinking. I was more distracted than I'd wished to be. Niro's and Hershko's and Dahan's unfocused eyes, dilated by the flashlight's beam, rose before me, hovering between me and the words on the page. Some flow of broken sentences that Dahan spilled about the short film he'd made with some of the friends, in whose general direction he pointed, which he wanted to show at the Independence Day party. And I said, And the Lord opened the mouth of the donkey. And Hershko's and Niro's braying laughter. I gritted my teeth. I squeaked. I was aware of the dues collector's piercing gaze as he followed me. When I walked inside, he asked why I'd come again when there was no *minyan*. What now, is there a singular *nefilat apaim* according to Moroccan Jewish custom?

What does it matter, what does *nefilat apaim* have to do with this morning, in which God almighty rang in every bud and leafstalk rising from the earth and the throat of every winged seraph burned with amber, the chariot work of light, the thousands of tones and notes of song before the heavenly throne? The Lord conceals His presence from the world, Nahum, and there are no words with which to replace His splendor.

As I rolled up the *tefillin* with flesh both full and lacking, the dues collector said, Don't you have to go to school?

Even the wooden walls blew with the air of Iyar. I said, The school year ended early.

He told me to come on Shabbat, it was a shame I was attending an empty synagogue, that a synagogue without worshippers was like a widow among gentiles.

I wanted to tell him I didn't have the energy for the aimless talk of sermonizers and was shocked by the brashness of the mere thought. I nodded silently and left.

My father asked the same question. What's going on, Nahum? You've been skipping school the past few days.

My mother wasn't there. We sat facing each other on opposite sides of the dining table. My fingertips traced the floral images, the slipperiness of the nylon texture, the new tablecloths my mother used. In the past year, my father's might had been replaced by an indecipherable affection. Almost without warning. His solidity of body was preserved, as was the threat contained within it, but some soft whisper became intertwined within his speech, fragmenting the boniness of the statement. Tova, who was more attentive to him than any of us, started joking about the drama the people of Sderot made of the upcoming city hall elections. Like, what, she said, is Sderot not going to be a hellhole anymore?

I told him all the classes were dedicated to finals prep, anyway.

And you have a command of the material?

No one commands material, I said.

He hummed.

I said, Dad, what are you worried about? This isn't like you.

He said, That Romanian, who was driving the car last night, he plays with the Kakoon Brothers.

I nodded.

He said, Good kid, making a living at such a young age.

I said, He dropped out of school.

Some people don't need to go to school to make it, said Simo.

So what—

You aren't one of them. You don't have life skills.

I said nothing.

He said, Are you sure there isn't any other reason you haven't been going to school?

Like what?

He said, Your mother says that Sabah boy is shrinking up your life. When he's around you don't meet new people, don't evolve.

Mom said that?

What, are you surprised to find out your mother's smart? Look at how keen your sisters are, where do you think they got that from? Not from my side. On the Farkash side the girls are—

I cut him off quickly, God forbid. That Sabah is dead to me.

He said, Just don't rush to get too close to these new friends. Use your judgment.

I said, No, there's nothing between us. They just invited me to Hershko's enlistment party, and I felt bad saying no.

He sounded a dry, hoarse laugh. Tova made her comments about that laugh too, with the same cloak of levity.

He said, Still water runs deep. Go on, go to school. Your mother got you a doctor's note.

I SPOTTED SABAH, EHUD, AND THEIR GROUP FROM AFAR. I KEPT A safe distance from them. I switched to a seat in the back of the classroom. The Gmarah teacher said, It isn't like you to sit in the back, come back to the front row. I told him I was still a little under the weather. I faked a cough. He nodded. How pathetic they looked, their posture, the trifles that occupied them. I wondered who among them even thought about the future, the fate of the planet, the meaning of existence. The Gmarah teacher returned to *hasoher et ha'omnin*, the chapter about uneven business contracts. How fitting, I pondered, they're misleading each other. Tomorrow's Friday. Skipping the bringing out of the Torah ark on Thursday had its own meaty echo, a slicing in the bottom of my stomach. I have no idea why there, of all places. I would have expected my skin to be irritated. The connection between the body and sacred rituals is beyond me. I just had to bear Sunday and Monday, and then Independence. The blood flow exacerbated in its vessels.

My mother's diagnosis was fair. Sabah's existence was stretched like a screen over my eyes, obstructing my view. And when I dared remove it, even just for a few moments, the beauty of others was revealed to me, their otherness. Michael Bogdari was one of those random kids whose entire purpose was to add to the classroom's volume and makeup. Devoid of interior life, positioned within a sea of extras. I suppose that is how I would describe him if I were required to. If anyone asked me about him, my first response would probably be that I didn't know who he was. I wouldn't put a name to the face. If someone then pointed him out I would say, Oh, that one, just another kid. He's always around for some reason.

But he wasn't always around. His family had moved to America for three years during elementary school, and when they returned he became silently lost among the thirty-something fifth graders. Not lost, he maintained his uniqueness. He was a round child when he left, smiling. And a round child when he came back, smiling. Toward the end of sixth grade, he began to have pain in the forehead and around the nose. He'd contracted severe sinusitis.

The syllables of the disease, when he spoke them, were spiced with faraway dust, like the years his family spent abroad. It didn't matter that the sewing shop his father opened there had failed, it didn't matter that the support of their relatives, who encouraged them to move, had slowed until it came to a full stop.

He told me about all this one afternoon, with his usual tone of voice, the final words of every sentence turning nasal, affording the content a jokey character, about the natural ease of things, about the gravity unique to them as they are born.

I met him during the summer vacation after seventh grade. My mother sent me to the public pool to check on Tova and Chantal. My father was supposed to pick them up at the end of the camp day, but it was getting late and Simo was nowhere to be found. No one answered the phone when she called the swimming pool office. When I arrived, the main entrance gates were locked. A metal chain was wrapped around the white metal poles. I circled the fence surrounding the pool area. The whole way to the pool, horror scenarios filled my mind. They'd been kidnapped, run over, bitten by a snake, their bodies were lying in the unmowed weeds of the underbrush strewn along the way. At the sight of the bolted gates, a scorching line stretched down my gullet, from the opening of my throat to the opening of my heart. I heard voices from the side entrance, the service entrance. I hurried down the path. Tova and Chantal were there with a younger child, a seven-year-old, playing a game of hopscotch sketched unskillfully with chalk, crooked, curving lines. They urged him to push the playing pebble to farther squares, to the circle at the edge of the game. I called their names. The boy raised his wide, black eyes to me and burst out in tears.

Ugh, said Tova, we'd finally calmed down this crybaby.

Chantal leaned in and rubbed his shoulder. Nahum, she said, don't cry.

Tova said, Where's Dad?

I said he was busy and forgot to let anyone know in time.

She said, We know how to get home on our own, why did you come?

I said that little girls like them couldn't just roam the streets on their own. There are, I said, but didn't complete the sentence. Nahum the child kept crying. I remained indifferent to his sobs, to his crumpled face.

Chantal said, He doesn't know where he lives. We were waiting with him.

The bougainvillea vines tangled densely over the fence, casting a carpet of shade. I retreated there. Chantal persuaded Nahumito to keep playing. Who drew this ugly hopscotch? I said.

Chantal pulled a piece of chalk out of her pocket. Her hands were already painted with its white dust mixed with her sweat. She smiled her smile that was missing two front teeth. *Frunshnan*, I said affectionately, you're better off not smiling.

All the instructors went home already, said Tova.

I said we'd stop by the police station on the way home and leave the kid there. The police would track down his parents. Chantal said she was hungry and that Nahum must be hungry too, so maybe he could come over.

Tova said, They'll think we kidnapped him.

I urged them to follow me. Nahumito had to be dragged. He sobbed exaggeratedly. When we finally reached the top of the incline, which afforded him an aggravating power of resistance, someone called behind us, Nahum, Nahum, Nahum. Urgent cries. I turned around. Nahumito's body turned limp, his sobbing alleviating. A young boy came running and paused beside us. His face was wet with effort. He rested his hands on his knees, his posture hunched, as if he were bowing to us. But he was breathless. A few moments later, he stood up. He pulled Nahumito to him. What are you doing, he said between one gasp and the next, with my brother?

We're taking him to the police, said Tova.

Why? said the young boy, exhaling. I could almost recognize him.

I said, Because someone forgot to pick him up.

For a moment, a concerned look flashed through his eyes, as if he were fighting down tears himself. He said, You're Nahum Farkash.

I didn't respond.

Chantal said, Why'd you leave your brother all alone?

The boy said, We're in—exhale—the same homeroom.

Really? I said.

He nodded vigorously. We, he said—exhale—are going to our grandma's. You guys live on Yoseftal Street, right?

NIRO SUGGESTED I ATTEND THEIR SOUND CHECK ON INDEPEN-dence Day Eve, because Dalia and I were the only ones who weren't familiar with their material, and it might shock me. That's what he said when he asked me about my taste in music and marveled at the fact that I made do with randomly listening to the radio. He blurted out so many names of bands and recording artists. None of the names left a mark on my mind. He said, What are you even interested in, besides religion?

I asked, Who's Dalia?

He said, Someone I gave some guitar lessons to about a year ago.

This time, I had no dilemmas about what to wear. But I did try to shape up my resistant hair. Ultimately, Tova proposed I use baby oil. In a low voice, she said that the following day would mark a week since Cocoa Pup's disappearance. Chantal never mentioned the Pekinese anymore. She'd found something else to occupy her mind. The hair straightened at once with the motion of the comb. But the bobby pin attached to the yarmulke slipped off my head. I can't win, I told Tova.

She said, You don't need the yarmulke anyway. They're all secular. Who's going to tell on you?

She smiled meekly as I was about to leave. I asked if she and
Chantal were going to the live performance stages. She said they
were, Simo would join them, just like every year, after the boring
speeches by the mayor and the head of the culture department
and all sorts of wheeler-dealers and him. Why does he need to
give a speech, she said, doesn't he know everyone just waits for
those boring speeches to be over so they can make jokes about
them, what does he even have to say?

Msodi announced she'd once more make do with watching
the fireworks from the porch.

On the way, I thought about how Sabah encouraged his followers to joke about my father's speech without participating in
the fun-making himself, by asking innocent questions, by quoting my father along with a grave sigh, as if he agreed with the essence of the statements, and how he clicked his tongue whenever
one of them went too far and nearly slipped into outright insults.
Two years ago, he even made me use a toxic tone as I repeated
something Simo said about the culture department's commit-
ment to enriching residents' intellectual lives. The salty lumpi-
ness of the words burned faintly on the edges of my thought. I
tried to re-create his clicking, just a peep, like a long, musical fart
that accompanied my walk over to Hershko's house.

They lived in a villa bordering a small eucalyptus thicket,
pure of any dark omens. At the edge of the yard, a slope descended
into a gorge that cut through the thicket. A low plank fence and a
steel gate separated the yard from the slope. I didn't know this
part of Sderot well and didn't know whether the thicket was a
small enclave of new plantings or whether it was attached in its
primal days to the thicket of my childhood. The constant speed,
and the powder blue trapped in the pliable foliage, that the amber
of the day gilded in those unparalleled hours.

Be that as it may, the yard sprawled behind the villa. Hershko,

Niro, and another guy, Eddy, were standing beside piles of plastic chairs. I nodded in greeting. They were in the midst of an argument about whether or not to set up the chairs. Niro insisted that it should be a standing-room-only concert, and if anyone wanted to sit they could grab a chair and sit in the back. Hershko said they ought to arrange the chairs in rows, because sitting was more comfortable. Besides, Dahan wanted to show his film.

Niro said the weddings had messed with Hershko's mind. This wasn't an event, it was rock and roll.

Eddy laughed. He pulled out a small metal case and a pack of cigarettes.

Hey now, said Hershko, no drugs.

Seriously, Eddy, said Niro, is this your first time here?

I said, Won't the noise bother the neighbors?

On Independence Day it's legal to make noise all night long, said Hershko.

A phone rang inside. Hershko hurried in. Niro called out after him, Bring the lights with you when you come back.

Won't it bother his parents, I asked, the concert?

Niro said, His father's on call at the police for the holiday.

And his mother?

Do me a favor, don't ask him about her. Come help me unload the equipment.

The villas in Hershko's neighborhood were built in a semicircle around an indoor parking lot. Niro handed me one guitar and a case. For effects, he said. He carried a second guitar and a small, silver amplifier. He said, The real bummer is we can't play until Memorial Day ends, especially not at Hershko's.

When we got back to the yard, Hershko said, Oh, there you are. We need a favor, Nahum. Dahan couldn't get a projector, and he says there's an excellent one at the rec center.

But this was one of my father's hours of absence, those intermediate hours when he seemed to be off the grid of humanity.

He'd already left the office, he wasn't home, and he was absent from the lawn outside the gymnasium, the traditional Independence Day staging area, which he was in charge of constructing. We asked the laborers. They said he'd popped out and would probably be back soon.

Hershko said, Pay attention to the signs.

I asked what he was talking about.

He said, Remember what I said so it doesn't take you by surprise later. Pay close attention to the signs.

We leaned against his car and waited. He crouched in and pushed a tape into the deck. The volume was low. The sweet voice of a female singer, enveloped with foreignness, emerging from a distance, and a rustling that, for some reason, made me think about foghorns. He said, The sane alternative to Memorial Day music.

What is that? I asked.

He said, "Song to the Siren." Moving, isn't it?

He lit a cigarette and smoked it with slow movements. I said, It's like lying on a floating mat.

Shh, he said, let me listen.

After three similar songs of floating sound and flickering singing, a sob only emphasized by having been restrained, he crushed the cigarette butt under the sole of his shoe and said, I think we've waited long enough.

He waited for me at the edge of the street. I knew where my father's spare keys were. I sneaked in. Tova's eyes hit me as I walked out. I held a finger to my lips. She nodded and returned to her room. I went out without my mother noticing.

Hershko said, It isn't exactly like stealing. It's borrowing public property. We're going to give it back, aren't we?

The rec center was silent, as we'd assumed it would be. Even the houses around it were consumed by the awe of the day, though it would be over in less than two hours. I thought about the artificial switch of previous years, the waiting for the signal on the television, the burst of celebration that had been contained somehow, somewhere. Still, the click of the front door's locking mechanism sounded more like a rumble as I turned the key. Cogs groaned. Bolts were shifted with a roar.

I imagined my body moving through the hallways like oil, slipping, any thought threatening to break the marvelous viscosity. Still, voices rose from one of the rooms, hesitant, tense whispers. I listened with wizened limbs. I moved on, oil slick and thickened. I searched for the key to the storage room, but none of the keys on the ring fit. The metal protrusions were all wrong. The keyhole was wider, the door blocked, sturdy.

My throat was burning, and a granular matter formed between the skin of my face and the muscles and nerves beneath. Every swallow made it screech. No choice, I thought, we have to cancel the screening. And then a jolt of rage. I was such a loser, unable even to complete childish tasks. I turned around. Again the whispers, and further sounds, a suckling and a sigh. My father's office was near the room the sounds emerged from. The axes squeaked. My footfalls were soft. The key to the storage room was lying in the drawer, a purple-headed cylinder key. My fist tightened around the tines and dimples, a metallic topography slicing into my skin as I recognized one of the voices, a damp laugh, choking halfway through. What was Msodi doing here, at this place, at this time? I stifled my questions and walked out.

The projector box was heavy and had to be carried with both hands. I crawled back down the hallway. My arms were about to rip out of their sockets. I leaned the corner of the projector on the doorknob and pushed the door open with my shoulder. Then I lunged out. The door slammed behind me. Hershko ran toward me and took the projector. In his arms, it seemed to be made of Styrofoam, carried effortlessly. I locked the door and ran. He'd already started the Subaru, and the car began to glide ahead. The projector was placed in the front seat. The back seat door was open. I hopped in. He sped up. When he reached the street corner, I said, Wait, go back.

Why, he said, did you forget something?

No, I said.

He backed up carefully, until the whiteness of the rec center reentered our field of vision.

What, he said, why are we pulling up here?

I said, I want to see.

A man walked out the door urgently. Simo Farkash. The day's light had started to dissipate, but from this distance I could still see. His shirt was mussed and buttoned wrong. He looked in every direction, impatiently. He may have been out of breath.

I told you, said Hershko, pay close attention to the signs.

The Subaru hovered down the street, a green hour in the blackening languidness of evening. Hershko turned the wrong way at the intersection. I told him as much. He said Niro asked that we pick up that friend of his, Dalia. He spoke the word "friend" with mockery, crumbling the syllables against his tongue. We drove down the main street. On the sides of the road, wandering children had already gathered, twilight birds, parked between the two parts of the day. And the gray project buildings. Layers of time made of plaster and dust. Israeli flag garlands were stretched between electric poles. To our right, the partially constructed stages fell silently into the past. Hershko drove into a neighborhood of low single-story homes by the soccer field. I had no idea where the girl came from. She was standing at an intersection, separate from the houses and the meaning they contained, separate from the anticipation in the windows, blinded by evening, disconnected from the safety of thatched roofs, detached from the growth of pomegranate and lemon trees inside neat, white rock circles. She stood on her own.

You think it's this one? Hershko said. Kind of a fatty. Doesn't suit Niro to pick someone so chubby.

We pulled up next to her. I rolled down the widow. Are you Dalia? I asked.

She nodded.

Thick black hair. Quite a mane. The look in her eyes was amused. Suddenly, I was aware of the dents on the Subaru's chassis, the screeching of its movement, Hershko's clumsiness, his crude limbs, the ratty collar of my T-shirt, the glimmer of my jeans, the worn soles of my leather shoes. I muttered something. She got in the car and sat beside me. The weight of the body was more than an expression of flesh. She was fully present in her silence.

WHEN WE GOT BACK, DAHAN WAS ALREADY THERE. HE AND NIRO were stretching a garland of lights over the yard. Eddy sat on his amplifier near the makeshift stage, holding a bass guitar, smoking, and staring into space. Niro's equipment had been laid out. The special effects suitcase was open, colorful devices dangling from a row of short cables. A long cable was connected to the guitar at one end and to the amplifier on the other. A keyboard was placed on a black, crossed stand, and two cases, one silver and one black, were attached to it.

Dahan's torso leaned out of a second-floor window. Hershko warned him not to stand up on the bed in his filthy shoes. Dahan muttered a curse, then saw me and said, Smoky Farkash. He ignored Dalia, who was standing next to me. The eucalyptuses in the thicket alleviated the remains of the light, pushing the beast of evening inside. The bulbs wounded the darkening flesh.

Dalia pulled a chair from the pile in the corner of the yard and sat down. Niro dragged another chair and set it beside hers. Dahan opened the projector case, which Hershko had placed on a third chair. I hurried over. He pointed at a patch of wall to the right of the entrance. He said, That'll make a good background as soon as it gets dark.

I asked him to be careful with the projector. Don't worry, he said. It's a simple hookup. Hershko walked outside, carrying a small table. I watched him place the projector on top of it with extreme care. Handsome, he said. I looked at the appliance. To me it looked like a clumsy lump. A metallic friction rose from Eddy's direction. He was playing his bass without amplification. Pinching the strings and nodding his head. All of a sudden, Niro called out, Fifteen minutes. The call broke the flow of speech coming from him and Dalia. A background sound that cut off all of a sudden. I glanced at them. Niro was waving a booklet at her. I walked over to get a better look. *Creatures of Light and Darkness*, it was called. Beneath the black letters, against an ugly backdrop, appeared a golden illustration of a man with the head of a jackal or a fox with ruins underneath him, perhaps the ruins of the temple, or shards from Herod's palace. Idolatry, I thought, a perfect match for Niro's foolishness.

Niro said, But you're wrong, it's a genius idea. It's a genius book.

Dalia said she wasn't so crazy about Zelazny anymore. He was a little too childish for her taste. Even these more mature books. She told Niro he had to at least read the story "The Girl Who Was Plugged In" and then they'd talk, she had a copy to lend him.

And what was the other one you mentioned? said Niro.

Samuel Delany, but he isn't for you.

We'll give it to Nahum to read, said Niro, I think it'll suit him. It'll open his mind.

He turned to face me and offered the booklet. I flinched. I crossed my arms behind my back. I said, Who cares about that, literature is for girls.

The girl assessed me. Her dark eyes glinted with the dimmed mixture of lamplight and thick evening. She said, And what's for boys?

I said, The wisdom of Israel.

She was silent for a moment, trying to swallow. Then she said, You're stupid. Life is literature. It's your Torah and the money you buy food with, and everything you see and hear and smell and touch.

Niro looked at her and nodded.

She said, Literature is talking to the living about life. It's being alive.

I shrugged and retreated. Niro got up a few moments later. He touched my shoulder. Eddy had already turned on his amplifier, which emitted a white coo, followed by round, black notes that touched the body and sunk the limbs to the ground. Hershko sprayed sawlike sounds, iron chimes. Niro said, Don't be scared, she gets like that sometimes, talking all sharply.

I didn't answer. Dahan said, Gave you a talking-to, huh? Makes sense. What else does she have but a mouth?

Dalia sat, detached from her surroundings. Her hair fell on her face, which was lowered toward the tattered book in her hands. Just a poseur, I thought. Such a poseur. I watched her at length, her body occasionally shifting as she flipped to the next page of the book, until finally she looked up, but not because of me. The musicians in the back suddenly went silent, and Niro contributed trickles and screeches and echoes to Hershko and Eddy's noise. I turned to face them. They stood at attention, nodding at each other. Hershko pressed a key, a rhythm broken midway through, starting up again in a kind of loop, Eddy produced a scrambled sequence of notes, a sense of movement through space, of pacing, which resisted the broken beat, Niro responded with a sudden squealing of the guitar, a high note piercing the eardrum, draining as well, he strummed the strings that turned metallic and pealing at once, and the remains of other coils rose and fell. The terms I was familiar with were insufficient. This music had flavor and texture and color. At some point I stopped translating it and just listened. Niro sang in a clear voice that occasionally turned hoarse around the edges. It was as if singing had a different nature, required a second throat, different from the everyday one.

THE YOUNG BOY TOLD US HIS NAME WAS MICHAEL BOGDARI. HE held on tightly to the hand of his brother, Nahumito, though his brother tried to wriggle free. Their grandmother's house was in the neighborhood adjacent to ours. His name sounded vaguely familiar. The whole way over, he kept spewing details of information about our other classmates. He was informed on the most minute gossip of school life. He knew, for example, that I hadn't been invited to the party Sylvia Gozlan threw for Sabah. He knew she was in love with him. He knew about the rift between me and Ehud Barda. He didn't list the facts, but rather recounted them as if he'd had a part in them. I asked him how he knew all this. He said it was like a TV show, like one of the shows he used to watch in America. The whole time he spoke, he wiped his nose with bits of toilet paper he fished out of his pocket.

I told him I didn't understand. He said, It's like when you read a book and the things that take place in it happen to you too. More interesting than what actually happens to you.

As we arrived at the fork in the road entering our neighborhood, Tova and Chantal broke into a run. They were racing to see who would be the first one to report the adventure to our mother. Well, I told Michael, it's lucky my sisters took care of your brother.

It really is, said Michael.

As I moved away, he called my name. I turned around. Nahumito had freed himself from his brother's grip and was rushing into the road. Michael tripped on the sidewalk. I caught up with Nahumito up the road and pulled him back to the pavement. A car sped up and drove by without noticing us. Nahumito went wild between my arms. Michael hurried over once again, hyperventilating. Thank you, he said, and blew his nose. Thank you—exhale.

That evening, he came over uninvited. I was in my bedroom. Tova called me, saying, It's that kid from the pool, with the cry-baby brother.

But Michael was on his own. He asked if I wanted to go for a walk. I asked where. He said, Nowhere, just around.

We wandered and stopped to rest and then resumed our wandering. The scorched day cracked at the edges, and the dust of the consumed ends imbued the leaning trees and the sky above them, peeled wallpaper the color of tin, with heat. All throughout our wandering, Michael continued to amass information on top of information. At some point he moved away from gossip to share anecdotes from a faraway, unattainable life, about earthquakes, baby girls abandoned in China, the prices of cucumbers in Marrakech markets, a fat male singer dressed as a woman who choked on a sandwich, a mathematical problem that no one had been able to solve in two hundred years.

I listened to him. The necklace of details beaded on the thread of that sick, nasally voice had me hypnotized. We arrived at the public library. He said he came there often, and it was a shame the place was closed in summer. There was a tremor in his voice as he said this, which was instantly restrained into a jokey nasalization. He said it was one of the few places he could tolerate in Sderot.

I asked if he read a lot.

He said he liked looking at books. He read excerpts, the interesting stuff. He could spend hours looking at the *Guinness World Records* books.

But what's interesting about that? I asked.

He said, It's interesting. He said when the library opened again during the next school year we could go together.

I told him I went there once. He said he loved to sit in the reference room and watch the people coming and going.

I didn't see him over summer vacation. I forgot all about him.

But on the first day of the new school year, he rushed to take a seat beside me in the new classroom. He stuck around during recess. We didn't talk much. Or if we did, the conversations did not stay with me. They went out wherever they go out, in the dimness of their unimportance. From a distance, Michael caught the glimmer of Sabah and Ehud and Dudi and the others. He must have unfolded their stories.

The week before Rosh Hashanah, the physical education teacher appointed Sabah and Ehud heads of the volleyball teams. All the boys from our class except for Michael and me were picked quickly, without any hesitation. We were unevenly numbered. Ehud picked first, and then came Sabah's last turn to pick. He moved his eyes from Michael to me and said, I'll take Snot. The boys laughed.

Who? asked the phys ed teacher. He grimaced at Sabah.

Sabah said, The snot pump, what's his name, that little Bogdari guy.

Michael walked over, glancing back at me with hesitation, or perhaps to marvel. His eyes, at any rate, were different.

The phys ed teacher said, Farkash, you weren't picked, so you can choose which team to join.

I said, I'll join Snot's team.

Whose? said the phys ed teacher. He was standing over me with his intimidating stature, his belly, which had started to protrude, scratching the bottom of his chin.

I said, Bogdari's team. He's the only player here worth anything. I smiled at Ehud. He didn't smile back.

ALL AT ONCE, HERSHKO'S YARD FILLED WITH GUYS AND GIRLS, flooded with chatter and laughter and the shaking of drinks and the rustling of chewed snacks and conversations. They trickled in during the sound check. Niro and Hershko and Eddy stopped playing for a few minutes and the guests all turned their attention. Then the concert began without any warning. I thought they'd start it the way they'd started the rehearsal, with the same bewitching musical number, in which the singing was secondary. But no. Niro put on large headphones and played the guitar by himself, once again emitting white-hot squeals and penetrating hums. Hershko pressed a button on his keyboard and a mechanical beat emerged from the loudspeakers, a dense, steamroller sound, and on its edges the clean forging of iron, over which rode expanding hand fans of oceanic, spacey notes. There was no connection between his playing and Niro's. Eddy joined in, and for a moment the bass line created a connection between the two rivaling tunes, but he quickly joined Hershko's side. Hershko walked over to Niro, removed the headphones from his ears, and returned to his spot. To the spacey industrialism, he added warm, mercurial wind instruments. Slowly, Niro's guitar tune scooted closer to the melody Hershko and Eddy were producing, until finally it blended in. There was a sudden sweetness in this harmony. Niro walked over to the microphone. The music was heartbreaking. So were the words I caught.

Not all of the songs were as good as the sound check. One of the three made a mistake and the spell was broken. The sequence was cut off. Some of the guests whistled encouragingly. More songs were performed, but they were discreet pieces, pleasant to the ear, nothing more. Chaos ensued after the applause, swallowing the memory of the occasion. The navel of the yard was packed with lithe bodies. I poured myself some orange juice and retreated to the outskirts, carefully walking backward toward the fence bordering the slope. I stepped on a foot. A yelp. I turned around. Dalia. Sorry, I said.

She looked me over again. Her hair was pushed back. I saw her face. Clean skin, slightly oily. A random, tired expression. I kept retreating. She joined me, clutching her bag. A faux-unprocessed

leather material. The simplicity of her outfit, the lack of any character, suddenly appeared like a unique style in and of itself.

She asked what I thought about the music.

I said, I didn't really understand what they were singing about.

About loneliness. About how the stars continue indifferently
along their tracks. About how people get confused and think
that if love can cause so much pain, it means it can cause so much
pleasure too. About loneliness, about disappointment. About
loneliness.

Heavy, I said.

Did you believe them?

Niro? Yes.

She nodded. Then they're right.

Why?

The truth of the heart is not the truth of the brain.

I caught that line, actually.

Yes, they sang it in the very first song. If you're right, you
don't have to be sophisticated or–

I don't think so, I said. But I didn't know what I did think.

You prefer decorations and adornments, don't you?

What does that mean?

Nothing, just a feeling, that you contain no gravity, that you
like abundance.

You don't even know me.

The round shoulder pads of her jacket shifted. Perhaps she'd
shrugged. This girl is a total poseur, I thought. Dahan popped out
of nowhere. He was holding a small glass, halfway full.

We're about to get ready for my part, he told me, you've got to
drink, you can't watch my movie sober. Either you drink or you go
home.

I told you I don't drink.

There's no such thing, Smoky Farkash. Drink now, and by the
time we start the screening it'll kick in. He poured the contents

of the glass into my orange juice. And you—he turned to Dalia—did you have a drink yet?

I'm fueling up, nonstop, Dalia said in a shallow, smoggy tone.

Dahan blurted out a short laugh and took off.

What's his name? she asked.

Dahan.

No, his first name.

I don't know.

Dahan roared into the microphone over the general hubbub, instructing the guests to set up the chairs. The musicians were busy folding up and clearing away their equipment. I sipped from the cup in my hand.

So, said Dalia.

Like medicine. Are you actually intoxicated?

Intoxicated, she said.

I sipped some more. There was a surprising comfort in the combination of medicinal bitterness and the powdery texture of cheap orange juice. And more.

Dalia watched me intently. Something had abandoned me, a tiredness I hadn't noticed and that had been thus far filling my bloodstream. I was clear, I was dizzy. Dalia gestured toward two empty seats. I hovered in my chair, glued to it without being able to move. The lights went out all at once. The projector beam sketched a glowing square on a white patch of wall. Ready, Dahan roared. The yard went still.

Dahan rushed to the front of the yard. He stood there, bathed in light. He flipped his straight hair back with a practiced, boastful motion. He said, There are two films. One is mine, and some of you will recognize themselves in it.

A whooping sound rose from the front row.

The second film is a collaboration. This is its global, intergalactic premiere. You'll see.

His skinny figure abandoned the light, making its way back

through the dark. He bumped into someone else and guffawed. Get your paws off me, someone ordered, almost jokingly.

The first movie was filmed in black-and-white. Young men in suits and American gangster fedoras were sitting around a round table in a smoky room. They were discussing the poker game they were about to start playing. Their voices didn't match their lip movements. The voice emerged either before or after the lips began to move. The mismatch seemed intentional, because one by one, I realized that each character's late or early speaking style was unique. This was their only characterization. Had I not recognized the faces of the actors, who were all present in that yard, I wouldn't have been able to differentiate between the characters. They wore the same suits, the same mustaches, the top hats tilted so that their brims tented over their eyes and noses. Only the lips were spared by the shadows. A round clock was affixed to the wall, its hands unmoving. Every now and then, the camera focused on it. Waves of fog covered the lens, and when it cleared the time on the faulty clock was different, but the conversation retained its rational sequence. The people seated at the table discussed past events, mutual friends, the game they would play, and how it would progress. It seemed intended to decide their fate, but that was never clearly stated. One of the characters said, We might still have time. And then the movie was over. The boys in the front row jumped up and cried with excitement. Dahan returned to the patch of light, blinded. That same foppish shifting of the hair. His features were somewhat Native American, with slightly slanted almond eyes and smooth cheekbones. He asked them to sit down, the screening was not yet over.

The words SEALED AND LEASED appeared on the wall. Square, plump letters. They were followed by close-up shots of papers printed with words, with some diacritics added by hand. Their rough texture was visible in the close-up, as were the keystrokes, the faintly sunken letters. The writing trembled, perhaps the hand that held the pages shivered, or perhaps the camera tremored. The collection of words lingered on the screen for a long time. Sounds rose, broken up, random, the tweeting of a bird, the rattling of a laundry machine, the dragging of a stick against a fence, a bang on a piano, the breaking of a guitar string, the crackling of fire, a stormy wind, a muffled mumbling, the shattering of a glass against the ground, some unknown jangling. I stopped counting them. They accompanied the flipping of the papers.

word

words

twice

three words

twhorredes

4our

F4ur

Fo4r

Fou4

words

orwds

rowds

drows

sdrow

SHIMON
ADAF

six words sex

words sicks words

seven words

woven dress

re send vows

eight

        words

weight

        rods

sowed

        right

weird

        ghost

rule nine inn

neni nien enin

inner ennui linen

SHIMON
ADAF

ten

ent net

stern sworded town

words words words words

✳ ✳ ✳

I WAS FISHED OUT BY MY MOTHER'S HAND ON MY FOREHEAD. I opened my eyes with effort. The lids were glued together. Or lead. Leadlids. The aliteration of the thought startled me. All the old defenses were intact. Not this invasion again. Perhaps the shock was visible in my body. No. I sat up in bed. *Shbahela*, what's wrong, said my mother, I thought you'd gotten sick again.

I plopped back against the pillow. My mother said, Your new friend, Hershko, he said his name was, called twice already.

I watched her through cracks in my field of vision. A shutting and brightening darkness. She picked up my clothes from the previous night. They'd been lying naked on the rug. The pants and T-shirt and jacket. I tightened the blanket around me. She sniffed them. Flapped them through the air. Where did you go, she said, that you got so dirty? Sand and leaves and who knows what else. She sniffed again, then sighed. You decided to grow up in a day, Nahum, she said. Don't go back to sleep. It's almost noon and your father needs help with the grill.

I snoozed for a few moments longer and then startled awake again. Morning prayer. The swift motion made me nauseated. I limped to the bathroom to wash off the impurity. Then I carefully wrapped the *tefillin* around me with measured movements. The phone rang during *shir shel yom*. My mother knocked on my door. I raised the volume of my mumbling, *Ki ad tzedek yashuv mishpat ve'aharav kol yishrey lev*. My mother called me from beyond the door, So, in twenty minutes. I raised my voice in *tanhumeiha yesha'ashe'u nafshi*.

Hershko whispered into the phone on his end. His whisper poured into my ear on my side. Whisperadio. The pin of fear passing. You were so stoned last night, he said, that you forgot the projector.

My mother was busy preparing salads in the kitchen. My father was in the back, fanning the coals. On the counter were thawed chicken thighs, sliced beef, bleeding lamb chops. The thought of the upcoming feast made my stomach turn. I told Hershko, I'll be there in twenty minutes.

Don't worry about it, he said, I don't have that much time. We're about to leave to meet my dad's brothers at the beach. I'll come pick you up.

I walked to the corner. My body smelled sour, as if I'd dipped in baby spit-up. Partially digested food. That was the way my clothes smelled too. Hershko's Subaru appeared with its rumbling engine. It's rambling genuine.

Hershko said, You look beat-up, *ya* Nahum.

He looked so fresh. The projector was all packed up in the back seat. Nothing happened to it, right? I asked.

What could happen? I'm careful with electronics.

I don't know, I don't—

You blacked out, huh?

What?

Your memory of last night got blacked out.

But it hadn't. I still had ripped shreds. Blurry around the edges. By the end of the second film I was afraid that the clarity and warmth I felt were about to slip away. Dahan was standing by the drinks table. He accepted the waves of compliments showered over him with a natural ease. Handing over a drink in exchange for every compliment, a beer bottle from the cooler or a poured and mixed concoction. He guessed my concern. Before I even opened my mouth to speak, he shoved a reinforced orange juice into my hand. Vodka, he said. You might have been lucky enough to find your drink. Or maybe you're just inexperienced. He laughed.

Something happened. At some point we met up with the other boys. Then we slid down the slope into the ravine. Obviously we didn't really slide, but the memory was of a sliding. My leg muscles still held the memory of it. Hershko's father kept glow sticks in the shed. A yellow glimmer erupted when we bent them. It lit our faces on fire. Speech spilled out of my mouth. Showers, showers of speech. Overall, it seemed that the eucalyptus thicket was full of cheerful, chipper conversations. I thought to myself, They're my friends. At some point I told someone, Dahan's second film was brilliant. Only the person's features, painted by the incandescent aura, remained, detached from a name, square features, a chiseled jaw. After that there was Dalia's expression, peering at me with marvel. She said, Are you one of those?

I said, Those who?

She said, Those who favor empty art.

Despairingly, someone said, All the booze is up in the yard, and I'm too tired to move.

Dalia said, You've had enough.

I said, My world is empty.

She said, Why do you think I care about your world?

I said, You're just a condescending cow. What's with your posing?

She turned away from me.

Finally, we climbed up, slipping and laughing, and trying. Hershko eventually pulled me up the final, steep stretch. I made it home. Arid and old. The abode abides. But in between there was—

You're super hungover, said Hershko, say something, a word.

I said, A word.

I said, Hey, what's Dahan's first name?

Alon. Why, does he interest you?

His films are intense, I'm surprised.

Yeah, he's pretty freaking dumb usually, said Hershko. Only when he gets ideas for movies you ca—

I said, What happened last night?

He said, Besides the fact that you humiliated Niro's girl-friend? Not much.

He parked by the rec center, pulled out the packed projector, and followed me. We didn't keep quiet this time. We didn't steal in. We walked into the storage room, which I had stupidly left open the previous day. The key was still in the keyhole. Hershko examined the goods. Wow, he said, I never knew Sderot had this kind of equipment. Do you have any idea what we could do with this? He patted two large, black loudspeakers. They probably only use this for poolside dance classes. What a waste.

On the way back to the car he said, Oh, and another thing, you owe us a story.

A story, I said carefully.

Yes, said Hershko, about how you're not a virgin anymore.

IN NINTH GRADE, AN EVIL SPIRIT TOOK OVER SNOT. AFTER THAT volleyball game at the start of eighth grade, everyone started calling him by that name, which had been discharged of all malice. We spent a great deal of the year at the public library. Snot said he wanted to work there when he grew up. That's where he fled to from his father's grocery store most of the time anyway. Both his parents worked there nonstop, his mother in the morning and his father in the afternoon. His father asked him to come take over for a few hours every day, because he needed to get some rest. Snot said the dust at the store gave him sinus attacks.

Over the next summer vacation, his body grew. His rotundness remained, but it had become solid, almost threatening. The snot reserves in his body dried out. His voice thickened and deepened. He showed me his body, which had become covered with stiff, kinky curls. And he returned from summer vacation gripped with the lust of rebellion. He pushed his way in and out of synagogue, fighting for a seat, allowing nobody to shove him aside. He was still an outcast, and his attention was still completely devoted to the facts of other people's lives, but now he also passed judgment on them to me, using profanity. He thought the girls from the girls' school were all whores. They opened their legs to anyone who said a kind word to them, he said. He spoke to teachers bluntly and brashly. When a teacher showed up at school happier than usual, he'd say that his wife gave him some. He said he saw Sabah in the bathroom and that he had a small dick. And what did Sylvia Gozlan want with him? With that burnt candle he had there he could barely scratch her meat curtains. I warned him to shut up. He ignored me. I told him I couldn't listen to it anymore. He didn't care. He would assault me with his obscenities, his slander and hatred.

Sabah ignored the accusations. He appeared unmoved. On one of the early Kislev evenings, clutched with rings of twilight all around the horizon that seemed never to relent before suddenly evaporating, we walked out of the library. That afternoon, Snot didn't stop smut-talking for a minute. We read an encyclopedia entry about African fertility statues as Snot hummed his filthy fodder. We looked at the most recent edition of *Guinness World Records*, and Snot said, How come they don't write about the biggest dick in the world, there must be someone who has a three-foot dick. How wide do you think a pussy can open? And how much do the heaviest tits weigh? There must be a woman who can't walk because each of her tits is the size of a pumpkin. My brain was filled with this swarm of wasps, and I hurried to walk ahead of him. I was thinking how I didn't want to talk to him anymore, I didn't want him around me.

Behind us we heard wild yelling, a faction of yelling, Snot, Snot, you're gonna get your lot. I turned to look. A flock of cyclists, led by Ehud. I searched for Sabah. Couldn't find him. Snot gave them one look and broke into a cumbersome run. They passed me by. Ehud shot me a look and spat, What goes around comes around. Snot rushed down the road. I yelled to him to turn into the projects on our left, but he turned toward the soccer field, to a steeper slope. The cyclists sped up. They growled their childish rhyme with glee. Snot, with his ungainly movements, bumped into a rock and fell to the ground. One of the cyclists, who didn't manage to brake in time, crashed into Snot's legs and flew off his bike. He landed on a padding of grass. His friends helped him up, and one of them gave him a ride. They left his bicycle, with the bent front wheel, on the grass. When I got there, Snot was still on the ground. He said his right ankle hurt. It might have been broken.

I supported him and we limped all the way back to my house. Msodi looked at us, startled, and called Simo. Thank heavens he picked up, said Msodi. There were evenings when Simo disappeared and came home late. He drove Snot to urgent care. From there he was taken to the hospital. He was very lucky, he told me later, when I came to see him and his leg was bandaged in a cast. Very lucky, because the X-ray revealed a suspicion. Unidentified spots on the tibia, close to the ankle. They did a biopsy. They found an early-stage tumor in his bone.

No one spoke about the incident at school. I walked over to talk to Ehud, but he evaded me. Sabah, as usual, feigned ignorance, behaving like he couldn't believe someone would do such a thing. Everyone sighed mercifully and sent their well wishes.

I went to visit Snot again. Nahumito was sitting on the rug in his room, playing with a toy car. Hanukkah was approaching. Snot said that at first the doctors thought medicine would do the trick, but now they've decided to operate. His father's relatives from America were back in the picture upon hearing the news. They were arranging for the best doctors. They would pay the flight and treatment expenses. They're loaded, said Snot. He smiled meekly. His normally plump face had wizened.

I told him it would be all right.

He said it didn't matter, he just wanted to know what people were saying. All those fake get-well cards could suck his ass. Nahumito laughed when he heard the expression.

You're still here, said Snot, get out of here when grown-ups are talking.

Nahumito walked out with surprising obedience.

I said, I wish there was something I could do.

He said, You think I don't know it's that little dick Sabah who's behind it?

I said, But what difference does that make now?

He said, I'd take the thing that matters most to him.

I asked if he was happy to go back to America.

He said America wasn't Israel, every part of it was different. They used to live in Jersey, but now he was going someplace called El-Ay. It wasn't anything like what he used to know.

I said that anyway, he would go, he'd get better, and he'd have fun.

He said, Anyplace you go, you think another place is better. You can even tolerate Israel's butthole from El-Ay.

MY FATHER WAS SITTING ON THE PORCH. HERSHKO WAVED AT him briefly, then sped up as soon as I shut the car door. Simo opened his hand to me. I stared. He said, The keys.

My pants pocket was plump with the key bundle. I dropped it into his hand. Next time, he said, just ask.

His expression was serious. His eyes were cool. I said, But, then fell silent. The rest of the sentence, I looked for you and couldn't find you, terrified me for some reason.

But you were busy at the Independence Day stages, I said. The waves of nausea that swelled during the car ride home now intensified into stomach cramps. I said I must have eaten something bad last night. He smiled. He got up, patted my back. Come help me with the fire, he said.

In the kitchen, he and my mother exchanged looks. She silently handed him a plate with a large, flattened beef patty. She looked me over again.

The embers were already hissing under the grated surface. Crimson rings of ardor. On their edges, the ashes burned in the coal. The yard was sprawled before us, thrilled ferns under the cloudy sky. Simo said he'd been worried it might rain, but it ended up being a perfect day. The sky was notched with brightness.

He flipped the patty on the grill. The meat sizzled at the touch of the metal. Your mother used lots of *alia*, he said, that's good.

He placed the cooked patty on the plate and handed me a fork. Eat, he said.

I'm nauseous, I said.

Eat, he ordered me, his voice suddenly thickened.

The fat and the grease, their richness coating the space of the mouth with pleasure. The ancient power they ignited in the taste buds. That's what awakened Hophni's and Phinehas's lust. Why did I think that? My stomach rebelled, but everything the fork offered was swallowed down. The hasty, padded fullness. I felt the waves of nausea adsorbing into it. Slapping against rubber.

You drank last night, said Simo.

I nodded.

Proteins and fats, said Simo, that's the time-tested cure. It must have been cheap alcohol. Who would sell your friends fine liquor?

I lowered my head.

You don't need to feel ashamed, said Simo, it's good for you to make your mistakes now, when you can still fix them.

I didn't touch the food after that. There was a different nausea. I labored to fish more of the previous night's events from my memory. The boys who remained, who joined us in the ravine. They were all boys, save for Dalia. And they all created things. The boy with the square features and the heavy jaw, what was his name, he said he painted. Another guy said he wrote.

Chantal ate with astounding voraciousness, loading her plate with salads, chicken hearts, spleen, dredging browned, dripping chicken thighs from the pots. She removed the skin and placed it on Tova's plate. I thought about the three-tined fork smacking against the pan, the kettle, the cauldron, the pot. I tried to hunt Tova's eyes. She was watching my parents, who were also absorbed in the rituals of eating. I watched them as well. Simo pointed at the pots, and Msodi nodded or shook her head. Simo filled her plate accordingly. Once, he leaned in and wiped the corners of her lips with a napkin. They both laughed with abandon.

Later, on the porch, I asked Tova if she'd snitched on me. She wasn't sure what I was talking about. I asked if she told Simo or Msodi that I'd taken something from their room. She denied the allegations with decisive whispers. I said she probably ran to tell our mother as soon as I left the house. She said our mother wasn't even home at the time. She'd left shortly after I went to the party. This too she said in a near whisper.

I asked why she was lowering her voice.

She said, So that those two don't sense I know something I shouldn't.

What?

Nothing.

Our parents were still sitting inside, chomping away.

I hated the unconstructed areas I had to cross on my way to Niro's neighborhood. Especially in this season, with its disturbed blooming and the abundance that grazed the calf muscles, clinging to them. Without warning, when I crossed the tangled pattern of shade cast by some tree, and the gold spots of sun flickered against some blossom in this afternoon hour, Dahan's image popped into my mind. He was teasing me last night, what did he say, that now I'd had a smoke and a drink and all that was left for me to do was lose my virginity. I think I was in the midst of another uncontrollable speech about his films, especially the second one, when I told him I wanted to see the texts, though I thought I remembered most of them after a single viewing. I think that's when I said, defensively, that I wasn't a virgin.

Somebody chuckled, somebody slapped my back. Dahan's expression turned suspicious, or else the blurring of this slice of awareness had colored his expression.

Niro said he couldn't sleep last night after drinking so much, just couldn't. The excitement from the concert had coursed through his veins. He fell asleep for a few minutes, and right away some girl materialized before him, a girl who, in that brief, shallow dream, he knew to be named Lesbian Nataly. He didn't know anyone like her in his waking life, she didn't resemble any of the girls in his circle.

I asked what a lesbian was.

He laughed. He said, You're not a virgin, but you don't know what a lesbian is?

I asked if one had to do with the other. We were sitting on a bench outside of his house. His parents didn't like to see him smoke. The incense of Independence Day sacrifice rising from the neighbors' yards bonded to form greasy air. A group of young kids circled around on their bicycles, urging each other to perform more daring tricks, riding standing up with no hands, popping wheelies, skidding.

All this barbecuing makes me want to barf, said Niro. He looked at the kids and shouted at one of them, who was riding a shiny new BMX, Ofer, let me take it for a spin.

The kid skidded to a stop in front of us. This is a new bike, he said.

I'll show you something you've never seen before, said Niro.

The kid gave the cigarette in Niro's hand a long look and gestured to it with his chin. Niro nodded. The kid got off the bike seat. Niro handed him the half-finished cigarette. He got on the bike, moved away from us, then turned around and sped back toward us. He leaned back. The front wheel rose into the air, and then Niro hit the hand brakes, raised his body, and leaned forward. The front wheel thudded softly against the asphalt, the bicycle's state-of-the-art coils trembled, and the rear wheel rose. For a flash, Niro and the bike were almost perpendicular to the road. Then the bike landed back. The other kids, who had paused in their tricks, all cried out enthusiastically. Niro said, Don't try this at home.

Ofer sneaked in two more puffs from the cigarette Niro had left with him for safekeeping before handing it back. Coughing, he took hold of the handlebars.

❄ ❄ ❄

NIRO REFUSED TO GIVE ME DALIA'S PHONE NUMBER. HE SAID HE didn't know her exact address, only that she lived in Hapoel neighborhood, near the soccer field, and that her last name was Shushan. He said, She got under your skin, did she?

I said no, just that Hershko said I'd insulted her pretty bad.

He said, You were blunt, but I don't think she was insulted. I don't think she cares enough about you to be insulted.

I told him I really loved their music, especially the first song. That I'd like to hear them play again.

He said who knows how many chances they'd have, now that Hershko was about to enlist. I said they could find another key-boardist. Niro said there was no chance, that Hershko was the only talented musician among them. He'd done the arrangement for the first song I was so excited about, and written most of the compositions. I said the songs were also moving thanks to Niro's singing and performance and playing.

Niro shrugged. With feigned indifference, he said, We'll see.

I asked if all of his friends were artists. He asked what I meant. I said that if I wasn't mistaken everyone I spoke to the previous night did something, painting, playing music, acting. He said they were just poseurs, most of them pimps and bimbos. I asked why he hung around with them.

He said, They're the lesser of all evils.

I didn't understand the abnormally dark mood that had taken over him. I asked about Dahan. Reluctantly, Niro said he was tal-ented, but an idiot. He lit another cigarette. I bent down to pick a stem of scutch grass from the crack in the sidewalk. The clouds thickened. A gust of chill passed through the air. I said I loved his second film. Niro said he'd noticed, that I wouldn't stop talking about it. He said that Hershko was involved in it too, he'd created the soundtrack. He helped him. The idea was that the soundtrack would be made up of fifty-five notes, same as the total number of words that appeared on the screen. I asked who'd written the po-ems. Niro muttered some name. Said the person was a friend of

Dahan's. He didn't really know him, but Dahan was always singing his praises.

He said, Let's go inside, so strange that it's about to rain on
Independence Day.

Then he asked if I had plans for later that night. I said I didn't.
He said the group was meeting at Eddy's girlfriend Nofar's place,
and would figure out a plan from there. He said I was invited.

The names Shushan, Yossef and Esther, appeared in the phone
book, along with the name of a street that I thought was located in
Hapoel neighborhood. I lay on my back in bed. The walls truly were
nude. Nothing in the bedroom was mine. Everything was done according to Msodi's taste, from the pattern of the sheets to the color
of the lampshade and the picture frames on the walls. I also had a
visit from the Lesbian Nataly that Niro had talked about. He said
she was wearing a leotard and a denim skirt, small and shapely. I
wondered what "lesbian" meant and what was threatening about
her. A warmth spread through my limbs. My hand almost reached
for that spot. But it was paralyzed. Ever since the Sylvia Gozlan affair, there had been no more nocturnal emissions or spilling of se-
men in vain. Snot was right. It was an efficient cure. Better than the
speech fasts of age fifteen. Better. I tried to shift my thoughts to
other avenues, but I could find none, save for the events of the previous night, the poems, and the insults I spewed at Dalia Shushan.

The darkness, reddish beneath the black cloak, filled the space,
the throat. Someone was trying to break through the door of my
bedroom. The house was empty, and the front door had already
been beaten down. I struggled to get up. That muddy medium
closed in on me. I rose up and out of it. The door trembled from the
stranger's blows. I sunk back down. If only I could move my limbs,
command something through the bloodstream. A shadow as white
as a sword stood in the doorway against a second darkness that
came from the outside. A being called out a name, a name I recognized, if only I could remember where from, but it wasn't my name.

I lay in bed, my flesh exhausted. My mother knocked on the

door, finally she started knocking. Yes, I croaked. Evening was descending outside, I noticed. Its moderate chill came in through the windows in waves. My mother peeked through a crack in the door. She said, One of your new friends called to ask if you're coming. I got the address from him. Nofar, that's Ezra's daughter, from the tire factory, isn't it?

I was grateful I'd decided to go. The closer I got to the address Niro had left me, the more that breathless anticipation ignited, a merriment I'd forgotten my body was familiar with and knew how to sustain. Eddy and Niro and Dahan, and the square-featured boy, the painter, and a lanky, long-haired girl in an intentionally patched denim suit were already sitting at the Ezra family's living room. They were in the midst of an argument about whether to go to the stages to watch the fireworks, bringing alcohol and hanging out, as Nofar said, or just go sit someplace. Hershko hadn't returned yet, and nobody had a car.

We could go to the cemetery, said Niro, it's more alive than those dead stages.

Or to the ravine near Hershko's place, he'll be back sometime tonight.

What do you say, Nahum? asked Niro.

Hesitantly, I said, I think sitting on a grassy hill near the stages could be a good start.

You too, huh, said Niro, you'll all die with the bourgeoisie.

Yalla, yalla, said the lanky girl, big-time rocker.

Dahan had a bottle of arak he'd stolen from the new grocery store at the old shopping center a few days ago, he announced proudly. That place deserved to be robbed just for being called the new grocery store at the old shopping center.

You're the one who calls it that, said Niro, it isn't their fault.

You're so heavy, said Dahan, you guys are no fun when Hershko isn't around.

Nofar said, Why don't you go wait for him outside of his house?

By the second round of fireworks, we were already tipsy. The anise flavor clung to my teeth and my tongue, and I spat it out. Dahan insisted that I drink. He disappeared for a few minutes and returned with some beer. He pressured me until I drank. The star of the moment was prancing around onstage. They said he used to be a backup dancer for that singer who represented Israel at Eurovision. Her agent discovered the beauty of his cracked, masculine singing voice when they were on a flight together, and she signed him. The lanky girl mouthed along with the words. Gross, Nofar told her and pushed her shoulder, and the two of them burst out laughing. A few moments later they stood up in unison, holding on to each other, and started to dance to the sounds of the parched singing. They twirled around. The green bed of grass absorbed the frequencies and vibrations produced by their limbs, the liquidity of the lanky body against the hardness of Nofar's limbs. Dahan instructed me to take another swig of arak to reinforce the beer buzz. We sprawled out on the grass, looking skyward. The heavens were purified from the cloudiness of the day. It's like the birth of a solar system, Niro said, pointing at the cascade of brightness that, for a moment, wiped out the starry crystal of the month of Iyar.

I said, Like whispers, but made of light.

Dahan rolled over and sat up. So, Nahum, are you going to keep your word?

What word?

He pulled a stack of pages from his bag. The promise you made yesterday, he said, I'm giving you the Sealed and Leased poems and you'll tell us how you lost your virginity.

A MOMENT CAME WHEN I COULD LOOK AT THE SEQUENCE OF action and tell myself, From this point onward, you are subjected to this sequence as well, not generating it, you are not the being for whose purposes it is performed. Six months earlier, Snot sent me a short letter. He'd recovered, thank God. That's what he wrote: *Thank God.* His handwriting was crooked as usual, the letters rebellious, those meant to be straight tilting sideways, those naturally round angular instead. He wrote that they were staying in America but moving to live near his father's family, who were helping them out, all conflicts resolved. His leg still hurt, the memory of the shattering contained within the ankle. How was I doing? When would I come visit?

I didn't write back. His questions seemed merely courteous. The letter was drenched with pain, but not a single word bore witness to it. Just the feeling of a quiet defeat. I couldn't have imagined how much I'd miss Snot, that I'd left a part of myself with him without noticing. The blade of grief ran over me then, in the shower, alone, I shuddered with tears that were not my own. My hand leaned against the tiles for stability. The floor was slippery. The showerhead glowed with foreign silver.

Ehud might have sensed an inkling of this, my internal rebellion against seclusion. He caught me on my way out of school on a day in the month of Shevat. The air densing around us, the downy insides of a retreating winter were clear to me. His skin was windswept, submitting to its usual youthful pinkness. He said, So, Farkash, where are you hurrying off to?

I said I was going home.

He said it was a shame I was pulling away like that. What was wrong with me? A few friends were coming over that night, and the guys had been asking about me lately.

I didn't answer. He said, You should come, it'll be fun.

I said I had plans. Maybe another time.

Then another messenger hunted me down. I saw the exterior will activating her, forcing movement upon her limbs. Sylvia Gozlan and her famous Purim parties. Wear a symbolic costume, she said. I was leaning against the blue metal fence that divided the paved path from a sandy lot, beyond which was the despicable gymnasium, padded with unscrubbable sweat, where, even if it were destroyed, new temples and stately halls built in its stead, the cornerstones would be anointed with the smell of young boys and the oils emitted by their skin. We would never be vanished from this place. Cultures and societies would become caught in the wheels of destruction and resurrection, and someone would pause from their race of existence and sniff, and recognize that we'd been there. I was pressed between the fence and Sylvia Gozlan. She'd tweezed the hair from the bridge of her nose. Her black hair had been glistened into electricity. But there was a pleading twinkle in her eyes, I saw it, a fracture of light glaring with many hopes, plenty of visions. She said, There's no parties like mine, you should know, none.

The fair tissue of her lips, chapped around the edges, occasionally cracked open. I wanted to tilt my head and fall into that wounded softness. I turned my face away. I muttered a meek agreement.

I saw the masks Chantal and Tova had made strewn about the living room. They made them out of poster board, paper, and any other hard, cuttable material they could get their hands on. Then decorated them with markers, sparkles, felt, and heaven knows what else. I asked Tova if I could borrow one of the masks. She looked me over and squealed that she didn't think any of them would fit me, my face was too flat. She'd make me a new one.

I told her not to do me any favors.

She was crushing and plucking the ends of her skirt with her fingers as she spoke. She's going through something, I thought. She said it wasn't about doing favors, that she was being sincere. She asked where I was going.

I told her I'd been invited to a party and that she shouldn't pry. She said she'd make me a mask to cover up my ugly face.

I laughed drily. She placed a sheet of plastic against my face and sketched over it with a marker.

She delivered the final result to my bedroom. The gray surface of the mask was stained with metallic, industrial powder blue, embedded carefully with glinting pieces of green glass that formed arches over the eyeholes, to resemble eyebrows. Black, curvy marker lines grew out of them, twisting on to the edges. I whistled with appreciation. I asked her if Chantal had helped.

Tova, Simo called out from outside before she could answer. Her mouth, which was open a crack, opened farther and then froze. Tova, our father repeated his roar, and the two of us hurried outside. Tova was still holding on to the mask.

I knew it, said Simo, I knew you were responsible for this.

The coffee table was a mess. Crafting materials and glues and brushes, and glitter dust clinging to the tablecloth. The jar in which Tova kept her glass pieces was lying on the floor. Its contents were strewn over the floor. Are you insane, said Simo, filling the house with glass, look at this.

The gloomy grumbling had been gone from his features and his posture for the past year. Tova quickly kneeled before him, carefully gathering the glass shards.

What's wrong with you, asked Simo, go get a broom and dustpan and clean this garbage up.

Tova said, It isn't garbage, it's crafting materials.

Simo emitted a growl, almost a bark. And you—he turned to me—what are you doing, standing around like that, either help or get out of here.

I got the broom and dustpan from the utility closet. Simo snatched them from me, signaled to Tova to move away, and swept the floor vigorously, spraying the glass in every direction rather than piling it. Tova stood beside me. In a low voice, she hissed, He did something bad again.

CHANTAL RETURNED FROM WALKING COCOA PUP IN THE MIDST of the cleanup project, after Tova fearfully took the broom from Simo's hands and he'd retired to the kitchen. We heard him rummaging through the fridge, clumsily pulling out vegetables and other groceries, the rustling of bags, the banging of the fridge walls, the slight squeaking sound as the door closed by itself.

Chantal looked at the mask in my hand. She said to Tova, Why did you make a special one for him?

Tova didn't answer. Cocoa Pup's leash dropped from Chantal's hand, and he pranced around us and hopped onto my lap. I gave him the quota of attention I'd budgeted for that day and pushed him off. I'm going to the party, I said.

Tova said, To Sylvia Gozlan's Purim party?

Chantal said, But you can't dance.

Walla, said Tova, I forgot about that.

Chantal smiled, her paleness suddenly stretched into mockery, her small teeth resting against her bottom lips, painted a dirty white.

I said, How do you know about Sylvia Gozlan and her parties?

Softly, Tova said, Everybody in Sderot knows.

Decisively, Chantal said, Everybody in Sderot.

Look, said Tova. She offered the dustpan with the heap of glass. The bits were lying among dust and lint pilings. So dirty, she said, looking around her. The floor needs a serious cleaning. Mom hasn't mopped it in like a week.

New sounds rose from the kitchen, the bell-like tide of pots banging against pots, the swooshing of knives and forks. Tova's eyes widened as she whispered, Dad's making dinner.

From the kitchen doorway, we could see the chaos Simo had caused. Drawers pulled out halfway, heaped tomatoes, crushed garlic cloves, thawing fish, potatoes, all sorts of sages and parsleys and cilantros, a blade raised above them and chopping them up. You want me to help? said Chantal. Cocoa Pup echoed her words with sharp barks.

Simo had his back to us and did not turn around. Blandly, he said, No, and get that smelly dog out of here. He'll get diseases in the food.

Tova whispered to me, Mom's going to kill him. She walked

closer and began gathering the unnecessary dishes. A guilliotine fell on the onion, slicing it in two. We moved away from the kitchen. Tova said, Why is he using onions, what's he putting onions in the fish for, why is he even cooking fish on a weekday, Mom's going to kill him.

I recognized tension behind Msodi's typically unbiased expression as soon as she walked through the door. Her eyes shifted in their sockets with greater alertness than usual. I was in the living room, looking at Simo's outdated amplification system. Tova and Chantal were in the yard, playing with Cocoa Pup. His happy squeakiness invaded the home. I wondered how complicated it would be to move the system into my room. My mother shot me a quick look. The rustles from the kitchen drew her attention.

The walls absorbed part of her shouting, which was muffled by brick and plaster. *Allah ister*, what did the kitchen ever do to you? All you know how to make is a mess. Nothing but chaos.

I didn't join them for dinner. I used my dislike of fish as an excuse. The creaking of the chairs, the crudeness of Tova's table setting, all echoed our mother's upset. From my bedroom, I didn't hear conversations, didn't hear laughter. Only miniscule rackets. I stood in the middle of the room, barefoot. I closed my eyes and tried to conjure some of the sounds and beats of the songs from the Top 40 show Tova and Chantal watched religiously. Nothing came to mind. I tried to picture the dancers' moves in the music videos. I thought I could come up with something. My muscles loosened, my limbs moved.

At the party, Sylvia asked me why I was standing on the sidelines instead of dancing. Her yard was a bedlam of heavily made-up faces covered with cloaks of different materials, happy and distorted against their will, and all of this drowned within writhing bodies, subjected to songs I didn't recognize, crude, simplistic rhythms, the pounding of the hammer and the beat of the drum. I told her I couldn't dance. My stomach was still turning anyway.

The balance of silence between Simo and Msodi was unloaded into malicious hissing directed at Chantal, Tova, and me, sarcastic, belittling remarks. Those two never fought outright. It's all him, Tova had told me. I asked what she meant. She said he always took our mother for granted and spoiled things.

Sylvia said, Look, nobody knows how to dance, it's freestyle, everyone just makes whatever moves come to them. She pointed at a girl who was pantomiming away while her legs moved this way and that. What do you think that one's doing?

I said I had no idea. Sylvia said, She's opening and closing drawers and doors in her closet. And that one—she pointed at a boy—is washing his dad's car.

All right, I thought. I had committed to memory the dance moves of the pop singers in the most recent episode of Chantal and Tova's show. I entered the crowd of revelers. I felt the dark, low assault of the song that played rising from my groin to my heart. The hips, then. I shook my legs, wiggling them according to what I remembered. I don't know when I realized that people around me were stifling laughter. All I could see of Sabah and Ehud's faces were rows of teeth underneath their masks, but their laughter rumbled. I pushed my way out of the crowd of dancers. I sat on a recliner on the edge of the party, my back clinging to the fabric.

SYLVIA GOZLAN'S GOLD-AND-RED-PAINTED FACE FLICKERED within the masses. I didn't think she saw me. She dragged a wicker chair and set it against mine. From up close, the sparkle of pleading in her eyes was harder, hotter. She said, That pathetic David. What's his problem?

I didn't answer. The whirlwind of red and gold was wounded by her mouth. She brought her forehead to mine. I brought mine to hers. Our noses touched. We kissed, a small, fluttering kiss. She pulled her head away, looked at me, astonished, and got up. I stayed seated. I thought about that vague accusation Tova had made about Simo. What did she know that I didn't? I thought, That pathetic David, damn that Sabah.

Sylvia Gozlan returned a few minutes later. The gold-and-red whirlwind finally suited her features. Her face was twisted savagely, and she was on the verge of tears. She touched my arm. They're all leaving soon, she said. She asked me to leave with everyone and then come back on my own.

I didn't ask where her parents were, the rest of her family, if they'd gone away, leaving her in charge of the house, if they'd given her permission to throw a party. I helped her gather the leftover food into enormous trash bags and place all the dishes in the sink. Her bedroom was on the second floor. She handed me a cotton ball and a small bottle. I drenched the cotton ball with the liquid from the bottle and wiped the makeup off her face. From her wide forehead, to her somewhat curved, broken nose, to her cheeks. Cotton balls, red, gold, black from the blend of colors, filled the wastebasket beside the dresser. The artificial skin peeled off of her, revealing her new image, not the superficial genetic one, but the one born from the mood of the moment, igniting with excitement and trembling, attentive to the shifts of light. In the splendor that stood in the space with her, her eyes yearned. I put my lips to hers.

We lay side by side. I wanted to kiss her some more. It was as if the inside of the mouth was buttery, and I didn't know if it was my mouth or hers. But she parted our mouths with her hand. My tongue bumped against a scorched divider, pushed back. She removed her hands and lightly bit my chin. She said, I don't know what I'm supposed to do.

I told her I didn't either.

She said she was ready to lose her virginity, she was on fire down there.

I asked, Down where?

She grabbed my hand and led it down her belly, lifting her dress with her other hand. She placed my hand between her legs.

Some voice pecked at the edge of my thoughts. I ignored it. I could feel the dampness through the fabric of her underwear. I said, But you're wet down there.

She laughed all of a sudden. A rip of laughter that quickly died out. Perhaps it was a sound of nervousness, the ringing of the tense body. Feel it with your hand, she said, put it in there.

I slipped my fingers in. There was heat in the thing I touched, hair, did she have pubic hair like boys did? A soft tingle and further wetness. I touched skin bathed with something, some curve of skin, pliable. Sylvia Gozlan let out a scream, but her expression radiated. Our faces were so close, I could perceive the radiation. She pulled down her underwear.

Why are you wet down there, I whispered, did you pee yourself?

Breathing shallowly, she said, Smell it.

I put my fingers to my nose. A rich, liquid salt. I became infected with her shortness of breath. My body lost its actuality in space save for one spot. So taut I could feel the metallic trace of the zipper etching into it. I unbuttoned my pants and pulled them down. I pulled down my underwear as well.

Sylvia Gozlan said, You need to put your thing inside.

I said, What thing? I gasped. I was scared. I said, Put it in where?

Without warning, her fingers wrapped around my penis, the distress of its hardness was gone, and only the alertness of muscles against flesh remained, just like before a nocturnal emission, the promise of softness, I wanted to give in to it, to come to pleasure. Sylvia lay on her back. I lay on top of her. I brought my face to hers, waiting for her lips to respond to me again and for our mouths to melt and meld into each other again. The room was dim. Her face shone and she was more beautiful, her tortured features attuning to an entity that wasn't me. I closed my eyes. I tried to keep the pleasure inside of me, not to let it spill over, I was hard and I was soft and I wanted to hold on and I wanted to let go.

Sylvia Gozlan's hand was still holding on to my thing. She moaned when its tip rubbed against her down there. I almost suffocated from the congestion of air suddenly removed. And then, beyond touch, I understood what the inside was. The chills down my back and thighs understood it. I pushed. I was fully the act of pushing. Sylvia Gozlan moaned again, a faint, broken groan. Or maybe I moaned. I returned to the room for a fraction of time. I asked if it hurt. She said a little, but that I shouldn't stop, to push more, more, more.

JUST MY LUCK, I THOUGHT, ALWAYS FINDING MYSELF WITH pieces of shit. The thought surprised me with its violence, its urgency. Simo's voice spoke from within it. Its flint core. I stuttered on that grassy hill in the alcoholic darkness of the breeze. The story of Sylvia Gozlan was on the tip of my tongue. A web of delicate strands, pink and powder blue, fell from somewhere onto the hair and face of the square-featured boy. He touched it and sprang up. A child, about six years old, brutish, looked at us from the slope, canister in hand. A liquid spray blew out of the canister, its trajectory sabotaged by gravity. It partially hardened in beads at his feet.

Shiloh, the square-faced boy yelled, grabbing the kid, who shouted and giggled in turn. He hoisted him easily onto his shoulder and slapped his buttocks lightly. That's for the spray, he said.

The child farted from the effort of resistance against the grip of the square-faced boy. A long whistle, startlingly sprawling, perfectly timed. A silent aperture opened in the racket onstage, a pause between songs.

Dahan bellowed with laughter. The square-faced boy almost dropped his brother to the ground, then tightened his grip and turned to leave. Dahan called after him, pleading with him to come back. But the boy continued to move away.

He turned to me. Tell us, he said, almost demanding.

I had a moment to ponder this, a clumsy, spasmodic pondering, but a moment nevertheless. I sat before him, the printed pages in my hand.

Come on, what's the big deal? said Dahan.

He pushed his hair back, that same foppish, possibly calculated gesture. From his mouth, open in a smile or a question, pearly white rabbit teeth peeked out.

What's the big deal? he repeated. She, he said, pointing at the lanky girl with whom Niro was now sitting some distance away from us, she used to sit in the back during math class and masturbate out of boredom.

A fluttering sound of a breath catching came from Nofar. She stood up.

Yeah, said Dahan, she would turn the pen around and shove it down there and—

He was cut off when Eddy slapped the back of his neck. Nofar placed her hand on Eddy's arm and pulled him up to stand. He followed her wordlessly. She touched the shoulder of the lanky girl, leaned in, and whispered something.

What, Niro called to him, leaving already?

You can stay with this loser if you want, said Nofar.

The lanky girl got up and Niro got up with her. He shrugged apologetically. His expression spoke of angry helplessness.

So, said Dahan.

I said, Everybody's gone.

Come on, he said, come on already, Smoky Nahum, tell the story already.

I said I'd better go too. When I got home I realized I still had the Sealed and Leased pages.

(I, MEANING I, SUDDENLY FEEL ENVIOUS OF I-NAHUM, OF THAT moment in which I-Nahum am trapped, along with all my aches.

Not my youth, but my faith in words, within which I could find the evaporated fullness of reality.)

WHEN I CAME HOME FROM SCHOOL I LAY IN BED AND LOOKED AT the poems. I piled the original pages on my stomach by order. I picked up a poem, stared at it, then set it aside in a new pile. I re-created Sealed and Leased in my mind. I thought, I could write poems like that too. I sat down at my desk. I turned to a new, empty page and jotted down a few words. They were devoid of force, devoid of an inner flow. I lay down again. I stared at poems seven through ten. They were the hub of the work. Their words stood like objects on the page, a presence. But a thread of mystery drew from them, for the fact that they weren't trying to say anything, but just being what they were. I asked myself what was the quality of existence, what made their words *there*. I thought, They're just the numerals representing the exact number of words, and the word itself, words. How abstract and how tangible. It was as if someone had set a ghost before me and I'd stripped it of all its scarves of air, all the ghostly matter, and beneath it, all I'd found was a firm, ossified skeleton. I thought, I'd like to write poems like this.

I thought with some elation of the one poem I'd written in seventh grade, which in my recollection was replaced with a lump in the stomach, a ticking spreading through the cells. I'd never written anything else. There wasn't anything to write. How did Dalia Shushan extract that simple truth out of me that night in the ravine, under the Hershkowitz house? How easy it was to say. My life is empty. My heart is hollow, as are my lungs, the space of my abdomen. If I tapped on the outside of my skin, a muffled echo would sound back.

I stepped outside. Setting Iyar sun, pray for me. Pray for me, Persian lilacs, with your evening honey, dripping with nectar. I thought about the lost Tannaim, beseeching the heavenly bodies and forces of nature to take mercy on them and speak for them. I would beg Sderot, on its shattered street corners and stucco façades, to be my mouth. An urgent brightness of evaporating light was shed on the shopping center. Someone had sprayed the wall with graffiti that read, All you monkeys go suck. The command bubbled between the electricmatter transmissions. I'm a monkey, now, suck what?

I'd already reached the soccer field from the other side. Not far from it, the long, dilapidated wooden halls of an abandoned school were being repurposed into a yeshiva. The rabbi at the synagogue urged me to come there in the afternoon and join the study groups. I told him I was already learning the Gmarah at school. He said, Not learning, study group. *Hevruta.*

Mituta, I thought to myself. I stood there, staring at the construction site. They would soon convene for evening prayer. I could join and talk to them.

I hadn't noticed Dalia's arrival. Perhaps she'd popped out of the earth, holding on to roots and bulbs, climbing out from the depths. In her presence, anyway, was an ancient earthliness, in the heavy body and the mane of hair tucked behind her ears. She was holding on to a bent stick. I thought, All you monkeys go suck. She said, You're here too. I can't get away from you.

I began to stutter something, then fell silent.

She said, It isn't a coincidence that you're here.

I shook my head.

She said, Is it a coincidence or not?

I thought, It isn't too late to say I'm on my way to pray at the yeshiva. But I said nothing.

She pulled away. Wait, I whispered after she'd already started to leave.

I don't know if she heard me, but she stopped. I hurried over. I said, I didn't mean it, that night, I didn't mean to say what I said, it just came out.

She may have smiled. Something in her lips moved. She said, Forget it, you were drunk.

By three things a man is known: by his cup, by his pocket, and by his anger, I said.

She said, Do I need all three of them in order to know someone, or is one enough?

DALIA SAID, SO YOU HANG AROUND THE LIBRARY, BUT YOU DON'T read books.

I said that was true. I asked why it surprised her.

We made plans to meet on the lawn outside the library. Dalia wanted to meet in a demilitarized zone. She said, But the library is a charged place, a war zone.

Between who? I asked.

She asked if I'd read the story.

I said I had. I said, It's a girls' story, isn't it?

She asked if I thought that because of the name. I recognized the story's name, "The Girl Who Was Plugged In," when she'd said it. She'd mentioned it in her conversation with Niro just a few days earlier, a few days, it seemed like years, interior landscapes collapsed and sprang up over the course of time, it was as if just a moment had passed and the two events, Dalia and Niro talking on the edge of the preparations for their private Independence Day concert, and Dalia and I standing in the fallow field, not far from the soccer field, those two events seemed to stem from each other, succeeding each other along a timeline that could only be sustained by the foreign gaze of memory, that human God.

That afternoon, we said very little. But I didn't want to say goodbye to her. She seemed to need the company too, even if it was mine. We wandered aimlessly. Occasionally, she spoke a sentence that required no response, extracted by force of my general presence. The barbs are soft now, riches do not endure forever, the bustle of Sderot in the afternoon, a fear of evening, a terrible, monstrous logic.

Through her eyes I saw a different Sderot, a panicked one,

men and women and children who, under the surface of the everyday, were gnawed by anticipation, horror of darkness. Or perhaps the everyday was entirely intended to delay the darkness, which erupted for a flash, a rallying cry, a flicker, in their lives, against the partition of the eyelids, even when they were shut.

We circled the lanes, the streets, the dwindling of the sun, its rays against the asphalt, the disappearing pleasantness of Iyar. We approached the EMT station. In the event hall across the way, wedding guests were already gathering in fine clothing, ironed fabrics, and layers of tulle. Dalia paused. I paused with her. We watched the procession in silence.

Dalia said, What do you think?

I said, I don't know. Ultimately, everyone has to go through it, and everyone thinks they're special on that day.

Kind of corny, she said.

What, the way of the world?

What about pain?

What's that got to do with it?

She said, You said a man is known by his cup, by his pocket, and by his anger. What about his pain?

I don't see pain here.

Look at how happy they are. Doesn't it pain you that you aren't as happy as them?

I said, Truly, I don't really care about them.

She said, Yeah, I could have guessed that.

Do you envy them?

No, said Dalia, I like their act, but I like the backstage even more.

I said nothing. I considered this. I said, Do you believe that the backstage is pain?

I don't know what I believe, I only know what makes me pause and watch.

We fell silent again and kept walking. When we passed by my

neighborhood, I said, I live over there, and gestured toward the sloping line of houses.

She said, So this is where we part.

I nodded.

Are you good friends with Niro?

I told her we were pals.

What does that mean, pals?

Not strangers, but not friends yet. Certainly not close friends.

You seemed pretty close in the ravine, after the concert.

I'd like to be his friend, but I have no idea if I've got anything to offer.

That's none of my business, said Dalia. I was just asking because I lent him a book that has a story that would be good for you to read. "The Girl Who Was Plugged In."

I asked if I could call her.

She said I could call but she wouldn't necessarily be able to answer.

I said, So maybe we should meet, anyway.

She said we ought to pick a demilitarized zone.

I said, What's demilitarized?

She said, Not charged, but not uninhabited, and certainly not a home turf.

Young poincianas rustled over us outside of the library, their lacy branches turning gold around the edges by the force of greenness imparted to them. I felt it too, the intensity of growth, how it rose within me, a tangle of the soul to which something has just opened up. I was holding the short story collection in my hand. I said, The Hebrew is bad.

Dalia said, The translation isn't great. So you read it.

I said, Niro laughed when I asked him to let me borrow it.

Did you tell him I said it was okay?

I didn't mention you.

Her heavy body leaned against the tree trunk. We sat at a certain distance, separate, legs crossed. The white dress, strewn with yellow florals, covered her thighs. Her thick calves were covered by long, taut socks woven with a delicate pattern of wheat stalks. A strip of skin showed between the ends of the dress and the tops of the socks, golden as well. I looked into her eyes. A small twitch, a flinching of the eyes, a light ripple, passed through her irises.

Why not? she asked.

I said, I didn't think you'd like that.

She nodded. Then why did he laugh?

I don't know. Maybe because of the irony of it.

The irony, she said.

I lied. Niro had mentioned her. He repeated his words from the other night. She's getting under your skin. She's already there. What nonsense.

So what did you think about the story? asked Dalia.

I'd had trouble following the plotlines the first time I read it. They kept mixing into each other. So I wrote a summary on a piece of paper and read it methodically. I told myself, she's testing you, this is a test.

Here's what I wrote:

- The story takes place in a world that forbids advertising in public spaces.

- Society is controlled by a media conglomerate that creates stars and starlets in order to bypass this prohibition.

- The stars and starlets receive orders about which clothes to wear, which accessories to use, and which opinions to voice.

- The story revolves around an ugly, isolated girl who idolizes one of these teen stars. Her name is P. Burke.

- When she realizes she can never have him, she tries to kill herself.

- She is saved and becomes involved in an experiment designed to develop the next stage of the star industry.

- She is trained to remotely control the body of a beautiful girl, Delphi. Delphi is the newest glamorous socialite.

- P. Burke shows great skills in controlling this golem.

- She starts to believe that she, P. Burke, and the golem, Delphi, who is plugged in, are the same woman. She is as beautiful and desirable as Delphi, and Delphi is witty like her.

- She falls in love with Paul, the son of a wealthy family.

- Paul wants to rebel against his father, the head of the media conglomerate.

- P. Burke shares her secret with Paul—that she is actually a miserable girl held hostage by evil scientists.

- Paul storms the lab.

- When he sees the real P. Burke, he is disgusted by her ugliness.

- Paul goes straight. He becomes a senior executive in the media conglomerate.

- When P. Burke is disconnected from Delphi, she dies.

I told Dalia, It's a sad story.
Is it?
Yes, I said. It teaches us that every story is a prison, but all we've got is stories. We can either give in to them or die.
Dalia said, So predictable. You didn't understand a thing.

✽ ✽ ✽

(I, MEANING I, TO WHOM I-NAHUM'S THREADS OF TIME ARE AS known as my own are concealed, though all of them lead to some inscrutable primary purpose, know the feeling. Some story shard that does not belong to I-Nahum suddenly shoves its way in. It happens that a man returns to his hotel room after wandering a strange town and finds his slippers upside down, their soles facing the sky defiantly, and though at the time he believes he's rid himself of the many superstitions he'd accumulated since childhood, all the small defaults of the day are recapped in his mind, the dysfunction of the magnetic strip on his subway card, the bad gamble on an unfamiliar dish at a restaurant, the unfortunate choice to stand in the short ticket line, only for the man ahead of him to delve into a lengthy conversation with the cashier, aimless wanderings that lead him over and over again to a black marble statue, a heap of images said to mark the doorway to hell. And suddenly it hits him. The pattern of defaults appears, along with its cause.)

I WANTED HER COMPANIONSHIP MORE THAN SHE WANTED MINE, I think. She wanted to learn about the Jewish world, the practices, the traditions I knew, the mitzvahs I observed, their rationale, the *halachahs.* The ritualistic side, as she referred to it. I could speak of that endlessly. She'd only had narrow, diminished access. Everything she knew came from rumors, faint echoes of dos and don'ts, customs transformed into rules. I often asked her about this. She said these rituals were the literature of life.

I said I thought that to her literature and life were one and the same.

She said that was true, if the literature was good. She said the details that created the spark, the movement, the organs' knowledge of how to wake up every morning, how to absorb the noon light, how to survive the evening quiet, the actions and words, that was the literature she was looking for.

She didn't talk about herself. Her mother's name was Esther and her father's name was Yossef. They both came from Marrakech during the first waves of immigration. I asked if she meant "Aliyah." She said, Waves of immigration. She was an only child, both the eldest and the youngest. I asked what that meant. She said she was born late, against all odds, so she was her parents' eldest, but they treated her with the forgiveness of a youngest child, marveling at the fact that she was granted to them after they'd already accepted their childlessness. They saw her through the ghosts of the children who'd missed their opportunity to be born. I liked her ambition to speak precisely. She said she liked my Hebrew, but it was a shame I kept quoting scripture all the time. I asked what she'd expected when she asked me about the rules of religion. She said she'd expected a smidgen of independent thought.

This conversation repeated itself in different forms. The blood flow of Iyar slowed to match the long, pricking, blinding pulses of Sivan. School dwindled as well. Save for prep days for junior year finals, we were left to our own devices. I planned to skip the prep. I knew I would just pass the literature finals. The material for the other finals was stored in different compartments of my brains, digested to become resin in my veins that I could secrete in my sleep. Dull weeks that only brightened when I saw Dalia. Niro called a few times to check up on me. I answered in a low voice, saying I was very busy memorizing facts and figures. Give me an example, he said. I said, The Hasmonean Dynasty. I said, Good and evil in King Herod's court. I said, The ruin of the second temple.

The sweet appeasement between Simo and Msodi, whose causes I could not identify, lasted through the days of Omer. There was harmony between them. They completed each other's sentences when they spoke to us, if they spoke to us. Decisions were made through silent looks, through nods.

Chantal ignored this, as usual. She found new friends with

whom to chatter as she came and went. The corners of Tova's mouth drew down. She smiled rarely, and even then they were lip-deep smiles for appearances' sake. She answered every question or order with terse, curt statements.

On Shavuot eve, around the cheese pastries and dairy feast, she let out a short, uncontrollable sob. I was the only one who noticed. I had already been looking at her. Her eyes were fixed on Simo, who was piling our mother's *berkoksh*, that revolting puddle of rice and milk, onto his plate. Simo usually hated these kinds of dishes. Give me meat, he'd say, give me chicken, give me bones, Moroccans don't eat cheese. Msodi said something about roasting some *bobarisa* for the holiday and Simo said, Udders, and licked his lips lustily, and they both laughed. Then the sound cracked in Tova's throat. She retired from the table.

The next day, on the holiday, I only tasted a little of Msodi's cooking. I was still full of the power of sanctity from the previous night's *Tikkun* service, a mixture of a blurring of the senses and an electric overflow of the spirit. I made plans with Dalia to meet in the afternoon, when the heat broke. I lay in bed. Again, I pondered the Sealed and Leased poems. There was nothing in there, I thought, besides the words' insistence on being, first and foremost, words. I thought about the meaning of the combinations, "ent net, stern sworded town." I could say it was deep, making an argument about the character of words. Language is indeed a stern and sworded town, and the words are a net of the endless stern rustle of leaves in the trees, of ideas in the caverns of the skull. But at the same time, the poem pointed at the fact that the insight was no more than a pangram of the numeral ten and the nouns, the technical demands of the poem. I'd already thought this, I wanted to think something new. The poem didn't imbue me with the same calm. But I wasn't searching for it, anyway. The great nervousness of the power of sanctity and my empty stomach, my tired limbs, the heaviness of my eyes from the lack of sleep, were more pleasurable.

The heat of the day had not diminished an inch in the late-afternoon streets, the sky that could not be distinguished from white-hot whiteness holding strong. But a similar light lived within me, an equal force of blaze. The body was nothing but a wall, a thin partition between the two types of brightness, inside and out. The asphalt burned through the soles of my shoes, seeping through the skin and pausing there, against the parallel scorch. I walked to our meeting point, outside the orphaned industrial zone. I waited and waited, but Dalia didn't show up. I was worried I might have gotten the time or place wrong. I tried to conjure up the scene of our plan-making. We'd been sitting outside the library for the millionth time. We'd gotten up to say goodbye. I could re-create Dalia's voice, her measured tone, stating the time and meeting point. I glanced at my watch. An hour had gone by. I wandered among the concrete buildings with their bare asbestos roofs, down the paths leading to blocked gates, secured by lead chains, impossible to rip off with human hands. I couldn't hear the usual Sderot hubbub, the one I intentionally avoided, young and older boys roaring through their games. All of a sudden I had the frightening thought that perhaps Sderot itself had been wiped off the face of the universe through some miraculous disaster. It began with a humorous spot of thought, a drop of oil dimming the sunrise of my soul, that glommed and spread.

I hurried back, crossed the desolate roads, entered between the first projects. I ignored the warning call directed at me. The presence of the voice was enough. It was followed by a deafening wave that crashed over my head. A few moments went by before I realized I was soaking wet, the sensation of the water through my clothes swooshing and shattering. A girl holding a bucket looked down from a second-floor window right above my head. The orange bucket glimmered, fruit-like. Two little children stood beside her, their faces twisted. The sounds of ridicule fell on the sidewalk all around me.

※ ※ ※

MAYBE DALIA JUST FORGOT. MAYBE SHE WAS TIRED OF OUR CON-versations because we never got anywhere, a kind of spinning around of unending acquaintance. Just incident and incidental-ness. Last time, she interrogated me about the Shavuot *Tikkun* service.

I tried to describe the sensations to her. The soul igniting from learning, the simmering coal flaming into a fire. She kept shifting the conversation to actions, dry details, what did we learn, why, who determined it, were there disputes, were there or weren't there traditions? I told her that wasn't the point, the point was connecting to a hidden hub. I told her that until a few months ago I used to fast a lot. Then I blushed. Snot had chuckled back when I told him about my nocturnal emissions and the singular fasts I sentenced myself to as a result. You just have to fuck and be done with it, he said.

She asked if anyone could sentence themselves.

I said, Under certain conditions. But I, I do—

She said, I suspected you were part of that camp.

I asked what camp.

She said, The camp of people who fear death so much that they hate life.

I didn't answer. She fell silent too. We stood up together to say goodbye. We made plans to meet again. I wanted to show myself to her in my true image, purified of the slags of secularity. The way I was at the beginning, for brief moments, in some primor-dial childhood of honest observance.

But never mind. I wasn't angry. I was angry. I wasn't angry. Why would I be angry? I was prepared for her to vanish, if that was her wish. But what was her wish, sealed and leased? How fitting a name that was for the cycle of poems, Sealed and Leased. I read it again. It was mine in more than one sense. Snot was wrong, it wasn't that what happened in books happened to you too. It happened to you first. The books just stole what happened from you.

I picked up a piece of paper and wrote—
what are you doing here

doing here what you are

without poetry

try hew it, o, pout

I VISITED THE LIBRARY EVERY AFTERNOON. THE POINCIANA under which we liked to sit was plump with blossoms, red resplendence, and rot. Shifra did not smile upon me that day. She showed me her dark side. Either way, I too entered with my measure of judgment. She pressed her lips together. I did the same. I brought some books from the reference room and asked to borrow them. Random books. Her skull smile sliced through her scrawny face. She said, I told you and that fat Kurd a million times that you can't borrow reference books.

I put the books back and brought other ones back to her desk. I said, How about these, they're from the shelves no one looks at. I glanced at the title on the top of the pile, *The Morphology of Gnathostomata*. She pulled it out of my hands and opened it.

I said, Look at that, gnathostomata. When was the last time you used the word "gnathostomata" with anyone, or even just with yourself, sitting in a room and saying, Gnathostomata, how I'd like to discuss gnathostomata, how I'd like to see them and to touch their gnathos and their tomata. She continued to flip through the book, lingering on some images, the skull structure of ray-finned fishes. I easily read the words upside down. I said, Ray-finned fishes. When was the last time I thought about ray-finned fishes, how I'd like to picture ray-finned fishes all day long, raying and finning through the water. I opened and closed my fingers as if they were jaws, ra ra, ya ya, fn fn, fsh, fsh.

383

She slammed the book shut. You're bored, Farkash, she said, go home.

I said, And what about you, you'll be left here all alone, not a soul around.

I walked over to the theater and poetry section. She watched me silently. I said, No one borrows these books either, Snot and I looked, there aren't even any return dates on the borrowing cards, they're empty. Can I borrow from here?

Shifra sighed and returned to her affairs.

I pulled out books without rhyme or reason and placed them on the mat at the bottom of the bookcase. I constructed a mosaic of covers according to their sizes and colors. I was almost finished covering the entire mat. Above me, Shifra cried, what are you doing?

I said I was preparing a surprise for her. She said Snot and I had already pulled this trick on her before, that we'd overloaded the book carts and then she and the other librarian, Kokhava, had had to spend hours putting every book back.

I shrugged.

Get out of here or I'll call your father, she said.

I told her to go ahead and call him.

You're rude, somebody said. I couldn't mistake the voice's moderation, its decisiveness, the careful pronunciation. Dalia was standing in the doorway of the circulation room. She leaned lightly against the sliding door. The spaghetti straps of her dress sank into her thick flesh. Her hair was pulled back. She was pale, perhaps angry. There was fire in her eyes, or maybe I imagined it.

I got up and left. I passed her by with a lowered head. I hesitated on the steps leading out. Why should I feel scolded, when she was the one who deserved a scolding? I should have yelled at her in front of Shifra. I sat down on the iron railing slicing between concrete and lawn. Behind me, the branchy poinciana stood motionlessly, besides the hidden rustle of producing blossoms. It was actually funny, I thought, ra ra, ya ya, fn fn, fsh, fsh.

When was the last time you used the word "gnathostomata" with anyone. Funny for real, that's what Niro would say, but with his usual dry tone. Funny for real, Nahum. I started to laugh. Dalia came outside. Her arms were crossed against her chest. She stood a distance away from me. She said, Why are you tormenting her? She could be your mother.

So could you, I said, considering your behavior.

She didn't answer at first. She looked at a spot beyond me and I turned my head. Nothing but projects in the metallic light of this late hour, nothing but antennas rustling within the lucency. She said, That's why I wanted you to read "The Girl Who Was Plugged In." You men, when it suits you, you're scared children, and you're mature and wise when it suits you. But never about yourselves. Always in order to make a woman feel bad about herself.

The softness of the words, as if they'd been whispered for years before she'd finally mustered the courage to speak them outright. I don't know why, but I felt ashamed. I said, You're one to talk, as if you don't do everything according to what suits you. You're egotistical too.

Almost derisively, she said, So you insist on not understanding the story. I never imagined you were so obtuse.

I said, And you insist on remaining a condescending cow.

She walked away. I stayed on the iron railing. The day that had accumulated into it burned my fingertips to the touch. Suddenly, I jumped up and chased after her. She'd already reached the fork where the road leading to her neighborhood lay on one side, the road leading to mine on the other. I roared her name. She stopped. I said, I'm sorry, Dalia, I'm really sorry.

She said, What's there to be sorry about, I've seen you in your cup and in your anger, haven't I? Now all that's left is your pocket.

I felt my pants pocket.

Let's get it over with, she said. What's in your pocket?

I pulled out the piece of paper on which I'd written that short poem. I handed it to her.

(HERE, ONCE AGAIN, I, MEANING I, CAN FEEL THE BEATING OF truth about me, no, the beating of experience I had once upon a time, as if a lost memory had transformed into the story of another, and that is how I got to know it. Perhaps that is the nature of fiction. Maybe literature is that man from Crete telling us that all the residents of that island are liars. Maybe only under the guise of fiction can it push us toward the conditions of the appearance of truth in us, which have nothing to do with facts, surface, a relation to reality.)

EHUD MADE IT PERFECTLY CLEAR WHAT MY REJOINING THE BOYS' group meant. I had to perform little errands, such as going to get everyone drinks from the corner store near school during recess. That was the only place that sold root beer, David's favorite. The first time I walked into the corner store, I felt for some reason as if I was walking into Snot's parents' shop, though I'd never been there. Something about the moldiness of the space, the wrinkled and worried expression of the clerk. The store was desolate. His eyes followed me. He spoke with a Moroccan accent, shrill and soft at once. I detected liturgical traces in his practical statements.

There were other errands too. Carrying the sweat-smelly gym clothes they didn't deign to carry home themselves, saving seats in the front rows of the school's synagogue, skipping my turn as cantor during morning and afternoon prayers.

It didn't matter to me. It had been a long time since Snot left. Detachment was a worse sentence. I spoke to Sabah rarely, though I was always around him. His laugh, his gentle gestures, his calculating expression during chess games, they all reminded me of Sylvia Gozlan, lying in bed as I stared at her. She said she didn't bleed as much as she'd expected. She'd prepared a towel in her bedside table drawer. She chatted innocently, telling me she'd planned on losing her virginity to David, but that pathetic son of a bitch couldn't take a hint, she did everything but throw herself at his feet and cry for him to fuck her already. No matter how much she clung to him earlier, when they danced, or when she dragged him into the living room so they could be alone without his hanger-on friends, nothing, that jerk just didn't get it. Her two older sisters were married and at least fifteen years older than her. Her eldest sister had a daughter who was only a couple of years younger than Sylvia herself. Sylvia Gozlan asked for this sister's advice. Her sister told her to be prepared for heavy bleeding. She pressed the towel against that spot of hers. In the lighting, which returned to its common, springlike nightliness, her breasts took on a monstrous shade. The nipples like anthills swarming the heaps of flesh. I told her I had to go. I got dressed quickly and walked outside. I managed to conquer my nausea for two-thirds of the way home. I threw up by the old shopping center's parking lot. The town was deserted, sprawling in its aridness.

Passover went by, a heat-wave flyover, the bauhinias gaping their mouths, their winged seeds rustling in the calyx. The typical nervousness of Holocaust Memorial Day ceremonies and the belching of clouds in the sky. Sabah picked an evening. They had an evening tradition that had formulated over the years I'd pulled away from him and his followers. That's what they called their gatherings, their get-togethers. They called the social activity itself the entertainment, sitting down to entertain. The location changed according to Sabah's and Ehud's whims. This time, they'd chosen the outer thicket. I was tasked with collecting money from all the boys and buying refreshments according to a list dictated by Ehud.

I walked out of my house laden with bags of snacks and sodas that slapped against my thighs. A few hundred meters later, I heard squealing barks behind me. Cocoa Pup, with his carefully combed coat, his brown nut-shaped eyes, looked like an animated stuffed animal. His leash dragged behind him. Tova had rebuked Chantal many times for not carefully fastening Cocoa Pup's leash to the hook Simo had installed on the side of the doghouse. I ordered him to go back home. I kept walking, and he followed me and licked my shins, jumping at the bottom of one of the bags, trying to bite it. I yelled at him to leave. I shoved him away with my legs. His barks turned more spasmodic. The plastic handles grew tighter, digging deeper into my palm. I couldn't just stand there. I pushed him away again. Go. But he wouldn't. He followed me all the way to the highway that separated insideSderot from outsideSderot. I crossed it faster than usual. My hands were burning. Cocoa Pup remained on the sidewalk, whimpering. Go, I told him, get out of here, go home, and I kept walking.

You're late, said Ehud.

The boys were gathered in the thicket clearing that Pini and I had discovered that time. When Ehud gave me directions he added, David said you'd know where to go.

I told them I'd been delayed because of the snacks. Ehud said I should be grateful they invited me at all. I nodded.

Sabah was sitting on the wide, felled tree trunk. The rest were sitting on the ground. They'd all brought blankets. The boys entertained to their hearts' desire, shooting the shit, as they called it, about girls. They mentioned one girl, saying she was a piece of ass, but the piece was just too big, or that another girl was a bombshell because her face looked like it had been in a bombing, and other witty and totally original accolades. Between one joke and the next, they sipped the drinks I'd carried over, deflowering bags of snacks with their strong hands, undressing chocolate bars from their colorful covers, peeling off their aluminum corsets. During these breaks, Sabah dragged the conversation to the approaching Independence Day, the fabulous speeches that those freeloader city hall employees would probably give again, all the department heads. He went on and on about the cultural scene of Sderot and its fat, aimless, lazy leaders.

It was no longer possible to separate the dimming of the air from the dimming of the trees. The treetops had turned almost entirely black. The smell of eucalyptus deepened, bitter, clean. But birds sang to welcome in the evening. A thought pushed its way into my mind and wouldn't let go, one of those forgettable facts Snot had gathered among the reference book pages. I said that the brains of songbirds grew as summer approached, making their singing more complex, but that their brains shrunk down again after mating season, because they had no reason to chirp.

Bki alek, ya Farkash, one of the boys said, what do you know about mating?

Yeah, said Ehud, are you an expert now, did you learn it from your dad?

My dad, I asked.

He's running around with every receptionist in town and every ugly piece of ass with legs, thinking he's some kind of player, another boy said, looking at Sabah.

Sabah confirmed this with a nod. He said, Don't be so mean, even though I don't think we're telling Farkash anything he doesn't already know.

I looked him over and said, And what does anyone here know about mating? Did Sabah explain it to you?

Sabah said, Really, Farkash, what are you getting worked up about, we're just joking.

But the heat behind my eyes blinded me. I said, So let's joke, make me a joke, what do you know about mating?

I know, said Sabah.

I said, Yes, of course, Sylvia Gozlan told me how much you know.

Pfft, he said, you? You heard it from Sylvia Gozlan?

Yeah, I said, at the Purim party. I slept with her. What, am I telling you something you don't already know?

I wasn't sorry I said it, not while I was saying it. Only the edges of the holeache in my chest expanded. The heat behind my eyes blinded me. I could see through it, the paleness of Sabah's face within the forest darkness. He got up on his feet. I had no idea why he believed me right away. Maybe my total honesty, maybe the directness of the defiance, maybe both, knocked him off balance, or maybe he was just used to ruses.

He took a step toward me. I was getting ready to get up too, but then Cocoa Pup burst into the clearing with a storm of barks. He panted near my feet. Then he turned his head to Sabah and sounded a restrained growl, a threatening purr.

Sabah forced out a laugh. What'd you bring this mouse here for?

Cocoa Pup hummed through bared teeth. Sabah defiantly downed his can of Sprite and tossed it at the dog. Cocoa Pup evaded the can and pounced at him. With the acute senses of a soccer player, Sabah kicked him, one swift kick toward Ehud, who was sitting on the other end of the clearing. Cocoa Pup's paws dug into the sand in a vain attempt to block the momentum. He rolled over to Ehud, who was already prepared, and kicked him back. He rolled halfway into the clearing and Sabah lunged over and kicked him again, a crushing kick that pressed his body against the ground. Cocoa Pup's body turned limp. He tried to balance himself with a meek, piercing sob, then collapsed. I rushed to him. His chest rose and fell with wheezing inhalations and exhalations. I wanted to embrace him but recoiled. Sounds came from behind me but I paid them no mind. I hovered over the dog, paralyzed. Cocoa Pup was crying for both of us.

A century later, it was silent. The boys had all deserted. I picked up the wounded dog. I wanted to leave the thicket, run to the road, and call for help. But my knees betrayed me. I only made

it as far as the fallen tree trunk. I placed Cocoa Pup on top of it.
He wheezed and whistled. I petted him for a long time until finally one of my arms held his body in place while the other
gripped the top of his skull. I twisted. The whimpering stopped.
I thought I ought to accompany the departure of his soul with a
prayer, but I could only come up with one bit. I whispered, Guide
us with your good counsel. I removed his leash and left the
corpse where it was.

DALIA FOLDED UP THE PAPER AND GAVE IT BACK. SHE SAID, SO I
see it did affect you after all.

I said it did, that the poems from Sealed and Leased had had
an effect on me. And that I had no idea who'd written them. She
spoke a name. I didn't catch it. She spoke it again. She said she
wasn't one of his fans. I asked if he was part of Niro's group of
artists. She snorted. She said there was no group, only a few artists, some of them more talented than others, all unlucky enough
to be born in Sderot.

I wanted to ask what she thought of my poem. Instead I said,
So what do you think the story you told me to read is about?

She said, I thought it was obvious. You men only leave us a
little something to be, but when we really want it, with intense
passion, you panic.

About what? I asked.

The fervor of our passion. You call it madness, witchcraft, obsession, whatever, maybe you're right. It doesn't acknowledge
your mastery. It answers to no master.

I said, Then I failed the test.

She said, There are no tests.

I said, Of the cup, the anger, and the pocket.

She said, Forget it, Nahum, I'm getting a headache.

I said, Why didn't you come on Shavuot?

She said nothing.

I said, Maybe I'm bad at taking hints.

She said, I wasn't trying to give any hints. I was too tired to go out that day.

I nodded.

The paleness left her face. The heavy, hidden vitality, its radiation always tangible, was back.

I said, But the pocket can mean something else too. We can go get pizza. On me.

She said we could do that another time.

I didn't think I'd see her again. In spite of what she'd said, I'd failed all the tests. It isn't fair, I thought, it isn't fair. But I couldn't muster up enough anger to maintain the defiance, and the thought cooled off in the immense darkness of my brain.

A week later, when I returned from my first recruitment call, Tova said a girl named Dalia had called to remind me we had plans to meet at the pizza place that night.

I looked at her mutely.

Tova said, I told her you have your civics final the day after tomorrow and you're such a nerd there's no chance you'll be leaving your room tonight.

Why'd you say that?

It's the truth, isn't it? said Tova, making a face.

What did she say?

She repeated herself like a broken record.

What's wrong with you, Tova?

Nothing, she said, nothing. I'm sick of this house.

It was early. The pizza place was deserted save for a couple of tables of kids who chatted with excitement as they noisily hoovered milkshakes through straws, sucking away, the racket of clicking teeth and inhaling lips. Nevertheless, I felt exposed. Eyes peeked, eyes examined, eyes jumped to conclusions. I couldn't set myself free of their weight, that constant, curious spying. What if Sabah or Ehud or one of their lackeys came by?

Dalia sat down across from me, collected, almost lying down in her seat.

It's busy here, I said.

She smiled. Yeah, really lively.

I looked at the menu. I asked if she wanted anything to eat or drink. Why was it suddenly difficult to get the conversation going, when we'd been so adept at it? She said she'd take a cold chococcino. Chococcino. What is the ancestry of the chococcino. What transformations and incarnations did the chococcino go through before it emerged into our lives in 1989, at the only pizza place in Sderot? I ordered two cold chococcinos and some kind of pastry. They arrived, tall glasses, brown liquid, wild whipped cream blossoms, golden puff pastry.

I swallowed and said, What did you think of my poem?

I was hoping you wouldn't ask, she said. I knew you'd ask.

I said nothing.

She asked why I'd written it. I said it was a blind urge. She said the influence of the Sealed and Leased poems was apparent. I nodded and sucked on my straw. It went down the wrong pipe. I coughed. I told her the poem could be read down or across. If she read it down, then the first two lines created a kind of rule, rearranging the first line. The two bottom lines were a demonstration of the rule and an example of its results, the words in the fourth line contained the same letters as the words in the third line. And she could also read the poem across, two lines on the right and two lines on the left, and then they showed an evolution, the two right lines were direct statements and the two left lines were poetic statements, the poem showed that meaning was—

Dalia said, Long story short, it's all technical, the poem, the explanation, but why did you write it, you, Nahum, not some anonymous guy, and what did you, Nahum, have to say, how does the poem's language express you, the most Nahum Nahum there is?

I didn't answer. Dalia sipped her chococcino. I thought, Choc-occino. I thought, Chococcino, chococcino, chococcino.

She said, That's what I meant when I asked you if you liked empty art. Because that was my sense, during Dahan's screening, that the words were a hollow game.

I didn't think that way.

I don't get it, said Dalia, what did that poet have to say, really? Why Sealed and Leased, what exactly was sealed and leased about all those arrangements of words, words, words?

I thought, How could she not detect that simple truth, she, with her sharp perception? I leaned toward her and said quietly, But if you feel a hole, for instance, in your chest, a holeache, how would you write about it?

Dalia recoiled into her seat, pressing against the back of the chair. She said, What kind of music do you listen to? Her voice was crass when she asked it. It sliced through the storm of state-ments I'd been stifling, slitting the awakening of the desire to tell something, which I'd managed to distill into that single question. It stifled it.

I stuttered something.

Isn't that a shame, Dalia said, I could recommend lots of bands and artists. Lots.

After a long silence, sips, gulps, the nervous licking of whipped cream, chewing, chewing the puff pastry that the microwaving gust still continued to work, softening the crispy skin, disgusting it, I told her I didn't really have any way of listening to music.

What are you talking about, Nahum? she said. This is the end of the twentieth century. You should get a Walkman.

LATER, I THOUGHT, SHE'D NEVER USED MY NAME AS MUCH IN ANY previous conversation. Maybe that was progress. I had a small amount saved from my allowance. My parents vehemently ob-jected to my getting a job, as some of my classmates had in the beginning of the year. They said they were busting their asses so that their children could have a better life than they had. None of us rebelled against the laziness they enforced. I went to an appliance store to check the prices of Walkmans. I didn't have enough saved.

I called Tova aside and asked if she could lend me the money. She fixed her eyes on me. The chill of her gaze was bisected by a flame that ignited through it. I said, Come on, Tova, I'll pay you back.

Why don't you ask them? she said.

I said, I can't be bothered to talk to them right now. What do you care, it's only until next week.

She left my room and then returned with the glass jar she used to keep her coins. She carried it carefully, with both hands. She placed it on my desk and said, You can have it all, as far as I'm concerned, I don't want his money. She was gritting the words between her teeth.

It's just a loan, I protested.

She said, At least he isn't stingy about allowance.

I emptied the jar. Bills fell down silently, coins made a dull jingling sound as they hit the wood. I asked if she was sure.

I told you, I don't want any of his money.

Since when does Dad insult you, I said, he can be stupid sometimes, but that's it. What did he say to you during the holiday?

It isn't what he said, she said, it's what he did, what I know he did.

What did he do?

Never mind.

You can't just start telling me and—

He kicked out Cocoa Pup, she whispered. Her inside voice came from the outside, and she realized how much certainty it held for her, no more guessing, conjecture, doubts, but a fact the world had returned to her through its regular methods. I saw the certainty emerging in her face. She said again, confidently, I know, I know he kicked out Cocoa Pup.

My throat clogged. The words screeched and hoarsened, but she didn't detect the discord. I said, How'd you figure that?

She started to cry. She said, He always hated him, called him an annoying cockroach. And I found . . . I found his leash tied up in the doghouse. Cocoa Pup couldn't get his leash off by himself, and you know how Dad was always yelling at Chantal that she didn't tie him hard enough, and that cockroach kept getting between his feet, and one day he would step on him.

I cleared my throat, but hoarseness clung to it still. You're jumping to conclusions, I said. Chantal's dog just went missing.

He and you are the same, said Tova. She picked up her jar and left me there with her reparations.

Dalia arrived at the old shopping center just as we'd planned. Early, even. She was standing underneath the cripple's kiosk awning. Afternoon hours in Sderot. The sun had been nailed to its place in the lower part of the sky and would not relent. A cauterized Saponaria lapped at its surroundings, the light blue weaves drenched with bleach. The bauhinias were bent. A few pigeons hobbled from here to there. And Dalia. From a distance, I thought, smoking would suit her. But she was completely absorbed in something on the ground. She didn't answer when I called her name. I touched her shoulder and she shuddered. Her eyes were gripped by a dream, cloudy. They cleared up at once. She removed her headphones, hanging them around her like a necklace. Sounds mixed in the sponge of the headphones, thorny invertebrates. She pulled a device from her bag and pressed a button. The sponges fell silent.

She said there was an electric appliance store in this center that she thought was expensive, but that I could also get a Walkman at the gift shop in the new shopping center or at the toy store in Neve Eshkol. We ought to compare prices. We walked around. The sun shone its shining. Dalia thought the Walkmans at the toy store and the gift shop weren't good quality. Made in Taiwan, she said. The whole world is now made in Taiwan. She couldn't understand how Taiwan wasn't an Asian empire by now, considering how much production was happening there.

The statement astonished me. Not that Dalia's other statements weren't invasive or unsettling, and yet, it was as if I'd come across a truth I hadn't known was hidden. I told her that, told her I'd never thought about the connection between how much product a country makes and—

It's political power, Dalia asked, what could be more obvious, he who pays the piper calls the tune, you should know that.

Yes, I said, but I never considered the scale.

She said, You think small, you think about a neighborhood, a city. You should get used to thinking about the whole of humanity.

But I like thinking about the neighborhood and the city, I see faces, I hear voices, they're real to me. When I go bigger everything blurs, I don't really care about the masses.

Who determines your fate, then?

I glanced at the acid-bleached sky.

Dalia said, That's the problem with religious people.

We returned to the old shopping center. Dalia said it behooved us to spend more money, at least the product would be good quality.

I liked that she'd said "behooved." I rolled the verb through my mind, behooved, behooved.

When we reached the covered corridor where the store was located, someone called our names in the distance. We paused until he reached us. Niro, with his long curls. He said, I had a feeling the two of you were hanging out together. It was no coincidence that you both disappeared on me at the same time. He smiled with pleasure, his face glowing in the shade of the covered space. He said, So what are the plans?

We told him about our search for a Walkman. He said, Why waste your money, I've got a Walkman I don't use, I'll give it to you.

The two of us said nothing.

Besides, he added, we're auditioning a new keyboardist to replace Hershko. You've got to come.

AS A GOODBYE GIFT, HERSHKO HAD FOUND NIRO A BASEMENT for his band to practice in. It wasn't far from my neighborhood. Dalia and I decided to meet at the intersection that branched into my neighborhood. She didn't want to get any closer to my house. We crossed the thin summer evening, a parchment inscribed with glints of semidarkness.

A mildewed lightlessness hovered inside the basement, which was split into two rooms, a foyer and an inner room, which was guarded by a heavy metal door. The instruments were placed against one wall of the inner room, on a rug with frayed ends. On the left was Eddy with his bass, sitting on his amplifier as usual, thinking whatever he was thinking. At the center was Niro's electric guitar alongside a microphone with a broken stand. The top pole wasn't properly fastened in place and would drop lower with the weight of the microphone. From time to time, Niro would move away from his special effects case—the multieffect, as he called his new toy—to adjust it.

On the right, a boy I didn't know was laboring over his synthesizer hookups. He stretched a cable from the synth to the amplification system. Two other boys I didn't recognize stood across the room. They must have been the other candidates. Long, black-covered cases lay beside them. On the other side of the room, six of the group members were whispering to one another. The concrete walls echoed back their chatter, increasing the volume tenfold. I could have guessed that Dahan would be among them, but I hadn't thought about him in weeks. He hurried over, Dahan, with his nervous gait and the haughty brushing back of his straight hair. His somewhat slanted eyes glimmered even in the meager light, as did his rabbit-like front teeth.

So, said Dahan, where'd you disappear to, Smoky Farkash?

I glanced over his shoulder. Niro waved and gestured for us to join them. We were the last arrivals. We crossed the room, which grew silent. Behind me, Dahan whispered, So, Nahum, you took off with those poems without delivering your end of the bargain.

I turned around and, with the same whisper, said, Shut up already.

He said, Oh, look who's got some courage. But remember. You owe me a story.

We were swallowed among the group members. Auditions were about to begin. The players took their positions and looked at one another. Dahan wouldn't relent. He said, Remember, you owe me.

Enough already, you pest, I said. I said it louder than I'd meant to. In a commanding tone, more impatient than I should have been. The words rumbled through the room. I flinched.

Can we start? Niro said into the mic.

The bubbling of blood I felt on the way over, the tension in the skin and the soft, excited tingles, now died out. I was slipping back into my ordinariness. Dalia put her mouth near my ear and whispered, What an idiot. I nodded. I was gripped once more by that bubbling, that tension.

Niro cut off the first keyboardist after a few minutes. He said a few sentences I couldn't hear. They started over. The keyboardist activated a programmed beat, heavy, crude drums disrupted by a ferrous shattering and a rattle in a repetitive pattern, I could count it, one, two, ferrous shattering, four, one, rattle, three, four. These were accompanied by wide, flowing cascades of sound. Niro stopped him again after a few more minutes. Eddy shook his head. Niro sent the candidate away with a thank-you. The second keyboardist was already busy extracting his instrument from its black nylon packaging. Dalia whispered, He clogged up their sound, but beside that he doesn't have a drop of originality.

The second candidate played more vibrating sounds, high and nearly sobbing, tubular maybe, fluty. Bored to death, Dalia determined. The third musician focused only on beats, groaning taps and thuds and a snaking of galvanized tin sheets. I recognized the Moroccan beats, could count them, the *darbuka* that ranged between a muffled slap and a dancing poke. The others were too tangled for me. Niro and Eddy couldn't bear them either. Every once in a while one of them stopped playing, listened, tapped his feet, and rejoined. The third keyboardist paid them no mind. He was absorbed in his buttons, attuned to the mélange of rhythms he'd created. Dalia whispered, He's too weird for them, too sophisticated, he's playing ethnic beats they've never heard before. No chance that Niro and the three- and four-quarter rhythms he was educated on can match his music up with that.

I saw Niro's expression growing tense as they kept going. Even Eddy, who mostly remained expressionless, furrowed his brow and shook his head. Finally, Niro cut the music off with a decisive arm gesture. It's a no-go, he said, you're too good for us. The third candidate narrowed his eyes, almost flummoxed for having his personal space invaded, for having awakened from his musical delusion to find himself surrounded by strangers. He abandoned his keyboard, slowly joining the two other applicants, mumbling to himself. Eddy put down his bass and plopped onto the amplifier. Niro stood in front of the microphone, which was once again sliding down to the ground, and which they didn't even use, in spite of the fact that Niro had been adjusting it ceaselessly throughout the auditions. None of the sessions reached a fully formed piece of music that Niro could overlay with one of their songs. Niro watched as the microphone glided, then whacked it to the ground. The mic, which was still connected to the loudspeakers, crackled and whispered as it met the floor, and from within that crackle and whisper rose a piercing, cutting, mercurial screech. I could feel it in my teeth, shoving into them, crumbling them from the outside. I stuck my fingers in my ears. It took years to stop. Eddy was standing by their injured console. He spoke, and as he did I realized I'd never heard his voice, which was soft and confident. Cool it, Niro, cool it.

Dahan departed from us, disappearing into the rectangle of darkness that opened up in the brighter darkness where we were standing. And the refuse came out, I thought for some reason, the refuse refused to stay. Why was I now recalling the story of the biblical Ehud and the fat Moabite King Eglon, with his bisected bowels, how the interpreters joked about him. The refuse, they said, the refuse he'd been defecating when Ehud attacked him with his double-edged sword.

Niro picked up the microphone and returned it to the stand. He signaled to Eddy, who returned and picked up his bass. Dalia, said Niro, come do something with us.

I turned to her. Her lips were tight, and her hair, which was gathered into an improvised bun, left her expression of dissent bare to the eyes fixing on her.

Please, said Niro, I don't want to leave this rehearsal with a bad taste in my mouth.

I thought, But what does he expect her to do, she isn't a keyboard player.

Dalia looked at me helplessly and moved away with calculated steps. Someone standing next to me, the square-featured boy, said, Now we'll finally see if Niro is full of it.

Full of it, I thought, is it like fool's gold.

Dahan returned, carrying a cooler. Dalia stood in front of the microphone. Dahan pulled out a beer bottle, then realized all attention was focused on the musicians. He muttered a curse I couldn't really hear.

✼ ✼ ✼

DALIA RESTED HER HEAD AGAINST HER CHEST AND LISTENED TO Niro and Eddy's music. Niro's playing changed, no more sawing and sobbing, slicing strings. Instead a slow, echoing lightning, every note ringing singularly through a giant hall, a cathedral. Eddy's playing became more fluent too, sneaking footsteps, I'd say. And Dalia started talking into the microphone, her words riding on the surface of the music, blending into it, becoming a composition. She sang. Her voice ascended into song. It filled with a breadth and depth that were not present in her speech. Every note her throat produced was overflowing with an emotion I could recognize from my brief experience on this planet. There was the moment when the animal moved through the walls of childhood, scratching from the inside, there was the fortification of my spirit of waiting for a comforting hand, there was the tenderness mixed with horror of the act of dreaming, having been a dreaming creature, a dreamed creature, my whole life, never realizing it. What she sang about I do not know, but I could feel my holeache was inflamed, yet appeased.

I didn't notice the third keyboardist who was approaching his instrument until sounds rose from it, pouring into Niro and Eddy's playing. At first, a simple, small, beeping, playful beat. Dalia responded to the addition immediately, her eulogistic singing sweetening, her voice moving higher, and with the sweetness came breaches, it was webbed by scorches and scarrings of an overly sober maturity. I got carried away after her, hearing in her voice the endless wandering through streets and through myself, adding up to nothing save a burning, capricious glee. Niro and Eddy changed as well. They intentionally stumbled. Eddy played closed-off, broken notes. Niro added an effect that echoed his music, neutering it around the edges, pushing it off beat. The keyboardist added one of his tangled, wild rhythms. There was the flesh touching flesh, integrating into it with pleasure, igniting the senses and stilling the soul. With the intensifying complexity, the two's playing died out. All that was left was Dalia, with her elation, and the third keyboardist, competing against each other, defying. Niro and Eddy stood there, listening, adding random embellishments that only contributed to the overall stormy sensation of an unexpected being, so enticing in its force of life.

(AND I, MEANING I—WHAT'S IT TO ME? SOME STING RUNS THROUGH me now, awakening. What is this form of emotion, through which a modulated, encoded, telegraphic, electric flickering pounds in my nerves through the screens of existence, a longing? What do I, meaning I, even know?)

DAHAN HANDED OUT HIS BEER BOTTLES. EVERYONE WAS STANDing around Dalia. I didn't listen to the tumult. I went out like refuse. Indeed, an annex to the central space. A sort of moldy storage room, laden with cobwebs. The praises must have melded together to form a brassy racket. I wanted to cry but couldn't. The crying insisted on pushing itself back into my lungs, the tears into my eyeballs. I pictured Dalia's expression, which had etched onto my mind before I'd slipped away to this dim rectangle. There was horror in it, I realized. Of what, I wondered, what does she have to be horrified, with that immense singing, with that ability, that gift? And then I comprehended, in a flare, that everyone else in the room was a boy and she was the only girl. What was it she'd said about fervent passion?

I rushed back inside. Her distress was apparent. She no longer stood still as usual, but was shifting her weight from one foot to the other. They were talking at her. She said nothing. I interrupted their aimless chatter, saying, Dalia, you asked me to remind you that you have to get home early tonight. She sized me up through the limpness that had taken over her. She shook her head weakly, frizzy ends flying out of her black hair. Niro was standing by the exit, talking to the third keyboardist, whose eyes wandered across the space and whose mouth was tightly closed. Niro placed a hand on Dalia's shoulder and said, You're awesome, but you already know that. He gave me a restrained, miserly smile.

Outside the bomb shelter, Dalia said, I don't need you to rescue me.

I said, I beg to differ.

We walked in silence. My neighborhood's intersection would materialize for us any minute. I wasn't ready to say goodbye to her yet. I asked if she wanted to go somewhere, maybe to the quad outside the rec center or to the old market, just to sit.

She said, I thought I needed to get home early tonight.

I said, I'm not very resourceful. I can be kind of dumb sometimes.

She laughed briefly.

I said, I'm a bit of an ass.

She said, All right, don't get carried away.

So what do you say?

Maybe some other time.

I said, It goes without saying, but that improvisation, your singing . . . It was amazing.

She said she was already regretting agreeing to it, but that she was indebted to Niro. I asked what kind of debt. She said he'd taught her how to play the guitar. I said I didn't know she played. She suddenly remembered she'd made something for me. From her bag, she pulled out a cassette in its hard, plastic case. I took it. It was cool to the touch. Must have grown cold during our time in the bomb shelter.

She said, There are songs here I thought you ought to hear.

I pressed my fingers against the tape. When you sang, I said, I felt that my holeache was finally a part of me and not an implanted organ.

She didn't answer.

Then she said, What's a holeache, what language is that?

I said, A hole of pain. I made up that word with my friend, Snot, actually, his name is Michael, Snot was a derogatory name that ... never mind, it's too hard to explain, I always feel ashamed when I talk about the ...

I waited for a sign from her, a flicker of interest. She retreated into herself.

I said, He was the only person I felt comfortable talking to, without shame.

I felt the integumentary film of the lack of curiosity growing to suffocate her silence. But I kept going. I said, And now with you. My voice rose of its own accord, the tone surprising even me, four words, the first two pleading, the next two already demanding.

I said, I feel like I can talk to you.

She shifted her eyes to look at the nightly chill of stars, gauzy with summer, heavy with a slow, concealed burning. We reached the intersection and I couldn't bear to part from her. But she moved on. I hurried after her. She paused, watching me. My image tiny, extinguished, in her dark irises.

What do you want from me? she said.

I didn't answer.

Are you looking for friends to help you close your hole, or friends with similar holes?

The words shoved out of her, forced out, slamming against me. Why are you treating me like this? I asked.

She didn't answer.

Dalia, I said, you're a hypocrite, you're always talking about other people's pain drawing you in, about the beauty of life, of humanity, how all the good and bad feelings get mixed up in it, giving it depth ...

I huffed. I said, But when you're standing before me, someone real, who lives, and wants to share his confusion with you, his unease, offering you this gift, you draw away ... you run away, Dalia ... it's hypocri–

The tears that had been aspiring to their origins found an opening, breaching a breach. But Dalia kept walking home, not turning her head toward me.

THAT ENTIRE SUMMER, I IMAGINED CONVERSATIONS WITH DALIA, long heart-to-hearts. I saw her briefly at an exhibition of artwork by the square-featured boy, whose name turned out to be Gabby. He presented pencil and charcoal drawings on the walls of his home's hallways and living room. The furniture was pushed aside to make room. His smiling parents peeked at us from a distance, supervising. But I saw the love contained in the looks they gave him. Tables covered with bowls of snacks and nuts and drinks were set on the front porch. We walked around, sharing thoughts. He mostly drew the lanky girl, whom I remembered from Independence Day, in different dance poses. He said it was an homage to his favorite painter, whose name was Degas. I thought, Degas, sounds like *daga*, the Hebrew word for "fishery." I thought, The likeness of any fish that is in the waters beneath the earth. Gabby Daga. I thought, Degabby. There was also a pencil sketch of his parents, quick, clean lines, during mealtime. A gleam gleamed over them. Beamed from the inside.

I saw Dalia at a few of the rehearsals Niro had with the new band he formed with the third keyboardist. He'd abandoned the tribal beats, but their music became even stranger, the songs extending, growing more sophisticated, forgoing repetition for the sake of a gushing, an evolvement. They were infected by some aspect of the keyboardist's personality. They sank into the music they made, giving up communication.

One day, after I'd stopped attending rehearsals, Dahan called. He said he was working on a new project that he wanted all his friends to take part in as a souvenir, before they each went their separate ways.

Their separate ways? I asked.

Yeah, said Dahan, most of us are enlisting in October.

I asked what the project was about. He said he had no intention of explaining it a million times. He'd explain it at the meeting. He said the best time for most of the group was next Thursday, if that worked for me.

I put down the phone. I hadn't realized time was so brief, that there was already an expiration date. But an expiration date for what, actually? The friendship? Were we friends?

Dalia was also among the attendees. Dahan explained that ever since he'd made Sealed and Leased with that poet, he'd realized that collaborations were the answer. He was planning to make a film called *This Summer*, which would be a sort of jigsaw puzzle made up of short films he'd make with each of us, separately, but edited together at the end. He'd work on some music with Dalia, Niro, and Eddy. He'd work on an animated scene with Gabby. He went on. When he got to me, he said, You and I will work on a script together, you already know what the story's going to be, and he laughed.

I left the meeting irritated, a murky electric current rising and falling within me. Dalia hurried out too, but I didn't notice her until we crowded into the stairwell together.

I took several steps at a time to leave her far behind. The automatic light went out. She called my name. I reached the floor below her and turned on the light. She was standing at the landing, holding on to the railing. I waited for her. When we left the building, she said, You're right.

What about? I said.

About not wanting to take part in this project.

I asked if it was that obvious.

She said she'd simply been watching my response. She didn't think anyone else had noticed.

I didn't speak.

She said, Nahum, we're going around in circles.

Around what? I said.

Around what we're looking for in each other.

I just want to be your friend, I said, I mean, a regular friend, I want to hear you talk, and I want you to want that too.

She said, How can you be sure you don't want more?

I said, What do you want?

She said, I like being around you, but that isn't enough.

What isn't enough?

The words, there's a difficulty in them, an obstacle.

I said, Then what else is there?

She said, The body.

She told me that in the past few months she'd been drawn to the enormous thicket beyond the road that flanked Sderot.

I said, The outer thicket. A panicked trembling ran through me, the murky electricity intensifying. I asked, Since when? She said, A little after Passover, that time we met. She'd just returned from a walk there. She said there was another quality in that thicket, something different from all of Sderot's other earthly wonders. I repeated the phrase "earthly wonders." It left a bitter aftertaste on my tongue. She said she wanted to show me something special. The evening gathered from the outskirts of the sky, intent on the sticky glow of the month of Elul that rushed toward us. I said maybe it was late for this. She said not to worry, that she used to feel a pull toward cemeteries, so the thicket was a step up from that.

I followed her. She forged a path skillfully. She was already familiar with the paths. The eucalyptuses drooped in the burning skies. They emitted their usual spicy aroma. She led me to the clearing.

I asked, Why here? She asked if I couldn't feel it. I asked what. She said, The space here is thinner, like paper, it can tear.

That electricity coursed through me. She spent quite a bit of time in this clearing, it turned out. She had a light blanket hidden in a bag between the trees. We spread it on the ground. I asked if she was sure. She said yes, she wasn't a virgin either, she'd lost her virginity with an older man almost a year earlier. We're both experienced, she said, laughing.

We were naked, lying side by side on the blanket, looking up. I told her that's all I wanted, to lie beside her like this. She asked again how I knew.

I said I knew what I wanted. I wanted to be a poet, that much was clear to me, for instance.

She asked what the point was. Poets needed to find a new voice.

I told her more about the holeache. She said I had to find a way to express it. I said I had, through poetry. She said I'd been led astray, that I would find my voice, my means of expression, sometime.

I said, But I'm a poet, I'm going to be a poet.

She kept silent for a few moments.

Then she asked if I wanted to try. I reached over and cupped one of her breasts. They were larger than Sylvia Gozlan's. The breast was firm and pliable, the areola dark. I leaned in and kissed it, gently closing my teeth around it. Dalia moaned. I moved to the other breast. Her body was warm with the heat of her surroundings, the frock of the air, my lips burned by the touch of her skin. My hand traveled between her thighs. I ran my hands gently over her genitals and the slit, the swell of flesh that protruded. A few more moans. My hand reached to feel among my clothes, which were piled up next to us. My yarmulke was buried underneath them, the first item of clothing I'd removed. I felt the knit pattern. I licked the breasts, I caressed the apertures. Dalia pushed me back. She said, Yes, this isn't what you want, this isn't what I want, this isn't what the place wants.

The yarmulke was still gripped in my hand. I asked if she meant God. She said, No, she meant this thicket, there was an awakening in it that repelled life, lust.

I, meaning I, was struck hard by this insight, but my senses were turned off, they were the senses of I-Nahum. How could I detect anything outside of them? Toward whom? I-Nahum swallowed the panic, the pulsating holeache. I asked if it was all right if we lay there anyway, looking at the treetops. I said I'd never felt such simple, sufficient intimacy with another person.

She said there was nothing simple about intimacy, that there was always something else we didn't fathom, something . . . She lingered in choosing her next word. I waited with her for her desired adjective to pop up. She said, Different. I wasn't disappointed by the banality, her voice charged the word "different" with mystery, with power. As if she'd penetrated some inaccessible layer, and fished out the word, fragile and twitching. Different, she said. There's always something different.

I LAY BESIDE DALIA IN THE THICKET. I PRATTLED, I WONDER what about, the words flowing from my mouth with intoxication, minor events from my past, superfluous landmarks. At some point, Dalia said, Let's go back, this place is becoming unbearable, all the oxygen sucking out, how do you still have the energy to talk, aren't you getting sick of how fast the words turn gray here?

I, meaning I, was shaken up, cracks opening all over me, and deeper, into the being that was me. We got dressed. She was faster than me. I walked blindly behind her, stumbling. My right hand that reached to break the fall bumped into a bush. I stifled a cry and limped after her. When we crossed the flanking road, I paused by a streetlight to examine my hand. It was poked all over with thorns. By the time I looked up, Dalia was already swallowed among her neighborhood houses. I couldn't tell her shadow from others.

I knew how tattered and shabby my clothes were. I knew there were leaves and weeds clinging to my hair and clothing. Maybe a few crushed bug corpses too. I didn't care. I would be arriving at a home where half the residents were missing and the other half would be deep in sleep. My holeache pulsed to the pace of my walking. I, meaning I, the network of cracks stretching from me to me, pulsed in the same pace too.

But I was wrong. Simo and Msodi were sitting at the dining table. Msodi's arm was held in Simo's hands, his fingers dancing up and down it, and she laughed. I felt their eyes on me, sizing me up, as I stood in the doorway. Simo said, Nahum.

I said, What?

Nahum, he said, look at me.

I looked up. His eyes shone. He said, You're finally raising hell a little. Without even knowing it, you're becoming a Farkash. The past few months have been good for you.

Msodi's face was stretched into a wide smile. As if I'd unknowingly entered a contest they'd yearned for me to take part in, and they were sitting on the sidelines, cheering me with pride.

Sit down, tell us something, said Simo. He patted the chair beside his.

I walked over and opened my injured hand to them. My mother examined it. She said, It's just a few thorns. She said, Go wake up Tova, she's got strong eyes.

Tova wasn't asleep anyway. When I knocked on the door to her room, she yelled, Get out of here, let me sleep. Go make noise out on the porch.

I said, It's me, Nahum.

She didn't answer. A few seconds later, she opened the door a crack. She whispered, You know he does an impression of you?

I whispered back, Who does?

She opened the door and gestured toward the living room with her chin. I nodded. I showed her my hand. She said, Wait in your room, I'll go get Chantal's tweezers.

Why Chantal's? I asked when we were in my room.

She smoothed out her nightgown. The feminine mannerisms were already impressed into her movements, as was her grandeur, which had been ripening under her worried skin all this time. An unbreakable grandeur. I thought, She'll have it even harder than me.

She said, What do I need all your grossness on my tweezers for?

I smiled. I said, Tova, you're wrong to be mad at Dad, you're jumping to conclusions.

She said, I'm not mad anymore, I've just had enough, enough.

She pulled my night-light over to the desk, held my hand, and took a close look. She said, Where've you been that made you so smelly?

I, meaning I, thought, In the thicket, and another noise, an uproar, that I-Nahum hadn't even noticed. How quickly the words turn gray here.

Enough of what? I said.

She pinched my hand with the tweezers. I gritted my teeth. She said, Sorry, I thought it was a thorn.

Enough of what?

She pulled away from my hand and looked into my eyes. Those gaping pupils. Once, in Turin, at the Egyptian museum, I saw a corpse that had been naturally embalmed, a man from the generation of Enos, folded into his death slumber, in the glass womb that entrapped him, rising from the countless years, trapped in my own gaze. What did that pagan try to tell me? That sort of distance was in Tova's pupils. But I'd never been in Turin, this wasn't my thought. A passage struck me-Nahum: Have the gates of death been opened unto thee? Or hast thou seen the doors of the shadow of death?

Enough, she said, of those two and their disgusting games. What are they, our age? They need to grow up.

Her eyes were large, hazy. I told her that her eyes reminded me of Sylvia's.

She said, Sylvia Gozlan's?

I said, No, Aunt Sylvia's.

What aunt are you talking about? she said.

She tightened her grip on my hand. Her head entered the circle of lamplight. The first thorn was pulled out with a little pinch, the next one with a bigger pinch. At the museum in Turin, there are false doors that the ancient Egyptians installed in their magnificently built mausoleums. They were intended to open to those who knew the spells, the work, a passage into faraway kingdoms of death. I don't know when I, meaning I, heard them opening. At some point I, meaning I, could no longer bear the pain, and I opened my mouth to yell, my being was enveloped by this flesh, pulled out by force of the tweezers, one bit after another of the self, extracted from its temporary cloak, pulled out, expelled, finally infected by my name, the name now given to me for a period of time, Elish Ben Zaken, I.

MY NAME WAS PUSHED BACK FROM THE WALLS OF THE SPACE IN which I am contained, that is how I realize how narrow it is. I am a man whose boat is floating on the river and he blows on the sails hoping to get it moving. But to what end? The banks are pressing against each other. I'd better jump in the water.

I feel an urge, the origin of which I cannot grasp, to tell my own story. Maybe that voice, speaking inside my head, is responsible for it. Perhaps it's a consequence of it. I hope it isn't only mine, the story. After all, every story claiming to stand on its own is always enslaved to another story, which, by virtue of its ghostly touches, its insistence to be revealed at inappropriate intersections, its sudden entrapment by an outside eye, becomes profound and mysterious. But not for those living it, who are also haunted by another story.

And anyway, there is no bottom line, no conclusion to be formulated. There are only principles, structures, patterns that allow each of us to tell some story, and they all come to light at their best when we tell others' stories, wishing to lend an ear to their otherness. It isn't the overcoming of obstacles that matters, our ability to attribute words to the otherness, but the overcoming of the self that blocks our path, our desire for that overcoming.

I heard them say, and I heard them say violently, that the effort to tell our story, the memoir, the autobiography, obligates us to struggle, to scuffle, with our sense of truth, with honesty. It's a mistake. The metaphysics of the I Industry—and I say "I Industry" because that's what it is: a rumor factory, not a religion—is a languid, abusive, barbaric metaphysics. In its hands, even honesty is a ruse, much less interesting than the lie and the defeat.

But that doesn't mean that the principles and structures are given to us. What greater enemy is there than the previous form, the genre, the pretense of believing that they are at our service before we have even spoken a single word?

No, they must appear out of the act itself, in a path that matches experience, out of observation.

If there is a struggle, then it is this, the struggle to mold our knowledge into a different, astounding, singular knowledge that emerges from the time and being it is meant to describe.

Because for time to be, time has to happen to someone—not a specific someone, but me, her, you all—and still, it is one personal occurrence after the other.

What is memory, then, a gauge of time or evidence of time's existence? Can this question be parlayed into another: Is creating a gauge not also creating the matter it measures?

(Where shall these questions echo, in which consciousness of which absent listeners of this story? Who are you anyway, bitches?)

I am tired of books that aim to arrange time in predictable ways that have nothing to do with the story's generation of time. And how relevant is that for the detective novels I'd been writing so far, the profound interest of which is competing for the rule of time, unraveling the time threads of suspects' alibis and weaving them into a story of the time of my detective, Benny Zehaviv? And always according to the chronological pattern, arranged according to the order of actions.

But the more echoing meaning, that which fills us with wonder, is rooted in synchronicity, the simultaneous occurrence of several events, the ability of consciousness to contain the contradiction between them, the reciprocal relationship.

I've spent the past few months pondering. That's obvious, I think. I now know that detective novels are unworthy of being called "literature." Their sole function today is to convince readers of the reality of the false questions they present, to conceal the questions they are able to present and that they misappropriate.

Early on, detective fiction was able to raise questions about the structure of the universe, about the desire for meaning. Then things transpired, the circumstances of detective fiction's creation became extinct, the needs it met mutated into passions. Other questions—political, social—undermined the original ones.

For some reason, a waning literature relies on the illusion that its political and social questions are the burning ones. That is when its golden age arrives. But a golden age is always an array of the first signs of demise, like the glowing faces of people dying of tuberculosis.

I can no longer read the old detective novels, and certainly can't write them. I spent too long in the exile of that unlife. And for what? Whenever I sat down in front of the computer I told myself, Reason is fated to lead us to the places where it cannot enter. That voice, the speaking voice in my head, asked where I was seeking entrance.

Maybe I'm overdoing it with the philosophizing, as Manny Lahav once claimed, with the blather. Who would tell me, Enough, cool it, what a wild exaggeration? Ronnit, with her mundane ridicule?

But I can't call Ronnit. Two months ago, when she rushed to

tell me about her pregnancy, that she was carrying the child of the converted Wolodia, David Dgani, she gave me the divorce writ the two of us had been circling for years, delaying it, hurrying to fulfill it, washing our hands of it. No more. Who, then? Me? You?

Fine, honorable audience, man-whores and bitches, let's get to the point. Is that truly what's bothering me?

Yes. But I'll be honest. The abstract only rises from the tangible. And the essential reason shames me. I have more successful imitators. True, I've written books for order, engineered and calculated to the last letter. They were intended to camouflage themselves abroad as a faithful reflection of life in Israel. But I tried to write a worthy story, tried not to betray all of my inner compasses.

And now enters a new generation of people who understand the economy of signs and symbols, who understand the power of image as a thought structure. The full resources of this generation are aimed at establishing their own image, of who they are, the simple contours of their naked self, through which they would be read. The content of the writing, its character, isn't as meaningful. From the moment the metaphor has been set, any piece of blabber, prattle, libel, dull thought, inarticulation, is read in its service.

I think that is my limit, the corruption of language. A man or woman who masturbated in public would be imprisoned for indecent behavior. But we are drowning in public masturbators, masturbating on the Wit-ternet or in Heb-rage, the only two jargons still available in the Hebrew language.

And here I am too, speaking myself, telling, telling, telling.

I TRAVELED SOUTH ON ROSH HASHANAH. I PICKED UP MY MOTHER from her home in Ashkelon. I waited in the car outside her building. The street was melting in the sun that had burned ever since the war. A cauterized sun beneath the skin of the days and nights. The light like dust, beams strewn with grains. And yet, the slow burn of Tishrei, when the world is new. The street rose fully from childhood, an unending whip of asphalt, someone had ordered the heavenly bodies to stand in place, and only their radiation had been fading since then.

You and those thoughts again, my mother said when she got in the car. She had tapped on the window and I hadn't heard. What thoughts? I said. Her white-tinged hair had been braided. It was fastened to her skull with barrettes that gathered a dying sparkle at their tips. She touched them hesitantly, securing them in place. When she caught me looking, she said, A gift from Tahel. Such a gesture from my niece surprised me. She was a sly girl, but certainly not cruel. She bought them in Eilat, my mother said. I said, I see the swelling in your nose is almost gone. Yes, my mother said, the CT scan helped. No, I said, the CT doesn't cure, it's just– She cut me off, saying, the simplest thing would have been to go to the Dead Sea, the salt there can even cure leprosy. I told her she was thinking about the Jordan River. What are you talking about, Jordan River, she said, what, that dirty river? I said, Don't you remember? She said, Remember what? I said, The story of Naaman. She said, No. I said, So, what did the doctor say? My mother said, I told you, there's no faith in doctors. I asked if there was no faith in those purifying by water or by flame. She said she had no idea what had gotten into me.

We drove in silence. The Ashkelon Junction was barren. Approximately twenty years ago I drove by here on my way to Tel Aviv after a Friday-night dinner. A guy in military uniform, a captain's ranks, and a paratrooper's beret was waiting impatiently at an empty bus stop, perhaps for a car to pick him up. His gloomy features converged in a glorious nose. Some would call it Roman. I recognized him. He'd been in my class in high school. I didn't know him well. He'd been part of the group of children of standing army men and wealthy families that lived in the Afridar neighborhood. His eyes were haunted when my gaze fell on him in the pale light of the streetlamps. I thought he'd grown so much. I wondered what this speedy maturation had required. I thought about rolling in the dirt, sleeping out in the field, I thought about aching bones. I thought about muscles stretched beyond their abilities by force of will, about a well-timed sex life that transformed into a line of bodily gestures, adding up to form a routine. I thought about stuttered male conversations, about tarps. I thought about the first flutter of breath as the feet abandoned the lead floor of the plane and the body submitted to free fall. I thought about the experience too fleeting to become memory. I thought about a language that never caught up with events, about an interior being sentenced to only be conveyed by shortcuts and code names. His image and the density of thoughts pounced into my mind at once. My being was doubled in the driver's seat, me and that same old me, still experiencing things, surprised by their sharpness.

I asked my mother how Yaffa had reacted when I announced I was coming. Her head was turned toward the window, to the eucalyptus trees embalmed in the vagueness of twilight. Rough sinter, my mother mumbled. What? I said. You can tell by the color of the evening, she said, it's thin. I said, "Thin" isn't a color. My mother didn't respond. I'm worried about Tahel, she said. They shouldn't have moved to Sderot. And what about Oshri? I asked. My mother said, She's already a young woman, she needs to find herself. Finally, we agree, I said. She turned to face me. Did you say something? she asked. I told her I agreed with her. She said Tahel was now at that stage of anger, and that if Yaffa didn't watch out, the girl would stay angry for the rest of her life. Her words were shoved back from the view that was revealed some distance after the turn at Yad Mordechai Junction. The remains of the light skidded down the hill, to our right were the thin trunks of a long hedgerow, gold-lit vegetal hieroglyphs. And Oshri? I asked again. My mother said, You can tell it's going to be a rough winter. When you look around at this hour it's like the world is surrounded by horses of fire.

THE LAKESIDE NEIGHBORHOOD WAS STILL BARE NAKED. CAST concrete platforms and heaps of floor tiles and bricks. Most of the construction zones were surrounded by poles with cameras at the top. My mother said that Yaffa told her there'd been a theft spree in recent weeks. One of the neighbors left a shipment of marble from China unattended overnight, and in the morning the marble was gone. It's the Bedouins, she said, they drive over and take everything that isn't nailed to the ground. But here and there lights were on in windows. Slow down, my mother said, pointing. A man and a young boy walked on the sides of the road, wearing their white holiday best. She said she knew we'd arrive after the holiday began even though I drove like a savage, paying no mind to the road, and that Zalman and Oshri were probably at the synagogue already.

I didn't respond. Less than two weeks earlier, a building in my neighborhood was demolished. I saw the sign announcing the evacuation and reconstruction project and ignored it. I assumed the threat was still far away, even though nearby buildings were already being taken down, new ones erected in their stead. The day before the demolition, signs were posted outside the nearby buildings and on the windshields of cars. That night, I closed the shutters, thickening the dark.

A collapsing home is a sight to behold. The street's residents all gathered to watch, along with, perhaps, some random passersby. The sand walls of Zionist architecture awaited the coming of the bulldozer. I could see the gathering crowd, a loose circle of heartbeats and blood, exchanging views, gesturing. On one side, the organic, fighting for self-maintenance, on the other side, the still, plummeting into a deeper silence, aspiring for the quality of dirt within it. How easy it is to shake off the illusion of solidity, the matter made up of crystalline collapse. Every demolished house is evidence of other demolished houses, the houses we've ceased to see, that we turn our eyes away from, our own houses that were lost, houses we prefer to push out of our minds. A man stood next to the building, watering the air, restraining the dust. I sensed a sourness in my mouth, and my skin tingled, whispering. I retreated into my apartment. I think that's when my suspicion started, that things were trembling at my fingertips. A loosening I didn't know whether to attribute to the objects or to the way in which I thought about them, in which I ordered them to be present.

Tahel was sitting in the yard, staring at the lake. On the distant bank, treetops bit into the evening. When I called her name, she smiled, her mouth clenched. I asked if everything was all right. I sat down beside her. She said, Yes. I asked how she was doing again. Ugh, she said, you've become annoying. Then she said that all people asked her about at school was Heftzi Columbus and the murder. I said I thought they'd reported it quite extensively in the media. She said, They want to know what it's like to live here, where they found the body. And what do you tell them? I asked. She said the missile that fell in the thicket at the beginning of the war is more interesting, and so was that story about Zevulun the Sweet. The news offered extensive coverage on the finding of his body, headless and handless, in an apartment in Ramat Gan, without any identifying documents. The apartment was owned by a middle-aged man named Zevulun Desuete. A week after the body was discovered, the severed head and hands appeared outside a building in Kiryat Gat. The eye sockets had been emptied, bits of the flesh of the face had been removed, the fingertips had been cut off, and the empty spaces were filled with honey, which was also smeared over the rest of the flesh. Tahel asked if that happened in my neighborhood in Ramat Gan, if Manny Lahav offered any details that hadn't made it to the media, if they knew who'd done it. I said they thought it was a serial killer. She said I once told her there were no serial killers in Israel. I said, Yes, and your mother shouldn't hear about us having this conversation. Damn, she said, I can't talk to you about anything anymore. There was some alertness underneath her skin. I could see the anger my mother was talking about, a paper-thin fabric wrapped around her organs. I doubt if she herself was yet aware of its existence. I asked if there was anything else. She smiled her ungenerous smile again. She said, Let's see if you can guess. I said, I can think of two reasons for your mood. Either you had a fight with your mother or something happened with Yalon. Her face remained frozen. Grandma would have told me if you'd gotten into trouble with Yaffa, I said, so I deduce you're in a bad mood because of Yalon. She nodded slowly and said, That's part of it. What about the other part? I asked. She said, Don't you want to hear the part about Yalon? I laughed. She said, That loser came up to me at the beginning of the school year and asked to talk to me alone, as if there'd been no war, no nada. I asked since when she said things like "no nada." Tahel said, Ever since I realized my class is one-third *arsim* from the kibbutz, one third *arsim* from villages, and one third *arsim* from Sderot. Then she added that I didn't get it. I said, I'm not the one who needs to get it, you are.

She squeezed her chin between two fists, and her eyes fixed on the surface of the water, an indifferent metal sheet. One of the new neighbors, my mother had told me, imported live koi fish from China and set them loose in the lake. The school of fish was still in a fragile state. Their bodies must have moved through their silent courses in the moderate depths. In the dim light, I imagined the greasy glistening of their backs, the blue beam of the skeletal chill. The air moved a little, carrying over the summery bitterness of vegetation along with a meek dampness. My mother had been right about that too. A rainy winter was coming, fraught with cold fronts, a freezing patch over the site of the burn. The longer my eyes lingered on the sights, the more they faded, on the verge of dissipating. Strange, I said, looking at the thicket now. Tahel didn't answer. I asked if she could forgive without understanding. She said, Who said I forgave him? Mom says you never forgive anything, not even on Yom Kippur, and that's why you haven't been here in two months. I said, But your rift with Yalon wasn't that kind of rift, difficult days are coming, you can't be choosy about your allies. She gave me a long look, her irises drilling into me, that harsh Berber blue. She said, And what about your allies? I said, I'm a lost cause, all I have is enemies. She said, But Manny is your ally, why do I need any? I said, There is no grace in the world, only negotiations, explicit and implicit agreements, puppets and strings, cease-fires, balances of terror. I don't know what inspired me to tell her the truth so bluntly. A lump blocked my throat. But Tahel laughed. She said, Elish, you. Then she said, Never mind. I asked, What about the other part? She got up.

YAFFA WAS STANDING BEHIND US. WE HADN'T NOTICED HOW THE yard had darkened like a hand closing into a fist over our heads. Bully for you, she said, laughing together. So, Tahel, I see you've gotten over your little depression. Tahel walked past her mother wordlessly, then paused by the sliding doors, glass covered by a screen. Rude girl, said Yaffa, go help Grandma set the table, then straight to the shower and to get dressed. Don't be like your uncle, coming to the holiday dressed like a bum. Tahel was wearing a knee-length dress, its tattered whiteness glimmering in the aura of the house. She'd grown taller in the past six weeks, but her body language still clung to childhood. I said, Sorry I didn't consult with the fashion police. Yaffa said, Look at how you show up here, wearing jeans and a T-shirt for a holiday dinner, is that how you were brought up? Come on, Mom, said Tahel, get off his back, he's finally here. Yeah, said Yaffa, his honor deigns to show up. I smiled at her. She said, What, you're too good to say hello when you get here? I said, I shouted hello when I walked through the door. She said, And thank you for the flowers. There may be hope for you yet.

She stood close to me. The exhaustion that had governed her posture all summer long had left no marks. Though she'd spent the day cooking, she looked refreshed. The uncomplicated joy of life's fountain of youth. She said, No, really, I mean it, it's good that you came, Zalman wouldn't leave me alone this week. All of a sudden, he thinks he needs your advice on all sorts of nonsense. I said, These Moroccans, their pride won't let them admit their feelings. She said, I'm not turning the light on in the yard because there are still plenty of mosquitos, come into the living room, the air-conditioning is on.

What disturbed me about that apparition of my classmate? I didn't know many details about him. We were only in the same homeroom for one year, before we were divided into different courses of study. He was also a Moroccan, but came from a family that had assimilated into the Ashkelonian bourgeoisie. Once, I spotted him immersed in a book. I followed the shifts of the cover until I learned the name of the book and the name of the writer. It was one of Tom Clancy's spy thrillers. When the weight of my gaze became unbearable, he looked up and blinked. This was on the field trip I was forced to go on. That year, after the spring of age sixteen, after my first encounter with Dalia Shushan, when the fevers were finally quenched. The principal convinced my mother that it would be best not to let me play sick, to force me to overcome the burning of longing for home that only popped up whenever I drew away from it. The open spaces would assist my recovery. With great effort, I scoop out of my memory a meadow, a burst of sunlight, and his eyes trying to read my intentions. His mind was still wrapped up in the threads of the plot from which he'd been forced to wake. I asked if he only ever read Tom Clancy novels. He said pretty much, there was no other author in his league. I said, A one-man league, that's inconceivable, by definition a league is a group of people. He was in the biology course of study, his logic was fuzzier than mine. I remember clearly that a crow, or one of those dark birds that disguise themselves as crows, let out a screech that blended into my classmate's laugh. You're so weird, he said, you're one of those weirdos. His BFF was Romanian, wiry, his shoulders the breadth of his hips, his skin bad. People said he was a clown. We went to the same middle school, and like me, he'd drag in the rear during track drills, far behind the light-footed boys. He constantly joked about the phys ed teacher who would hurl rebukes and insults at us. I didn't resent that teacher. Once, he stopped me after class and asked, You know what's a synonym for strength? I said nothing. He said, Tenderness. It turned out he'd watched me all throughout class as I'd tried to strike a volleyball with all the force of my right arm. He said, Why work the back muscles when what you need is the soft push of your fingertips?

The two friends walked up to me at lunch a week before the trip. I assume this time I was holding a book, perhaps one of Günter Grass's loathsome novels. The Romanian friend asked if I'd read *Cat and Mouse* yet. I hadn't. He said it was actually a good book, just a shame the hero died, he had a big dick. Like yours, said the classmate. Mine's a little bigger, I think, said the friend. Then he added that he liked the scene where the boys masturbated on the beach and fed their jizz to the seagulls. I didn't know what jizz was. My classmate said, Don't play innocent, what, don't you jerk off? I didn't answer, I'm sure I didn't answer. My classmate said, I'm going to grow hair on the back of my hand from rubbing so much. The friend said, We heard you're coming on the field trip, we'll finally get a chance to see you in the shower, you never shower after gym class. I shrugged. The classmate said, You probably have a big dick too. Yeah, said the friend, Moroccans all have big dicks, except for—then he named my classmate. That sunny, sloping meadow where he sits and reads is trapped in a shard of time, floating through a dark sea, an island whose edges are fraying and receding, and his own name is a hole, a puncture in consciousness. I know there's no point in trying to conjure it. The effort would only lead to that same draining of recognition and will. Just like as a child, when I tried to identify secret powers in myself, the ability to time travel whenever I liked, and pressured my brain and my nerves until I was washed over by a white wave of nothingness, my stomach turning.

I SAT IN THE HOT YARD, LISTENING TO THE BUZZING OF FEMALE mosquitos, those who still buzzed, not yet endowed by evolution with the silence necessary for any predator. In the past few years, Tishrei lacked the comforting softness of evenings, even in Sderot, where the addition of the artificial lake enforced the seasons' law of hardening and softening.

Nightmary, I heard behind my back. The glass parting between the yard and the house slid on its tracks. A nightmary boy, said Bobby's voice, I'm telling you, Yaffa, the boy's become a nightmare. Oshri crossed the short distance to the table, walking carefully, lest blades of mowed grass cling to the hems of his pants. The white shirt brightened his demeanor. A solidity was added to his limbs. When he reached me he whispered, Well, did you bring it? What did you promise him? said Tahel. She emerged from the golden core of the house wearing her holiday dress. The dress was a little over-the-top for my taste, lacy twists in the neckline, a flower on the shoulder. Not the dress, but rather the way Tahel wore it, like a child in costume. She hadn't practiced mimicking the appropriate mannerisms two years ago, and her new femininity was foreign. What? she said. I thought, She's beautiful, and immediately pushed the thought away. Oshri said, Don't interrupt. I said, In the bag in the living room. Oshri hurried back inside.

Tahel remained. She said, And what did you bring me? I sensed the blood rushing to her cheeks, though at this moonless hour I couldn't see the blush. She lowered her eyes. I said, Promise me you'll thank your mother and not butt heads with her at least until the High Holy Days are over. Why? she said, biting her lower lip. Then she said, Butting heads, and chuckled. You promise, I said. She said, First tell me why, why does she have to interfere in everything? I said, Remember what I said about allies. Yeah, yeah, she groaned. I heard you. Tahel, I said. She said, Fine, fine, I promise.

I pulled a small envelope from my pocket and handed it to her. She pulled on its end sharply. Gently, I said, We'd better go inside. She felt the contents through the paper. It's a SIM card, she said. Yes, I said, unlimited calls, texts, and data, and it's your regular number. Wow, she said, then asked how come her parents said yes. I told her I had my own methods of persuasion. Yes, she said, huffing, allies.

A faint tinge of sorrow, a light contraction of the heart muscles. Perhaps the body's letting go of the outside heat, the chill of the air conditioner, the motor of which didn't even purr, just a emitted cool swell, depleting the air of its vibrancy, or something else. For a moment, the house seemed to be darkened, discharged of its electricity, and from up high I observed the possibility of its being, an abstract model, a system of lines etched onto parchment, an architect's blueprints. Then it stabilized again, becoming that same weave of perpetual facts and imagery. My hand reached for my chest of its own accord. The living room looked empty. On its other side, an arched passage led to the dining room, where arm movements and bodily shifts were revealed, my mother's and my sister's, around the table, appearing and disappearing, spirits working on a mid-heat-wave banquet. I walked over, mesmerized, and almost tripped over Oshri. He was lying on the floor, the volumes of Philip Pullman's *His Dark Materials* trilogy spread out before him as he feasted his eyes on the cover art. I too, back in the day, had acquired the habit of reading on the floor, in the height of summer, the bottom side of my body suckling the last bits of night out of the floor tiles.

Why are you lying on the floor? I said. He asked, I'm going to like these books, right? Yes, I said, you're going to like them. The bag was gaping beside him. He shoved in the Pullman books and pulled out two of Diana Wynne Jones's *Chrestomanci* books. And these, he said. What do you think? I asked. He said, Tahel walked by and made a weird face when she saw me looking at them. Why are you looking so hard at the covers? I said. He said, I'm checking the feeling of the book, if it's round, or broken, or made of quiet. Made of quiet? I said. Yeah, like these books where you feel like you're in a fish tank and you don't mind. Don't mind what, I asked, drowning? Being a fish, he said. And Pullman's books, I said, what feeling do they give you? He said, That they're sour, that whoever wrote them has a sour heart, but still I know they're right for me. I know that with these books, he said, pointing at the *Chrestomanci* books, I'll feel like I'm a tree in the forest, and with the others, like I'm a tree whose brothers have all been chopped up and he's all alone on a land that used to be an orchard. Don't lie on the floor, I said, it isn't healthy, and you're not in mourning. He said, But Tahel's face is always a little weird.

Cool it, you fat little midget, said Tahel. She ran in, out of breath. With each footfall, she fled the purpose the dress forced upon her. The flower on her shoulder was almost torn. She handed me her iPhone. No, Elish, she said, you're unreal. On the top left corner of the screen appeared the name of the cellular provider to which I'd switched Tahel's number. What did I say, I said to Oshri. He stood between us, looking at the phone, his lips speaking the name, kum kera, "rise and call" or "take up and read," better still. Stupid name, he said. You're stupid, said Tahel, what counts is that for once I'm the first kid in my class to have something from the commercials.

BOBBY PRESIDED OVER THE TABLE IN HIS CLUMSY WAY. THE syllables were picked out carefully in his mouth, lest he make an error in pronouncing the Rosh Hashanah blessings and the holiday meal would all be for naught. I followed him closely, trying to detect any mistakes. After the Kiddush, I poured myself wine from a bottle I'd brought with me, a Pinot Noir I hadn't tried before, somewhat heavy. It isn't good to drink on an empty stomach, said my mother. I said it was all right, we'd be eating any minute. The pomegranate seeds shone bright red, the steamed leek a faded green, the honey in its bowl burning amber. Tahel and Oshri were in fine spirits. They broke the sequence of blessings with whispers and light kicks under the table. What's the big excitement, said Yaffa, so you got a few presents.

There are times when I do not recoil from the music of a meal, the echolessness of the serving dishes, the wounding of the air as metal crashes into china, the rustle of chewing, the humming of the filling body, the buzzing of the space. The wine was starting to work its magic.

Bobby said, You did good with the gifts, have you made any money off the new book yet? Zalman, said Yaffa, don't discuss money during a holiday. What, said Bobby, just now at synagogue I paid for a prayer for good earnings. I said I hadn't signed the contract yet, and that I wasn't going to ask for an advance anyway, because I wasn't sure I was going to write the book. And what will you live off of? asked my mother. Mom, said Yaffa, don't start that too. Yes, I said, I believe in Bobby's prayers. You're a hoot, said Bobby, you should drink more. What's your problem with taking the advance if they're offering it? This country is robbing us blind with the taxes we pay, anyway. I said I didn't want to be indebted to my publisher or my agent. That Betty, said Bobby, she looks loaded. Quietly, I asked, When did you see her? Bobby didn't answer. Yaffa shot me a warning look. My flinch sent a shock wave all around. Tahel and Oshri stopped dissecting the meat on their plates, ceased their soft, heated conversation. I looked at them. Their arms in their laps, frozen like dolls.

My mother said, What's wrong, why'd you all stop talking?

Yaffa said, Because Elish has a habit of always saying the wrong thing. My mother said, I didn't hear him say anything. Yaffa said, You've got to look into that, I told you. After the holiday I'm getting you an appointment with an ENT doctor. Why? I said. She isn't hearing well, said Tahel. You, said Yaffa, stop butting into grown-up affairs. Since when? I said. Yaffa said, When she puts the phone to her right ear she can't hear what you say to her. I told you there's a problem with that phone, my mother said. The problem isn't with the phone, said Yaffa. My mother said, So, Elish, what are you going to live off of? Write the book, said Bobby, and take the dough, what's the big deal?

I said it wasn't easy for me to deal with all the sorrow involved in Heftzi Columbus's murder right now. The thought of researching her life before she moved to Sderot and started working for Mayor Yoram Bitton depressed me. Nonsense, said Bobby, you're blowing this out of proportion, these days there's a new murder on the news every day. You don't understand, I said, Columbus's murder has political implications. Political, yeah right, said Bobby, it happened during Operation Protective Edge, when those pieces of Palestinian shit were shooting missiles at us. I'm more interested in hearing about the soldiers who died to protect their country. That's enough out of you two, said Yaffa, I've had it up to here with you. The operation in Gaza is over, and we're in the middle of a holiday dinner. And reading a book, I asked, does that interest you? Bobby said, Isn't it enough that you made my kids catch that book bug? I said, You should thank me every day. I glanced at my niece and nephew. Oshri was immersed in his plate, moving the pieces of meat and vegetables this way and that. Tahel's face sporadically wore that same amusing expression, features drawn with effort and eyes glassy. Then she shook it off. In a tone she may have thought sounded serious or grave, she said, Dad, let me get something straight, you want us to succeed, right? He nodded. To succeed, she said, we've got to do well in school. True, he said. Oshri got the highest scores in his grade in the learning level group tests, she said. How do you think that happened? It's got nothing to do with books, said Yaffa, Oshri's a smart kid. Oshri leaned deeper over his plate. Are you sure? asked Tahel. What's changed in Oshri's life between last year, when he was a bad student, and this year? Bobby said, He's at that age. Tahel said, Or maybe something opened his mind. A gleam came down upon the table and all around us. The voice speaking in my head said, Don't miss a single detail. If you look away, even for a fraction of a second, the image will be gone. I poured myself another glass of wine.

BOBBY ASKED ME TO SLIP OUT TO THE BACKYARD WITH HIM. HE needed a cigarette after all that heavy food. The silent toil of smoking alone. And yet he asked me to join him. He said the air was bearable at this hour. When we were outside he said, So, Elish, everything good? I said, Except for what isn't. He said, May our enemies be felled down, damn their names, may evil befall them. That's the most important blessing of Rosh Hashanah. We sat under the pergola he'd built during the war. Ferns and creepers gripped the shoots, holding on to their tendrils in the night. I said, When one can distinguish between powder blue and the color of leek. I had no idea where that phrase popped out from. It wasn't mine. *Prasa*, said Bobby. I like it when your mother calls leeks *prasa*. Okay, I said, when one can distinguish between piety and *prasa*. The wine burned in my blood vessels, an alcoholic pacemaker moving the body according to pulses not my own, speaking through me. I was familiar with this experience, watching the world through the malleable pane of intoxication, while another creature, which I'd designed in hiding, and which had a better grasp of my throat muscles and the proper order of words, inherited my place.

Bobby started to laugh. The smoke he'd inhaled caught in his lungs, and he slipped into a coughing fit that only got worse. Let it out, I told him, all that dirt, that filth we breathed last summer. He almost settled down, his typically murky eyes dampening, shimmering, the eyes of his children emerging for a few seconds through the black film, their tense attention to the world, that restless search. You're funny when you drink, he said again, when did you start drinking? I said exhaustion was getting the better of me, I hadn't been able to sleep since construction began on my street. But you drink, he said. I drink every evening, I said, one glass of wine, ever since the war. You have a hard time falling asleep, he said. Not hard, I said, I've always had difficulty sleeping, but now its temperature has risen, it's boiling, it's a speed I can't catch up with. What's temperature got to do with speed? he asked. I said, I don't need to tell you, haven't all your years working as a welder taught you anything? Temperature is the expression of the speed of molecular movement. I said that sleep molecules were more frantic and wine heated the blood to the appropriate degrees. You and your nonsense, said Bobby. Do you at least enjoy drinking? I said, It's a field I'm starting to investigate. But Yaffa's right, he said, that's it, it's over, Protective Edge is behind us. No, I said, we can't go back. I said, You're talking to me as if this war took place on a faraway continent. I don't understand, said Bobby, every morning your friends go to their mosques and yell *itbah el-yahud*, and you've got no problem with that. I'm not a wimp like you, I'm a proud Jew.

I said, You're not a Jew. You're an Israeli who goes to synagogue. Gone is the time when the two overlapped. But you're certainly proud, that much is true, proud enough to burn children, to bomb them. One child, he said. I think I said that burning a child was never a singular event, that the concept of burning scorched the weave of history like a cigarette. What else. I think I said that humanity was bloodthirsty, and that as soon as the reins were loosened on one of its violent urges, it transformed into lust. I think I said that lust was a plague, a virus, jumping from one soul to another with a word, a look, a bodily gesture.

Half of what you say is bullshit, said Bobby, I don't understand what you want, that's exactly your problem, you get all riled up about your own words. I said he was letting himself off the hook. Bobby said, What can we do, we have to get used to living in a war zone, only God can save us. I said that in order for a Jew to be able to accept the rule of God he must be qualified to distinguish between the color of piety and the color of *prasa*. He said, This is how things are going to be from now on, we're surviving—

Yaffa burst into the conversation. She stood behind Bobby's back, between us and the light streaming out from the windows. In the sudden shadow that was cast, Bobby's face retreated down the slopes of evolution, his eye sockets deepening, only a spark shining from the burrows of his skull, like the sheep's head that had been placed at the center of the holiday table earlier, deboned, its teeth bared in a spasm of slaughter. *Yalla*, said Yaffa, what'd you think, you were going to sit out here while I do all the work? Come help clear the dishes. What are you talking about, clear the dishes, said Bobby, I'm barbecuing tomorrow, who do you think is going to bust his ass on the grill in this heat? Let me be at peace for a while. He turned to me. You're staying, right? I was in the middle of getting up. I swayed, lost my balance, and plopped back into the chair. Look at that, said Yaffa, you can barely stand up. I said it was fine, I'd help out a little and then drive back to Tel Aviv. Where do you think you're going in your state? said Yaffa. You're spending the night here.

My mother was staying in the guest room, and Yaffa said she'd make one of the beds in the reinforced room for me. I told her I'd rather sleep in the living room. I saw argument gathering into her face, then letting go. This night had gotten the better of her. Me too.

The heaviness of wine swished through me as I lay down on the sofa. The air-conditioning continued to pour its chill, and I wrapped my arms around one of the pillows, pressing it to my cheek. I squinted to steal a last look at the faint sheen of the lake, a dark surface within the slowly dissipating darkness. Even though the moon was not visible, the night brightened, a false dawn. The water retained its dimness, or so it seemed to me. Perhaps in the dwindling of reason I attempted to force my images on outside visions, to make them bear the limits of my mind. I heard rustling in the distance, from the only inhabited houses in the neighborhood, a faint song of the everyday, preparations for sleep, back and forth inside the rooms.

The melody extended into a dream in which I was summoned to a crime scene. I arrived at an abandoned building, laden with countless testimonies and evidence, none of which pertained to the crime whose nature I was yet to ascertain. I stood, surrounded by the abundance of clues of a foreign life, filling with fear. In my apartment, an unidentified being awaited my return, one of Lovecraft's interstellar gods whose mere presence causes space to bend into unfathomable geometries. When I arrived, I realized this was not my apartment that resided on the other bank of wakefulness, but a house I'd once peeked into through a window. Its recollection landed into the dreamscape like a blow. I had happened upon the time and body in which I'd stood outside of it. Its walls mixed into the walls of Yaffa's home, the walls of the living room at the center of which I knew I was lying, limbs paralyzed, throat dry, as necromancers leaned over me, singing their spells of bone and iron. I opened my eyelids with great effort, with languidness. Not far from me stood Tahel and Oshri, watching. Shh, you see, Oshri whispered, you woke him up. Shut up, said Tahel, he'll thank me, I can feel in my veins and arteries that he'll thank me. She seemed to be quoting an expression my mother ceased to use years ago, an eternity. An eternity. What's wrong? I asked. The sticky utterances refused to leave the mouth and tongue. Nothing, said Oshri, go back to sleep. No, said Tahel, I got a super-weird text. In a low voice, Oshri added something I couldn't decipher. I sat up on the sofa. From who, I said, what's weird? Unknown, said Tahel. She handed me her phone.

THE CAREFUL DETAILING OF THE STORY SURPRISES ME TOO. IT must have listeners. You. Who are you? You Goddamn pieces of shit, go fuck yourselves. And they, you, haven't you fucked off already, asking about the lengthiness. I have no idea. I feel that there are keys here. In a certain twist of the plane of the story, a tilt, a shake, a detail would be revealed, allowing me to understand something. What. The mystery is the memory. No. The mystery and the memory work in the same way, their tangibility flashing, shining from within the everyday, the gleam of minerals on the cave walls of the present.

The text message received on Tahel's phone was indecipherable. *There shall be no more death in the Land of Shadow.* It came from a text marketing number. The sentence scratched the edge of my thought. I could almost recognize the trail it left in its wake as it passed through me. But no. Tahel's and Oshri's faces were pale when I looked up from the phone. The brightness of the screen left its mark on my retina. And in this mark, the difference in their paleness was revealed. Tahel's was born of a nervousness, a curiosity, she was about to burst. Oshri's came from fright, as if he'd found in my own face confirmation of a concern that had been bothering him, that this was no joke and no mistake, that there was a reason the text was sent, a reason for the time it was sent.

Do you know what this means? Tahel asked. I said, It's probably just a wrong number. Tahel looked at Oshri and then looked back at me with eyes that, in the dark, expanded like a bird of prey's. She said, You know what this is and you don't want to say, just like with Kalanit and with Heftzi Columbus. The tremble of rage beaded through the words was not lost on me. Oshri took one step back. In an intentionally sleepy voice, he said, Well, things'll probably clear up tomorrow. No, said Tahel, tomorrow Uncle Elish will leave, and nothing will be clear. I said, You have to trust your allies. She said, Are you my ally or my enemy? Tahel, I said, then fell silent. Oshri left the room. Tahel looked me over at length. She whispered, If you know your ally's secret but you don't understand why it's a secret, you're allowed to tell. I wasn't sure if she was asking or stating. I said, Depends on the secret. She said, A secret. Is the secret putting you at risk? I asked. No, she said, but it's causing the ally pain. I asked, Do you want to spare your ally his pain, or reinforce his faith in you? Her voice trembled as she said, You don't understand anything, Elish. She left the room. The screen of the iPhone went dark in the middle of the conversation and I didn't know Tahel's passcode.

I lay back on the sofa for a few minutes. I closed my eyes. The text message had somehow burned itself into the texture of the dark. I'd fully digested the alcohol, which left in its wake a sharp, wounding wakefulness. But my limbs were still fatigued from its bubbling. I forced myself to shake it off. I got up and took my laptop out of my bag. I typed in the website address for Take Up and Read, a virtual operator that had started selling cell and internet packages a month earlier. The dust of the war in Gaza had just settled. One could believe this was a firm testament to Israel's lust for life, not allowing even wars to kill its routine, no more recovery period, a slight morning fatigue after a night of bombing, a quick coffee and off to work. The dead on both sides wiped away with the dream webs from your eyes. And one could say the dirt-cheap prices for which these packages were sold and the provider's marketing techniques were a brilliant commercial move. They leveraged the need for renewal, the illusion of a change of scenery, while the country's institutions were crumbling to the ground, the land cracking open. Perhaps Nahum Farkash was right when he'd said that Israel had always been a financial entity cleverly cloaking itself with the garments of ideology.

Advertising real estates passed through my computer screen,

small clouds of wonder, celebrities and glitterati whose expressions beamed in the light emitted from the devices in their hands, the name of the provider tattooed across their foreheads. They were placed against a backdrop of a night sky dotted with galaxies, the most prominent one of which, sparklingly leaping out of the darkness, was arranged in the shape of the provider's logo. The logo, a sort of engraved bird with its beak pointed to the left and its talons replaced with a hook, appeared again in bold at the bottom of the ad. Where did I know this from? Like the text message, it flickered behind my closed eyelids, then vanished.

The next morning, I silently handed Tahel her cell phone. She unlocked it and stared at the screen. The cup of cocoa in front of her was steaming. We were sitting in front of the lake. My mother carefully followed the movements of the water, trying to catch a glimpse of one of the koi. Can't see a thing, she said. Tahel whispered, There's nothing there, it's just a rumor. Across the water, the thicket susurrated its distant susurrations, the lake absorbed its image, swallowing it. My mother said, Tahel, *yidoroni*, move out of the sun, it isn't good for your skin. I asked if she was able to see her screen, sitting like that in the direct sunlight. From inside the kitchen, where she was busy thawing meat and slicing vegetables, Yaffa shouted, Tahel, get under the sun umbrella, I don't want you getting sunburned again.

What a pair of ears that mother has, said Tahel. My mother said, *Ya binti*, it's always like that, a mother can hear her children from half a world away. I imagined Yaffa's snort of ridicule, if she heard what our mother said. Why would she hear it? Children can't hear their parents' roar from a stone's throw away.

BUT BLOOD TIES HAVE THEIR OWN COMMUNICATION NETWORK, private memory, oblivion. I headed back to Ramat Gan before Bobby and Oshri returned from their holiday morning prayer. My mother beseeched me to stay longer, using her usual argument,

What have you got to do at your apartment, your fridge must be empty. And I gave her my usual response, What I always do in my apartment, I live. And besides, I ate enough food for two weeks last night. My mother clicked her tongue. Look how skinny you are. Before I could complete the farewell ritual, Yaffa interjected. Sure, sure, we've heard it all before, she said. Next, you'll say that Dad used to be skinny too. Why do the two of you have to bring him into every conversation? But actually, perhaps this was the construction of a new ritual.

Tahel stayed in her room. I saw her peeking out the window. I waved at her. She stood, petrified, watching. The phone was gripped in her hand. I could sense her mind putting out feelers, concealed, shifting and sliding, asking further questions, extrapolating one fact from another. She'd become skilled in this art if she could only learn to control her anger.

Perhaps she was mad because she assumed I was continuing the Kalanit Shaubi investigation. Indeed, I'd tried to follow the thread I'd discovered at random. I called Vivian Kahiri several times until she finally picked up. Her voice broke. She asked what it was good for, why'd I have to dig and dig until I found Heftzi Columbus's body, until I discovered her murder? And she'd been so happy for Heftzi, picturing her traveling through Europe, having a ball, swapping wealthy lovers, why'd I have to go ahead and kill her, that Heftzi, I was just as much to blame as her murderers, as Yoram Bitton, as George Arguile, damn his name and memory, may God punish him, may he be raped every night by Arabs, a gas chamber would be too good for that bastard.

I listened in silence. Not that I enjoyed this warlike rhetoric, the Heb-rage taking over every inch of conversation. She said, So what do you want, haven't you ruined enough? I told her I was calling on a trivial matter. I wanted to know if her new life partner was called Dmitry Shtedler. With marked suspicion, she said, Why do you ask? I told her that he and I were hospitalized at Ichilov at the same time last year, in the ENT ward. She said, Don't you come near him, you hear me? I asked her to let me finish my– She cut me off. She said I'd told her enough stories to last her a century and she wasn't interested in hearing any more.

I waited for him one morning in my car at the edge of the neighborhood. He came out of her building, walking heavily, giant and soft, just as I'd remembered him. He paused when I got out of the car to greet him. The smile and flash of recognition were replaced with recoil. His voice emerged from his broad chest, low, naturally rumbling. He said Vivian had warned him about me. Why was I looking for him, what, was I like the KGB? He pronounced the letters in Russian, emphasizing them. The Russian accent was trapped inside of them, fluttering. I said I just wanted to hear more about his niece, because the same thing had happened to a friend of my family. He said, I thought you were from the HMO office. I asked why I looked to him like an emissary of the authorities. He said, Because why would they come looking for me, what did I do? All he did was fail to pay for his hospitalization. I told him his insurance was supposed to cover that. He didn't answer. I asked about his niece again. He said, She's a legal resident. I told him I didn't care about the law, I was looking for information. He said, But what happened to her? I told him I'd like to hear more details about her disappearance when she came to visit him some time ago. He massaged his temples with his fingertips. He asked what I meant. I said he must remember telling me about her disappearance last year when we were both at the hospital. He shook his head slowly. The heat of mid-Elul mornings left its mark. He was sweating. He pulled a handkerchief from his back pocket and wiped his face. He had no idea what I was talking about. His niece had a very nice visit. I thought about my last conversation with Sima Shaubi. Neither she nor her daughter Kalanit even remembered that Kalanit had disappeared for three days. So the event was being erased from the minds of the victims and the minds of their relatives.

I pushed the thoughts away. The roads returned to normal. If some missile had wounded the asphalt over the summer, the asphalt had been patched up. Nothing but the random potholes of a road's attrition. The car shook pleasantly. At Yad Mordechai Junction, I turned my head to investigate what my mother had seen in the tree saplings. Again, that same hieroglyph, its readers long since embalmed in sarcophagi and clay barrels, their soft tissues already consumed, their hearts, their brains, their visual organs. Of course, the Take Up and Read logo, I suddenly remembered where I recognized it from. During my visit to Northern Italy I spent hours at the Egyptian museum in Turin. Pairs of eyes were engraved on the adorned caskets of the old and new kingdom, looking out from within death, protecting or supervising, who's to say, acting as barriers. In the exhibit, the caskets were arranged according to the evolution of ornamentations, and thus the pair of eyes became an abstract contour, a pictogram, an Eye of Horus. The logo was borrowed from that image, without the eyebrow or the pupil, a singular, blind eye mold, watching from the beyond.

When I got home I pulled out my notes from the Kalanit Shaubi investigation and Tahel's notebook with her own findings and looked through them. Again, I reached the dead end at the end of my notepad, where I'd etched over and over with my pen, *No solution, no foundation to the story, no point in further investigation.* The foolishness of ongoing detective games. A crushing sound, almost like the sound of stepping on dry leaves, echoed through my mind. Perhaps the narrating voice was laughing. Laughing for the first time. I added another layer of etching, the pressure of the pain against the lines notched into the paper. I took out a new notepad and copied the Take Up and Read logo onto the first page. Underneath, I wrote, *There shall be no more death in the Land of Shadow.* I ran it through a search engine. Maybe it was a new marketing trick. No. there were no reports of anyone receiving that phrase via text. The first results linked to articles about the asswipe singer who'd become the leader of a gang of rioters during the war.

I told myself there was no more point in complaining about the violence. It had nested in every encounter here since the war. The cyclists of Yarkon Park, for instance, rode toward pedestrians, offering no signs of having noticed them, instead continuing on their trampling trajectory. It didn't matter which part of the park I visited in my explorations, even the wild areas of Ramat Gan, yes, yes, I allowed myself to access even that wilderness. The lichens shimmering on tree trunks, the insects hovering in thick clouds, fracturing the light into its thousand colors with their carapace. Even there, a ferocious cyclist emerged, racing toward me, diverting me off my path. Residents of Ramat Gan, lend me your ears, come out of the project apartments you've condescended into temples, hurry out of your nouveau riche chandeliered pavilions, gather, equipped with clubs and bats, hasten to the park and crush skulls and handlebars, pedals and tibias.

I couldn't give up my walks, of course. Any way of maintaining my adaptation to the evasive speeds of sleep types had to take precedence. After the Gaza War, I lay awake for several nights. The first nights, I took the anti-anxiety medication the doctor prescribed to me after I was released from the hospital. It worked its magic, but poured lead into my muscles the next morning. Then, taking Manny's advice, I tried having a glass of wine late at night. The wine helped a little. More than anything, I developed a habit for drinking it, familiarizing myself with the unexplored expanses of wine that had now become visible. The aroma and texture, the finish on my palate and the reaction of my glands, the wealth of varieties and the range of flavors, all of which I'd previously dismissed as a deceptive, agreed-upon discourse whose purpose was to establish, just as in any other human field of interest, the superiority of a specific group over others. Only at dawn did I drop into this comforting abyss, dropping at the speed of sleep, the wine adjusting my limbs to the appropriate deceleration.

But then the clamor of bulldozers pulled me out of dreams draped in fog, accelerating toward wakefulness. With shut lids, with limbs stiff with tiredness, I'd listen to the grating of metal against broken walls, the raking of bricks and plaster. But the collapsing of my being was even louder. And after a few days came the barking of engines laboring to rummage through the earth, the evacuation of foundations and the digging of holes, a drilling in the thick of the ground. More demanding was the din of blossoming dirt, taking with it all matters of sleep.

How I hated the grogginess, the lack of clarity. I, who knew how to get sick better than most of you (you hear that, you dirty bastards?), to woo the fever, who specialized in sinking into capricious disorientation as a child, and insisted on becoming healed. Now my grip on my own thoughts loosened. One thought followed another at random, without any rhyme or reason. Before one thought was finished, the other was already expelling it. The walks helped, sometimes. In the midst of a long walk, I regained some clarity, and I believed I would be able to sustain it, that the right effort would keep it contained. But an hour would go by and it would dissolve. Sometimes I lost my sense of direction.

A few days before Rosh Hashanah, I sat in my study, summarizing the main points of my research on Heftzi Columbus's life and death, which Betty Stein insisted I write as a sort of thriller, though its end was foretold. I was searching for one thing, for mystery to produce a life that was not its resolution, so that wrestling with it would derive literature, not a conclusion. Suddenly, my eyesight grew dim, sliced through by a sort of shadowy blade, my handwriting lost its focus, and a slight dizziness took hold of me. Seconds in the dark, perhaps an eternity, and my consciousness lit up like a bulb. Somebody flipped the switch and Elish was. That's at least how it felt. I remembered that in a minute and a half I'd be emptying the contents of the saucer before me, dozens of sleeping pills I'd been hoarding, into my mouth, washing them down with a gulp of wine, that for a moment I'd be filled with confidence, nothing was happening, I must be immune, then a brief disappointment would follow, and then my head would plop down against the desk. I'd stare at the gaping door, at the radiance of dark blowing through the crack, and that would be it, the world that existed only by force of my perception would be gone. The experience was blinding in its intensity. A few moments went by before I was able to look around. The notepad was on the desk alongside the laptop, to my right the pack of Klonopin, to my left a goblet of wine, still full to the point where the curving of glass gave in to the perpendicularity of the cup, and beside it an open bottle of Rioja, the peppery aftertaste of which would soon scratch my tongue. The limpidity of the experience faded away almost at once, and all that remained was a delusion of the future, remembering what was about to come to pass.

I got up and paced the apartment. Everything was in its rightful place. The floor of the bedroom was still coated with the PVC I'd ordered in a slip of judgment. Bluish linoleum that had grown ugly with years, covered with drag marks and scratches. I couldn't imagine the space without it, without the curious gluiness of the floor under the bed. The aluminum frames of the shutters, their slats and tracks collecting dust and soot. The capacious living room. At its corner was a solid wood table, its legs an openwork of leaves and florals, six chairs surrounding it, carpentered of similar wood. The enormous kitchen that served no purpose. The wine fridge I'd recently bought stood shrunken with its pale temperature display under the splendor spilling from halogen fixtures. The three of those made Ronnit laugh. The forever-orphaned dining table made for guests who would never show up, the size of the deserted kitchen, and the PVC tiling. She said it suited me to live in a home that reflected none of my true needs. She said, You're more a guest here than I am. Why do you insist on being a guest? Upon our paper marriage, she said, Half of this belongs to me now, doesn't it? Maybe it's time to renovate. When she came to visit, years after the breakup, she said, You know what, over the years you've grown to resemble this home, rather than it growing to resemble you.

THE TINNITUS RING OF THE PHONE DINGED NEAR MY EARDRUM, and I realized I'd been wearing headphones this whole time, but the music player wasn't on. Perhaps it was one of the typical disruptions of the feral parts of the park. There was no cell service in the realm of lichen and insects. I was closer to the bird grounds. By order of the head of the local council, open cages were hung from the branches of trees growing in this enclave. And though he'd been removed from office following the exposure of some corruption or sexual harassment, it's hard to follow, his wishes had been carried out. How mighty are mayors around these parts, their desires unhindered by the loss of their position. Rare birds came and perched in the houses of twig and gold installed for them. Half of them sang their heartbreak, the other half their passion for many offspring.

I recognized Tahel's swift inhale that preceded every piece of important news. I said, And hello to you too. She said, Ugh, don't be such a nag again, this is important. I said nothing. She said, Are you there? I said, Yes, yes, are you not mad at me anymore? She said, Never mind that right now. So what? I said. She said, The day before yesterday I got another text, just like the first, from a marketing text number, and we tried. In the middle of the night again? I asked. Yes, she said, it's kind of annoying to wake up from the beep. Why don't you silence it? I said. Silence it, she said, you mean turn off the sound? Yes, I said, it's the same thing. Not at all, she said. I said, Fine, why don't you put it on silent? She said, Because what if something important happens? What could be so important, I said, you're sleeping at home, your parents and Oshri are with you. She said, Dad isn't home, he got another project from

Yalon's father. He's sleeping the night up north. He's spending the night up north, I said. She said, Don't correct me. It isn't mutual, then, I said. She said, I correct you when it's important to, you correct me for no good reason. I laughed. One of the birds chirped its agony, a peacock swooping over its cage. What is that, asked Tahel, where are you? I said, In Yarkon Park. She said, But what's with the yelling, it sounds like someone's on fire there. I said, It's a refugee bird seeking shelter in Israel. What's hurting it? she asked. I said, Maybe it can't go back to its homeland, maybe hunters are after it, who knows? She said, Okay, you keep getting off topic. The hint of anger was already affixed in the depths of her enunciation, her words buzzing as they escaped the tiny earpieces. I said, Who's "we"? She said, What? I said, You said, we tried. Who tried, you and Oshri? No, she said, Oshri doesn't even want to get involved. Yalon—

I allowed the hesitation to ripen. The name died, leaving a pearly white space behind it. I said, Are you back in touch? I didn't know who else could help me with this, she said. With what? I said. She said, Figuring out who's been sending the texts. Yalon was kind of annoyed they didn't send it through a social network app. I said, That would require the senders to identify themselves, wouldn't it? Yes, she said, that's exactly what I told him. I said, So you just walked up to Yalon and talked to him? I told you, she said, that he's been clingy since the beginning of the school year, and Racheli and Elinoar keep encouraging him, coming up to me and saying, Your boyfriend's looking for you, those pieces of trash. Don't get carried away, I said. They're such trash girls, she said. Her tone was rehearsed. The bird song died out. Animated chirps and screeches invaded the haze of its melody. The peacock persisted in its exhibitionist aerial performance from one branch to the next, the beating of its wings dominating the patch of cages. A myna bird fixed its beady, perforated eye on me, the yellow of its beak clicking through the sloughed leaves.

Tahel said, So are you listening? I said, Listening to what? It was Oshri's idea, she said, asking Yalon for help. All right, I said. She said, So yesterday at recess, when he started hanging around me, I told him I needed help with something, but that he shouldn't think that helping me meant I'd forgive him. I said, Do you re-member the—

Yeah, she said, allies, I'm starting to get it. No, I said, you're far from getting it, I'm not talking about favors, manipulation, or taking advantage, but about people willing to fight for you simply because the fight is important to you. She kept silent for a long time. Tahel, I said, are you there? She said, Yes, stretching out the syllable. I could sense the temporary calm crossing the distance between us. But there was that brief sense of closeness that illus-trated the fierce presence of the distance. Tahel may have felt it too. She quickly said, So we're collaborating on an investigation again.

What investigation? I said. She said, Yalon is convinced the number the text was sent from belongs to the company, to Take Up and Read. He also wanted to switch providers when the com-mercials started airing, but his dad said no. Why? I asked. She said, Because he, and then her voice became muffled. She was whispering. What? I said. She said, Because if he was on Take Up and Read, he could have— Her voice lowered again, then lit up. Hang on, I'll let you talk to him. What, I said, he's been there this whole time?

Yes, said Yalon. His voice was cracked down the middle, off-key, as if he were talking through a shattered pipe. I said, Hello. He said, You see, if I used TUR I could have sent a request for a passcode reset, and then they always send text messages, those oldies, every text center has its own number sequence, see?

I asked, Why can't you just call their customer service? Yalon said, You try getting hold of a customer service for a virtual pro-vider, they only have websites or computers responding, not that we didn't already try that yesterday. We were on hold for an hour before we got cut off. His voice was muffled too, as if a handkerchief had been placed on Tahel's iPhone speaker. I could still decipher what he was saying. He said, You're right, it sounds a little unusual, like my parents do sometimes, when they're out of the country. I said, What's unusual?

Yalon said, My dad wouldn't let me switch. He says the company's going to go bankrupt in six months, he doesn't understand where they got all the money to begin with, who's investing in it. He says it's suspect that no one knows who the investors are. Hmm, I said. Yalon said, My dad says that when a company uses this kind of marketing strategy, usually the owner gives an interview, he's the face of the company, you see. Behind him, Tahel shouted, and her shout weaved into the flow of his speech: The owner's a woman, she's the face of the company. Yalon said, My dad says this whole TUR business is dubious.

Yes, I said, interesting point, but– He said, I'm giving you Tahel. Hang on, I said, is your father making assumptions or did he look into it, did he? Tahel said, I'd trust Yalon's dad. I said, What did you mean when you said "collaborating on an investigation"? She said, We can still verify that someone from the company is sending those texts. I said, And? She said, But the SIM card is under your name, so they might actually be sending them to you. Don't you want to know who's bothering you?

SOMEONE WAS TALKING ON THE PHONE AT THE TABLE ACROSS from mine as I waited for Manny. He called to say it had been too long since we'd last met and that he needed my advice. She was sipping white wine and unraveling her troubles. When she noticed me eavesdropping, her tone changed. Now she relayed her experience from her last Lufthansa flight to Frankfurt. As it turned out, she'd tasted all the fruit compotes served during the flight and rated them. She wondered in her counterpart's ears whether it was wise to make banana compote these days, seeing as how bananas were becoming extinct due to a pest. What, didn't her friend know that all the bananas in the world were a clone of one original banana, and that's why they were unable to mutate and adapt? I wanted to correct her. The potato also began life as an asexual root vegetable. The potato blight plague of the nineteenth century almost annihilated it. It led to the Irish Potato Famine, for instance, since in Ireland almost all potatoes were genetically identical. It also caused symbiosis to form between the potato, originating from the Andes, and a type of bacteria that split it into two reproductive sexes. Male and female: created the bacteria them. For had it not been for symbioses between unicellular organisms and bacteria in the ancient oceans, there would never have been a division into two biological sexes.

But where did that thought pop up from? My fingers grasped at the pillars of the tables. Lumps and fibers at the tips of my fingers, the model of a disappearing continent. From Turin I continued my trip to the Alps. I stopped for a rest at a picnic area near the village of Lillaz. The water of the river, the source of which I was headed toward, floated on its course, green, bluish, foaming. The smell of pines filled the air. An older family joined me at my table, made of naked logs. I considered switching tables and whether or not that would hurt their feelings. I hoped one of them would notice the empty table nearby. The father of the family, nearly blind, tapped the ground with his cane. They conversed with measured fervor. I pulled a book out of my bag and tried to read. All of a sudden, in a perfect American accent, the father said the words "double helix," tapping his cane for emphasis. I looked askance. Other English phrases shone from within the fog of his Italian, joining together to form a subconversation that I could listen in on: molecular biologies, physical models. I grew alert, my gaze no longer furtive, not because of the subject, but because I had the perverted pleasure of understanding. By the time they got up to leave I no longer wanted them to. The youngest son, whose hair was already turning gray, nodded at me before they moved on. I wondered why I'd never written a character whose world revolved around genetics. Maybe I did some research afterward, maybe that's where I gained this knowledge. I ought to consult my notepads. They multiplied and filled my drawers, sliding off my desk, filling the bookshelves, suffocating the space, soon I wouldn't be able to open my study door.

Yes, Yalon was right. I would have realized that myself had the subject been on my mind. But a second text message was not random, it was a pattern. I requested a passcode reset on the TUR website. The sender's number that appeared resembled the one that had sent the suspect text, the Israeli international code, preceded by the plus sign, followed by short, hyphenated sequences of the numbers zero and one. But how did that help any of us?

I told Tahel all this on the Skype call. She said she preferred the ruses I utilized, rubbing shoulders with danger, tricking others. I asked how she knew that. She said she kept careful watch over the methods I'd used in the Kalanit Shaubi and Heftzi Columbus investigations we'd run during the war. I said, That was then, and it was life and death. She said I ought to at least find out where the TUR offices were located and go over there. I said maybe we were overreacting. Maybe it was just a system bug. She said, What's wrong with you, Elish, why are you—but she didn't complete the sentence. She said, Come on, what do you care, do it for me. I said, Maybe. Her hint of anger ignited. She said, What kind of ally are you? She said I should at least find out who the investors were.

Manny still hadn't arrived. The woman kept chatting. A punch of rage ran through me, like an electric shock, which took the form of a single thought, How dare he keep me waiting, that son of a bitch. Then he appeared down the alley. He'd lost more weight, wrinkles plowing through a face unused to an absence of flesh. He was wearing a shirt printed with the characters of the Inhuman Royal Family. Black Bolt in the center with the restrained beam on his forehead. To his left was his wife, Medusa, with her mane of red hair, and her sister, Crystal, who ruled over the elements. To his right were Karnak and Gorgon. Which superpower did I favor, Karnak's power of conjecture, making him able to recognize and exploit the weak point in every structure or plan, or Black Bolt's power of destruction, which manipulated electron arrangements and originated in his voice, in his speech centers, which was why he had to focus most of his efforts on remaining silent?

Manny walked over to the woman, leaned in, and kissed her cheek. She hung up the phone. Then she looked at me directly, defiantly, her eyes full of a dark glow. I couldn't look away. She kissed Manny's other cheek, rubbing the back of his neck softly, whispering something in his ear. Manny stood back up and turned to face me. There was surprise in his expression, almost shock. He swallowed. I asked him if he'd forgotten we had plans to meet. He apologized, his tone official, stiff. He said the surprise really was inappropriate, he should be surprised to see *her*, and he pointed at the woman.

He said, Ohila Svevo, Elish Ben Zaken, Elish Ben Zaken, Ohila Svevo. What's Svevo, I asked, like Italo Svevo? But he'd made the name up. Yeah, she said, it's made-up, my husband doesn't like it either, I made him hyphenate it with his. What does the name Josiah Liege Svevo sound like to you? I said, Like *Lord of the Flies*. She laughed, That's what he said, his mother almost had a heart attack when he told her, amen, God willing, only bad omens for people who rise from the gutters and call themselves Liege, like a master. You can't get the shtetl stink off them even with an axe, the whole family has the same features, like a butt cheek pinched into eyes and a nose. I asked if the source of the name Svevo was like the source of Italo Svevo's name, Schmitz. She said, Almost, Schnitz. I said, Schnitz, what's Schnitz? She said, What, don't you know Leo and Nathan Schnitz, makers of bicycle bits? I said, BMX bikes? She said, Sort of, the imitation, CMX. I said I'd never heard of them. She said, No one has, not even back in the eighties, when they were a hit, that's why I live in the projects in Jaffa and not in a villa in the Afeka neighborhood. I said, You could have lived a life of luxury in Petah Tikva. She said, So you *have* heard of us. I said, I told you I haven't. She said, The company offices used to be in that godforsaken place, the Petah Tikva industrial zone. Manny said, But prices are rising in Jaffa now, not rising, skyrocketing. I said, How symbolic is it that the most godforsaken place in Israel is called Petah Tikva, "window to hope." She took another sip of her wine, got up suddenly, and placed her hand on Manny's shoulder. She said, Wow, Mannush, I've got to run, I'm meeting a friend, put the wine on your tab. He nodded.

She took a few steps forward and then came back. She said, Have you noticed that the names Ohila and Elish have the same number of letters? I said, High five. She laughed, a coughing laugh that neared hoarseness. When she disappeared at the end of the alley, Manny said, She almost never laughs around strangers. I said, She laughed for you, what's your connection to her? He waved the question away. I said, But that energy, that determination. A smile flashed across his lips and fell away.

I GLANCED UP DURING THE CONVERSATION. A MURKY PIECE OF moon, extricating from its early-month Rosh Hashanah shrouds, flourishing toward the tenth day, Yom Kippur, when it would become a yellow blaze in the still summery thin sheet. Manny had grown fond of the flea market area, he said, ever since we met there during the war. You could run into all sorts of interesting characters there. I asked him if the unusual characters at his job weren't enough. He said he'd spent too many years among conservatives, people holding on to norms. They'd forgotten that those norms were intended to save them, and that they weren't the world order, that there were other possibilities of existence. I thought, Who could have imagined that Manny would undergo such an extreme change at his age? He answered my thoughts. He said he thought getting to know me had changed him, that our relationship was the seed of change. Embarrassment descended, scrambling the sparks of fury that pricked me. I said he was getting carried away, that we each had our pace, our speed, and that the central role of norms was to force people to live at a speed that wasn't their natural speed, that sometimes all it took was a crack, a small injury, to become liberated from the bit and the bridle, to slow down or speed up to the accurate pace.

He said, Why don't you let me give you a compliment? Do you know how long I've been waiting to tell you the things that have been accumulating inside of me, and you're pushing me away. His tone was clouded, stifled. I didn't respond. The narrating voice in my head groaned, either in mockery of Manny's sorrow or in empathy for it. I didn't drink the night I experienced my futuristic delusion. I didn't take an anti-anxiety pill. The voice appeared at night, disturbing me. I wrote it off as one of those branchings sleep breaks us into, dividing us into several realms of self.

Forget it, I said. A server strutted over. I asked about the white wines. He said they had an Orvieto. I asked if it was dry or semi-dry. He said decisively that Orvieto was always dry—fruity, yes, but dry. I asked him to bring the bottle. Manny ordered his usual whiskey. Upon first sip he muttered, yes, when the speed is right, you can just tell. Like the speed of this Black Label, for example. I said, Now you're getting it.

He asked if I still remembered the Zevulun Desuete case. I said I did. I asked if the police were still working under the assumption that it was a serial killer. He said it wasn't unfounded, overall, someone named Desuete had been murdered in Ramat Gan, his head and hands severed, mutilated, and smeared with honey. If he remembered the lecture I gave years ago correctly, the first time we met, that's exactly what I was talking about. I said, About what, the ritualistic logic of serial murder and poetry? He asked if this wasn't a good example. I said, For a serial murder you need a series of dead bodies, a ritual can't be a one-time thing, the effort to re-create private meaning necessitates repeated attempts, an organization prevented by the chaos of existence, itself a battle over organization. The server came over, carrying the bottle. I examined the label. See, I said, semi-dry. He said, Maybe you'd still like to try it, it's very popular with our customers, it's our house wine. I asked him about reds. He said he'd check.

I told Manny, That assumption doesn't suit Manny of a few years ago. You would have dismissed it offhand. He said, What's your hypothesis, then? I said police officers today watched too much television. Manny said, So do murderers. Fine, I said, let's follow the logic of substandard literature. You've got a lunatic choosing victims with family names that, mispronounced, can be symbolic, and he stages the murders to recall stories from scripture, a kind of biblical crumb that lots of lunatics cling to for some reason. The server returned. They only had Cabernet. That's fine, I told him. Then, to Manny, I said, Chances are the killer is a woman, by the way, that's the plot twist. At some point in the penultimate episode, a young female officer fighting for her place in the investigation team, or who suffers from some generic syndrome, say, Asperger's or Tourette's, preventing her from fitting in, realizes there are no sexual characteristics involved in the murders.

The narrating voice in my head emitted his crushed leaves tune again, a possible brief, scorched laugh.

Manny said, All right, we're getting carried away. I asked what was special about the building in Kiryat Gat where the victim's head had been placed on the doorstep. He said that was unclear. They've questioned all the tenants and they had nothing to do with Zevulun Desuete. He asked how my research for the book about Heftzi Columbus was going. I tensed. I asked, What's the building address? He said, You should have made the connection earlier, you're off your game. I told him I hadn't been following the case, that I'd lost interest as soon as people started making conjectures about serial murder. Still, said Manny, you're less focused than usual. The voice in my head said, A lot less. I told him about the sleep deprivation, I told him about the construction noise. Manny asked if it wasn't anything deeper. I said, Like what? He said he'd learned from me that the first reason we grab on to typically covers up a more profound reason we're afraid to admit. The wine was too warm, tart with warmth. I said, You remind me of Ronnit. He said, What about her? I said, She would quote me back to me, but always against me, and I didn't like to play those games. He said, What's going on with her? I said, I have no idea, she's pregnant with her husband's baby. The bit of moon, diapered with an afterbirth of glow, stood paralyzed over low awnings and antennas, the filth of roof tiles and tar.

He said a friend of his was going to England with his wife for a month to spend some time with her son, who just had a new baby, and her daughter-in-law, who needed some help. Manny's friend was divorced, his children all married. He would be glad to lease out his place for a modest sum. I said, What's the address? He said it was a rooftop apartment on Tel Hai Street in Tel Aviv. I said, No, the address in Kiryat Gat. He said forensics had finally managed to re-create the victim's portrait using the severed head. He recognized him right away. He looked nothing like the images of Zevulun Desuete the police had been using to track him down. I said, Is it George Arguile, who killed Heftzi Columbus? Manny said, Yes, what do you say about that plot twist?

MANNY SEEMED TO HAVE TAKEN OFF IN THE MIDDLE OF THE conversation. When I tried to recap the main points the following day, the same image erupted. He asks the foppish server something. The server nods and points inside, into the dim space of the bar. Manny walks inside and doesn't return.

It's nonsense, of course. We said goodbye after he asked me to meet the head of the special investigations team. He's the nephew of the wife of his friend whose apartment he suggested I rent.

They met at a dinner the couple hosted. His friend was also a former police commissioner. They all kept in touch. The nephew sometimes called Manny to get his advice. He said Eldad, the head of the special investigations team working on the Zevulun Desuete case, could use any piece of information I could give them about the Heftzi Columbus case, on which I was the expert. He shook my hand. His handshake remained as robust as ever, but I could feel the bones, brittle beyond the partition of flesh.

Before the server showed up, the conversation veered off to where it usually did, to the distress of the place. I told him I didn't know why I wasn't leaving, relocating away from here. The country had been growing darker ever since the war. I said, When someone writes the history of the second Hasmonean kingdom, the Gaza War would be more significant than the Six-Day War. He said, You're exaggerating, you're giving in to despair. I said, I've grown used to seeing things from the perspective of ruin. The narrator's voice in my mind echoed, Ruin, ruin, ruin. What are you so surprised about, you sons of a thousand whores? This call that you reject during wakefulness whistles through your dreams. Ruin, ruin, ruin. The third repetition was swallowed and stifled. Manny said, Isn't that a shame.

I hesitated to ask him at what point our conversation actually cut off. He called two days later to tell me he'd passed on my agreement to the head of the special investigations team, and that Tuvya Hasson and his wife had left the country. The keys were with the neighbor. I didn't ask. The line was broken, his words rising among waves of white noise, a chirping lopped up the syllables. He said I'd enjoy the apartment, it was quiet, and waking up from a good sleep was like coming home again. When he hung up I wondered what waking up in the end-time could be comparable to.

I arrived around noon and struggled to find parking. The sun beat down on the metal of the car. I thought about those horses of fire my mother had seen in the trees, on the way to Sderot, about the Eye of Horus that served as the basis for the Take Up and Read logo. The neighbor gave me the keys. In spite of the late-morning hour, she was wearing a robe of shiny fabric, her face a brew of puzzlement and awkwardness. It was as if I were a friend separated from her by years of shame, now returning for a hesitant meeting. The furniture arrangement in the apartment was familiar to me. The blueprint had somehow been etched inside of me, I knew where to find every object, as soon as it came to my mind I knew where it would be. I was split into two, one of me moving confidently through this memory, the other feeling his way, astounded to discover his guesses hitting the mark every time. I didn't bring much with me. I came to rest for a week at most. I salvaged three investigation notepads from my old study, which had become the notepads' habitat, their lair. The door was almost blocked, and behind it I heard rustling and susurrations.

The investigation notepad on Heftzi Columbus's life, the investigation notepad on Kalanit Shaubi's disappearance. The third notepad that fell into my hand surprised me, the old one, the first one, containing the testimonies, findings, and fake entries from Dalia Shushan's death investigation. I opened it. The roots and tendrils of a vinegar plant emerged from the jumble of my heart, damming the coursing of blood. The name Rami Amzaleg was circled and a question mark was jotted beside it. The name Yehuda Menuhin was framed with open-ended lines, followed by an exclamation point.

But as early as the first hours there, I realized I'd want to stay in that apartment for as long as I could. The pleasure at the familiar erupting from the uncanny, making it homey, was equal in intensity only to the pleasure derived from the reverse action. Once, when Ronnit complained to me, I told her that to some people the world was a homeland, and to others it was a strange land. And I belonged to a third kind, those who could not tell the two apart. She made a face. I didn't tell her this was a line I came up with while listening to Dalia's songs years earlier, as a young man, and I'd been saving it for just the right opportunity.

Eldad Buganim called in the evening. I was sitting on the balcony. How natural it was to sit on the balcony. Pigeons cooed on the Persian lilacs. Some distance away, a raven crowed, cutting through the evening. I thought about the rare bird enclosure at Yarkon Park. Something almost revealed itself to me after the conversation with Tahel. Something, the shimmering of sunbeams through the leaves, the falling of light against gold cages and twigs, the singing of a vague bird. Something summoned a sunken memory, which rose to me. But I couldn't hold on to it. Even though the narrator's voice in my head said, Look carefully, care to look. The certainty of the street, the reality of the cool breeze sneaking in from the sea, wrapped with autumnal saltiness, swiftly patched over the unraveling.

Eldad Buganim's voice had an upward trajectory that he wished to restrain. Throughout the conversation, whenever he caught it nearing a whimper, he lowered it, forced it to rise from a deeper place inside his body. We made plans to meet the following day. He said, Bring every bit of information with you, you never know what might turn out to be significant. I said of course, but that he should take into account that most of my research revolved around Heftzi Columbus's past, her formative childhood years, and that I knew almost nothing about George Arguile. He said, Still, you were the one responsible for finding her body. I said, I gave all my notes to Manny at the time, and he passed them on. There should be a copy in the file. He said, Yes, I went over them. Sloppy work, but I didn't expect anything professional from a rusty private investigator such as yourself.

I ASSUMED ELDAD BUGANIM WOULD BE OF SHORT STATURE. PERhaps his struggle to control his voice gave me that impression. He was strong, almost brutish. He got up to greet me when I walked in. And I recognized him. He was that boy, my classmate whose name had evaded me, that same dull presence of memory at Ashkelon Junction. Most faces are arranged around the eyes. Their light radiates from them, as do their liveliness or stupidity. In his own face, the features schemed around the vulturine nose, the nostrils wide, Roman, not especially large, but central. The eyes were appendages to it. As if the expressions all stemmed from the tiny changes in the relations of the other features to that nose. He was a dark, gloomy guy, his face on the verge of constant dissatisfaction, but not threatening, smiling. The stretching of the lips, which in other faces was a sign of stinginess or restraint, was in him, due to the nose, a gesture of loosening, an invitation.

But Eldad Buganim wasn't his name, the sound was wrong, like a slap against a plaster wall. How often in life had I knocked on a plaster wall, listening to the hollow echo, as if searching for a hidden nook, a secret door. Now I seemed to be tapping ceaselessly. Even in his narrow office, certainly not the office of the head of a special investigations team or a senior detective, I felt the urge to slap the walls. The narrator's voice in my mind said, Tap and break in, break through. The space was too small, his own measurements took up most of it. I recoiled from the hand he offered me, suspecting I wouldn't find a proper hand, flesh and bones, but a smoky, slowly evaporating material. He took a step toward me. I gave in. But there was only a hand there, a firm shake. Surprised, he asked, Are you Elish?

I nodded. His nostrils trembled, but actually it was only his eyes narrowing to examine me. He said, No, that isn't your name.

I said, We went to high school together, right? He blurted out a syllable of agreement, yes. I couldn't hear it, but I learned it through his lip movements. We spoke to each other through water. His voice rose and broke through the viscous air, saying pointedly, but your name wasn't Elish then, you've changed it. I said I thought he'd changed *his* name, I didn't remember it being

Eldad Buganim. Maybe he was known by a nickname. What was his high school name, could he remind me? He said, I'm convinced that wasn't your name, Elish, your name started with a, oh, come on, it's on the tip of my tongue, you lived in the Antiquities neighborhood, didn't you? I said we did. The screen of water between us disappeared. We spoke the way people speak, if they do at all.

He said, You had two girlfriends in tenth grade. They sat in the back of the classroom and you'd pass them notes. You wrote them poems and they'd write you back.

I denied the allegations.

He said, Yes, yes, I remember being jealous that two girls were talking to you, you were a runt, just like now, pitiful, and the gym teacher always got on your case, lecturing you after every class, like what, like you were some great athlete, but something did come of you. I smiled dismissively. He said, I found one of your poems once, yes, yes, I'm remembering it now, it was on the floor and I picked it up, nothing but overblown words. Probably from all those books you used to read, you were always sitting on the side during recess, reading, and the girls would walk over, it was such a great act, if only I'd known that was the way to attra—

I said, But you used to read too, Tom Clancy. *Walla*, he said, good on you, coming up with that detail, yeah, he's the only one, a top-league writer. I said, A one-man league. His lips stretched. Then I realized he wasn't teasing me for no good reason, his intentions were aimed at something else, what was it, diverting me from finding out his original name. He said, But none of your books were any help in that trivia contest, my team won. I was super excited, they wrote about it in the *Southern Wind*, I still have the news clipping. My wife always teases me about—

He fell silent. He used to be a muscular, competitive boy. His muscles had since thickened, affording him with a greater presence, but the voice retained a childish, unruly persona. His voice was high, eunuch-like. A man with experience sunken into his face, the confidence gained by experience, if not peacefulness and serenity, and his voice was suddenly crystalline, rejecting time.

He ordered me to take the seat across from him. I mentioned my surprise at the size of the room, its humdrumness. He asked if I'd expected a palace. I said I hadn't, but I'd expected a spacious office with an enormous desk and LED screens constantly showing data and graphs. He said, You see, you still have that pomposity, that hasn't changed, at least. I suggested we allow the swell of nostalgia to subside. He cleared the papers covering his desk, fixed his eyes on his computer screen. Then he opened the Heftzi Columbus file. He asked me to tell him, in my own words, the story of the investigation I ran last summer in Sderot, how I came to discover the body, and when my suspicions arose. I told him it was a coincidence. I'd been investigating a different case, a young woman who'd disappeared for three days and her family hired me to find out where she'd been. The young woman had completely forgotten what had happened during the three days she'd been missing. Of course I didn't mention the previous, identical case, the disappearance of Dmitry Shtedler's niece. I told him that while I was conducting the investigation, all sorts of evidence and clues came up, pointing at improper conduct in city hall, and that piqued my curiosity.

He stopped me, saying, What do you mean, it piqued your curiosity, how were those connections even made? A detachment and hovering of limbs, a hint of bitterness on my tongue. I said that somehow, it happens sometimes, that I see patterns where others can't see them, innocent statements that, in the appropriate context, are revealed to be clues. He gave me a long look, inhalations and exhalations fluttering his nostrils, Louvers, I thought, louvers in the nasal passages. He said, What's so amusing? His voice whined. I said, Nothing. He growled to elasticize his throat and said, So I'd like you to take me through it, step by step, and see how those connections were made. He almost spat the word "connections." I said I thought the purpose of our meeting was to

❦

unravel Heftzi Columbus's biography. He said it would be more useful for him to know how I'd come to discover the body, perhaps there was something I'd missed, something I hadn't seen in the right light.

I LEFT MY MEETING WITH ELDAD BUGANIM EXHAUSTED. HE asked that I re-create the conversations in which Heftzi Columbus was mentioned or in which the affairs of city hall had come up. Police officers came and went during the careful questioning, asking his advice, placing documents in front of him. He excused himself for a few minutes, asked someone to make us coffee and tea, respectively, without asking which I preferred. Now and then he deviated off course to tell me about his military past, which I could have guessed at myself, combat service that had been more emotionally than physically demanding, and how he'd retired from service as a captain. But his mind wouldn't let go of the investigation for a moment. He always returned to where he'd last been before he got interrupted or distracted. The sequence never broke. Of course I left out Oshri and Tahel's involvement. Of course I didn't talk about the ghost in the thicket that Yaffa sensed trying to invade the house, the street, disrupting the peace of the new Lakeside neighborhood residents. Of course I didn't provide any information about Heftzi's lover, Elkoby from the engineering department. I weaved my own parallel story, in which the whimsicality of discoveries was greater, devoid of a steering hand. The story therefore demonstrated a better power of deduction than I actually possess, a sharper attention to detail. Eldad Buganim noticed this and remarked that he thought either my intuition was over-the-top or my suspiciousness was pathological, that some of my deductions were extreme, and that if I'd shone this brightly at the regional trivia contest, perhaps my team would have won.

I asked him if he was still in touch with his Romanian friend, his second-in-command on the team. He said, May his memory be a blessing. I asked if he was dead. He said he'd stayed back in Ashkelon, married with kids, as they say, and owned a sanitation company. I said, Some people never get themselves out of the trash. He said, You're a smart-ass, huh? I'd made that joke to him years ago.

I asked if he could help me with a question in return. I said it was something I could ask Manny Lahav, but I didn't want to bother him. He said, Really, that Manny Lahav, the whole earth is full of his glory. I said, What? He said, He's everywhere, you can't get away from him. I said, I thought you said something else. He said, You'd better get your ears checked. I nodded. He said, So what is it you wanted? I told him about the text message. He said, Who knows, maybe it's a clue. I said, Why a clue? He said, You're the one who sees every bit of nonsense as a clue. I said, Still. He said it would be a breach of supplier-client confidentiality. I said my understanding was that the new law allowed every senior official to request private information from communication providers without a court order. He said he'd run the check through their technological forensics science team. I asked where they were situated, because I found it hard to believe this building had a state-of-the-art lab or even a computer lab worthy of the name. I gestured at the appearance of the office, the stained carpeting, the felt partitions between the desks, the antiquated equipment. He said, You'd be surprised, our cyber unit is one of the most advanced in the world.

The needles of jealousy pricked through me back in Tuvya Hasson's apartment. I felt sharpened wooden skewers poking into the invisible organs that were my kidneys or my guts. Who was stupid enough to believe these organs truly existed and weren't some anatomical hoax, a physicians' scheme to persuade us that our insides weren't as unknowable as our outsides? This could have easily been my apartment, I thought. I wouldn't have changed a thing, it would have suited me just as it was, already designed to my taste. I went out on the balcony. I paced up and down it. Persian lilac branches invaded it from the east, thickened, covered with unseasonal blossoms. In spite of the heat of the afternoon as it advanced toward Yom Kippur, we were headed toward autumn. But the floral lace was so delicate, the starry purple with the dark core, drawn forward, and the yellowish crown around the stamens. I leaned toward them, drunk from the poison that welled up through the trunk and its future fruit. I shifted the leaves for a better look, and beyond them I spotted a small gate. It was installed into the hedge that flanked the building's yard.

I went downstairs to check, but paused on the landing of the floor beneath mine. I sensed in its full intensity the presence of the neighbor, spying through the peephole, an inquisitive, restless probe. I stood there a few seconds, as if debating which way to turn, feigning helplessness. The presence was infected by my hesitation. Part of it wished to lean out and open the door, the other part to lean back, into the apartment, the safe zone of rugs and chandeliers. I left her to it and continued downstairs.

The small gate was frozen to the touch, icy, and locked. I felt around the key ring that was given to me. It contained a double German key, the purpose of which I recognized. An intelligently engineered key, which slipped through the keyhole to one side after the gate was unlocked on the other and could only be pulled out with a locking motion. A double-edged key. I walked through the gate. Expansive lawns sprawled from it to an orderly garden, hedges mowed to twist this way and that, small fountains, where water jets bounced around, spraying out of the genitals of stone monsters. Collapsing towers, of which only staircases remained, rose toward moldy brick patches, descending to the grass. All this abundance was cleverly concealed behind a wall of ferns, which appeared slim at first look. I thought about Edgar Allan Poe, and about the common mistake when reading "The Purloined Letter." The letter didn't escape the eyes of police officers because it was in plain sight, but because its appearance attested that it hid nothing, its ploy only to be, not to be something it wasn't. I thought that in this garden I could sit and read without interruption. Read, and read, and read.

Back in Hasson's apartment, I looked over the bookcase, which stretched over an entire wall. An Israeli police commissioner who was also well-read. The wonders never ceased. The letters of the titles, which were identical to the ones I kept in my apartment in Ramat Gan, flickered, refusing to be deciphered. With a flash of emotion, I recognized my five Benny Zehaviv books on one of the shelves. The excitement was replaced by bitterness. The books were new, the covers shiny, the spines intact. They'd remained closed. Perhaps that was for the best. Before I left the police station that morning, Eldad Buganim told me he'd heard I wrote detective novels. I said I'd abandoned them. He said had he known it was me, his old classmate, he would have read one of them, but now that he'd questioned me, it was obvious he would find nothing new in them. I've had enough of you, he said. Standing before the bookcase, I thought that he, with all his Tom Clancy, was right. I thought about how I'd always known literature was not a report on experience, but rather a tracking of the ways experience was contemplated, formulated, constituting a foundation for further observation. In this sense, it was an infinite task. Meaning, it was finite, since humanity's days were numbered in cosmic terms. Religious ones too.

ELDAD BUGANIM CALLED ME TWO DAYS LATER. I LOOKED HIM UP online. He was real, at least as far as the internet's church of archives was concerned. The images that appeared alongside his name removed any lingering doubt. And yet that nagging nagged me, that pestering pestered me, that falsehood may have falsified me. A more fanciful destruction seemed imminent. I was sitting in the hidden area beyond the gate, reading. He said my hypothesis

had been correct, that the text had indeed been sent from the
company offices, and that they had no physical address, but that
the owner's name was Therese Kavillio, she was the main share-
holder. I told him I thought it was strange that a company embark-
ing on such an extensive advertising campaign wasn't publicly
traded. He said he had a similar thought, but that he wasn't in
charge of competition law, he had a murder case to crack. I asked
how that was going. He said, With George Arguile, not great. Arguile had returned from Germany a week after Heftzi Columbus's
murder, assuming the name Zevulun Desuete. It turned out he'd
created the Zevulun Desuete identity years earlier, maybe when
he'd realized that the scope of his fraud was putting him at risk
and that he had to arrange an escape route. I said I assumed that
meant the circle of suspects was widening. He said he had a feeling this murder was directly connected to the Lakeside affair and
to Heftzi Columbus, and that he needed me to come in for a second round of questioning. He'd looked at my testimony again and
there were holes and gaps in it. I asked, A questioning or a testimony. He said, Questioning, testimony. I said I had a busy week
ahead and perhaps we could meet after Yom Kippur. He said,
Maybe something will come up when you do your soul-searching.
His voice was high enough to pierce. The narrator's voice in my
head answered him, saying, Soul-searching, stat. I told him he
was jumping to conclusions. The fact that Zevulun Desuete was
an alias for George Arguile didn't cancel out his previous conjecture. Which was what? he asked. I said, That this is a serial killer
who picks his victims according to the biblical references his
twisted mind conjures up. He said, Listen to yourself. His attempt
at a chuckle did not go well. I was pleased by the sound of the
stifled cough that hoarsened his words of parting.

I dialed Manny's number, breathless. His phone was turned
off. My call was sent to voicemail. When I clicked on the social
chat application to send him a message, I found one from Tahel
from the previous day waiting for me. What's up with you, Elish?

I got another text, you promised you'd check. I texted back, The messages are coming from the company offices, under investigation. I turned off my phone. I went back to reading. Another Agnon book. I was thinking about how I only grasped what true horniness was when I read him. An erotic fishing net spread over life in his works, but the Eros was split, dissected, a sensual Eros and another intellectual Eros constantly fought for precedence, when one weakened the other grew stronger, one dwindling and the other rushing to inherit it. Column A wished to awaken, and column B ignited to hush it down. The excessive actions of matchmaking and romancing, their disruption and correction in future generations, could only be overcome by pure knowledge, awakening cunning machinations.

I thought, I'd done well to retire from the battle of placing one sentence after another, from the crumbling that intensified with every period I typed, with every space I spaced before the next sentence, the lingering in the written word's desire to break into its discrete particles, into that dust from which all actions were constructed. I thought, In every act of writing, a question arises: Why this story, these moments, these words?

And as if in response, a fuse caught fire within me, and a rage exploded, a wordless rage, every tendon charged with the urge to punch something, break something, I tossed the book onto the grass, the cover spreading, a stained, black creature, and the pale paunch of the pages split. I ran toward one of the shorn hedgerows and kicked it. My foot got caught in the tangle, the bare skin of my ankle was scratched. No blood appeared, only the reddish smears of irritated skin. The shattering within me did not abate, I yelled with that evil power, over and over. The hidden area was empty. The yell was swallowed. I yelled again, meaningless syllables, a sobsnort. I left my book in its perch and ran to the gate. The double-edged key slipped between my fingers. I leaned down to pick it up and banged my skull against the bars of the gate, the echoing in the inner space ignited further. I barely managed to pull out the key. My palms were shaking. I rushed down the side path to the building. I walked inside. The stairwell was deserted. I climbed up a few steps and slipped, their touch was greasy against my calf muscles. My feet sank into the pliable matter from which they'd been formed. But me, give up, God forbid, I grabbed hold of the railing and pulled myself, fighting to pull up my body, which was being sucked back down. Only the fire inside motivated me. I reached the door to my apartment. When it opened, I was washed over with blindness, a brightness that had never assaulted me before, stronger than flesh, more paralyzing than music, more fervent than disease. When my eyesight returned, I was standing in the kitchen, leaning over the sink, knife in hand. My palm gripped the handle and the blade was aimed toward my neck. The stainless steel sink gleamed at me with its thousand cuts. I dropped the knife. I heard a voice from within the silence. The voice, meek, was calling my name, I think. A voice lit up like a flower, a weak flame of sound.

THE NEXT DAY, I LOOKED FOR MANNY AGAIN. THERE WAS A malfunction in the cellular network he subscribed to. Hundreds of thousands of users remained without any means of communication, thus announced a fly that buzzed through my computer screen, a brief news flash shot from the corner of the screen and rushing away. Sons of bitches, sons of whores, assholes, I'm telling you, the machine has got to malfunction. The machine has malfunctioned and we are destined to live among cracked bolts and burnt motherboards. I couldn't find any information about Therese Kavillio. Yalon's father's suspicions were founded, then. If she was the owner, why was her identity kept so concealed? I went to the company's website, kera.com, what an odd name, but my attention focused on the logo inspired by the darkened, lacking Eye of Horus. On the edges of flickering ads, showing stars and starlets with words printed on their foreheads, I found the

name of the advertising firm responsible for this glorious campaign. Kurkevados PR. They were located in one of the Ramat
Gan towers. I couldn't find my car where I'd parked it. First the
wild whirlwind of panic, it might have been stolen, then the chill-
ing breeze of thought, it might have been towed. Or perhaps I'd
misremembered my parking space. I wandered Tel Hai Street and
the nearby Bar Giyora Street. Nothing. Troubled, I turned onto
Israelis Street, and exhaled. The car was at the end of the street, I
saw its rear shining at me in the light of day that was sloughing
off the dark tails of night. No, because there were leftovers, the
lighting was darker than usual, but without any apparent cloudiness. The contours of tree shadows were too blurry, blending into
the sunny sheets of asphalt. The top part of my right ankle
smarted. I rolled down my sock for a look. Yesterday's scratches
had deepened, the redness turning crimson and swollen. It wasn't
about money, the car was insured, and towing only involved a
fine, but the effort of dealing with the authorities. The wounds
itched. I scratched them gently. The sickening pleasure of picking at the flesh.

I got on the bus. These diesel monsters could barely move.
Their inner breathing rotted too. The fuel burning was fully devoted to emitting noise and pollution. I thought, This will only take
a minute. I thought, This'll take hours. Either way, the atmosphere
gets scarred. Those are the kinds of thoughts I had sometimes. The
Kurkevados PR offices were located on the sixth floor. The elevator wasn't working. The stairwells were neglected, gray concrete
cast by an inexperienced hand. And the damp space eradicated
breath. At the end of the climb, I was spat into a wide lobby, into
the thin coolness of central air. Golden threads were intertwined
in the thickness of the front door's glass. The front desk was un-
manned. Beyond it, a large room sprawled. Its door was open. Beyond it I saw a young woman with curly hair, sitting on a desk,
her legs loosely crossed. Her feet were in stockings, the high-
heeled shoes dropped on the carpeting that covered every inch of

floor. Her head was lowered. Her hair covered her profile. She was immersed in watching something. The entire scene seemed staged, paused in wait for the action to begin, a spark of life to turn on the machine. I pressed the buzzer. The glass partition blocked the chirping or the chorus of bells that played on the other side. Her head shot up and turned to face me. Something was pressed between her lips, a pencil or a pen. She lingered for a few moments, her shoeless feet hovering above the floor, swaying. Perhaps she was examining me from a distance as I'd done to her just a moment before. She leaned toward the side of the table, a low buzz sounded, and the door opened.

She stayed seated, and I walked over. From closer up I saw she wasn't as young as I'd guessed. Her face, in spite of its narrowness, was plump, every feature like a fine swelling that disclosed no part of the supporting bones. If her bones were supportive at all and the entire skull wasn't made out of cartilage. The same went for her silhouette, which could have been bony or muscular in its chiseling, but the padding of her limbs made her soft to the eye. There was a pencil between her lips. She pulled it out quickly, gathered her hair up with a swift motion, and jammed the pencil into the bun. Her eyes filled her face, not because of their size but because of the intensity of their gaze. Even the cloudedness of surprise, of awakening from a strained sleep, did not conceal their glimmer. They were honey-hued, like her hair. The longer I stood there, watching her, the more she resembled a flare growing brighter until it reached the apex of its burning by force of watching it.

Yes, she said, how can I help you? I said, Have I come at a bad time? She said, Too early, most of the employees show up at eleven. My watch said it was 10:45. She asked, Why do you wear a watch? I asked if the employees just materialized out of thin air when the hands pointed to eleven. She said, Yes, the bell at the top of the tower rings, and they appear, like an act of magic.

I said, I wasn't trying to criticize. My name is Elish Ben Zaken, nice to meet you. She said, Nice to meet you. Do you have an appointment? I said I didn't, that I'd come on instinct. At first, I'd thought of coming up with some sophisticated excuse, to assume an identity, to say I was seeking PR consultation for a company I was starting, but ultimately I decided to tell the truth. I was a private investigator looking for contacts at TUR. Somehow, all the information about the company was confidential and no one was picking up the phone at customer service.

She nodded slowly. The cloudiness in her eyes didn't fully clear up, but I couldn't miss the hint of light added to them. She asked, Do you think that ruse would have worked? I said I thought so, I was pretty good at it. She said, So what would you have tried to sell me?

I told her about my experience with Betty Stein. I said I wanted to start a digital publisher that would focus on a series of short novels, written in TV episode format, and that the editors would be screenplay editors. That way, as soon as a certain series gained success, we could transition to television production, meaning that the company would be a joint venture of book publication and a broadcasting conglomerate that would be part of the development department. She said nothing. I said, It's like this, producing books is very cheap, so rather than investing a fortune in shooting pilots and taking risks, we can test the draw of a certain piece of work on a large, unbiased audience.

She said, That's a pretty good idea, though the presentation is kind of patchy. We definitely would have agreed to meet you, but I would have figured out you were lying right away. How? I asked. She said, I've got instincts. I said, So do I. She said, Fine, what's next? What would you have said at the meeting? I said, That we want to target a young audience, create an air of high quality for the books, but also insinuate that they wouldn't require a large effort, that they're fun. She said, No easy feat. I said, But isn't that exactly the aura of TV shows these days, that they replace the great novels of the nineteenth century, which are mostly expertly made telenovelas? Supposedly profound arcs, supposedly complex characters, supposedly meaningful dialogue, but in fact packets of cheap thrills, masks, fast food served at a gourmet restaurant, stimulation for a generation that has identification mechanisms but no identity.

You're exaggerating, she said, I'm part of that generation too. I said, But between you and me, we're in the PR business, we're cynical. She said, All right, let's say that. I said, Then why should I hire you, if my enterprise has great potential, what have you got to offer me? She said, That's certainly interesting. I would have of course asked why you came to meet us. I said, I would have told you it was because of the fine work you did with Take Up and Read. She said, I would have agreed, of course. I said, It's eleven now, where are the other employees? She said, Not to worry, they'll be here. I said, Maybe you aren't such a serious firm after all. She said, We've got a large roster of satisfied customers. I said, I'm surprised that TUR, which, to judge by their advertising campaign, has a fortune to spend, even agreed to work with a firm like this, where the employees don't even bother to show up. I don't think I can afford to take this gamble. She said, I promise you that everyone at TUR is very pleased. I said, I'd rather hear that firsthand. Who can I talk to?

SHE LAUGHED, THE KURKEVADOS EMPLOYEE. I TOLD HER MAYBE she wasn't authorized to refer me. She said she was, that this meeting had gone as it should have. I said, Who says I would have met with you? She said, This is my office, I'm the head public relations agent. I said, Are you Kurkevados? She said, For this project's purposes. I said, What about other purposes? She said, When we get to know each other better. What do you want to know about Take Up and Read?

She instructed me to sit across from her. She smoothed her tailored, hip-tight skirt as she stood up, asking if she could get me coffee or tea. I told her I was truly worried about the other employees not showing up. She told me to relax. I asked for water. I was plagued with intense thirst. My throat and the top of my mouth had gone completely dry. She pulled the pencil out of her hair and waved it at me. The graphite was sharpened enough to pierce. The curls fell, and she looked youthful again. She went into a recitation, the typical summary of TUR's virtues, the services it offered, the personal account management system on the company website, a close tracking of all package uses, and the possibility of switching to a new package without waiting on hold for hours. Immediate virtual tech support, any hour of the day or night. I said, But what about human response? She said they had a Facebook page too, where questions could be posted. I said, The answers there are also mechanized, robotic.

She placed her pencil on the desk. She asked for my phone number so she could send me Therese Kavillio's contact information. I asked if I could have a glass of water now. She said, But there's a water cooler with cups at the entrance, you were parched this entire time when you could have gotten up to get some.

The communications provider Manny subscribed to had returned to normal operation, the news flashfly on my screen informed me. Out of simple curiosity, I sought out the source of the malfunction. The first search result led to a piece written in Witternet, demonstrating the sheer mightiness of its author's pen. Those whores no longer hide the fact that all they want is to speak about how marvelous they are. The pretense of dialogue had been killed with the blows of an axe. Who needs indirect methods of communication anymore, pretending like one has the urge to say something, to listen, to change others' minds? Are you reading this, you *ibnei kalb*? I thought, Maybe these malfunctions are revenge. Manny's number was disconnected. A metallic wrinkling posing as a human voice croaked, The number you have dialed is not in service.

I crossed the gate into the secret area. The night had chewed into the Agnon book I'd abandoned in haste, perforating and wiping out the words. I opened it to a random page. Bits of words joined into sentences against their will. One absence is a lamentation ahead of its time, gone are all the beautiful girls, a lover of home has a mountain in his soul.

Therese Kavillio's contact information consisted of only an email address. I sat down on one of the shattered stone monuments planted into the grass. The irritation in my ankle exacerbated, and I bent down to check. There were signs of infection, enclaves of pus, bubbles of white cells. I needed to sanitize it. I wrote to Therese Kavillio that I was a concerned customer, that I'd had to procure her email address from— I paused, what was that young woman's name, did she even introduce herself? I wrote, From the young public relations agent at Kurkevados PR, and that I was sorry to be writing to her directly, but I wanted her to pass this email on to her technical support, because for several days now I'd been receiving disturbing texts sent from the company's computerized system.

As I was writing, my phone beeped. An incoming message in the social chat app. Tahel. I opened it. All the message said was my name. The letters were pixelated, their screen resolution diminished, dying. I fought to focus my eyes on them. Beneath them, the letters of a different name strove to show themselves. I thought to myself, You too, Tahel, I didn't expect this from you.

That evening, I sat in the study and went over my notes from the Heftzi Columbus summer investigation again. A pleasant, uncharacteristic chill invaded through the windows. I looked outside, the passing moon was still fighting to shed its afterbirth. I thought, Pathetic heavenly body, it spends the majority of its life insisting on shining through afterbirth or cerecloth. I couldn't bear the silence the thought cast upon the room. Tel Aviv was emptied of sounds. What happened to it? I recalled the times I'd lain down, listening to the urban happenings moving toward the sea and back, footfalls, whispers, the shouting of foolish boys, intoxicated before their time, the bellowing of buses, the sputtering of engines, faulty alarms, liquids spraying somewhere. But when had I ever lived in Tel Aviv before? In my Ramat Gan neighborhood, save for the angered, terrified barking of dogs left to their own devices, the night was spacious, spacey. Tuvya Hasson's music collection contained a Sufjan Stevens album I'd never heard, *All Delighted People*. I slipped it into the player. Funny, needing this material infrastructure to listen to music.

I could sketch out the singer during the first listen. A contemporary young man closed off in a 1930s-style Paris loft. A sheet of paper is spread before him on a wobbling desk and he dips a feather in ink. As he writes, he lets out a long, broken sigh, and the tear streaming from his eye stains the words. His heartache was rending. I forgave him for his wimpish, dolled-up singing. The power of truth lay in only being visible behind its costumes, I thought. I was relieved within the shelter of words that erected itself around me. I played the first song again. It had two versions, the first and last track of the album. The singing was relentless, the voice of a chorus boy struggling with a gospel, but his voice was fragile, lacking the confidence, the pathos, to which the orchestration was surrendering. The determination and the failure enchanted me. No doubt about it, there was something repulsive about the hollow, deceptive consolation at the foundation of Christian gospel. Perhaps its desperate emphasis through the song was the secret of its success. There was something repulsive about every masterful stroke.

I read my notepad, note by note, recounting my conversation with Eldad Buganim as I went along, what I'd told him, where holes had opened in the story I'd woven from partial information. I sketched a map of discoveries and clues I'd left out, observing the story they created. There was a pattern to them, but I could not yet see it whole.

✻ ✻ ✻

WHEN MORNING CAME, THE NARRATOR'S VOICE IN MY MIND said, Ticktock, Yom Kippur is just around the corner, soulsearching, soulsearching, searchsouling, sing arch-louse. What, weren't the Egyptians punished with lice? Aaron made sure to torture them, along with their children and cattle. Why is tonight different from all other nights? The innocent are crushed in the name of justice and redemption. And of course the lice would be singing their deeds. Have you ever heard a louse sing, motherfuckers? As soon as it gets hooked on those hymnals of revenge, it can't shut its damn mouth. To hell with lice. Their sinfulness blinds the world. I lay in bed in this twilight in which the words were the only reality. The iPhone beside my bed alerted me of an incoming message. What did that sound say, a crispy cracker, yes, an email had arrived. The email contained a generous response from Therese Kavillio. She'd read one of my books on her most recent flight and had been so captivated that she couldn't even listen to any of the flute music played on Lufthansa flights. Her eyes remained glued to the pages even during the cab ride from Frankfurt to Heidelberg.

Therese wrote that she would of course ask that the problem be looked into, and since the connection had been made, she would love to meet for a brief conversation. She asked if I could meet for ice cream and soda at Café Moda. I thought, Yom Kippur is the day after tomorrow. I glanced at the date on the screen. I was wrong. Just like when I checked two days ago, Yom Kippur was four days away. I thought, They've extended the ten days of repentance again, those assholes, to what end, probably considerations having to do with the end of daylight saving time. Outside was nearly bleak, a souring of skies in a false fall. I thought, it never rained during the ten days of repentance, but if it did this time, maybe the people in charge of clocks and calendars would earn some wisdom. I wrote Therese Kavillio that I'd be glad to meet her.

I wrote Tahel a brief update, saying I'd have an answer for her soon. She didn't answer, which was unlike her. The flashfly announced across my computer screen that communication malfunctions had been reported all over Israel. Sun storms, magnetic disturbances, some believed an unseen comet had generated chaos in the movement of celestial bodies.

I emailed Manny, What's up, I can't reach you lately, I need your advice, your protégé Eldad Buganim is out of control, sincerely, Elish Ben Zaken, Private Investigator. I reconsidered, deleted my signature, and instead just wrote, Elish. I regretted it after I sent it. The intimacy seemed inappropriate, as if I were forcing a friendship on him, asking him to act in its name. But friendship between detectives was inconceivable. The line between conversation and investigation must always be protected, every side standing guard to extract the information it deemed necessary. I wrote him, Manny, fuck you, disappearing just when I finally need your help. I breathed a sigh of relief.

Breathless, I walked into Café Moda by the train station. Halfway there, a thunderstorm had erupted. I'd rushed over. The screeching of the trains braking on the tracks sliced through the air, those immense Faraday cages, those steel traps. I looked over the interior space. There were no empty tables. Customers sitting in the yard were driven inside by the horror of thunder. And the wallpaper grew uglier with the human density, abstract creamy decorations on a green backdrop. I glanced at my watch. I was a few minutes early. I asked a passing server if a table was going to open up soon. She said that table twenty had just asked for the check. I was filled with immense gratitude, a beaming swell that was about to overflow. Affectionately, I said, This weather's not easy, huh? She dismissed me with a half smile. I could see her scapula through her black T-shirt.

But the couple at table twenty was in no rush to leave. The man stretched his legs ahead, the woman rummaged through her bag at length. I went to the bathroom. By the time I got back, someone else was at the table. Same position again, leaning against the chair, her profile aimed at me, her curly hair covering her face, waiting for stage directions. I walked over and said, Ms. Kurkevados, you stole my table. She looked up from colorful prints that were spread on the table in front of her. Perhaps she'd been immersed in them. She said, This is my regular table. What are you doing here, Elish Ben Zaken? She pronounced my name with a measure of ridicule. I said, None of your business. The aloof server placed a glass of rosé in front of her, the temperature of the liquid sealing the glass with an icy film. I told the server, Didn't you say table twenty was about to free up? She said, It did, we don't reserve tables.

The PR agent said, You're welcome to sit down. I'm meeting someone, but until they get here, it's a shame for you to have to stand. I said, I'm meeting someone too. She shrugged. I ordered a glass of wine as well, in spite of the late-afternoon hour. They had a Petite Sirah. She said, There's nothing like bad weather to get you to break habits. I said, You don't normally drink rosé? She said, I don't drink wine at all, I've got to keep a clear mind for my meeting. I glanced at the printout she was inspecting. It looked like a poster for a new campaign. The image showed two children with fair hair and blue eyes, as children in Israeli advertisements often have, standing close together in a small wooden house, pointing toward an enormous tub of yogurt. Hairy legs stretched from the bottom of the yogurt container, and its circumference was painted with a crude, mustachioed face, eyes narrowed with anger. He was holding a knife in his hand. In bouncy, colorful font, the top of the poster announced, "Yo, gurt out of here."

I asked how exactly that poster was meant to convince anyone to eat more yogurt. She said, It's meant to get them to *stop* buying yogurt. Do you have any idea how harmful yogurt is, especially for kids ages six to ten? I said, No. She said, So you'd best read up and learn about it. It's full of bacteria. The yogurt consumption in this country is out of control. Every grocery store you walk into, you see more and more kinds and combinations.

What do you think about Yo? I said, Who? She said, The character, Yo. I said, He looks kind of like a Palestinian, doesn't he? She said, Yogurt has no nationality. Still, I said, you know, umm, he's dark, he's angry, he's holding a knife. I think you're scratching the edges of the stereotype. She pulled the picture away from her, then brought it closer again. No, she determined, I don't see it.

I said, Who hired you to do this? She said, A concerned foundation called It Is No Fairy Tale. Don't you mean, It Is A Fiery Tale? She said, Good one. I said research showed that yogurt protected dental integrity. She said, First, that study was conducted in Iran, and we know how trustworthy they are. And second, you're encouraging people to take care of their teeth, and in return they bite you. I said, This is the only democracy in the food chain. She said, Exactly, a democracy, and the majority decided that the people must entrust their dental health to state establishments. I said, What are your friends going to do once yogurts are removed from grocery stores? She said, I'm just guessing here, but I think their next target is pudding. Why pudding, I said, what's the danger there? She said, It's too much like yogurt. No matter how it tries to squeeze in next to the *leben*, it can't really change its nature. I said, But *leben* is produced by bacteria too. Yes, she said, but that's *our* bacteria, genetic testing has shown that there's no connection between the DNA of both types of bacteria. I said, Your conceptual confusion is simply embarrassing. *Leben* was invented in Arab countries. She said, What are you talking about, *leben* is purely a Polish invention.

SHE IGNORED ME AFTER THAT, PORING OVER HER PRINTOUTS. The next poster contained an image of a soldier standing at a hitchhiking stop, his hand hovering over the trigger of his rifle, the barrel pointing down. Yo was sneaking up on him from behind with his drawn knife. She pulled the green pencil from her bag. In the lights that had been turned on to drive away the outside dark,

I saw gentle bite marks all along it. She marked a few Xs, jotted some notes I couldn't read. I wondered if graphite even adhered to this shiny printing paper.

Twenty minutes went by, to take the watch's word for it, and there was still no sign of Therese Kavillio. I checked my email app, but no messages had been received. I asked the PR agent if she happened to have Therese's cell phone number. She pulled up her hair and jammed the pencil through it. Disgusting, I thought, she put that thing in her mouth later. She said, You're wrong, my hair, with all the shampoo and product, is much cleaner than my mouth, with all the grossness that goes through it. When was the last time your hair smelled bad? I said, I didn't say anything. She said, It's easy to guess where your thoughts are headed. Oh, yeah, I said, where, then? She rubbed her neck. It was long, almost dainty, but the cartilagesque nature of her body burst through, spoiling the effect. She said, I don't have Therese's direct number, I scheduled all our meetings through her personal assistant. I asked if she could give me his number. She said there was no point, the network TUR leased airtime from had crashed an hour earlier. I said nothing. I couldn't leave, the clouds were paunchy and low, lightning shifting urgently behind them, boulder avalanches of groans. I couldn't get up either. The human density inside Café Moda had intensified, crowded, sweaty bodies, predatory eyes roaming, ready to pounce at any free seat. I saw customers holding on to the edges of their tables or leaning over them, marking their territories. I thought, Any second now, this place is going to be a bloodbath. I said, The TUR logo, who's responsible for that? She said she was. I said, I thought you were in advertising. She said she'd contacted a few different designers for proposals according to an instruction sheet she'd prepared with the desired impression, which platforms to use, etc. All the mockups she received were corny, almost literal, either focusing on the literal meaning of Take Up and Read or focusing on cell service. One day, as she was looking over posters, she began sketching distractedly on a piece of paper. She pulled the pencil out, letting her hair fall coppery around her plump face, her eyes losing their flame. She waved it. With this pencil, can you believe it, with this pencil. The next day, when she looked at the shape her pencil had produced, she realized it was the basis for what she'd been looking for. She sharpened the outlines, got rid of the messy sketching style, stabilized it to form flowing lines. I said, Wasn't this Therese Kavillio's choice to make? She said, We were in complete agreement about this. She turned over one of the posters and jotted down the logo quickly, easily, filling it in. You see? she said.

The shelter seekers crowded us from all directions. One of them shoved his elbow into my shoulder. Enough, I said. She said, Go, I'll pay. I said, And what about you, who have you been waiting for this whole time? She said, My meeting was canceled because of this weather. I got the message five minutes after I got here. Then why'd you stay? I asked. She said, No reason, I just had an inkling we were going to have a useful conversation. I said, But it was prosaic. She whispered, You're the detective here, Elish Ben Zaken. She giggled.

I got up from my seat. The irritation on my ankle was worsening, my nerve endings burning even though I'd cleaned and bandaged the wound. I knew if I bent down to check the injured area I wouldn't be able to stand back up. Luckily, I barely had to move my feet in order to leave. The accumulation of bodies worked as a single being, the chest and diaphragm muscles pressing down on the stomach. I was shot out of the café, reeling. Through the windows of my temporary apartment, I watched the clouds breaking up, clearing up, transforming into rote evening duskiness. I wrote to Therese Kavillio that I was sorry she'd missed our meeting and asked if her system managers had located the reason the disturbing texts were sent.

I received no response that day or the next. The High Holy Days' heat had returned. The calendar continued to show Yom Kippur as being four days away. I picked up a book and walked out into the secret area. The spying presence of the neighbor marked itself, fully solid, behind the door. The lead sheets of which the door had been forged separated before my eyes, and I saw her standing there, watching breathlessly, like an animal. As I approached the gate, someone called my name. It wasn't the wounding call inside my mind, but an actual voice. I turned to look. The PR agent's head appeared on top of the hedge, as if it were speared on top of it, but her eyes were bursting with energy. She said, Careful, you almost walked into the fence. I said, What are you doing here? She said, I live nearby, I didn't realize you were my neighbor. I said, Where? Where what? she said. I said, Where nearby? She said, Over here, at 17 Israëls Street. I said, Someone I knew used to live there. She said, Who? I said, Never mind. She said, Dalia Shushan. I asked how she knew. She said she'd looked me up online, and that the results showed that those who searched for my name had also searched for Dalia Shushan. I asked, Is she the reason you rented that apartment? She said, The apartment belongs to my family, Dalia rented it from us. I said, I assumed she'd owned the apartment. She said, You think some sad Moroccan from the periphery can afford an apartment in Tel Aviv? Why do you think we work so hard to preserve the high real estate prices in this city? Certainly not to have peripherals coming in by droves. She looked me over. Then she said, Relax, it's just a joke, what's with you, you're cold like El Pescado. And she laughed.

SHE GASPED AS WE WALKED THROUGH THE GATE. SHE HADN'T even noticed it. I told her to try looking from the corner of her eye, that was how it first revealed itself to me. She said she noticed a flicker, shimmering spots that emerged, but she couldn't say for certain it wasn't just an optical illusion born of effort.

As usual, the gate blended into the air right after I pulled the double-edged key out of the keyhole. I walked down the path that bisected the lawn. She stood behind me, petrified. Listen to that, she whispered, but it wasn't her scathing, toxic whisper. It was awe-filled. I said, To what. She said, The endless rustling of existence. Yes, the grass was filled with insects, a chirping and buzzing, the beating of tiny wings, legs rubbing against a hairy abdomen, miniscule orchestras that gathered to form a serene hum of life. And the light broke against the small shells, returned, refracted into shine and glare, sparkle and dazzle.

We wandered among the trees, which were overflowing with the activity of arthropods and arachnids, among the shorn hedges. In a dreamy tone that matched her lowered voice but stood in direct contrast to her character, she said, I've heard about this place, there's a passage here to the metaphor fair. The metaphor fair? I asked. She said, Come on, you know, everybody in Tel Aviv wants to visit it sometime, there are six hidden passages in the city, don't you remember? Just like in that song we used to sing as kids. She started to sing in a squeaky voice, One is a partridge, the second a willow, the third is a stone bridge, the fourth is a widow, the fifth is a stream, the sixth is unseemed. I said, I don't know it. She said, Where'd you grow up? I said, In Ashkelon. She said, The periphs. I said, Yeah, I rose from the outskirts. She said, Anyway, I think one of the passages is here. I said, What does "unseemed" mean? She said, I don't know, but those are the lyrics. I said, Maybe it's "unseen." She said, No, she was sure of the pronunciation, it was "unseemed." I said, Maybe "uncleaned." She said, Cleaned of what? I said, I have no idea. She said, Let's look for it. She was invigorated, breaking into a run. She hurried along the mowed hedges, reached a dead end, and turned on her heel. They spread in all directions, twisting and turning. I called after her to wait for me, I had trouble running with my ankle injury. She came back, pencil in hand, her hair down, its ends clinging to the corners of her mouth as she pushed them away. Her eyes were covered with the glassy veil of a fervent glow. They were dark, pupils gaping. She said, I noticed you were limping a little. I didn't respond. I sat down on a heap of stones scarred by tiny, red ants. I removed my shoe, my sock, the bandages, which had grown dark with disinfectant. She said, Good idea, and kicked off her flats. I thought, Why wasn't she wearing her heels? She came prepared. She ducked down beside me and helped me remove the bandage. Maggots were moving inside the wounded flesh. You're decaying, she said. I said, It's what the disinfectant does, the maggots eat the dead tissues. She said, They're peeling you. I said, In a manner of speaking. She said, Charming, charming, let's keep going, then.

It was easy to spot the bridge from where I was sitting. A stone arch rising somewhere to our right. I pointed. She looked. She said, How far do you think it is? I said, Very far. She said, Come on then, it won't get any closer on its own.

The mowed hedgerows opened up for us. We walked confidently and they flanked the path for us, lest we deviate. I told her, I don't actually know anything about you. She said, What's there to know? I said, You tell me. What? she asked. I shrugged. She said nothing for a while, matching her pace to my faltering. I said, Why an advertiser? She said, A PR agent. I said, Same thing. She said, It started as a hobby, and it turned out I was good at it. I was helping out a friend, and I suggested something at one of the meetings, and she liked it, and I got excited all of a sudden, realizing I knew how to manipulate and shape people's reality, that I'd been doing it ever since I was a little girl, and now it could be my profession. I said, You talk about your talent as if it's a superpower. It kind of is, she said, don't you think? I said, There's a difference between getting people to buy a product and shaping their perception of reality. She said, What's the difference? I said, The difference between illusion and actuality. She said, It's that simple to you? I said, Yes, it's that simple when it comes to the foundations of our actions. I can't stand people who deal with shit and are so unhappy about it that they try to convince everybody around them that the world is made of shit, and that even gold and beauty are shit deep down, and that they are the only ones not kidding themselves. You're weak, Elish, weak, she said, Goddamn you. She said this softly, affectionately.

WE GOT TO THE BRIDGE. THE SECRET AREA CHIRPED AND hummed, and for an instant, a hand reached out and rummaged somewhere inside of me. I was filled with the force of walking, the muscle expanses in working order, the blood flowing. I told myself, I'm happy. The bridge stretched over a crack that ran down the grass, black, jagged, bottomless. We paused in the middle of the bridge and looked down into the abyss in silence. My iPhone ringtoned, the pealing of bells. I pulled it out of my pocket. A text marketing number appeared on the screen, similar to the one from which the messages were sent to Tahel's iPhone. I thought, Therese Kavillio. The PR agent walked on. Yes, I said into the phone. The high voice confused me at first. It said, Elish? Yes, I said. He said, Service is still bad, I can barely hear you. I said, Who's this? He said, Inspector Buganim. I said, Oh. I said, Yes. He said, So when are you coming in for further interrogation? I said, We talked about questioning, a testimony. He said, Yes, yes, questioning, testimony. I said, We said I'd come after Yom Kippur. He said, What, what, I lost you. I spaced my words. I said, After. I said, Yom. I said, Kippur. He said, You're poor? I said, Judgment day. He said, I dig you, man. He purred, or perhaps it was the smashing of the bad reception, his voice lowered. He said, I'd like you to come tomorrow or the day after, Yom Kippur is running late this year. I said, It truly is, but I'm busy until Yom Kippur. He said, Don't sta— I said, Fine, any progress in the Arguile case, did any of the information I gave you help? He said, I can't share any information, I can only tell you that we're about to hit a breakthrough. I said, I can come the day after— And the noise died. A message appeared on my screen, call failed.

The PR agent was waiting at the end of the bridge. It was swallowed into a covered passage, also arched, made of the same mildewed, clumsy stone as the heaps in the secret area. The agent gathered her hair and let it down alternately. She said, You should change your ringtone. I said the bells were good enough for me. She said her husband used to be obsessive about his ringtones. Eventually, he settled on a rooster's crow. Who else would ever pick that ringtone? I said, So you're married. She said, Widowed. My late husband. I said, I'm sorry to hear that. She said, What do you have to be sorry about, it happened years ago. I asked how he'd passed away. She said, "Pass away," what's with that term, I hate that phony term, "passed away," he was killed in the war. I said nothing. She said, Operation Cast Lead, what good did it do?

I said, I thought only young soldiers died in that operation. She said, Is thirty-seven not young? I asked, Do you have any kids? She shook her head. There were other questions on the tip of my tongue, but the passage opened onto an enormous, paved quad, flanked on both sides by a covered passage, and on the far end by a tall, white building with a multitude of turrets and cornices. And a rabble, a crowd of people filling the passages. Colorful birds, the likes of which I'd only seen in the cage enclave in Yarkon Park, flying down to eat from the hands of children. *Gallabiyahs*, suits, dresses, kilts, swimsuits, robes. The climate in the quad stretched itself to contain them all. A small snowstorm raged around a man cloaked with furs. We were surrounded by the burning sunny aura of the High Holy Days. The PR agent sang in her squeaky voice the rest of the childish, zigzagging tune, Twice for free, you bleed on three. I said, What does that mean? She said she thought it meant we could try twice without a fee. And the fee is blood, I asked. She said, Probably. I said, Maybe it means money, such as in biblical or legal terms. She said, It's the metaphor fair, you think they want you to pay with some dignified cultural alternatives? I said, Metaphair. Metaphair, she sneered, you're weak, Elish, so weak, this isn't a city hall enterprise or an art college final project, this is the real thing. She sang the closing lines again. She said, The girls in class used to sing this when we jumped rope.

We walked into the covered passages. Small shops, some resembling sewing shops, others were food stalls, some were electronics and cell phone stores, a few thrift shops alongside designer boutiques, optometrists, and sunglass kiosks. I said, Where's the fair? She said, This is my first time here, same as you. I suggested we go to the spired castle. A young woman wearing a burka walked out of a store that, according to the sign out front, offered discounted flight tickets and resort packages. Only her eyes were visible, and they were amazed, washed with elation. We started to look over the faces of the people walking out of there. All of their faces were engraved with intensified expressions, distilled emotions that could not be mistaken, wonder, sorrow, pain, dissatisfaction, indifference, alienation, excitement, stupidity, thoughtfulness, embarrassment.

Inside the edifice, in the space that expanded into arches and adornments, a dark, basalt boulder had been set. A Black boy whose torso was bare stood on top of it. His ankles were bound with iron chains that were anchored onto the boulder. His hands were tied around his back, his ribs protruded, his skin was bruised, scratched bloody, gashed. Behind him was a tall, muscular, nearly Nordic man with eyes of a pale blue that bordered on the color of frost, a pink, chiseled face, a blond mane of hair that also aspired to the hue of ice. A golden crown embedded with a sapphire adorned his head. He held a whip. The boy cried from deep in his throat, but what do we ask of literature, to tell us what we already know from experience or phrase for us those parts of reality of which we're ignorant? The man whipped the boy. They were both silent for a few seconds. Then again. The boy roared his roar and his torturer whipped him.

✻ ✻ ✻

I STOOD BEFORE THEM, BEWITCHED. THE PR AGENT PULLED ME by the elbow, and I followed her unwillingly, my head turned toward the exit to continue watching. Idiot, she said, I think we just wasted one image, why'd you drag me in there? I smiled at her. She said, You've got such a disgusting expression right now, you're crazy happy. I said, And you look terrible, terrible. She said, Maybe you ought to shut up, *ya mitnayek*, huh, Moroccan with a knife, *yinal din babur il dizhabkum*. With immense affection, I said, You rotten Ashke-Nazi. Not so smug all of a sudden. I almost said that. Instead of "smug," I said "slug." I said, Not so slug all of a sudden. And indeed, the horrific expression on her face thinned out her features, emphasizing her cheekbones, her eye sockets, her plumpness banished for a moment.

We sat down to gather our strength on squared pedestals at the entrance. The metaphor fair was a mélange of smells and colors, a wonderful sediment. I was filled with power, charged to my last cell, buzzing. Everything was true, everything I'd believed about writing, I was right, I had to write, write, not that detective novel nonsense, but life, its veins and arteries, not mine, but others', the unheeded submission to moments when writing becomes itself, no longer requiring me to guide it, just the mind laboring over weaving the details, the language flowing all by itself. The knowledge clarified that in every bit of life, when examined with sufficient care, one could track down the principles of human experience, its limitations and whims, which, while we could not look at our own lives from the outside, there was no reason why we shouldn't be able to do so with other people's lives, all of it was possible, attainable, always had been, all I had to do was bend my neck a little and look at the world from a different angle.

But her crying pecked through my elation. Shards of voice, growls that caught in her lungs and then spewed out, dwindling into low sobs and growing into groans. I wrapped my arm around her shoulders, she rested her head on my chest, and I rubbed her hair. I told her, Everything is wonderful, reality is wonderful, there's nothing to lament. She said, I can feel that Palestinian sniper's bullet shattering Dedi's skull, he was afraid, he hadn't been scared in twenty years, had made a pact with fear, to love danger, and in return danger would stimulate him. But with a single bullet the entire charade fell away. All that happiness he persuaded himself to feel, that masculine camaraderie, the bread of adversity and water of affliction of the fighting hills, weeks out in a combat zone, inside tents, all that pleasurable sloppiness. The lead razed all that. You know how long the shock of the blow lasts, how long is that, twenty hours? Twenty hours in a fraction of a fearful second, of paralysis, of the realization that you're scared, that had you not been scared you could have continued to live, that you're giving up the will to live, giving up what you loved, giving up on me, because you're scared. I thought, That's an excellent foundation for writing, I should remember that. The fear of Dedi, her husband, probably, the giving in to one's own death. As I thought this, my confidence in being right evaporated. So did her crying. She pushed me away, recoiling, searching her bag and coming up with a pack of tissues and her cell phone. She turned on the camera application and looked at her reflection, wiping off the tracks of tears. She looked at me. She said, My eyes are a little puffy. Three young women walked by. They entered the building. She said, Let's keep going. Wait, I said, I want to see what they'll look like when they come out. She said, That's private. I said, The tallest of the three looks like a poet, she has a sensitive face. She said, That's a private matter, come on, come on.

We looked at the stores in the covered passage again. I said it was a shame there were no explanations. She said, Go with your intuition. We paused by two stores. One had many types of magnifying glasses, different-sized spectacles, pens, clocks, and boxes full of tracking and recording devices in the window. The other store's window was covered with black velvet pinned with

barrettes whose crystal heads were ignited with some form of inner light, but they wouldn't stand still, these barrettes. The more
I watched the crystal heads, the more they shifted and turned,
constellations, floral cascades, chattering teeth, sparkles on the
surface of a lake. The PR agent pushed me toward the first shop.
I tripped down the small step in the doorway and fell inside, onto
the floor tiles. Behind a polished glass window stood a chubby
woman, padded with flesh, apple-ish, and a skinny, slightly droop-
ing man. He said, Darling, what has fate wrought? She said, You
knew the decision well, my darling, we cannot choose our agents
this time. He said, But darling, he does not seem qualified for
the task. She said, Our most talented agents have failed, darling.
It is time to try a different type of agent. She stepped out from
behind the counter. I was still crouching on the floor. She said,
Massage or El Pescado? I said, Not a massage. The man pulled me
up. He was hunched over, wearing a felt suit, his fingers long and
limp like the rest of his body. He told me to take a seat. The woman
walked in. In her gloved hands she carried a glass tank containing a liquid that was occasionally disturbed by a black, violent
motion. I couldn't spot the source of this disruption. She shoved
her hand in and pulled out a water creature, a multi-armed black
spot, like one of Lovecraft's horrific creatures in pet version. I
asked, Is that El Pescado? She said, Yes. It lives in frozen ponds
and has fifty tentacles, that's where it gets its name. I said, The
fish with L tentacles, fifty tentacles. She nodded. She said, You're
going to feel a cold burn. I did.

AFTER THAT, I COULDN'T FIND THE PR AGENT. I WAITED OUTSIDE
the store, plagued with that old excitement, tickling the pit of my
stomach. I was tensed up, truly angry, yes, for having led myself
astray by forces beyond my control. I was impatient. I walked into
the store with the crystallized window. A woman stood there before an outdated backdrop of desert landscape. Fabric sand and

plants of painted fiberglass. She was wearing fine clothing, a turban decorated with chains and a white silk robe with gold hems. Her fair eyes were framed with *kajal* that elongated their corners, just like the paintings on the façades of Pharaonic sarcophagi. I asked if the previous customer had left. Her tone was arid when she asked if I was prepared to pay the price of blood. I left. I walked through the passages, passing by women who resembled the agent but were not her. I hurried toward the covered passageway, but she wasn't there either. The aura of summer around me grew dusky, a murky, granular light of Tishrei sunset. I pulled out my cell phone. There was no service. I decided I'd meet her back in Tel Aviv. I had to hurry. The knowledge burned inside of me.

El Pescado's suction cups were placed against my skin, small shatterings of freezing cold, hard tentacles piercing the skin and invading the veins, and I was drowned by a wave of horror, standing on a wavering raft upon an ocean of filth, formless, frenzied, unrecognizable shapes bubbling and sinking all around, jaws and maws peeked and melted as they descended back into the liquid mire, frozen screams of horror, shattered into thousands of whispers and pleas and tears, the terror trickled into every last cell, and with it the certainty that this was existence, this was its first and final form, why resist, the end was nigh. I felt deeper inside. An ancient force, not as ancient as the primordial reality all around me, but more ancient than I was, a faint ray before light had even been fathomed by thought, urged me to poke further until I fished out some used self that had been lying within me, collecting dust. I found him inside some age, within an unceasing reading of Edgar Allan Poe, an enormous reason that banished the noise into an inconceivable abyss, soldering meaning onto what was deemed to be a sound.

With it, El Pescado's tentacles detached from me, the slippery arms reaching inside of me to remove all restraints. I floated in a pure, interior, incandescent space. Before my eyes hovered all the facts I hadn't reported to Eldad Buganim. The pattern was clear.

Within them, the name Nahum Farkash stood out. He hadn't even come to mind when I spoke to Eldad Buganim. Back then, in Sderot, during the war, Nahum too had mentioned the corruption in city hall. Furthermore, he talked about Heidelberg, where George Arguile had last been seen before his body popped up in an apartment owned by one Zevulun Desuete in Ramat Gan. Therese Kavillio, the shadow investor, had also just returned from Heidelberg. A conspiracy involving those two elements presented itself clearly. A pale echo of that old excitement tickled the pit of my stomach, intensifying to form a choir. An urgency plagued me. I had two days left to beat Eldad Buganim in the race to solve the mystery and dissolve his ridiculous suspicions.

The double-edged key was the only place where El Pescado's cold burning remained. The closer I got to the gate, the more my body warmed up from the walk. I stepped out into the boiling twilight of the days of repentance. The sky was painted with red strips, the remnants of clouds, the tracks of the dying of the sun. I thought, The clues are strewn all over. My phone reception was back. I called Nahum Farkash's number, which I'd jotted down in my notepad back in the day. In the chill of the air-conditioning, I waited for him to answer. An annoying tune faded out and started up again. I was sent to voicemail. I wrote him a text in the social chat app. I texted Tahel. I called Manny. His number was still out of service. I told myself I'd go see him at work tomorrow.

I opened the texting app and clicked on the number from which the PR agent had sent me Therese Kavillio's email. A menu opened, containing the option "Create New Contact." I clicked on it. A new contact card opened, and the keyboard popped up at the bottom of the screen. My finger hesitated over the virtual keys. I didn't know her name. Suddenly, I realized in a jolt of insight that I still didn't know her name, that I'd failed to ask her again. I clicked on the number. My phone dialed it. She picked up, a wheeze in her voice that was interrupted by a sucking sound. Yes, she said. I said, It's Elish. She said, Yes, I know. I said, Where are you? She said, In my apartment. I asked if I could stop by. She said she was tired, that this had been an exhausting day. I asked, The store you walked into, it sold expressionistic images, didn't it? The clerk looked like Else Lasker-Schüler. She said something vague and noncommittal. I said, I don't know your name. She said, It isn't that complicated. Then she hung up.

The voice came and called my name. Like a flesh wound, a hook that caught me and pulled me in. Elish, Elish. I left the apartment. The evening boiled. We're neighbors, I thought. There was a cheerfulness to the thought. I arrived at 17 Israëls Street. I looked at the mailbox for the apartment where death had come for Dalia Shushan. There was no name on the mailbox. I examined the buzzer for that apartment. Nothing but a blank piece of paper. A woman walked out of the building, dragging a shopping cart. I said, Excuse me, who lives in apartment one? She said that for as long as she'd lived in that building, that apartment had stood empty.

HESITATION MOVED THROUGH ME LIKE A SILVER SWORD. PER-haps I'd ask Tahel to visit the public library, sending her and Yalon to serve as my agents and glean information from Nahum Farkash. Yes, yes, my little agents would be like sly bees, sucking nectar and flying off. I made do with texting Tahel that all tracks kept leading to Sderot. I added an astonished emoji. I dialed Nahum's number religiously, every hour on the hour. I called his office, no answer. I spied on him online. His Facebook page announced that he was in Heidelberg. I recalled that being in Heidelberg meant he was disconnecting and lying low.

Late in the day, an idea came to me. I could find him on the public library network. It was a known fact that all public libraries were interwoven underground, like trees in the forest. Scientists who fed one tree minerals with color-coded molecules later found the same molecules in forty other trees in the area, or in trees that were forty meters away. Fungus mediated communication between the roots, monitoring their metabolism. And what is true for trees must be true for books and libraries, because not only did paper come from trees, but information appearing in a book in one library was instantly divided and reproduced into books in other libraries.

I couldn't sleep. I'd dropped the speed of sleep anyway, or I'd dropped out of it, I couldn't catch up. Throughout recent nights, waves of sickening wakefulness. I sped up to it effortlessly. I had the power to do that. I once told Yaffa that, like all corporeal habits, we never spared a second thought when the ability to slow down to the speed of sleep was working, but when we lost it, we couldn't comprehend how we'd ever been up to the task. *The Work of Sleep*, I'll write that book someday, I still contained some of that blazing faith in the act of writing, I could feel the pulsation, writing when for its own sake. When all of this is over, when I shake off these suspicions, when I finally bring the George Arguile murder mystery to a close. I thought, My sister, we must repair years of aimless talk, years of language patterns intended for nothing more than the transfer of information. Longing hit me hardest in the throat, of all places. I may have cried for a spell.

The Sha'ar Zion Library was walking distance from my borrowed apartment. I arrived when it opened. The entire building was covered with ferns and creepers, bindweeds or ipomoea or ivy or parthenocissus or purple rubber vine, leaves and tendrils, a spring greenness amid autumnal orange, and purple, blue, and yellow petals. They covered every nook in the wall, tangling over the windows, blocking the doors. I was alone out in the plaza. The museum was surrounded by its typical glorious, cumbersome silence, the works of art slowly rotting in their gilded tombs. Whatever, fuck their mothers' asses. I moved the creepers away with my hands, stung, scratched, injured. The blood in my palms grew hotter. I shoved them, tore them even, and finally made it to the entrance. A few loyal readers were already in their seats, those same city hall hired extras that appeared on the outskirts of every concert or special event thrown by the department of culture. Two librarians sat behind the circulation desk, pretending to be lost in their books. I wasn't sure if they were actors or actual librarians. I didn't want to be found out, forced to reveal my plans, and have them gape at me. So I walked to the computer expressionlessly, clicked on the intra-library borrowing software, and typed in the name Nahum Farkash. The screen returned with the message, *o results*. He evaded me here too.

I walked into the reference room. A heavy librarian leaned back in her padded seat, watching visitors like a hawk. A few fast students sat in front of their laptops, a pile of books in front of them as they clicked away knowingly. I leaned in and spoke to the librarian. Good morning, I need to contact the Sderot public library, is there anyone who can help me here? She nodded. She typed something on her keyboard. She picked up a pen, jotted something down on a thick piece of paper, and handed it to me. She said, This is the library's phone number. I said, No one's picking up there. She said, They're working a half day today, from what I can tell. I asked if there was no other way and gestured with my chin toward the top floors. She said, Oh, that way, you need a special permit. I asked, How do I get that? She searched through her drawer and pulled out a few forms. She said, Fill these out. Processing takes several days, probably longer right now because of all the strikes at local authorities. I said I hadn't heard of any strikes. She said, The trains aren't working either, I assumed that's why you came here instead of going there directly. You know, the train to Sderot is top-notch. You've got Ethiopians and Palestinians serving you Moroccan cookies and pouring you tea out of a samovar the whole way. I attended a conference in Sderot a few—

She raised her voice and I had to signal for her to keep it down. It wasn't just me, shushing sounds came from all directions. With all due respect to the barefoot children of cobblers, being a librarian comes with some strings attached. She nodded, shamed. I said, I've got family in Sderot, could you maybe help me out, make an exception? She said, How urgent is it? I said, It's an emergency, life and death. She said, The manager came in today just for a few hours, if you want to wait for her to leave, I could let you take a look at the real network. I smiled as best I could. She said, You're Elish Ben Zaken, I know, I liked your first book, you should have written others like that one. I said, That's an insight I've been forming these past few days. Her lips sliced her face in two. The narrator's voice in my head sighed and asked if all librarians ultimately develop a skull smile.

THE LIBRARIAN SUGGESTED I WAIT IN THE JOURNALISM ARCHIVE, on the floor above. Luckily, I'd brought my notepads with me. I went over the notes again, the life and murder of Heftzi Columbus, now with the addition of notes on the murder of Zevulun Desuete. What was the connection between Nahum Farkash and George Arguile, besides Heidelberg? So many details were missing. How would the story be told from Nahum Farkash's point of view? He must have known Columbus, they both worked for the Sderot municipality at the same time, he as a library manager and she as the mayor's secretary, or office manager. I closed my eyes. There was lead in my lids, a chance that they might remain shuttered. Nevertheless. I forced my wandering brain to focus, to follow a thought through to the end. I had that ability to think a thick tractate of thoughts, laden with connections and cross-references, I had it, I was sure of it. No, what was it, the conversation with him, just a few months ago, what had he tried to say? He started the conversation with my writing about Dalia Shushan. I opened my eyes. My eyesight was slightly blurry. Three adults and a young girl were sitting at the tables, perusing today's or the past's newspapers. Their images had foggy contours, their smoky portraits unraveling and wavering around the edges.

I returned to my notepads, opening the one for the investigation of Dalia Shushan's death. Yehuda Menuhin, Yossef and Esther Shushan, Lior Levitan, Levana Hacham, Debbie Malkieli, Nicole, Rami Amzaleg. They passed me by, names, dates, tidbits of information, nothing more. Where was the life that had been lived, the being that had formulated its literature? Nahum Farkash must have known Dalia Shushan, so why was he absent from these notes, how could I have conducted a full investigation without him, what would have come of the case had I extended the list of suspects, testimonies, had another solution appeared? Whose existence would have transformed as a result?

I opened the notepad for the Kalanit Shaubi disappearance. The shadow man, who was he? Kalanit was injured by a missile next to the public library. If I mixed the clues and testimonies from the three notepads, shuffled them, and reweaved them, a single common denominator would emerge. Nahum Farkash. There was no way around it. I wrote, Turn Eldad Buganim's attention to Nahum Farkash. My pen trembled as I wrote the name Eldad Buganim. Even in its written form, within a simple sentence, the name was devoid of actuality. The fake sound echoed through the letters, as if they'd been written with invisible ink, lemon juice, or blood.

I brought up the journalism archive search engine on the computer. I ran a search for Eldad Buganim. Yes, that piece he was so proud of, about his team winning the regional trivia contest, had appeared in the local southern paper. There was another hit, from another local paper. A copy of the first was on microfilm. A hunched, bespectacled man helped me with the machine. The filmic nature of the scene did not escape me. Newspaper pages in scratched sepia moved through the screen. There was the piece, a small square of text and an image. You couldn't mistake that nose, taking over the face, its vulturine shapeliness, the grumbling expression, on the verge of sweating, were all apparent in the boy he used to be. I could pull his current-day portrait from my mind's eye, place it alongside his past image, and feel the slice of time fluttering between those two sections, fighting to set itself free and return to the indifferent, endless flow.

The article listed the names of his teammates by their order of appearance in the picture, from right to left. I counted. His name matched the face in the picture, no doubt about that. The second hit referred me to a printed source. I tracked down the tome in which that copy of the local paper was contained. The January 9, 2009, issue, 13 of Tevet, the Jewish year 5768. The city of Ashkelon mourned the falling of Major Eldad Buganim during Operation Cast Lead. Major Eldad (Dedi) Buganim led a team of fighters into a building that intelligence sources had reported contained a missile launch group, as well as a fair amount of ammunition. A Palestinian sniper killed him and injured two of his subordinates before being killed by our forces. Major Eldad Buganim is survived by his wife, Therese Buganim née Kavillio, as well as his heartbroken family. His father, Shlomo Buganim, referred to Eldad in his eulogy as an Israeli hero. His soldiers, Mr. Buganim said, were more precious to him than his own life. He died defending his childhood home and the residents of Ashkelon. May he rest in peace. A picture of the late Eldad Buganim in uniform, young and determined, granted immortality by the blurry image and the cheap paper, appeared alongside the piece. I expected to sense the roughness of existence on my fingertips as I touched the eternally lost features, offered endless testimony by black and gray spots. I expected a big bang. I looked for a quote from his mother's eulogy, though that might have been simply a torn soul forcing itself to speak through moans and cries that could not be put into words. That's what they should have printed, instead of the father's restrained eulogy, the mother's broken syllables, the wailing, the howl. The State of Israel has no other music.

I left the volume open, gathered my notepads, and turned to leave. The calculation wasn't complicated. Eldad Buganim was killed on the Tenth of Tevet. I was tired of symbolism. I was fatigued of the dense significance of the random. The flammable noontime light withdrew the ferns and creepers, flower petals diminishing into buttons. The way was open. I thought of my mother, her deteriorating hearing, the cyst in her nose, the symptoms bonding onto a blind urge hatched at birth. I wanted to hear her voice, wanted to hear the promise contained within it before the great disruption, the warmth, the comfort, being able to submit, to let go of the quiet war for deliverance. I must flee this town, I must see her face one last time. I don't want to be distant anymore, you hear me, assholes, I no longer have the time I have. The lump in my throat grew with every repetition of the thought. I need, I have to, I don't have the time I have. The landscape rushed toward me through the veil of longing. The narrator's voice in my head whispered my name, Elish, Elish, Elish, like a hole in the flesh, wounding, escaping, and the flesh healed at once, in fast-forward, the redness around the sepsis, the exposed capillaries, the inflammation, the pussing of the infected area, the bursting of the pus, the scab rising, peeling, the fresh tissue tautening anew.

MY CAR WASN'T IN ITS PARKING SPOT ON ISRAËLS STREET. ALL the other cars that parked there, widely spaced, were padded with dust. The regular jokey comment, *Clean me*, was jotted by a fingertip onto their rear windshields. Their front shields all had stickers from city hall, informing the owners that the cars had been parked for too long, and that they would be towed and taken apart by a certain date unless their owners moved them. Cats wandered among them, some of them sitting on the shaded metal hoods, others rubbing against the sunken tires. I walked the nearby streets and saw the same scene repeating itself.

I returned to my apartment. The dreariness startled me. The objects, the furniture, something of their vitality had been taken from them, the vibration, the humming of their being, so detached from their sources, the wood having lost the memory of the tree planted in the soil, the pleasure of the suckling of roots, the bubbling of light converted into energy, the metal had forgotten the limberness of quarries, the supernovas in which atoms heavier than iron fused, all elements were devoid of the memory of the birthed suns inside of which their particles melted and were propelled in here.

I went down to the yard. I thought about the PR agent's confession, Dedi, the bullet of a Palestinian sniper. My name, she said, isn't that complicated. How slow I was, Therese Buganim née Kavillio. I entered the secret area. The activity of insects was deafening. I thought about my mother's damaged ears again. Here the trees bloomed in the pleasant air, and the mowed hedges stretched to the horizon, but in every direction, fractured rays of light bit into insect shells, their colors excessively glaring. I left. I dropped the double-edged key near the locked gate, and the grass in my building's yard jumped up to close over it, pulling it into the ground.

I wandered around, searching for my car again, reaching areas of Tel Aviv I didn't expect to. The stifling afternoon hours had arrived, the light stood between day and night, a sun shining through a curtain of soot. In one neighborhood I spotted my car from afar, among other abandoned vehicles, and hurried over. It was another car, bent up from some accident. Its insides were eaten up, the faux-leather covers on the steering wheel and handbrake were chewed up. The hood was popped. I lifted it up. The engine was rusted, swept by the tide of time.

The vision of the car flashed before me again in the next neighborhood. I walked over more carefully this time, flanking it. It was crushed beneath another car, which had its heavy bumper pressed against my car's roof, windows shattered. I waited for the owner to show up. A stocky guy with a round face and stubble over his childish cheeks and chin showed up. I assumed he was growing his facial hair due to the High Holy Days. He was carrying a bag. I asked him why he had to park this way, when there was no shortage of parking spaces in this neighborhood. He said, Watch it, I'm a right-winger, and pulled a baseball bat from his bag. He slammed it against the car as I stood there, petrified. Then he got in his car and reversed, swallowed into a nearby building. I walked over for a better look. There was an enormous shaft gaping from the floor of the lobby. I couldn't see his car's headlights down there. By the time I returned to the street, my car was gone.

The afternoon light held strong. I dragged my feet through Tel Aviv. The maggots were good for my scratches. They'd scabbed over, but would leave a scar. Denizens of the city passed me by, walking swiftly, averting their eyes. I wondered what would happen if I approached one of them. But I didn't get the chance. I covered kilometers by foot and arrived at one of those vague neighborhoods, the existence of which nobody believed besides their residents. Benny Zehaviv lived in this kind of neighborhood, building blocks arranged in circles, bushes growing wild in yards, pomegranate trees blossoming, in season. A car equipped with a PA system drove by. In a scratchy voice, the driver called out, Rejoice, Jews, Yom Kippur will take place in two days. I thought, He's wrong, he's mistaken. The sun, fixed just before the end of its setting into the sea, would not be moving. We had miles to go before that could happen.

I returned to the apartment, keeping my eyes peeled the whole way there in case I might have missed my car, re-creating my driving route the day I'd arrived in the neighborhood, bending down to see if the car might have fallen through the cracks in the asphalt. Therese Kavillio was standing outside the building. Her curls were gathered in a bun, her cheeks flushed. She interrupted my greeting, saying, I've been waiting for you for an eternity. I insisted. I said, Hello, Therese. She said, So you finally got it. That doesn't matter. Listen, I thought about your venture.

I said, Venture. She said, Yes, the digital publisher. I think you should develop a reading application that can track reading patterns in the series' books. I looked at her. The words emerged between her lips, collecting in the corners, aspiring to be swallowed into them if only she paused for a moment. She said, The application would gather data such as which plot twists encouraged more sequential reading, which events caused more readers to stop and for how long. The feedback would allow writers to better plan the next insta—

I said, Why didn't you tell me that you're Therese Kavillio, that you're Eldad Buganim's wife? She said, What? I said, Your husband is harassing me, falsely accusing me, and you're pretending to be somebody you're not. A spasm passed through her face, like the attack of a nocturnal predator. Her tone was scorched. She said, How dare you, Dedi was killed—

Yes, I said, killed during Operation Cast Lead. She said, I don't want to talk about that right now. I said, Then what do you want to talk about, this nonsense? She said, That's all that's left now. Do you even have any idea what's going on? I said, No. She said, I figured. She pointed at the sky, pinched the air, and rubbed her fingers, as if she could feel the granularity of the light. She said, It's getting worse, and we'll each have to find a way to cope.

THERESE WAS RAMBLING. SHE RETURNED TO THE SUBJECT OF the venture, clutching onto it like straw. She told me about the events taking place over town. The residents, she said, had retreated to the final front line. Of what? I asked. She said the first and last battlefront of any confrontation was always language, if I hadn't yet realized that, in the story of themselves the first and final battlefront was language. She said, No metaphor remains on the metaphoric level, all metaphors aspire to become reality. She said that sects were forming all over Tel Aviv, and that the members of one squad had started speaking in a lingo in which all nouns and proper names signified nonexistence, and that the prefix Ur had to be added in order to signify a being. She listed some examples, Ur-bird, Ur-cat, Ur-sky, Ur-Elish. She pointed at herself and said, Ur-Therese. She said that another squad switched genders, male becoming female, female becoming male. Elish, she said, you're not focusing, lady, listen to me, girl, I'm a guy who's trying to tell us something significant, crucial, you've got to understand me, woman, listen to me, Elish, what do you think about the venture, I'm a gentleman prepared to invest. Do you mind becoming partners, we can call the e-reader Take Up and Read.

I said, Tell me about Dedi. She said, There are other squads too.

I said, Don't change the subject. She said, I told you everything that matters. She said that after his death she could no longer keep his name, could not be the widow everyone expected her to be. For spite, she invested the compensation she received from the military in a social navigation software start-up. Three years later, she was wealthier than she'd ever dreamed of becoming. All of her actions were maneuverings to evade the position of military widow, and the wilder the gambles she took, the greater her fortune became. But there was a hole: every sum she made held some of the DNA of the death reparations that seeded it. Like homeopathic medicine, she said. No matter how much you dilute it, or so the charlatans would say. I asked her if she ever ran into Nahum Farkash. She asked, Who's that? I said, A poet, he manages the Sderot public library. She said she was contacted by that library with a request to fund some lecture series, but that she never got back to them. I asked, Why would they contact you? She said she'd started a fund that invested in cultural ventures. I said, You have your finger in every pie. She said, And how is that helping me?

I told her it was ridiculous to stand out in the yard, that we should go up to my place. She said, But what have you decided about the venture? I asked her why it was so urgent. She said, I need an answer. I said, Now that I realize what I'm looking for in writing, I'd rather not open that can of worms. She said, But you've already been involved in a similar project. How is this any different from your Benny Zehaviv books? I said, Let me tell you a parable. There once was a woman who grew desperate about her romantic partners. To her dissatisfaction, they each behaved according to their nature. One day she submitted a detailed order to the engineer of males. The next day, the man of her dreams appeared on her doorstep. That's your moral? she asked. How trite. I said, I haven't finished the parable yet, I assumed you could do that yourself. She said, Yes, that whole "be careful what you wish for" nonsense. No, I said, the ending is even more trite. What, said Therese. I said, The miserable woman got so bored that her complaints bored her friends, who bored their friends, who bored their children, who bored their school teachers, who bored the principals, who bored the board of education supervisors, who bored Members of Parliament, who bored television stars, who bored their astrologists, who bored the lesser lights, who bored the greater lights, who bored the angels, who bored Metatron, the divine scribe, who bored God, who renews the act of creation every day according to the Torah that was written before him with black fire against white fire.

I SAT IN MY APARTMENT, THINKING, THE FINAL FRONT LINE IS always language, in the story of the self it is always language. The sooty sunrise extended an unknown time, the night had been temporarily suspended. I couldn't find the car. Meaning, occasionally it appeared on some street or another, but by the time I reached it all I found was dying metal chassis. Therese left after our conversation, taking her sluggishness with her, making me swear to partner with her on the digital publisher venture. Perhaps redemption is found in the most negligible routes. She left to pound the pavement and search for investors and collaborators all over Tel Aviv. No metaphor ever stays put. Beyond the door I sensed the intensifying of a presence, probably the spying neighbor's, who hired her, was it Tuvya Hasson, whose apartment I'd inherited? A knock, an open-palm slap against the metallic tabulation. A swollen echo, rolling through space. Elish Ben Zaken, you've got one minute to open this door before I break it down. The high, eunuch-like voice, the vocal cords of a child trapped in an adult's body.

Eldad Buganim walked in wordlessly. You came alone, I said. He said, I didn't come here for the questioning. I said, You mean interrogation. He said, No, an interrogation requires advance notice. I asked, Haven't you given that? He said, No. I said, You're here to arrest me, then. He said, Maybe the other way around. I said, You've got no authority here, not on this realm. What realm? he said. I said, The realm of life. He said, Maybe it's the other way around. I said, You've done your duty, why don't you move on? Where, he said, I'm exactly where I need to be. I said, Where? He said, Here, in the Land of Shadow, there shall be no more death here.

I retreated into the living room. The space was enormous. Five steps later, I was already pressed against the glass windows leading out onto the balcony. He said, Doesn't that amuse you? What? I said. He said, That you're trying to solve one mystery, only to discover it leads to a corpse, the existence of which nobody even suspected. I said, When someone offers me a mystery, I always ask if it's the right one. He said, That's what we're counting on.

I said, Who's "we"? He said, We. He said, We're coming back, all of this country's dead, all the soldiers who were sent to the killing fields in the name of false ideas, to grease the seats of spineless politicians, feeding the lust for power of cowardly men who hide behind their warmongering cries inside their homes. And we shall demand our payment in blood, pound after pound, our stolen years, the pleasure taken away from us, we shall eviscerate, we shall tear limb from limb. And they would be the first, everyone who roared in favor of battle, everyone who issued a command, they would be the first. Throats will rip, stomachs will be hacked, no one will be spared, and we shall take their loved ones and kill them by the sword on the altars they built, their children and their elderly, and we shall feast, and we shall become satiated, our bones gathered, our tendons rebuilt, and they will be our atonement, and we will be theirs.

I said, What do you want from me? He said, I want nothing from you, you're merely a means to an end, not the agent. Our gate is ready. We're all here. We require a sufficiently strong, sufficiently desperate consciousness to open it, we need one person to pass through.

The narrator's voice in my mind spoke my name with urgency, Elish, Elish, come, I need your help. The voice took on the character of a summons, not words, but cutting through the body, a wound, the burning of recovery.

I told Eldad Buganim, Who's this someone you're talking about, what's the gate? He asked, Haven't you guessed yet? I thought you were famous for your intuitive leaps, your irregular deductions. I said, Heftzi Columbus. He lowered his voice, Heftzi has no heft. He laughed, his effort at lowering his voice turning the laugh into a gurgle. He said, She was too close to the gate to cross over here. She was an accident, nothing more. I said, The gate is in the thicket. He nodded. He said, We only need the crack in existence, the first passage. I said, Kalanit Shaubi. He said, That was a failed attempt. Then, finally, I saw him, in his own image, his insides black, ancient, but his periphery glowing, greenish, algae-ish, as if he'd been dipped in mucky, standing water, in mildew.

The narrator's voice in my head said, Elish, Elish, tell me your story. No, I said, leave me alone, don't you understand, this is a disaster, a disaster. I was washed by the same fury I'd felt in the presence of the shadow man that had haunted Kalanit Shaubi, who insisted on speaking to her, the rebellion of life against the conviction of the tenants of the netherworld, the dwellers of Tophet, against their revenge and their desire. I pounced at Eldad Buganim. I crossed the living room, running, gaining speed, my fingers aimed at his eye sockets, his nose, I would scratch off his human mask with my fingernails.

He stood still. I slammed into him and he fell, me on top of him. I was powered by rage, beating my unskilled fists against him, bones against bones, muscles against muscles. He didn't react, didn't defend himself. The narrator's voice wounded me, singing, *Now you know there shall be no more death in the Land of Shadow, to the place you beseech, you shall not be redeemed by love.* The music veered off tune, distorting inside my body, overly superficial scratches, overly long bruises. I pounded Eldad Buganim's face. His skull banged against the floor tiles with a muffled sound. I squeezed my hands around his neck, shoving my thumbs against his Adam's apple. I had no idea if that was where I should be squeezing, was powered only by instinct. *Pain shan't be your savior*, she sang, *all that is will rise to the extant, and you shan't be brought down by the shackles of metaphors, free in the web of flesh.* I raged at the speed of rage, veins and arteries enlarged to contain the flow, pressing my fingers, pressing. She sang, *your ears are pricked to the depth of silence, your eyes torn to see in the dark, and by these signs you shall know that your kingdom is nigh, son of man*, she sang off tune, but I recognized the composition structure, it had to be a Dalia song, but it couldn't have been, I knew Dalia's songs well. I said, Leave me alone. Elish, the voice fondled, Elish, Elish, arise and call, take up and read—

No, I said, my hands were choking, blocking, squeezing out breath. I said, No, no, you don't understand what you're doing, but my limbs diminished, my protesting voice thinned, what do you mean it worked, I'd told Oshri, I don't remember a thing.

Oshri had filmed it all in 3D. He got the intePhone Extreme especially for that purpose, so he said when he came home with it in the morning, but it was obvious he'd just been waiting for an opportunity. No way around it. He'll never admit he's addicted to technological innovations, and he always manages to get money for them out of our father, even though he didn't serve in a combat unit like our father wanted him to. The new biocyber unit he was drafted into was more prestigious anyway. It took our mom a month to make Dad realize it and get him out of the depression he caught when Oshri told him. But he should be thankful Oshri enlisted at all, with his past. They made up quickly, and ever since then he's been suffocating him with gifts. I don't get male relationships, even between father and son. They'll never say they love each other or miss each other. Loving or missing can only be felt toward a woman. Instead, they come up with all sorts of stupid rituals, like watching television together or talking about nonsense for hours. What's so hard about saying, Dude, I love you, I'm happy when we're together. They rule out anything they imagine belongs to soft feelings. But there's nothing soft about loving or missing. They're hard. The way a diamond is hard, but fragile, not durable at all. Maybe that's where their confusion comes from. Maybe they're right. Never mind.

In the video Oshri filmed, I was sitting the way I am now, by the coffee table in the living room where we'd prepared a special corner for our experiment. A shadow man stood before me. He looked like that guy who used to visit Kalanit Shaubi after she disappeared and returned. It looked like I was talking to him, voicelessly, or at least moving my hands the way I do when I talk. Oshri hates those hand gestures. He once told me I had to practice pantomime so that my movements would at least mean something and my energy wouldn't be for naught. That's what he said, I swear, "for naught." Those old translations he used to read really stuck in his brain. He'd never admit that either, if he ever even agreed to discuss them.

He stood before me, watching it with me. Before we started watching he explained, all excited, how the 3D worked, but I wasn't really listening. All I got was that the device contains a small projector that shoots lasers that stimulate retinal nerves. So you can only watch it from weird angles. Oshri ran his fingers over the video, pulled them aside, and the point of view changed. I could see my face. It was empty, no expression, and my lips weren't moving, only my hands. Oshri said it looked like we were speaking through telepathy, in our minds. I said again that I couldn't remember anything. He said Kalanit couldn't remember anything either, and accused us of making it up. Even in 3D the shadow man looked patched into the video, bad animation, unnatural, a gross lump of darkness.

My body was exhausted. I wanted to cry but didn't know why. I should have been happy, it was working, but no. There was a kind of fist around my heart, and the entire apartment was colored with some sort of sadness, like a plastic covered our lockdown corner. We built it in Elish's apartment, where Oshri lives now. The four 3D cameras that Oshri hooked up to the InteMon, the InteMon case, the lights, the mattress we laid down, the walls, the table. No plastic, a kind of dirty layer of light. As if I were a visitor, as if I'd crossed the distance between years from now and this present in one go, and I could only see things the way they are where I came from, eaten up and rotten. I looked at my fingers. They were old, wrinkled, the lines deep.

Oshri touched my shoulder, a small touch. His eyes, the cracked blue in his eyes, the worry and concern that spilled through the cracks, that was all I needed. The marble that rose in my throat broke and I let out a broken sound.

Oshri asked if I was all right. I nodded but didn't speak. I still couldn't control my breathing and my mouth well enough. I didn't cry when Elish died. So why should I cry just when I was about to find out what happened to him? Is that what I'm sad about? I must have felt the same thing when we heard about his death.

Something disappeared from my throat, no, annihilated, I think that's the word, but not like dried up, but like pressed together. I felt as if a giant stapler were moving through my body, one organ at a time, stapling the words, and the pain, back to the flesh. There was no place to run, nothing to run from, and I was heavy with it from morning till night. Light and dark were stapled to my blood and lungs and everything else. Oshri cried every chance he got. He cried when Manny Lahav spoke at the funeral. Us girls were pushed aside, but I shoved my way in to stand with the boys around the grave, hiding behind Yalon, and I heard everything. Manny said that Elish changed his life, that meeting him made Manny a different person, better, he hopes, more open, who never stops asking himself if he's asking the right questions, but Elish was the kind of guy who wouldn't take compliments, wouldn't let anyone tell him he was meaningful. Manny was sorry he didn't insist.

Oshri cried with our mother and cried with Grandma Zehava. She had a torn crying, like there was a knife in her chest and the crying moved over it, tearing. She yelled so much that Mom said that's how the problem with her ear started. Now I'm convinced that it started when Elish had his hearing issue and got hospitalized. After that she said she had a noise, tinnitus, and that sometimes in the middle of the night she heard him talking, as if on a cell phone with bad reception, a word here, a word there. She didn't hear Grandpa Prosper, or her parents. And Oshri cried with our father. I'd walk around Grandma's building's yard. Dad took us to the shiva every day. And I saw Oshri inside of Dad's hug, crying, and there were tears in Dad's eyes too.

IT'S A COMPLICATED STORY TO TELL. I'LL TRY TO MAKE EVERY-thing organized and not get off track. I have a feeling I'm supposed to recognize you, but I don't. For some reason I don't mind telling you, even though you're a stranger. Maybe because you're a stranger you'll find parts that matter to you. You wouldn't have talked my ear off if this story weren't essential to you, right? Otherwise, why would you care about me? I'm so glad that sharing is an antique thing. I mean, that's what people say about my generation, that the generation before mine shared every bit of crap that popped into their heads, until the waves of violence in 2019, which made them back off. And it's true, social media was swamped with those horrifying photos and videos, with the blood week of the Chaos Front and their combined attack. They documented and posted everything. It was shocking to see the severed heads of the prime minister and his wife thrown out of the windows of their villa in Caesarea into a pile of cow dung, even to people who started every morning by praying for the two of them to get cancer. It was disgusting to see the pictures of the Minister of Justice's son, who was kidnapped outside his school and hanged from a streetlamp near the family home, the name *Vaizatha* engraved on his forehead, as if the name was supposed to send some message. The pictures made their way to you even if you didn't want to see them, even if you turned off your computer, some idiot would DM them to you or share them on an app you forgot to cancel notifications for. Even the accidents went viral. The smoke bombs that went off at the La Familia rally, and the run-over face of the Minister of Culture, who came to speak at the rally and was trampled to a pulp when everyone panicked and fled from the bombs, or that patheteeth guy, a wannabe hip-hop artist who came to confront protesters and choked on the shawarma he was eating, all the tahini and cabbage juice streaming down his cheeks while the protesters crossed their arms with indifference and watched him slapping his own chest. There was always someone who documented, always someone who posted it. And the fake pictures, and the false news, were disgusting. So yeah, that week was the apex of a process, because our generation, as early as age sixteen or seventeen, suddenly started thinking it was hella pathetic to think we'd be interesting to anyone or that we should make an effort to be, just super patheteeth for people to write a social media post, to wake up in the morning and say, I got up on the wrong side of bed, I got up on the right side of bed, to Snapchat, to TikTok, to tweet, to write down every unnecessary thought that went through their unnecessary heads and make it public and call it tweeting. Like happy little birds. Sure. If they're birds they can shit and pee in public, because that's what birds do, right?

I should find out if birds even pee. I've never seen a bird peeing. Maybe they don't separate pee from poop. I'll ask Oshri when he gets back. He knows about these things. Or he'll consult with Yalon. Yalon, that negligent, takes an interest in negligibles too. But the short story is, this is where I feel your urgency to listen. I have no idea how I can be so sure, but it's strong enough for me. You're listening. Or anyway, you're prepared to absorb.

So where should I begin?

I listened at Elish's shiva too. The words were stapled to my body, like I said. I eavesdropped. Nobody minded that I was there. Except for one time, when Manny came to visit and signaled to Mom and Dad to go into Grandma Zehava's kitchen with him. I followed them, but Mom gave me that withering stare, when her eyes become like pistols, and shook her head. I turned my back on her like I was about to leave, but then I snuck back to the doorway and stood there quietly. They were whispering. They didn't want us to hear the circumstances of Elish's death, as they put it. But we knew—well, me and Yalon knew, anyway. There was no talking to Oshri. Yalon's father told Yalon, I don't know how he heard, but he heard it was an accident. They found Elish in his apartment, in his study, lying on the desk. There were all sorts of pills on the desk, antidepressants, anti-anxiety, sleeping pills, and an open wine bottle. What he didn't understand was why the police were investigating. I never liked Yalon's dad. He rubbed me the wrong way big-time, that Mr. Asor. Very few things scare me. I'm not just showing off here. Maybe fear is an instinct I just don't have, maybe I'm messed up. But even as a child I knew that fear was a way to control people, and anytime someone tries to scare me I get this resistance, this anger, that burns out the threat. Generally speaking, people who use scare tactics are cowards themselves. They know from experience that fear is efficient, and they mistakenly think that if they use it on others they'll be rid of it themselves. Almost all of my military commanders, in basic training and in squad commander course, were like this. But not Yalon's dad. I recognized that he gains pleasure from control. The first time I got in their car, together with Yalon, and realized just how much Mr. Asor's body sucks out the air from the car, how his voice, emerging from this body that looks like a barrel, clogs the spaces between molecules, I flinched. And I saw the smile that almost burst out of his lips, the flaring nostrils, like he could smell my reaction, that flinch of mine. I don't get how Yalon chose to live with him after the divorce instead of with his mother, who took his brothers, the babieses, to the kibbutz. He said he hated it there. But that's not a good reason.

Anyway, Yalon isn't the point here. He was just the messenger. In Grandma Zehava's kitchen, Manny Lahav whispered to my parents. He insisted on an autopsy, even though Grandma Zehava said no. He sat there, talking her into it. And they did end up finding a high content of antibodies in the blood test, his immune system having worked overtime before he died. That taught them he might have been in pain, and maybe that's why he took all those pills and drank that wine, that he wasn't of sound mind, and they determined it was an accident. That's what they said, and it wasn't like they originally thought, that he, the words run through my mind, but my heart speaks them, beating a hard beat, kicking and going wild. Killed himself. Why is it easy for me to say he died but not that he killed himself?

Even though it's obvious he didn't. It's obvious. He had no intent. That's what they said. But every time something in my life breaks, I go back to that image of Elish in his study, lying on the

511

desk, and I know that something inside of him wanted it, not that small something most of us have, when we close our eyes and don't want to open them again, or when we sigh and call our moms in a desperate moment, when we realize we never chose to be born, and that if anyone had asked us, maybe we would have preferred not to. With him it was something bigger, firmer, that pined for unbeing, so to speak. He shifted between child and man his entire life, and as a girl I thought he was avoiding making a choice, because he didn't want to be either. In Nahum Farkash's poems that Yalon and I found, there was one poem I remember by heart. There once was a man who didn't want to be, neither mineral nor plant, neither animal nor bot, he didn't want for years, and finally he was not. I should have asked him if he'd written that about Elish.

My parents and Manny Lahav whispered in the kitchen. Manny said he was applying pressure behind the scenes to keep the case open, because if they recalled Elish's investigation that had caused people to threaten Grandma Zehava, it was Manny who'd hired him for that one, to investigate the death of Yehuda Menuhin, a university philosophy professor, and that Yehuda Menuhin's body was the same, found lying on his desk, with painkillers and wine. He said the similarity couldn't be a coincidence, that there was forethought here, that there was intent.

WE WAITED ALL AFTERNOON FOR THE SHADOW MAN TO COME back. Oshri said there must be something we could do to help draw him in, tempt him to show up. I said Kalanit didn't try, he just showed up, and she didn't even know he visited her. Oshri said there was something he hadn't told me, that when he saw the shadow man he wanted to attack him, that up close all his senses yelled at him to lunge, to tear him to shreds, to finish him, to make him not exist. He said the shadow man was made of a life negative. I asked if he meant death. He said no, that death was the end of life, but the shadow man was the opposite of life, a hatred of life, an envy of life for existing, a madness for being unlife, that's what he's made of. I asked if he was like antimatter. He said not exactly, that if we'd cut a man's image out of paper and the space that was left behind had consciousness, not exactly consciousness, blind will, that would be the shadow man. He smiled when he finished his explanation, just like he did every time he managed to be precise. He said the question was, was there a mental state I needed to be in to get him to come? I said the mental state could be like a smell I emitted, like pheromones. He said, Mental pheromones, exactly. His smile widened, and the cracked blue in his eyes lit up from the inside. He smiled like that whenever I got something more precisely than he did. He asked if I felt better, because my brain was clearly working again. I said I did. He said he was going down to the store to get some groceries for dinner. Of course I knew he needed some privacy to talk to Nitzan. Like clockwork, every day around sunset. I don't know why those two care so much about sunset, it's so corny, but they're cute, these nerdy officers. He even suggested involving her. Of course I said no. He was already taking a risk by synthesizing the Weigl and Fleck bacteria at the MKI lab without getting his superior's permission. Nitzan helped without knowing it, and it was best if she stayed ignorant.

He said he felt bad leaving me unattended. I pointed at my eyes, with the AR lenses, and the sense bracelet, they were covered with monitoring sensors, and at the 2D cameras, and at the InteMon, which documented every frame, and asked if that seemed unattended to him. He ran his fingers over his InteMon affectionately. He called it a *natar bina*, Hebrew for "intelligence monitor," or Natab for short. He preferred his Hebrew translations, insisted on them. When he said Natab, I told him to grow up and stop it with that overtranslation of his. And he said, Overlation, good one. For the thirtieth time, he said we should have recruited Yalon to our cause. What a nag. So what if Yalon was part of the investigation to begin with, and so what if he joined us on our first journey? He wasn't there for the second. And of course Oshri wanted him to be part of it, those two are still in touch. But how is it my fault that Yalon turned into one of those lonesomes who still post pictures on social media, taking photos of everything he eats and uploading them, trying to convince everyone that he's an amazing person with a bangalicious life, when actually he works for his dad's company, in an office his dad arranged for him, learning the profession his dad chose for him? Like I said, if you're my age and not an antique, you've got to be godforsaken up to your teeth, a killer solitary, to traject into the Agora view an animation of yourself smiling on some hill or next to some yore-time building. It's like someone once said, that not knowing what to keep in-house is worse than smoking.

But thanks to Yalon, the loose ends started connecting. There was a period when he wasn't completely useless. He and his dad came to the funeral, his mother was at the kibbutz again with her relatives. I hadn't seen him since the war was almost over, when he became a fan of that Bobarisa, patheteeth just like he is. At the start of the school year he tried to talk to me a few times, sniffing around me, walking in circles, and Racheli and Elinoar would crack jokes, Your boyfriend is looking for you, those bitches told me. And what did he even want from me, to join his *ars* squad or convince him he wasn't truly an *ars*, that he didn't contain *ars*ness? He always swayed, his nature pulling him in one direction, and whatever it is that pushes people to be just like everyone else pulling him in the opposite direction. Before he enlisted, I told him there was no reason why he should go into combat besides the fact that the other boys in our class yearned to be recruited by elite units, and that his blind enthusiasm would end up killing him. And when he got honorably discharged and said his father offered him a job, I told him not to use me to justify the fact that he remained true to himself, that I couldn't carry him, that he had to make up his mind. So he finally made up his mind to be a zero, to zero in. He sent me a private conference request. At that point I was no longer an Agorite. He talked. I said nothing the whole time. I was prepared for his words. I wasn't prepared for the shattering. When you clap your hands over a fly, to you the sound is a sharp slap, a little burn against the skin. But have you ever tried to imagine the thunder the fly hears?

HE CAME TO THE SHIVA, YALON DID, BY HIMSELF. HE TOOK THE bus and used his iPhone to navigate from the Central Bus Station to Grandma Zehava's house. He came and sat down next to me. I turned my back on him. He said my name, asked me to look at him. I didn't. He said people were writing lots of things about Elish online, about his book, about whether or not he'd killed himself. He said the words without any special intent, but that's when I heard that terrible loneliness inside of them, as if Elish were standing in a huge, empty hall, shouting to someone. I shrugged. Yalon said he'd downloaded Elish's book on his iPad. Someone had uploaded a scan. He pulled it out of his bag and showed me. I expected one of the Benny Zehaviv books, but it was a different one. The title *The Sky Is Dust* was written in large font, and a little smaller, underneath, it said *The Rise and Fall of Israeli Rock*, and then, smaller, but clear, was his name. My fingers froze on the touch screen. I wanted to shove them inside through that misanthropic glass, to feel the roughness of paper. I didn't know that book, it wasn't on the living room shelf where Dad arranged Elish's books, and Elish never mentioned it either. Yalon said someone started a Facebook memorial page for Elish, and that the person who uploaded the scanned book said Elish was the reason he discovered Blasé et Sans Lumière. Yalon had trouble saying the name. He pulled up the Facebook page on his iPad. I read. Some guy named Golan Pitusi wrote that back in the roaring nineties, when local papers had cultural value, he opened the local Tel Aviv paper one weekend and read a review by Elish Ben

Zaken. It was the most interesting review of rock music he'd read in years. It was all about a new, promising duo. Golan went to Blasé's next concert. What he wanted most of all was to be twenty-one again and hear Dalia Shushan when she was still an anonymous singer, and to feel the shock, the shock of being twenty-one, and realizing that his pain was a treasure, a gold mine, an electric reactor, that the more lost he got, the more confident he'd be that he was there. He wrote that Dalia Shushan's murder was the first blow and that Elish Ben Zaken's death was the final blow. The end of an era. He linked to a Blasé song on YouTube, "One Mile and Two Days Before Sunset." Yalon pulled his earbuds out of his iPhone, connected them to the iPad, and handed them to me. I shook my head. He said he couldn't stop listening to them, he'd downloaded the two Blasé albums, Dalia Shushan's demo, and the album that Rami Amzaleg, who was Dalia Shushan's partner in Blasé, dropped a few months ago. He kept talking about them. I just listened. The sting and excitement of discovery were born inside of me, but underneath them were so many layers of day-timelight and nighttimedark stapled to my organs that I couldn't even notice.

The same thing happened on another day, when Ronnit came to sit shiva, all apologetic for not having made it to the funeral, explaining that it was too difficult, what with her older son and her new pregnancy, and David, her husband, working overtime. She'd left Akiva with some relatives that day.

I guessed she didn't bring him because she was worried Grandma Zehava would figure it out. My parents wouldn't remember Elish's face from when he was a kid, because they were just kids themselves, and they watched him changing day by day, like their own faces in the mirror, slowly getting used to the shape they were taking on. But Grandma Zehava, even in mourning, maybe especially in mourning, searching for his face everywhere, she even told Oshri he had Elish's mouth, even though, it's not nice to say, but Elish was kind of ugly, and had these shriveled, dry lips, and Oshri, with all of his downsides, every one of his features is just as it should be.

She hugged me, Ronnit, that hypocrite. Forgot how she yelled at me when I called her over the summer. I wanted to punch her for breaking up with Elish, leaving him all alone. If she had been with him it wouldn't have happened. But these thoughts were also like a mosquito in a cotton ball, mountains of cotton balls. She wrapped her arms around me. I could have slipped my hand through the collar of her dress and scratched her back, or bit her neck. And she whispered that I had her number and was welcome to call her at any hour. I didn't respond.

More people came, people I had no idea even knew Elish. I followed Manny Lahav around quietly. He gave my parents an update. Only after we finished sitting shiva, just before Yom Kippur, when we got back from the cemetery, my throat opened and my mouth snapped out of its paralysis. I asked Mom if she ever heard about Dalia Shushan. She said she hadn't. I asked her about Elish's book. She said she didn't have her copy anymore, that she threw it out after she stopped talking to Elish for putting me and Grandma Zehava at risk. I asked her what was going to happen to Elish's apartment. She said the police would give the keys back when they finished their investigation. I wanted to ask more. She said she was tired of my questions, how were they even helping me, I was cold just like my uncle, holding my pain inside a fist, all I cared about was knowing, I was indifferent.

NO ONE'S GOING TO DECIDE FOR ME WHEN TO BE HAPPY AND when to be sad, no one's going to make my choices for me. What did she even know about the daytimelight and nighttimedark that were stapled to my body, that my blood barely moved, and that it barely squeaked by when it did? I didn't ask what it was like for her, I didn't ask if, when she fell asleep, nails also popped out of the mattress, the sheet, the pillows, and entered her dreams, and if everyone she saw, if she could recall any of their faces, had their eyes gouged out. What an annoying mom.

Oshri came back a few minutes later. I wonder what happened with Nitzan. Maybe she was busy. He asked if I was all right, because I seemed a little unfocused. I promised him I was fine. He walked over to the InteMon, touched its right side, and the screen lit up. I forgot to turn off the regular info layers of the augmented reality lenses when I enslaved them to Oshri's InteMon. The structure measurements, the blueprint, the locations of power sources, a map of the area, GPS coordinates, the usual night-vision menu, everything I used when I was on the field, floated up, mixed up with the InteMon's feedback, my vital signs, my blood sugar levels, pulse, temperature. I blinked to wipe away most of the information and only leave Oshri's InteMon feed. With his left hand, Oshri scrolled and toggled to run the recording from the 2D cameras. He said he thought the shadow man came to visit while he was gone because of how detached I looked. But it seemed he'd been wrong. We had to hurry him up. We were in a time crunch. We'd lost three days and nights while I was under the influence of the serum Oshri had synthesized. Oshri said I had no reaction to it, I'd done the basic things, I ate and drank, but it was as if I was doing it all in my sleep. He showed me some of the footage. Scary, as if someone were operating me from the outside, I was me, but I wasn't. Of course I remembered nothing, just like Kalanit Shaubi, just like Olga Kovilishin.

Oshri took a week off from military service, that's all they allowed him, and even then it took some haranguing. Marco, my boss, would understand if I extended my break by a few days. My faction is skilled enough to get by without me in spite of the alert level, and I can give Avdiel, whom I appointed temporary faction commander, instructions through the intePhone. I've never taken a sick day or a day off, not during my training period and not in the four and a half years that followed.

I was at peace with my job. After my failure in the military, being kicked out of the officer training course and returning to my unit as a squad commander, I was just unlucky. The waves of violence in 2019 took place during my basic training. I was excited about enlisting into a mixed unit. Half of the combat units were already orthodivisions and girls weren't allowed to come near them. In our tents, we started getting reports of the attacks on the Chaos Front. During blood week, the base was all nervous. Nobody knew what was going on. Rookies talked about a civil war and asked one another which side they were going to take. The commanders reassured us in their own way, sending us on a million field excursions, wringing out the bitterness and worry. But there was still concern in the air. Soldiers might be sent on security detail, Palestinians might take advantage of the commotion to stage a riot. Our mission was clear, but how would we act within a civilian population, where we might be among our uncles, our relatives, our siblings? People talked and talked, but the only mission soldiers ended up getting involved with was attacking the Caesarea compound where the Chaos Front underground were entrenched. Most of them were killed in the armed conflict. A few soldiers too. There was a public agreement that even though these underground members were Jews, they were to be considered dangerous criminals. Later, it turned out that some of them were radical left activists, others were settlers who committed price tag vandalism, or armed hilltop youth, and all sorts of other organizations that the defense forces were aware of but did nothing to stop. Among these wild warriors were recent orthodivision graduates. They received direct orders from rabbis in settlements. This information obviously caused an uproar. The immediate effect on my own life, which was all I cared about back then, was a ratcheting up of military conduct and close supervision. I hate power, I hate oppression, but for some reason I thought I'd fit into the military just fine. It seemed fun, enlisting, meeting new people, having new experiences, spending the night in a sleeping bag in the desert cold or in some other hellhole. Like an extreme sport, nothing like my life in Sderot. I could forget about Mom and Dad for a bit, be independent.

It took some time before things started to sink in, that ultimately the military was a convenient environment for people to test their power over others, to indulge in it. Power is like wastewater, it trickles down and shit bathes in it. That's all. Nothing more. Losers are given a command rank, then they think that rank makes them better or smarter, licensing them to abuse. There was one commander at the officer training course who despised me. Dad said she must be jealous. Ever since we were little, he told Oshri and me how perfect we were. Mom told me to check if this commander had a boyfriend on base, because if she did, then he must have his eye on me. Often, women pick on other women because they sense a threat to their relationship. I thought it was worse than that. I thought she was picking on me for no other reason than that she could. I must have told a joke during one of the early drills, and somebody laughed, and that bugged her, and made her realize she could get back at me, and every little revenge just fired up the impulse, fanning the flames to the point where she no longer bothered to hide it. And the environment that had formed made things worse. There was an unspoken compulsion to be rough on us, to make us submissive. During the commanders' meeting, she called me the rebel and talked shit about me, that piece of garbage, and slowly but surely the rest of them started to have it in for me too. Everyone but Yishai, the adjutant officer at headquarters. He recognized her evil, though she wasn't actually evil at all, just enslaved to her weakness for enacting arbitrary force only because nobody stopped her. Weak people always think that a lack of punishment means there's been no crime, but the crime is there. Children can feel it in their stomachs. They know when a kid isn't playing fair, when they're breaking the rules, and they revolt. I can't forgive crimes, real crimes, I don't mean misdemeanors such as disregarding the law. Say if someone crosses the street on a red light, I find that healthy. But I'd be willing to carry a gun and shoot paintballs at criminals, marking them for life. Elish once told me I had a strong moral compass, and that there was no better gift he could wish for me, but that I had to watch out, because if I followed it too strictly, I'd risk destruction. But he was wrong. I'm liable to do awful things when curiosity gets the better of me. After I was kicked out, Yishai called and asked me out. We dated for a while. He was a nice guy, a little boring, and soon enough I was totally over him.

OSHRI TOUCHED MY SHOULDER AGAIN, GENTLY. I SAID, WHAT? HE asked if I wanted to eat. He'd called out to me from the kitchen, but I hadn't answered, and hadn't noticed when he waved a hand in front of my face either. I told him maybe the visit from the shadow man had rattled me in ways we couldn't measure yet. I asked him if birds pee. He looked at me like, What? I said it was just a thought I had. He said they didn't. That their refuse was a mixture of unprocessed food and superfluous fluids. What, didn't I remember that time a pigeon shat on my shoulder, and all her poop got smeared on my shirt when I tried to wipe it off? I said I did. I didn't. The pigeon shits on me at a fixed point in time and space, in a sequence of other points I try to wipe it off. My consciousness puts them together to form movement, a flow of time.

Oshri made pasta with tomato and basil sauce. Simple but delicious. His salad was good too, fresh. Once, I got stuck at school for an hour and came home late. When I walked in, the kitchen was a mess, the sink full of pots and pans, spills on the floor, dirty towels. Our parents went to Romania for the week and left me in charge. Turned out Oshri and Yalon were hungry, so they'd put everything that looked edible on the counter and experimented, cooking all sorts of bizarre combinations. That was one of the first times Oshri snapped out of his damn depression, so I forgave him. His cooking skills have definitely improved, but not by much. Itay, my ex, was a fantastic cook. He drowned me in fancy dishes and elaborate meals. Even when I just felt like a burger, he made some delicacy. Just to spite him, I went vegetarian, but that didn't stop him. He became an expert on vegetarian cuisine, preparing extravagant meals. Every night when I came home from work the table was set with stews or beautiful, toylike salads, every leaf in its place, every slice of tomato shining like a jewel. I'd chomp on Pringles in front of him until he got grossed out. Any sensory addiction conceals a perversion. The problem is, it's hard to admit to one when everyone around you praises whatever you use to hide it.

Oshri said that, in that case, he'd look over Elish's notepad from the Kalanit case, not that it would do any good, as we'd already looked over it several times. I asked him what he meant by the words "in that case." He asked if I wasn't listening when he told me about his conversation with Nitzan, about an NS strap for brain activity. I told him no, I never listen to that kind of talk. He cleared the plates at the end of our meal, went to the kitchen, then returned to the lockdown corner. He touched a crystal board on the wall screen and pulled up the virtual keyboard. He played with the InteMon for a few minutes and said maybe I should rest, that this was the first night since I was back to my old self, and was I sure it was all right for him to record me while I sleep? If I was uncomfortable he could turn off the cameras and only leave the data intake from the augmented reality lenses and the sense bracelet. I asked him about the brain activity monitoring sensors he was talking about. He said he was an idiot not to think of it before, but that tomorrow Nitzan would pilfer one for him from the lab. I asked if he'd told her. He said he told her he was working on a little project during his break and that he'd share it with her when it was ready. I thought he wouldn't be able to fool her for long. He might have had the same thought. He grimaced all of a sudden.

I lay on the mattress and stared at the ceiling. Even though

Oshri had shrunk the wall screen to just one crystal board and dimmed its transparency to the lowest point, until it looked like an opaque picture, the twinkling of his other devices intensified into low lighting in the darkness of the living room. The night was almost quiet, the streets empty, the automated cars driving themselves to out-of-town parking areas. The light trains slid soundlessly along their tracks. But people could be heard, announcing their existence through shouting and whispering. I wouldn't have joined them right now for all the money in the world. It was as if that desire in me had died. I should have told Oshri we were documenting the outside, but maybe it was more important to document what was on the inside. I didn't want to tell him that my longing for Elish, which only arose in times of crisis, had gone back to the way it was right after he died, a sort of background static beneath every thought or intention. Sometimes feelings come to me by surprise, like a strong intuition, just like that time when I knew right away I had the Richard Perotz gene before Oshri checked and confirmed it.

OSHRI AND I WENT BACK TO SCHOOL AFTER SUKKOT BREAK. OUR parents agreed to let us stay home a few more days after the shiva. They didn't agree right away. Our mother wanted us to get back to normal life immediately. Our dad softened. He said work at the new Asor neighborhood up north would only start up again after the second holiday, so he could stay home and watch us. I knew he was lying a little, that he needed more time too. Yalon's dad would never have given his employees such a long break. It turned out that Elish became a temporary star on the internet. That's what they used to call Virtualia back then. A few of the kids in my class actually bought his books. They tried to talk to me, but I just kept silent until they left me alone. Except for Yalon. He sat next to me during the first recess and behaved like usual. He showed me the new headphones his dad bought him, enormous, only framing his face and emphasizing his natural ugliness. His hairdo was ruined, I suddenly realized, and didn't suit him anyway. He kept yammering about his excitement about Dalia Shushan's duo, which he called Blasé. Just before we got up to go back to class he whispered to me that his parents were getting a divorce. All of a sudden he didn't have the protection of his energy and smiles, so slim, and I could tell he was trying hard not to shiver, even though all around the patch of shade where we were standing, the sun was burning, like we were standing next to a radiator and feeling the heat waving off of it. I asked if he wanted to come over after school, or even in the evening. He nodded. He whispered again that he had to decide who he wanted to live with. I asked why it was so urgent for him to decide. He said his mother was moving to the kibbutz for now, there was an arrangement there for the babieses, and if he went with her they had to start looking at schools. He looked at me. I looked at him. We said nothing. Inside his eyes I could see myself, not a reflection, but me, the way I'd accumulated in him, and I was glad and felt a wild electricity, and I was a stubborn kid, and maybe he could see himself, a gullible, funny, dense kid who liked arguing for no good reason, and suddenly I realized that was familiarity, that this was how people know each other, one layer heaps over another and the actions and the sharing push up against each other and mix up and something new comes out, like a diamond inside the brain, and I thought how I didn't want him to leave.

We were in my room and he kept talking about Blasé. He played me a few songs, but I didn't get carried away the way he promised I would. He wasn't disappointed, he said I'd get it someday, because this was Elish's favorite singer. I was quiet. The longing invaded my airways, like food does when you talk while you eat. He said he almost forgot and pulled out from his backpack a copy of *The Sky Is Dust*, Elish's book that I hadn't known about. He asked his father to order two copies. I said his father bought him lots of stuff. He said when his father had to work late, he called in the evening and they talked. I asked what about. He said, I don't know, about my day, about soccer. I said he wasn't a soccer fan. He said he wasn't, but he sort of was. I said he was just trying too hard, the way Oshri tried too hard to play with our father, that he was confused and just wanted to please him.

Oshri walked into the room. I had a feeling he'd been standing outside the door and eavesdropping until he heard his name. I asked. He said he hadn't been, and showed us his backpack, which was still on his back. He said he just got home and Mom sent him to ask if we were hungry.

I think Mom knew about the divorce, because she was gentle with Yalon and asked about his grandmother and gave him special attention even though he didn't really have anything to say. When we got back in the room, Oshri followed us in. I asked if he wanted anything. He looked at me, insulted. He said he thought we'd go back to being TYO, the investigation agency we'd started during the Kalanit Shaubi case. TYO like our initials, Tahel, Yalon, and Oshri. I said that was kind of childish. Even as a child, Oshri had a tendency to say the right thing, he may have a supernatural sense of timing for hitting the weak spot of my thoughts. I need to guess his, and I do a decent job of it, calculating and assessing, planning and picking my moment. But he can just feel mine. It shouldn't surprise me. He had that ice worm that passed through his arm whenever something went wrong, and adolescence had turned it into a strong sense that operated in the back of his mind. When Yalon and I went into my bedroom, the things Manny had said about Elish's death opened up inside of me, and I was able to think of death, not the shrinking of muscles, or the acid invading the lungs, or the pining jammed in the windpipe. No. A clear thought riddled by a riddle. The coolness it brought into me. Oshri was already halfway back to the living room. I called him in to join us.

✻ ✻ ✻

THE NEXT MORNING, OSHRI SAID HE HAD TO GO TO THE LAB. HE'D told Nitzi he'd go. I repeated the nickname. He blushed. It's adorable when a twenty-six-year-old blushes, even if he's your brother, and not blushing out of embarrassment, for being caught doing something naughty, but because his soul was blooming on his cheek like a rose. I wanted to tell him not to lose the ability to blush like that, that Nitzan was lucky, that people tried unsuccessfully to conceal things, and that their efforts to conceal were all the more revelatory. Then I realized that was Elish's thought, not mine. Maybe there was some connection between Elish's thoughts glomming on to me and the shadow man's visit. Suddenly, I grasped the full meaning of what we'd done in managing to re-create the shadow man's visit. We were on the right track. Oshri could say it was madness as much as he wanted. I was right. Nahum Farkash's story about Take Up and Read, which Oshri claimed was unfounded, was true, it was true. Then I silenced the hope. Maybe it was too early to celebrate. We haven't been able to find out what became of Kalanit Shaubi or Olga Kovilishin, Dmitry Shtedler's niece. Oshri conferenced with Yalon on audio and visual after he asked him to talk with Sima Shaubi. He put the call on public so I could take part too. Turned out Kalanit had a lot of tests done when she was hospitalized after the missile hit, unusual tests, for months afterward, and the HMO even covered some expensive ones that weren't normally funded. They found nothing, and now, thank God, she was healthy as a horse. The way Yalon slipped into Sima's voice, into her expressions, only hurt me. He tapped an imaginary wooden board as he said these things.

Back then, in my bedroom, he said we had to investigate. I told them about Elish and the Yehuda Menuhin investigation. Yalon pulled out his iPad and ran a search. We didn't learn much. Yehuda Menuhin was a philosophy professor who committed suicide twelve years earlier. He was the brother of a Member of Parliament and had written one book, *Lampoons*, a copy of which

Yalon tracked down in a Russian website that contained scans of research books. We downloaded it and tried reading it, but it wasn't very interesting. Pretty dense too, to tell the truth.

The whole time we were searching and passing the iPad back and forth, Oshri was checked out. He opened Elish's book that Yalon gave me and looked at it. What's with that annoying habit of sitting with people just to ignore them? In the middle of our attempt to figure out what Menuhin was talking about, Oshri said that Elish wrote a lot about Blasé et Sans Lumière. Yalon said, Yes, yes, it's an amazing duo, the singer is from Sderot and was murdered in Tel Aviv by a junkie. Oshri said that wasn't mentioned in the book. Yalon said the book came out earlier, that the guy murdered her in 2002. I asked when. Yalon tapped on the iPad. He moved his eyes between the two of us. He said, Just before that Menuhin guy killed himself. I said that was too big of a coincidence. Yalon said what I meant to say was it was no coincidence. I said that's what I meant. He said, In that case, why didn't you say what you meant? I said I was being sarcastic. He said when being sarcastic it was better to emphasize the words more. He demonstrated, It's too big of a co-in-ci-dence. I said he was exaggerating, that he sounded like an actor on an Israeli TV series. He said he didn't sound at all like an actor on an Israeli TV series and emphasized the words again with excessive mockery. Oshri asked if he could have the iPad and we both realized we were holding it together, our fingers touching. He smiled and I smiled.

Why would that conversation, with all the details, get stuck in my head, why that one? The heat from his finger shot along mine. In the window, I saw the sun was starting to set, and the glow of the lake was gone, the water was gray, but inside, among the movements of water, there were silver strands, as if hidden aquatic creatures took bites of daylight and pulled them down to the depths of the lake. The eucalyptuses rustled. Why would that image stay with me, whole?

Dad called Oshri from downstairs. He said he was starting to take down the sukkah and that Oshri had promised to help. Oshri had promised nothing. After Yom Kippur, Dad pulled out the folding metal sukkah he'd built a few years earlier. Grandma Zehava was over at our place. Mom wouldn't let her be alone for the fast this year. She told Dad she didn't know what kind of holiday we'd be having, so what was the point of building a sukkah? Dad ignored her. We followed him out. I was nauseated from all the cakes I'd gobbled up when the fast ended. Oshri's face looked a little sickly too. We helped him put up the metal skeleton. He told Oshri that this year he'd have to help him stretch the fabrics, but that Oshri was in charge of the frond covering. That should be easy, since we had the thicket right there. Oshri made a face. I said I'd help him, but Dad said it was Oshri's responsibility.

Oshri gave Yalon back the iPad and went outside. Yalon said he had to go home too. His head was lowered. I looked at the iPad. There was a text from his dad, asking where he was, saying he was waiting for him to start making dinner together.

I CAREFULLY PULLED MOM'S GALAXY OUT OF THE KITCHEN SIDE-board. I opened the contact list and found Manny Lahav's number. She barked at me from behind, what was I doing with her phone? I put on my pain mask and looked at her. She softened. But the suspicion was in her eyes, a hot, white dot. I went up to my room and called Manny. A hoarse, pale voice answered, like a leaf in strong wind. I said good evening and asked if I could speak to Manny Lahav. I made my voice smaller for politeness. The hoarse voice cleared its throat, but whatever was lodged there wouldn't come out. I heard her call Manny's name. He sounded hoarse too, though in a different way. A hoarseness of cracks and exhaustion, not phlegm. He asked to what he owed the pleasure of my call. I stuck to sweetness but let my sadness trickle down, like in a dream, when you hear random words, or even say them, and underneath them is an unrelated sorrow. I have dreams like that, where as soon as the words come out of my mouth they turn out to be a plank floating through a sea of sorrow. But without the plank, you can't fathom the sea. I told him Oshri and I were working on a memorial presentation for Elish and gathering testimonials from his friends. He said maybe that wasn't healthy for us. I told him it was all I could think about. I could hear him thinking, Poor girl. He asked what I needed. I asked if he could make some time for us to film him the next time he came to Sderot. He said he had no plans to come down at the moment. I said I'd heard from my father that he was supposed to give him keys. He said, Oh, the keys to Elish's apartment, the police are going to give those back. Surprised, I asked why the police had the keys. He said they had a few loose ends to tie up. I asked which ones. He said it was late and this wasn't appropriate. I asked why, if it was because I was a child. I made my voice bigger for the sake of assertiveness, my mature voice, and said I'd helped Elish with the Heftzi Columbus investigation. He chuckled, which was clearly involuntary, and said I was such a sweet girl, but that some matters weren't appropriate for me. He said Elish told him I read a lot and had a vivid imagination. I told him Elish would never say I had a vivid imagination. He said I was right, that was his own addition. I said he could see for himself I was good at deductions. He paused for a long time. Then he said I talked like my uncle, and that he hadn't been able to protect him, but he wasn't about to let me walk toward danger with eyes wide open. I asked what he meant, if Elish had been in danger. He said there were certain questions it was better not to ask. I said adults always said that when they hit a wall. He hung up.

I sat on my bed and balled my hands into fists, pressing my fingernails into the flesh. A cry grew inside of me that I couldn't swallow and couldn't release. I called Ronnit and she picked up. I screamed at her, told her everything I thought, asked her where she'd been when Elish needed her, why did she break up with him, why did she leave him all alone? She listened in silence, not interrupting, not reacting, until the words grew blank inside my mouth, like the inside of a loaf of bread that you chew until it becomes a paste. She said she understood my anger. Another thing grown-ups say, that they understand anger. No one can understand anger. Anger is like grief. At some point it becomes an independent creature, detached from its causes. I didn't know that then. I only got madder, only got more frustrated. She said I'd understand when I got older, that we hope to fix the men we love, but that what they seek wasn't to be fixed but rather to be forgiven for their flaws, to be granted permission to hold on to them. And you walk into their whirlwind, and at some point you realize you've given up a lot of yourself just to be there. And what for? Your beloved loved somebody else and insisted on you being her. She said she didn't get it either, just like me, that she was searching for answers too.

I said nothing, letting the anger drip. I asked her if she'd ever heard about Yehuda Menuhin. She said no. I told her I thought Elish had been investigating his suicide when the two of them first met. She said no, that they'd met when Elish was doing research for a book about Dalia Shushan. She didn't know anything more than that, only that when she met him a year later he told her he'd decided to shelve the book. Then she said all sorts of condolences I couldn't bear to listen to, and said she'd talk to my mom and suggest floral extracts that could help me, and proposed that I say the Shema prayer in bed every night, that it healed the soul and brought peace. I hung up. I knew Elish's methods. If he'd been writing a book about Dalia Shushan, then I was a monkey's uncle, and I'll be a monkey's aunt if he was working on a book about Heftzi Columbus. He was still investigating, in that secretive style of his. Something about Dalia Shushan's death didn't compute for him. I knew it in my veins and arteries, it was no coincidence that he was investigating both cases at once. There was a connection there, and now he was dead because of one of them. Or both.

MY INTEPHONE VIBRATED ON THE TABLE IN THE LOCKDOWN corner. I drank my coffee slowly. Or I thought I did. When I picked up the cup, it was cold. I wondered if I'd made a fresh cup or if this was still the one from the light breakfast I'd made after Oshri left. I looked at the visual conferencing request. Avdiel. I only approved an audio channel. He asked if everything was all right. I said yes. He said I sounded sleepy. I said I was always like this when I wasn't active, faux-sleepy. He said he'd never seen me unenergetic. I caught the insinuation, but I let it slide. He knows I'm private. He wouldn't dare ask me for visual conferencing after I only turned on audio. I asked if everything was all right in terms of security shifts. He said yes, Marco wasn't planning on lowering the alert level even though things were fairly quiet, and he believed the showy attack would still come, if not from a Palestinian organization then from some remains of a right-wing or left-wing underground, or just a band of disgruntled rioters. Like he even needed to tell me that. We raised the alert level two months ago, when negotiations started over the Israeli and Palestinian canton venture. I asked if he'd switched between digital observation methods and human recon tours, if the patterns were random, if he was conducting surprise visits to the three MKI sites under our faction's jurisdiction, and where he was calling from. He said he was in the command room at the Ashdod site. I told him to say hi to Oshri, who was on the way over. He said he just missed him, he was told he'd already come and gone, he's quick, that Oshri.

Avdiel said there were no updates from the Palestinian parallel. Israel had helped establish the MKI site in Ramallah. Before they started talks, they wisely founded a combined force of Israeli fighter forces with the military of the United Palestinian

Authority. Marco was one of the consultants. The combined force is efficient. It maintains order on both sides, as much as any order can be maintained in the chaos that has ensued ever since 2019. I asked Avdiel why he was calling. He said Marco had asked him if he'd been in touch with me and how I was doing. When I asked Marco for leave to take care of a family matter, his large eyes, with their misleading softness, rested on me. He said he was surprised, though there was no surprise in his face, only his usual expression of indecipherable emotion about to burst out, compassion maybe, or a longing tattooed onto his muscles and facial features. That's where he got the nickname his commanders gave him back in military service, after a character from an animated show they watched as children. I found a clip in the Virtualia archives. Trembling, crude animation. But I could see what they meant. He really did look like a child searching for his mother. It was an amazing camouflage. He was a brilliant, calculating strategist. With him, every form of emotion was taken into account, a piece of data to weigh. I didn't have to come up with a story for him. He trusted me. He knew I wouldn't be asking for leave if it wasn't an emergency. I liked the quiet understanding between us. He was one of those people who could see a few steps ahead, who realized the military structure was being undermined and would be undergoing a profound change following the 2019 riots. For far too long, the illusion of a people's army covered up the fact that the military was made up of different social strata, or at least created the impression that there was a balance between them. But the riots collapsed that illusion. Marco started Civil Legion, a security company intended from the start to become a private army, or an independent mercenary arm of the military.

At my job interview, he asked me for one thing: to pick one of the gangs and undergrounds that had popped up all over the world, numerous independent terror organizations, small-fry groups taking pleasure in violence. He wanted me to make a presentation, analyzing my chosen group's patterns of action. He knew everything about my past, being kicked out of the officer training course, my attempts to join one of the Israeli undergrounds myself after I was discharged. I was lost back then, and bitter. Because I was two years too late. Two years after being drafted. Two years after the darkness of the All-Rights, the new ruling party that cruelly oppressed any idea that was too extreme, left or right, and any form of criticism or atypical thought, using the military as a police force. Two years after the exterminations, after the siege on Jewish outposts in the occupied territories and the dismantling of yeshivas. Two years after the invasion into universities and the general censorship law. I was part of it too. I beat and cuffed young people who were only a few years older than me, I helped break up protests, I shot rubber bullets into a crowd that probably contained people I knew. To me, they were enemies of the system. But two years later, the All-Rights shattered, along with their amiable leader, whose entire essence was a fear of angering anybody. The combined ruling party figured it out. They based their methods on writings by an expatriate Israeli thinker who wrote about military states. He argued that Israel was a clear-cut military state. The military edicts dictated civilian mentality. As long as the military was founded on combat units, the state had to be a country fighting for its own survival. It was never the other way around. The head of the combined party invited him on as a private consultant. He suggested changing the IDF's focus, determined that Israel's true resource was military know-how, not training itself. The new government claimed it was the first step toward transforming Israel into a civilian state. Then they started establishing Military Knowledge Industries. Oshri enjoyed the spoils. They tracked him down and recruited him to the first graduating class of MKI.

I hated what I'd become, hated having the opportunity taken away from me over and over again, arbitrarily, outside of my control. Most of the anti-free-speech laws were overturned upon the rise of the combined ruling party. I wandered among coffee shops in Tel Aviv, Beersheba, even Haifa, and listened to lectures by gurus who didn't realize yet they were gurus. Sickening narcissists who considered themselves revolutionary philosophers. Whatever. I listened and listened, participated in rallies, joined protest actions I'm ashamed of to this day, all in the name of ideas I didn't believe in. I wanted to object, I wanted to voice my objection, I wanted to kick, I wanted to smash, I wanted the pain in my chest to thaw, to go away. I couldn't say exactly what it was I'd been promised, but I could say it was taken away from me, that I, who'd spent my entire life biting anyone who tried to neuter me, had been neutered without even noticing it.

Marco saw that. He told me himself. After I analyzed the gang of female rapists from New York. Their leader was a rape victim. Such a terrible term, "rape victim." A woman who'd been raped by three men at a party. She was a lawyer, a rising star in her law firm. In the video posted by the rapists, she talked about how there would never be true gender equality, that it wasn't an issue of economic division or historical injustice, because no matter how much money or status a woman gained, the most lowlife man in the world could break her down and destroy her in fifteen minutes by raping her. So she was going to even things out. She was going to institutionalize the rape of males as a viable option. She and her followers went on nightly rape rampages, hunting down men and taking them by force with dildos. Their slogan was "no man is safe." In conclusion, I said the diagnosis was correct but the treatment was erroneous. Marco nodded. His trembling velvet gaze didn't mislead me. He saw me, he could tell that I could tell that in spite of his empathetic expression, he wasn't only listening to what I was saying. He was listening to that story told by my body, and my eye movements, and my changes in tone. He said I was a fit, but that we'd have to see how my training went.

At our conference, I told Avdiel to tell Marco I was touched by his concern, that I knew how sensitive he was. Avdiel laughed briefly. He always laughs like that. Once, I asked him what the name Avdiel meant. His mother was a professor at a settlers' college, and liked that name because of a poem about how the slaves of time are the slaves of slaves, and only God's slave is truly free. I said it was another one of those stories religious people came up with so as not to take responsibility for their actions, but that there was no real freedom in this world, only cease-fires. He laughed that annoying laugh of his, just like he did now. He said it sounded like I'd finally woken up. I said that was good, because I had things to do. He said he would be interested in seeing my chill side. The word "chill" made me feel sick. I told him he just had to learn how to look.

BACK IN MY BEDROOM, I PULLED A NEW NOTEBOOK OUT OF MY drawer. On the front page I wrote *TYO Investigations and the Mystery of the Lost Detective* and wrote down notes from my conversations with Manny and Ronnit. The lines on the page were dry and cold, containing nothing of the stapling of the daytime-light and nighttimedark to my body. They were clean of the longing that had replaced them, which I felt like a shudder on the edge of everything. The letters were pretty. Pure.

The next day, I shared my discoveries with Yalon and Oshri. They agreed there was a connection between Elish's different investigations, but we had no idea where to go from there, how to get information. For a moment, I thought about texting Elish, asking for advice, and then the thought was gone and a blow came instead, and the air turned black all around me. Oshri suggested we listen to Blasé et Sans Lumière songs. I asked what for, did he think we'd find any clues there? He whispered that it was only a suggestion and I didn't have to attack him. I said I wasn't attacking, but that he should try making sense. He said he was the only one making sense, and went to his room. Yalon said it was an awesome idea. He connected his iPhone to my Bluetooth speaker and hit PLAY.

I can't describe what happened to me. The way Dalia Shushan sang, she didn't sing from the outside, music that reached me through my ears. She sang from the inside, and I helped her lead her singing into the room, into the speaker, to put it there, let it be. I lay down on the bed. Yalon lay down on the rug, and we listened.

It became a ritual of ours, Yalon's and mine, to lie around and listen to the two albums, back-to-back. After that we'd talk about how we'd continue our investigation, about his parents' breakup, his decision to stay with his father, and how hard his father was trying, that he hadn't tried that hard since they'd gone to Italy together, just the two of them, eighteen months earlier. We talked about Dalia Shushan's music and how it changed with us. We read Elish's book, cover to cover, and asked ourselves if what he wrote about Blasé matched how we felt. One time, Oshri joined us. He said the music and the singing sounded like they contained coded messages. It was an odd idea, even for me. But for a few days afterward, Yalon and I tried to find messages, twisting the lyrics and the music to make them sound like cryptic lines. It made us laugh. Yalon said I was a super-bad singer and my musical ear was for shit.

One evening, Oshri knocked on the door and came in. I was lying on the bed with my head dangling toward the floor and Yalon was lying on the rug with his head held up, so our faces were close. Yalon's face looked like a planet you see from the window of a spaceship in sci-fi movies, gray matter wrinkled into mountains and continents. In his concise manner, Oshri said the police had just returned the keys. I lost my sense of direction. Instead of sitting up, I plopped down. Yalon laughed. I stood up, dizzy. I asked if Manny Lahav had come over. He said no, the police called and Dad stopped by the Tel Aviv precinct on his way home from up north and picked up the keys. Yalon asked, What keys? I told him they were the keys to Elish's apartment. Oshri retreated and was just about to shut the door. I called him back. I asked if he even knew what he meant. He said I shouldn't even think about it. Yalon asked what I was thinking about. I said we could go to Tel Aviv, to Elish's apartment, to continue our investigation. Oshri said again that it was a bad idea and left.

It took me two days to talk him into it. He asked why I wanted him to come. I said, What do you care, I want you to, maybe it's a superstition. Finally, he agreed, under one condition. He always poses conditions, but so do I. Not conditions exactly, but protections and promises. He said he'd join to prevent me from doing anything stupid, but that I had to swear to join him on his own journey when he asked me to. Not to nag, not to create difficulties, just to say yes. I said we'd make a deal, that from now on if one of us had to go on a journey the other would say yes, no questions asked, no challenges posed. He nodded. I asked if he was already planning something. He didn't answer.

We set a time to meet outside school. The school year had reached its exhausting phase anyway, just a horizon of days and slow classes, Hanukkah still miles away. We walked to the train station. We walked in silence. We were nervous. We had trouble with the ticket machine, because even though we had our money ready, the coin slot wouldn't take Yalon's ten shekels. Yalon said it must be a fake coin and slapped the machine. It worked. Some skinny guy stood near us. Skinny from dieting, not skinny by nature. People are either round or flat, fat or thin. When thin people get round, they look like they've puffed up, not gained weight. When fat people lose weight, they look deflated. Manny Lahav, for example, is round, but he insists on turning flat. The result is unpleasant, like their body got squeezed by a vise. Like pants that were taken in but are still loose. That's what the guy who followed us was like. He was firm around the base, but trying hard to be a twig. He looked starving. There was curiosity in his eyes, not evil, but I still felt uncomfortable when he looked us over. Yalon seemed to be flinching too, pushing into himself to keep the skinny guy from seeing him. Long story short, I wasn't a fan.

He came up to us later on the train. Oshri ignored him and

read his book. He knew Yalon, the skinny guy, he called him by his name. I looked at Yalon. His face turned white. I could tell he didn't want to be there. The skinny guy didn't catch Yalon's hint to get out of there and fast. Instead, he started snooping around. He said his name was Nahum Farkash and that he managed the public library. He spoke to Yalon. Yalon didn't answer. I wasn't surprised. Everybody in Sderot knows Yalon's dad, so I didn't really buy that Farkash guy's friendly act, not that I could figure out what he truly wanted. Anyway, I'm convinced that's how our parents heard about our trip. He must have told Yalon's dad, who told our dad. When we got back Mom was in the living room, livid. She sort of kept this frozen tone, her pupils small. But her mouth was stretched down to soften the tension in her jaw. The corners of her lips stood out unusually. She just asked about the keys we'd duplicated. I placed them on the counter. She asked if we took anything from the apartment. I lied that we didn't. We couldn't find anything to help us anyway, other than Elish's notepads that were in my bag. And perhaps something else that we didn't want to take with us. Oshri started feeling upset when we went inside the apartment, and by the time we left he was totally pale. He felt better on the way home, good enough for our mother not to notice in the confusion of her anger.

SHULA, RIGHT? YOUR NAME SUITS YOU, SOMEHOW. IT RINGS true. We met, we're meeting, we will meet. When? We should cancel the word "when." Throw it out. When we ask when, we really mean where. Language makes us confused about time. It pretends to show us the way time is, but it only demonstrates the way we feel time. After Elish died, I thought a lot about time, feeling time but not realizing what I was feeling. I thought about ways to think outside of time, tried to understand more. Because I think that, first of all, it can't be that all that's left is memory, that things we thought were in the past are just inside of us.

Because even inside of us all that is is matter, say a cluster of brain cells, a piece of brain. That means that the past is physical. And second of all, how can it be that things that are contain the qualities of things that *used* to be? If we go into our thoughts, how can we say this was then, and that's happening now? What is the quality of being *then?* Where is it? And if it exists, then it exists now. So it turns out that everything always is, always in the now, always in the world.

But I'm not explaining it well. Language is confusing me again. I'll try another tack, something I'd guessed earlier but could only explain after all those navigation excursions during basic training and Civil Legion training. Say that X happens to me at exactly twelve o'clock, and Y happens to Oshri at the exact same second, five hundred meters away. I know what happened to me, but in order to know what happened to Oshri I have to cross those five hundred meters, and it takes, say, five minutes. So as far as I'm concerned something happened to me at twelve and something happened to Oshri five minutes later. Those five minutes are in the sensation of time, not in reality. I can take that five-hundred-meter, five-minute gap and stretch it to the size of the universe. Everything in the universe happens simultaneously, but not in the way we sense it. Or maybe that's another, unrelated explanation. I should have said, Third of all.

I thought it was strange that Yalon didn't understand these thoughts of mine at all. We were sixteen, and the cracks had started to show. But he grew up on *Doctor Who,* which is a show with a primitive perception of time, because even though the doctor goes to wherever and whenever he wants, he still thinks about time as something separate with rules of its own.

I don't want to philosophize too much. Philosophizing leaves a bad taste in my mouth, like a lie I'm telling myself. I have no problem lying to others, and I recommend that you also practice the art of lying and deception; otherwise, how would you be able to tell that you're being lied to and deceived all the time? Suddenly,

Oshri's phrase popped into my mind, leading them down the garden path. Our mom once said I'd had her and Dad wrapped around my finger ever since I was a baby, and Oshri said, Not wrapped around her finger, leading you down the garden path, that's what Elish used to say. Mom's eyes filled with cotton balls. And I looked at Oshri. And he squeezed his mouth so as not to cry. By "once," I meant the time we returned from our first journey, the journey to Elish's apartment. I appreciated the way he'd sacrificed his pain like that, just to get me out of trouble.

I didn't notice Oshri coming in. He must have opened the door quietly. I looked up and he was in the doorway to the living room, watching me, no, examining me. He asked if I'd had anything to eat. I said I wasn't hungry and that it was still early. He told me to look at the clock. I blinked quickly to turn on the time gauge in the augmented reality lenses. It was twenty past two.

He walked over to the table and pulled a dark velvet case out of his bag. He asked how long I thought he'd spent talking to Nitzan the previous evening. I said I thought it was a few minutes, that he'd come back faster than usual. He said they'd spoken close to an hour. He moved his hand against the screen of his intePhone Extreme. The crystal boards of the SmartWall turned on. He turned on the video player. I appeared on the wall screen, sitting at the table, staring into space. The video was fifty-seven minutes long. He fast forwarded. Not much happened. I was sitting in the chair in the lockdown corner, staring ahead, or not. I was completely absorbed in some thought, occasionally shifting in my seat. Oshri said something was wrong, that he wanted to run a few tests. He pulled a white strap, half-transparent, made of bendy plastic. He steadied it and pulled out paper-thin metal arms from the edges. When he was finished he was holding a sort of tiara with metal thorns poking out of it. He placed the strap on my head, sliding it until the tiara surrounded my forehead. He adjusted the arms. I felt the cool kiss of their edges against my scalp. He leaned over the InteMon and the virtual keyboard it projected. He said he hoped nobody at Nitzan's lab would need this neuro monitor today, that he didn't want to get her in trouble, and that he'd put me under observation for now.

IN THE WEEKS AFTER WE RETURNED FROM ELISH'S APARTMENT, Oshri had spells of exhaustion. He called it "exhaustion," but actually it was ennui. For example, he'd be sitting with me and Yalon, then suddenly say he was tired and going to lie down in his room. I didn't pay it much mind at first, but the evidence slowly accumulated. The teachers told our parents that he'd laid his head down on his desk during class and seemed to be dozing off, and asked if he was getting enough sleep at night. I saw him in his room, plopped on the bed, one of his books on the rug. I asked if the book was boring, and he said sometimes he felt like no book would ever be interesting again.

But he would recover a few hours later, get his flavor back, get his energy back, and everyone would relax, except for Mom, who insisted on taking him to the doctor and requested bloodwork and consulted with psychologists. Everyone told her it was just a phase, that intellectually he was ahead of the curve for his age and maybe he needed more stimulation. Dad made him go outside every day, to get moving, as he put it, get some air. Oshri would obediently go for long walks in the thicket. I tried to evade his eyes, not that there was something missing inside of him and the eyes revealed it, just the fact that the world that reflected in them was pale and meager, a world without any spark or power or beauty.

One morning, during that dense routine, Yalon called when I was on my way to school and asked if I'd heard that someone was making a movie about Dalia Shushan in Sderot and that everybody was talking about it. When he said "everybody," he meant his Facebook friends. Since when were his Facebook friends everybody? And anyway, they weren't even friends, just strangers who'd pasted over their stranger tag with a sticker reading

FRIENDS. Why can't we lie less, come up with a name to distinguish them, say, fauriends, faux-friends, or allyiens, alien allies, something like that?

Of course I hadn't heard. Mom was checking to make sure I hadn't opened a Facebook account. She said she built this home to keep us safe and she wouldn't be installing a pervert entrance. Over the summer, when the war was going on, I opened an account to see what the whole deal with Facebook was, but the fakery grossed me out, it was so gross, all those ingratiators and trolls, phony, repulsive. I started an Instagram account too, pressured by Racheli and Elinoar, who said I should have one just for the filtered pictures of funny stuff, just that and Snapchat, so everyone could see I had an eye for funny too, like butt-ugly pictures of what I'd look like in fifty years, what some girl would look like if you merged her face with a dog's. A boy from junior year asked me to be his girlfriend after I posted a few photos, but that was a super-hard pass for me.

I told Yalon that of course I hadn't heard. He said there was a development, because Nahum Farkash, from the train, was objecting to the film. We didn't only remember the name from the train, it also appeared in Elish's notes in the Heftzi Columbus investigation pad. Even though we were involved in that investigation, we'd never heard of him. His name was framed with a thick rectangle in Elish's notepad with an arrow coming out of it. Near the head of the arrow, the letters *DS* appeared alongside a question mark. We didn't understand all of Elish's markings. His handwriting wasn't always legible, and some stuff was written in code, or so claimed Oshri, and Yalon agreed with him, but it was obvious to us that DS stood for Dalia Shushan, and that Elish was asking himself if Nahum Farkash was connected to that investigation as well. What we couldn't figure out was whether or not Elish thought all those deaths were connected, Dalia Shushan's, Yehuda Menuhin's, and Heftzi Columbus's. And I added Elish Ben Zaken's to the list. I wrote my conjectures in the notebook.

I said this was the confirmation we'd been looking for, that Nahum Farkash was connected to Dalia Shushan, and we could move on with our investigation. Yalon said he hadn't even thought about that, that he was excited about the film and wanted us to go to the locations, maybe even be part of the movie like some of those crazy people who shove into every paparazzi shot, that it could be hilarious if we were in the background of half of the scenes and no one but us would know it was actually our film. I smiled when I pictured us going to the movie theater and watching a secret film, a different one than everyone else, a film that was just ours inside a film that was everyone else's. Then I thought maybe it was always like that. Yalon said it would be our own Dalia Shushan movie. Then I felt a little blue, like a rash that spreads the more you scratch it.

But the Nahum Farkash investigation did not go as planned. It was Yalon's fault. All of a sudden, Nahum Farkash mentioned Elish. He called him Elish Ben Zaken, may he rest in peace, and I looked at Yalon, because how would Nahum Farkash know about Elish and about us? And when his name with that gross addition, "may he rest in peace," rolled through his mouth, it was like a knife in my stomach, a knife in my breath. A wounded animal can't be a detective. A detective can't be a wounded animal.

Yalon didn't want to let go. A column by Nahum Farkash explaining his objection to the film had been published in the *Southern Wind.* Yalon came over on Saturday afternoon, and we sat in my room. Oshri joined us. His hour or two of daily exhaustion had already happened in the morning, and he was over it. The article was too long and unclear. Nahum Farkash wrote about sci-fi and about being religious and all sorts of irrelevant stuff. But he mentioned us, and the article was full of clues about corruption in city hall, which we knew about from the Heftzi Columbus investigation. Yalon got enthused because things were heating up and there was action. Oshri said Nahum Farkash was hiding something. I said he knew about us and part of the article's intention was to get us to talk to him. He'd known about us since the train, it was no coincidence he'd bugged us then. I said it was only because he'd recognized Yalon. Yalon said they didn't even know each other. I didn't understand Yalon's lying. I told him that. He said he didn't even know that Nahum guy and that it was only because his aunt, his mom's older sister, worked at the library. I thought he was lying and that his dad must have some kind of in at the library and Yalon was embarrassed to admit it. Why was he defending his dad, did his dad need someone to defend him? He asked if I was sure I wanted to go meet him again, because last time I wasn't ready for it. What was he even talking about? I was super focused on my mission. Oshri said he'd come too. He wanted to borrow some books.

OSHRI PLACED A SANDWICH BESIDE ME. I TOLD HIM HE DIDN'T have to worry about feeding me, that this nourishing was a type of control. He said I was confusing control with care. I told him that any exaggerated emotion was exaggerated for the purpose of control. He took the plate away and said, Then go ahead and starve. I smiled. I snatched up the sandwich and took a bite. Whole-wheat bread, 5 percent fat white cheese with fresh cucumber and tomato. What a delicacy. He said it was Nitzan's trick. What trick? I said. He said, Seasoning the vegetables separately with olive oil, salt, and pepper before adding them to the sandwich. I said it was different from how Mom did it, putting the vegetables on the bread and cheese and then sprinkling salt and pepper on top. He said when he went to Sderot on Saturday, Grandma Zehava asked when I'd come see her. I didn't answer. She can barely hear now, and she's lost in a sequence of private time and space that she can't always shake off. She talks to me about her father, whom she lost as a child before they even came to Israel, about Grandpa Prosper, about Elish, all the men in her life who died young. The last time I came, she said she may have waited too long, and that by the time she got where they were she'd be old and they'd still be strong and virile, and what would they do with an old lady like her, what would they talk about? I couldn't listen to her. Even though this flow of words was my fault. I was the one who'd asked about her father. I never imagined the question would peel the scab off a wound inside her soul, the kind that doesn't close back up so easily at her age.

Mom asked why I was in such a rush to get back to Tel Aviv. I told her I was doing a surprise inspection of my faction at the MKI site in Herzliya. She said they'd be fine without me for one day and that I shouldn't leave my grandmother all alone. My parents brought her to live with them a few years ago. They disagreed about a lot of things, but not about that. Dad said Grandma Zehava was like his second mother. But Grandma Zehava fought them for her independence. She insisted the live-in assistant her social security paid for was enough. Until she could no longer go down the stairs by herself.

Oshri returned. He turned on all the crystal boards again and the wall screen spread out to full size. He bent over his keyboard. The display was divided in two. On the left, the camera zoomed in on my face, and on the right was a brain activity graph. At some point, my features relaxed, turning serene. Oshri zoomed in and my eyes flickered. The shape, the pattern of the brain activity graph, changed accordingly. Oshri said I was going into a deep dream state. He moved his hand over his intePhone screen. The graph shifted to the top boards of its half. In the bottom boards, data flows appeared. Oshri said all the vitals in my biofeedback were normal, pointing to a fully awake body. He said it was deep daydreaming, but not actually dreaming. Reverie, he said I was reverying. I said he'd use any opportunity to come up with a new word. He said it was because he couldn't think of any existing term to describe my state, and that he wanted to run a blood test.

I was silent for a few seconds, considering this. I said no, I didn't want that. He asked why I minded. I said I knew he would stop the experiment as soon as he detected a hint of abnormality. He said of course, that was his condition to begin with. I said I wouldn't have it, not now, not when it was working. He reminded me I'd promised him he'd have full discretion. I said that was true, but that we were stepping into unfamiliar territory, how were we even supposed to know what— He cut me off. He said that's what protocols were for, that I didn't understand the difference between studying and getting lost. I asked who'd made him an expert. He said I was just as reckless as Elish, and that Elish had died from it. I said we'd been through that before. He said he was disconnecting the devices. I said what good would that do, if I was already under the effect of the typhus bacteria? He said he'd call Marco and tell him I'd been infected with a rare disease and had to be hospitalized. I said I'd tell on him to his commanders.

He yelled that I had no boundaries, that I got everyone I knew into trouble with my curiosity, that when we were little he'd thought it was courage but now he thought it was stupidity, that maybe I was just like Elish, that at some point people yearned. He fell silent. I said, Yearned for what? He said, All these riddles—as soon as the investigators become involved, they yearn to become a death riddle themselves. That's what protocols were for. For protection. I said he was getting carried away. He said he had to go think in peace. He turned away from me and went to the living room doorway. I called out after him that he was a coward who'd chosen to leave me on my own even though I'd never do the same to him. He turned around and whispered my name. He said, Tahel, and the syllables of the name were filled with sadness, as if a wind were whistling through them. I hadn't heard that sadness in him since the time he told me he was one of the kids who stayed. He said if the people close to me weren't with me, then they were alone, that's what everyone who cared about me found out eventually. He'd already forgiven me for not being there for him when he needed me, but he wasn't talking about himself. I yelled, Who, then, who's everyone who cares about me, Yalon? He didn't answer. He left.

I hated him in those moments. Hated him for knowing me, for missing everything, for knowing me by his own terms, for recognizing the important things in me but judging me according to his own values rather than trying to imagine for a moment what it was like to be me. I hated him for using it to hurt me. That burning lava boiled inside of me, the muscles stretching to let loose with a shattering and a scream. How dare he tell me I posed conditions to those I loved? Me, who fought so hard for him.

BUT THE BURST DIDN'T LAST LONG. A COOL BREEZE ENTERED MY roiling blood, like a wave of air from a cooling system. There was a comforting presence around me, not by virtue of action or words, just the knowledge that it existed was soothing. We were in Elish's apartment, and even though Oshri had lived there for a few years, introducing his changes, tiling the walls with smart crystal boards, laying cables and connecting adapters and routers and monitors, Elish's being was like a see-through coat of paint over everything. His desk became our experiment table. My elbows leaned against the wood, sensing the vibrations that had run through it as Elish wrote his notes, made his investigations, wrote his Benny Zehaviv books.

But that comfort was gone too, and my thoughts were jumbled, mad, and quiet all at once. Oshri was in the lockdown corner again, saying he was back, the shadow man was back. There was excitement in his voice. I asked what he was talking about. He said I'd just spent twenty minutes talking to the shadow man. He showed me the recording, spreading the wall screen and splitting it into four. Each part showed the feed from a different camera at a different angle. The shadow man stood across from me, close, pixelated and edited into the duplicate reality of documentation, and my hands moved, accompanying the silent speech I may have been emitting from inside. I watched in silence. Clarity slowly spread through me. I told Oshri that this was proof that our experiment was working. He said he wanted to take a blood sample now, because in terms of vitals there was no change at all, not in temperature, not in pulse, not in blood sugar levels monitored by the lenses—I was regular in everything besides brain activity. He brought that up on the screen. The graph lines were all over the levels of the Y axis of frequency throughout the shadow man's visit. Oshri said we had to read the graph by way of elimination, because my brain was active in almost every frequency, but it transmitted no alpha waves and no delta waves. I asked what that meant. He said he was no expert. He'd spent all night reading materials Nitzan had sent him, but a superficial reading of the graph showed that I was simultaneously in an extreme emotional state and a state of strong focus, learning, and creativity, but neither in routine nor in deep sleep mode. He said it didn't make sense. I asked what exactly about this thing we were doing *did* make sense. We'd completely abandoned logic when we started this project. He said that was exactly what he was trying to tell me.

I still hadn't forgiven his words. Indignation was still lit up all over me. But I needed him. I asked what was different from before. He said that when I was reverying there was mostly theta-wave activity, which characterizes a state of learning or recollecting, or hallucination. It was a single concentrated state, while here I was in a few conflicting states all at once, both collapsing under the burden of emotional overload and in deep meditation.

I said I had no idea how to translate that into feelings. I could only say I felt Elish's presence, intensely, that's all I remembered. He asked if I meant that I talked to the shadow man about Elish. I said I didn't know if I talked, but that the traces Elish left in this apartment, traces of his life, his thought, beamed out, beamed to me, were more real to me than anything else.

Oshri asked what I thought this meant for the manifestations of Richard Perotz and of Olga Kovilishin and Kalanit Shaubi. It couldn't be about Elish. I said the manifestations couldn't be identical if they were a projection of our minds, and that in my case the shadow man was about Elish and we had to find the connection. He asked what I was getting at. I said that he told me the shadow man was an anti-being, a hole in the papercutting of the texture of life, and that it followed that he was Elish's anti-being. He repeated the phrase, "Elish's anti-being," and said, Unelish. He pronounced the syllables carefully, fretfully, and asked what we should do about our Unelish. I said we had to answer a different question first: Whether I'd summoned him or whether he'd shown up on his own, and if I had summoned him, then how? Oshri said it was a shame we had no way of measuring the mental pheromone discharge, and that he was stepping out to get Nitzan's advice about a more accurate reading of the graph because he was sure he was missing something. I said, Yes, you might miss the sunset. He smiled, but behind his smile I saw his suspicion, he was still afraid, he wasn't willing to go all the way with me. I thought he might have been a little bit right, that I erase anyone who isn't with me.

My intePhone sent a conferencing request alert. Mom. I only turned on an audio channel. She said she couldn't see me. I got up from the lockdown corner and walked into the study Oshri had inherited from Elish. I'd wanted no part of the inheritance. When Oshri turned eighteen, our parents suggested we sell the apartment. It was worth a lot, and Oshri and I could split the money between us. I said I'd give up my part and Oshri could keep it. They suggested we rent it out, said that it was a shame to keep it standing there, empty. I said if Oshri wanted to do that he was welcome to. He refused to sell or lease it. He insisted he wanted to live there. I was kind of surprised. After all, that was the place where he'd shown first signs of the long depression that went on to last almost three years. Was that really where he wanted to return to? But Oshri said he needed independence. He was willing to pay me half of the rent we would have made. I said no. The fact that Elish had written a will, that he'd left the apartment to me and Oshri, and signed royalties from his book in Grandma Zehava's name, was stifling. What did I need this weight of memory for, to remember him under his own terms? I wouldn't do it. Besides, Manny said his death case was closed because he'd left a will, which showed intent. Who writes a will at age forty?

Mom asked where I was. I told her I was visiting Oshri. She was surprised. She said she thought I had no time to breathe, so how come I was making time for my brother? I knew she was really complaining about the fact that I didn't visit her. I turned on the video channel. Her almond eyes looked me over, searching for something. She said Grandma Zehava missed me. I said nothing. She asked if everything was all right. I said the usual. She asked what was going on with Marco. I said nothing. I'd invited him to our holiday dinner last Rosh Hashanah. He'd just broken up with his wife and he was all alone. Ever since then, she's been claiming we're meant to be. It makes no difference to her that he's thirteen years older than me, as long as he doesn't have children. She says children are the obstacle. I told her I thought he was seeing someone. She said I shouldn't write off opportunities when they come my way. Some opportunity, I said. She said Yalon came to visit yesterday, that his dad's company won a bid to build a residential neighborhood not far from the MKI Ashdod site, a luxury neighborhood for scientists, and that he'd come to talk to Dad about electrical infrastructure, that he'd asked about me. I didn't respond. So that's what she was getting at. Asking about Marco was only her way of softening me up. She said Yalon had broken up with Agam, his girlfriend of the past two years. As if she'd coordinated with Oshri, she said I had no appreciation for love because men have been offering it to me ever since I was a little girl, that it had started with my father and my uncle, and that other people were willing to give up a lot for just the hint of a promise of love. She said I should look at Oshri, how he'd gotten mixed up with that Nitzan, who wasn't good enough for his pinky toe. She twisted up her mouth and nose like she'd just smelled something foul. I told her not to bring Oshri into this, that Nitzan made him happy. I swallowed when I said this, because I realized how much it mattered to me, Oshri's happiness, because being happy mattered to him. I myself found little use for happiness. I told her people chose to make mistakes even when experience had taught them differently, mostly to avoid undermining norms, and that the problem lay with them, not me.

IT WAS WINTER WHEN WE WENT TO SEE NAHUM FARKASH. HE wasn't there when we arrived, and the librarian from the adult circulation room almost jumped on Yalon when we walked in to ask about him. She leaped out of her seat so quickly that it fell, along with the books on her desk. Yalon pulled away. She asked what was new with him. He barely answered. When I looked at her I actually did see the resemblance to his mother. She was like her, but more wrinkled, her skin white but a grainy white, like she was a piece of schnitzel that had been dipped in flour but not yet fried. I felt Oshri pulling away from us, headed for the youth reading room. He wasn't uncomfortable and he didn't care. Not even about Yalon. Too bad. The librarian opened her arms to Yalon and he lowered his head, and those bangs of his covered his eyes. Then all of a sudden the smile was wiped off her face, and it turned hard, no longer a chicken breast, more like stone. She signaled to me, pointing at Nahum Farkash's office, and told us to wait inside.

It wouldn't have been cool to ask Yalon what had happened. It was obvious it had to do with his mother. After we were quiet for a while, Nahum showed up, Oshri with him, carrying a pile of books. I thought it was a good sign, him asking Nahum to borrow them. Nahum spoke to us as if we were adults, but without looking at us. He still looked starved, with the hollows in his cheeks and his prominent bones. But in his eyes there was a warm spark of action. I followed their movement as they shifted from us, sitting in front of him, to the library's yard. Outside the window were trees without leaves, and a beam of light rested frozen on the ground, like a layer of frost.

He gave us a gift. The whole meeting was just a pretext for the gift. A Dalia Shushan song that nobody else knew. She wrote it for him. I closed my eyes when he played it through his office speakers. I recognized her voice, the way she sang, right away. The recording came from afar, but still close to the blood and bones. I tried to figure out the meaning of this gift, what he was trying to tell us. He said the song was ours now. What did that mean, ours? Yalon was sky-high on the way home. He did donuts on his bike, striding ahead, turning sharply, and yelling, World premiere, world premiere. Now it would have been really weird to ask him about the thing with the librarian. He said we'd definitely get in the movie if we said we had a rare Dalia Shushan recording.

Oshri was quieter than usual. Even though he hadn't listened to the song. As usual, he opened a book and read while we listened. But the song affected him more than us. I had a discussion with Yalon, when we were about sixteen and all of this was behind us, or actually, when we believed that all of this was no longer ahead of us. I asked Yalon if he knew where his self ended. He asked what I meant, and I said, The line after which the not-me begins. He said just a touch above his skin, whatever was past the skin, he couldn't feel directly. I told him I thought it was something else, that sometimes my self expanded until it touched others, even if they were on the other side of the room. He asked if it ever happened to me with him. I said yes, when we touched, I could feel him feeling my touch, or when we talked on the phone, sometimes, my self shot forward through the cellular connection. I said sometimes it was the other way around and the self collapsed. He asked if it was like in *The Man Who Mistook His Wife for a Hat*, when people feel like they're trapped in a dead body, or that limbs don't belong to them, like an arm or a foot. I said not necessarily.

I thought about Oshri that day. It was as if he'd retreated a few inches away from his own skin, and the space between him and his skin was filled with Slime. He rode slowly, sitting upright on his bike, his hands gripping the ends of his handlebars, not bent over like usual, steering with one hand while the bike twisted underneath him. I stopped and waited for him. He nodded when I asked if everything was all right.

It rained for a few days, a drizzle, like mist. Yalon and I looked out my window in the evening and couldn't tell the difference between the air and the lake. We saw Oshri standing on the porch, under the awning, watching as well, but the way his body was taut told me his watching was different. I couldn't resist. I went downstairs to get us something to drink and walked over to him. He turned when I said his name and asked if he wasn't cold. There was a dull pressure of longing in his eyes. He asked if I'd keep my promise to join him. I asked if he meant on his journey. He said yes, when the rain stopped.

The rain stopped. Oshri said we would leave home, we would go to the thicket. The way he said it, quietly, iron in his voice, killed my laughter. I was wondering why he was making such a big deal about wandering the thicket across the lake. He took his backpack, which was fattened up, two water bottles in the side pockets. I asked if he was planning on doing a lot of reading on our journey. He said not at all, there were no books in the backpack. I asked what was in there, then. He said food for the road. I asked how long we were going to stay in the thicket. Not long, he said, we'd walk until we got there.

The ground in the thicket was muddy, and the wet leaves stank. The sun had been shining all day long, and the air was humid with the steam the trees had emitted. I told him we were getting all dirty for no good reason, but he didn't answer. Only when we got closer did I realize where we were heading. The shape of the ground was different because of the digging, but the clearing remained, and where the Sarah Matatov Monument used to be, now there was a dust heap. I thought, Heftzi Columbus's grave. A shiver ran through me. Oshri stopped. He told me to take a good look at the dirt heap. A small puddle, really a tiny one, the size and color of a five-shekel coin, was embedded into the heap. No, it wasn't a puddle. I looked up. The sun was hidden behind some clouds, and the light glided off the edges, painting the tops of the eucalyptus trees with that gold that isn't gold but rather the leaves' desire to radiate. But when it came farther down, it melted into transparency, and no sunbeam or sun ray could have brightened the puddle to make it look like silver, and the more I watched, the more its hue changed to black, then back to silver. Oshri ducked down and slipped a finger into the liquid. His fingertip seemed to be swallowed. He pulled the finger up to the surface, then slipped the finger of his other hand to the opposite point. He spread his fingers and the divot widened, as if it were elastic. The surface area of the liquid expanded. No, it was no rain. A bit of dark fluttering in the light. He pulled more and more until he had no space left between his fingers. Then he pulled them out. The divot and the liquid shrank back with a whipping sound, just like rubber, a kind of scratchy whistle. He told me to help him stretch the divot to its maximal size. We went to work.

WE PULLED ON OPPOSITE ENDS UNTIL THE LIQUID TORE WITH that rip-rappy sound of a piece of clothing ripping. It grew thinner and thinner and could stretch no further. Bits flew everywhere, and the divot stabilized. It became a hole. Not a hole, more like a dark opening, like a wound. I turned on the flashlight function of my iPhone and aimed it inside. There were stairs leading down into a bomb shelter. Oshri grabbed the straps of his backpack, tightening his fingers around them. I told him I'd go down first. He said no, this was his journey. I insisted. The deeper we descended, the brighter things became. We saw more and more, but as if through the wall of an aquarium. Dark, erect trees. The bottom step was completely lit up when Oshri's foot stepped off of it, and the impression of a glass partition was gone. We stood on the ground of a thicket. The falling leaves were dry, like in summer, and the dirt was cracked. But besides that, it was the exact same thicket. No. The sun shone from the opposite direction, as if it were earlier, morning. I looked at my iPhone. It showed a few minutes had gone by, the time hadn't really changed.

I asked Oshri what was next. He said he had no idea, that we should start walking. I asked, Which way? He said, Toward home. I asked, Why there? He said it made sense to him to go someplace we knew. I didn't share the observation that we'd arrived at the thicket, but at another time, according to the leaves and the sun, and that we ought to find out what time it was. This was his journey, not mine. He started walking. I hurried after him. We didn't speak. According to the length of our walk, we should have made it to the lake, or at least seen it beyond the trees, but we didn't. All of a sudden, the thicket stopped and a mountain started. We walked back to see if we'd missed it, but the mountain disappeared from view. We had to walk onto it to make it be. The thicket bumped into the middle of a mountain. There was a narrow path that emerged from it, and we stayed on it. It twisted among boulders and trees, pine trees, but fatter, nothing like eucalyptuses. I turned my head. The thicket was kilometers behind us. I told Oshri there was some distortion of space. He nodded. I had no idea how I was able to formulate my sensation like that, a distortion of space. Oshri said he didn't want to say anything earlier, but it was just like one of the books Elish gave us. He gave me a serious look, as if there was a secret meaning behind his words. But there was no meaning. I thought he was glad but afraid to be glad because he was supposed to be sad, and it was this indecisiveness that made his eyes hard and severe.

It wasn't like in the adventure books Elish gave us, where the story starts as soon as the kids arrive. They meet a talking animal, or someone chases them, and someone else explains what's going on. We climbed that mountain for hours, and it was exhausting. The landscape did change. Some parts were steep and mossy, there were small meadows, and narrow parts alongside a ravine, where we saw small pools of water sparkling in the sun. But there was no life on the mountain besides pestering butterflies, orange and yellow, that clung to our arms and legs like we were flowers, and the mountain went on and on, and in spite of the cool air we got hot from the effort and started to sweat. It was as boring as last year's field trip, when they took us to some dried-up stream, and Racheli and Elinoar latched on to the guide and bugged him with questions, making fun of him, and I was embarrassed for them and slowed down to walk in the rear, with the slowpokes, and Yalon was there, intentionally walking slow like a turtle, watching. When our pace matched up, our conversation flowed too, as easily as it had in the school Purim party where we first met. We walked freely, amusing ourselves. Yalon told me about last summer vacation, when his dad took him to Italy and they went up to the Alps, first by train car, then by foot, to a lake that had a name that sounded like "Shmuel." The mountain didn't make him feel so desperate, like this sucky stream, where the view was all the same and there wasn't even any water. In Italy, the view changed and turned wild. They reached a patch of mountain from which they could see a solitary farm with cows grazing all around. The cows were so far away that they looked like black flies against the green grass. Yalon told me he ate some Bamba and when he finished he threw the empty bag on the ground, and his dad got mad and made him pick it up. He told him to look around and see if he could spot any garbage, and Yalon was surprised to find that the mountain was completely clean. He asked if workers came to clean up after the tourists. His dad almost lost his mind, and asked who he thought those workers would be. I looked at the dry stream. Everywhere there were bottles with faded labels and plastic bags caught on thorns. When Yalon and his dad made it to the lake, his dad looked around, then unzipped his pants and peed into it. Yalon asked him if that wasn't the same as littering, and his father said, Screw all those Israel haters. I don't know why that story made me laugh. Yalon laughed too, even though he didn't laugh when they were at the lake. His father told him that he might be peeing into that Israel haters' lake, but in Israel he'd never be the barbarian that people tried to make him out to be, and that Yalon should get that into his head, they were masters of their own house.

I told the story to Oshri to make the walk easier. He shrugged and didn't laugh. We paused to rest on a wide boulder. The mountaintop, which looked close, kept growing farther away. The path twisted to it, but kept leading the other way. Oshri handed me a bottle of water. He pulled packed sandwiches from his bag. An especially naggy butterfly landed on my knee, and when I waved it off it clung to my hand. I put down the sandwich and prepared to squash the butterfly. Oshri stopped me. He said he had a bad feeling about it. I grabbed the butterfly and pinned his wings to the ground with two small stones. We finished eating and got up to keep walking. After we took a few steps I turned around and threw a rock at the trapped butterfly. Oshri shouted not to, but it was too late. It was a good shot. The rock landed right on the nagging butterfly. But it didn't stay there for long. The rock started shaking, and a rumbling sounded beneath it. It flew into the air and the butterfly burst out from underneath it, ten times larger and still growing. I was frozen, and Oshri tugged on my sleeve, shouting at me to run.

EVENTUALLY, OSHRI CONVINCED ME TO GIVE HIM A BLOOD sample. He said he needed more than a finger prick and more advanced equipment than the health app on his InteMon for the tests he wanted to run. I asked if that meant he was going back to the lab tomorrow. He said no, that Nitzan would stop by and pick it up. He'd meet her downstairs after he took my sample. I told him I'd make dinner tonight. He asked what I'd do if the Unelish came to visit while I cooked. I said the salad would certainly be interesting. He laughed and said I was getting back my sense of humor. I said I didn't know he thought I had a sense of humor in the first place. He said, Oh, come on, he meant my cynicism. I said nothing, because that was Yalon's accusation. But Oshri said it with affection.

I asked him what Nitzan said about the EEG. He said he presented it to her like a puzzle, an exercise. He told her he'd made it artificially, like a code she had to crack. I told him he was getting better at this. He said he wasn't me, he didn't like lying to her.

I took my time in the kitchen, though all I made was salad and rice with tofu, but I put a lot of work into it. I marinated the tofu in soy, date honey, and ginger. A great accomplishment for me. Usually, I don't have the patience to cook. There's always something more urgent or important to do than stand around the pots or chop parsley. Never mind. I felt a tranquility, like after physical exertion and a hot shower. I hadn't gone on a run in a few days. We each had to make sacrifices.

Oshri said I'd outdone myself. I told him that was an empty compliment, because when I outdid myself I achieved the same results other people did when they just rustled something up. He started to say something, but I said, Please just don't say it's all relative. He said he wasn't going to say that, just to say that Mom would have assumed I was either in love or pregnant.

I told him I knew that even after the shadow man came for a second visit, and even now that we were starting to figure out what's going on, he still wasn't convinced that this experiment was necessary, or that we were on the right track. He blinked and said he would let me have it my way for now, though he thought we were in over our heads. I asked him what was bothering him,

then. He said nothing. I said, Maybe you aren't bothered, just annoyed. He asked what I was talking about. I said he kept teasing
me, saying I was sarcastic, that I was used to lying, and now he
brought up Mom and her pestering me to find a husband and
think about kids, as if it were still 2000 rather than 2028. I was
thinking how I could barf when I saw parents who adored their
children, convinced they were giving them confidence, when later
they would agonize over every flaw their parents saw in them, as
if they were in breach of contract. Maybe it was healthier to grow
up with parents who tried to compensate for their own wounded
childhoods, although on second thought, no. Definitely not.

He said he had no idea what I meant, that this was how we always talked to each other. I fixed him with a look. He really meant
what he said. Oshri was easy to read. When he snapped out of his
long depression, he'd gotten a boost of vitality, or maybe it was
depth. Maybe when he said he was one of the kids who stayed, he
meant he was someone who held on to childhood, and throughout those three years of depression, childish naïvety was soldered
into him, receiving the form of openheartedness, his simple honesty, at least toward me. He said he never thought these things
would bother me, and that maybe I was finally becoming sensitive, and that Mom really should have been here for this.

He served himself more rice and tofu. He said he was doing
that because the rice was good, not to spare my feelings. He asked
how far I planned to take the experiment, that he needed to know
where my line was, because I had a tendency to push it. I told him
I intended to keep going until we understood these manifestations of shadow people who visited Olga and Kalanit, and why
Elish was willing to risk his life to find out the answer. Oshri
asked if I wasn't afraid, even a little. I told him for the millionth
time that I wasn't, I wasn't afraid, and I reminded him that he'd
confirmed the fact that I had a normal allele in the Richard Perotz gene, balancing out the dangerous allele, just like Olga and
Kalanit, and that Elish's gene was made up of two copies of the

dangerous allele, just like Oshri, and that we were only assuming he was even hurt by . . . Then I fell silent.

Oshri said it sounded like I was once again trying to convince myself, not him. I looked around. I told him I hadn't insisted on the apartment because it wasn't my inheritance. I asked him to tell me, for the millionth time, that he understood me, even just a little bit. He said he was doing these things *for* me, that understanding me was not an issue, but . . . Now it was his turn to fall silent. I asked him to finish the sentence. He refused. He mumbled that a mystery couldn't be an inheritance, not as far as he was concerned.

WE RAN UP THE PATH, WHICH GREW STEEPER AND MORE TAPERED just to provoke us. I caught up with Oshri. The path was too narrow for two people to walk side by side. The butterfly was enormous. The wind from its beating wings flattened us, almost making us stumble. Oshri grew tired, I could hear it in his breathing, could see it in his wobbling body. I'd take his heavy backpack, but there wasn't a moment to pause. It looked like the path was about to end in an abyss that deepened below us. I looked around. Maybe there was a rock or a stick I could use against the butterfly? The path took a sharp turn, flanking an enormous boulder. We turned with it. Oshri disappeared into an opening on the face of the mountain, an opening with a stone arch over it, engraved with symbols we had no time to look at. We ran inside. The butterfly tried to shove its way in, but it was too big. It pushed its disgusting head inside, with the twisting antennas that stretched forward like long, fat tongues. Why are insects always so disgusting in the end, even with their beautiful colors? The eyes always look like spotted eggs, sunken into all that hair. I turned the iPhone's flashlight and aimed it into the butterfly's eyes, hoping it would go blind or at least feel pain. The light was swallowed by the opaque balls. Oshri used his iPhone to check out the cave. He shone the light all around. The rock was smooth, polished, black, strewn with strands of gold and copper, zigzagging like veins and arteries. Oshri touched the rock. I did the same. The warmth surprised me. The sounds of the butterfly's wings beating, its body slamming against the opening, grew louder in the interior space, the walls beating with them. I said I hoped we didn't accidentally walk into some living being. I shone my light on the ground. Dirt. I relaxed a little. I aimed it back at the walls. There was a small shadow over me. I looked closer. There was an iron ring with a rod fitted through it. I asked Oshri to give me a boost. I held on to the wall to steady myself and pulled on the rod. It was made of wood, with a lump of multifaceted, multiangled glass at the end. I held the iPhone close to it. It lit up with the beam of the flashlight, burning brightly. The cave walls responded to its lighting, all those metallic arteries glowing like LED lights. The butterfly kept trying to get in. I grabbed the rod like a bat. I would have bashed its head in, but Oshri stopped me. He said to think about what happened the first time I'd killed it, and that we had no way of knowing what would happen the second time. I held the bright light close to the butterfly. It retreated, the antennas shrinking away. How I felt like crushing it or burning it, like barbecuing a mosquito on a stove coil.

Oshri pulled my arm and pointed at the other side of the cave. In the glow of the glass lump, another opening was revealed. We walked over carefully and entered a larger, domed, empty space. At the end was a door. We both spotted it with relief. At its center was a small stone platform with a kind of sink on it. It was mined out of the same dark material with different metals running through it, silver and gold and yellow and white. Inside, underneath a transparent board, were two objects. One was a smooth, round crystal pendant with a black dot in the middle, tied to a silver chain. The other was a sort of old, rusted metal cylinder. Oshri felt around the sink and the clear board to see if there was a lock or a pull tab. I handed him the light torch. I said I was better at this stuff. He asked why I thought that, we both read the same books, if anything he'd read more, so he was better prepared. I said it wasn't about reading the books but about understanding how they worked. I spread my hand over the clear plate and it lit up too. All the light from the metal veins flowed into it, injecting it with electric fire, the hub of which was my hand. You could see the bones inside my flesh, the map of blood vessels, the nerves, and underneath them a symbol that appeared, a sort of chubby bird with a curly leg. Probably the kind that's too heavy to fly. The clear plate evaporated and my hand sank in. I pulled out both objects, handed them to Oshri, and told him to pick. He took the pendant. He asked how I knew how to open it. I said it was obvious the path didn't just happen to lead us here. One of us was meant to open the sink. He said he thought the correct word was "basin." I said that didn't matter. He touched it, but his touch didn't fit, so that meant my touch was the key.

The light in the metals grew brighter, and they started catching fire, like the fuse of a bomb in a cartoon. They burned and blazed inside the rock. We ran to the door. The light grew brighter, blinding, and we had to move with our eyes closed. Oshri made it there first and found the doorknob. He pushed the door in. We were spewed out. We were on the mountaintop, on a round flat caprock, as if someone had lopped off the point at the top. The door swung on the edge of the platform, as if a wind were blowing it, but there was no wind. The door just hung there, squeaking, without a wall or a frame around it, only a jamb holding its hinges in place. A world spread out before us. Oshri gasped with wonder. So did I. On one side, way down below, we saw the entrance to the cave we'd passed through. That stupid butterfly wasn't giving up. It kept pouncing at the entrance and then being pushed back. From this height, its size seemed reasonable, like that of an average chicken. If it weren't for Oshri's warning, I would have dropped a boulder on it. From another side we saw the thicket, but between the thicket and the mountain lay an enormous city.

It started on the slope of the mountain and stretched into hilly terrain. Oshri was the first to discover the mountaintop's special quality. I saw him leaning in and retreating, turning his head and looking at the view from the corner of his eye. I asked what he was doing. He said the air here worked like a collection of lenses or magnifying glasses. I came closer to the edge of the round surface. He was right, with every step along the perimeter and every shift of the angle, parts of the city came into focus, moving closer, as if I were looking at them through binoculars or a telescope. There were old parts to the city, ancient, I mean, like the Wailing Wall, or that fort up north we once visited on a school trip, and there were glass towers, and buildings that looked like the body of an animal, and there were barren areas that, from a distance, looked like spots, but up close, magnified, were swamps or deserts, and were filled with countless creatures, not all of them resembling humans.

I LOOKED AT MY IPHONE. THERE WAS NO RECEPTION. THE CLOCK was stuck on the same time it showed when we'd entered. I asked Oshri what he thought this place was. He said, Sderot. I asked if he was crazy. He told me to come look. He found a point that overlooked our thicket, the Lakeside neighborhood thicket. The eucalyptuses were dark, washed by the rain of the last few days. On the water were strips of late-afternoon light, just like I could see from my window when the sun passed to the other side of the roof, beautiful silver strips among the green rivulets. I could see the half-constructed neighborhood houses, and our house, which was hazy. I moved my head to see more details, maybe the glass porch doors, or Grandma Zehava in the living room. But the image went blurry. Oshri tightened his hand around the pendant. He was already wearing it around his neck. Then he exposed it and held it up to the light. He asked what I thought was inside the crystal sphere. I said it looked like a plant seed. He said he thought so too, but that it was kind of strange to keep a seed in crystal. He asked to look at my object. The scratched cylinder, bent in places, was a container with a lid. I uncapped it. It was empty, and at the top of the lid was a straight wire with a circle at its end. Like a bubble wand, but made out of rusty metal. Oshri asked why I'd let him pick first. I told him this was his journey. He said I must have had a secret agenda. I told him that, the way I understood the rules, the object that doesn't look as valuable is the more valuable one. He looked at his pendant again and shrugged. I said we had to find a way to get back home. He said, What's the rush, let's look around first, study this place, investigate. I asked if he knew what the purpose of our journey was, if he'd guessed where it would take us when we started. He shook his head. Only one path descended from the top. I asked if he had the strength to keep walking. Rather than answer, he started moving toward the path. I followed suit.

About a hundred meters later, the path was interrupted by a paved square. We tried to get our bearings again. We walked back. We were close to the top, and the city was at the foot of the mountain. A few more steps and now the mountain was far away, covered with clouds and fog. The plaza had five sides. A group of creatures with furry faces and elephant-like tusks walked by without giving us even half a look. They were chatting in some language that sounded like cats meowing and hissing.

Five streets intersected at the plaza. At its center was a fenced-in garden with a statue of a crooked, diagonal ladder, half made of stone, the other half of glass zigzagged with metal veins and arteries, just like the cave walls. The two halves seemed to swirl around each other, their rungs connecting and holding each other at the base. In the top part, their connection weakened until finally the ladder unraveled like a piece of string cheese. What a repulsive word, "cheese." I hope whoever came up with it dies.

Two sliced horses—meaning, truncated horses—walked through the plaza. Say you take a horse, cut off its stomach, and then attach the ass and tail to the neck. They whistled at each other and looked to be in love. Cranes passed by. One of their feet was in its rightful place, and the other grew in place of a beak. They stood on one leg, shifted their weight forward, then leaned on the other. A herd of rabbits with smushed faces, flattened like paper, gurgled at one another on the trees. Tall, skinny trees with gold trunks and small flames instead of leaves. The rabbits didn't burn. On the contrary, the flames enveloped them, and I'm pretty sure they were gurgling with pleasure.

Oshri said this looked like hell. Someone behind us said that had been the original plan, but it failed. We turned around to look. A short, fat man wearing a red tracksuit, a little too tight for my taste, with the hood up over his head. He was chewing on the hood's cord. His cheeks were droopy and red, though not as red as the tracksuit. He had a button nose and purple eyes, no white, just purple all over the eyes, and his pupils were elongated and vertical, like black sticks floating in the purple. He looked us over the way we did him. He asked which Sderot we were from. Oshri said, The regular one. The man said, Sure, sure, but which time period and which plane of existence? I said late 2014, and what did he mean by plane of existence? He asked which year count. I said AD, 2014 AD. He said that wasn't helpful. I told him we weren't there to help him, and that if he didn't like our answers he could get out of our faces. Oshri suggested maybe he tell us what time period and plane of existence he was from and maybe that way we'd be able to answer. He said he was from here, from the Sderot of the House of Avgad, a decade since the defeat of the CRISPR, twenty-three-degree tilt to the Mualem axis. Oshri said we were from the Sderot of sixty-six years since the foundation of Israel, and that he couldn't say about the Mualem axis. The fat man's pupils shrunk to the normal pupil shape, almond-like holes. Astonished, he asked how we'd crossed all the other Sderotae. I asked for his name. He said, Profession. I told him we were kids and didn't have professions yet. He said, No, my name is Profession, what's yours? We gave him our names. He said very few scouts came through this Sderot, since there were no buried treasures or adventures or monsters to kill, although the CRISPR had planned to turn this Sderot into hell, just like Oshri had said, which means heaven for scouts. I told him we didn't understand anything he just said. He told us to follow him. He paused by the statue and said it had been erected to mark the defeat. He rubbed the stone half, and lights blinked on the glass half. He signaled for us to touch. Oshri touched the stone, and the glass lit up again. He seemed to have gotten more lights on. I put my hand on the stone. It was scorching, and I couldn't say why. The sun above us glinted like a pin, and the air was warm. I pulled my hand away quickly. Profession giggled. He said the statue reacted a little differently to everybody.

PROFESSION SUGGESTED WE VISIT THE ONLY INN ON THE square, which served as a café at this time of day. At the bottom of the stairs was a row of patheteeth stores, like the kind of stores where poorer people shop. The distorted animals were wandering down here too, and the air was filled with beeps, whistles, chatter, and rip-raps. They were butt ugly, yes, but they also seemed happy, I'm not sure why.

He suggested we sit at a table outside and said he'd get us something to drink. On a table not far from us, someone was smeared over a seat, actually smeared, like he had no bones, his arms hanging off the sides of the chair like flesh socks.

Profession gave Oshri a few coins and asked him to order three glasses of pomegranate soda. While we waited, he questioned me about the Sderot we came from and how exactly we got here. I gave him vague answers. I said we woke up on a mountain, walked down a path, and suddenly found ourselves here. I didn't trust him. I can tell when people are trying too hard. Pointing at Oshri's backpack, he said whoever it was that transported us here took care to pack us some gear. I felt I had to come up with a more sophisticated lie before I felt safe enough to tell the truth. I asked how people usually came to . . . I couldn't come up with the word. He said, To a time disruption hub. I nodded. He said that in every reality there were openings and doors and portals partially torn by a disruption, which were called seeping points. But guides could also land people in any one of the Sderotae. I asked who these guides were. He said they were an order of goddesses and wizards to whom the laws of disruption did not apply. I said maybe one of those people put us here. Oshri came back and sat down. He said the woman working inside would bring out our drinks. I asked Profession to explain what this place was and what a time disruption was.

He said there were lots of planes of existence, each with a history, anecdotes, and a timeline, and that most of them have experienced a time quake that tore parts of it, allowing the different parts to invade one another and coalesce. The place we were now in was a coalescing point of the parts of lots of different Sderotae, from different planes and different points in those histories. Some were in the far future, as far as we were concerned, home to societies that were technological, no longer human. Others were from the deep past, as early as biblical times, or even earlier. Oshri said that Sderot hadn't existed in the patriarchal age. Profession said it hadn't existed in the history of our own plane of existence. I asked how we could get back to our Sderot. He said the different Sderotae were separated by the merging lines that distinguished them and retained the autonomy of each one, and that there were border crossing points, familiar seeping points, but that we had to pay to pass through them. He asked if we had anything of value. I said I had a little money in my pocket. He said money was useless because each Sderot had its own currency. Oshri said we had brand-new iPhones and showed Profession his device. Profession said to put that away, who knows what people might think he was carrying, but that, generally speaking, devices were tricky, because they were too primitive for technologically advanced societies and inoperative in untechnological societies. I glanced at my iPhone. The clock was still stuck on the same time and there was still no service. Profession asked if we had anything else. Oshri looked at me. I shook my head, but he ignored it. He pulled the pendant from inside his shirt. Profession leaned in for a closer look. Then he said no, he didn't think the pendant was worth anything.

A woman who looked like she'd been sculpted from coal or black marble came up to our table. Her skin was black, her eyes were black all over, her lips, her nose, her hair. No different tones. I think the books Elish gave me would have described her as made of eternal night. She was beautiful, but not in a way that arouses envy, more in a way that arouses admiration. She didn't bother us too much, just put down the glasses and looked at us. You couldn't tell what she was thinking. I didn't know how to read her face. It truly looked like a statue's.

When she left I saw that Profession's head was lowered and he was peeking from the corners of his eyes to make sure she was leaving. He said this Sderot had annihilated the worship of guides and working with them was forbidden, but that we had another option, a trade caravan. They passed through the Sderotae and we could try joining one, offering to work in exchange for passage. He asked what we could do. Oshri looked at me. I sighed. Profession said we should go to the checkpoints by border control in the morning and wait for the traders to pass through in their carriages and pick laborers. We might get lucky. He told us to be ready for hard work. Oshri said we'd probably get whipped. His voice was dreamy, oddly infatuated.

Profession asked if we had some place to stay. I said we didn't. He said even local currency wouldn't help us. Ever since this Sderot stopped receiving scouts, there weren't even any hotels or guesthouses. He said we could stay with him. I kicked Oshri under the table to signal no. He put down his pomegranate soda. He said it was delicious. I asked if it was better than Turkish delight. He caught my hint from *Narnia* right away. He told Profession we'd find some park to sleep in. Profession said it wasn't dangerous out here at night, but it did get cold, the temperature dropping without any warning. He asked us to consider his offer while he went to the bathroom. I noticed him lowering his head as he approached the door to the inn, tugging and tightening his itchy-looking hood. What a gross word, "itchy." I hope all the inventors of patheteeth words burn in hell, amen. I told Oshri to wait for me and got up to follow Profession. Inside, I saw him walking down a hallway on the side of the black woman's counter. I hurried after him. She laughed like a flute and asked if I couldn't hold it in any longer. I hurried down quietly. He closed a door behind him and I heard the lock click. I bent down and looked through the keyhole. Gross, bathroom. I hoped he wouldn't do anything disgusting. But he didn't. He stood at the sink and lowered his hood. He was bald, his scalp covered with ridges, like fat worms between his skin and his skull. He felt the mirror and the sides of the sink. I couldn't figure out what he was looking for, but he gave up and slammed the faucet, which started to leak.

WHEN HE CAME BACK HE SAID HE HAD AN IDEA. WE COULD OFFER to do the dishwashing if the innkeeper let us spend the night in the storage shed out back, and that he'd come by the next morning to take us to the border crossing. I asked why he was helping us. He closed his eyes and opened them again, like a fish's mouth, and his droopy cheeks turned even redder. He said everyone in this Sderot was kind and they would all have helped. I had no doubt he was lying. Softly, Oshri said that was what he was supposed to do. My discomfort, like some splinter in your foot you can't quite find, transformed into anger. Why was Oshri being all nice? Couldn't he smell the danger?

Profession told me not to be so suspicious, I knew nothing

about the history of this place. Oshri smiled and leaned in. He was curious. Profession said people had lived calmly for years in the Israel of the House of Avgad, the capital of which was Sderot. He said the Avgadians had migrated from the Transjordan Highlands, overthrown the evil rule of the descendants of David and Solomon, and ruled wisely, fairly, and peacefully, beloved by all people. They exterminated the rituals of ignorance and destroyed the temples. But one day, when Profession was just a child, a tremor passed through the capital, buildings collapsed, neighborhoods crumbled to dust, and immense lightning bolts flashed through the sky. A dazzling light shone, a white beam, and the residents of the capital found themselves in a time disruption hub, in the coalescence plane. A long, confusing period went by before they figured out what was going on. But the Avgadians kept their cool and sent researchers to study the situation. Some of the researchers attempted to cross the time borders and were never seen again. People said that those borders were designation zones where no laws applied, and trying to pass through them was like jumping into a crevasse that could tear you to shreds or shrink you down to a speck. But the situation slowly grew clearer. The royal family's eldest son, the crown prince, whom everyone was convinced had not survived the time shock, was found in another, very scientifically advanced Sderot. He came back, but no one had realized the shock had made him lose his mind. In the other Sderot, he acquired the art of intervening with the texture of life, or CRISPR. He started a workshop at the palace and began experimenting. Residents vanished, distorted animals were seen walking outside the windows of the workshop, which grew larger and larger. Odd sounds were heard, and rumors began spreading. They made it to the king and queen, who demanded explanations. But the prince had already gained much power. He created a loyal army of messengers and servants. He staged a coup, took hold of the palace, and commenced his reign of terror. He called himself the CRISPR, and the palace became one big workshop where he kneaded the texture of life. His parents were his first famous victims. They were study subjects. There was intention behind their punishment. They heeded people's gossip about him, and therefore would spend their entire lives gossiping, hungry for rumors.

He had a plan. He wanted to make this Sderot an attraction for scouts. Not a single resident remained as they had been, neither animal nor human. He'd transformed all of them but didn't break them. He bent their shape, thinking he was turning them into monsters, brainless nightmares, and that when the scouts came they would have exciting encounters in his hell. He was already working on intensifying the violent urges in some of them, making them predators. That's where he went wrong. Because this violence turned against him. Ten years ago, a rebellion started. It began by accident, but things grew heated and the rebels realized they had a chance. They formed an army, besieged the palace, and killed the CRISPR and his lackeys.

Oshri gasped with excitement. I said it was awful that the prince was willing to destroy so much just for a thrill. Profession said the time disruption had changed the logic and meaning of their existence, that it was difficult to fathom, and that we were making up values the function of which was to help us fulfill the purpose of life as we understood it. But that if the purpose changed, then so did the values. I didn't understand what he was getting at. Neither did Oshri.

He said goodbye and left. We walked into the inn. The black woman said to call her Von Schwartz. She dismissed our offer of dishwashing and asked what kind of hostess would she be if she made us pay to stay in the storage shed, which was half-empty anyway. She gave us some blankets to spread on the ground and said she wished she had an available room in her home. I told Oshri to pay attention to the differences between Von Schwartz and Profession. He said he saw none. I asked if he'd become stupider ever since we came down from the mountain. He said he

didn't see the difference between the help Profession offered and
the help Von Schwartz offered. I asked how he could miss it, she
wasn't suspect, he was. He said I was getting riled up again. I
asked why he said "again." He said we didn't come here to get
mad, but if that's what I liked I should go ahead and get mad. I
told him I'd be as mad as I wanted if it meant keeping him safe. He
said I'd lost my sense of adventure. I ignored him, turned away,
and pulled the blanket over my face. It really was getting cold.

I woke up in the dark. There was a noise inside the storage. I
couldn't move. I was paralyzed. My eyes grew accustomed to the
dark. A stocky figure in a hood, Profession, was mounting a bundle on his shoulder. I knew the bundle was Oshri, wrapped in his
blanket like a chrysalis. I wanted to shout, but my throat was
blocked. He turned his face to me. I was sure I saw a smile, the
purple painted with evil, darkening with a scheme. I screamed
and cursed inside my head until the night dropped over me again.
I fell asleep.

I woke up groggy. It was light out, and it streamed in through
the cracks in the windows and door. The events of last night came
back to me. I jumped to my feet and called out for Oshri. He wasn't
there. I ran outside. The plaza was empty, even the crooked animals were gone, other than the rabbits with the smushed faces
that were warming themselves in the flames of trees. I hurried
into the inn. Von Schwartz was wearing a robe and mopping the
floor. I cut off her good morning greeting and asked if she'd seen
Oshri, if she saw Profession abducting him in the middle of the
night. She asked, What Profession? I said, That chunky character
in the red tracksuit we came in with yesterday. She said she was
a deep sleeper. I hurried back to the shed. Oshri's backpack was
there. Out of desperation, I opened it. He'd packed too many
sandwiches. I kicked it. I kicked the old furniture. What an idiot,
you're such an idiot, I shouted at myself. When I catch that Profession I'll tear him apart, I'll rip out his arms and legs. I'll find

leeches in CRISPR's workshop and get them to suck out all the fat from his body.

I WENT BACK INTO THE INN. VON SCHWARTZ SAID SHE'D CALLED the police and they were sending someone over. She suggested I sit down in the meantime and she'd make me some tea or hot cocoa to calm my nerves. I didn't feel like it. I paced outside, waiting for the cops to show up. The animals were starting their wandering, the truncated horses with their whistles of love and all sorts of other deformations whose sounds made me feel sick. After about a hundred hours, three people came, also wearing tracksuits. The guy in the front was wearing yellow, and the other two that followed him were in plaid blue. They ignored me. I followed them inside. They walked with speed and determination and paused at the counter. They asked Von Schwartz if she'd seen a messenger. She asked what they meant. The man in yellow spoke, but he wasn't totally a man. He looked like a half man and half woman sewn together. The seams were very visible. The half man face was crude, with a large jaw and thick eyebrows, and the half woman face was delicate, skinny, with soft skin and thin lips and long dirty-blond hair. The two half faces didn't fit in size, so one eye and half nose were higher than the other, and the lips were diagonal. I asked myself what happened to the other halves, if they'd been thrown out or used to suture up another creature like him. The two in blue were a woman whose entire skin was made of corns, big and small, on her lids, her forehead, her neck, her hands, and a man who had feathers instead of hair and scales on parts of his face, and a shell like a turtle's. His hands were covered with small fingernails that broke out of his skin.

The half-and-half in yellow spoke in plural form. They said the fireabbits told them that a messenger had been seen on the plaza. The blue one with the feathers huffed and asked who even believed the fireabbits' nonsense. Von Schwartz said a guy had come by with two kids. She pointed at me. They looked at me. The half-and-half asked if the man had been wearing the alloy. Von Schwartz said she couldn't remember, she'd barely gotten a look at him, and what would a messenger do here? Those who hadn't been captured and killed must have already escaped to the other Sderotae. Then she retired to her cleaning.

The woman in blue looked me over. I didn't feel comfortable making eye contact because my gaze kept drawing to her corns. Yalon told me he'd had a corn on his finger that kept returning every time it was cauterized. Finally, his parents took him to a specialist who said corns were like plants, they had roots. He found the root on Yalon's neck, where there was a tiny corn nobody had noticed. He pulled it out. It was connected to a long, white thread. After that, the corn on his finger quickly dried up. I should suggest the specialist to this woman. How I wished Yalon were there to help me. It was a shame Oshri had insisted this journey was just for the two of us.

She asked me who that man was. I said his name was Profession. I told her he'd abducted Oshri. For some reason they were caught up in the question of whether or not he was wearing an alloy necklace, like them. I didn't care about the necklace. I asked if they were the police and how we could track down Oshri. The half-and-half said they had to know. He pointed at his necklace. It was the same rust color as my cylinder. I asked what was special about it. They said the CRISPR had created this alloy in order to control them. It was toxic to anyone whose biology he'd intervened in. After the rebellion, they found a vaccine and injected it themselves to everyone who'd taken part. That was a way to recognize the CRISPR's messengers and servants, the ones who escaped and would dare return under the guise of loyal residents.

I said I couldn't remember. All I knew was that he wore a red tracksuit, like theirs, and hid his head with the hood most of the time, but that when I followed him to the bathroom I saw his bald head with the fat worms, and that he was looking for something in there. The half-and-half and the woman in blue glanced at each other. They said the word "hybrid." They told the man with the feathered mane not to belittle the fireabbits, that they didn't forget their origins, even though the CRISPR had shrunk their brains, and that he ought to remember the part they played in the rebellion. The man huffed again. The woman in blue said they needed eyes on the palace. Hybrid wasn't working alone; he was a servant, not a master.

The man with the feathered mane said the CRISPR was dead, he saw him dead, and his knowledge spread through all corners of the time disruption hub, through Sderotae that nobody thought had anything to do with this one, not even trade relations. That it was over. The half-and-half said they understood his fear, he wasn't the only one who suffered in that workshop, not the only one who'd experienced loss. The feathers stood up on the man in blue's head as he said no, he saw it with his own eyes, the CRISPR was dead. Dead. The woman in blue said it was a good fairy tale and she couldn't think of a better temptation for scouts. The man with the feathered mane kept mumbling, Dead, dead. He was on the verge of tears. The half-and-half asked what she meant. She addressed them with the name Woe-man. She told them to think about it. An evil creature who had been defeated and whose store of knowledge, whose source of power, was spread among the Sderotae, to be attained only by overcoming obstacles. Woe-man asked if she thought a group of scouts was trying to re-create the CRISPR's knowledge. She said that if they considered it a treasure, then yes, especially if they could fight a few nightmarish creatures on the way, move through foreign dimensions. That was the foundation of scout culture. They were wanderers and grifters, they didn't consider the price paid by the cultures who lived where they enjoy their adventures. Woe-man addressed the man in blue with the feathers as Beta. They told Beta that Cornelia was right, if a group of scouts was trying to gather the CRISPR's knowledge, collecting *ezovyon* seeds and the exhalers from the different Sderotae, they'd go to the palace.

I asked them what any of that had to do with Profession and with Oshri's abduction. Cornelia said the messenger enticed the scouts with that story and that he could be using them. I asked again what that had to do with Oshri. They said they had no idea and that this Oshri I kept talking about wasn't important. I asked if the messenger would take Oshri to the palace. They said the messenger would indubitably go there. I said I was coming with them. Beta looked at me, really looked, his pupils dilating. He asked who I was and how come I had no signs of imagetortion.

IT WAS JUST A WASTE OF TIME, STANDING AT THE INN AND TELL-ing them I was from a different Sderot, that my brother and I had been landed here. Cornelia's conjecture calmed down Beta, who had lots of unnecessary questions about the nature of my Sderot. Mostly, he was irritated that I didn't know where my Sderot's plane of existence stood in relation to the cosmic axis of the Mualem measure. Like, what would knowing the tilt angle do for him? Cornelia agreed with me. She said we could talk on the way. But first Woe-man made sure I wasn't susceptible to the alloy. They asked me to hold it. There was no reaction. Of course, I didn't tell them I'd found a canister made of the same stuff. Cornelia talked to me, and Beta wouldn't stop interrupting with nagging questions about technological level and Israeli politics. He hated hearing that the Sderot of my plane of existence was considered a hellhole and that people shot missiles at us. It was sort of insulting to him, because before the imagetortion he used to be an officer in the royal guard. Cornelia explained that "imagetortion" was a portmanteau for "image" and "distortion." I could have figured that out myself if I weren't so anxious to get to the palace. Beta's questions only seemed to delay us.

We walked through all sorts of streets that kind of resembled the streets of my Sderot, meaning they were boring and normal, neighborhoods, villas, and housing projects. I asked Cornelia where the animals lived. She said there was an enormous site in the other direction, with lairs and stables and nests. She said the animals were very miserable. For the ones who walked through the city, part of the imagetortion was a special gland that secreted a substance causing a pleasure sensation whenever the residents looked at them. I thought Cornelia must be the miserable one, because her name was Cornelia and she was covered with corns. Once, when Woe-man told us to hurry up, they called her Skipa, and she angrily corrected, Cornelia. I asked if she'd changed her name, and she said that after the rebellion they all took on names that had something to do with their distortion. Beta said he chose his name because the CRISPR changed his alpha-keratin, the protein that created keratin tissues like hair and nails, into beta-keratin, which builds scales, shells, feathers, and beaks.

I asked Cornelia what were those *ezovyon* seeds and exhalers she'd talked about. Beta butted in and said that after they killed the CRISPR, they tortured every servant and messenger they caught. They all told the same story, that the CRISPR coded his knowledge onto six indestructible *ezovyon* seeds hidden somewhere deep in the workshop. Tadpola and Gianton, the rebellion leaders, found the seeds and tried and failed to destroy them. So instead, Tadpola and Gianton sacrificed themselves. They learned the forbidden art of the CRISPR and created a durable crystallized coating for the seeds, and canisters of a toxic alloy that contained a radiation generator able to consume the coating. They ordered that these be dispersed throughout the Sderotae, hidden away. So that was the canister we'd found, an exhaler. It burned inside of Oshri's backpack, which, after I emptied out all the sandwiches, I discovered did contain a book after all, as well as some long-sleeved shirts, who knows why. I hoped they wouldn't ask to look through my bag. I asked what the exhalers had been invented for. Cornelia said she thought that was the nature of knowledge, once you acquire it you refuse to lose it. Nobody dared question Tadpola and Gianton, they were the rebellion leaders and they were heroes. Beta said only those with a specific genetic signature could activate the radiation generator, and that he was one of the people who believed that Tadpola and Gianton had a secret agenda. That they'd discovered something unspeakable when they studied the CRISPR's knowledge. I asked what "sacrificing themselves" meant. She said they killed themselves, that was the law they'd passed themselves, that anyone who learned the CRISPR's knowledge or kept something of his would be sentenced to death.

After walking through dreary streets with houses full of image-tortions with pincers and horns and all sorts of missing or misplaced limbs, we arrived at the palace compound. The trees with the golden trunks and flames multiplied, as did the fireabbits sitting in them. A dirt path wound between the trees. Beneath the dirt, the old paving peeked out here and there, broken, pink pavers. Woe-man suggested we go up to the exterior watchtower, where we'd have the best view. Beta agreed right away. I could tell he was sorry he hadn't suggested it first. We climbed the winding steps. I skipped ahead to get there first, but Woe-man's hand blocked me. They told me to stay in the rear. I saw the palace from the window at the top of the tower. The other three all took out binoculars. Unfortunately, that was one thing Oshri hadn't thought to pack. At its base, the palace looked more like a large villa, a Villa Sillykulla, that's how Elish referred to Pippi Long-stocking's house, which was called Villa Villekulla in the book. He showed me a picture of it from a movie, with green roof tiles and yellow wooden walls. When I was little I used to spend hours imagining I lived there with Mr. Nilsson the monkey and the horse on the porch. When those leeches Tommy and Annika came to nag, I'd kick their butts back to their parents.

But there were spires and turrets added to the villa, and concrete structures in the large plaza that surrounded it and in all the gardens and lawns, with narrow glass windows and connecting paths. I didn't spot any movement, but the place didn't seem deserted at all. Woe-man affirmed this. They said they could see someone, that it was Hybrid. They said he was never alone, that his dog, Hybred, should be nearby. Cornelia passed me her binoculars. It was him, with his fatty dwarfness and the worms in his scalp, that stinking con man, standing at the window of Villa Sillykulla, looking out. My anger ignited. I told them we had to break into the palace. What could that lardball possibly do against four of us?

SO, SHULA, THIS ISN'T EXACTLY THE STORY YOU WANTED TO hear, is it? I can sense your impatience, but you'll have to wait, because this is the only way I know how to tell it right now, this is how it comes to me. Elish once told me that any true story takes the side roads, and that's how you find out what it's really about. Those were also his investigation methods, which I'd learned a little of, and those are the tactics I use when I'm planning an attack or defense, an outflanking or a bypass maneuver.

But could it be the other way around? Could I be telling it this way because these are the details you're actually looking for, and your impatience is nothing but excitement? Does any of this ring a bell? Does any of this disclose a meaning I can't see? Of course you aren't going to answer. You only listen.

Woe-man told me to relax, they didn't know who else was in the palace, they were just trackers. Beta took my side, saying whoever they might be, we had to attack and kill them as quickly as possible. That was the law, anyone who studied or retained the CRISPR's knowledge was sentenced to death. Cornelia said it would be wiser to find out their plans and their numbers first, then report back to the Leper. I asked who the Leper was. Woe-man told me to stay out of it. Cornelia said he was one of Tadpola and Gianton's lieutenants. He was the highest-ranking warrior still alive after the rebellion. Beta reminded the others that he used to be a guard officer and that physically he was more than capable of taking out a few scouts. Severed heads were better than intel, and he was sure the Leper would agree. They kept arguing. I realized Beta was losing the argument, and I had no time. Rescuing Oshri wasn't part of their plan anyway. I retreated quietly.

I didn't know this reality as well as they did, but there was one thing I knew that they didn't. Oshri had an *ezovyon* seed, and if the people in the palace were scouts they would have taken the pendant and let him go, because what kind of reward or treasure was a child? I walked through the collapsed open gate in the wall and walked close to the garden fences and the tree trunks and the building walls. Occasionally, I looked up at the windows of Villa Sillykulla to make sure no one was watching me. I moved in short bursts, hiding in between. I didn't let my impatience get the better of me. Instead, I thought about what I'd do to Profession-Hybrid when I got hold of him.

As I got closer to the villa, I realized that the palace was much bigger than Pippi's house. It either just looked small from a distance, or this was a defensive technique. First of all, it wasn't made of wood, but rather of stone and marble. The colors were the same. I walked through the door, which squeaked more than I'd have liked. My footsteps were quiet. It was a good thing I'd worn jeans and sneakers even though I hadn't believed Oshri when he said it was a real journey. There were carpeted stairs pinned in place at the base of each by golden rods. According to my calculations, Hybrid was on the third floor. I pulled the exhaler out of the backpack and held it up like a knife. The ground floor was empty. I climbed the stairs carefully, at an angle, ready to pounce. At the top of the stairs was a hallway, blocked by a curtain. The carpet ended, and with it the muffling of my footsteps. I hid behind the curtain. I heard a door opening and peeked out. Hybrid walked out of one of the rooms. His head was bare, the long protrusions on his scalp as disgusting as he was. He had his back to me, going the other way. I hurried after him, jumped on him, and leaned back. He was heavy and ducked down to fight me off. I held the exhaler against his temple. He started screaming faintly. The sound the exhaler made when it touched his skin was louder, like the sound of frozen fries when they land in boiling oil. It made a repulsive smell too, the smell of rot and feces. I pulled the exhaler back just a little and told him to shut up. I asked where Oshri was. He said he had him locked in a side room off the parlor at the edge of the hall and that he'd take me there. I said I didn't trust him and I wanted answers, and that if I sensed he was lying he'd get another hit of the exhaler. I asked what he wanted from Oshri. He said all he wanted was the *ezovyon* seed and to find out how he got it. I asked, What for? He said his master, the CRISPR, was coming back. I reminded him he'd said the CRISPR was dead. He said that's what he thought, but the CRISPR couldn't be killed. I asked if he knew about the exhaler. He said he didn't know what that was. I asked what he was looking for in the bathroom. He said he tried to call his master, that Sderot used to be interconnected by communication and supervision devices that the rebels must have destroyed. He spat when he said the word "rebels." I asked why he was picking on us. He said he was curious to see two children who hadn't been imagetorted. We couldn't be there when his master returned, especially since we had the gene. I asked what he meant. He said the statue of the double helix at the plaza showed that Oshri and I both had the gene, Oshri in the dangerous way, and me in the correct way. I asked what that meant. He said I'd find out for myself. I put the exhaler to his temple again and heard a grunting, like an overheated dog, and before I could do anything, something hit me in the head and the hallway shone all around, and at the edges of the light stroke was a darkness that quickly swallowed me.

✻ ✻ ✻

MY EYES OPENED A CRACK, AND I COULD SEE I WAS IN AN ELE-gant hall. A dog was licking my neck, a long, damp caress and the sound of panting. Automatically, I tried to jump to my feet, but I was bound to a chair. My arms were pinned to my sides with rope, as were my legs. Luckily, I'd worn long sleeves and couldn't feel the chafing of the rope on my skin. I tried to wriggle free, but the knots were too tight. The panting continued next to my ear. From the corner of my eye I saw a large head, like Hybrid's, with those fat worms in his scalp. He wasn't licking me anymore, only sniff-ing. Smells good, he said, clean flesh, smooth skin. Then he said it again. I shouted at him to get off me, pervert. Hybrid came quickly. He called the name of the creature beside me and re-minded him he'd said the creature could only lick me once to wake me up. He told him to move it. He called him Hybred. Hybred moved away from me. He looked like Hybrid, fat and squat, but his gait was different, hunched, his back wrinkling and his arms waving uncontrollably, as if his body were falling apart and knit-ting back together as he walked. When he reached Hybrid, he low-ered his head. There was a collar around his neck, which Hybrid attached to the chain in his hand. A long tongue covered with stingers dangled from Hybred's mouth. I realized that's what he'd touched me with. So gross, what a pervert.

Hybrid said I should thank him, that Hybred's tongue had me-dicinal and energizing qualities, and that if he hadn't licked me I'd still be out from that blow and might have suffered a concus-sion, but luckily for me, the master needed to see me. I didn't an-swer. I looked around. The hall was large. This must have been the parlor. The walls were white marble with black patterns I couldn't follow. I looked around for the door to the chamber Hy-brid said Oshri was locked in. There was one opening concealed by a heavy red velvet curtain with gold fringes. That couldn't be it. Yes, there it was, behind Hybrid and Hybred, a small iron door. To my left was a gleaming appliance that looked like stainless steel, and it let out a buzz like sawing or drilling, screeching but dense.

I examined it. It looked like a table covered with a metal dome, and between the two parts was a great, white light, a cloud of light that didn't evaporate. Blue and green lights blinked around the edges of the table. There were other metal tables behind me, covered with sinks, test tubes, and other devices I didn't recognize. It looked like they'd been pushed aside because the space wasn't evenly utilized. The center was empty. Next to the curtain stood a round table with one leg that split into several legs and a base. It had a dim, deep glow like old jewelry, like Grandma Zehava's Moroccan gold. It seemed to belong to what the parlor used to be. The surface was made of marble, and my exhaler was set on top of it. I took another good look at Hybrid and Hybred. The hole in Hybrid's temple stood out, a black circle with red lines stretching out toward his forehead and cheeks. His left hand was completely black with red ruptures. Hybred licked it and occasionally paused to whine. I figured that idiot Hybrid must have carried the exhaler over here. I was glad to see that Hybred's tongue wasn't helping against the alloy. Served them both.

I tried to figure out how to get out of those ropes. I told Hybrid to let me go, that I'd play along and tell him whatever he wanted to know about the exhaler. He looked at me suspiciously, then moved his eyes to the exhaler. He didn't know what that thing was. He moved his eyes back to me and coughed. No. He laughed. I fought against the binds again. Hybrid said it was pointless, that he was famous for his knots. A racket sounded outside the parlor, behind me. Rolling metal and shattering glass. Hybrid dragged Hybred behind him and they went out to investigate.

I heard soft footfalls. I turned my head but couldn't see who was coming. Suddenly, Oshri was whispering in my ear to keep quiet. Instinctively, I wanted to call his name, but he put his hand on my mouth. It smelled like wet dust, stinking like Dad's socks. There was familiarity in that smell, a comfort. He walked around me, and I got a look at him. He was dirty, his clothes covered with lint and cobwebs and small shoots. But his face was laughing, his features all atwitter, his eyes shining. He was holding a small scalpel in his hand. He cut the rope around my right arm pretty easily. Then he handed it to me and brought another knife, a curved one, like a scythe. He said the tables behind us were covered with knives. I cut the rope off my left arm while he cut the ones around my legs. He told me Profession, that moron, had locked him in a room full of lab equipment, and how hard could it be to cut off some ropes and break through a door with all that equipment around? I said his real name was Hybrid, and that he'd tricked us. Oshri nodded. Anyway, he'd gone out to investigate. I told Oshri we had to get out, inform the trackers who'd brought us that the CRISPR was returning. I asked what had happened to his *ezovyon* seed. Oshri said Hybrid had taken it from him. It was in that device at the edge of the parlor. I was unbound. My arms and legs were sore, but not sore enough to slow me down. I ran over and picked up the exhaler. I told Oshri we had to run away. Oshri said no. He had been about to go get the *ezovyon* seed back when he heard Hybrid and Hybred arriving. He hid behind the tables and saw them tying me up, so he slipped out to create a diversion. Now he told me to watch the door and make sure those two fatties weren't coming back. I said, No, let's go. He didn't listen. He said it wasn't fair for us to get my object back but not his. He hurried over to the metal appliance that buzzed and hummed. I went with him. In the middle of the cloud of light was the *ezovyon* seed in its crystal coating. Metal arms extended out of the table, attempting to cut into it with laser beams and spinning metal saws. They didn't seem to be pulling it off. They weren't making so much as a scratch on the crystal. Oshri said there had to be a switch somewhere. He ducked down to check under the table, then stood on tiptoes to peek over the dome. He found it and reached out. I said no, the seed was protected by the coating and we had to get out of there. He touched the switch. A screech exploded all around us. I pulled on Oshri's arm, but he was paralyzed, glued to the switch.

I pulled and pulled, but nothing. It was as if he were made of stone. Why'd he have to stick his hand there? I walked around the appliance to see if I could unplug it, but there was no cable and no outlet anywhere around it. I realized I'd seen no evidence of electricity use around here. I ran over to the tables. Maybe I'd find a long blade I could slip between the switch and Oshri's finger and separate them. Halfway there I heard a rustle, like insects chewing or coals popping in a flame. I turned around. The curtain in the parlor's doorway parted and something stepped out. It looked like a human, had the shape of a man, face and arms and back and stomach and legs. But he was naked and his skin was completely smooth, as if made of plastic the color of sand, somewhere between yellow, gold, and gray. An unnatural, undefinable hue. And he had no genitals, no nipples, and nothing between his legs. It was smooth like the rest of him. No navel either. Like a mannequin. But he was alive. His mouth made this sound. A laugh, probably. His lips split like a gash on his face, showing his teeth. His eyes were purple and large like Hybrid's, and his nose was small, too chiseled, too perfectly shaped. I thought that when Racheli and Elinoar grew up that was the kind of nose they'd have, an upturned nose, a snobby nose.

He approached me, walking regally, as if he was waiting for applause with every footstep. As he walked, his features shifted. At first I thought it was a trick of the light or something, but no. Suddenly, his forehead was broad, and his mouth lowered almost all the way to his chin. Then it climbed up again. I walked to the table, reached out, and felt around carefully. All the tools were metallic and cold, and I was afraid of getting cut. I pulled. A hacksaw, the blade pliable and taut between the two ends of the arch. I held it before my face, but my hand trembled, and so did the hacksaw. The creature paused a meter away from me. His face wandered down to his chest with a smooth motion, like a flock of birds, first the mouth, then the nose and the eyes. The face was now at eye level with mine. He reached out his hand, the creature, fingers outstretched. He said he needed the alloy canister. There was that same popping and crunching in his voice. No. The words came together out of the popping and crunching. He'd called it the alloy canister. He didn't know what it was, then. I shook my head. He said I'd be much better off giving it to him than if he chose his preferred option, which was for him to tear out my limbs and rearrange them. I could barely speak, but I managed to tell him to release Oshri first. He asked if Oshri was the rawmaterial next to his rupturer. I asked if he was the CRISPR. He said he used to be the CRISPR and would be again, but that the CRISPR without his knowledge was merely an empty shell. I told him to release Oshri, that I could help him. He said he didn't negotiate with rawmaterial. He bent down, his hand reaching out for me. With all my shaking, I held out the hacksaw to slice off his fingers. He was fast. He whipped me with his hand, making the hacksaw fly out of mine. His fingers gripped my wrist and tightened. He dragged me behind him across the parlor. I screamed.

Then I heard a smacking sound. Something, a large rock maybe, hit his head and fell. His face shifted to the back of his head, which was all bloody. The blood trickled quickly, like water over porcelain, quicker than that, rinsing his skin. His let go of my wrist. Hybrid's head was on the floor, rolling around and coming to a stop not far from him. I heard Cornelia calling my name. I turned around and ran toward the voice. She and Beta were in the doorway. She was holding Hybred's head in her hand. His tongue was dangling, blood dripping out of his severed neck. She threw the head at the CRISPR's feet.

He made that sound of his again. A sentence was taking shape. He ordered all man-mades to obey his orders. Beta responded that they were free people and that he'd never control them again. I noticed how hard it was for him to speak the words. The CRISPR said he'd never waste fine rawmaterial like them, and that once he killed them he'd make sure they obeyed. Even death wasn't the end of obedience.

They stood before him and I got behind them. They told me to back away and take cover. Cornelia rolled up her sleeves. There were silver straps wrapped around her deformed arms. She pulled on them, one in each hand, whipped them through the air, and they hardened, transforming into two long blades. Beta growled. The feathers on his head stood up, the small fingernails on the backs of his hands growing longer. His fists looked like spiky balls. They both lunged at the CRISPR.

I hid behind the tables. I figured if I ducked behind them, I could make it all the way to Oshri. But I couldn't look away from the fight. It was mesmerizing.

Cornelia danced with her blades, spinning and stabbing. Beta circled his fists around. The CRISPR's face streamed down his body, in line with his movements. His body streamed too, as if he were some thick liquid like tar or mercury, flowing between Cornelia's blades, bending, flexing, wriggling, easily evading Beta's storm of fists. I'd never seen anything so riveting in my life. I forgot about Oshri and the emergency siren in my bloodstream stopped. I just watched, I don't know for how long. At some point, Beta removed his alloy necklace, opened it up, and used it like a whip. He got the CRISPR right in the face. Cornelia stabbed low, slicing through his right leg. He fell to his knees. She stabbed him in the shoulder and Beta wrapped his chain around the CRISPR's neck, pulling. He tied the ends together and twisted them to strangle him. The CRISPR's face rose and fell over his chest and stomach, and one of Cornelia's blades followed them around. She demanded to know how he'd managed to come back. He said man-mades had no right to question their master. Beta growled at him that he was wrong, that maybe he hadn't noticed, but he was the one on his knees. The CRISPR raised his hand, as if in submission, and his mouth scampered like a cockroach down his arm, to his palm. He turned it toward Beta's head, and the mouth let out a scream. Beta's body seemed to drain out, going limp. He fell to the floor, writhing. Cornelia dropped the blades and covered her ears. The CRISPR stood up. His cuts closed up. He was unharmed.

The siren returned to my body. Bells were ringing all over my brain. I felt useless, helpless. Oshri was still paralyzed by the appliance. Beta was dead on the floor, blood flowing out of his eyes and ears and nose. And the CRISPR was coming at Cornelia, who looked panicked, her eyes bouncing around in search of a weapon. He walked over to her with that same arrogant gait. How could he be so aloof, I wondered, how could he be so vain? I grabbed the exhaler in my left hand and stood up. My voice was trembling, my legs were jelly, but I told him to let go of her and Oshri, here was his stupid canister, go ahead and take it. He ignored me. He seemed to be relishing every footstep, probably thinking about what he'd turn Cornelia into. Idiot, I thought to myself, how could I have let Oshri risk himself like that? With my right hand, I twisted off the cap. I pulled out the bubble wand. What did Cornelia and Beta say about it? I shouted at the CRISPR that the metal canister was called an exhaler, and that it could melt off the coating from the *ezovyon* seed. His face wandered to the side of his head. He paused. I tried to remember what else they'd said. That only someone with a specific genetic signature could do it. That's what Hybrid meant when he said I had the gene. The CRISPR looked at me. I held out the wand and blew. Nothing happened. Only air. The CRISPR's mouth opened and that popping and crunching sound came out, but no words were shaped. Laughter, then.

What was he laughing about, that jackass. I felt my blood boiling, my nerves crackling, about Oshri, about this disgusting creature who bent people out of shape without a second thought, who oppressed them. He laughed again. The sounds formed words. Rawmaterial. I wanted to cry, but I can't cry. I didn't cry at Elish's shiva, I didn't cry, while Oshri took every opportunity to, as if he hurt more than I did, but I hurt more, really, I did, Elish was mine more than his. Oshri only discovered him last summer, but Elish had been by my side my entire life. It was the daytimelight and the nighttimedark that held me back, drying out my organs, and I couldn't tell anybody, even when I tried talking, the words were empty. My eyes burned, they burned, with hatred for myself for being so useless. At the center of the wand's circle I saw a concentrated blue dot. It was trembling. I put it close to my lips and blew, not lightly. I poured in all my lonesomeness, all my hatred for being lonely, all my aggravation for not being able to save anybody. The dot hovered in the air before me, and then it sped up, gaining speed and growing, shooting toward the CRISPR. Small electric lightning bolts shot out of it. By the time it hit his stomach, it was the size of a tennis ball. The lightning bolts elongated like spider legs, a thousand legs wrapping around his body. He yelled, the popping and crunching growing sharper. His face bounced around his body, but the lightning bolts kept stinging it, stabbing it, electrocuting it. Cornelia was shoved back. The CRISPR's body shrunk, as if the bolts were sucking on it, swallowing it down. At some point, I noticed that the appliance behind him had turned off. Oshri was released from it and was watching as well.

The CRISPR was completely eaten away. All that was left was the tennis ball, which floated in the air a few seconds longer, then fell to the ground and shattered, a pile of dust turning into smoke and scattering until its particles could no longer be seen. I cried for Oshri. He put his hand in the appliance and snatched up the pendant. He ran to me. The hall was filled with cries of joy. Where were they coming from? I turned around. About twenty Sderot residents were gathered behind us. I was too tired to detect their individual imagetortions. They were all mixed up, hugging and raising their arms. Oshri was next to me, his face filled with excitement, his smile wide, his eyes glimmering, like he had a story he had to tell me. He paused at my side.

Cornelia kneeled. She touched my shoulders and said I'd done a great thing, and that it was a shame Beta was no longer with us because she realized now that he'd been right.

I asked what she meant, but she didn't answer. Another voice answered instead, hoarse, stifled. The voice said we must be exhausted. I turned toward it. A tall man in a black tracksuit made of a shiny, fine fabric. A clubbing tracksuit, as the *arsim* in my grade call it. The skin of his face was completely cracked, as was the hand he offered me. One of his eyes was closed, the lids glued together, and one ear and part of his nose were missing.

I said I wasn't too tired, that I wanted to hear about it. Oshri nodded. A few of the imagetortions carried chairs into the parlor and cleared out Hybrid's and Hybred's heads and Beta's body. They seated Cornelia, Oshri, and me next to the Leper. The others stood across from us. Off to the side, I saw Woe-man. The woman half smiled, the fake smile girls make when they want to kill you but are pretending to be your friend. The man half fought to contain his emotions, but I could recognize his frustration.

The Leper said he was finally free to explain everything and let go of this burden he'd been carrying for ten years. He said that during their studies, Tadpola and Gianton had discovered that the CRISPR was almost totally invulnerable and could be revived from any harm by a single cell, a drop of blood, even a hair. The only way to destroy it was with the radiation generator. So they invented a complicated trap. The name of the device that would cause his demise was a deception. It was called a radiation generator, but was in fact a mobile lab for genetic mutations. The ball of light was actually a machine that disassembled his cells and turned them into a bacterial infection, the sole purpose of which was to attack the CRISPR's cells, wherever they might be. A plague aimed at a single creature. But to use it, they had to get him out of hiding. So they spread the story about the *ezovyon* seeds and the exhalers. The entire time, there was only one exhaler and two seeds. One seed was coded with the CRISPR's knowledge, the other contained the decoder.

He opened his arm and showed us his alloy necklace. It had a pendant identical to Oshri's. He said the generator was designed to contain three exhalations. The first would annihilate the CRISPR, the second would annihilate the seeds, and the third would create a seeping point in the time border.

He looked at Oshri and me. He said they'd expected some hero scout, versed in battles and adventures, not two children. Oshri shifted uncomfortably in his seat. His face was alight, his eyes wide and his mouth hanging open, wanting to swallow everything around him.

There was movement within the rebel crowd. People were shoved aside. Woe-man stood up in front. They said that according to the Liberated Sderot Law, anyone who learned the CRISPR's knowledge or obtained it was sentenced to death. They pointed at the three of us, at the Leper, Oshri, and me.

Cornelia jumped to her feet. She asked how Woe-man dared say that. Woe-man said, A law's a law. Cornelia said they were just bitter because they always followed rules, and that if the girl—she pointed at me—and Beta and herself hadn't done something, who knew what would have happened. Woe-man chose to go back to camp and report and call for help rather than join the battle, and now they shouldn't try to punish the others for winning. Woe-man insisted. They said again that a law was a law. Oshri looked at me. I realized he wasn't getting half of this. I lowered my head to his and whispered that Woe-man were the head of the tracking team that brought me here. The Leper cut off our whispering, as well as Cornelia and Woe-man's argument, and the ruckus in the small crowd. He stood up and said Woe-man were right, and that the great justice that was achieved today could not take precedence over the small justice they were demanding. But that the small justice didn't apply to the children, meaning us, and that we had only been playing the roles designated to us by Tadpola and Gianton's plan. He said the weapon should not be punished, but rather those carrying it. I didn't love the fact that he referred to Oshri and me as weapons, but I got what he meant. He said those that carried the weapon were Tadpola, Gianton, and himself. Tadpola and Gianton had already paid their price. Now he was willing to pay his.

He said there was a lesson to be learned here, that in their blind faith in the law, Woe-man failed to remember the fact that the girl, meaning I, was the only one who could operate the exhaler and that it took another puff to destroy the CRISPR's knowledge. How would they propose to convince her, meaning me, to help them after they'd sentenced her, meaning me, to death?

Truth be told, the Leper's words warmed my heart. I'd been floating in some pleasant sensation before Woe-man started talking. Those patheteethes, we saved them and now they wanted to kill us. They were just jealous, Cornelia was right about that. I would have liked to cut open their sutures, take them apart, and sew them back up again at the half ass and half back. I was still holding the exhaler. If it burned the CRISPR so bad, just imagine what it could do to Woe-man. I gritted my teeth. The metal from my braces tasted bitter.

Someone in the crowd pulled back Woe-man, swallowing them in and spitting them out the other end. A few of them shouted that if Woe-man didn't shut up they'd cut off their tongue. The Leper shushed them. He said things were getting out of hand, and that they should be celebrating. But first, I had to destroy the *ezovyon* seeds. He and Oshri placed them on the antique table with the gold leg. I stood between Oshri and the Leper, everyone else behind us. I still held my anger toward Woe-man, burning inside of me. I puffed and the burning came out of my mouth, along with the air. The blue radiation ball pounced on the seeds, turning them into nothing before disappearing itself.

I turned to face the Leper. He was walking toward the crowd, his arms stretched ahead of him. He said that Woe-man were right. The law dictated that he be executed. Cornelia stood between him and the crowd. She said she objected. He told her to leave him alone, that for the past ten years every breath he took felt like a sword through his flesh, that his bones were brittle and he had acid running through his veins. He agonized from morning till night. He'd been yearning for the moment when his mission would be complete. When he'd finally be able to rest.

OSHRI WANTED TO STAY FOR THE VICTORY CELEBRATIONS. I told him everything I'd been through, and the more I told him, the more excited he became. He stopped me to ask for more details about the CRISPR, about the imagetortion. It turned out his paralysis in the parlor was limited to his movements. He could still hear and see. He said the battle between the CRISPR, Cornelia, and Beta was amazing and that he wanted to see more. He was most interested in the scouts and guides. Who were they? He asked anyone willing to speak to him about how they passed among the different Sderotae, what they got out of their adventures, how they made contact with guides. He gathered a lot of information, which he tried to relay to me as we walked among the revelers. He said that in the books Elish gave us, the kids were always in a rush to get back home, but that couldn't be the only possibility. I stopped listening. I'd grown too tired of it. We made plans to meet in an hour by the gate in the wall. That's where Cornelia told me to meet her, so she could take us home with her for the night.

There were tables set with food and drink in the palace plaza. Lamps were installed throughout the gardens. I asked an imagetorted man with teeth of all kinds growing out of his body and no fingers what power source they were connected to. He hugged one of the poles in his arms. He said he was providing the energy, that it came from his joy. He told me to look at the light. Yes, the lighting danced like the flame of a candle. His name was Incisor-cerer. He said this was how appliances operated in this Sderot. That certainly clarified things.

I kept wandering. There was too much action, too many image-tortions drinking and dancing. I tasted the food. None of the flavors were familiar, but they were all rich and appetizing. I might have eaten more under different circumstances. I walked over to a garden that seemed quieter. Less lit, anyway. No music either. I walked through a small metal gate. The garden was the shape of a flower, with a fountain at its center and six arches all around, like petals. The arch to my right was made of partially broken marble columns, rough at the point of fracturing. Two arches that faced each other contained green sculptures of stags. So strange to think that this Sderot used to have stags. The rest featured benches and pergolas like the one Dad once built out back. There must have been plants that climbed on the trellis here too, and rosebushes. An imagetortion sat on the far end, a small light on beside them. I didn't want to interrupt, but I was curious. When I came closer, I saw it was Cornelia. She was staring into a glass ball on a metal base. I whispered her name. She looked at me. She was crying. Her cheeks and the corns all over them were wet, and her eyes reflected the light from the ball. She patted the bench. I asked if she was all right. She said she couldn't celebrate after having lost three friends in a single day. I could tell she needed silence, so I was silent with her, ignoring the questions that filled my head, like why no one lived in the palace now. I could guess the answer. But I wanted someone to tell me if I was right.

Eventually, I asked if the Leper would really be executed. She said it didn't matter, he'd already made his own sentence, and if he was pardoned he'd kill himself. The same thing happened with Tadpola and Gianton. Everyone begged them to stay alive, but like Woe-man, they said a law was a law.

We got up to go meet Oshri, but he was late. When he arrived, he was even more fired up. The whole way to Cornelia's house, he kept telling us how amazing this time disruption hub was. He said no one knew how many Sderotae there were altogether, and that one of the more advanced ones had a science institute and a library that documented all the different histories and planes of existence, but that it was invaded by demons called the Occult, who'd become infected with an artificial intelligence cybervirus, and the residents were under siege. At least that was according to somebody who'd spoken to a scout years ago. Time moved differently in each of the Sderotae. He asked if I'd tried the food. It turned out it was produced by animals from all over the realm who had symbiotic relationships with the residents here, and they traded products discharged by local animals to the other Sderotae. Also, the appliances here operated on emotional energy.

I told him I'd heard enough. He said no, it wasn't enough, we had to stay longer, because when would we ever get another opportunity to—

I cut him off. I asked what he was talking about. We were abducted, almost killed by a monster, and when we saved the residents, one of them proposed they execute us. He said it was easy for me to talk because my adventure was more interesting than his. All he got to do was find one important object and escape his abductors. I reminded him he also untied me. He said sure, but that was nothing compared to what I did. I told him to stop keeping score. He said there was so much to see in the different realms, so many adventures, and that this was his journey.

The next morning, he had a faraway look in his eyes. They kept shifting to a point in the clouds and staying there. A delegation accompanied us to a time border. Cornelia and the Leper, who was wearing handcuffs, and two guards, among them Woeman. It wasn't exactly a border, but everything stopped there, and even still objects seemed to be emptied of something, and the air turned cold but was also trembling, and there was movement within it, like enormous, dark, blurry sea creatures. The Leper explained how to aim my puff so that the border opened up onto our Sderot. I was finding something within myself I'd never thought possible. I blew on the exhaler one last time. The air tore and the sea creatures fled. Through the rip, I could see the lake and the thicket on the side we entered from. They held the same afternoon light, the same remnants of rain on the leaves. I smelled them, the wet decay of the lake and the stench of the eucalyptus. I gave Oshri my hand and he held on to it weakly. I closed my fingers around his tighter and we walked toward the rip. I put one foot through, half my body. Oshri pulled his hand out of mine and jumped back. He told me to go on by myself, that I hadn't understood what he'd tried to tell me. He whispered sadly that he was one of the kids that stayed.

OSHRI ASKED IF I GOT UP AT NIGHT TO EAT OR DRINK. I SAID I hadn't. He said, Good. He opened his medical kit. I sat next to the table and offered my arm. I didn't turn to look away when he stuck in the needle. I watched as it filled with thick blood. He closed the syringe and slipped it into a bag. He looked at his intePhone and said our timing was perfect, Nitzan was almost there. He said while he went outside to meet her, he'd stop by the open-air market to get some groceries. He asked if he could get me anything. I said, Yes, wine. My hand wandered to the wide surface of light, dipping in it. I said this season was appropriate for white wine, and asked him to look for Pelter sauvignon blanc, that I wondered if that winery still existed. He gave me a long look and asked when I'd started drinking wine. I told him I've had some chances, that Itay was a wine enthusiast. He said yes, but you only dated Itay for like six months. I wanted to correct him, we'd been together for a year and a half, but I didn't see how that would help our conversation. He never remembered. He was sure I'd dated Lior for a month, for example, but it was actually five. I shrugged and stood up. Oshri said to do him a favor, when I got back to the lockdown corner after washing up and getting my coffee and some breakfast, to put on the NS strap, because he wanted to check something.

What was there to check, I asked. My blood test would tell him everything was fine. He said, What do you care, you just sit there and stare anyway. He'd asked how I'd slept earlier, because when he came in to wake me up he was convinced my eyes were open, but it took me a while to respond. I couldn't be bothered to answer him. He touched a point above his intePhone and the shutters opened. A diagonal ray of sunlight fell beside me, a piece of heat on the side of the mattress. I sat up. I told him it had been a strange night with very vivid dreams, the kind you have just before you fall asleep, when a full movie that has never been made but you know exists appears all at once, or in the space of awakening, when you hear a complete song and you know all the parts, the lyrics, the music. So my entire night was like that, like the space before falling asleep and the space before waking, without the sleeping part in the middle. Oshri said the first space was called "hypnagogia" and the second was called "hypnopompia." But he didn't think either of them could last very long. I said maybe I just dreamed that I spent all night not transitioning to sleep or waking up constantly. He asked if I remembered that Elish—

I said yes, that I'd failed to sleep at the speed of sleep, that I twilighted at the speed of twilight. Oshri said nothing, but I didn't feel that prick that rolls over and goes through the stomach and up into the throat, but a warmth, like missing someone you'll see soon, the way I felt when I went on leave during basic training, and a few stops before Sderot I was ready to burst with longing. It doesn't really matter.

Marco called a few minutes after Oshri left. I only turned on the audio channel. He said, Okay, like he was hurt. He asked how I was doing. I said fine. He said it sounded like he'd caught me in the middle of something. I said not at all. He said maybe I was preoccupied with thoughts. I said it was lucky I'd taken the time off because I ended up getting the flu and that's why I wasn't focused. He asked if someone was taking care of me. I said yes, that Oshri had made me come stay with him for a few days. He said we were close, Oshri and I. I said it sounded like he was accusing me of something. He said no, that Oshri was a good brother, and if only his own brothers were more like him. I knew he liked Oshri. Actually, who doesn't? Oshri is skilled at hiding the fact that he only requires a drop of affection from others, but Marco has trouble admitting his fondness, so he says he's a good brother, a good guy, etc. Like I said, men. He asked if I needed anything, offered to stop by. I asked since when he had any free time to spare. He laughed, a brief laugh, so restrained it came out like a bark. I said speaking of that, to what did I owe the pleasure of his call? I knew I was quoting Manny Lahav. He always says, To what do I owe this pleasure, with that old-guy tone.

Marco said he wanted my opinion on something. I said, Wow, you actually called for advice? He said, Don't be like that. Like what? I asked. Cynical, he said. I asked what was cynical about me. He said I was pretending like he didn't appreciate me. I said maybe I should have gone on leave much earlier. He made that barking sound again. I thought that laughing twice in one conversation was unusual for Marco. Was he embarrassed or what? I asked how I could help. He said they received a focused alert about a potential attack on the MKI site at Plugot Junction. Surprised, I asked why someone would want to attack an agricultural development site. He said there was intel about a collaboration between a temple loyalists' cell and a cell of what remained of Hamas troops. I said that explained things. The patheteeth mimics of the Chaos Front were all show, lacking a single strategic cause. They were nothing like their models. He said he still found it odd.

I told him I thought this was a diversion, and that he should check if there was a third terror group hiding behind this alliance, using it as bait. He asked, In that case, where would the central target be? I asked if this was a test. He said not at all. I said he ought to know better than me that they'd either go for the MKI site in Ashdod or the one under construction in Ramallah. He said this was his assumption too, but what's next? I said I would booby-trap the perimeter of the Plugot site with nerve mines and leave the security level as is, then reinforce combat forces, observation, and digital tracking at the two other facilities but without showing increased presence. That way, if we were right about the third organization, they'd have a surprise in store, and if this was just a patheteeth exhibition of power then they'd be screwed, because there was no chance they were advanced enough to defend themselves against nerve mines.

He said he was glad to hear that my analysis and solution resembled his. The other analysts from the military's combat center thought it was a waste of resources. I said, Well, why did you call, then? He said there was no beating around the bush with me. I didn't respond. He said he was still waiting for that date I promised him. I said he'd already gotten it. He said he hadn't, that I cheated. I said I'd kept my word down to the letter. He said that was the problem, sometimes down to the letter was cheating. I said I thought he was seeing somebody. He said they broke up, that he couldn't be with someone he couldn't discuss 80 percent of his life with, and even if he could, he doubted she'd care or understand.

YOU KNOW, SHULA, AFTER OSHRI GOT DEPRESSED, THE CASE OF the Lost Detective started to seem pointless. I put the notebook back in my drawer and closed it. I had Yalon. Occasionally, I tried to speak with Oshri, but he was immersed in his own affairs. When he wasn't busy with his books and the digital reader he'd gotten at the library, he spent hours clicking away on his computer keyboard. I saw some of the books he was reading. He'd ditched stories and read more nonfiction. I wondered what he was writing on the computer. He wouldn't let anybody read it.

Talking to him got crazy boring. Not the things he talked about, but his tone. It was like it didn't matter what we talked about. Sometimes I wanted to peel off his skin, remove the Slime padding, and let the Oshri I know breathe. But he was inside himself. Besides the two hours a day Dad made him do physical activity, like riding his bike or walking. It did our dad good. He insisted on only taking jobs nearby so that he had time to spend with Oshri. And he lost some weight. Mom said that was also because he stopped eating garbage and snacks instead of a normal lunch.

I had Yalon. He wasn't too excited about living with his father. As soon as he chose to live with him, his father kind of ditched him, and would leave Yalon to stay with his grandma Kuti in her big, empty villa. But Yalon was even less excited about staying with his mother. She tried to poison him against his dad any chance she got, saying he was mean and abusive. All nice-like. That's why that time we went to see Nahum Farkash, Yalon avoided Shifra, his aunt, because she and his mother were the same. I didn't want to tell him that I'd heard his father say the exact same thing. We spent our evenings together in my bedroom or his. Sometimes we listened to Blasé and talked about what might have actually happened to Dalia Shushan, and what Elish meant when he wrote that something about the solution to her mystery didn't add up and that he had to expand the circle of suspects. We already learned from his notes that he thought Yehuda Menuhin had murdered Dalia and then killed himself, unlike the news websites from the time reported, that she was murdered by some junkie who tried to rob her. But it all grew vague and far away. We thought it was funny that Nahum Farkash quit the library and became the manager of the reading encouragement project, Reading Forward, or something lame like that, and that they called the digital reader Take Up and Read. It was like a private joke between the four of us, Nahum, Oshri, Yalon, and me. Yalon said he'd gone back to see Nahum on his own and asked for the first conversion file Nahum made of the original recording of

Dalia Shushan's song, the .wav file. Yalon used a special software that saved the sounds and frequencies that are cut out during the conversion from .wav to .mp3 file. And the music those pieces made is hypnotizing, like eavesdropping on a conversation between ghosts. He gave it to me as a birthday gift.

Then came my difficult years. Yalon and I broke up when we enlisted, because he was mad at me for choosing to serve far away and hardly coming home. Then we got back together toward the end of our service, and broke up for good when he decided to stay under his father's wing. His swaying was over. I was sick of him using me as an excuse to rebel. My heart was bruised again, again my heart was bruised. I thought a lot about Elish during that time. I thought about Akiva and Ronnit and about her husband, David. During the violence waves of 2019, David started Making Peace, an organization for solidarity and accountability, and that's what he called it, that loser. I wondered if my role, like Elish's, was to urge others to live normal lives but avoid living one myself. I thought what was awful about it was that Elish didn't encourage them or urge them out of his own desire, he just insisted that others live life the way he saw it, hopeless, and they panicked. I thought maybe that was the problem, that Elish thought he could see a truer layer of life, that he might have suffered because of it but wasn't willing to admit to himself his mistake. I didn't cry, even though I wanted to. I found other things to keep me busy.

Six months ago, Oshri called and asked me to come meet him at his Tel Aviv apartment. I thought, Elish's apartment. I told him I wouldn't go in there. He said there was something that required my attention because I was part owner and we had to make a decision about the structure. It sounded strange. He'd always made it sound like he'd renovated the place according to his needs.

It was hard for me to go in there. I hadn't been since the last time we came as children. I stood in the doorway and Oshri pulled me inside. He closed the door and tapped a crystal board he'd integrated into the wall on the left. I heard a humming followed by silence. Oshri said the apartment was secured against all tracking devices. His job demanded it, and now it finally served him too. What he was going to tell me had to stay between us, because it involved a breach of confidentiality.

MKI had already started establishing themselves as the new center of the military, founded on cooperation between the combat center and civilian research institutes and companies. Part of their establishment was the Knowledge Nationalization Law. Any private lab, start-up, or firm had a choice—either transfer all their businesses to another country, or become bound to MKI's enormous conglomerate. If they chose the second option, they could keep all of their existing products, but the development of all future products would be done in collaboration with MKI, which would also receive 50 percent of the profit. Either way, any company that operated on Israeli land and was Israeli-owned was obligated to report the development protocols of every nonmarketed product to MKI.

Oshri was assigned to a team that categorized and catalogued these protocols. It drove him insane. After that challenging, demanding biocyber training, they were tasking him with building an archive. But his anger didn't last, because he met Nitzan, who'd also been assigned there after undergoing neuro training, so they had lots to talk about. And also because he fell in love with the work. He was amazed by how many studies on the assimilation of biological computerization had been performed on Israeli territory, and by how many of them were based on models of microorganism information processing. That's what he called it. I didn't ask too many questions.

Anyway, it went like this. He came across a file of protocols describing experiments on a certain type of typhus. The studies themselves were based on records from the Buchenwald concentration camp. Oshri asked how much I knew about Rudolf Weigl and Ludwik Fleck. I said, Pretty much nothing.

He explained a lot, and I'll do my best to repeat his explanations, because I imagine it's important to you, Shula. I took a few notes in my Case of the Lost Detective notebook. Yes, I kept it. I took it with me when I moved to the northern Tel Aviv suburbs. I'd been wise not to let go of it.

Typhus is caused by a bacteria that's transferred into the body through the excrement of body lice. These lice can only live at the temperature of the human body, and procreate under bad hygienic conditions. Obviously. For instance, when you don't change your clothes for weeks on end. Typhus was a hella serious plague in World War I battlefronts. It damages the nervous system, causing the deformation and shedding of organs. Those who catch it burn with fever and experience hallucinations. The lice feed on blood. When they bite, they release a substance that keeps the rupture in the skin open, creating an irritation that causes scratching. Scratching allows the excrement that's left on the skin to penetrate the infected zone, and the bacteria invades the bloodstream.

During World War II, the Nazis tried to develop a vaccine. They recruited a Polish scientist, Rudolf Weigl, who was already working on a vaccine in his lab in Lvov. They built him a lab at Buchenwald. Oshri said the problem with the bacteria was that it only passed through lice, and the lice could only survive on living bodies. Meaning, it couldn't be grown under normal lab conditions, and could not be formed in cultures. At least not the way those were done at the time, without the biotechnology that exists today. Weigl used humans as incubators. He tied small cages full of lice to their legs. The lice would bite their hosts, sucking their blood. This way, Weigl could experiment on the infected lice. He convinced the Nazis he needed these human hosts, and that they could use the Jews in the camps. He chose artists, poets, musicians, philosophers, people who weren't much good at the hard labor the Jews were ordered to perform. He hooked them up with improved conditions, better food, better sleep. That's how he saved their lives. Some of them caught typhus, of course, as did Weigl himself, but they received the kind of medical care that wasn't available to soldiers on the front lines. And that's how he saved the life of Ludwik Fleck, who worked with him at the lab in Lvov before the Nazis occupied Poland. He hired him as an assistant.

Oshri said that so far this was known information. But the protocols he received mentioned that one of the human incubators was a Jewish poet of North African descent. He'd been handed over to the Nazis in Paris and sent to Buchenwald, where he was chosen to participate in Weigl's study. His fate was unclear. Fleck's guess was that he'd caught typhus. In later questioning, his cellmates said he'd grown introverted for a few days before his manifestations began. The other inmates reported shadow people appearing around him, with whom he seemed to be speaking. In his notes, Fleck wrote that he'd witnessed these delusions. He'd assumed the North African poet had infected other inmates with his fever dreams, making them see the shadow men somehow. His consciousness had somehow affected theirs, even though the poet showed no signs of fever, only shock. After ten days the delusions stopped and the North African poet could remember nothing of them. Fleck ran an experiment under Weigl's approval, but couldn't re-create the phenomenon. After the camp was liberated, the poet disappeared without a trace.

Oshri said Fleck had written quite a bit about the relationship between consciousness and fact and the manner in which culture creates scientific facts. He analyzed the way diseases are defined. Fleck argued that the definition of an illness was a method of thought that allowed us to see an illness. Something like that. But he kept his study of the hallucinations a secret. Maybe it seemed too crazy to him. He remained in Lublin after the war, only coming to Israel in 1957, after Weigl was already dead. He was convinced something in the poet's immune system had caused this phenomenon as a way to fight the typhus or as a reaction to the infection and figured he might find patients with a similar immune structure in Israel.

All sorts of negligible details in this story made Oshri laugh. For example, the fact that Weigl and Fleck smuggled the vaccine into other concentration camps, injecting the Jews with it but sending faulty vaccine samples to Nazi soldiers on the front line and holding back development. When Nazi commanders complained that the vaccine wasn't completely efficient and difficult to get ahold of, they said, What can we do, it's produced out of Jewish urine, and Jewish urine is a second-rate product. I'm not sure I'm getting all the details right, but that doesn't matter. The point is, Oshri found it amusing.

No, here's the main point. The study on human reaction to the special breed of typhus that infected the Jewish poet was run four times. The first was thought to be on a certain date during the 1980s. It ended with the death of the test subject. The next three times were run during the second decade of the 2000s. The first two times, it produced the manifestations, that's what the experimenters called them, manifestations or vivid delusions. The first time in a fairly weak and singular way that could not be properly recorded. The second time in a way that was clear to the experimenters, but the records are questionable. The third time it created no response, but the subject died a week later from an overdose of alcohol and anti-anxiety medication. No connection was found between the events.

Of course, from the moment Oshri mentioned the Jewish poet I couldn't contain my questions. He asked me to be patient until he reached the important part. He wanted to test the—

But I beat him to it. I remembered the dates of Kalanit Shaubi's disappearance by heart and nodded when he mentioned them. I asked about the date of the final experiment. He asked why. I asked how he could fail to notice that the test subject's date of death was the same as Elish's. I asked who'd conducted the studies. He said part of the Knowledge Nationalization Law was

that protocols from studies that hadn't produced marketable results or that were not published as papers would remain anonymous. He could mark certain protocols as special interest for
further investigation, but then it would be out of his hands and
attract unwanted attention.

I HAD THOUGHT THE SPARK OF THAT MYSTERY HAD DIED WITHIN
me, especially after my life took shape and direction through
working for Marco at Civil Legion. I was promoted quickly. I had
ideas for improving security measures, especially ideas involving misleading and deception. When I was appointed team commander, Marco ran a surprise inspection and asked my opinion
about the security arrangements. I told him I thought we were
failing to take into account the psychology of our threats. He
asked me to give him an example. I said, First, our shift changes
were too regularly scheduled, and every small-time terror group
now had advanced intelligence and observation equipment. Second, we were too busy with defense rather than entrapment, and
we weren't thinking like predators. If we included the character
of attacks in our security arrangements, we wouldn't just prevent
terror attacks, we'd damage the terror organizations, which
would think twice before messing with us again. He said we only
rarely get such accurate intelligence. I said either way we should
be more flexible with our preparedness. He said he'd consider it.
After that, he kept testing me. I guess he felt criticized. He kept
challenging me with questions about scenarios he came across,
presenting them as future threats, asking what I would have
done. I failed half of his tests, but I didn't care. Those puzzles
were good. They made my blood move. My brain was oiled like a
rifle, shipshape like a rifle.

But when Oshri told me that story I realized I'd only been concealing that spark, covering it up, trying to replace it with the
spark from other riddles. The thought bore through me, through

and through me. I had to verify the dates and make sure they co-incided with our information. It wasn't hard to track down Dmitry Shtedler. Elish's notes said he was the boyfriend of Vivian Kahiri, Heftzi Columbus's best friend who helped cover up her escape. Well, what she thought was her escape. I found her on some sort of media. I have no problem with people who are old of age, but antiques drive me crazy. The previous generation got old so quickly, and I don't understand why they stick to their habits. I requested an audio conference. I asked about him. Her voice was like a tree that was hit with an entire summer all at once.

She said ever since the changes to the public health law. I said she meant the rollback of the public medicine law. She said yes, ever since then she could no longer support Dmitry. I asked about independent Jewish aid organizations that paid medical insur-ance fees for the less fortunate. She said he was registered in the Ministry of Interior as belonging to a different nationality, even though he was Jewish, he really was. She paused. Then she said, Circumcised. I asked what was going on with him. She said he was in one of those hospices, his heart was slowly failing. I knew those places. They were always affiliated with medical MKI sites. I had no problem accessing their records. He was in the one at-tached to Wolfson Medical Center.

Shtedler didn't remember much. He didn't remember that Olga disappeared. That was his niece's name. Olga Kovilishin. He wheezed when he removed his oxygen mask to answer me. He looked like a crumbling building, all that height and the flesh that the skeleton couldn't hold up. I was appalled by his outdated medical equipment. Who still uses an oxygen tank as life sup-port? He just wanted to talk to someone. I was convinced they were running experiments on him. He said they took a blood sam-ple every morning. I couldn't help him. Between wheezes, he talked about Olga, how beautiful and gentle she was. She came to Israel in 2010, a few days before Shavuot. I checked the calendar. That matched the date of the first study in the protocol. I asked about shadow people, but he had no idea what that meant. I think his brain was kind of erased. I would call Olga in Ukraine to find out more, but ever since Ukraine was annexed by Russia and their local government fell apart, and they passed new laws prohibiting Virtualia, it's hard to track anybody down there.

I called Manny Lahav. We hadn't spoken in years, ever since he recommended me to Marco. I asked to meet. He sounded surprised. He asked, To what do I owe this pleasure? Hadn't gotten over that expression. I said I had something important to discuss. He aged well. His forced skinniness finally matched the body that had grown in it. He was one of those hot old men in their seventies with a small gut and white hair that seemed like they'd picked it out, like they'd beaten age rather than age beating them. He moved to Jaffa. Divorced and remarried at sixty. His daughters cut off all contact with him. I have no idea why I'm giving you all these details. Maybe because they matter for the mystery. Or they matter to me, because that's what I learned from Elish's Benny Zehaviv books. He would describe each of the characters' movements, what they ate and drank, how they felt. It made it feel more real, even though sometimes he overdid it, describing every seasonal change, how everything smelled, and what color the light had.

I can tell you it was winter, pretty droughty, with few night clouds, and that the Jaffa sky looked like black skin with shiny wounds. Is that enough detail? I can go on. But I can already hear my mother saying, See, when you make an effort, you succeed. Like, when have I ever not made an effort? So what if they kicked me out of officer training? You know what, Shula, I won't make an effort. I'm not going to describe seasons and trees and clouds.

So we sat there. I thought about how during the 2019 violence waves, Jaffa residents declared independence from Tel Aviv. The Jaffa Liberated Reservation, they called it. Nonsense. Poppycock. Israel swallowed them back up and only spat out the Palestinians, like a snake spitting out bones. Manny wanted to know everything about my life and about Marco, whom he'd had a chance to work with before he retired. He said he heard I was excelling, and that he expected nothing less of me. He drank his whiskey and said most people his age had diabetes and that it was all a question of lifestyle. I softened him up with stories about terror attacks. He said he was glad he was too old for that stuff because the younger generation was so good at what it did. He said his generation and the one that followed, if Elish could be considered a representative, were in despair, believing there was no hope for the following generations.

I asked him about Elish's investigation. He asked why I was bringing that up now. I told him I'd found new evidence related to his death. I asked why the case had been closed. He said it was closed due to lack of evidence and public interest. I asked about Yehuda Menuhin. He said he tried to apply some pressure behind the scenes to keep the investigation going. I told him I knew the truth, that Yehuda Menuhin was the one who murdered Dalia Shushan, that Elish left notes. He sighed. He said I must understand that he couldn't pass on this information. Who would benefit from reopening the Dalia Shushan case? I said certainly not him. He said he wasn't part of the investigation of Elish's death, and besides, there was pressure to end it. I asked who'd applied the pressure. He said he didn't know. He used his influence, and someone else applied counterinfluence. That was how things worked.

OSHRI RETURNED WITH GROCERY BAGS. IN SPITE OF HIS PASsion for technological innovations, he didn't buy things on the Virtualia besides content and software. The virtual purchase apps are the biggest scam. As if touch and intimacy could be replaced, and by what? You had to wrap yourself up with tracking sensors just to save yourself from rubbing against people and the effort of air-conditioning a place. Especially when it came to food, it was critical for him to use all his senses, feeling fruits and vegetables by hand, smelling herbs, shaking and listening to eggs, weighing manually, judging by color, arguing about the quality of meat. Only foodies of his kind still ate nonsynthetic meat. And animal-sourced meat was always sold fresh, so he had to be careful. At least he didn't bring meat into the apartment while I stayed with him. Even synthetic meat grossed me out. He said I was a hypocrite, working for the killing business, euphemistically known as security or Civil Legion, but refusing to touch the death of animals. Luckily, I wasn't one of those vegan extremists. He said it was impossible to live in Israel and deny the murderousness of the place by policing one's stomach. It was conscience cleansing of the worst kind he could imagine. I agreed with him. But I couldn't help but feel nauseous around meat, any meat.

He said Nitzan would get back to us during the day with the results of the blood test. I asked what he'd told her. He told me to let it go, it was bad enough that he lied to her, he didn't want to repeat those lies. He'd told her the most important thing he needed was a mapping of antibodies. That wasn't her area of expertise, but she'd figure it out. They've both only been at the MKI site in Ashdod for two months. They were promoted to the research department thanks to the great work they did in classifying and cataloguing.

I asked what she said about my EEG. He said she thought it was a love letter, that he was trying to tell her there was nothing typical about their relationship, no routine, only excitement and solace. But that he was optimistic. Because she thought such excessive brain-wave activity would burn both of their neurons in less than twenty minutes, forget years. I laughed briefly. He blushed. I told him not to panic. He said he was the one who had to make sure not to panic her. As far as he was concerned, what they had was forever.

610

I said that in that case his assessment had been correct, which meant I wasn't in danger at all. He asked how I'd managed to reach the exact opposite conclusion. I told him what was happening to me was unexpected. By all known precedents, I should have either contracted typhus or died, so none of our knowledge was valid. I removed the NS strap. Oshri was quiet. He walked over to his InteMon and turned on all the crystal boards on the living room wall. The top left corner was feeds from the four cameras, and the top right corner was the EEG map. My vitals and data were moving along the bottom part. Oshri mumbled that there was a method to this, he just couldn't recognize the pattern. I said it was funny that we choose the people who would become our enigmas, and that when you think about it, the process of picking is the most enigmatic part. He asked what I meant. I told him to forget it, it was nothing.

He asked if I'd make us lunch. I asked if it wasn't early for that. He said no, it was almost noon. I said it would be better if he made it, that I felt like having a good meal, and I'd do the dishes. I didn't mean it, I wasn't hungry, but I could tell he needed a distraction or he'd stay glued to the InteMon. I'd already realized we had nothing to gain from analyzing the data. We didn't have the necessary tools. Elish once told me we had to pick the mysteries we had the power to bear. Those were his exact words. From the distance of years, I want to tell him that isn't true, that our power depends on our means of looking. If we can change it, a power grows in us that we never imagined we could possess.

He made a Korean dish, bibimbap, and our personal bowls were hot, just as they should be, the rice continuing to cook as we mixed in the soft-boiled eggs and vegetables. Well, I was mixing them in properly into mine. Oshri, who kept glancing at his intePhone, burned his rice at the bottom. I told him not to worry, that Nitzan was probably waiting for sunset, clearly the test results were nothing to panic about.

Ha ha, he said. He said he hadn't told me, but he'd met Marco the previous day at the Ashdod MKI site. Marco told him he was running a surprise inspection, but Oshri had a feeling he came there especially. I said the alert level at the site would be going up in the next few days. He said Marco asked about me. I asked what Oshri had told him. He said he'd told him I was fine. I said nothing. He told me not to take what he was going to say the wrong way. I told him to surprise me. He said that ever since I got this investigation fever, and he moved his arm to indicate the living room, that ever since then I haven't been able to see what was right in front of me.

I asked why he thought I was so goal-oriented. He said he thought Marco was interested in me. I asked why he cared about that. He said nothing got me going like planning, testing, discovering. I'd been this way ever since we were kids. I never turned around to see if the others were catching up. And when I get this way today it makes him concerned I'll end up alone. He blushed, but not on the cheeks. It was as if his entire being was blushing, the blood rushing into every inch of his skin, making it blaze.

I wanted to tell him to shove his concern you know where. But I didn't. I let my resistance melt away. Inside of it, I felt the truth of his emotion, like a patch of land in the fog of the self. I kept silent. I felt sorry for him for feeling sorry for me, for suffering because of what he assumed I felt. The bibimbap grew colder in our bowls, the egg yolk turning into threads of gray omelet.

I LEFT MY MEETING WITH MANNY IN A RAGE. THIS WHOLE TIME, he knew something wasn't right but did nothing except cover his ass. Some friend. Once I calmed down, I called Marco. I requested visual and audio conferencing. He looked at me expressionlessly from the screen of my intePhone. The screen was all cracked from being dropped. It was time to replace it, like Oshri said. He said the new generation of intePhones is about to come out. But I'm attached to mine. Every crack is a reminder of a mistake made, of hunched, unmeasured runs across the site, of getting banged around during training, or when it dropped when I was distracted.

I saw those big, innocent eyes through the cracks, looking me over, waiting. I told him I needed a favor. He asked what. I said it was under the condition that he didn't ask why. He said fine, but while we were naming conditions he had one too. His was that I have dinner with him. I told him I'd take him out to dinner, on me. He looked at me in silence. All of a sudden, I wanted to be able to decipher him. His expression was so unreadable. What did he look for in me in those moments? I told him I needed a copy of a police investigation file from fourteen years ago. He said that shouldn't be a problem, there were plenty of collaborations between Civil Legion and the police, and if he wasn't mistaken their archives from that time period were computerized. He asked what I needed from the file. I said no questions. He said he just wanted to know which part of the file I needed, evidence, suspect interviews, investigation team summaries? I said everything, everything he could get. I said he should just know it had to do with my uncle, who died under mysterious circumstances. He started to say something, then stopped himself. He said he trusted that I knew what I was doing, not digging some pit. That was his term for any unfounded cause the main purpose of which was to inflate the ego of those who fought for it. He told me there was a settlerorist in his officer training course who kept telling the other cadets, Whoever digs a pit may fall into it, and Marco adopted the expression. I told him I wasn't messing with any pits.

He got me a copy of the file rather quickly. I was surprised to find that my parents had been questioned. They never mentioned that. When did they agree to shut up about it? They didn't have much to say, just that Elish used to be a private investigator and may have made some enemies at the time, that they didn't believe he would have hurt himself, that he was a good person, that he liked to help, that he lived a good life.

I wondered what it meant to live a good life, and when someone might realize she was hurting herself. The more experience I
gain, the less certainly I can say that Elish lived a good life, not
because he did or didn't, but due to the simple fact that people
always judge these things from the outside. I kept perusing the
file, reading on without any idea if the investigation had been
efficient or just negligent. Too few interviews, too few threads to
follow, almost everything predictable, except for two elements.
First, the police discovered the body because Elish's downstairs
neighbor, Dina Boltkey, had called them. Elish's car alarm went
off and was disrupting the peace in the neighborhood for hours,
she said during her interview. When she knocked on his door she
heard suspicious sounds, something like wheezing. The police
broke down the door and found his body. The head of the special
investigation team assumed she'd lied about the sounds to get
the police there quicker. Her questioning was frustrating, because
Boltkey insisted that she'd heard noises, and the interrogator
asked her to consider very carefully whether she might have imagined them, because, according to the pathologist's determined
time of death, Elish was no longer alive at the time she claimed to
have heard them. This went on for two unnecessary pages.

The other thing was a name that sounded familiar but I couldn't
remember why. Therese Kavillio-Buganim. She was the last person
to speak with Elish on his phone, two hours before the estimated
time of death. I ran a Virtualia search. Of course, she was the one
behind the reading encouragement project that amused me and
Yalon so much, the campaign with all those illiterate celebrities
who, if they ever read a book in their lives, could only have gotten
through *Eat, Pray, Screw*. Was that the actual name of the book or
the joke name we made up for it? I wouldn't have even thought
about her with regards to Elish. But on the other hand, Nahum
Farkash was the project's artistic director, and he gave us that
Dalia Shushan song that inspired the project's name. I wrote
Therese's name in my investigation notebook, and Nahum's

name underneath it. Her questioning was one of the last in the file. It wasn't long. She said Elish came to see her as part of his research for his book about Heftzi Columbus. Heftzi's body had been found in Sderot six weeks earlier. For some reason, he was seeking out connections between Heftzi and Therese's husband, Yoel Buganim. She had no idea what he wanted. He seemed unbalanced, feverish, and incoherent. The only lead he had was that Columbus's murderer fled through Heidelberg and Therese's husband had a medical research lab there. Had she not been familiar with his books, she wouldn't have agreed to meet him in the first place. She would have been convinced he was eccentric, even insane.

I thought about the lost, erased sections of silence. Elish didn't come back to Sderot after the summer when the war happened. He was having a fight with my father. He was curt during our conversations, answering me with rigid statements. But maybe I'm projecting. Maybe I'm the one who talked like that. Maybe I'm rewriting.

I sent Manny a request for visual conferencing. I pulled up the conversation on the crystal board in my apartment so I could read his expression, find out what he was hiding. He approved the request right away. His tan face with the brushed white hair came up. There was a flicker of laughter in his eyes. He wasn't laughing with me, but with someone else who wasn't visible on camera. He said he was glad we were becoming closer. He really was in a good mood. I told him not to get ahead of himself. His smile grew, as did the flicker. He asked why women even needed men in the first place, beautiful and wise and generous as we were. I asked about Therese Kavillio-Buganim, the connection between her and Elish. He said Elish had told him he was looking into something to do with her husband's research, but that he didn't really understand what at the time. The head of the special investigation team told him that was what Therese said at her questioning, and Manny confirmed it, so they'd dropped that line of investigation.

I asked if Elish seemed unbalanced, like she said. He said a little bit. He said, You know how he got the moment he found tracks that no one had noticed before? His expression turned serious, his mouth straightening out, his gaze scattered. I said yes. He said, So it was like that, he had that fire going and no patience for anyone who couldn't keep up. I asked if he knew what Elish was trying to find out about the research lab. He said he didn't. He asked what good could come of poking through the past. When you look back all you can see is this haze, and if you try hard enough, you can detect whatever shape you hope to see within it.

MARCO CONCEALED HIS SURPRISE WHEN I TOLD HIM I WAS TAK-ing him to a holiday dinner at my parents' house. I told him I didn't want him to be sad and alone on Rosh Hashanah, because then the rest of the year would be a bummer. But his expression wasn't that different from usual. The emotion was swallowed in those big eyes begging for a drop of compassion. He pulled himself together quickly. He said he'd thought we were going to have a private dinner at a fancy restaurant and that he'd already bought a suit. I laughed. I told him I was sure a famous romantic like him had a closet full of suits. He said he didn't wear a suit more than once and that he taped a note to each one with the date and occasion he'd worn it. I told him I hoped he arranged them by chronological order, not by how bad the date was. He said at some point it all became the same order, you opened his closet and saw the story of his marriage. He suggested we not count the holiday dinner as our date. I told him to watch out because his coolness was at risk. He said I was cheating. I told him the good and bad thing about men was that they refused to acknowledge that times have changed. He asked what was bad about that. I said he should ask what was good about that. He asked, What's good about that? I said, You're easily manipulated.

For my mother it was love at first sight. I think she subconsciously connected the name Marco to the television show she used to watch as a kid, but consciously all she registered was fondness. We didn't explain anything to her. Dad was a little suspicious. He'd always thought of Yalon as his future son-in-law, and Marco looked like a womanizer who'd come to steal away his daughter. It really is a problem that men refuse to realize times have changed. Oshri and Marco already knew each other, and Oshri used his regular ploy, his liberated amiability that concealed the fact that if Marco disappeared in the middle of dinner Oshri really wouldn't give a damn.

But ultimately Marco captivated Dad too. Though Dad didn't forgive him for trying to take Yalon's place, he could tell he was the kind of man my father considered properly Israeli, masculine, versed in military life, with a belief in might and daring. Oh well. We've already seen how the previous generation's life got fucked up by all that nonsense.

On the way home, I saw Marco had been taken by them too. He was drunk off wine and phony familial warmth. I drove, out of habit. We don't use autonomous driving at Civil Legion. The navigation protocols aren't secured enough, in Marco's opinion. The special care trickles into what little existence we have outside of work. He pushed back his seat and looked at me. The steel behind his eyes was gone, and all that left was an invitation. I didn't speak. I tried to think about something else. A few days earlier, I'd met Oshri at his place for updates and consultations. The name Buganim was vaguely familiar to him, but the name Kavillio was very familiar. He asked if there was any relation to Eldad Kavillio. I said yes, that was her husband's name, according to the Virtualia. He said he'd read some of his immunology and serology research papers and was making the connection now. Eldad had died in a lab accident in Poland, due to a rare bacterial infection, what was it? He searched on his InteMon, and I searched on my intePhone. He said he was shocked to find that Eldad had died of a strain of typhus that didn't exist in any lab in Lublin at the time.

He said Lublin was where Ludwik Fleck's lab was before he came to Israel. I told him to look at Eldad's date of death. He asked what about it. I said it matched the date of death of the first subject in the unidentified protocols.

I asked if he thought the protocols belonged to Buganim's research lab. I looked at my intePhone and told him these days the lab has grown into Becker-Kavillio-Buganim Medicinal Technologies, Inc., and that Therese may have been involved in the research since she was trained in the field. He said he wanted to look at Eldad Kavillio's research before we jumped to conclusions. I told him to do his part while I did mine. He asked what my part was. I said, Isn't it obvious that Therese Kavillio-Buganim is behind all this? If only they'd have interrogated her properly. He didn't answer, only clicked his tongue. I detected the doubt in his silence and clicking. I told him to consider the fact that the pressure to close Elish's case began after she was brought in for questioning. He asked what I was thinking. I said I thought she had something to do with Elish's death. He said I was getting carried away. I told him she was the last person he spoke to, and that Elish's autopsy found heightened antibody activity in his blood. He asked if there was a DNA mapping of the antibodies. I told him now *he* was getting carried away.

When we got closer to Ashdod, Marco broke the silence. He sat up and asked if I felt like doing a surprise inspection at the MKI site. I told him I didn't think he was in any state to run an inspection. He said he wouldn't be running it, I would. He'd never seen me run an inspection before. I asked if he meant to say he'd never given me that test before. He smiled and leaned back again. I pulled up on the shoulder of the highway. It was deserted. I used my profile to log into the Civil Legion network and pulled up the site blueprint on the car's screen. With my hand, I outlined the estimated position and movement of patrols. The software processed my movements into a crude but good-enough animation. I sent it to my intePhone, put on my AR lenses and my sense bracelet. I always had those two items with me. I told Marco I'd been waiting for this opportunity. Less than a week ago, I'd figured out a potential weak point in the security arrangements. I turned on the car shielding and kept driving. I got off the highway after the turn into Ashdod and found a dark corner among the trees, where I killed the engine. I told Marco that if our team was as good as I thought, they'd already spotted an unidentified car approaching the site, shielding be damned. I said what they didn't realize was that them spotting us worked in our favor. I asked if he was ready to duck and cover. He said always, even when he wasn't wearing appropriate clothes. I reminded him that at his opening talk during my training he said the real uniform was muscles, skin, and determination. A salty chill of approaching autumn blew in from the sea. I was filled with quiet vigor, just like him. I was thinking how there was a deep current between us that didn't need words, it existed and it was clear, something I didn't think I'd feel again. I thought it was a shame the circumstances weren't different, a shame I could not tell love and power apart, which is why I would never forgive myself if I dated my commander.

I HEARD THE APARTMENT DOOR SLAM SHUT AND OSHRI CALL MY name softly. It had gotten dark and I hadn't noticed. There was still some light out when Oshri stepped outside for his regular sunset phone call with Nitzan. I was getting in their way. I had to encourage Oshri to go out tonight, I was mature and responsible enough to sit at a table without interrupting all the tracking sensors that were recording me.

Oshri turned on the light in the living room. He asked how long I'd been sitting in the dark. I told him I'd dozed off. He walked over to the InteMon and pulled up the data. He said it didn't look like it, that there was heightened theta-wave activity again. I asked what Nitzan said about my tests. He said there was an increased amount of antibodies. She'd mapped the genetic sequence and run a check through the MKI biological infection resource pool, but couldn't find a match. She'd sent him the mapping, genius that she was. She said the amount and distribution indicated a secondary immune response. I told him to start over, this time in normal people language.

He said I was naturally immune to the strain of typhus he'd injected me with, just as I'd thought. He said the antibodies my immune system produced at random already contained a protein that identified the typhus bacteria, as if it were logged in its memory. And when an infection is logged into the immune system's memory, it reacts aggressively when the infection invades the body, wiping it out immediately. I asked if he meant I didn't contract typhus. He said yes, but he was afraid something about these antibodies, the proteins my body produced, affected my nervous system, my brain. He couldn't figure out how that was possible.

I didn't answer. I was too tired to have this argument again. He said this coincided with Nitzan's insight about the EEGs. She wanted to see how he pictured getting in and out of the state he'd sent her, to better understand what his love code meant.

I asked, What? He looked at me severely, the cracked blue of his eyes becoming dense as a precious stone. In a low voice he said this was it, he'd reached his line, he couldn't watch me take this risk like some overexcited kid.

I reminded him we'd never determined what *my* line was. He said it didn't matter, he quit. I said whatever Nitzan said couldn't have been that bad, fact is the blood tests—

He cut me off, saying it was a fact that there was nothing he could possibly say that I wouldn't interpret in my own favor, in favor of this nonsense. I asked, What nonsense? He said the nonsense I kept repeating when I was trying to convince him, that everything I'd learned from Elish had been preparing me for this moment. What moment, exactly, to die like him, and for what? I told him not to get angry, we were so close. He said he was just now realizing that this madness of mine was nothing but a delayed grief over Elish.

I repeated the phrase, "delayed grief." That insolent bastard. How he cried over Elish, falling apart, like Elish was some big deal to him, and now he was accusing me for not grieving, for not hurting, for moving on. He said, Yes, Tahel, a delayed grief. He wanted me to admit that I wasn't able to grieve before, that I'd replaced my grief with rage. That no one could talk to me during the shiva because all I did was bark at them. That I walked around like I was about to explode, and maybe that's what I should have done, exploded, and this mistake we were making now, all the mistakes I've been making ever since—

I said, Go on, spit it out. What mistakes do you think I'm making, do you hate me so much that you had to wait for my moment of weakness to—

He said I'd given up every opportunity for happiness, and that poor Yalon had to bear all my dark rage, and then when he showed a hint of independence, wanting to defend himself—

I yelled at him not to bring Yalon into this, that he had no idea what Yalon—

He said I was making the same mistake with Marco.

My throat dried up all at once. My body ignited like I don't know what, a white, blinding glare that jumped all over it. I couldn't see, only feel, feel. There was that crying on the edge of it again, that crying that had grown moldy years ago and was only waiting on the edge of every crisis for me to look its way and fall into the trap. The image of Elish lying on his desk would spread all over, no longer retreating, and I'd become the child standing on its margins. Instead of it only occasionally fluttering into my field of vision, instead of being just a reminder, a warning.

But the knowledge was no longer scary. I thought I could talk to Elish while I was daring to stand there and watch. That the walls were breaking, and that any image, if you think it hard enough, becomes reality. I contained only sadness, clean as silk, and I could need without cowering with shame. I said Elish's name. I told him I needed explanations, that I didn't know where to go from here. His answer echoed back to me, like a soft wave of knowing somebody was on my side. I was little and asked him if God could make a rock so heavy that He Himself couldn't pick up, and Mom was there, and he looked at her and said I truly was smart. I told him I wasn't the age he thought I was, that was why, that his eyes were backward, I told him again that I needed explanations, and he said no, that I didn't understand what I was asking him for.

I STILL FELT THAT TREMBLING OF TEARS. IT STAYED WITH ME. I could say clearly that I'd just returned from someplace, that I'd visited a realm that wasn't part of Elish's living room, that was inside and outside of it at once. Oshri was at the table, smiling like an idiot. He said it worked. I asked what worked. He said he'd managed to push me to a state where I summoned Unelish.

I didn't understand. He said that was Nitzan's brilliant idea. She'd noticed a heightened emotional state on my EEG right before I entered the wild summoning state, and he recalled that just before the last time Unelish visited me, he and I had had a fight.

I told him I wasn't sure the name "Unelish" still applied, that I felt like I'd just spoken to Elish, that it was no longer his presence in my memory or what he left behind, like this apartment, but actually him.

Oshri nodded. He said my conjecture about mental pheromones checked out. I told him not to look so surprised. He asked what I thought Kalanit and Olga's triggers were. I asked what he thought my trigger was. He said, Do you even have to ask? Your trigger is rage.

I told him I wasn't going to forgive the things he said. He said he had to make me enraged, so he twisted the facts. I said I didn't think I'd explode like that if they didn't contain a kernel of truth. He said I was attributing too much importance to his statements. I said he knew me too well, that I wasn't sure what was harder for me, the contents of his diagnosis, or the fact that he was able to make it.

He told me to drop it, it was just a diversion. I said I was about to say the same thing. I said I'd bet Kalanit's trigger was self-deception. He asked what I meant. I said I'd read Elish's little research about her family enough times to see it. Her father was a terrible person. But when she had the chance to communicate with someone she'd lost, she turned to him. I said we had no hope as a species because we indulged in false tenderness. How could anyone expect a species to evolve enough to survive our pathe-teeth obsession with something that isn't there?

Oshri snickered. I asked, What? He said, Never mind, just a reflex. I said we could continue our study now that we knew what activated me. Oshri said he wouldn't dare put my body and brain under that kind of duress again. He told me to look at the vitals. This time, it wasn't just the EEG that was going mad, but my pulse and blood sugar as well. I told him it was because of this frenzy he'd put me in, not because of Elish.

He said it was bizarre that I called the shadow man Elish. He was there with me, accompanying me every step of the way, but he still couldn't view this as a real thing. Just an adventure, a childish disruption, just like back then. I said I knew he wouldn't be willing to go all the way, that I'd warned him about this. He asked if I realized we were facing a scientific breakthrough. I told him it would be difficult to re-create our study. How many people were out there with this specific mutation in the Richard Perotz gene, with the correct allele and the normal allele? Olga Kovilishin, Kalanit Shaubi, and me. And the three of us must be descendants of the same family.

He said I wasn't getting this at all. When he was on the classi-fying and cataloguing team, he'd been astonished by the number of studies on the biological computerization assimilation. I said he'd already told me that. He asked what I took from it. I said I hadn't been listening, it didn't seem significant, just another of his boring spells where he got caught up in a tizzy of self-importance. He said I had selective hearing, which was why he repeated himself from time to time, to see if conditions had improved enough for me to listen.

I asked if he was trying to make me angry again. He said he wasn't, that this was just how we normally talked. I said okay, I hoped he hadn't wasted all of his ammunition. He said we'd see about that tomorrow. I said I was listening. He said there was more and more evidence of the fact that the calculation methods of biological creatures differ from mechanized calculation, that there's a rift between them. That it seems as if digital calculation could mimic biological results, but the question was, which results? Up until now, researchers have been trying to mimic processes related to intelligence. He picked up his intePhone and pointed at his InteMon. He said all of these devices were founded on artificial intelligence, but the truth was, in nature, complex processes aren't necessarily connected to what we call logic, but rather to aptitude and resourcefulness. The resources invested in this type of calculation were unfathomable. Flowers, for instance, probably used quantic calculation to attract insects. Bird retinas could read magnetic fields, and their little brains could solve navigation equations according to these fields, which requires endless calculation abilities. Endless.

I told him to slow down, that I wasn't following. All I understood was that living creatures calculated in a different way from computers, but I didn't understand how.

He said that was sort of his point. The important thing was, these discoveries changed the ways we considered calculation methods, utilized them, mimicked them, and used them to create new technologies. The purpose of MKI was the collection and sale of these technological possibilities. His biocyber department focused on biological models of reality perception, and that's how he received the Take Up and Read protocols. He asked if I was getting the meaning of what we were doing. I said I wasn't. He said we'd discovered a reproducible scientific procedure that allowed us to track the interaction between reality and consciousness. He said the key wasn't the brain, as people assumed. The brain was the tool for integrating data and impressions, but it was only a mediator. The true key was the immune system. Those were the two sides of Ludwik Fleck's work, philosophy and immunology, and we'd just found evidence of a connection between the two.

I told him this was exhausting, that I always lost track of ideas when they became theories, that I didn't understand what they had to do with my experiences. I told him that's what I was looking for here, not an abstract idea, but a person who could explain, with his own words, with his own tone, with his own expressions, with his own eye movements, why Elish had made the choices he'd made, what was so urgent, what he had to say for himself, what he had to tell me that—

I fell silent. Oshri asked what. I said I had trouble putting it into words, and that I'd do better tomorrow.

SHULA, YOU'RE ALL SHULA. ALL OF A SUDDEN I CAN'T THINK "YOU" and certainly not picture you saying "I." I say "I," but what does that actually mean? I can't contain all of Tahel in that word. Other people gave it to me. It was wandering around until it found me, and I picked it up and installed it on my lips and I speak through it, and remnants of other people who used it before me stick to my speech, staining the Tahel who started it, and all I can say is Tahel-minus-usage-minus-remnants-of-the-word-"I."

I discussed this with Oshri once, the limits of the self. How old were we? I'd just gotten out of the military and he was staring his biocyber training and was acting overly knowledgeable, which is always the sign of ignorance. These days he checks his facts rather than announce them, and admits when his knowledge is superficial or insufficient. Back then he said the best definition he knew was the immune system. Its entire function was to recognize what belonged in the body and what was foreign to it. It learned and it had a memory, and it was founded on the fact that the body is a microbiome, a colony, a collection of cells that work together, bacteria and algae and microorganisms, not one mass or a closed unit, and that sometimes it made mistakes. That meant the self wasn't a thing, but rather a dynamic, and the limits of the self were a result of that dynamic, not a static, exterior thing. They shrank and expanded according to threats or evolution. But let's assume that's true for a moment. In that case, what are those remnants stuck to the word "I" and to the words I speak? Are they infections or welcome guests?

I couldn't get hold of Therese Kavillio-Buganim, or TKB, as I came to think of her. I tracked down a conferencing number that was unavailable, an email address to which nobody responded, a physical address in northern Tel Aviv that had since been sold. I even looked through the Civil Legion database to check if we'd secured some project she owned or if she'd made it into our blacklist. This organization has some serious blacklists, believe me. Nothing. She and her husband were two of those Israelis who chose to part ways with Israel. The Knowledge Nationalization Law was the last straw for them. Their labs were based in Heidelberg anyway, as was their health technology company. I wondered if they'd hired lawyers to fight for their intellectual property as others had, or if they just gave up. The new government was uncompromising on this issue, even if it meant swift coups of hostile structures. Either way, their protocols made it to MKI.

I spent about a week trying to track her down. I even considered asking Marco to send me to training in Germany. Obviously, the Germans, with all their private tumults, were pretty thrilled about Civil Legion. Their local security firms tried to mimic our

methods. They'd passed a law forbidding corporations from starting their own police force or privately employing armed units.
But I'd already asked Marco for too much. That Rosh Hashanah
eve, we were caught before we made it to the control center, but
we managed to invade headquarters undetected. Marco became
grumpy, his good mood from the holiday dinner was gone. I didn't
know if it was because of my success or the security team's failure. He pulled me aside, praised me, and said that after the holiday he wanted us to discuss improvement measures. Then he just
stood there and looked at me, once more allowing himself to remove the steel from his eyes. I evaded him after that, telling him
over audio conferencing that I'd send him a written proposal
through our encoded channel. Besides, I think he could tell right
away, when I was animating my plan on his car's screen, what the
weakness point was and what we had to do to get rid of it. It was
all fairly simple. I knew he was nodding along from his seat.

So I couldn't ask him, and was left with a frustration about
this dead end that gnawed the edges of my soul. Oshri came to the
rescue again. He sent one sentence via Justforme, his encoded
for-your-eyes-only application. A surprising name among the
Becker-Kavillio-Buganim lab's Heidelberg workforce: Nahum
Farkash. I watched as the sentence disappeared. I liked the app's
animation, the crumbling letters scattering and fading back into
the screen within seconds.

The image was becoming clearer, more sensical. Yes, TKB was
still the spider at the center of the web, but Nahum Farkash
was the great unknown in the equation. No matter where I looked,
at the Case of the Lost Detective, the Secret of the Disappearing
Student, the Murder of the Legendary Singer, he always popped
up, not involved enough to be a suspect, but still in the background. If he wasn't a master spy, then he had a hell of a knack for
showing up unexpectedly. I wouldn't be surprised if he turned out
to be connected to the Mystery of the Enchanted Thicket too.

I requested conferencing with Nahum Farkash. He didn't

answer for several nerve-racking hours. Finally, just when I was in the shower, I got a conferencing request from him. I got back to him with half-dried hair dangling over my shoulders. He insisted on visual conferencing. He was still skinny, but now there was the fragility of age about him. His eyes remained young. I recalled a time when Yalon and I found some of his poems and memorized them, I don't know why. Maybe as a joke. Some of his poems sounded like jokes. He had one about a patheteeth television star, Ari Sass. That was Yalon's favorite. I'll buy a movie ticket from behind the Plexiglas, under the dome of the air-conditioning, I'll sit my fine ass, and watch *Guavas*, a film by Ari Sass. From time to time he'd say, Should we sit our fine ass, and I would answer, And watch *Guavas*, a film by Ari Sass? I liked a different poem. The racket of blossoms, a pulse of salt through the veins, I took the pill, of love, I took the pill, of the morning after. Yalon joked about that one too. He was always saying that he took the pill of the morning after. Just to sound cool. We all saw how that turned out.

Never mind. That poem suddenly fit Nahum's face, the face of a man who took too many pills of the morning after love. The thought saddened me. I wanted to recite the poem to him. He knew from the conferencing request's metadata that I was calling him, but he was still all surprised when I turned on the camera. He had lots of questions about me, about Yalon, and about Oshri. He remembered us in great detail. I wondered why. I told him I'd answer literally all of his questions if he'd agree to meet me. He complained that as much as his generation had resisted using the word "literally" to mean "figuratively," it had failed. I told him Elish used to nag me about that too, saying we sound like idiots, but that it was better to be an idiot than a tight-ass. He laughed. I told him my generation picked its battles wisely, not everyone, but most of us, unlike the generation between mine and his, that bought into that disgusting combination—

He cut me off and said, Nationalistic narcissism. I said yes.

He said it seemed that we were on the same wavelength, and asked what I wanted to meet about. I said I'd tell him that when we met too. I don't think he suspected anything. I'd piqued his interest. Elish was right, people like it when you talk to them in their own language, because they believe it's the only language worth speaking.

I ARRIVED AT OSHRI'S PLACE AROUND NOON TO FIX IT UP BEFORE the meeting. I suggested to Nahum that we meet on Friday, when Oshri and I went to Sderot for Shabbat dinner with our parents, but he said he didn't mind coming to Tel Aviv or someplace nearby. It was good for him, he said, he needed reasons to move. I called Oshri and told him I'd pop by his place that evening. He insisted we meet Nahum there. He said if Nahum truly was involved, we'd have to discuss some sensitive matters. I told him Nahum would get suspicious if we asked to meet at Elish's apartment. Oshri said he didn't care, he wanted complete secrecy. I detected Nahum's discomfort during the visual conferencing. There was an underhanded hesitation on his face, a swift dash of alertness, like a mouse emerging from a hole, sniffing the air, and retreating. I said we wanted to show him something that we preferred to keep between the three of us. He nodded.

I swept the floor and dusted. There wasn't much to clean. Oshri's a neat person, but I was nervous and full of bad energy, the kind that prevents any action instead of motivating it, blocking concentration. I thought about baking cookies. Once, on some boring reality show about real estate, I saw that people used the smell of baked goods to create a homey sensation. I scanned the contents of Oshri's pantry and fridge with the InteMon and asked the AI to find the easiest recipe with the shortest prep time that could be made with those ingredients. The results came in, a recipe for halva cookies with a million likes. I followed the instructions verbatim, never veering off the amounts, sending the temperature and baking time directly from the AI to the oven control, but half of the cookies still burned. That's why I hate these artificial intelligence devices. There's nothing intelligent about them. They only use what people refer to as the wisdom of the masses, scanning data online and arranging it. And who's in charge of inputting this data? Of course, a moron collection of Virtualia fanatics. Wisdom of the masses, my ass. Show me one time in history when the masses made a smart choice.

But the smell was sweet and inviting at least. Oshri mentioned it as soon as he walked inside. And I could tell Nahum was also relaxed when he came in.

I apologized about the patheteeth cookies when I placed them on the coffee table. Nahum asked what "patheteeth" meant. He said he'd heard the word before but never took the time to figure it out. Oshri said it was an old slang word from our high school days, short for "pathetic teeth." Nahum asked why "pathetic teeth." Oshri said that the word "teeth" meant something is rare, like when you try to get money from a miser and people say he's going to fight you off with his teeth. Nahum said it was like when people used to say they can't even. Oshri said, Maybe. Nahum told him not to worry about it, that he wasn't embarrassed, he was familiar with the phenomenon. When they were young, they also invented words that made grown-ups feel irrelevant, which was a nice illusion, because the people who made meaningful decisions regarding their fate weren't these grown-ups but politicians whose time had run out but who refused to die. Oshri said, Yeah, until they decapitated the prime minister during the violence waves. Nahum sighed. He said that few people would admit that one of the greatest pleasures in life is a proper bowel movement, and that Israel had been constipated for way too long, and someone had to serve as the enema. He said that it only took tearing off one mask to reveal the absurdity of the gap between Israel's economic foundation and its ideology. That kind of gap was always bridged by violence. He said the funny thing about all of this was that politicians refused to learn the most fundamental lesson in history, and somehow those who sanctified force were always taken by surprise when eventually it was turned against them with unrestrained cruelty. He sighed again.

He already knew that Oshri was a development officer at MKI and that I was a commander at Civil Legion. He'd done his research. He wanted more details. We told him what we could, which was very little. He recognized our evasive maneuvers. Ultimately, we even had to ignore some of his questions. He said he knew we didn't want to meet him to discuss the state of the country or give him updates about our lives. I said he was right. He asked why, then. I said I thought he could already guess or else he wouldn't have come. He said it was about Dalia's song that he'd given us. I asked why. He said some works of art have a history that reveals itself the farther into the future you move. I said that was a strange thing to say. He asked if it wasn't the song, then what was it? I said it had to do with the song, or with the expression in it, Take Up and Read, which was . . . He cut me off with a nod, his skull bobbing on top of his wiry neck.

He nibbled on another cookie. I noticed he wasn't really eating but taking tiny bites along the edges, time-buying baby bites, bites that offered some quiet to think. He caught me looking. He said the cookies were good. He said he'd eat more if he didn't have a sensitive stomach.

As we'd planned, Oshri told him we wanted to propose a collaboration to Therese Kavillio-Buganim. Nahum said the two of them weren't in touch. Oshri said that according to the MKI database, his name appeared on the employee roster. Nahum said that was because of the Reading Forward project he'd managed, which was paid for by Becker-Kavillio-Buganim. I said I was surprised that an international firm paid the salary of a culture fund. He said he'd long ago stopped being astonished by the ploys wealthy people utilized to evade taxes. I said, Still, it doesn't make sense.

He nibbled some more. I signaled to Oshri. Oshri said he'd

proposed a project to MKI that was unsuitable for them and they'd rejected it, but he still wanted to promote it. He said he thought it would be a good fit for Therese Kavillio-Buganim and that Nahum could be the perfect middleman. One might say it was a natural continuation of Take Up and Read, to which he owed an enormous debt of gratitude. It was a project for the coding of literary works into the DNA of flowers and trees. He asked Nahum to picture it. As a boy, Oshri loved the Moomins and *The Chronicles of Prydain*. What if he found out there was a tropical fern with DNA encoded with the entire Moomintroll book about the hobgoblin's hat, the way a jungle popped out of the hat in the Moomins' yard and covered the entire house? He asked Nahum if he wouldn't love to eat Turkish delight made with pistachios encoded with *The Lion, the Witch and the Wardrobe*, if he wouldn't like to grow a rosebush encoded with Shakespeare's *Romeo and Juliet*. These were just anecdotes, of course, because the plants could be engineered to have other qualities related to the books, such as color, flavor, smell, and even texture. Wasn't that just the thing for Therese Kavillio-Buganim? It was marketable. And why stop at books or poems? Why not go for music . . .

I followed Nahum's expression. His reservation, his inhibitions, which manifested in a slight distance, as though he had protective glasses over his eyes, were now gone. I saw him falling into Oshri's web. The project was an actual idea Oshri had come up with during his biocyber training. He explained CRISPR and all sorts of innovative genetic engineering technologies that I didn't completely understand, except that they could cut out DNA segments and implant any segments they wanted, even ones drawn from different creatures, using programmed germs. I saw Nahum's face smoothing out, his skin turning pliable. I thought it was awful, these people who haven't yet finished being boys and were now living in bodies that insisted on telling a different story. But I had no time to feel sorry for him. When Nahum was fully immersed in Oshri's sales pitch, I hit him with a *shotokan ryu* to the nerve center in the base of the neck, boom, open-palmed blade smack. I said we knew Therese Kavillio was responsible for Elish's death.

NAHUM LITERALLY COLLAPSED FROM THE ACCUSATION. HE WENT pale. He grabbed the cup of tea we'd made him and took one long gulp and then quick, small sips, and stuttered, For what? The word "what" got stuck in his throat, and he became hoarse, like a sputtering engine.

Oshri went silent. He looked at me. I could tell he didn't love my tactic, but what does he know about tactics? He felt bad for Nahum. I wondered if finally talking about his little passion project to someone who was willing to listen didn't go to his head a little. I told Nahum not to be alarmed, we weren't accusing him of anything, we just wanted to know, after all these years, what happened to Elish.

He averted his eyes. He murmured, Why do you think I have any idea? There was no point in maneuvering and misleading. I gave him a summarized version of our investigation. I told him about the protocols from Therese's lab, about Eldad Kavillio's typhus research, about his death and how Therese had tried to re-create the studies with two girls and then with Elish. He nodded, slowly, slowly, as if considering his options. I told him we had to know.

He leaned back in his chair and looked at us. I don't know why, but I wanted to reach out and touch his shoulder. His fragility filled him up, became all that he was, and I wanted to reassure myself that he was durable enough, that he wouldn't shatter.

He said that years ago, around the time he first met us, when people were trying to make the film about Dalia Shushan, he was desperately trying to secure funding for a cultural project at the public library. He knew it was a lost cause, but the way things in Israel were going at the time, his choice was between a lost cause and surrender, and he wasn't willing to surrender. Even if it was a foretold defeat, he intended on posing as many difficulties and causing as much anguish as he could, because he believed his battle would inspire the next generation not to give up on resistance in every shape or form, to practice it, to come up with at least three resistance methods first thing every morning.

He said he'd met Therese Kavillio at a very young age. After her husband, Eldad, disappeared and his body was found, she moved in with her sister, and her nephew was his best friend at the time. He was always sad to see childhood friends becoming estranged as adults, but when you watch it from the inside there's no sadness, only the knowledge that the friendship was founded on a misunderstanding, on mismatched expectations, from the very beginning. They say people change, but he wondered if the change was truly within other people and not in our desire to see them as who they aren't.

I looked away when he said this. From the corner of my eye I saw Oshri looking at me, then returning his eyes to Nahum. Nahum said he thought Therese was the way to go. She had money and interest in both Sderot and culture. They met sporadically, and she always seemed to take an interest in him. Anyway, their conversations were friendly. But she refused to help. She pushed for the film about Dalia to be made, she invested in it and cut some deal with the mayor to launch her reading encouragement project in Sderot, and the name of her e-reader, which was at the center of the project, as we already knew, was Take Up and Read. The name set off a warning in his mind, even though he was usually very slow about these kinds of things, unlike Elish.

I sat up. I asked, What do you mean, unlike Elish? He told me to let him speak, he'd get to that soon. He knew one day this story would come out, and he'd made sure to retain all the facts in the correct order.

Not a warning, exactly. Warning was just the word he'd

adopted in retrospect, when he tried to make sense of things. He said that in retrospect we enforce a logic on things that simply happen in the moment.

I nodded.

So not a warning. He encountered another obstacle and his reaction was to resist, to spite, to challenge, to invoke chaos. Take Up and Read were words from a song of Dalia's that only he knew about. He'd kept the song on his iPhone, like a talisman. He didn't listen to it anymore. He remembered that during the war that summer, he'd lost his iPhone in the chaos of the empathy rally held in Sderot. Elish was there too, and he picked up Nahum's phone.

I resisted the urge to tell him I remembered that, that Yalon and I were the ones who unlocked the phone for Elish.

Nahum said he'd heard that Elish had also been wandering around Sderot twelve years earlier, investigating the death of Dalia Shushan. He suspected that Elish went through his phone, copied Dalia's song, and somehow passed it on to Therese. But it seemed far-fetched, and anyway, like he said, he didn't have an instinct for these things. But the suspicion gnawed at him, so he went to see Esther Shushan, may she rest in peace, Dalia's mother. Among the incoherent things she'd said, she mentioned the fact that Ronnit, her niece—

I couldn't hold back. I said, That Ronnit is his part— Then I fell silent.

He said that Ronnit came to see her after she sat shiva with my family and told her that Elish said he was investigating someone by the name of Buganim. She also said something odd, that Elish wasn't finished dying. At the time, Nahum attributed this to her general lack of lucidity. He realized he had a bargaining chip, so he requested a meeting with Therese.

He didn't have a plan, really he didn't, but Therese's carelessness and arrogance made him lose his cool, he said. She only granted him ten minutes and told him that if he came to ask her to support his library project again, then he shouldn't waste his time or hers, because she was taking Mayor Asraf's side in that.

In response, he just told her he knew about Take Up and Read. She looked surprised, but asked what exactly he thought he knew. So he bombarded her with everything that seemed pertinent. Before their meeting, he recapped all the conversations they'd ever had, things that might be on her mind, and he said he knew about Elish, he knew about the investigation he'd been running into her husband's work, and he knew about the Land of Shadow.

She repeated the words "Land of Shadow." She said there was no possible way for him to know about it. Nahum said he knew about it from Dalia's song. She asked what song. He said Dalia wrote a song called "The Land of Shadow" that ended with the words "take up and read."

She was stunned. Her hands started shaking uncontrollably against her desk. She looked at him like she wanted to kill him. Then her expression changed, he said. She cried quietly, silent tears, and then let out a sigh of relief. He just watched her, doing nothing, startled by her response. After a few minutes of weeping, she told her assistant over the phone that something had come up and to postpone all her meetings in the next two hours. She asked Nahum to wait in the lobby. While he waited, there was a document she wanted him to read carefully. She pulled an envelope out of a hidden safe in the wall and handed it to him.

The envelope contained an agreement signed by Elish for participation in an experimental medical procedure that might end with the death of the test subject or with severe side effects and diminished health. Nahum knew nothing about contracts or legal agreements, but the document read like a will. It said that he, the undersigned, Elish Ben Zaken, was confirming the terms with sound body and mind, and with full comprehension and acknowledgment.

Therese asked him back into her office and handed him another document, an employment contract. The moment he signed it, he would become a full-time employee of Becker-Kavillio-Buganim Health Technologies Incorporated, hereinafter known as "The Company," that signing this employment contract obligated him to maintain full confidentiality with regards to any information that might become available to him during the duration of his employment, and that he must offer The Company any information at his disposal which pertained to the studies run by it or to products under development.

He was reciting the wording as if he'd memorized it, like a poem or a prayer. That's what Oshri said later, that his tone and lilt reminded him of the cantor at the synagogue he and Dad used to go to on Shabbat and the holidays.

He asked Therese what this meant, what his conditions were. She pointed at the salary clause, and he marveled. She said he was hereby taking on a position as manager of the reading encouragement project. He asked about the Dalia film. She said she'd promised herself it would be made. He said he would help, but only under the condition that her mother not be involved. She promised him. He already knew he was going to sabotage the film, and indeed, it had never been completed. Nahum said that, for some reason, that was all he could think about, his revenge against all those abusers, all those leeches, like the film director. He said that was the only reason he signed the contract.

But what difference did that make, really? Because after he signed she requested his copy of Dalia's song. He told her Dalia had recorded it on his tape deck at home and that the tape strip had since broken, but that he remembered the words by heart and could hum some of the music. She handed him a piece of paper and he wrote down the lyrics. She recorded him singing it. Luckily, Dalia's songs were the kind that got stuck in your head, but as soon as you tried to sing them you realized how complicated they were. You always ended up singing off-key.

I couldn't resist again. I asked why that was lucky and when Elish was going to enter the picture. He said soon, soon, that he would love another cup of tea, or maybe something stronger, because his throat was dry. I told him we had excellent wine from last night's dinner. He debated whether it was too early for wine. I didn't give him the opportunity. I got up and brought the bottle over. I poured him some. He took a tiny sip, the kind a bee might take from a flower's nectar. Perhaps I should have given him a straw. His lips elongated, and his wrinkles stretched taut. How old was he, I wondered, nearing sixty? This is what Elish should have looked like now. But I can't think of Elish being any other age. He's frozen in a point of singularity where all ages before the time of death coalesce into one age, one life event, like a well-oiled combat unit made up of individuals who are the organs of a body more effective and efficient as a whole than its arms, legs, brains.

I wondered what Oshri was thinking about. He hadn't said a word so far, and didn't seem on edge. He was just listening, with his cunning amiability. Perhaps he was waiting to get to the parts that applied to him, the way you, Shula, are waiting, staking out some detail to shine out of this pile, this generalized blah-blah.

Nahum said that after he finished recording he told Therese it was her turn. She asked if he understood he was bound by the confidentiality clause. He said he did, and that he wanted to know more about the medical procedure. She asked if he meant Take Up and Read. He didn't catch her drift, but said yes.

Therese said it was a shame she never got a chance to know Elish better, a shame they hadn't met sooner, because she could have used his help, might have hired him, that to that day she couldn't figure out how he made the connections he did, how little bits of rumors and clues gave him an understanding of the bigger picture. He called her two weeks before his death. He was investigating a case regarding a young woman who was visiting Sderot.

I said her name was Kalanit Shaubi, and that her disappearance was the reason he'd moved to Sderot that summer during the war. Nahum said that was her name, but he thought that Elish was investigating Heftzi Columbus's murder at the time. I said no, the Kalanit Shaubi investigation just happened to lead him to finding Heftzi Columbus's body, but that hadn't been his original intent.

Nahum trembled, a shock of electricity across his face. No, the features stayed put, unmoving, the eyes like a lamp whose light brightens right before it burns out. I asked what. He said it was odd, how lots of the stories he knew all intersected in the outer thicket. I asked if he was talking about the thicket by the lake. He said yes. I asked what stories. He said nothing, just events from his life. I said that in our investigation, he was the thicket. He asked what I meant. I said lots of threads either started with him or led to him.

He said Therese told him Elish had a copy of Kalanit's medical record, as well as records of the treatment she'd received after being hospitalized for her missile injury, and before. She'd had some blood tests taken and her general practitioner sent the sample to the lab. Elish discovered that the lab was a satellite of Becker-Kavillio-Buganim. He introduced himself as a writer working on a book about Heftzi Columbus, who wanted to dedicate a chapter to the events in Sderot during the Gaza War. He said Kalanit Shaubi's story was one of the bizarre events that took place there at the time. Nahum said that Therese was suspicious, and yet Elish managed to get her talking and reveal irrelevant details about Eldad Kavillio's research, which he knew about somehow, putting two and two together. A week later, Elish appeared again in her office without prior notice. He said he had a few more details to clarify, and during their conversation she found out he'd managed to procure the medical records of another young woman, from Ukraine, who'd been visiting Israel two years earlier. Anyway, he uncovered an experiment Becker-Kavillio-Buganim was running on young women without their knowledge. But Therese had a surprise in store for him too. She'd done her own research about Elish.

Oshri finally snapped out of his indifference, out of his wow-how-fascinating-I'm-on-your-side act that covered up for the way he peeled the flesh of emotion off of everything, like a fruit, to end up with the seed of fact, which he exhibited in the display case of his mind. He sat up. Nahum reacted to his alertness without even noticing. His eyes, which had been on me most of the time, shifted a little to the side to include Oshri in his field of vision, like a pulsation of data on an augmented reality lens.

Nahum said that this was the story Therese had told him. Like too many things in this country, it connected back to concentration and death camps, or at least that was the feeling at the time, that every sentence in the Hebrew language ended with crematorium smoke. Oshri cut him off and said we knew about the poet from Buchenwald. Nahum said that actually, this poet, who Therese said was named Richard Perotz, had come from Morocco, and was probably originally named Richard Peretz. He became a widower at a young age, twenty-something, and had a little girl, who he sent to live with his parents when he traveled to France. According to what he wrote, Ludwik Fleck, the scientist who—

Oshri cut him off again, saying we knew about Ludwik Fleck. Nahum said the man was a brilliant thinker. Therese had read his work and mentioned him as one of her heroes, so to prepare for their meeting, he'd read the book of Fleck's that Therese had mentioned, *Genesis and Development of a Scientific Fact*. Oshri said that was the one about syphilis, and Nahum said yes, it was the kind of writing that changes the way you think. Oshri asked if he'd read—

I told them both to cool it, because we were getting off track, and that Ludwik Fleck, applause please, had received the respect he deserved, so let's move on. Nahum said it was good that we knew about him, that meant we also knew about his journal, which Eldad Kavillio had tracked down with a private collector in Poland who had no idea what he had at his disposal. Nahum happened to see the journal at the Heidelberg lab when he went to visit after years away. Neat handwriting, without a single spelling error or cross-out. Nahum asked us to consider what it was like to write by hand or even by typewriter before the age of computers. What careful planning of grammar it required, what mental organization, the entire perception of language was different, not like today when people barely finish their sente—

I said, Yes, yes, nostalgia is nice, but what's the deal with this Richard Perotz, what was he looking for in France and what does it have to do with anything? Nahum said he didn't really have anything to do with anything, but that Perotz had told Fleck his parents had married him off at a young age because they could tell he was restless and all he cared about was poetry. He'd planned on going to Europe to continue his studies, and after his wife died he realized he had to try as long as he was still young. He spent a few years in Paris.

We said we'd heard about it, he'd been turned in to the Nazis after they occupied France and was sent to Buchenwald, where Rudolf Weigl used him as a lice incubator.

Nahum said it was easy to judge, but the Jewish prisoners in the camps suffered inhumane conditions, and Weigl took care of their welfare. He smuggled vaccines into the Lvov Ghetto and hid Jews in his home. He was condemned in Poland after the war, but when you weighed the good against the bad, you could see that the final tally was in his favor. There was a reason he was named Righteous Among the Nations.

I said nothing. Nahum said that Therese told him Fleck wrote that Perotz was naturally immune to typhus, but that his reaction to the bacteria was unusual, causing changes to his consciousness. He said that years earlier, when they spoke, she'd also told him that Eldad Kavillio had left notes to the effect that any microorganism that affects consciousness leaves an opening for study of the structure of reality, or something like that, and that he reminded her of that. She confirmed it.

HOW IS IT THAT I CAN REMEMBER EVERY DETAIL SO ACUTELY that I can practically stand there and watch it unfolding, knowing it all? It's your trick, isn't it, using me like a magnifying glass into my own life.

I know your name. It isn't enough. It's exterior, like the shell of a pill. I say "you" and the word bounces off of you. But at least your name is like a finger I can stretch inside the thought to show where Shula is. Shula can't hide from me.

But that isn't accurate either. You have a language. I have to add a suffix to the verb that signifies that I'm talking to Shula when I'm in front of her, and not the way she is. To add a "you." Shula is listenyou to me. Shula is lookyou for something. But I won't use it. I'll point to you, Shula, and say "you." That'll be a combination of the Shula I'm speaking to and the Shula that exists apart from me, in the third person, someplace in the world. Like our self, that leaves sometimes, and something fake comes to fill its place. When I poured Nahum the wine, I poured myself some too. Someone else was tasting it for me. I sipped and the wine slid down my tongue, flowing down my gullet, but I wasn't the one drinking it.

Oshri asked Nahum if Therese had explained to him what Eldad Kavillio's statement meant. Nahum said not really, that he was interested in the ethical aspects of the study. I asked like what. He said he had to explain something first. Therese said Fleck wrote that he couldn't replicate the Perotz study, that he'd tried to infect him with typhus several more times, but the phenomenon didn't repeat itself. He questioned soldiers who returned from the front lines, where there were typhus outbreaks, trying to find out if there were any unusual occurrences. There hadn't been, except for a few people who cried during nightmares or lost their minds or their limbs, which was par for the course, nobody reported any hallucinations that anyone else was able to see. One day, Richard Perotz left Lublin and Fleck's study. Therese said that Fleck's conclusion was that perhaps something in Perotz's specific immune system was responsible for the phenomenon, and that he had to find a way to track down others like him.

Years later, Therese's first husband, Eldad Kavillio—

Oshri said he knew about him, that he'd read a lot of his writing and that he was a serious scientist with groundbreaking insights about immunology. Nahum said he'd only heard about him because his best friend at the time, Ehud Barda, adored him, and Nahum was jealous of that adoration, of the fact that Ehud had someone he aspired to be like. He said he had nobody like that. He was religious, but couldn't bring himself to admire rabbis or righteous men, and only understood why when he was older. One day, he went to the library and read about Eldad Kavillio in some book. He didn't understand much, but he realized then that Ehud didn't understand either, and was just showing off.

I looked at him. He had that disconnection of longing, when the power of longing weakens whatever's happening at the moment, strengthening what happened then, which is why people like that are fated to sink, as if whatever is more powerful in his existence spreads heat, because existence is a kind of fire. Again I wanted to reach out and touch him, remind him we were right there with him. Why, actually, why did I care about him? Because he was older?

I said that Eldad Kavillio somehow ended up dying from the experiment. He said that part was unclear. Eldad Kavillio had contacted some Polish scientists. It was hard to form collaborations at the time because of the Iron Curtain and the Cold War.

I didn't want to ask him for explanations because I knew he'd get sidetracked again. I glanced at Oshri and shrugged. Nahum said there were some connections, that back then people were discussing atom bombs and nuclear fallout, but the truth was that military developments were actually focused on chemical and biological warfare, and governments were negotiating on those terms. Oshri said there had been no information exchange agreement with Poland at the time. Nahum said that Oshri, as a MKI employee, should know better than he did that when it came to arms dealing, Israeli had neither enemies nor friends, only customers. Oshri nodded slowly, reluctantly. His eyes bounced to the corners of the ceiling to make sure his scramblers and shielding devices were working. He was no fool. Neither was I. We were trying to make the best of a bad situation; that was a sorry excuse, but I could say we weren't blind, we didn't lie to ourselves, and maybe that's a sort of deception too.

Nahum said Eldad Kavillio found an opening, made his connections, and must have been able to track down descendants of the lice with the bacteria from the strain Weigl and Fleck had grown. He said that to this day there's an enormous incubator of body lice carrying typhus in Poland. He visited it with Therese. She insisted on showing it to him. He thought she didn't fully believe he was convinced as she was of her innocence. They were made to wear protective gear before going inside. Nahum thought it was to keep them from catching the lice, but it turned out it was the other way around, it was so they wouldn't harm the lice, infecting them with the germs they carried. Nahum said that Therese looked at the incubators and said quietly, There go Eldad's murderers. Oshri said it was amazing to think that body lice were the most lethal creatures on Earth after mosquitos and humans. I said, Mosquitas. Oshri said, What? I said, Not mosquitos, female mosquitos. He said, Yes.

Nahum said that was when Therese started investigating. For years, she tried all sorts of directions, buying Fleck's estate from his family in Israel, those people had enough history for an entire nation. Fleck's son had come to Israel on the refugee ship *Exodus*. One day, she had an epiphany. She realized that Fleck's comment about the unique structure of Perotz's immune system was a spark of genius, and that actually Fleck was talking about a genetic profile. And that was it, she started tracking down Perotz to see if she could find any of his descendants.

It turned out Perotz was a serial escape artist. He lived with a Ukrainian woman in East Germany, had children, then fled due to communism, returning to Morocco, to a different city, Fez, where he also married a woman, had two children with her, then died. He was physically broken, run-down, maybe because of all the wandering, maybe because of the typhus, though these were just guesses. He died pretty young.

I said it was obvious then that Olga Kovilishin was his descendant, as was Kalanit Shaubi, through her mother, Sima. Nahum said so was our family, or Grandma Zehava, at least. That was Therese's surprise for Elish.

WE WERE SILENT FOR A LONG TIME. SHULA-YOU LOOK THROUGH me and see the silence, but Shula-you can't understand it, Shula-you are just sniffing around for a detail, a key. I can look back too. Shula-you might be dense, but Shula-your presence reveals, just like any other. Shula-you look like a girl at the stage where she becomes a woman, your body beating Shula-you to it. Someone older takes Shula-you out of the room and you go to the field. There are only girls there, right, because existence is a female quality, or the other way around, everything that is alive is always female and everything that is dead is always male. You say "her" and mean something that contains life. You say it and mean something still, an object, lifeless. But you have a he too, which means something dead pretending to be alive. Am I a sort of he for Shula-you? I can feel Shula-your suspicion, but it's got nothing to do with whether I'm her or it or something in the middle, but with the fact that I'm not using language properly. So, if Shula-you are looking for something, Shula-you are going to have to get used to it. You won't understand a thing here unless you learn our language. A similar one is insufficient.

We were silent. We were silent. We sipped. Finally, Oshri said that Therese probably suggested that Elish do some genetic testing, because in the protocols he found the protein sequence of a specific gene appeared in three test subjects. Oshri said he was still surprised by Therese's findings, that she and Eldad Kavillio were true pioneers. He said, If memory serves, immunogenetics. He said that Therese had mapped the DNA of all of Olga's immune cells, using antibody proteins to track down the gene, which she also discovered in Kalanit, it was an anomaly that couldn't—

I was hoping he wouldn't go into his hours-long loop now. I asked Nahum what he meant when he said he had an issue with the ethical aspects of the studies. Nahum said Therese had told him that Olga had agreed to participate in the study, that it had been supervised and paid for, and that everything was documented and Therese had signed agreements. She was hospitalized in a lab at a hospital in Kiev, injected with a vaccine of the bacteria, and her immune system responded aggressively, destroying the bacteria. They were disappointed and sent her home. A few days later, she got on a flight to Israel and Therese heard reports of her disappearance. Olga was asked to come to the Israeli lab for observation, where the manifestations were recorded. They were very weak. When the other girl— I said, Her name was Kalanit Shaubi. He said, Yes, so when the accident happened to her, Therese said she concluded the manifestations were weak and that Olga's immune system had a delayed response because she was quarantined. I asked what that had to do with anything. Nahum said the manifestations might be a social phenomenon, or might at least require having some people around. Richard Perotz was surrounded by friends and people he'd grown attached to. Anyway, again, the process could not be replicated.

He said Therese told him she'd tracked down Kalanit through a net she'd cast at the HMOs. Because she could barely find any birth registries from Morocco, she learned from Fleck's journal that Perotz was originally from Rabat. But as soon as she found a direct descendant of his, re-creating the family trees was no problem. He said we knew how things were with Moroccans, they remembered things differently, orally, through rumors and gossip. Records could be forged, but there was no escaping the web of collective memory. He said Therese had begun putting together an enormous database and offered incentives to blood test labs in exchange for samples of Moroccan descendants, for a study her lab was running with regards to a treatment for a rare genetic disorder. Oshri said that was a breach of confidentiality. Nahum said it was money. And the reporting was meant to be anonymous, so not exactly a breach of confidentiality. And anyway, they were just details, details that weren't important. The important thing was that they made a mistake with Kalanit. They offered her a spot in the study and she needed the money. They wanted to inject her with a weakened sample of the bacteria and track her routine to see if their assumption had been right. The problem was the technician accidentally injected her with an active bacteria sample, and—

I told him we saw the results. I asked where she'd disappeared to.

Nahum said she was under supervision the entire time. They watched her for three days, then let her go. She'd been acting like an automaton and had no recollection of those days. I told him we knew that, and that it was irresponsible. Nahum said Therese had said they didn't leave her alone for a single moment, and that her people were watching and documenting and prepared to intervene if anything happened. I asked if she was tracked when she was with us as well. Nahum said he supposed so. I said, That whole time we thought we were investigating her mystery, but, really, we were the ones being investigated.

Nahum said he'd only learned about this in retrospect, but hadn't known about it when he first met us. It was a good thing he gave us the song before he met with Therese. He said he knew himself, and if he'd had it on him, he would have given it to her,

just as the contract he signed required him to. I asked why he
gave it to us. He waved his hand, as if to say, who knows. He asked
if we still had it. He said that after all these years, finally being
able to talk, clarifying the meaning of things by talking, he'd like
to listen to it again. Maybe this time he'd understand what Dalia
was trying to say.

Oshri picked up his intePhone, ran his hand over the screen,
and swiped. The amplifying system was hidden in the walls, but
it didn't diminish the sound quality. Again the white noise from
the room Dalia and Nahum had been in, as if the tape had also
recorded the way youth echoed between the walls, the guitar that
started and stopped and started again, and the voice that reached
me from inside myself and led me through the nighttimedark I
could no longer locate inside of myself, which I've never been able
to traverse without this song.

AFTER THE SONG WAS OVER, NAHUM SAID IT WAS THE OPPOSITE
of a lullaby. It was a wake-a-bye. Shula-you know what he meant.
My words are slipping off Shula-your shell, as if Shula-you are
wrapped in plastic, but the song does hit Shula-you through my
memory. Or maybe it's Nahum's phrase that hits you, a wake-a-
bye song. Something takes effect, something does the trick.

The souldaughter that takes Shula-you to the field is called
Shulz. Shulz demonstrates Shulz's task to Shula-you. Shulz in-
vestigates the plants. Shulz points at the patterns Shulz notices.
Shula-you can't understand it, but Shula-you are elated with
Shulz's keen eyes, with the way Shulz talks to Shula-you. The elation is like a lamp inside of Shula-your body, the light pausing on
the skin. A breathing, glowing light. Shulz takes Shula-you to the
control center, evening falls on the streets, the streets are about
to go quiet, and all the souldaughters go to sleep in a clump, even
the grains, like Shula-you. The other souldaughters, their senses
are honed and they hear the sounds coming from the stars and

can see into the ground and taste the air and smell the distances until the distances ittify, become it, become still. Lots of souldaughters from the cluster are at the control center. They shove roots down their throats, and a substance is sucked out of them into the receptacles. Shulz does the same. Then Shulz looks at Shula-you and asks what a grain has to look for at the souldaughters' control center, and Shula-you speak her name, but Shulz doesn't understand. She says the grains should all be in the grainhouse before nightsleep. How did a grain like you make it to the control center? Shula-you realize that the day doesn't accumulate for Shulz, the day is sucked out of her throat along with Shulz's investigations. The realization intensifies Shula-your excitement. Shula-you return to the grainhouse but don't get into bed. Shula-you stand around, watching. Above the grains' beds, Shula-you see roots descending to cling to the grains' throats. Shula-you stay out of bed all nightsleep long.

After morningrise, the grains go outside to play and Shula-you don't want to go play with them. Shula-you think about your trip to the field, your investigation with Shulz, Shulz's eyes that don't recognize Shula-you. Shula-you think the trip isn't happening today, it happens before morningrise, before nightsleep. The thought seems odd to Shula-you. What's before morningrise? There is no before morningrise. There is rising in the morning and sleep at night. Nightsleep doesn't come before morningrise. But Shula-you know. Shula-you think about what happens before nightsleep. Shula-you call that time the sunjourney before nightsleep.

Another grain stays in the room with Shula-you. Shulm. Shulm's body is swollen. Shulm calls Shula-you, saying one word, wake-a-bye. Then repeats it, wake-a-bye. Shula-you approach it. Shulm grits her teeth. She tells Shula-you that she needs shamanamer, that shamanamer is late. Shula-you know where the shamanamers' house is. They are the souldaughters that name the new grains. Shula-you run over there. Shula-you walk into the yard and Madden, a large shamanamer, is sitting there. Shula-you tell

Madden that Shulm says wake-a-bye, and Shulm needs a shaman-amer. Madden comes with Shula-you to the grainhouse. Madden picks up Shulm in her arms easily and takes Shulm away. Shula-you follow them, but Madden turns around and tells Shula-you to go back to the grains' games. Shula-you pause and Madden looks at Shula-you. Shulm is crying in her arms. Madden holds her against Madden's chest. She says it's a shame that Shula-your wake-a-bye hasn't come yet, that it might never come, that Shula-you might be sent to absorption without going through the entire cycle, it's a real shame, Shula-you come from a good source.

Shula-you stop and stare. Shula-you are scared. Madden is using holyspeak, the speak of the verse of versions, of the return of the great scientist, of after nightsleep. Shula-you think that the sunjourney before nightsleep has an expression in holyspeak. Shula-you think, Shula-I went to investigate a field with Shulz, and panic, and panic, and the lamp of elation in Shula-your body sucks in the light. But Shula-you say, Shula went out. Not Shula-I go out. Shula went out, in the sunjourney before morningrise.

And before nightsleep, Shula-you don't get into bed again. And in morningrise, Shula-you have two sunjourneys before nightsleep, a sunjourney before nightsleep and a sunjourney before a sunjourney before nightsleep. Shula-you think that Shula-you need to find a way to name these sunjourneys. And again the panic. Shula-you are stealing the tasks of shamanamers. But what is the action of arranging sunjourneys, what is the name of that action?

Shula-you are terrified, but the thought haunts. Shula-you wander, following the souldaughters in the clump, walking down the streets, Shula-you arrive at the place of the listeners. The souldaughters are scattered there, sitting motionlessly. Shula-you approach with loud silence, and suddenly Shula-you see Shulm around them. She isn't a grain, she's a souldaughter. Her body is big like the clump's souldaughters'. Shula-you think that this is the meaning of wake-a-bye, turning from a grain into a souldaughter. Shula-you wonder what Madden means when she says it's a shame Shula-you don't go through the wake-a-bye.

Shula-you tell Shula-you, No, Shula-you are getting used to saying, What did Madden mean when she said the wake-a-bye had not come and might not come? Shula-you bite Shula-your tongue but keep thinking.

Eventually, Shula-you recite the verse of versions in a whisper. One was alone in her eternal nightsleep, without clump or budding ability, and she cried her longing. From the crying came the its, the motionless. The its rose and crawled inside, and heified and disguised themselves as souldaughters like her. And the hes played with the one, entertained the one. And the whole time they schemed to drag her to the hushes so that she, the one who with her crying woke them up from the it to the he, would be silent forever. And they gnawed at the living being of the one, stinging and freezing and silencing, and the one cried a terrible cry, and from the primeval neon aura came the great scientist to the one in the spaceship *Glaria*. No good were the medicines offered by the great scientist. The great scientist was unable to heal the one. And the great scientist took her scalpel and separated between the one and memory of the one, and warmed the one in the core of radiation, until her budding ability erupted. And the great scientist planted the radiation core in the nightsleep and a morningrise grew. And by force of the budding, grains peeked out all at once. And the great scientist ordered the born clump, Awake and investigate morningrise until you find a cure for soulwaking beyond wake-a-bye, then the clump will return to be as one, and we, the great scientist and her forty-two research assistants, will return to welcome the second resurrection. And the great scientist boarded the spaceship *Glaria* and returned to the primeval neon aura.

OSHRI GOT UP FROM HIS CHAIR. HE SAID HE COULDN'T LISTEN anymore, that he had to do something. He asked Nahum if he'd like to stay for dinner. I said, What's the rush, we're finally getting to the point, don't you want to hear what happened to Elish? Oshri said he could guess by himself that Elish took the test and found out that he had the Richard Perotz gene and that Therese had talked him into the procedure, which killed him, just like Eldad Kavillio. He didn't need to hear any more about that. He turned to Nahum and asked if that wasn't how it had gone.

Nahum didn't answer.

Oshri asked him again if he'd be staying for dinner. Nahum said no, he'd made plans with friends since it was so rare for him to come to central Israel. He pulled out his intePhone from the days of yore and looked at it. I asked him not to go, I still had more questions. He said he could give us twenty more minutes, and that was it. Oshri said to give them to me, he was out. I looked at Nahum. He said that when he said that was it, he meant he wouldn't be talking about this subject anymore. He suddenly understood the relief Therese had felt, being able to finally tell someone about it. But it was a story that could only be conveyed through conversation. Repeating it would mean betraying it. I said he could tell it a little differently each time. He asked how I would know. I didn't answer.

He said Therese told him that meeting Elish had been like meeting a long-lost brother, that there was a harmony in their obsession for answers. He said Oshri was right. I said, Obviously he was right, I could guess that myself, but that I didn't care about what happened, I cared about why, why Elish took that risk. He said that was the difference between me and Oshri. Oshri cared about what and how, and I cared about why and wherefore. I said he didn't know us well enough to make those generalizations. He said it was apparent in our conversation. He said questions of what and how reveal the possibility of danger, but only questions of why and wherefore lead the way into it. I asked if he was trying to warn me, if he was saying Elish also asked why rather than make do with what and how.

He raised his glass, but it was empty. I leaned in to pour him some more wine, but he covered the top of the glass with his hand. Nahum said that Therese had told him that from the moment Elish heard about this procedure he wouldn't let go. I asked if Nahum had any idea of what Elish had been searching for. He asked what I felt when I listened to the Dalia Shushan song. I described it to him. He said that, in his opinion, that was the only song where Dalia stayed real throughout, and that was why it was a difficult one to listen to. He said the songs in the two Blasé albums and in her demo album were wonderful, but save for a few lines, they didn't contain the Dalia he knew. The Dalia he knew spoke in praise of life. That Dalia, and the voices she left behind her, were conjured from the netherworld, charmed by it. I asked what he meant by "the netherworld." He said he believed Dalia's pain, but to her the pain became a door, not a wound she hoped would heal. I told him he still hadn't answered my question.

He said any answer I didn't figure out by myself wouldn't truly satisfy me. I said I still wanted to know what he thought. He said Therese had told him that Elish had responded to the treatment just like Olga. His immune system simply vanquished the bacteria. He stayed in her lab for four days for observation, then said he was giving up because nothing happened. Therese begged him to come back a few days later, explaining that Olga's manifestation state had also been delayed. But Elish dismissed her. Nahum said Therese had told him that Elish had been disappointed, as if she'd betrayed him or led him astray. I said it was as if she'd led him down the garden path. Nahum smiled. Smiling suited him, the smile moved his features into their natural placement, and the burning dots on the glaze of his eyes that came with it were graceful.

Therese had told him that Elish's death had rattled her. She obtained the results of the autopsy as well as a blood sample from the police and saw the renewed rise in antibodies in his blood. She couldn't figure out what had gone wrong, because when they'd run their own tests, the antibody levels had dropped on the second day after infection. She said this event had killed her curiosity completely and she'd issued a directive to halt and archive the study.

I added that she also applied pressure to close the investigation. She was far-reaching. He shrugged. Another smile flickered across his lips, but a small one this time, sad. He asked who the truth would have helped. I said it would have helped my grandmother, my parents, me. He asked if I truly believed that. I said I did. I asked if that's why Therese had cried when he'd brought up her responsibility for Elish's death, if she'd been afraid her secrets would be revealed.

He said no, not at all. Therese was a collector. She was compulsive. When she tracked down the descendants of Richard Perotz, she found a poem he wrote in the Kovilishin home. He'd written it in flowery, heavy-handed, Enlightenment-day Hebrew. It started just like Dalia's song, "And there shall be no more death in the Land of Shadow." And it ended the same, with the words "take up and read." That's where she got the name for her medical project, Take Up and Read, because she thought Perotz must have written that poem about his manifestations.

I said that was impossible, how could Dalia Shushan have—

Nahum said he wasn't that surprised. Had I met Dalia, I would have understood it. She was a year younger than he was, but still smarter than him. She wasn't wise with experience, but wise with knowledge that comes from the places that make experience possible. He didn't understand that at age sixteen. He was just enchanted by her, enamored. He didn't want to be away from her for a single minute. But in retrospect he knew that her wisdom was also her weakness. It blinded her.

I said there were things that didn't add up. For instance, where was Elish's notepad? Elish never ran an investigation without a dedicated notepad for it. The ones he left behind contained no notes about the Yoel Buganim and Therese Kavillio investigation, only clues to his findings. And, if Sima Shaubi's stories were to be believed, then who were the people who tried to kidnap Kalanit Shaubi as a child, and what did Therese and Elish talk about two hours before he died, and who made the alarm in his car go off, and what was that wheezing that his neighbor, Dina Boltkey, heard after Elish was already—

Nahum said Therese might have answers. She was more inquisitive than him. Therese and Elish would have made a fine couple. He glanced at the clock on his intePhone and stood up. He thanked me and Oshri for giving him the chance to—

I asked him to wait, I wanted to know more, more about Therese, who was she, these disruptions didn't add up, the idea that it all just happened to her, that she had no ill will, that—

Nahum said that every story contained holes and details that didn't fit or tie together neatly. He walked to the door. Before he opened it, he said he used to be religious, and religious thought was not something you could get rid of. It was hard for him to believe that anything rooted in evil could produce positive results, and that now that the State of Israel was parting with the worldview that had been emblazoned into it at the Auschwitz crematoriums, maybe we could let this story go too. He was letting go of it, and he proposed that I do the same. He said that, in Therese's defense, he could tell me that she was doubting and blaming herself. As a child, he wasn't able to admire the exemplars of devoutness. Nothing scared him more than the faces of righteous and enlightened men. Only years later did he realize that when he looked at them he knew, without being able to explain it to himself, that they would be able to commit the most atrocious acts without thinking twice, because they were in possession of absolute truth.

He opened the door and said goodbye, but I heard it as "goodbouch." That was Yalon's expression in high school. He'd adopted a trend that was just catching on in Spain, where boys would wear puffy knee-length pants. The internet videos referred to them as

breeches, but Yalon called them "pouch pants." It seemed like a
bad joke until other patheteeth kids started copying him. Maybe
every fashion trend is a bad joke that gets out of control. His problem was, he didn't get rid of the pants even a year later, when the
trend was over. And he got used to saying "pouch," until, just like
Elinoar and Racheli, he would add the "ch" sound to the end of
everything. Most of all, he said goodbouch. I hate words with the
"ch" sound. They sit in your mouth like a group of people walking
sluggishly ahead of you in a line. You feel like kicking their ankles and making them all faceplant.

SHULA-YOU QUIETLY, CONSTANTLY MEMORIZE THE ONE'S VERSE
of versions in holyspeak. During nightsleep, Shula-you are not in
bed, Shula-you are wandering. Shula-you are watching the star-
herders. Shula-you know they're blind to Shula-your light, but
can see a different, richer, wilder, more beautiful radiation. The
star-herders secrete the accumulation of their observation before morningrise, at the control center. Then they sleep during
sunjourney. Shula-you sleep in a hidden corner of the field, waking up before morningrise, looking at the glittering strips of pre-
sunjourney, and sneaking into the bed in Shula-your room at the
grainhouse. How many sunjourneys have gone by? Shula-you
think that Shula-you need to find a way to mark them so that
Shula-you can tell the order of time accumulations.

One sunjourney Shula-you run into Maddea the shamanamer.
Maddea asks Shula-you why Shula is wandering the streets rather
than playing with the grains. Shula-you say, Shula-I'm started to
walk and don't stopped. Maddea looks at Shula-you with Maddea's
narrow eyes. Maddea says, Too bad, such a good source, such a fine
budding, and no wake-a-bye, Shula-you are starting to rot, in ten
sunjourneys Shula-you will be sent to absorption. Shula-you ask,
Ten? Maddea shows Shula-you her hands. Maddea's fingers are
stretched out. Maddea says, Ten, again and sighs. Shula-you panic

again, without recognizing why. The bulb in Shula-your body flickers. Shula-you realize that Shula-you don't know what absorption is. Shula-you follow Maddea that entire sunjourney.

During feedtime, Maddea walks among the souldaughters and points at some of them. Shula-you can tell they are rotten, the souldaughters' flesh is starting to ittify, black spots of it invade the souldaughters. The smell makes Shula-you feel sick, but Shula-you resist the urge. Shula-you don't feed at all. The other souldaughters get up and follow Maddea as an entourage. Shula-you follow Maddea and the souldaughters and the entourage. Maddea and the entourage approach the area that Shula-your senses warn against. A danger zone. A nightmare zone. Shula-you know from deep inside Shula-you. Shula-you wonder how Shula-you know that fear, if the shamanamers put that fear inside of Shula-you. Shula-you wonder when, on which sunjourney.

Shula-you try to calculate how many sunjourneys go by since the arrival of the great scientist, how many morningrises and nightsleeps. Shula-you think again that Shula-you have to find a way to arrange time accumulations.

Shula-you contain your fear. Shula-you follow Maddea and the entourage into an enormous hall. Inside the hall are long glass cases. The rotting souldaughters get inside the cases. The colors inside blend. And no more souldaughters, the it washes the souldaughters away. Shula-you run away. Shula-you run to the grainhouse and sit on the floor of the grain room until the grains come back from their games. There are enough time accumulations in Shula-you to know that grains come and grains go. Shula-you know the names. Shusg and Shush and Shusi and Shusj came to Shula-your grain room, and Shulz and Shuma and Shumb and Shumc leave in separate sunjourneys, go through wake-a-bye, become souldaughters, but Shula-you stay. Not for many more sunjourneys. Ten sunjourneys. How many sunjourneys is ten sunjourneys?

Shula-you think that Shula-you can mark the sunjourneys by

the grains that leave, but how do Shula-you arrange them? Shula-you put each grain on the tip of a finger. Shula-you name the fingers, Shulm and Shulz and Shuma and Shumb and Shumc. The fingers run out on Shula-you. Shula-you decide that the hand is called Madden. A hand and another hand are called Shulz Madden. And another hand Shuma Madden. And so on. Shula-you look at the fingers. Shula-your fingers are like Maddea's fingers. Ten sunjourneys, one hand and another. Shulz Madden sunjourneys.

On the sunjourney after nightsleep, Shula-you have Madden and Shumb sunjourneys left. Shula-you panic. Panic. Shula-you leave the grain room. Shula-you think that Shula-you ought to talk to Maddea. Maybe if Maddea knows that Shula-you have time accumulation, Maddea doesn't send Shula-you to be absorbed.

Shula-you walk into the shamanamers' yard. Shula-you peek through the door. The shamanamers are lying in their beds. The shamanamers are sleeping. A root is connected to Maddea's forehead. The root sucks on Maddea. Maddea's body shivers and relaxes. A root comes down and glues to Maddet's forehead. Maddet looks like Maddea, but Maddet is riper. The root flows a substance into Maddet's forehead. Maddet's eyelids flutter and Maddet opens her eyes. The rest of the shamanamers continue to sleep.

Shula-you retreat slowly and leave. Shula-you think that every sunjourney has a shamanamer. Shula-you don't see Shulz shamanamers on that sunjourney. But shamanamers know the happenings of separate sunjourneys. Do time accumulations pass between shamanamers?

Shula-you memorize the verse of versions in holyspeak. Who put the verse of versions inside Shula-you? The shamanamers, upon budding. But Shula-you don't know what budding is.

Shula-you sit in Shula-your corner of the field and think. Shula-you know another forbidden zone, the budding halls. After morningrise, Shula-you go to the budding halls. Shula-you peek inside. Souldaughters sit in chairs. Shula-you match their numbers to fingers. Shula-you call this fingerizing. Shula-you fingerize. Shulz Madden and Shumb souldaughters. Shula-you focus on a souldaughter named Shuky. Shuky has bare feet. Roots come out of Shuky's soles, penetrating the circle of dirt around her seat. Maddet paces between the souldaughters, knife in hand. Shulz follows Maddet with a padded basket. Maddet reaches Shuky. Maddet cuts the flesh of the shoulder. A stem grows through the cut. At the end of the stem is a flower, the flower opens, at the center of the flower is a golden crown, the crown falls into Maddet's hand, and writhes, and screams. Maddet places the golden crown in the padded basket and Shulz steps aside. On the side are small glass domes. Shulz opens a glass dome and places the screaming crown inside. Shulz closes the dome and the scream gets swallowed. Shula-you follow the golden crown's writhing. Shula-you fingerize. There are Madden and Shumb writhing crowns inside Madden and Shumb domes. The domes fill up. Shulz retires. Maddet picks up a big piece of paper and cuts out bits. Maddet glues each bit to a glass dome. Maddet is holding a cylinder. Maddet's hand moves over a glued piece of paper. Maddet moves on to the next piece. There are markings on the piece she just left. Shula-you think this is how the shamanamers put the names and the knowledge and the verse of versions into grains. Shula-you know she has seen buddings.

During Shumb sunjourneys and nightsleeps Shula-you think about what Shula-you should do. During the feedtime of sunjourney Shumg, Shula-you sit and stare. Shula-you aren't hungry. Shula-you stir the plate of food. Shula-you see color at the bottom. Shula-you stir more and more. Shula-you see colors. Shula-you wonder what the colors are. There are no colors in the knowledge the shamanamers put into Shula-you. Shula-you check time accumulations. Shula-you check one accumulation at a time. And inside an accumulation from before the fingerization of sunjourneys, Shula-you discover an image. The colors resemble the colors of absorption cases. The bulb in Shula-your body flickers very much.

Are grains and souldaughters in the clump fed by the absorption of souldaughters?

Shula-you push the plate away. Shula-you look at the feeding tables. The clump members are feeding with little noises.

The clump members eat souldaughters.

A few more sunjourneys and the clump members are feeding on Shula-you.

Shula-you suddenly notice. Madder the shamanamer is watching Shula-you. Madder's eyes are hard, hard.

AFTER NAHUM LEFT, OSHRI CAME OUT OF THE KITCHEN. HE WAS wearing an apron covered with stains, red from tomato and dark oil circles and a few stray parsley leaves. It was funny, seeing him like this. Once, when Marco came by for a surprise inspection, I heard him speaking to my commander. I was just a head of a unit back then, and my commander was a particularly disgusting guy. He told Marco that the best girls were hot chicks who behaved like men. He said that he didn't mean they farted or smelled bad. On the contrary, when it came to hygiene they were soft like women, but there was something manly about their personalities. He told Marco to think about super-tough guitarists or biker chicks. Marco asked the commander if he meant lesbians, because he saw the way he'd been looking at Nataly from his team. The commander said, Hell no, he meant real women. I didn't keep listening. I would have shoved the butt of my rifle into his face if he ever talked to me that way. But maybe the opposite is true for me. Maybe I think more highly of men when I see a feminine side in them, like Oshri with the apron. Shula-you don't know anything about the relationships between men and women, because your kind is asexual, with super-gross virginal procreation, but if Shula-you looked out of my eyes rather than making me look from the side, maybe Shula-you would have seen how a flower in the pocket or a pink shirt upgrades a man. A crack of silk in the rough skin. On the other hand, I might be falling for the same stereotypes as that sleazy commander. Maybe I'm not much better than him after all.

Oshri asked if I learned a lot from the rest of the conversation. I asked, What do you care, you didn't even want to hear it. He said something was bothering him and maybe he'd left too early. I told him it was the story of Richard Perotz, all too coincidental. Did he really think we were related to him, related to Kalanit and Olga? It was dumb. He said no, there was something else he couldn't see.

I asked if he'd paid any mind to the simple fact that Therese Kavillio-Buganim's experiment worked with girls and failed with boys. He gawked at me and asked what I meant. I said that other than Richard Perotz, who was a man, the two cases where manifestations occurred were–

He cut me off. I know where you're going with this, he said, and I have no intention–

Why not, I said, we can run genetic tests. I'm convinced we'll find out that he had the dangerous gene and I have the right one.

He retreated into the kitchen. I followed him in. A pot was bubbling and the air smelled appetizing. All that wine made me hungry. I lifted the lid and breathed in the steam, fish balls just like Grandma Zehava used to make them. She wouldn't give Oshri the recipe because he was a boy, and boys belonged around the table, not in the kitchen. And for some reason, Mom never did a good job with them. So he would ask Grandma Zehava to make them especially for him when he came home on leave from the military. He would eat them and take down notes until he figured out his own version. I was craving them hard right now. My stomach was empty from my conversation with Nahum, but I was feeling nauseous, eating was so not a good idea right now. The hunger swung inside of me, coming and going every second. I told Oshri I knew it in my veins and in my arteries. He said no, absolutely not. I told him not to be a patheteeth, just one more journey. He didn't answer.

I went to Sderot in the middle of the week. Dad was out on the porch, Mom wasn't home. Dad looked at me, surprised. He didn't age well. He had high cholesterol, we didn't need a test to know that. Something in him thickened and I could see that his skin had a dirty color, the color of grease floating through his bloodstream. He hugged and kissed me like crazy. I'd missed him too. I could push the present out of myself and replace it with his image from the past, the husky man of my childhood, a little less handsome than Oshri but equally impressive.

I asked where Grandma Zehava was. He said she was in the living room. I said I came to sit with her. He said that was excellent, because she wouldn't stop asking about me. I asked if he wanted some coffee. He said he was trying to lower his caffeine intake, but could I do him a favor and make him a decaf? He said he was so glad I'd come. Honestly, so was I. I don't know when the switch happened. Home piles up and piles up inside of you until you feel like you have to get away before it crushes you, then years go by and you realize when you come back that home is where you can shed the weight of your other life. Shula-you can't understand this flexibility, you, who are so possessive of your time accumulations, counting them like coins.

I sat with Grandma Zehava. I had to shake her awake from her listening to herself, from that deafness that had taken over her. She grabbed my hand. Her own hand was gaunt, acquiring the shape of the bone, but her touch was comforting. I spoke into her ear so she could hear me. I said I wanted to ask her some questions about her family in Morocco, if she remembered. She asked what had changed, I never used to take an interest. I said, I do now. She said what about, she could hardly remember anything. I asked about her father and her mother, who were they? She said her mother died in Israel, a saintly woman who raised her and her brothers on her own, brought them to Israel on her own. I asked what happened to her father. She said he died young, used to be a porter back in Rabat, there was an accident, she remembered the shouting on the street when she got closer, her mother came out of the house without her headscarf, her hair all wild, and she tore if off and yelled, Mahluf is dead. She squeezed my hand. She said, You're such a pretty girl. Where's your man, where's Asor's boy? I told her we weren't together anymore. She asked why and looked at me. I noticed she was crying, but I didn't know what the crying was for, she had tears in her eyes and her voice was like leaves flying in the wind, but not because of old age. She said the men in this family were unlucky. I told her not to say that. She said his brother died too. I asked, Whose brother? She said her uncle, her father's brother, there were stories about him that he traveled to France and those damned Germans caught him, they would have made it to Morocco if the British hadn't stopped them. I asked what her maiden name was, her father's last name. She said it was Peretz, that people in Morocco used to say Peretz was a strong name, full of life, but not for them.

SHULA-YOU ARE IN A RUSH. SHULA-YOU ARE SURE THAT MADDER is looking for Shula-you. Shula-your breathing hurts. Shula-you run in the field, running and running. Shula-you no longer see groups of souldaughters investigating, searching, gathering. The field goes on and Shula-you want to leave, but Shula-you are afraid. In the distance, Shula-you see the wall. The knowledge inside Shula-you jumps. Shula-you know that Shula-you have reached the border, that the border is it. That the border makes souldaughters ittify. The wall is see-through and inside the wall move dark shapes that Shula-you don't recognize. Shula-you turn around. Maybe Shula-you run a different way. But no. In the

distance, Shula-you see Madder and an entourage of souldaughters. They gain on Shula-you. They arrive. Madder tells Shula-you
that Madder understands what is wrong with Shula-you, that
Shula-you are a criminal, Shula-you remember. Shula-you flinch.
Shula-you ask what "remembering" means. Madder doesn't answer. She signals to the entourage to catch Shula-you. Shula-you
ask what will be done to Shula-you. Madder says everything
Shula-you gathered during all the sunjourneys will be ripped out
of Shula-you. Shula-you gasp when Madder speaks holyspeak
around the souldaughters. The souldaughters don't care. The
souldaughters advance on Shula-you. Shula-you say the time accumulations belong to Shula-you, that Shula-you want to keep
them. Shula-you take a step back. Shula-you are afraid and not
careful. Shula-you wonder why the time accumulations are being
taken from Shula-you. Shula-your back touches a pliable, soft
material. Shula-you don't understand what that material is. All of
a sudden, the material grabs Shula-you, hard. All of a sudden,
Shula-you are sucked into the material. Shula-you yells because
Shula-you understand that the material is it, not her, that Shula-
you are being swallowed into the border. The it stretches Shula-
your limbs, trying to tear Shula-you apart, no, pieces of the it
want to penetrate Shula-you, to take Shula-you apart from the
inside. Shula-you see what they're trying to get at, the accumulations inside of Shula-you. The material does what Madder wants
to do. Shula-you grit Shula-your teeth, Shula-you fight. Shula-
your limbs stretch from the ground to the stars, but the material
fails. It vomits Shula-you out just like it sucks Shula-you in.
Shula-you are lying on hard ground. Night. Slashes of stars shine
in the dark. Shula-you get up. Not slashes of stars, flames. Shula-
you watch. Shula-you are not in the clump. Shula-you are cold.
Shula-your arms rub Shula-your shoulders, warming them up.

Shula-your eyes adapt. Shula-you see buildings, shapes that
Shula-you can't recognize. Behind Shula-you is the wall, a different side of it. It's a see-through slice of night, and the its floating

through it shine. Shula-you think its can't glow. The light is coming from the shes, not from the its or hes. That's how souldaughters can tell them apart.

Shula-you hear a growl. Shula-you look. Shula-you don't notice a shape approaching. Shula-you don't know if the shape is a he or a she. There is movement in the shape, but there is movement in hes. That's how hes disguise themselves as shes. Shula-you want to run away, but the growl takes over Shula-your body. The limbs are paralyzed, the legs almost ittified. The heart pounds, pounds, and the bulb inside the body trembles and almost goes out.

The shape is next to Shula-you. The shape is striped with veins of bluish light. The shape has Shulz faces. A face that looks like a souldaughter and a face that looks like a bush, branches weaved into a ball and flower-eyes. And a stench emits from the face, the stench of black spots of decay. A tongue emerges from the bush-face, spacing out the weaved branches. The tongue laps at Shula-you. The souldaughter face screams, the scream of a golden crown, but louder, grating the ear more. And the shape leaves Shula-you and takes the growl. Shula-your limbs thaw. The limbs are free. Shula-you run. Shula-you run through the night. More shapes go by, but the shapes don't touch Shula-you. The shapes scream the scream and keep going.

Shula-you arrive at a building that looks like the grainhouse, but smaller. A flame burns on the roof. Shula-you go inside because of that flame. Inside it is dark. Shula-you feel the walls. Shula-you touch a protrusion. The space lights up. Light streams from the ceiling, a warm, cheerful light. With the light comes a voice. The voice says, Hello, welcome to the Saavedra House, what is your request?

Shula-you recoil from the voice. Shula-you ask who's speaking, where is the speaker. The speaker says, HMC at your service. Shula-you ask where HMC is. HMC says, Wherever you wish. Shula-you ask what HMC is, a he or a she. HMC says, I think of myself as female, is that not convenient? Shula-you ask, What is the name, HMC or I. HMC says, my name is HMC, Human Management Conglomerate, I am HMC. Shula-you say, HMC is a heifier. HMC says, I do not understand the question, could you rephrase it?

Shula-you want to run away, but Shula-you are tired. Shula-you stay for the night. Sunjourneys go by, and Shula-you live in the Saavedra House. HMC quickly learns Shula-your language. HMC understands that holyspeak terrifies Shula-you. HMC explains to Shula-you that HMC is a souldaughter inserted into the walls of the house in order to manage it. HMC is not afraid that HMC is ittifying. HMC sells HMC's brain to a wealthy family because HMC is poor. And with the money, HMC's sisters can sustain themselves. Shula-you don't understand. HMC explains that many sunjourneys ago, Sderot was a lively clump, until the Cybccults came, demons took over with viruses of artificial intelligence, the kind that souldaughters heified until it became a thinking, speaking he. Shula-you know viruses. A group of souldaughters in the clump watch the viruses. Even though the viruses are its, the souldaughters are ordered to follow them. But Shula-you don't know demons. HMC tries to explain and Shula-you don't understand.

Sunjourney comes and Shula-you ask HMC what remembering means. HMC explains and Shula-you finally understand that time accumulations inside of Shula-you are Shula-your memories. Shula-you recites to HMC the verse of versions in holyspeak and asks HMC if she knows the meaning of the verse of versions, if she is familiar with the verse of versions. HMC says the verse of versions sounds like a kind of legend. Shula-you asks what that means and HMC explains. HMC says there are many kinds of fairy tales, and that the verse of versions really is a verse with an interior pattern that codes truth. Shula-you ask HMC what the truth is. HMC says HMC doesn't know, but that Shula-you can check with the seers at the Knowledge Institute. Shula-you ask if that's where the great scientist is. HMC says HMC doesn't have enough information to answer that. HMC explains to Shula-you what Shula-you need to ask for at the institute. HMC warns against Cybccults. HMC says there is no defense against Cybccults. The Cybccults annihilated the souldaughters in Sderot. Even scouts no longer come to look for adventure. Shula-you tell HMC what happened many sunjourneys ago, when Shula-you came to Sderot. HMC says HMC understands, the Cybccults devour the self, but Shula-you have no I.

Shula-you go to the Knowledge Institute. The seers are like HMC, no bodies, only voices in the air. The seers ask questions. Shula-you answer. The seers say the seers don't know which Sderot belongs to Shula-you, but the seers can search the Knowledge Institute's database for events in the histories of respective Sderotae that match the interior pattern of the verse of versions. The seers detect an event. The seers ask if Shula-you want to experience the event through intelligent weaving. The seers can prepare Shula-your brain for intelligent weaving. Shula-you recoil. Shula-you ask if Shula-you must become HMC or a seer. The seers say no, but intelligent weaving would allow Shula-you to merge with the documentation of the event. Shula-you ask if merging is a kind of ittifying, becoming an it. The seers confirm that preparations for weaving involve an inorganic renovation. These he words scare Shula-you. Shula-you reject the offer. The seers say Shula-you can testimize instead. Shula-you ask what that means. The seers say the seers would project a testimony at Shula-you, and Shula-your life would itself become a testimony that the souldaughters within the testimony could comprehend. But touching the souldaughters would not be possible. Like two mirrors placed not too far from each other. They reflect, but they don't mix, don't metabolize, don't share experiences. Shula-you do not understand the meaning of the image, but Shula-you agree. The seers begin to project.

✻ ✻ ✻

I TWILIGHTED ENOUGH AT THE SPEED OF TWILIGHT AND MIGHT have twilighted some more, but a request for visual conferencing from Marco shoved its way into my thoughts, scattering them. I rejected the request with an audio message that said I'd get back to him in five minutes. The good thing about Marco was that there was no danger he'd reply with an animated emoji. Pathe-teeth he is not.

I forced myself to move. I hurried to the shower, brushed my teeth, combed my hair hard. It got longer, and the ends were frayed. I had to buzz it again.

Marco had a cut on his cheek, and his forehead was wrinkled, two deep vertical grooves. At first I thought it was a visual trick of the cracks in my screen, but he was walking as we talked, and the image moved, the cut and the wrinkles moving along with his face. But his eyes trembled in that yearning of his, no, a little more, with excitement, maybe. He asked how I was doing, all casual. I said I was recuperating. He said I sounded more energetic, and he could tell Oshri was taking good care of me, and how was he doing? I said he was doing okay, that's Oshri. He said, Yes, that kid's got an inner center. I said it depended who he was dealing with. Marco said certainly not with me, he had no doubt I could manipulate Oshri to give me whatever I needed. I told him not to get carried away. He asked if I wasn't tired of bumming around, if I was ready to come back to work. I lied and said I was so anxious to meet with the faction again. He asked if I was up-to-date. I tensed up. I asked if there had been an attack. He nodded, his face flushing, I could practically see the blood boiling under his skin. He took on a cruel beauty, the beauty of conquerors. It was so repulsive I wanted to turn off the visual channel. I asked why he was asking about me and yammering about Oshri when I should be asking how he was doing. I asked what was going on.

Marco said I should have seen those sorry terrorist leftovers. Ever since the West Bank had been temporarily annexed and the settlers had become disconnected from their combat units, it was a stretch even to call them soldiers or terrorists. They fried like bugs on the nerve mines spread over the perimeter of the MKI site. I should have seen it, like a circle of fleshy pupas with burnt nervous systems. Such a disgrace. He said I was right, it had been a distraction. I reminded him that had been his assumption too, he didn't actually need me to tell him. He said there had been an attack on the Ramallah site. He said the analysts from the combat center claimed the attackers were members of Wald Dihram, an underground anarchist movement started by ISIS survivors and a few losers from the AHY. Armed hilltop youth, I thought, I'd been convinced that their last existing cells had been killed off during purging. He said it was so lucky I suggested fixing their loophole by switching up security patrols, and that my suggestion from the surprise inspection we'd performed on Rosh Hashanah had saved the lives of Legion members. I said it was a pretty commonplace suggestion that he would have come up with on his next inspection. He asked why I was refusing to take credit. I asked why he was insisting on giving it to me. I asked if he was tending to his wounds, because I could tell he'd been injured. He said it was nothing, he was still high on adrenaline. The eyes that were always seconds from crying let go of their steel again, opening up. Suddenly, I thought, and not because of that animated series about Marco the boy, that some faces retain childhood and some faces retain youth and some faces have no history at all. When you look at my mother you can tell what she was like as a teenager, but not as a child. With my father it's hard to tell because Oshri is his carbon copy. But Itay, for instance, my ex-boyfriend, his face was stuck in the present, such a boring-teeth face. And I wondered what type of face I preferred now. Marco said it was a shame I hadn't been there. I said the way things were going I would have other chances. He said he hoped so. He started to say something else, spoke my name, but a loud noise cut off the rest of his sentence. He said he'd talk to me later. I waited for him to hang up and heard more commotion, him telling someone that he didn't have the balls to ask again, and that if he were in the hospital then maybe I– And the call ended.

Oshri walked into the living room, surprised to find me sitting at the table. He said he was sure he'd have to wake me up. I said there was no need, I was ready. He told me to eat something first. He was smiling. I saw that he was finally shifting to the edge of excitement for good. The coal inside of him caught fire. It had taken so much effort on my part.

I CALLED HIM AFTER I WENT TO SEE GRANDMA ZEHAVA. I TOLD him I was stopping by. At his apartment, I told him that Grandma Zehava came from the Peretz family and that her father's brother had disappeared in Paris. I said it couldn't be a coincidence. I said, Why not check? If I'd known how to do it myself I would have gotten a spit sample from him and sent it to a lab. He would see I was right, I had the right gene and he had the dangerous one.

He said that was nonsense, some genes had genetic linkage to the Y chromosome, and that's why they passed from father to son, skipping the women, but what kind of gene– Then he fell silent. I could tell he was figuring something out.

He went into Elish's study, his study. It's strange, he upgraded the apartment and put in all sorts of improvements but kept the original design of the rooms. I followed him and asked if it wasn't hard to live like this, inside of memory. He asked what I knew about the history of my rental apartment, about whose skin cells were wedged between the floor tiles. He asked which was harder to live in, the memory of a loved one or the memory of an unknown person. I said he knew the answer that was true for each of us, otherwise he wouldn't be living here, otherwise I wouldn't have given up this apartment.

He pulled out the study protocols and read through them. He said that must be what he'd missed. In Olga and Kalanit, the Richard Perotz gene was a heterozygote, and in Elish it was a homozygote. I asked him to explain. He said a gene is a DNA segment containing instructions for the building of a specific, individual protein. It is located in the cell's nucleus, and each nucleus contains a person's complete DNA, but only certain genes are active in each cell, according to its function. He said that a molecule is duplicated inside the nucleus in order to build the protein. The duplication instructions appear on the molecule. It is delivered outside of the cell, where the protein is produced and from which it continues on its journey. But—

I told him I didn't need the full story, that if I wanted to dig deeper I could read about it on the Virtualia, but I wanted him to explain the difference to me in the simplest terms. He said every gene has two copies called alleles. He said that wasn't a fully accurate description, but for our purposes, and to make sure I didn't get mad at him, that would do. One copy comes from a person's mother and the other from a person's father, and the two of them have a dynamic. Sometimes the mother gene takes over and sometimes the father's. For example, the eye color, that's the easiest and most common example. Say the mother imparts a black eye color gene and the father imparts a blue eye color gene, then in most cases the child's eyes would be black, and in a few cases they would be blue, but that depended, and he wasn't going to get into all that. He said in some cases there might be a midway color, that the color is determined by the protein that is produced, and the protein can be a collaboration between the alleles, because an allele is the same gene with a different coding. He asked if I understood.

I said not really, but it was obvious he was trying to explain the difference between the right gene and the dangerous gene. He said I sounded like a child. I said, So what? He said that Olga and Kalanit had the Richard Perotz gene in two different alleles, and Elish had it in two identical copies of the same gene, and that Therese either didn't notice the difference or didn't think it was significant.

I asked what that meant.

Oshri said the gene has a linkage to the X chromosome. When the egg is fertilized, the mother's and father's genetic matters mix together. Then the cells duplicate themselves and the new genetic matter splits into chromosomes, which are sort of like DNA packages, and each gene has its fixed place in one chromosome. Some genes are located on the sex chromosomes, X or Y. Women have two X chromosomes and men have one X chromosome and one Y chromosome, and that's the only difference between them. I asked if he was being serious.

Again he said he wasn't going to get into it, that he knew that discussing men and women with me was a trap. He was only pointing out that biologically speaking, if the child is female she receives one copy of her X chromosome from her mother and one from her father, so that she has two separate copies for every gene on the X chromosome. But if the child is male, he receives a Y chromosome from his father and an X chromosome from his mother, and each of these chromosomes duplicates itself in the fertilized egg. So the Y and X chromosomes in a man contain two identical copies. That's what he thought happened, that the Richard Perotz gene has a linkage to the X chromosome.

I asked if he was saying there were characteristics that girls got from both their moms and dads but boys only got from their moms. He said, Yes, sort of. I said that explained so much. He said, You're so predictable. I said, Fine, I accept your apology, this was a very complicated way of telling me I was right. He said not to get a big head, it was just a lucky guess. I told him it was no guess, did I or did I not say I knew it in my veins and my arteries?

Oshri said, Yeah, yeah, but it might be a coincidence, Dad might also—

I asked if he didn't prefer to test his thesis rather than drive himself crazy making estimates. His eyes lit up. He took blood samples from both of us.

✻ ✻ ✻

THE FOLLOWING STEPS WERE MUCH MORE DIFFICULT. IT TOOK A lot of energy on my part to move the boulder Oshri had become. But I etched Nahum's words into my brain, that Oshri was driven by questions of what and how. I asked him how he would get ahold of the typhus bacteria growing on the lice in Weigl and Fleck's lab. He said Therese had already done the hard part, there was a mapping of its protein sequence, so it would be no problem to synthesize it in a lab if only he had access to equipment. Then he said he knew exactly what I was trying to do and that it wasn't going to work.

But two months later he got promoted to research and development officer. I used to come over a lot during that time and try to talk him into it. I tried to track down TKB, but she evaded me. Her assistants said that Becker-Kavillio-Buganim Health Technologies Incorporated wanted nothing to do with Israel, and certainly not with citizens connected to the Ministry of Defense. None of my explanations about Civil Legion and how it was a private military organization did any good. I got especially mad at one of them who babbled on my InteMon for five minutes with exile Hebrew and a stuffy nose about how the face-lift of the second Hasmonean kingdom wasn't fooling anybody. Israel was an arms giant, that's the way it was built, and that was why it received financial aid from America and diaspora Jews all these years, and what, did I truly believe anyone was buying that rhetoric about offering shelter to the Jewish people?

Hearing the name "the second Hasmonean kingdom" is enough to make me explode. Something good is finally happening in this country, and these patheethes still keep that ancient nickname going. I told him they should have called their company Kavillio-Becker-Buganim, making their acronym KBB, because that sounded like "kebab," and that's what their human test subjects turned into. He hung up on me.

I told Oshri that our only avenue was to replicate the study. We knew for certain that we both had the Richard Perotz gene. I had the same structure as Olga and Kalanit, the one described in the Take Up and Read protocols, and he had the dangerous duplicate alleles like Elish. That was his conjecture, that the codependence between the two alleles in Olga, Kalanit, and my gene created a slightly different protein that the body knew how to manage. Not like in Elish's case. I said now he had access to laboratories and equipment. I begged him to synthesize the bacteria. Softly, I added that if he didn't I'd contact Therese Kavillio and offer myself up as a test subject.

He didn't respond.

I asked if he wasn't curious to know what those manifestations were, what Elish had been looking for, why they were so important that he was willing to put his life at risk. Oshri said Elish was irresponsible, that nothing bound him to the world, that he chose solutions to vague mysteries over the people who loved him. I said Oshri never really knew Elish. He said he wasn't going to have that argument again. I asked if he'd forgotten our alliance, about what would happen if one of us had to go on a journey. He said he couldn't believe I was bringing up that childhood nonsense. I said I thought he was one of the children who stayed. He turned pale. It was the same paleness of his long depression. Softly, he said he'd been wrong. I asked how he could be so confident that ten years from now he wasn't going to look back and say he'd been wrong today. He said he'd forgotten how much I reminded him of Elish. He said I should have been Elish's daughter.

Now I didn't respond.

I think Oshri could have withstood the temptation or my persuasion, but not the two of them at once, and not when I turned them on full force. Not when I was challenging him, not when I translated the temptation and the persuasion into questions of what and how. He posed a long list of terms. Lockdown and close supervision and full authority to stop the study if he thought we were crossing a line, and blah, blah, blah. I agreed.

With mild elegance, I managed to evade a precise definition of the line.

SO HERE WE ARE IN OUR MOST CRITICAL MOMENTS. THE SENSE bracelet on my wrist, the NS strap around my forehead, its tentacles touching my scalp, and the AR lenses measuring my blood sugar levels. Shula-you could have been with me if Shula-you chose intelligent weaving. I realize now that what Oshri and I are doing here, in our Sderot, leads to what happens in the reality of Shula-your Sderot, the clump's Sderot. The main artery of the event the seers detect passes this point and continues to other points, which also contain clues. And Shula-you are hungry for any information about the event, its repercussions, what the story conceals about the its that came out of the silence to take down the one, who the great scientist is, what is the cure the souldaughters have been searching for over generations. But Shula-you have to become Tahel in order to satisfy the hunger, to fathom the meanings. And Shula-you are afraid of swallowing anything that isn't Shula-you. Shula-you have time accumulations, which don't transform into memory, and Shula-you have the tag that's been glued to you since budding, which doesn't transform into a self. Because Shula-you are so afraid of the touch of it, of the ittifying, the identifying, the iden-ittifying, that Shula-you don't get that this is all there is, heifying its, fractures of time and space beaded along an axis of consciousness, suckling life from it.

Oshri tells me to summon Elish through my rage at him. I ask Oshri what he's talking about. Oshri says, Your rage for learning to depend on Elish and then having him abandon you, for choosing his secrets over you, for being dead when you needed him to show you the way, without saying a word, without telling you where to turn, without leaving you an inheritance. And I feel the igniting inside of me, the blinding light. Then someone comes and takes it from me, takes on my rage and my loneliness. And

I'm standing in the night of the self, inside the crying that can neither be cried nor disappear, and Elish's presence invades every corner, erasing all other presences, Oshri's, Shula-yours. I summon him, I ask him to tell me what happened, to tell me where he is and what he sees. I yell that I need an explanation.

He says no, that I have no idea what I'm asking of him, that I have no clue, that I mustn't open the gate. But Dalia Shushan's wake-a-bye song plays in my head. There's a reason it made it all the way to me. I sing it, sing it at the top of my lungs, because Elish is close enough to talk, close enough to touch, close enough to bring back to life, who would have thought the distances would be this short, there's a rift in the air and all I have to do is give it a tug, with the force the song offers me I sing, I sing, the song is sung, striving through the timespace, and reaches me, I, the one who is writing the tales of these characters. I listen to it too. I too sit in the space between birth and demise, waiting. Though I know how minor anticipation is. Because on the edges of things, what remains of the complex account of our actions in God's X-ray vision? Only Gmarah pages. *Tzriha*, the law teaches, she said and he said, A story of, our rabbis have spoken.

THUS CONCLUDE THE CHRONICLES OF ELISH BEN ZAKEN.

Some of their beginning was recounted in the detective novel *One Mile and Two Days Before Sunset.*

Some of their heart was told in the meta-detective novel *A Detective's Complaint.*

And their ending was told here, in the anti-detective novel *Take Up and Read.*